KT-456-031

The Valley of Horses

Jean M. Auel

coronet

CORONET BOOKS
Hodder & Stoughton

Copyright © 1982 by Jean M. Auel

First published in Great Britain in 1982
by Hodder & Stoughton
First published in paperback in 1984
by Hodder & Stoughton Ltd
A Coronet paperback

This edition 2002

The right of Jean M. Auel to be identified as the
Author of the Work has been asserted by her in accordance
with the Copyright, Designs and Patents Act 1988.

20 19 18 17 16

All rights reserved. No part of this publication may be
reproduced, stored in a retrieval system, or transmitted,
in any form or by any means without the prior written
permission of the publisher, nor be otherwise circulated in
any form of binding or cover other than that in which it is
published and without a similar condition being imposed
on the subsequent purchaser.

All characters in this publication are fictitious and any
resemblance to real persons, living or dead, is purely coincidental.

A CIP catalogue record for this title
is available from the British Library

ISBN 0 340 82443 3

Printed and bound in Great Britain by
Clays Ltd, St Ives plc

Hodder & Stoughton
A division of Hodder Headline
338 Euston Road
London NW1 3BH

The Valley of Horses

'A panorama of human culture in its infancy . . . THE
VALLEY OF HORSES is great fun.'
New York Times Book Review

'Magic'   *Daily Telegraph*

'A remarkably vivid fictional recreation of what life was like
for early cave man and woman'
Daily Express

Also by Jean M. Auel

The Clan of the Cave Bear
The Mammoth Hunters
The Plains of Passage

About the author

Jean Auel is an international phenomenon. With the
publication of THE CLAN OF THE CAVE BEAR, the
first novel in her Earth's Children® sequence, in 1980,
she achieved unprecedented critical and commercial
success and this has continued to the present. Her
extensive research has also earned her the respect of
many renowned scientists, archaeologists and
anthropologists around the globe. Jean Auel lives
with her husband, Ray, in Oregon.

ACKNOWLEDGEMENTS

In addition to the people mentioned in *The Clan of the Cave Bear*, whose help has been of continuing assistance for this Earth's Children book, and for which I am still grateful, I am further indebted to:

The director, Dr Denzel Ferguson, and staff of Malheur Field Station, in the high desert steppes country of central Oregon, and most especially to Jim Riggs. He taught, among other things, how a fire is made, how a spearthrower is used, how bulrushes make sleeping mats, how to pressure flake a stone tool, and how to squish deer brains – who would have thought that could turn deer hide into velvety soft leather?

Doreen Gandy, for her careful reading and most appreciated comments so I could be assured this book stands alone.

Ray Auel, for support, encouragement, assistance, and doing the dishes.

EARTH'S CHILDREN

PREHISTORIC EUROPE
DURING THE ICE AGE

Extent of ice and change in coastlines during 10,000 - year
interstadial, a warming trend during the Wurm glaciation
of the late Pleistocene Epoch extending from 35,000 to
25,000 years before present.

Mother figurines are examples of many similar
small sculptures found throughout prehistoric Europe,
dated c. 30,000 years before present.

SEE OVERLEAF FOR DESCRIPTION

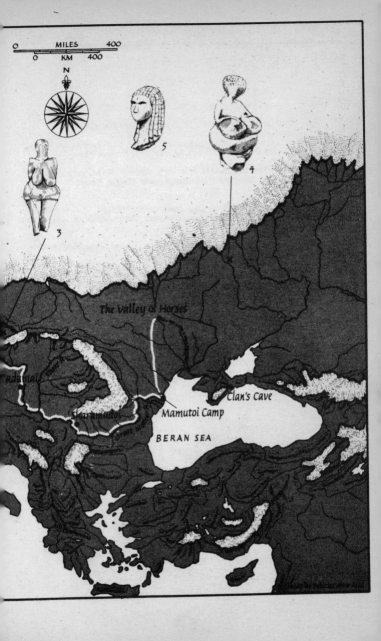

EXPLANATION OF FIGURES AS SHOWN ON MAP

1. "Venus" of Lespugue. Ivory (restored). Height 14.7 cm/5¾ in. Found Lespugue (Haute-Garonne), France. *Musée de l'Homme, Paris.*

2. "Venus" of Willendorf. Limestone with traces of red ochre. Height 11 cm/4 in. Found Willendorf, Wachau, Lower Austria. *Naturbistrorisches Museum, Vienna.*

3. "Venus" of Vestonice. Fired clay (with bone). Height 11.4 cm/4½ in. Found Dolni, Vestonice, Mikulov, Moravia. Czechoslovakia. *Moravian Museum, Brno.*

4. Female Figurine. Ivory. Height 5.8 cm/2¼ in. Found Gagarino, Ukraine, USSR. *Ethnographic Institute, Leningrad.*

5. Lady of Brassempouy. Ivory (fragment). Height 3.2 cm/1¼ in. Found Grotte du Pape. Brassempouy (Landes), France. *Musée des Antiquités Nationales, Saint-Germain-en-laye.*

1

She was dead. What did it matter if icy needles of freezing rain flayed her skin raw? The young woman squinted into the wind, pulling her wolverine hood closer. Violent gusts whipped her bearskin wrap against her legs.

Were those trees ahead? She thought she remembered seeing a scraggly row of woody vegetation on the horizon earlier, and wished she had paid more attention, or that her memory was as good as that of the rest of the Clan. She still thought of herself as Clan, though she never had been, and now she was dead.

She bowed her head and leaned into the wind. The storm had come upon her suddenly, hurtling down from the north, and she was desperate for shelter. But she was a long way from the cave, and unfamiliar with the territory. The moon had gone through a full cycle of phases since she left, but she still had no idea where she was going.

North, to the mainland beyond the peninsula, that was all she knew. The night Iza died, she had told her to leave, told her Broud would find a way to hurt her when he became leader. Iza had been right. Broud had hurt her, worse than she ever imagined.

He had no good reason to take Durc away from me, Ayla thought. He's my son. Broud had no good reason to curse me, either. He's the one who made the spirits angry. He's the one who brought on the earthquake. At least she knew what to expect this time. But it happened so fast that even the Clan had taken a while to accept it, to close her out of their sight. But they couldn't stop Durc from seeing her, though she was dead to the rest of the Clan.

Broud had cursed her on impulse born of anger. When Brun had cursed her, the first time, he had prepared them.

He'd had reason, they knew he had to do it, and he'd given her a chance.

She raised her head to another icy blast, and noticed it was twilight. It would be dark soon, and her feet were numb. Frigid slush was soaking through her leather foot coverings despite the insulating sedge grass she had stuffed in them. She was relieved to see a dwarfed and twisted pine.

Trees were rare on the steppes; they grew only where there was moisture enough to sustain them. A double row of pines, birches, or willows, sculptured by wind into stunted asymmetrical shapes, usually marked a watercourse. They were a welcome sight in dry seasons in a land where groundwater was scarce. When storms howled down the open plains from the great northern glacier, they offered protection, scant though it was.

A few more steps brought the young woman to the edge of a stream, though only a narrow channel of water flowed between the ice-locked banks. She turned west to follow it downstream, looking for denser growth that would give more shelter than the nearby scrub.

She plodded ahead, her hood pulled forward, but looked up when the wind ceased abruptly. Across the stream a low bluff guarded the opposite bank. The sedge grass did nothing to warm her feet when the icy water seeped in crossing over, but she was grateful to be out of the wind. The dirt wall of the bank had caved in at one place, leaving an overhang thatched with tangled grass roots and matted old growth, and a fairly dry spot beneath.

She untied the waterlogged thongs that held her carrying basket to her back and shrugged it off, then took out a heavy aurochs hide and a sturdy branch stripped of twigs. She set up a low, sloping tent, held down with rocks and driftwood logs. The branch held it open in front.

She loosened the thongs of her hand coverings with her teeth. They were roughly circular pieces of fur-lined leather, gathered at the wrist, with a slit cut in the palms to poke her thumb or hand through when she wanted to grasp something. Her foot coverings were made the same way, without the slit, and she struggled to untie the swollen leather laces wrapped around her ankles. She was careful to salvage the wet sedge grass when she removed them.

She laid her bearskin wrap on the ground inside the tent, wet side down, put the sedge grass and the hand and foot coverings on top, then crawled in feet first. She wrapped the fur around her and pulled the carrying basket up to block the opening. She rubbed her cold feet, and, when her damp fur nest warmed, she curled up and closed her eyes.

Winter was gasping its last frozen breath, reluctantly giving way to spring, but the youthful season was a capricious flirt. Amid frigid reminders of glacial chill, tantalizing hints of warmth promised summer heat. In an impulsive shift, the storm ceased during the night.

Ayla woke to reflections of a dazzling sun glinting from patches of snow and ice along the bank, and to a sky deep and radiantly blue. Ragged tatters of clouds streamed far to the south. She crawled out of her tent and raced barefoot to the water's edge with her waterbag. Ignoring the icy cold, she filled the leather-covered bladder, took a deep drink, and ran back. After relieving herself beside the bank, she crawled inside her fur to warm up again.

She didn't stay long. She was too eager to be out, now that the danger of the storm had passed and the sunshine beckoned. She wrapped on foot coverings that had been dried by body heat and tied the bearskin over the fur-lined leather wrap she had slept in. She took a piece of dried meat out of the basket, packed the tent and hand coverings, and went on her way, chewing on the meat.

The stream's course was fairly straight and slightly downhill, and the going was easy. Ayla hummed a tuneless monotone under her breath. She saw flecks of green on the brush near the banks. An occasional small flower, bravely poking its miniature face through melting patches of snow, made her smile. A chunk of ice broke loose, bumped along beside her for a pace, then raced ahead, carried by the swift current.

Spring had begun when she left the cave, but it was warmer at the southern end of the peninsula and the season started earlier. The mountain range was a barrier to the harsh glacial winds, and maritime breezes off the inland sea warmed and watered the narrow coastal strip and south-facing slopes into a temperate climate.

The steppes were colder. She had skirted the eastern end of the range, but, as she travelled northward across the open prairie, the season advanced at the same pace, retaining the chill of early spring.

The raucous squeals of terns drew her attention. She glanced up and saw several of the small gull-like birds wheeling and gliding effortlessly with wings outstretched. The sea must be close, she thought. Birds should be nesting now – that means eggs. She stepped up her pace. And maybe mussels on the rocks, and clams, and limpets, and tide pools full of anemones.

The sun was approaching its zenith when she reached a protected bay formed by the southern coast of the mainland and the northwestern flank of the peninsula. She had finally reached the broad throat connecting the tongue of land to the continent.

Ayla shrugged off her carrying basket and climbed a craggy outcrop that soared high above the surrounding landscape. Pounding surf had cleaved jagged chunks of the massive rock on the seaward side. A bevy of dovekies and terns scolded with angry squawks when she collected eggs. She broke open several and swallowed them, still warm from the nest. She tucked several more into a fold of her wrap before climbing down.

She took off her footwear and waded into the surf to wash sand from mussels pried loose from the rock at water level. Flowerlike sea anemones drew in mock petals when she reached to pluck them from the shallow pools left stranded by the receding tide. But these had a colour and shape that were unfamiliar. She rounded out her lunch with a few clams instead, dug from the sand where a slight depression gave them away. She used no fire, enjoying her gifts raw from the sea.

Surfeited on eggs and seafood, the young woman relaxed at the foot of the high rock, then scaled it again to get a better view of the coast and mainland. Hugging her knees, she sat on top of the monolith and looked out across the bay. The wind in her face carried a breath of rich life within the sea.

The southern coast of the continent curved in a gentle arc towards the west. Beyond a narrow fringe of trees, she could see a broad land of steppes, no different from the cold prairie of the peninsula, but not a single sign of human habitation.

There it is, she thought, the mainland beyond the peninsula. Where do I go now, Iza? You said Others were there, but I don't see anyone at all. As she faced the vast empty land, Ayla's thoughts drifted back to the dreadful night Iza died, three years before.

"You are not Clan, Ayla. You were born to the Others; you belong with them. You must leave, child, find your own kind."

"Leave! Where would I go, Iza? I don't know the Others, I wouldn't know where to look for them."

"North, Ayla. Go north. There are many of them north of here, on the mainland beyond the peninsula. You cannot stay here. Broud will find a way to hurt you. Go and find them, my child. Find your own people, find your own mate."

She hadn't left then, she couldn't. Now, she had no choice. She had to find the Others, there was no one else. She could never go back; she would never see her son again.

Tears streamed down Ayla's face. She hadn't cried before. Her life had been at stake when she left, and grief was a luxury she could not afford. But once the barrier was breached, there was no holding back.

"Durc . . . my baby," she sobbed, burrowing her face in her hands. Why did Broud take you away from me?

She cried for her son, and for the clan she had left behind; she cried for Iza, the only mother she could remember; and she cried for her loneliness and fear of the unknown world awaiting her. But not for Creb, who had loved her as her own, not yet. That sorrow was too fresh; she wasn't ready to face it.

When the tears had run their course, Ayla found herself staring at the crashing surf far below. She watched the rolling breakers spout up in jets of foam, then swirl around the jagged rocks.

It would be so easy, she thought.

No! She shook her head and straightened up. I told him he could take my son away, he could make me leave, he could curse me with death, but he could not make me die!

She tasted salt, and a wry smile crossed her face. Her tears had always upset Iza and Creb. The eyes of people in the

Clan did not water, unless they were sore, not even Durc's. There was much of her in him, he could even make sounds the way she could, but Durc's large brown eyes were Clan.

Ayla climbed down quickly. As she hoisted her carrying basket to her back, she wondered if her eyes were really weak, or if all the Others had watering eyes. Then another thought echoed in her mind: find your own people, find your own mate.

The young woman travelled west along the coast, crossing many streams and creeks that found their way to the inland sea, until she reached a rather large river. Then she veered north, following the rushing waterway inland and looking for a place to cross. She passed through the coastal fringe of pine and larch woods which boasted an occasional giant dominating dwarfed cousins. When she reached the continental steppes, brush of willows, birches, and aspens joined the cramped conifers that edged the river.

She followed every twist and turn of the meandering course, growing more anxious with each passing day. The river was taking her back east in a general northeasterly direction. She did not want to go east. Some clans hunted the eastern part of the mainland. She had planned to veer west on her northward trek. She did not want to chance meeting anyone who was Clan – not with a death curse on her! She had to find a way to cross the river.

When the river widened and broke into two channels around a small gravel-strewn island with brush clinging to rocky shores, she decided to risk a crossing. A few large boulders in the channel on the other side of the island made her think it might be shallow enough to wade. She was a good swimmer, but she didn't want to get her clothes or basket wet. It would take too long for them to dry, and the nights were still cold.

She walked back and forth along the bank, watching the swift water. When she decided upon the shallowest way, she stripped, piled everything into her basket, and, holding it up, entered the water. The rocks were slippery underfoot, and the current threatened to unbalance her. Midway across the first channel, the water was waist high, but she gained the island without mishap. The second channel was wider. She wasn't sure if it was fordable, but she was almost halfway and didn't want to give up.

She was well past the midpoint when the river deepened until she was walking on tiptoe with the water up to her neck, holding the basket over her head. Suddenly the bottom dropped. Her head bobbed down and she took an involuntary swallow. The next moment she was treading water, her basket resting on top of her head. She steadied it with one hand, trying to make some progress towards the opposite shore with the other. The current picked her up and carried her, but only for a short distance. Her feet felt rocks, and, a few moments later, she walked up the far bank.

Leaving the river behind, Ayla travelled the steppes again. As days of sunshine outnumbered those of rain, the warming season finally caught up and outpaced her northward trek. The buds on trees and brush grew into leaves, and conifers extended soft, light green needles from the ends of branches and twigs. She picked them to chew along the way, enjoying the light tangy pine flavour.

She fell into a routine of travelling all day until, near dusk, she found a creek or stream, where she made camp. Water was still easy to find. Spring rains and winter melt from farther north were overflowing streams and filling draws and washes that would be dry gullies or, at best, sluggish muddy runnels later. Plentiful water was a passing phase. The moisture would be quickly absorbed, but not before it caused the steppes to blossom.

Almost overnight, herbaceous flowers of white, yellow, and purple – more rarely a vivid blue or bright red – filled the land, blending in the distance to the predominant young green of new grass. Ayla delighted in the beauty of the season; spring had always been her favourite time of year.

As the open plains burgeoned with life, she relied less on the meagre supply of preserved food she carried with her and began to live off the land. It slowed her down hardly at all. Every woman of the Clan learned to pluck leaves, flowers, buds, and berries while travelling, almost without stopping. She trimmed leaves and twigs from a sturdy branch, sharpened one end with a flint knife, and used the digging stick to turn up roots and bulbs as quickly. Gathering was easy. She had only herself to feed.

But Ayla had an advantage women of the Clan normally did not. She could hunt. Only with a sling, to be sure, but even the men agreed – once they accepted the idea of her hunting at all – that she was the most skilled sling-hunter in the Clan. She had taught herself, and she had paid dearly for the skill.

As the sprouting herbs and grasses tempted burrowing ground squirrels, giant hamsters, great jerboas, rabbits, and hares from winter nests, Ayla started wearing her sling again, tucked into the thong that held her fur wrap closed. She carried the digging stick slipped into the thong, too, but her medicine bag, as always, was worn on the waist thong of her inner wrap.

Food was plentiful; wood and fire were a little more difficult to obtain. She could make fire, and brush and small trees managed to survive along some of the seasonal streams, often accompanied by deadfall. Whenever she came across dry branches or dung, she collected that, too. But she didn't make a fire every night. Sometimes the right materials were not available, or they were green, or wet, or she was tired and didn't want to bother.

But she didn't like sleeping out in the open without the security of a fire. The extensive grassland supported an abundance of large grazing animals, and their ranks were thinned by a variety of four-legged hunters. Fire usually held them off. It was common practice in the Clan for a high-ranking male to carry a coal when they travelled to start the next fire, and it didn't occur to Ayla to carry fire-making materials with her at first. Once it did, she wondered why she hadn't done it sooner.

The fire drill stick and flat wood hearth-platform didn't make it any easier to start a fire, though, if tinder or wood was too green or damp. When she found the skeleton of an aurochs, she thought her problems were solved.

The moon had gone through another cycle of its phases, and the wet spring was warming into early summer. She was still travelling on the broad coastal plain that sloped gently towards the inland sea. Silt carried down by the seasonal floods often formed long estuaries, partially closed by sand bars, or sealed off completely to form lagoons or pools.

Ayla had made a dry camp and stopped at a small pool at midmorning. The water looked stagnant and not potable, but her waterbag was low. She dipped in a hand to sample it, then spat out the brackish liquid and took a small sip from her waterbag to wash out her mouth.

I wonder if that aurochs drank this water, she thought, noticing the bleached bones and skull with long tapering horns. She turned away from the stagnant pool with its spectre of death, but the bones would not leave her thoughts. She kept seeing the white skull and the long horns, the curved hollow horns.

She stopped at a stream near noon and decided to make a fire and roast a rabbit she had killed. Sitting in the warm sun, spinning the fire drill between her palms against the wood platform, she wished Grod would appear with the coal he carried in . . .

She jumped up, piled the fire drill and hearth into her basket, put the rabbit on top, and hurried back the way she had come. When she reached the pool, she looked for the skull. Grod usually carried a live coal wrapped in dried moss or lichen in the long hollow horn of an aurochs. With one, she could carry fire.

But while she was tugging at the horn, she felt a twinge of conscience. Women of the Clan did not carry fire; it was not allowed. Who will carry it for me if I don't? she thought, jerking hard and breaking the horn away. She left quickly, as though thinking of the prohibited act alone had conjured up watchful, disapproving eyes.

There had been a time when her survival depended on conforming to a way of life foreign to her nature. Now it depended on her ability to overcome her childhood conditioning and think for herself. The aurochs horn was a beginning, and it boded well for her chances.

There was more to the business of carrying fire than she realized, however. In the morning she looked for dry moss to wrap her coal in. But moss, so plentiful in the wooded region near the cave, was not to be had on the dry open plains. Finally she settled for grass. To her dismay, the ember was dead when she was ready to make camp again. Yet she knew it could be done, and she had often banked fires to last the night. She had the necessary knowledge. It took trial and error, and many dead coals, before she discovered a way to preserve a bit of the fire from one camp to the next. She carried the aurochs horn tied to her waist thong, too.

Ayla always found ways to cross the streams in her path by wading, but when she came upon the large river, she knew another way would have to be found. She had followed it upstream for several days. It doubled back to the northeast, and did not decrease in size.

Though she thought she was out of the territory that might be hunted by members of the Clan, she did not want to go east. Going east meant going back towards the Clan. She could not go back, and she didn't even want to head in that direction. And she could not stay where she was camped in the open beside the river. She had to cross; there was no other way to go.

She thought she could make it – she had always been a strong swimmer – but not holding a basket with all her possessions over her head. Her possessions were the problem.

She was sitting beside a small fire in the lee of a fallen tree whose naked branches trailed the water. The afternoon sun glinted in the constant motion of the swiftly flowing current. Occasional debris floated past. It brought to mind the stream that flowed near the cave, and fishing for salmon and sturgeon where it emptied into the inland sea. She used to enjoy swimming then, though it had worried Iza. Ayla didn't remember learning how to swim; it just seemed she always knew.

I wonder why no one else ever liked to swim, she mused. They thought I was strange because I liked to go so far out . . . until the time Ona almost drowned.

She remembered everyone had been grateful to her for saving the child's life. Brun even helped her out of the water. She had felt a warm sense of acceptance then, as though she really belonged. Legs that were long and straight, a body too thin and too tall, blonde hair and blue eyes and a high forehead hadn't mattered. Some of the clan tried to learn to swim after that, but they didn't float well and had a fear of deep water.

I wonder if Durc could learn? He never was as heavy as anyone else's baby, and he'll never be as muscular as most men. I think he could . . .

Who would teach him? I won't be there, and Uba can't. She will take care of him; she loves him as much as I do, but she can't swim. Neither can Brun. Brun will teach him to hunt, though, and he'll protect Durc. He won't let Broud hurt my son, he promised – even if he wasn't supposed to see me. Brun was a good leader, not like Broud . . .

Could Broud have started Durc growing inside me? Ayla shuddered, remembering how Broud had forced her. Iza said men did that to women they liked, but Broud only did it because he knew how much I hated it. Everyone says it's the spirits of totems that make babies start. But none of the men have a totem strong enough to defeat my Cave Lion. I didn't get pregnant until after Broud kept forcing me, and everyone was surprised. No one thought I'd ever have a baby . . .

I wish I could see him when he grows up. He's already tall for his age, like I am. He'll be the tallest man in the Clan, I'm sure of that . . .

No I'm not! I'll never know. I'll never see Durc again.

Stop thinking about him, she commanded herself. She got up and walked to the edge of the river. Thinking about him won't get me across this river!

She had been so preoccupied with her thoughts that she didn't notice the forked log drifting close to the bank. She stared with detached awareness as the outstretched limbs of the fallen tree snared it in its tangled branches and watched, without seeing, the log bumping and straining to break loose for long moments. But as soon as she saw it, she also saw its possibilities.

She waded into the shoal and dragged the log onto the beach. It was the top portion of the trunk of a good-size tree, freshly broken by violent flooding farther upriver, and not too waterlogged. With a flint hand-axe, which she carried in a fold of her leather wrap, she hacked off the longer of the two forking branches fairly even with the other one, and trimmed away obstructing limbs, leaving two rather long stubs.

After a quick look around, she headed for a clump of birch

trees draped with clematis vines. Tugging on a fresh woody vine loosened a long tough strand. She walked back pulling off the leaves. Then she spread her hide tent out on the ground and dumped out the contents of her carrying basket. It was time to take stock and repack.

She put her fur leggings and hand coverings in the bottom of the basket along with the fur-lined wrap now that she wore her summer wrap; she wouldn't need them until next winter. She paused for a moment wondering where she would be next winter, but she did not care to dwell on that. She paused again when she picked up the soft supple leather cloak she had used to help support Durc on her hip when she carried him.

She didn't need it; it was not necessary for her survival. She had only brought it with her because it was something that had been close to him. She held it to her cheek, then carefully folded it and put it in the basket. On top of it she put the soft absorbent leather straps she took along to use during her menstrual flow. Next her extra pair of foot coverings went in. She went barefoot now, but still wore a pair when it was wet or cold, and they were wearing out. She was glad she had brought a second pair.

She checked her food next. There was one birchbark packet of maple sugar left. Ayla opened it, broke off a piece, and put it in her mouth, wondering if she'd ever taste maple sugar again after this was gone.

She still had several cakes of travelling food, the kind the men took when they went hunting, made of rendered fat, ground-up dried meat, and dried fruit. Thoughts of the rich fat made her mouth water. The small animals she killed with her sling were lean, for the most part. Without the vegetable food she collected, she would slowly starve on a diet of pure protein. Fats or carbohydrates in some form were necessary.

She put the travelling cakes in the basket without indulging her taste, saving them for emergencies. She added some strips of dried meat – tough as leather but nourishing – a few dried apples, some hazelnuts, a few pouches of grain plucked from the grasses of the steppes near the cave, and threw away a rotten root. On top of the food she put her cup and bowl, her wolverine hood, and the worn foot coverings.

She untied her medicine bag from her waist thong and

rubbed her hand over the sleek waterproof fur of the otter skin, feeling the hard bones of the feet and tail. The thong that pulled the pouch closed was threaded around the neck opening, and the oddly flattened head, still attached at the back of the neck, served as a cover flap. Iza had made it for her, passing the legacy from mother to daughter when she became the Clan's medicine woman.

Then, for the first time in many years, Ayla thought of the first medicine bag Iza had made for her, the one Creb had burned the first time she was cursed. Brun had to do it. Women were not allowed to touch weapons, and Ayla had been using her sling for several years. But he had given her a chance to return – if she could survive.

Maybe he gave me more of a chance than he knew, she thought. I wonder if I'd be alive now if I hadn't learned how a death curse makes you want to die. Except for leaving Durc, I think it was harder the first time. When Creb burned all my things, I wanted to die.

She hadn't been able to think about Creb; the grief was too new, the pain too raw. She had loved the old magician as much as she loved Iza. He had been Iza's sibling, and Brun's too. Missing an eye and part of an arm, Creb had never hunted, but he was the greatest holy man of all the clans. Mog-ur, feared and respected – his scarred, one-eyed old visage could inspire dread in the bravest hunter, but Ayla knew his gentle side.

He had protected her, cared for her, loved her as the child of the mate he never had. She'd had time to adjust to Iza's death three years before, and though she grieved for the separation, she knew Durc was still alive. She hadn't grieved for Creb. Suddenly, the pain she had kept inside since the earthquake that killed him, would stay inside no more. She cried out his name.

"Creb . . . Oh, Creb . . . Why did you go back in the cave? Why did you have to die?"

She heaved great sobs into the waterproof fur of the otter-skin pouch. Then, from deep within, a high-pitched wail rose to her throat. She rocked back and forth keening her anguish, her sorrow, her despair. But there was no loving Clan to join their wails with hers and share her misery. She grieved alone, and she grieved for her loneliness.

When her wails subsided, she felt drained, but a terrible ache was relieved. After a while she put her medicine bag inside the basket. She didn't need to check the contents. She knew exactly what it contained. Then anger welled up to replace the grief and added fire to her determination. Broud will not make me die!

She took a deep breath and willed herself to continue packing the basket. She put the fire-making materials and aurochs horn into it; then took several flint tools out of the folds of her wrap. From another fold she took a round pebble, tossed it in the air, and caught it again. Any stone of the right size could be hurled with a sling, but accuracy was better with smooth round missiles. She kept the few she had.

Then she reached for her sling, a deerskin strap with a bulge in the middle for holding stones, and long tapered ends twisted from use. No question about keeping it. She untied a long lace of leather that was wound around her soft chamois-skin wrap in such a way as to create the folds in which she carried things. The wrap came off. She stood naked except for the small leather pouch fastened to a cord around her neck – her amulet. She slipped it over her head and shivered, feeling more naked without her amulet than she did without her wrap, but the small hard objects within it were reassuring.

That was it, the sum total of her possessions, all she needed to survive – that and knowledge, skill, experience, intelligence, determination, and courage.

Quickly, she rolled up her amulet, tools, and sling in her wrap and put them in the basket, then wrapped the bearskin around it and tied it with the long thong. She enfolded the bundle with the aurochs-hide tent and tied it behind the fork of the log with the vine.

She stared at the wide river and the far shore for a while, and thought of her totem, then kicked sand on the fire and shoved the log with all her precious possessions into the river downstream of the entangling tree. Lodging herself at the forked end, Ayla grabbed the protruding stubs of former branches and launched her raft with a push.

Still chilled by melt from the glacier, the icy water enveloped her naked body. She gasped, hardly able to breathe, but a numbness set in as she became inured to her frigid element. The powerful current grabbed the log, trying to finish its job of transporting it to the sea, and tossed it between swells, but the forked branches kept it from rolling. Kicking hard, she struggled to force her way across the surging flow, and veered at an angle towards the opposite shore.

But progress was agonizingly slow. Every time she looked, the other side of the river was farther than she expected. She was moving much faster downstream than across. By the time the river swept her past the place she had thought to land, she was tired, and the cold was lowering her body temperature. She was shivering. Her muscles ached. It felt as though she had been kicking forever with rocks tied to her feet, but she forced herself to keep on.

Finally, exhausted, she surrendered to the inexorable force of the tide. The river, taking its advantage, swept the makeshift raft back in the direction of the stream, with Ayla clinging on desperately as the log now controlled her.

But ahead, the river's course was changing, its southerly direction swerving sharply west as it curved around a jutting spit of land. Ayla had traversed more than three-quarters of the way across the racing torrent before giving in to her fatigue, and when she saw the rocky shore, with a resolute effort she took control.

She forced her legs to kick, pushing to reach the land before the river carried her around the point. Closing her eyes, she concentrated on keeping her legs moving. Suddenly, with a jolt, she felt the log grate against the bottom and come to a stop.

Ayla couldn't move. Half submerged, she lay in the water still clinging to the branch stubs. A swell in the turbulent stream lifted the log free of the sharp rocks, filling the young woman with panic. She forced herself to her knees and shoved the battered tree trunk forward, anchoring it to the beach, then fell back into the water.

But she couldn't rest long. Shivering violently in the cold water, she made herself crawl onto the rocky spit. She fumbled with the knots in the vine, and, with that loosened, she hauled the bundle to the beach. The thong was even more difficult to untie with her trembling fingers.

Providence helped. The thong broke at a weak spot. She

clawed the long leather strap away, pushed the basket aside, and crawled on the bearskin and wrapped it around her. By the time her shivering stopped, the young woman was asleep.

Ayla headed north and slightly west after her perilous river crossing. The summer days warmed as she searched the open steppeland for some sign of humanity. The herbal blossoms that had brightened the brief spring faded, and the grass neared waist high.

She added alfalfa and clover to her diet, and welcomed the starchy, slightly sweet groundnuts, finding the roots by tracing rambling surface vines. Milk-vetch pods were swelling with rows of oval green vegetables in addition to edible roots, and she had no trouble distinguishing between them and their poisonous cousins. When the season for the buds of day lilies passed, the roots were still tender. A few early-ripening varieties of low-crawling currants had begun to turn colour, and there were always a few new leaves of pigweed, mustard, or nettles for greens.

Her sling did not lack for targets. Steppe pikas, souslik marmots, great jerboas, varying hares – grey brown now instead of winter white – and an occasional, omnivorous, mouse-hunting giant hamster abounded on the plains. Low-flying willow grouse and ptarmigan were a special treat, though Ayla could never eat ptarmigan without remembering that the fat birds with the feathered feet had always been Creb's favourite.

But those were only the smaller creatures feasting on the plain's summer bounty. She saw herds of deer – reindeer, red deer, and enormous antlered giant deer; compact steppe horses, asses, and onagers, which resembled both; huge bison or a family of saiga antelope occasionally crossed her path. The herd of reddish-brown wild cattle, with bulls six feet at the withers, had spring calves nursing at the ample udders of cows. Ayla's mouth watered for the taste of milk-fed veal, but her sling was not an adequate weapon to hunt aurochs. She glimpsed migrating woolly mammoths, saw musk-oxen in a phalanx with their young at their backs facing down a pack of wolves, and carefully avoided a family of evil-tempered woolly rhinoceroses. Broud's totem, she recalled, and suitable, too.

As she continued northward, the young woman began to notice a change in the terrain. It was becoming drier and more desolate. She had reached the ill-defined northern limit of the wet, snowy continental steppes. Beyond, all the way to the sheer walls of the immense northern glacier, lay the arid loess steppes, an environment that existed only when glaciers were on the land, during the Ice Age.

Glaciers, massive frozen sheets of ice that spanned the continent, mantled the Northern Hemisphere. Nearly a quarter of the earth's surface was buried under their immeasurable crushing tons. The water locked within their confines caused the level of the oceans to drop, extending the coastlines and changing the shape of the land. No portion of the globe was exempt from their influence, rains flooded equatorial regions and deserts shrank, but near the borders of the ice the effect was profound.

The vast ice field chilled the air above it, causing moisture in the atmosphere to condense and fall as snow. But nearer the centre high pressure stabilized, creating extreme dry cold and pushing the snowfall out towards the edges. The huge glaciers grew at their margins; the ice was nearly uniform across its full sweeping dimensions, a sheet of ice more than a mile thick.

With most of the snow falling on the ice and nourishing the glacier, the land just south of it was dry – and frozen. The constant high pressure over the centre caused an atmospheric chute funnelling the cold dry air towards lower pressures; wind, blowing from the north, never stopped on the steppes. It only varied in intensity. Along the way it picked up rock that had been pulverized to flour at the shifting border of the grinding glacier. The airborne particles were sifted to a texture only slightly coarser than clay – loess – and deposited over hundreds of miles to depths of many feet, and became soil.

In winter, howling winds whipped the scant snowfall across the bleak frozen land. But the earth still spun on its tilted axis, and seasons still changed. Average yearly temperatures only a few degrees lower trigger the formation of a glacier; a few hot days have little effect if they don't alter the average.

In spring the meagre snow that fell on the land melted, and

the crust of the glacier warmed, seeping down and out across the steppes. The meltwater softened the soil enough, above the permafrost, for shallow rooting grasses and herbs to sprout. The grass grew rapidly, knowing in the heart of its seeds that life would be short. By the middle of summer, it was dry standing hay, an entire continent of grassland, with scattered pockets of boreal forests and tundra nearer the oceans.

In the regions near the borders of the ice, where the snow cover was light, the grass supplied fodder the year around for uncountable millions of grazing and seed-eating animals who had adapted to the glacial cold – and to predators who can adapt to any climate that supports their prey. A mammoth could graze at the foot of a gleaming, blue white wall of ice soaring a mile or more above it.

The seasonal streams and rivers fed by glacial melt cut through the deep loess, and often through the sedimentary rock to the crystalline granite platform underlying the continent. Steep ravines and river gorges were common in the open landscape, but rivers provided moisture and gorges shelter from the wind. Even in the arid loess steppes, green valleys existed.

The season warmed, and, as one day followed the next, Ayla grew tired of travelling, tired of the monotony of the steppes, tired of the unrelenting sun and incessant wind. Her skin roughened, cracked, and peeled. Her lips were chapped, her eyes sore, her throat always full of grit. She came across an occasional river valley, greener and more wooded than the steppes, but none tempted her to stay, and all were empty of human life.

Though skies were usually clear, her fruitless search cast a shadow of fear and worry. Winter always ruled the land. On the hottest day of summer, the harsh glacial cold was never far from thought. Food had to be stockpiled and protection found to survive the long bitter season. She had been wandering since early spring and was beginning to wonder if she were doomed to roam the steppes forever – or die after all.

She made a dry camp at the end of another day that was so like the days that had gone before it. She had made a kill, but her coal was dead, and wood was getting more scarce. She ate a few bites raw rather than bothering with a fire, but she had no appetite. She threw her marmot aside, although game seemed more scarce too – or she wasn't keeping as sharp an eye out for it. Gathering was more difficult as well. The ground was hard-packed and matted with old growth. And there was always the wind.

She slept poorly, troubled by bad dreams, and awoke unrested. She had nothing to eat; even her discarded marmot was gone. She took a drink – stale and flat – packed her carrying basket, and started north.

Around noon she found a streambed with a few drying pools of water, which tasted slightly acrid, but she filled her waterbag. She dug up some cattail roots; they were stringy and bland, but she chewed on them as she plodded. She didn't want to go on, but she didn't know what else to do. Dispirited and apathetic, she wasn't paying much attention to where she was going. She didn't notice the pride of cave lions basking in the afternoon sun until one roared a warning.

Fear charged through her, tingling her into awareness. She backed up and turned west to skirt the lions' territory. She had travelled north far enough. It was the spirit of the Cave Lion that protected her, not the great beast in his physical form. Just because he was her totem did not mean she was safe from attack.

In fact, that was how Creb knew her totem was the Cave Lion. She still bore four long parallel scars on her left thigh, and had a recurring nightmare of a gigantic claw reaching into a tiny cave where she had run to hide when she was a child of five. She had dreamed about that claw the night before, she recalled. Creb had told her she had been tested to see if she was worthy, and marked to show she had been chosen. Absently, she reached down and felt the scars on her leg. I wonder why the Cave Lion would choose me, she thought.

The sun was blinding as it sunk low in the western sky. Ayla had been hiking up a long incline, looking for a place to make camp. Dry camp, again, she thought, and was glad she had filled her waterbag. But she would have to find more water soon. She was tired and hungry, and upset that she had allowed herself to get so close to the cave lions.

Was it a sign? Was it just a matter of time? What made her

27

think she could escape a death curse?

The glare on the horizon was so bright that she nearly missed the abrupt edge of the plateau. She shielded her eyes, stood on the lip, and looked down a ravine. There was a small river of sparkling water below, flanked on both sides by trees and brush. A gorge of rocky cliffs opened out into a cool, green, sheltered valley. Halfway down, in the middle of a field, the last long rays of the sun fell on a small herd of horses, grazing peacefully.

2

"Well then, why did you decide to go with me, Jondalar?" the brown-haired young man said, unstaking a tent made of several hides laced together. "You told Marona you were only going to visit Dalanar and show me the way. Just to make a short Journey before you settled down. You were supposed to go to the Summer Meeting with the Lanzadonii and be there in time for the Matrimonial. She is going to be furious, and that's one woman I wouldn't want angry at me. You sure you're not just running away from her?" Thonolan's tone was light, but the seriousness in his eyes gave him away.

"Little Brother, what makes you think you're the only one in this family with an urge to travel? You didn't think I was going to let you go off by yourself, did you? Then come home and brag about your long Journey? Someone has to go along to keep your stories straight, and keep you out of trouble," the tall blond man replied, then stooped to enter the tent.

Inside it was high enough to sit or kneel comfortably, but not to stand, and large enough for both their sleeping rolls and their gear. The tent was supported by three poles in a row down the centre, and near the middle, taller pole was a hole with a flap that could be laced closed to keep out rain, or opened to let smoke escape if they wanted a fire in the tent. Jondalar pulled up the three poles and crawled back out of the opening with them.

"Keep *me* out of trouble!" Thonolan said. "I'm going to have to grow eyes in the back of my head to watch your rear! Wait until Marona finds out you're not with Dalanar and the Lanzadonii when they get to the Meeting. She might decide to turn herself into a donii and come flying over that glacier we just crossed to get you, Jondalar." They started folding up

29

the tent between them. "That one has had her eye on you for a long time, and just when she thought she had you, you decide it's time to make a Journey. I think you just don't want to slip your hand in that thong and let Zelandoni tie the knot. I think my big brother is mating-shy." They put the tent beside the backframes. "Most men your age already have a little one, or two, at their hearths," Thonolan added, ducking a mock punch from his older brother; the laughter now had reached his grey eyes.

"Most men my age! I'm only three years older than you," Jondalar said, feigning anger. Then he laughed, a big hearty laugh, its uninhibited exuberance all the more surprising because it was unexpected.

The two brothers were as different as night and day, but it was the shorter dark-haired one who had the lighter heart. Thonolan's friendly nature, infectious grin, and easy laughter made him quickly welcome anywhere. Jondalar was more serious, his brow often knotted in concentration or worry, and though he smiled easily, especially at his brother, he seldom laughed out loud. When he did, the sheer abandon of it came as a surprise.

"And how do you know Marona won't already have a little one to bring to my hearth by the time we get back?" Jondalar said, as they began rolling up the leather ground cloth, which could be used as a smaller shelter with one of the poles.

"And how do you know she won't decide my elusive brother isn't the only man worthy of her well-known charms? Marona really knows how to please a man – when she wants to. But that temper of hers. . . . You're the only man who has ever been able to handle her, Jondalar, though Doni knows, there are plenty who would take her, temper and all." They were facing each other with the ground cloth between them. "Why haven't you mated her? Everyone's been expecting it for years."

Thonolan's question was serious. Jondalar's vivid blue eyes grew troubled and his brow wrinkled. "Maybe just because everyone expects it," he said. "I don't know, Thonolan, to be honest, I expect to mate her, too. Who else would I mate?"

"Who? Oh, just anyone you wanted, Jondalar. There isn't an unmated woman in all the Caves – and a few who are –

who wouldn't jump at the chance to tie the knot with Jondalar of the Zelandonii, brother of Joharran, leader of the Ninth Cave, not to mention brother of Thonolan, dashing and courageous adventurer."

"You forgot son of Marthona, former leader of the Ninth Cave of the Zelandonii, and brother of Folara, beautiful daughter of Marthona, or she will be when she grows up." Jondalar smiled. "If you're going to name my ties, don't forget the blessed of Doni."

"Who can forget them?" Thonolan asked, turning to the sleeping rolls, each made of two furs cut to fit each man and laced together around the sides and bottom, with a draw-string around the opening. "What are we talking about? I even think Joplaya would mate you, Jondalar."

They both started packing the rigid box-like backframes that tapered outward towards the top. They were made of stiff rawhide attached to wooden slats and held on with leather shoulder straps made adjustable by a row of carved ivory buttons. The buttons were secured by threading a thong through a single centre hole and knotting it in front to a second thong that passed back through the same hole and on to the next.

"You know we can't mate. Joplaya's my cousin. And you shouldn't take her seriously; she's a terrible tease. We became good friends when I went to live with Dalanar to learn my craft. He taught us both at the same time. She's one of the best flint knappers I know. But don't ever tell her I said so. She'd never let me forget it. We were always trying to outdo each other."

Jondalar hoisted a heavy pouch that contained his tool-making implements and a few spare chunks of flint, thinking about Dalanar and the Cave he had founded. The Lanza-donii were growing. More people had joined them since he left, and families were expanding. There will be a Second Cave of the Lanzadonii soon, he thought. He put the pouch inside his backframe, then cooking utensils, food and other equipment. His sleeping roll and tent went on top, and two of the tent poles into a holder on the left side of his pack. Thonolan carried the ground cover and the third pole. In a special holder on the right sides of their backframes, they both carried several spears.

Thonolan was filling a waterbag with snow. It was made of an animal's stomach and covered with fur. When it was very cold, as it had been on the plateau glacier over the highland they had just crossed, they carried the waterbags inside their parkas next to the skin, so body heat could melt the snow. There was no fuel for fire on a glacier. They were over it now, but not yet at a low enough elevation to find free-flowing water.

"I'll tell you, Jondalar," Thonolan said, looking up, "I am glad Joplaya is not my cousin. I think I'd give up my Journey to mate that woman. You never told me she was so beautiful. I've never seen anyone like her, a man can't keep his eyes away from her. Makes me grateful I was born to Marthona after she mated Willomar, not while she was still Dalanar's mate. At least it gives me a chance."

"I guess she is beautiful at that. I haven't seen her for three years. I expected her to be mated by now. I'm glad Dalanar has decided to take the Lanzadonii to the Zelandonii Meeting this summer. With only one Cave, there are not many to choose from. It will give Joplaya a chance to meet some other men."

"Yes, and give Marona a little competition. I almost hate to miss it when those two meet. Marona is used to being the beauty of the bunch. She is going to hate Joplaya. And with you not showing up, I have a feeling Marona is not going to enjoy this year's Summer Meeting."

"You're right, Thonolan. She's going to be hurt, and angry, and I don't blame her. She has a temper, but she's a good woman. All she needs is a man good enough for her. And she does know how to please a man. When I'm with her, I'm all ready to tie the knot, but when she's not around. . . . I don't know, Thonolan." Jondalar frowned as he pulled a belt around his parka after putting his waterbag inside.

"Tell me something," Thonolan asked, serious again. "How would you feel if she decided to mate someone else while we're gone? It's likely, you know."

Jondalar tied the belt on while he was thinking. "I'd be hurt, or my pride would – I'm not sure which. But I wouldn't blame her. I think she deserves someone better than me, someone who wouldn't leave her to go off on a Journey at the last moment. And if she's happy, I'd be happy for her."

"That's what I thought," the younger brother said. Then he broke into a grin. "Well, Big Brother, if we're going to keep ahead of that donii that's coming after you, we'd better get moving." Thonolan finished loading his back-frame, then lifted his fur parka and slipped an arm out of the sleeve to hang the waterbag over his shoulder under-neath it.

The parkas were cut from a simple pattern. Front and back were more or less rectangular pieces laced together at the sides and shoulders, with two smaller rectangles folded and sewn into tubes and attached as sleeves. Hoods, also attached, had a fringe of wolverine fur around the face since ice from moisture in the breath would not cling to it. The parkas were richly decorated with beadwork of bone, ivory, shell, animal teeth, and black-tipped white ermine tails. They slipped on over the head and hung loosely like tunics to about midway down the thigh, and were cinched around the waist with a belt.

Under the parkas were soft buckskin shirts made from a similar pattern, and trousers of fur, flapped over in front and held on with a drawstring around the waist. Fur-lined mittens were attached to a long cord that went through a loop at the back of the parka so they could be quickly removed without dropping or losing them. Their boots had heavy soles that, like moccasins, went up around the foot, and were fastened to softer leather that conformed to the leg and was folded over and wrapped with thongs. Inside was a loose-fitting liner of felt, made from the wool of mouflon that was wetted and pounded together until it matted. When it was especially wet, waterproof animal intestines, made to fit, were worn over the boot, but they were thin, wore out quickly, and were used only when necessary.

"Thonolan, how far do you really plan to go? You didn't mean it when you said all the way to the end of the Great Mother River, did you?" Jondalar asked, picking up a flint axe hafted to a short, sturdy, shaped handle and putting it through a loop on his belt next to the bone-handled flint knife.

Thonolan stopped in the process of fitting on a snowshoe and stood up. "Jondalar, I meant it," he said, without a hint of his usual joking.

"We may not even make it back for next year's Summer Meeting!"

"Are you having second thoughts? You don't have to come with me, Brother. I'm serious. I won't be angry if you turn back – it was a last-moment decision for you anyway. You know as well as I do, we may never get back home again. But if you want to go, you'd better do it now or you'll never make it back across that glacier until next winter."

"No, it wasn't a last-moment decision, Thonolan. I've been thinking about making a Journey for a long time, and this is the right time for it," Jondalar said with a tone of finality, and, Thonolan thought, a shade of unaccountable bitterness in his voice. Then, as though he were trying to shrug it off, Jondalar shifted to a lighter tone. "I never have made much of a Journey, and if I don't now, I never will. I made my choice, Little Brother, you're stuck with me."

The sky was clear, and the sun reflecting the white expanse of virgin snow before them was blinding. It was spring, but at their elevation the landscape showed no sign of it. Jondalar reached into a pouch hanging from his belt and pulled out a pair of snow goggles. They were made of wood, shaped to cover the eyes completely except for a thin horizontal slit, and tied around the head. Then, with a quick twist of the foot to wrap the thong loop into a snowshoe hitch around toe and ankle, he stepped into his snowshoes and reached for his backframe.

Thonolan had made the snowshoes. Spearmaking was his craft, and he carried with him his favourite shaft straightener, an implement made of an antler with the branching tines removed and a hole at one end. It was intricately carved with animals and plants of spring, partly to honour the Great Earth Mother and persuade Her to allow the spirits of the animals to be drawn to the spears made from the tool, but also because Thonolan enjoyed the carving for its own sake. It was inevitable that they would lose spears while hunting, and new ones would have to be made along the way. The straightener was used particularly at the end of the shaft where a hand grip was not possible, and by inserting the shaft through the hole, additional leverage was obtained. Thonolan knew how to apply stress to wood, heated with hot stones or steam, to straighten a shaft or to bend one around to make a snowshoe. They were different aspects of the same skill.

Jondalar turned to see if his brother was ready. With a nod, they both started out, and tramped down the gradual slope towards the timberline below. On their right, across forested lowland, they saw the snow-covered alpine foreland and, in the distance, the jagged icy peaks of the northernmost ridge of the massive mountain range. Towards the southeast, one tall peak was shining high above its brethren.

The highland they had crossed was hardly more than a hill by comparison, a massif that was the stump of eroded mountains far more ancient than the soaring peaks to the south. But it was just high enough and just close enough to the rugged range with its massive glaciers – that not only crowned but mantled the mountains down to moderate elevations – to maintain a year-around ice cover on its relatively level top. Someday, when the continental glacier receded back to its polar home, that highland would be black with forest. Now, it was a plateau glacier, a miniature version of the immense globe-spanning ice sheets to the north.

When the two brothers reached the treeline, they removed their goggles, which protected the eyes but limited visibility. Somewhat farther down the slope, they found a small stream that had begun as glacial melt seeping through fissures in the rock, flowed underground, then emerged filtered and cleared of silt in a sparkling spring. It trickled between snowy banks like many other small glacial runoffs.

"What do you think?" Thonolan asked, gesturing towards the stream. "It's about where Dalanar said she would be."

"If that's Donau, we should know soon enough. We'll know we are following the Great Mother River when we reach three small rivers that come together and flow east; that's what he said. I'd guess almost any of these runoffs should lead us to her eventually."

"Well, let's keep to the left now. Later she won't be so easy to cross."

"That's true, but the Losadunai live on the right, and we can stop at one of their Caves. The left side is supposed to be flathead country."

"Jondalar, let's not stop at the Losadunai," Thonolan said with an earnest smile. "You know they'll want us to stay, and we stayed too long already with the Lanzadonii. If we'd left much later, we wouldn't have been able to cross the glacier at all. We would have had to go around, and north if it is really flathead country. I want to get moving, and there won't be many flatheads this far south. And so what if there are? You're not afraid of a few flatheads, are you? You know what they say, killing a flathead is like killing a bear."

"I don't know," the tall man said, his worry lines puckered. "I'm not sure I'd want to tangle with a bear. I've heard flatheads are clever. Some people say they are almost human."

"Clever, maybe, but they can't talk. They're just animals."

"It's not the flatheads I'm worried about, Thonolan. The Losadunai know this country. They can get us started right. We don't have to stay long, just long enough to get our bearings. They can give us some landmarks, some idea of what to expect. And we can talk to them. Dalanar said some of them speak Zelandonii. I'll tell you what, if you agree to stop now, I'll agree to pass the next Caves by until the way back."

"All right. If you really want to."

The two men looked for a place to cross the ice-banked stream, already too wide to jump. They saw a tree that had fallen across, making a natural bridge, and headed for it. Jondalar led the way, and, reaching for a handhold, he put a foot on one of the exposed roots. Thonolan glanced around, waiting his turn.

"Jondalar! Look out!" he cried suddenly.

A stone whizzed past the tall man's head. As he dropped to the ground at the warning cry, his hand reached for a spear. Thonolan already had one in his hand and was crouching low, looking in the direction from which the stone had come. He saw movement behind the tangled branches of a leafless bush and let fly. He was reaching for another spear when six figures stepped out from the nearby brush. They were surrounded.

"Flatheads!" Thonolan cried, pulling back and taking aim.

"Wait, Thonolan!" Jondalar shouted. "They've got us outnumbered."

"The big one looks like the leader of the pack. If I get him, the rest may run." He pulled back his arm again.

"No! They may rush us before we can reach for a second spear. Right now I think we're holding them off – they're not making a move." Jondalar slowly got to his feet, keeping his weapon ready. "Don't move, Thonolan. Let them make the next move. But keep your eyes on the big one. He can see you're aiming for him."

Jondalar studied the big flathead and had the disconcerting feeling that the large brown eyes staring back were studying him. He had never been so close to one before, and he was surprised. These flatheads did not quite fit his preconceived ideas of them. The big one's eyes were shaded by overhanging brow ridges that were accentuated by bushy eyebrows. His nose was large, narrow, rather like a beak, and contributed to making his eyes seem more deep-set. His beard, thick and tending to curl, hid his face. It was on a younger one, whose beard was just beginning, that he saw they had no chins, just protruding jaws. Their hair was brown and bushy, like their beards, and they tended to have more body hair especially around the upper back.

He could tell they had more hair because their fur wraps covered mainly their torsos, leaving shoulders and arms bare despite the nearly freezing temperature. But their scantier covering didn't surprise him nearly as much as the fact that they wore clothing at all. No animals he'd ever seen wore clothes, and none ever carried weapons. Yet each one of these had a long wooden spear – obviously meant to be jabbed, not thrown, though the sharpened points looked wicked enough – and some carried heavy bone clubs, the forelegs of large grazing animals.

Their jaws aren't really like an animal's, Jondalar thought. They just come forward more, and their noses are just large noses. Their heads are the real difference.

Rather than full high foreheads, like his and Thonolan's, their foreheads were low and sloped back above their heavy brow ridges to a large fullness at the rear. It seemed as though the tops of their heads, which he could easily see, had been flattened down and pushed back. When Jondalar stood up to his full six foot six inches, he towered over the biggest one by more than a foot. Even Thonolan's mere six feet made him seem a giant beside the one who was, apparently, their leader, but only in height.

Jondalar and his brother were both well-built men, but they felt scrawny beside the powerfully muscled flatheads. They had large barrel chests and thick, muscular arms and legs, both bowed somewhat in an outward curvature, but they walked as straight and comfortably upright as any man. The more he looked, the more they seemed like men, just not like any men he'd seen before.

For a long tense moment, no one moved. Thonolan crouched with his spear, ready to throw; Jondalar was standing, but with his spear firmly gripped so it could follow his brother's the next instant. The six flatheads surrounding them were as unmoving as stones, but Jondalar had no doubts about how quickly they could spring into action. It was an impasse, a stand-off, and Jondalar's mind raced trying to think of a way out of it.

Suddenly, the big flathead made a grunting sound and waved his arm. Thonolan almost threw his spear, but he caught Jondalar's gesture waving him back just in time. Only the young flathead had moved, running back into the bushes they had just stepped out of. He returned quickly, carrying the spear Thonolan had thrown, and, to his amazement, brought it to him. Then the young one went to the river near the log bridge and fished out a stone. He returned to the big one with it and seemed to bow his head, looking contrite. The next instant, all six melted back into the brush without a sound.

Thonolan breathed a sigh of relief when he realized they were gone. "I didn't think we were going to get out of that one! I wonder what that was all about?"

"I'm not sure," Jondalar replied, "but it could be that young one started something the big one didn't want to finish, and I don't think it was because he was afraid. It took nerve to stand there and face your spear, and then make the move he did."

"Maybe he just didn't know any better."

"He knew. He saw you throw that first spear. Why else would he tell that youngster to go get it and give it back to you?"

"You really think he told him to do it? How? They can't talk."

"I don't know, but somehow that big one told the young one to give you back your spear and get his stone. Like that would make everything even. No one was hurt, so I guess it did. You know, I'm not so sure flatheads are just animals. That was smart. And I didn't know they wore furs and carried weapons, and walked just like we do."

"Well, I know why they're called flatheads! And they were a mean-looking bunch. I would not want to tangle with one of them hand to hand."

"I know – they look like they could break your arm like a piece of kindling. I always thought they were small."

"Short, maybe, but not small. Definitely not small. Big Brother, I've got to admit, you were right. Let's go visit the Losadunai. They live so close, they must know more about flatheads. Besides, the Great Mother River seems to be a boundary, and I don't think flatheads want us on their side."

The two men hiked for several days looking for landmarks given them by Dalanar, following the stream that was no different in character at this stage than the other streamlets, rills, and creeks flowing down the slope. It was only convention that selected this particular one as the source of the Great Mother River. Most of them came together to form the beginning of the great river that would rush down hills and meander through plains for eighteen hundred miles before she emptied her load of water and silt into the inland sea far to the southeast.

The crystalline rocks of the massif that gave rise to the mighty river were among the most ancient on the earth, and its broad depression was formed by the extravagant pressures that had heaved up and folded the rugged mountains glistening in prodigal splendour. More than three hundred tributaries, many of them large rivers, draining the slopes of the ranges all along her course, would be gathered into her voluminous swells. And one day her fame would spread to the far reaches of the globe, and her muddy, silty waters would be called blue.

Modified by mountains and massifs, the influence of both the oceanic west and the continental east was felt. Vegetable and animal life were a mixture of the western tundra-taiga and the eastern steppes. The upper slopes saw ibex, chamois, and mouflon; in the woodlands deer were more common. Tarpan, a wild horse that would one day be tame, grazed the sheltered lowlands and river terraces. Wolves, lynxes, and snow leopards slunk noiselessly through shadows. Lumbering out of hibernation were omnivorous brown bears; the huge vegetarian cave bears would make a later appearance. And many small mammals were poking noses out of winter nests.

The slopes were forested mostly with pine, though spruce, silver fir, and larch were seen. Alder was more prevalent near the river, often with willow and poplar, and rarely, dwarfed to little more than prostate shrubs, pubescent oak and beech.

The left bank ascended from the river in a gradual grade. Jondalar and Thonolan climbed it until they reached the summit of a high hill. Looking out over the landscape, the two men saw rugged, wild, beautiful country, softened by the layer of white that filled hollows and smoothed outcrops. But the deception made travelling difficult.

They had not seen any of the several groups of people – such groups were thought of as Caves whether they lived in one or not – who referred to themselves as Losadunai. Jondalar was beginning to think they had missed them.

"Look!" Thonolan pointed.

Jondalar followed the direction of his outstretched arm and saw a wisp of smoke rising out of a wooded copse. They hurried ahead and soon came upon a small band of people clustered around a fire. The brothers strode into their midst raising both hands in front of them, palms up, in the understood greeting of openness and friendship.

"I am Thonolan of the Zelandonii. This is my brother, Jondalar. We are on our Journey. Does anyone here speak our tongue?"

A middle-aged man stepped forward, holding his hands out in the same manner. "I am Laduni of the Losadunai. In the name of Duna, the Great Earth Mother, you are welcome." He gripped both of Thonolan's hands with his and then greeted Jondalar in the same manner. "Come, sit by the fire. We will eat soon. Will you join us?"

"You are most generous," Jondalar replied formally.

"I travelled west on my Journey, stayed with a Cave of

Zelandonii. It's been some years, but Zelandonii are always welcome." He led them to a large log near the fire. A lean-to had been constructed over it as protection from wind and weather. "Here, rest, take your pack off. You must have just come off the glacier."

"A few days ago," Thonolan said, shrugging off his back-frame.

"You are late for crossing. The foehn will come any time now."

"The foehn?" Thonolan asked.

"The spring wind. Warm and dry, out of the southwest. It blows so hard trees are uprooted, limbs torn off. But it melts the snow very quickly. Within days, all this can be gone and buds starting," Laduni explained, moving his arm in a broad sweep to indicate the snow. "If it catches you on the glacier, it can be fatal. The ice melts so quickly, crevasses open up. Snow bridges and cornices give way beneath your feet. Streams, even rivers, start flowing across the ice."

"And it always brings the Malaise," a young woman added, picking up the thread of Laduni's story.

"Malaise?" Thonolan directed his question to her.

"Evil spirits that fly on the wind. They make everyone irritable. People who never fight suddenly start arguing. Happy people are crying all the time. The spirits can make you sick, or if you are already sick, they can make you want to die. It helps if you know what to expect, but everyone is in a bad mood then."

"Where did you learn to speak Zelandonii so well?" Thonolan asked, smiling at the attractive young woman appreciatively.

The young woman returned Thonolan's look as frankly, but rather than answering, looked over to Laduni.

"Thonolan of the Zelandonii, this is Filonia of the Losa-dunai, and the daughter of my hearth," Laduni said, quick to understand her unspoken request for a formal introduction. It let Thonolan know she thought well of herself and didn't converse with strangers without proper introductions, not even handsome exciting strangers on a Journey.

Thonolan held out his hands in the formal greeting ges-ture, his eyes appraising and showing approval. She hesi-tated a moment, as though considering, then put her hands

41

in his. He pulled her closer. "Filonia of the Losadunai, Thonolan of the Zelandonii is honoured the Great Earth Mother has favoured him with the gift of your presence," he said with a knowing grin.

Filonia flushed slightly at the bold innuendo she knew he intended with his allusion to the Gift of the Mother, though his words were as formal as his gesture seemed to be. She felt a tingle of excitement from his touch, and the sparkle of invitation was in her eyes.

"Now tell me," Thonolan continued, "where did you learn Zelandonii?"

"My cousin and I went across the glacier on our Journey and lived for a while with a Zelandonii Cave. Laduni had already taught us some – he talks with us often in your tongue so he won't forget it. He crosses every few years to trade. He wanted me to learn more."

Thonolan still held her hands and smiled at her. "Women don't often make long and dangerous Journeys. What if Doni had blessed you?"

"It wasn't really that long," she said, pleased with his obvious admiration. "I would have known soon enough to get back."

"It was as long a Journey as many men make," he insisted.

Jondalar, watching the interplay, turned to Laduni. "He's done it again," he said, grinning. "My brother never fails to single out the most attractive woman in sight and have her charmed within the first three heartbeats."

Laduni chuckled. "Filonia's young yet. She only had her Rites of First Pleasures last summer, but she's had enough admirers since then to turn her head. Ah, to be young again, and new to the Gift of Pleasure from the Great Earth Mother. Not that I don't enjoy it still, but I'm comfortable with my mate and don't have the same urge to seek new excitement often." He turned to the tall blond man. "We're just a hunting party and don't have many women with us, but you shouldn't have any problem finding one of our blessed of Duna willing to share the Gift. If none suits you, we have a large Cave, and visitors are always a reason for a festival to honour the Mother."

"I'm afraid we won't be going with you to your Cave. We've just started. Thonolan wants to make a long Journey and is anxious to get moving. Perhaps on our way back, if you'll give us directions."

"I'm sorry you won't be visiting – we haven't had many visitors lately. How far do you plan to go?"

"Thonolan talks about following Donau all the way to the end. But everyone talks about a long Journey when they begin. Who can tell?"

"I thought the Zelandonii lived close to the Great Water; at least they did when I made my Journey. I travelled a long way west, and then south. Did you say you just started out?"

"I should explain. You're right, the Great Water is only a few days from our Cave, but Dalanar of the Lanzadonii was mated to my mother when I was born, and his Cave is like home to me, too. I lived there for three years while he taught me my craft. My brother and I stayed with them. The only distance we've travelled since we left is across the glacier, and the couple of days to get there."

"Dalanar! Of course! I thought you looked familiar. You must be a child of his spirit; you look so much like him. And a flint knapper, too. If you are as much like him as you look, you must be good. He's the best I've ever seen. I was going to visit him next year to get some flint from the Lanzadonii mine. There is no better stone."

People were gathering around the fire with wooden bowls, and the delicious smells coming from that direction made Jondalar conscious of his hunger. He picked up his back-frame to move it out of the way, then had a thought. "Laduni, I have some Lanzadonii flint with me. I was going to use it to replace broken tools along the way, but it's heavy to carry, and I wouldn't mind unloading a stone or two. I'd be happy to give it to you if you'd like it."

Laduni's eyes lit up. "I'd be happy to take it, but I'd want to give you something in return. I don't mind getting the better side of a good trade, but I wouldn't want to cheat the son of Dalanar's hearth."

Jondalar grinned. "You're already offering to lighten my load and feed me a hot meal."

"That's hardly enough for good Lanzadonii stone. You make it too easy, Jondalar. You hurt my pride."

A good-natured crowd was gathering around them, and

when Jondalar laughed, they joined in.

"All right, Laduni, I won't make it easy. Right now, there's nothing I want – I'm trying to lighten my load. I'll ask you for a future claim. Are you willing?"

"Now he wants to cheat me," the man said to the crowd, grinning. "At least name it."

"How can I name it? But I'll want to collect it on my way back, agreed?"

"How do I know I can give it?"

"I won't ask what you can't give."

"Your terms are hard, Jondalar, but if I can, I'll give you whatever you ask. Agreed."

Jondalar opened his backframe, took out the things on top, then pulled out his pouch and gave Laduni two nodules of flint already prepared. "Dalanar selected them and did the preliminary work," he said.

Laduni's expression made it obvious he didn't mind getting two pieces of flint selected and prepared by Dalanar for the son of his hearth, but he mumbled, loud enough for everyone to hear, "I'm probably trading my life for two pieces of stone." No one made any comment about the probability of Jondalar ever returning to collect.

"Jondalar, are you going to stand around talking forever?" Thonolan said. "We've been asked to share a meal, and that venison smells good." He had a big grin on his face, and Filonia was by his side.

"Yes, the food is ready," she said, "and the hunting has been so good, we haven't used much of the dried meat we took with us. Now that you've lightened your load, you'll have room to take some with you, won't you?" she added with a sly smile at Laduni.

"It would be most welcome. Laduni, you have yet to introduce me to the lovely daughter of your hearth," Jondalar said.

"It's a terrible day when the daughter of your own hearth undermines your trades," he mumbled, but his smile was full of pride. "Jondalar of the Zelandonii, Filonia of the Losadunai."

She turned to look at the older brother, and suddenly found herself lost in overwhelmingly vivid blue eyes smiling down at her. She flushed with mixed emotions as she found herself drawn now to the other brother, and bowed her head to hide her confusion.

"Jondalar! Don't think I can't see that gleam in your eyes. Remember, I saw her first," Thonolan joked. "Come on, Filonia, I'm going to get you away from here. Let me warn you, stay away from that brother of mine. Believe me, you don't want to have anything to do with him, I know." He turned to Laduni and said in mock injury, "He does it every time. One look, that's all it takes. If only I had been born with my brother's gifts."

"You've got more gifts than any man needs, Little Brother," Jondalar said, then laughed his big, lusty, warm laugh.

Filonia turned back to Thonolan and seemed relieved to find him just as attractive as she had at first. He put his arm around her shoulder and steered her towards the other side of the fire, but she turned her head back to look at the other man. Smiling more confidently, she said, "We always have a festival to honour Duna when visitors come to the Cave."

"They won't be coming to the Cave, Filonia," Laduni said. The young woman looked disappointed for a moment, then turned to Thonolan and smiled.

"Ah, to be young again," Laduni chuckled. "But the women who honour Duna most seem to be blessed more often with young ones. The Great Earth Mother smiles on those who appreciate Her Gifts."

Jondalar moved his backframe behind the log, then headed towards the fire. A venison stew was cooking in a pot that was a leather skin supported by a frame of bones lashed together. It was suspended directly over the fire. The boiling liquid, though hot enough to cook the stew, kept the temperature of the cooking container too low to catch fire. The combustion temperature of leather was much hotter than the boiling stew.

A woman handed him a wooden bowl of the savoury broth and sat down beside him on the log. He used his flint knife to spear the chunks of meat and vegetables – dried pieces of roots they had brought – and drank the liquid from the bowl. When he was through, the woman brought him a smaller bowl of herb tea. He smiled at her in thanks. She was a few years older than he, enough to have exchanged the prettiness of youth for the true beauty brought by maturity. She smiled back and sat beside him again.

"Do you speak Zelandonii?" he asked.

"Speak little, understand more," she said.

"Should I ask Laduni to introduce us, or can I ask your name?"

She smiled again, with the hint of condescension of the older woman. "Only young girls need someone say name. I, Lanalia. You, Jondalar?"

"Yes," he answered. He could feel the warmth of her leg and the excitement it raised showed in his eyes. She returned his gaze with a smouldering look. He moved his hand to her thigh. She leaned closer with a movement that encouraged him and promised experience. He nodded acceptance to her inviting look, though it wasn't necessary. His eyes returned her invitation. She glanced over his shoulder. Jondalar followed her gaze and saw Laduni coming towards them. She relaxed comfortably beside him. They would wait until later to fulfil the promise.

Laduni joined them, and shortly after, Thonolan came back to his brother's side of the fire with Filonia. Soon everyone was crowded around the two visitors. There was joking and banter, translated for those who could not understand. Finally, Jondalar decided to bring up a more serious subject. "Do you know much about the people down the river, Laduni?"

"We used to get an occasional visitor from the Sarmunai. They live north of the river downstream, but it's been years. It happens. Sometimes young people all go the same way on their Journeys. Then it becomes well known and not so exciting, so they go another way. After a generation or so, only the old ones remember, and it becomes an adventure to go the first way again. All young people think their discoveries are new. It doesn't matter if their ancestors did the same thing."

"For them it is new," Jondalar said but didn't pursue the philosophical lead. "Can you tell me anything about their customs? Do you know any words in their language? Greetings? What should we avoid? What might be offensive?"

"I don't know much, and nothing recent. There was a man who went east a few years ago, but he hasn't returned. Who

46

knows, maybe he decided to settle some other place," Laduni said. "It's said they make their dunai out of mud, but that's just talk. I don't know why anyone would make sacred images of the Mother out of mud. It would just crumble when it dried."

"Maybe because it's closer to the earth. Some people like stone for that reason."

As he spoke, Jondalar unconsciously reached into the pouch attached to his belt and felt for the small stone figurine of an obese female. He felt the familiar huge breasts, her large protruding stomach, and her more than ample buttocks and thighs. The arms and legs were insignificant, it was the Mother aspects that were important, and the limbs on the stone figure were only suggested. The head was a knob with a suggestion of hair that carried across the face, with no features.

No one could look at the awesome face of Doni, the Great Earth Mother, Ancient Ancestress, First Mother, Creator and Sustainer of all life. She who blessed all women with Her power to create and bring forth life. And none of the small images of Her that carried Her Spirit, the donii, ever dared to suggest Her face. Even when She revealed Herself in dreams, Her face was usually unclear, though men often saw Her with a young and nubile body. Some women claimed they could take Her spirit form and fly like the wind to bring luck or wreak vengeance, and Her vengeance could be great.

If She was angered or dishonoured, She was capable of many fearful deeds, but the most threatening was to withhold Her wondrous Gift of Pleasure that came when a woman chose to open herself to a man. The Great Mother and, it was claimed, some of Those Who Served Her could give a man the power to share Her Gift with as many women as he desired as often as he wished, or make him shrivel up so that he could bring Pleasure to none, nor find any himself.

Jondalar absent-mindedly caressed the pendulous stone breasts of the donii in his pouch, wishing for luck as he thought about their Journey. It was true that some never returned, but that was part of the adventure. Then Thonolan asked Laduni a question that snapped him back to attention.

"What do you know about the flatheads around here? We

ran into a pack a few days ago. I was sure we were going to end our Journey right there." Suddenly Thonolan had everyone's attention.

"What happened?" Laduni asked, tension in his voice. Thonolan related the incident they had had with the flatheads.

"Charoli!" Laduni spat.

"Who is Charoli?" Jondalar asked.

"A young man from Tomasi's Cave, and the instigator of a gang of ruffians who have taken it into their heads to make sport of the flatheads. We never had any trouble with them. They stayed on their side of the river; we stayed on ours. If we did cross over, they kept out of the way, unless we stayed too long. Then all they did was make it obvious they were watching. That was enough. It makes you nervous to have a bunch of flatheads staring at you."

"That's for sure!" Thonolan said. "But what do you mean, make sport of the flatheads? I wouldn't invite trouble from them."

"It all started as high spirits. One would dare the other to run up and touch a flathead. They can be pretty fierce if you annoy them. Then the young men started ganging up on any flathead they found alone – circle around and tease him, try to get him to chase after them. Flatheads have a lot of wind, but they have short legs. A man can usually outrun one, but he'd better keep going. I'm not sure how it started, but next Charoli's gang were beating up on them. I suspect one of those flatheads they were teasing caught someone, and the rest jumped in to defend their friend. Anyway, they started making a practice of it, but even with several against one flathead, they didn't get away without some good bruises."

"I can believe that," Thonolan said.

"What they did next was even worse," Filonia added.

"Filonia! It's disgusting! I won't have you talking about it!" Laduni said, and his anger was real.

"What did they do?" Jondalar asked. "If we're going to be travelling through flathead territory, we ought to know."

"I suppose you're right, Jondalar. I just don't like talking about it in front of Filonia."

"I'm a grown woman," she asserted, but her tone lacked conviction.

He looked at her, considering, then seemed to come to a decision. "The males started coming out only in pairs or groups, and that was too much for Charoli's gang. So they started trying to tease the females. But flathead females don't fight. There's no sport in picking on them, they just cower and run away. So his gang decided to use them for a different kind of sport. I don't know who dared who first – probably Charoli goaded them on. It's the kind of thing he'd do."

"Goaded them to do what?" Jondalar asked.

"They started forcing flathead females. . ." Laduni could not finish. He jumped up, more than angry. He was enraged. "It's an abomination! It dishonours the Mother, abuses Her Gift. Animals! Worse than animals! Worse than flatheads!"

"Do you mean they took their Pleasure with a flathead female? Forced? A flathead female?" Thonolan said.

"They bragged about it!" Filonia said. "I wouldn't let a man near me who took his Pleasure with a flathead."

"Filonia! You will not discuss such things! I will not have such filthy, disgusting language coming out of your mouth!" Laduni said. He was past rage; his eyes were hard as stone.

"Yes, Laduni," she said, bowing her head in shame.

"I wonder how they feel about it," Jondalar commented. "That might be why the young one went for me. I'd guess they'd be angry. I've heard some people say they could be human – and if they are. . ."

"I've heard that kind of talk!" Laduni said, still trying to calm himself. "Don't believe it!"

"The leader of that pack we ran into was smart, and they walk on their legs just as we do."

"Bears walk on their hind legs sometimes, too. Flatheads are animals! Intelligent animals, but animals." Laduni struggled to get himself under control, aware that the whole group was uncomfortable. "They're usually harmless unless you bother them," he continued. "I don't think it's the females – I doubt if they understand how it dishonours the Mother. It's all the baiting and beating up. If animals are annoyed enough, they'll strike out."

"I think Charoli's gang has made some problems for us," Thonolan said. "We wanted to cross over to the right bank so we wouldn't have to worry about crossing her later when she's the Great Mother River."

Laduni smiled. Now that they were on another subject, his rage left as quickly as it had come. "The Great Mother River has tributaries that are big rivers, Thonolan. If you are going to follow her all the way to the end, you're going to have to get used to crossing rivers. Let me make a suggestion. Keep to this side until after the big whirlpool. She separates into channels as she goes across some flat land, and smaller branches are easier to cross than one big river. By then, it'll be warmer, too. If you want to visit the Sarmunai, go north after you cross."

"How far is it to the whirlpool?" Jondalar asked.

"I'll scratch out a map for you," Laduni said, taking out his flint knife. "Lanalia, give me that piece of bark. Maybe some of the others can add some landmarks farther on. Allowing for river crossings and hunting along the way, you should make it to the place where the river turns south by summer."

"Summer," Jondalar mused. "I'm so tired of ice and snow, I can hardly wait until summer. I could use some warmth." He noticed Lanalia's leg next to his again, and put his hand on her thigh.

3

The first stars pierced the evening sky as Ayla carefully picked her way down the steep rocky side of the ravine. As soon as she cleared the edge, the wind ceased abruptly, and she stopped for a moment to savour its absence. But the walls cut off the failing light as well. By the time she reached the bottom, the dense brush along the small river was a tangled silhouette seen against the moving reflection of the myriad shining points above.

She took a deep refreshing drink from the river, then felt her way into the deeper black near the wall. She didn't bother with the tent, just spread out her fur and rolled up in it, feeling more secure with a wall at her back than she had on the open plains under her tent. She watched a gibbous moon show its nearly full face over the edge of the ravine before she fell asleep.

She woke up screaming!

She bolted upright – stark terror charging through her, pounding in her temples, and racing her heart – and stared at vague shapes in the black-on-black void in front of her. She jumped as a sharp crack and a simultaneous flash of light blinded her. Shuddering, she watched a tall pine, struck by the searing bolt, split and slowly, still clinging to its severed half, fall to the ground. It was surreal, the flaming tree lighting its own death scene and casting grotesque shadows on the wall behind.

The fire sputtered and hissed as drenching rain doused it. Ayla huddled closer to the wall, oblivious still to both her warm tears and the cold drops splattering her face. The first distant thunder, reminiscent of an earth-shaking rumble, had kindled another recurring dream from the ashes of hidden memory; a nightmare she never could quite remember when she awoke and that always left her with a nauseous sense of uneasiness and overwhelming grief. Another bright shaft, followed by a loud roar, momentarily filled the black void with eerie brightness, giving her a flashing glimpse of the steep walls and the jagged tree trunk snapped like a twig by the powerful finger of light from the sky.

Shivering as much from fear as from the wet, penetrating cold, she clutched her amulet, reaching for anything that promised protection. It was a reaction only partly caused by the thunder and lightning. Ayla didn't like thunderstorms much, but she was accustomed to them; they were often more helpful than destructive. She was still feeling the emotional aftermath of her earthquake nightmare. Earthquakes were an evil that had never failed to bring devastating loss and wrenching change into her life, and there was nothing she feared more.

Finally she realized she was wet and took her hide tent out of her carrying basket. She pulled it over her sleeping fur like a cover and buried her head beneath it. She was still shaking long after she warmed up, but as the night wore on the fearful storm abated, and she finally slept.

Birds filled the early morning air with twitterings, chirpings, and raucous caws. Ayla pulled back the cover and looked around her with delight. A world of green, still wet from the rain, glittered in the morning sun. She was on a broad rocky beach at a place where a small river took a turn towards the east in its winding, generally southward course.

On the opposite bank, a row of dark green pines reached to the top of the wall behind them but no farther. Any tentative strivings above the lip of the river gorge were cut short by the slashing winds of the steppes above. It gave the tallest trees a peculiar blunted look, their growth forced to branching fullness. One soaring giant of near perfect symmetry, spoiled only by a spire growing at right angles to the trunk, grew beside another with a charred, jagged, high stump clinging to its inverted top. The trees were growing on a narrow strip on the other side of the river between the bank and the wall, some so close to the water that bare roots were exposed.

On her side, upstream of the rocky beach, supple willows arched over, weeping long, pale green leaf-tears into the stream. The flattened stems on the tall aspens made the leaves quiver in the gentle breeze. White-barked birches grew in clumps while their alder cousins were only high shrubs. Lianas climbed and twined around the trees, and bushes of many varieties in full leaf crowded close to the stream.

Ayla had travelled the parched and withered steppes so long she had forgotten how beautiful green could be. The small river sparkled an invitation, and, her fears of the storm forgotten, she jumped up and ran across the beach. A drink was her first thought; then, impulsively, she untied the long thong of her wrap, took off her amulet, and splashed into the water. The bank dropped off quickly and she dived under, then swam to the steep opposite side.

The water was cool and refreshing, and washing off the dust and grime of the steppes was a welcome pleasure. She swam upstream and felt the current growing stronger and the water chilling as the sheer walls closed in, narrowing the river. She rolled over on her back and, cradled by the buoyant water, let the flow carry her downstream. She gazed up at deep azure filling the space between the high cliffs, then noticed a dark hole in the wall across from the beach upstream. Could that be a cave? she thought with a surge of excitement. I wonder if it would be hard to reach?

The young woman waded back to the beach and sat down on the warm stones to let the sun dry her. Her eye was drawn by the quick perky gestures of birds hopping on the ground near the brush, pulling on worms brought close to the surface by the night's rain, and flitting from branch to branch feeding on bushes heavy with berries.

Look at those raspberries! They're so big, she thought. A flurry of wings welcomed her approach, then settled nearby. She stuffed handfuls of the sweet juicy berries in her mouth. After she had her fill, she rinsed off her hands and put her amulet on, but wrinkled her nose at her grimy, stained, and sweaty wrap. She had no other. When she had gone back into the earthquake-littered cave just before she left, to get clothing, food, and shelter, survival had been her concern, not whether she would need a change of summer wraps.

And she was thinking survival again. Her hopeless thoughts on the dry and dreary steppes were dispelled by the fresh green valley. The raspberries had stimulated her appetite rather than satisfying it. She wanted something more substantial and walked to her sleeping place to get her sling. She spread out her wet hide tent and damp fur on the sun-warmed stones, then put on her soiled wrap and began looking for smooth round pebbles.

Close inspection revealed the beach held more than stones. It was also strewn with dull grey driftwood and bleached white bones, many of them piled in a huge mound against a jutting wall. Violent spring floods had uprooted trees and swept away unwary animals, hurled them through the narrow constriction of sheer rock upstream, and slammed them against a cul-de-sac in the near wall as the swirling water tore around the bend. Ayla saw giant antlers, long bison horns, and several enormous, curving ivory tusks in the heap; not even the great mammoth was immune to the force of the tide. Large boulders were mixed in the deposit, too, but the woman's eyes narrowed when she saw several medium-sized, chalky grey stones.

This is flint! she said to herself after a closer look. I'm sure of it. I need a hammerstone to break one open, but I'm just sure of it. Excitedly, Ayla scanned the beach for a smooth oval stone she could hold comfortably in her hand. When she found one, she struck the chalky outer covering of the nodule. A piece of the whitish cortex broke off, exposing the dull sheen of the dark grey stone within.

It is flint! I knew it was! Her mind raced with thoughts of the tools she could make. I can even make some spares. Then I won't have to worry so much about breaking something. She lugged over a few more of the heavy stones, flushed out of the chalk deposits far upstream and carried by surging current until they came to rest at the foot of the stone wall. The discovery encouraged her to explore further.

She walked around the wall and stopped. Spread out before her was the valley she had glimpsed from above.

The river broadened beyond the bend, and bubbled over and around rocks exposed by shallower water. It flowed east at the foot of the steep opposite wall of the gorge. Along its near bank trees and brush protected from the cutting wind grew to their full luxuriant height. On her left, beyond the stone barrier, the wall of the gorge veered away, and its slope decreased to a gradual incline that blended into steppes towards the north and east. Ahead, the wide valley was a lush field of ripe hay moving in waves as gusts of wind blew down the north slope, and midway down its length the small herd of steppe horses was grazing.

Ayla, breathing in the beauty and tranquillity of the scene, could hardly believe such a place could exist in the middle of the dry, windy prairie. The valley was an extravagant oasis hidden in a crack of the arid plains; a microcosm of abundance, as though nature, constrained to utilitarian economy on the steppes, lavished her bounty in extra measure where the opportunity allowed it.

The young woman studied the horses in the distance, intrigued by them. They were sturdy, compact animals with rather short legs, thick necks, and heavy heads with overhanging noses that reminded her of the large overhanging noses of some men of the Clan. They had heavy shaggy coats and short stiff manes. Though some tended to grey, most were shades of buff ranging from the neutral beige of the dust to the colour of ripe hay. Off to one side stood a hay-coloured stallion, and Ayla noticed several foals of the same shade. The stallion lifted his head, shaking his short mane, and whinnied.

"Proud of your clan, aren't you?" she motioned, smiling.

She started walking down the field close to the brush that hugged the stream, noting at one spot the leaves and the dried umbelled flower stalk that pointed to wild carrots a few inches below the ground. Soon her sharp eyes had picked up the trail of a hare, and with the silent stealth of an experienced hunter, she followed fresh droppings, a bent blade of grass, a faint print in the dirt, and just ahead she distinguished the shape of the animal hiding in camouflaging cover. She pulled her sling from her waist thong and reached into a fold of her wrap for two stones. When the hare bolted she was ready. With the unconscious grace of years of practice, she hurled a stone and the next instant a second one, and heard a satisfying *thwack, thwack*. Both missiles found their mark.

Ayla picked up her kill and thought about the time she had taught herself that double-stone technique. An overconfident attempt to kill a lynx had taught her the extent of her vulnerability. But it had taken long sessions of practice to perfect a way to place a second stone in position on the downstroke of the first cast so she could rapid-fire two stones in quick succession.

On her way back, she chopped a branch from a tree, sharpened a point on one end, and used it to dig up the wild carrots. She put them in a fold of her wrap and chopped off two forked branches before returning to the beach. She put down the hare and the roots and got the fire drill and platform out of her basket, then began gathering dry driftwood from under larger pieces in the bone pile, and deadfall from beneath the protective branches of the trees. With the same tool she had used to sharpen the digging stick, one with a V-shaped notch on the sharp edge, she shaved curls from a dry stick. Then she peeled loose hairy bark from the old stalks of sagebrush, and dried fuzz from the seed pods of fireweed.

She found a comfortable place to sit, then sorted the wood according to size and arranged the tinder, kindling, and larger wood around her. She examined the platform, a piece of dry clematis vine, dug a little notch out along one edge with a flint borer, and fitted an end of the previous season's dry woody cattail stalk into the hole to check the size. She arranged the fireweed fuzz in a nest of stringy bark under the notch of the fire platform and braced it with her foot, then put the end of the cattail stalk in the notch and took a deep breath. Fire making took concentration.

Placing both palms together at the top of the stick, she began twirling it back and forth between her hands, exerting a downward pressure. As she twirled it, the constant pressure moved her hands down the stick until they nearly touched the platform. If she'd had another person to help, that would have been the time for that person to start at the top. But, alone, she had to let go at the bottom and reach quickly for the top again, never letting the rhythm of the twirling stop, nor letting up the pressure for more than an instant, or the heat generated by the friction would dissipate and would not build up enough to start the wood smouldering. It was hard work and allowed no time to rest.

Ayla got into the rhythm of the movement, ignoring the sweat that formed on her brow and started running into her eyes. With the continuous movement, the hole deepened and sawdust from the soft wood accumulated. She smelled woodsmoke and saw the notch blacken before she saw a wisp of smoke, encouraging her to continue though her arms ached. Finally, a small glowing coal burned through the platform and dropped onto the nest of dry tinder beneath it. The next stage was even more critical. If the ember died, she'd have to begin all over again.

She bent over so that her face was so near the coal she could feel the heat, and began to blow on it. She watched it grow brighter with each breath, then die down again as she gulped another mouthful of air. She held tiny curled shavings to the bit of smouldering wood and watched them brighten and turn black without igniting. Then a tiny flame burst out. She blew harder, fed it more shavings, and, when she had a small pile burning, added a few sticks of kindling.

She rested only after the large driftwood logs were blazing and the fire was firmly established. She gathered a few more pieces and piled them nearby; then with another, slightly larger notched tool, she shaved the bark off the green branch she had used to dig up the wild carrots. She planted the forked branches upright on either side of the fire so that the pointed branch fitted comfortably between them and then turned to skinning the hare.

By the time the fire had died down to hot coals, the hare was skewered and ready for roasting. She started to wrap the entrails in the hide to dispose of it as she had done while travelling, then changed her mind.

I could use the fur, she thought. It would only take a day or so . . .

She rinsed the wild carrots in the river – and the blood off her hands – and wrapped them in plantain leaves. The large fibrous leaves were edible, but she couldn't help thinking of their other use as sturdy, healing bandages for cuts or bruises. She put the leaf-wrapped wild carrots next to the coals.

She sat back and relaxed for a moment, then decided to stake out the furry hide. While her meal cooked, she scraped away the blood vessels, hair follicles, and membranes from the inside of the skin with the broken scraper, and thought about making a new one.

She hummed a tuneless crooning murmur while she worked, and her thoughts wandered. Maybe I should stay here a few days, finish this hide. Need to make some tools anyway. Could try to reach that hole in the wall upriver. That hare is starting to smell good. A cave would keep me out of the rain – might not be usable, though.

She got up and turned the spit, then started working from a different side. I can't stay too long. I've got to find people before winter. She stopped scraping the skin, her attention suddenly focused on the inner turmoil that was never far from the surface of her mind. Where are they? Iza said there were many Others on the mainland. Why can't I find them? What am I going to do, Iza? Without warning, tears welled up and overflowed. Oh, Iza, I miss you so much. And Creb. And Uba, too. And Durc, my baby . . . my baby. I wanted you so much, Durc, and it was so hard. And you're not deformed, just a little different. Like I am.

No, not like me. You're Clan, you're just going to be a little taller, and your head looks a little different. Someday you'll be a great hunter. And good with the sling. And run faster than anyone. You'll win all the races at the Clan Gathering. Maybe not the wrestling, you might not be that strong, but you'll be strong.

But who will play the game of making sounds with you? And who will make the happy noises with you?

I've got to stop this, she scolded herself, wiping tears away with the back of her hand. I should be glad you have people who love you, Durc. And when you're older, Ura will come and be your mate. Oda promised to train her to be a good woman for you. Ura isn't deformed, either. She's just different, like you. I wonder, will I ever find a mate?

Ayla jumped up to check on her meal, moving just to be doing something to take her mind off her thoughts. The meat was more rare than she liked it, but she decided it was done enough. The wild carrots, small and pale yellow, were tender and had a sweet tangy taste. She missed the salt that had always been available near the inland sea, but hunger provided the right seasoning. She let the rest of the hare cook a little longer while she finished scraping the skin, feeling better after she ate.

The sun was high when she decided to investigate the hole in the wall. She stripped and swam across the river, scrambling up the tree roots to climb out of the deep water. It was difficult scaling the nearly vertical wall, making her wonder if it was worthwhile even if she found a cave. She was disappointed anyway when she reached a narrow ledge in front of the dark hole and found it was hardly more than a depression in the rock. The scat of hyena in a shaded corner let her know there must be an easier way down from the steppes, but there wasn't room for anything much larger.

She turned to start down, then turned farther. Downstream and slightly lower on the other wall, she could see the top of the rock barrier that jutted towards the bend of the river. It was a broad ledge, and at the back of it there appeared to be another hole in the face of the cliff, a much deeper hole. From her vantage point, she saw a steep but possible way up. Her heart was beating with excitement. If it was a cave of any size at all, she'd have a dry place to spend the night. About halfway down, she jumped into the river, eager to investigate.

I must have passed by it on the way down last night, she thought as she started up. It was just too dark to see. She remembered, then, that an unknown cave should always be approached with caution, and she returned for her sling and a few rocks.

Though she had very carefully felt her way down, in good light she found she didn't need handholds. Over the millennia, the river had cut sharper into the opposite bank; the wall on this side wasn't as steep. As she neared the ledge, Ayla held her sling ready and advanced with caution.

All her senses were alert. She listened for the sounds of breathing or small scufflings; looked to see if there were any telltale signs of recent habitation; smelled the air for the distinctive odours of carnivorous animals, or fresh scat, or gamy meat, opening her mouth to allow taste buds to help catch the scent; let her bare skin detect any sense of warmth coming out of the cave; and allowed intuition to guide her as she noiselessly approached the opening. She stayed close to the wall, crept up to the dark hole, and looked in.

She saw nothing.

The opening, facing the southwest, was small. The top cleared her head, but she could reach her hand up and touch it. The floor sloped down at the entrance, then levelled out. Loess, blown in on the wind, and debris carried in by animals that had used the cave in the past had built up a layer of soil. Originally uneven and rocky, the floor of the cave had a dry, hard-packed, earth surface.

As she peered around the edge, Ayla could detect no sign that the cave had been used recently. She slipped in, silently, noticing how cool it was compared with the hot sunny ledge, and waited for her eyes to adjust to the dim interior. There was more light in the cave than she expected, and when she moved in farther, she saw sunlight through a hole above the entrance and understood why. She also understood a more practical value to the hole. It would allow smoke to get out without filling the upper reaches of the cave, a distinct advantage.

Once her eyes adjusted, she discovered she could see surprisingly well. Light coming in was an advantage, too. The cave was not large but not small either. The walls angled back from the entrance, widening until they came to a fairly straight back wall. The general shape was roughly triangular, with the apex at the mouth and the east wall longer than the west. The darkest place was the east back corner; the place to investigate first.

She crept slowly along the east wall, watching for cracks or passageways that could lead to deeper recesses holding hidden menaces. Near the dark corner, rock cleaved from the walls lay on the floor in a jumbled heap. She climbed the rocks, felt a shelf, and emptiness beyond it.

She considered getting a torch, then changed her mind. She hadn't heard, smelled, or felt any signs of life, and she could see a little way in. Putting her sling and stones in one hand, wishing she had stopped to put on her wrap so she would have a place to put her weapons, she hoisted herself up on the shelf.

The dark opening was low; she had to stoop to move inside. But it was only a recess that ended with the roof sloping to meet the floor of the niche. At the back was a pile of bones. She reached for one, then climbed down and worked her way along the back wall, and along the west wall back to the entrance. It was a blind cave, and, except for the small niche, had no other chambers or tunnels leading to unknown places. It felt snug and secure.

Ayla shaded her eyes against the bright sunlight as she

walked out to the far edge of the cave's terrace and looked around. She was standing on top of the jutting wall. Below her on the right was the pile of driftwood and bones, and the rocky beach. To the left, she could see far down the valley. In the distance, the river turned south again, curving around the base of the steep opposite wall, while the left wall had flattened into steppes.

She examined the bone in her hand. It was the long legbone of a giant deer, aged and dry, with teeth marks clearly imprinted where it had been split to get at the marrow. The pattern of teeth, the way the bone had been gnawed, looked familiar, and yet not. It had been made by a feline, she was sure. She knew carnivores better than anyone in the Clan. She had developed her hunting skills on them, but only the smaller and medium-sized varieties. These marks had been made by a large cat, a very large cat. She spun around and looked at the cave again.

A cave lion! That must have been the den of cave lions once. That niche would be a perfect place for a lioness to have her cubs, she thought. Maybe I shouldn't spend the night in it. It might not be safe. She looked at the bone again. But this is so old, and the cave hasn't been used for years. Besides, a fire near the entrance will keep animals away.

It is a nice cave. Not many are that nice. Lots of room inside, a good dirt floor. I don't think it gets wet inside, spring floods don't reach this high. There's even a smoke hole. I think I'll go get my fur and basket, and some wood, and bring up the fire. Ayla hurried back down to the beach. She spread out the tent hide and her fur on the warm stone ledge when she returned, and put the basket inside the cave, then brought up several loads of wood. Maybe I'll get some hearthstones, too, she thought, starting down again.

Then she stopped. Why do I need hearthstones? I'm only staying a few days. I've got to keep looking for people. I've got to find them before winter . . .

What if I don't find people? The thought had been hovering for a long time, but she hadn't allowed herself to frame it precisely before; the consequences were too frightening. What will I do if winter comes and I still haven't found any people? I won't have any food put away. I won't have a place to stay that is dry and warm, and out of the wind and snow. No cave to . . .

She looked at the cave again, then at the beautiful protected valley and the herd of horses far down the field, then back at the cave again. It's a perfect cave for me, she said to herself. It would be a long time before I found one as good. And the valley. I could gather and hunt and store food. There's water, and more than enough wood to last the winter, many winters. There's even flint. And no wind. Everything I need is right here – except people.

I don't know if I could stand it, being alone all winter. But it's already so late in the season. I'm going to have to start soon to get enough food stored. If I haven't found anyone yet, how do I know I will? How do I know they'd let me stay if I did find the Others? I don't know them. Some of them are as bad as Broud. Look what happened to poor Oda. She said the men who forced her, like Broud forced me, were men of the Others. She said they looked like me. What if they are all like that? Ayla looked again at the cave, and then at the valley. She walked around the perimeter of the ledge, kicked a loose rock off the edge, stared off at the horses, then came to a decision.

"Horses," she said, "I'm going to stay in your valley for a while. Next spring I can start looking for the Others again. Right now, if I don't get ready for winter, I won't be alive next spring." Ayla's speech to the horses was made with only few sounds, and those were clipped and guttural. She used sound only for names or to emphasize the rich, complex, and fully comprehensive language she spoke with the graceful flowing motions of her hands. It was the only language she remembered.

Once her decision was made, Ayla felt a sense of relief. She had dreaded the thought of leaving this pleasant valley and facing more gruelling days of travelling the parched windy steppes, dreaded the thought of travelling any more at all. She raced down to the rocky beach and stooped to get her wrap and amulet. As she reached for the small leather pouch, she noticed the glitter of a small piece of ice.

How can there be ice in the middle of summer? she wondered, picking it up. It was not cold; it had hard precise edges and smooth flat planes. She turned it this way and that, watching its facets sparkling in the sun. Then she happened to turn it at just the right angle for the prism to separate the sunlight into the full spectrum of colours, and caught her breath at the rainbow she cast on the ground. Ayla had never seen a clear quartz crystal.

The crystal, like the flint and many of the other rocks on the beach, was an erratic – not native to the place. The gleaming stone had been torn from its birthplace by the even greater force of the element it resembled – ice – and moved by its melted form until it came to rest in the alluvial till of the glacial stream.

Suddenly, Ayla felt a chill colder than ice crawl up her spine, and sat down, too shaky to stand thinking of the stone's meaning. She remembered something Creb had told her long ago, when she was a little girl . . .

It was winter, and old Dorv had been telling stories. She had wondered about the legend Dorv had just finished and asked Creb. It had led to an explanation of totems.

"Totems want a place to live. They would probably desert people who wandered homeless for very long. You wouldn't want your totem to desert you, would you?"

Ayla reached for her amulet. "But my totem didn't desert me even though I was alone and had no home."

"That was because he was testing you. He found you a home, didn't he? The Cave Lion is a strong totem, Ayla. He chose you, and he may decide to protect you always because he chose you – but all totems are happier with a home. If you pay attention to him, he will help you. He will tell you what is best."

"How will I know, Creb?" Ayla asked. "I have never seen a Cave Lion spirit. How do you know when a totem is telling you something?"

"You cannot see the spirit of your totem because he is part of you, inside you. Yet, he will tell you. Only you must learn to understand. If you have a decision to make, he will help you. He will give you a sign if you make the right choice."

"What kind of sign?"

"It's hard to say. Usually it will be something special or unusual. It may be a stone you have never seen before, or a root with a special shape that has meaning for you. You must learn to understand with your heart and mind, not your eyes and ears; then you will know. But, when the time comes and you find a sign your totem has left you, put it in your amulet. It will bring you luck."

Cave Lion, are you still protecting me? Is this a sign? Did I make the right decision? Are you telling me I should stay in this valley?

Ayla held the sparkling crystal cupped in both hands and closed her eyes, trying to meditate as Creb always did; trying to listen with her heart and her mind; trying to find a way to believe that her great totem had not deserted her. She thought about the way she had been forced to leave and of the long weary days travelling, looking for her people, going north as Iza had told her. North, until . . .

The cave lions! My totem sent them to tell me to turn west, to lead me to this valley. He wanted me to find it. He's tired of travelling and wants this to be his home, too. And the cave that was home to cave lions before. It's a place he feels comfortable. He's still with me! He hasn't deserted me!

The understanding brought a relief of tension she hadn't known was there. She smiled as she blinked back tears and worked to loosen the knots in the cord that held the small pouch closed. She poured out the contents of the small bag, then picked them up, one by one.

The first was a chunk of red ochre. Everyone in the Clan carried a piece of the sacred red stone; it was the first thing in everyone's amulet, given to them on the day Mog-ur revealed their totem. Totems were usually named when one was a baby, but Ayla was five when she learned hers. Creb announced it not long after Iza found her, when they accepted her into the Clan. Ayla rubbed the four scars on her leg as she looked at another object: the fossil cast of a gastropod.

It seemed to be the shell of a sea creature, but it was stone; the first sign her totem had given her, to sanction her decision to hunt with her sling. Only predators, not food animals that would be wasted because she couldn't return to the cave with them. But predators were more crafty, and dangerous, and learning on them had honed her skill to a fine edge. The next object Ayla picked up was her hunting talisman, a small, ochre-stained oval of mammoth ivory, given to her by Brun himself at the frightening, fascinating ceremony that made her the Woman Who Hunts. She touched the tiny scar on her throat where Creb had nicked her to draw her blood as sacrifice to the Ancient Ones.

The next piece had very special meaning for her and nearly brought tears again. She held the three shiny nodules of iron pyrite, stuck together, tight in her fist. It was given by her totem to let her know her son would live. The last was a piece of black manganese dioxide. Mog-ur gave it to her when she was made a medicine woman, along with a piece of the spirit of every member of the Clan. Suddenly she had a thought that bothered her. Does that mean when Broud cursed me, he cursed everyone? When Iza died, Creb took back the spirits, so she wouldn't take them with her to the spirit world. No one took them back from me.

A sense of foreboding washed over her. Ever since the Clan Gathering, where Creb had learned in some inexplicable way that she was different, she had occasionally felt this strange disorientation, as though he had changed her. She felt a tingling, a prickling, a goosebump-raising nausea and weakness, and a deep fear of what her death might mean to the entire Clan.

She tried to shake off the feeling. Picking up the leather pouch, she put her collection back in, then added the quartz crystal. She retied the amulet and examined the thong for signs of wear. Creb told her she would die if she ever lost it. She noticed a slight difference in weight when she put it back on.

Sitting alone on the rocky beach, Ayla wondered what had happened before she was found. She could not recall anything of her life before, but she was so different. Too tall, too pale, her face nothing like those of the rest of the Clan. She had seen her reflection in the still pool; she was ugly. Broud had told her often enough, but everyone thought so. She was a big ugly woman; no man wanted her.

I never wanted one of them, either, she thought. Iza said I needed a man of my own, but will a man of the Others want me any more than a man of the Clan? No one wants a big ugly woman. Maybe it's just as well to stay here. How do I know I'd find a mate even if I did find the Others?

4

Jondalar crouched low and watched the herd through a screen of tall, golden-green grass, bent with the weight of unripe seed heads. The smell of horse was strong, not from the dry wind in his face carrying their hot rangy odour, but from the ripe dung he had rubbed on his body and held in his armpits to disguise his own scent if the wind shifted.

The hot sun glistened off his sweaty bronzed back, and a trickle of perspiration ran down the sides of his face; it darkened the sun-bleached hair plastered to his forehead. A long strand had escaped from a leather tie at the nape of his neck, and the wind whipped it, annoyingly, in his face. Flies buzzed around him, landing occasionally to take a bite, and a cramp was starting in his left thigh from holding the tense crouch.

They were petty irritations, hardly noticed. His attention was focused on a stallion nervously snorting and prancing, uncannily aware of impending danger to his harem. The mares were still grazing, but in their seemingly random movements, the dams had put themselves between their foals and the men.

Thonolan, a few feet away, was crouched in the same tense position, a spear held level with his right shoulder and another in his left hand. He glanced towards his brother. Jondalar lifted his head and flicked his eyes at a dun mare. Thonolan nodded, shifted his spear minutely for better balance, and prepared to spring.

As though a signal passed between them, the two men jumped up together and sprinted towards the herd. The stallion reared, screamed a warning, and reared again. Thonolan hurled his spear at the mare while Jondalar ran straight for the male horse, yelling and whooping, trying to spook him. The ploy worked. The stallion was not accustomed to noisy predators; four-legged hunters attacked with silent stealth. He whinnied, started towards the man, then dodged and galloped after his retreating herd.

The two brothers pounded after them. The stallion saw the mare fall behind, and nipped her in the flanks to urge her on. The men yelled and waved their arms, but this time the stallion stood his ground, dashing between the men and the mare, holding them off while trying to nudge her on. She took a few more faltering steps, then stopped, her head hanging. Thonolan's spear stuck out of her side, and bright scarlet rivulets stained her greyish coat and dripped from matted strands of shaggy hair.

Jondalar moved in closer, took aim, and cast his spear. The mare jerked, stumbled, then fell, the second shaft quivering in her thick neck below the stiff brush of a mane. The stallion cantered to her, nosed her gently, then reared with a scream of defiance and raced after his herd to protect the living.

"I'll go get the packs," Thonolan said as they jogged towards the fallen animal. "It'll be easier to bring water here than carry a horse back to the river."

"We don't have to dry it all. Let's take what we want back to the river, then we won't have to carry water here."

Thonolan shrugged. "Why not? I'll get an axe to break the bones." He headed for the river.

Jondalar pulled his bone-handled knife out of the sheath and made a deep cut across the throat. He pulled out the spears and watched blood pool around the mare's head.

"When you return to the Great Earth Mother, thank Her," he said to the dead horse. He reached into his pouch and fondled the stone figurine of the Mother in an unconscious gesture. Zelandoni is right, he thought. If Earth's Children ever forget who provides for them, we may wake up someday and find we don't have a home. Then he gripped his knife and prepared to take his share of Doni's provisions.

"I saw a hyena on the way back," Thonolan said when he returned. "Looks like we're going to feed more than ourselves."

"The Mother doesn't like waste," Jondalar said, up to his

68

elbows in blood. "It all goes back to Her one way or another. Here, give me a hand."

"It's a risk, you know," Jondalar said, throwing another stick on the small fire. A few sparks floated up with the smoke and disappeared into the night air. "What will we do when winter comes?"

"It's a long time until winter; we're bound to meet some people before then."

"If we turn back now, we'll be sure to meet people. We could make it at least as far as the Losadunai before the worst of the winter." He turned to face his brother. "We don't even know what winters are like on this side of the mountains. It's more open, less protection, fewer trees for fires. Maybe we should have tried to find the Sarmunai. They might have given us some idea of what to expect, what people live this way."

"You can turn back if you want, Jondalar. I was going to make this Journey alone to begin with . . . not that I haven't been glad for your company."

"I don't know . . . maybe I should," he said, turning back to stare at the fire. "I didn't realize how long this river is. Look at her." He waved towards the shimmering water reflecting the moonlight. "She is the Great Mother of rivers, and just as unpredictable. When we started, she was flowing east. Now it's south, and split into so many channels, I wonder sometimes if we're still following the right river. I guess I didn't believe you would go all the way to the end, no matter how far, Thonolan. Besides, even if we do meet people, how do you know they'll be friendly?"

"That's what a Journey is all about. Discovering new places, new people. You take your chances. Look, Big Brother, go back if you want. I mean it."

Jondalar stared at the fire, rhythmically slapping a stick of wood into the palm of his hand. Suddenly, he jumped up and threw the stick on the fire, stirring up another host of sparks. He walked over and looked at the cords of twined fibres strung out close to the ground between pegs, on which thin slices of meat were drying. "What do I have to go back to? For that matter, what do I have to look forward to?"

69

"The next bend in the river, the next sunrise, the next woman you bed," Thonolan said.

"Is that all? Don't you want something more out of life?"

"What else is there? You're born, you live the best you can while you're here, and someday you go back to the Mother. After that, who knows?"

"There ought to be more to it, some reason for living."

"If you ever find out, let me know," Thonolan said, yawning. "Right now, I'm looking forward to the next sunrise, but one of us should stay up, or we ought to build more fires to keep scavengers away if we want that meat to be there in the morning."

"Go to bed, Thonolan. I'll stay up; I'd lie awake anyway."

"Jondalar, you worry too much. Wake me when you get tired."

The sun was already up when Thonolan crawled out of the tent, rubbed his eyes, and stretched. "Have you been up all night? I told you to wake me."

"I was thinking and didn't feel like going to bed. There's some hot sage tea if you want some."

"Thanks," Thonolan said, scooping steaming liquid into a wooden bowl. He squatted down in front of the fire, cupping the bowl in both hands. The early morning air was still cool, the grass wet with dew, and he wore only a breechclout. He watched small birds darting and flitting around the scant brush and trees near the river, chirping noisily. A flock of cranes that nested on an island of willows in midchannel was breakfasting on fish. "Well, did you do it?" he finally asked.

"Do what?"

"Find the meaning of life. Isn't that what you were worried about when I went to bed? Though why you'd stay up all night for that, I'll never know. Now, if there was a woman around. . . . Do you have one of Doni's blessed hidden in the willows . . .?"

"Do you think I'd tell you if I did?" Jondalar said, grinning. Then his smile softened. "You don't have to make bad jokes to humour me, Little Brother. I'm going with you, all the way to the end of the river, if you want. Only, what will you do then?"

"Depends what we find there. I'm glad you've decided to

come along. I've sort of got used to you, bad moods and all."

"I told you, someone has to keep you out of trouble."

"Me? Right now I could use a little trouble. It'd be better than sitting around waiting for that meat to dry."

"It will only be a few days, if the weather holds. But now I'm not so sure I should tell you what I saw." Jondalar's eyes twinkled.

"Come on, Brother. You know you will anyway . . ."

"Thonolan, there's a sturgeon in that river so big. . . . But there's no point in fishing for it. You wouldn't want to wait around for fish to dry, too."

"How big?" Thonolan said, standing up and eagerly facing the river.

"So big, I'm not sure both of us together could haul it in."

"No sturgeon is that big."

"The one I saw was."

"Show me."

"Who do you think I am? The Great Mother? Do you think I can make a fish come and show off for you?" Thonolan looked chagrined. "I'll show you where I saw it, though," Jondalar said.

The two men walked to the edge of the river and stood near a fallen tree that extended partway into the water. As though to tempt them, a large shadowy shape moved silently upstream and stopped under the tree near the river bottom, undulating slightly against the current.

"That must be the grandmother of all fish!" Thonolan whispered.

"But can we land it?"

"We can try!"

"It would feed a Cave, and more. What would we do with it?"

"Weren't you the one who said the Mother never lets anything go to waste? The hyenas and wolverines can have a share. Let's get the spears," Thonolan said, anxious to try the sport.

"Spears won't do it, we need gaffs."

"She'll be gone if we stop to make gaffs."

"If we don't, we'll never bring her in. She'd just slip off a spear – we need something with a back hook. It wouldn't take long to make. Look, that tree over there. If we cut off

71

limbs just below a good sturdy branch fork – we don't have to worry about reinforcing, we'll only use it once," Jondalar was punctuating his description with motions in the air, "then cut the branch off short and sharpen it, we've got a back hook. . . ."

"But what good will it do if she's gone before we get them made?" Thonolan interrupted.

"I've seen her there twice – it seems to be a favourite resting place. She'd probably come back."

"But who knows how long that would take?"

"Have you anything better to do right now?"

Thonolan made a wry smile. "All right, you win. Let's go make gaffs."

They turned around to go back, then stopped in surprise. Several men had surrounded them and looked distinctly unfriendly.

"Where did they come from?" Thonolan said in a hoarse whisper.

"They must have seen our fire. Who knows how long they've been out there. I've been up all night watching for scavengers. They could have been waiting until we did something careless, like leaving our spears behind."

"They don't look too sociable; none of them has made a gesture of welcome. What do we do now?"

"Put on your biggest, friendliest smile, Little Brother, and you make the gesture."

Thonolan tried to think self-assured and smiled what he hoped was a confident grin. He put both his hands out and started towards them. "I am Thonolan of the Zelan . . ."

His progress was halted by a spear quivering in the ground at his feet.

"Any more good suggestions, Jondalar?"

"I think it's their turn."

One of the men said something in an unfamiliar language and two others sprang towards them. With the points of spears they were urged forward.

"You don't have to get nasty, friend," Thonolan said, feeling a sharp prick. "I was going that way when you stopped me."

They were brought back to their own campfire and pushed down roughly in front of it. The one who had spoken before barked another command. Several men crawled into the tent and hauled everything out. The spears were taken from the backframes and the contents spilled on the ground.

"What do you think you're doing?" Thonolan shouted, starting to get up. He was reminded to sit, forcibly, and felt a ·trickle of blood running down his arm.

"Relax, Thonolan," Jondalar warned. "They look angry. I don't think they're in a mood for objections."

"Is this the way to treat Visitors? Don't they understand rights of passage for those on a Journey?"

"You were the one who said it, Thonolan."

"Said what?"

"You take your chances; that's what a Journey is all about."

"Thanks," Thonolan said, reaching for the stinging cut on his arm and looking at his blood-smeared fingers. "That's just what I needed to hear."

The one who seemed to be the leader spat out a few more words and the two brothers were hauled to their feet. Thonolan, in his loincloth, was given only a cursory glance, but Jondalar was searched and his bone-handled flint knife was taken. A man reached for the pouch fastened to his belt, and Jondalar grabbed for it. The next instant he felt a sharp pain at the back of his head and slumped to the ground.

He was stunned for only a short while, but when his head cleared, he found himself stretched out on the ground, staring into Thonolan's worried grey eyes, his hands bound with thongs behind his back.

"You were the one who said it, Jondalar."

"Said what?"

"They're in no mood for objections."

"Thanks," Jondalar remarked with a grimace, suddenly aware of a bad headache. "That's just what I needed to hear."

"What do you suppose they're going to do with us?"

"We're still alive. If they were going to kill us, they'd have done it, wouldn't they?"

"Maybe they're saving us for something special."

*

The two men lay on the ground, listening to voices and watching the strangers moving about their camp. They smelled food cooking and their stomachs growled. As the sun rose higher, the glaring heat made thirst a worse problem. As the afternoon wore on, Jondalar dozed, his lack of sleep from the night before catching up with him. He woke with a start to shouts and commotion. Someone had arrived.

They were dragged to their feet, and gaped in amazement at a burly man striding towards them carrying a white-haired, wizened old woman on his back. He got down on all fours, and the woman was helped off her human steed, with obvious deference.

"Whoever she is, she must be pretty important," Jondalar said. A bruising blow in the ribs silenced him.

She walked towards them leaning on a knobbed staff with a carved finial. Jondalar stared, sure he had never seen anyone so old in his life. She was child-size, shrunken with age, and the pink of her scalp could be seen through her thin white hair. Her face was so wrinkled that it hardly looked human, but her eyes were oddly out of place. He would have expected dull, rheumy, senile eyes in someone so old. But hers were bright and intelligent and crackled with authority. Jondalar was awed by the tiny woman, and a little fearful for Thonolan and himself. She would not have come unless it was very important.

She spoke in a voice cracked with age, yet surprisingly strong. The leader pointed at Jondalar, and she directed a question to him.

"I'm sorry, I don't understand," he said.

She spoke again, tapped her chest with a hand as gnarled as her staff, and said a word that sounded like "Haduma". Then she pointed a knobby finger at him.

"I am Jondalar of the Zelandonii," he said, hoping he understood her meaning.

She cocked her head as though she had heard a sound. "Zel-an-don-yee?" she repeated slowly.

Jondalar nodded, licking his dry, parched lips nervously.

She stared at him speculatively, then spoke to the leader. His answer was brusque, and she snapped a command, then turned her back and walked to the fire. One of the men who had been guarding them pulled out a knife. Jondalar glanced at his brother and saw a face that expressed his own emotions. He braced himself, sent a silent plea to the Great Earth Mother, and closed his eyes.

He opened them with a surge of relief when he felt the thongs cut away from his wrists. A man was approaching with a bladder of water. Jondalar took a long drink and passed it to Thonolan, whose hands had also been freed. He opened his mouth to say a word of appreciation and then, remembering his bruised ribs, thought better of it.

They were escorted to the fire by guards who hovered close with menacing spears. The burly man who had carried the old woman brought a log, put a fur robe on it, then stood to the side with his hand on his knife handle. She settled herself on the log, and Jondalar and Thonolan were made to sit in front of her. They were careful to make no moves that might be construed as endangering to the old woman; they had no doubt of their fate if any man there even thought they might try to harm her.

She stared at Jondalar again, not saying a word. He met her gaze, but, as the silence continued, he began to feel disconcerted and uncomfortable. Suddenly, she reached into her robe and with eyes blazing anger and a spate of acrimonious words that left no doubt of their sense if not their meaning, she held out an object towards him. His eyes widened in wonder. It was the carved stone figure of the Mother, his donii, she held in her hand.

Out of the corner of his eye, he watched the guard beside him flinch. There was something about the donii he didn't like.

The woman ended her tirade, and, lifting her arm dramatically, flung the statuette to the ground. Jondalar jumped involuntarily and reached for it. His anger at her desecration of his sacred object showed in his face. Ignoring the prick of a spear, he picked it up and cradled it protectively in his hands.

A sharp word from her caused the spear to be withdrawn. He was surprised to see a smile on her face and the glint of amusement in her eyes, but he wasn't at all sure if she smiled out of humour or malice.

She got up from the log and walked closer. She was not much taller standing than he was seated and, facing him at eye level, she peered deep into his startling, vivid blue eyes.

Then she stepped back, turned his head from side to side, felt the muscle of his arm, and surveyed the breadth of his shoulders. She motioned for him to get up. When he didn't quite understand, the guard prodded him into comprehension. She tilted her head back to look up at all six feet six inches of him, then walked around him, poking the hard muscles of his legs. Jondalar had the feeling he was being examined like some prize goods offered for trade, and he flushed to find himself wondering if he measured up.

She looked Thonolan over next, motioned for him to stand, then turned her attention back to Jondalar. His pink flush turned to deep crimson when the meaning of her next gesture dawned on him. She wanted to see his manhood.

He shook his head and gave the grinning Thonolan a dirty look. At a word from the woman, one of the men grabbed Jondalar from behind, while another, with obvious embarrassment, fumbled to unfasten his trouser flap.

"I don't think she's in any mood for objections," Thonolan said, smirking.

Jondalar angrily shrugged off the man who was holding him and exposed himself to the old woman's view, glowering at his brother who was hanging on to his sides, snorting, in a futile attempt to constrain his glee. The old woman looked at him, cocked her head to one side, and, with a gnarled finger, touched him.

Jondalar's crimson turned to purple when, for some inexplicable reason, he felt his manhood swell. The woman cackled, and there were sniggers from the men standing near-by, but a strangely subdued note of awe as well. Thonolan burst out in loud guffaws, stomping and bending over double as tears came to his eyes. Jondalar hastily covered his offending member, feeling foolish and angry.

"Big Brother, you must really need a woman to get a rise over that old hag," Thonolan quipped, catching his breath and wiping away a tear. Then he burst into uproarious laughter again.

"I just hope it's your turn next," Jondalar said, wishing he could think of some witty remark to squelch him.

The old woman signalled to the leader of the men who had stopped them, and spoke to him. A heated exchange followed. Jondalar heard the woman say "Zelandonyee" and

76

saw the young man point to the meat drying on cords. The exchange ended abruptly with an imperious command from the woman. The man shot a dark glance at Jondalar, then motioned to a curly haired youth. After a few words, the young man dashed away at full speed.

The two brothers were led back to their tent and their backframes were returned, but not their spears or knives. One man was always a short distance away, obviously keeping an eye on them. Food was brought to them, and, when night fell, they crawled into their tent. Thonolan was in high spirits, but Jondalar was in no mood for conversation with a brother who laughed every time he looked at him.

There was an air of expectancy in the camp when they awoke. About midmorning a large party arrived, amid shouts of greeting. Tents were set up, men, women, and children settled in, and the spartan camp of the two men began to take on aspects of a Summer Meeting. Jondalar and Thonolan watched with interest the assembly of a large structure, circular, with straight walls covered with hides, and a domed, thatched roof. The various parts of it were pre-assembled, and it went up with surprising speed. Then bundles and covered baskets were carried inside.

There was a lull in activities while food was prepared. In the afternoon, a crowd began to gather around the large circular structure. The old woman's log was brought and placed just outside the opening, and the fur robe draped over it. As soon as she appeared, the crowd quieted and formed a circle around her, leaving the place in the centre open. Jondalar and Thonolan watched her speak to a man and point to them.

"Maybe she'll want you to show off your great desire for her again," Thonolan gibed as the man beckoned.

"They'll have to kill me first!"

"You mean you're not dying to bed that beauty?" Thonolan asked, feigning wide-eyed innocence. "It certainly looked that way yesterday." He began to chuckle again. Jondalar turned and stalked off towards the group.

They were led to the centre and she motioned for them to sit in front of her again.

"Zel-an-don-yee?" the old woman said to Jondalar.

"Yes," he nodded. "I am Jondalar of the Zelandonii."

She tapped the arm of an old man beside her.

"I . . . Tamen," he said, then some words Jondalar couldn't understand, ". . . Hadumai. Long time . . . Tamen . . ." another unfamiliar word, "west . . . Zelandonii."

Jondalar strained, then suddenly realized he had understood some of the man's words. "Your name is Tamen, something about Hadumai. Long time . . . long time ago you . . . west . . . made a Journey? To the Zelandonii? Can you speak Zelandonii?" he asked excitedly.

"Journey, yes," the man said. "No talk . . . long time."

The old woman grabbed the man's arm and spoke to him. He turned back to the two brothers.

"Haduma," he said, pointing to her. ". . . Mother. . . ." Tamen hesitated, then indicated everyone with a sweep of his arm.

"You mean like Zelandoni, One Who Serves the Mother?"

He shook his head. "Haduma . . . Mother. . . ." He thought for a moment, then beckoned to some people and lined them up in a row beside him. "Haduma . . . mother . . . mother . . . mother . . . mother," he said, pointing first at her, then to himself, then to each person in turn.

Jondalar studied the people, trying to make sense out of the demonstration. Tamen was old, but not as old as Haduma. The man next to him was just past middle age. Beside him was a younger woman holding the hand of a child. Suddenly, Jondalar made a connection. "Are you saying Haduma is mother's mother five times?" He held up his hand with five fingers outstretched. "The mother of five generations?" he said with awe.

The man nodded vigorously. "Yes, mother's mother . . . five . . . generations," he said, pointing again to each person.

"Great Mother! Do you know how old she must be?" Jondalar said to his brother.

"Great mother, yes," Tamen said. "Haduma . . . mother," he patted his stomach.

"Children?"

"Children," he nodded. "Haduma mother children. . . ." He began drawing lines in the dirt.

"One, two, three . . ." Jondalar said the counting words with each one. ". . . Sixteen! Haduma gave birth to sixteen children?"

Tamen nodded, pointing again to the marks on the ground. ". . . Many son . . . many . . . girl?" He shook his head, doubtful.

"Daughters?" Jondalar offered.

Tamen brightened. "Many daughters . . ." He thought for a moment. "Live . . . all live. All . . . many children." He held up one hand and one finger. "Six Caves . . . Hadumai."

"No wonder they were ready to kill us if we so much as looked cross at her," Thonolan said. "She's the mother of all of them, a living First Mother!"

Jondalar was as impressed, but even more puzzled. "I am honoured to know Haduma, but I don't understand. Why are we being held? And why did she come here?"

The old man pointed to their meat drying on cords, then to the young man who had first detained them. "Jeren . . . hunt. Jeren make. . . ." Tamen drew a circle on the ground with two diverging lines making a broad V from the small space left open. "Zelandonii man make . . . make run. . . ." He thought for a long time, then smiled, and said, "Make run horse."

"So that's it!" Thonolan said. "They must have built a surround and were waiting for that herd to move closer. We chased them off."

"I can understand why he was angry," Jondalar said to Tamen. "But we didn't know we were on your hunting grounds. We'll stay and hunt, of course, to make restitution. It's still no way to treat Visitors. Doesn't he understand passage customs for those on a Journey?" he said, venting his own anger.

The old man didn't catch every word, but enough to understand the meaning. "Not many Visitors. Not . . . west . . . long time. Customs . . . forget."

"Well, you ought to remind him. You were on a Journey, and he might want to make one someday." Jondalar was still annoyed at their treatment, but he didn't want to make too much of an issue about it. He still wasn't sure what was going on and he didn't want actually to offend them. "Why did Haduma come? How can you allow her to make a long trip at her age?"

Tamen smiled. "Not . . . allow Haduma. Haduma say. Jeren . . . find dumai. Bad . . . bad luck?" Jondalar nodded to indicate the correctness of the word, but he didn't understand what Tamen was trying to say. "Jeren give . . . man . . . runner. Say Haduma make bad luck go. Haduma come."

"Dumai? Dumai? You mean my donii?" Jondalar said, taking the carved stone figurine out of his pouch. The people around gasped and drew back when they saw what he had in his hand. An angry murmur rose from the crowd, but Haduma harangued them and they quieted.

"But this donii is good luck!" Jondalar protested.

"Good luck . . . woman, yes. Man . . ." Tamen searched his memory for a word, ". . . sacrilege," he said.

Jondalar sat back, stunned. "But if it's good luck for a woman, why did she throw it?" He made a violent gesture of casting the donii down, bringing exclamations of concern. Haduma spoke to the old man.

"Haduma . . . long time live . . . big luck. Big . . . magic. Haduma say me Zelandonii . . . customs. Say Zelandonii man not Hadumai . . . Haduma say Zelandonii man bad?"

Jondalar shook his head.

Thonolan spoke up. "I think he's saying she was testing you, Jondalar. She knew the customs were not the same, and she wanted to see how you would react when she dishonoured . . ."

"Dishonour, yes," Tamen interrupted, hearing the word. "Haduma . . . know not all man, good man. Want know Zelandonii man dishonour Mother."

"Listen, that's a very special donii," Jondalar said, a little indignant. "It's very old. My mother gave it to me – it's been handed down for generations."

"Yes, yes." Tamen nodded vigorously. "Haduma know. Wise . . . much wise. Long time live. Big magic, make bad luck go. Haduma know Zelandonii man, good man. Want Zelandonii man. Want . . . honour Mother."

Jondalar saw the grin lighting up Thonolan's face, and squirmed.

"Haduma want," Tamen pointed to Jondalar's eyes, "blue eyes. Honour Mother. Zelandonii . . . spirit make child, blue eyes."

"You did it again, Big Brother!" Thonolan blurted, grinning with malicious delight. "With those big blue eyes of yours. She's in love!" He was shaking, trying to hold his laughter in, afraid it might offend, but unable to stop. "Oh, Mother! I can hardly wait to get back home and tell them. Jondalar, the man every woman wants! Do you still want to go back? For this, I'd give up the end of the river." He couldn't talk any more. He was doubled over, pounding the ground, holding his sides and trying not to laugh out loud.

Jondalar swallowed several times. "Ah . . . I . . . um . . . does Haduma think the Great Mother . . . ah . . . could still . . . bless her with a child?"

Tamen looked at Jondalar, perplexed, and at Thonolan's contortions. Then a big grin cracked his face. He spoke to the old woman, and the whole camp erupted into raucous laughter, the old woman's cackle heard above all. Thonolan, with a heave of relief, let out a great whoop of glee as tears squeezed out of his eyes.

Jondalar did not see anything funny.

The old man was shaking his head, trying to talk. "No, no, Zelandonii man." He beckoned to someone. "Noria, Noria . . ."

A young woman stepped forward and smiled shyly at Jondalar. Hardly more than a girl, she showed the fresh sparkle of new womanhood. The laughter finally subsided.

"Haduma big magic," Tamen said. "Haduma bless, Noria five . . . generations." He held up five fingers. "Noria make child, make . . . six generations." He held up another finger. "Haduma want Zelandonii man . . . honour Mother . . ." Tamen smiled as he remembered the words, "First Rites."

The worry lines on Jondalar's forehead smoothed out.

"Haduma bless. Make spirit go Noria. Make Noria . . . baby, Zelandonii eyes."

Jondalar exploded with laughter, as much with relief as pleasure. He looked at his brother. Thonolan was not laughing any more. "Do you still want to go home and tell everyone about the old hag I bedded?" he asked. He turned to Tamen. "Please tell Haduma it will be my pleasure to honour the Mother and share Noria's First Rites."

He smiled warmly at the young woman. She smiled back, tentatively at first, but, bathed in the unconscious charisma of his vivid blue eyes, her smile grew.

Haduma motioned for Jondalar and Thonolan to stand,

and looked the tall blond man over carefully again. The warmth of his smile still lingered. She chuckled softly and went into the large circular tent.

The two brothers stayed to talk to Tamen, even his limited ability to communicate was better than none at all.

"Tamen, this is my brother, Thonolan, and my name is Jondalar, Jondalar of the Zelandonii. I am honoured, to be chosen for Noria's First Rites."

"Haduma say big Zelandonii man make . . . big . . . strong spirit, make strong Hadumai," Tamen said.

Jondalar's forehead knotted. "Noria might not make a baby of my spirit, you know."

Tamen smiled. "Haduma bless, Noria make. Haduma big magic. Haduma touch, woman make baby. Woman no . . . milk. Haduma touch, woman make milk. Haduma make Jondalar . . . big honour. Many man want Haduma touch. Make long time man. Make man . . . pleasure?" They all smiled. "Pleasure woman, all time. Many woman, many time. Haduma big magic." His face lost its smile. "No make Haduma . . . anger. Haduma bad magic, anger."

"And I laughed," Thonolan said. "Do you suppose I could get her to touch me? You and your big blue eyes, Jondalar."

"Little Brother, the only magic touch you ever needed was the inviting look of a pretty woman."

"So. I never noticed you needing help. Look who's sharing First Rites? Not your little brother with his dull grey eyes."

"Poor little brother. A camp full of women and he's going to spend the night alone. Not on your life." They laughed, and Tamen, who caught the drift, joined in.

"Tamen, maybe you'd better tell me about your customs for First Rites," Jondalar said, more serious.

"Before you get into that," Thonolan said, "can you get our spears and knives back? I've got an idea. While my brother is busy beguiling that young beauty with his big blue eyes, I think I know a way to make your angry hunter happier."

"How?" Jondalar asked.

"With a grandmother, of course."

Tamen looked confused, but he shrugged it off as problems with the language.

*

Jondalar saw little of Thonolan that evening or the next day; he was too busy with the purification rituals. The language was a barrier to understanding even with Tamen's help, and when he was alone with the scowling older women, it was worse. Only when Haduma was there did he feel more relaxed, and he was sure she smoothed over some unforgivable blunders.

Haduma didn't rule the people, but it was obvious they would refuse her nothing. She was treated with benevolent reverence and a little fear. It had to be magic that she had lived so long and retained her full mental faculties. She had a knack for sensing when Jondalar was in difficulty. On one occasion, when he was sure he had unknowingly broken some taboo, she waded in, eyes flashing anger, and beat the backs of several retreating women with her staff. She would brook no opposition to him; her sixth generation would have Jondalar's blue eyes.

In the evening, when he was finally led to the large circular structure, he wasn't even sure it was time, until he went inside. As he stepped through the entrance, he paused to look around. Two stone lamps, with bowl-shaped wells filled with fat in which wicks of dried moss burned, lit one side. The ground was covered with furs and the walls were hung with bark-cloth weavings in intricate patterns. Behind a raised platform covered with furs hung the thick white fur of an albino horse decorated with the red heads of immature great spotted woodpeckers. Sitting on the very edge of the platform was Noria, nervously staring down at her hands in her lap.

On the other side, a small section was partitioned off with hanging leather hides marked with esoteric symbols, and a screen of thongs – one of the hides cut into narrow strips. Someone was behind the screen. He saw a hand move a few of the strips aside, and looked into Haduma's wrinkled old face for a brief moment. He breathed a sigh of relief. There was always at least one guardian, to bear witness that a girl's transformation to full womanhood was complete, and to make sure a man wasn't unduly rough. As a stranger, he had felt some concern that there might be a bevy of disapproving guardians. With Haduma he felt no qualms. He didn't know if he should greet her or ignore her, but he decided on the latter when the screen closed.

When Noria saw him, she stood up. He walked towards her, smiling. She was rather small, with soft, light brown hair hanging loosely around her face. She was barefoot, and a skirt of some woven fibre was tied at the waist and fell to below her knees in colourful bands. A shirt of soft deerskin embroidered with dyed quills was laced together tightly up the front. It conformed to her body enough to reveal that her womanhood was well established, though she had not lost all her girlish roundness.

She got a frightened look in her eye as he approached, though she tried to smile. But when he made no sudden moves, just sat down on the edge of the platform and smiled, she seemed to relax a little, and sat down beside him, far enough away so that their knees did not touch.

It would help if I could speak her language, he thought. She's so scared. No wonder, I'm a total stranger to her. Appealing, so frightened like that. He felt protective, and a few twinges of excitement. He noticed a carved wooden bowl and some drinking cups on a nearby stand and started to reach, but Noria saw his intention and jumped up to fill the cups.

As she gave him a cup of amber liquid, he touched her hand. It startled her. She pulled it back a little, then left it. He gave her hand a gentle squeeze, then took the cup and drank. The liquid had the sweet, strong taste of something fermented. Not unpleasant, but he wasn't sure how strong it was, and decided to drink lightly.

"Thank you, Noria," he said, putting the cup down.

"Jondalar?" she asked, looking up. By the light of the stone lamps he could tell her eyes were a light shade, but he wasn't sure if they were grey or blue.

"Yes, Jondalar. Of the Zelandonii."

"Jondalar . . . Zelandonyee man."

"Noria, Hadumai woman."

"Wo-man?"

"Woman," he said, touching one firm young breast. She jumped back.

Jondalar untied the lace at the neck of his tunic and pulled it back, showing a chest of light curls. He smiled a wry grin and touched his chest. "No woman," he shook his head. "Man."

84

She giggled a little.

"Noria woman," he said, slowly reaching towards her breast again. This time she let him touch without pulling back, and her smile was more relaxed.

"Noria woman," she said, then got a mischievous glint in her eye, and pointed a finger towards his groin, but didn't touch. "Jondalar man." Suddenly she looked frightened again, as though she might have gone too far, and got up to refill the cups. She scooped out the liquid nervously, spilling some, and seemed embarrassed. Her hand shook holding the cup to him.

He steadied her hand, took the cup and sipped, then offered her a drink. She nodded, but he held the cup to her mouth so that she had to cup her hands around his to tip it up to drink. When he put the cup down, he reached for her hands again, opened her palms, and kissed each one lightly. Her eyes opened wide with surprise, but she didn't pull back. He moved his hands up her arms, then bent closer and kissed her neck. She was tense, with anticipation as well as fear, waiting to see what he would do next.

He moved closer, kissed her neck again, and his hand slipped down to cup one breast. Though she was still afraid, she was beginning to feel her own responses to his touch. He tilted her head back, kissing her neck, flicked his tongue along her throat, and reached to untie the lace at her neck. Then he moved his lips up to her ear and along her jaw, and found her mouth. He opened his, and moved his tongue between her lips, and, when they parted, he exerted gentle pressure to open them more.

Then he backed off holding her shoulders, and smiled. Her eyes were closed, but her mouth was still open, and she was breathing faster. He kissed her again, cupping a breast, then reached up to pull the lace out of one hole. She stiffened a little. He stopped and looked at her, then smiled and deliberately pulled the lace out of another hole. She sat stiffly unmoving, looking up at his face as he pulled the lace out of yet another hole, and then another, until the deerskin shirt hung loosely, open all down the front.

He bent down to her neck as he pushed the shirt back to bare her shoulders and reveal her upright young breasts with their swollen aureolae, and felt his manhood throb. He kissed her shoulders with open mouth and moving tongue and felt her quiver, and caressed her arms as he pushed her shirt off. He ran his hands up her spine, and his tongue down her neck and chest, circled her aureole, felt her nipple contract, and sucked gently. She gasped but didn't pull away. He suckled the other breast, ran his tongue back up to her mouth and, as he kissed her, pushed her back.

She opened her eyes and looked up at him from the furs. Her eyes were dilated and luminous. His were so deeply blue and compelling that she could not look away. "Jondalar man, Noria woman," she said.

"Jondalar man, Noria woman," he said huskily, then sat up and pulled his tunic over his head, feeling the surge as his manhood strained to burst free. He bent over her, kissed her again, and felt her open her mouth to taste his tongue with hers. He caressed her breast and ran his tongue down her neck and shoulder. He found her nipple again, sucking harder as he heard her moan, and felt his own breath heaving faster.

It's been so long since I've been with a woman, he thought, and wanted to take her that instant. Go easy, don't scare her, he reminded himself. It's her first time. You've got all night, Jondalar. Wait until you know she's ready.

He caressed her bare skin below her swelling mounds down to her waist, and searched for the thong that gathered her skirt together. Pulling the tie, he reached in and rested his hands on her stomach. She tensed, then relaxed. He reached lower for the inside of her thigh, brushing over her pubic rise of soft down. She spread her legs as he moved his hand along her inner thigh.

He pulled his hand away, sat up, then worked her skirt down below her hips and dropped it on the ground. Then he stood up and looked at her soft, rounded, not quite full-blown curves. She smiled up at him with a look of trust and longing. He untied the thong from his trousers and lowered them. She gasped when she saw his upright swollen member, and a hint of fear returned to her eyes.

Noria had listened with fascination to stories other women told of their Rites of First Pleasures. Some women didn't think they were such a pleasure. They said the Gift of Pleasure was given to men, that women were given the ability to give men pleasure so men would be bound to them; so men would hunt and bring food and skins to make clothes when a woman was heavy with child or suckling young. Noria had been warned there would be pain in her First Rites. Jondalar was so swollen, so big, how would he fit himself in her?

Her look of fear was familiar. It was a critical moment; she would have to get used to him again. He enjoyed awakening a woman for the first time to the pleasures of the Mother's Gift, but it took delicacy and finesse. Someday, he thought, I wish I could give a woman pleasure for the first time and not have to worry about hurting her. He knew it wasn't possible. The Rites of First Pleasures for a woman were always a little painful.

He sat down beside her and waited, giving her time. Her eyes were drawn to his throbbing member. He took her hand and led her to touch him, and felt a surge. It was as though his manhood had a life of its own at a time like this. Noria felt the softness of his skin, the warmth, the firm fullness, and, as his member moved eagerly in her hand, she felt a sharp, pleasurable, tingling sensation within her, and a dampness between her legs. She tried to smile, but fear still lurked in her eyes.

He stretched out beside her and kissed her gently. She opened her eyes and looked into his. She saw his concern, and his hunger, and some unnameable irresistible force. She was drawn, overwhelmed, lost in the impossibly blue depths of his eyes, and felt the deep, pleasurable sensation again. She wanted him. She feared pain, but she wanted him. She reached for him, closed her eyes, opened her mouth, and pressed herself closer to him.

He kissed her, letting her explore his mouth, and slowly worked his way down her neck and throat, kissing, moving his tongue, and gently caressing her stomach and thighs. He tantalized a little, coming close to the sensitive nipple, but backing off, until she moved his mouth to it. At that instant, he moved his hand to the warm slit between her thighs and found the small throbbing nodule. A cry escaped her lips.

He suckled and gently bit her nipple as he moved his finger. She moaned and moved her hips. He went lower, felt her indrawn breath as his tongue found her navel, and tension in her muscles as he moved even lower, backing off the platform until his knees felt the ground. Then he pressed her legs apart, and took his first taste of her tangy salt. Noria's breath exploded with a shuddering cry. She moaned with each breath, tossed her head back and forth, and raised her hips to meet him.

With his hands, he spread her open, licked her warm folds, then found her nodule with his tongue and worked it. As she cried out, moving her hips, his own excitement was hard upon him. He struggled to contain it. When he heard her gasping in quick pants, he raised up, still kneeling so he could control his penetration, and guided the head of his engorged organ into her untried opening. He gritted his teeth for control as he pushed into the warm, damp, tight well.

As she wrapped her legs around his waist, he felt the blockage within her. With his finger, he found her nodule again and moved himself back and forth just a little, until her gasps came with cries and he felt her hips lift. Then, he drew back, pushed hard, and felt himself penetrate the barrier as she cried out in pain and pleasure, and heard his own strained outcry as he released his pent-up need with shuddering spasms.

He moved out and in a few more times, penetrating as far as he dared, feeling the last of his essence drained, then collapsed on her. It was over. He lay for a moment with his head on her chest, breathing hard, then raised himself. She was limp, her head turned to the side, her eyes closed. He withdrew himself and saw bloodstains on the white fur beneath. He lifted her legs back onto the platform and crawled up on it beside her, sinking into the furs.

As his breath started to come easier, he felt hands on his head. He opened his eyes to see the old face and bright eyes of Haduma. Noria moved beside him. Haduma smiled, nodded with approval, and began a singsong chant. Noria opened her eyes, was pleased to see the old woman, and even more pleased when she moved her hands from Jondalar's head to her stomach. Haduma made motions over them, chanting, then pulled out the bloodstained fur from beneath them. There was special magic for a woman in her blood of First Rites.

Then the old woman looked at Jondalar again, smiled, and reached a knobby finger to touch his spent member. He felt a moment of renewed excitement, saw it try to spring to life again, then go soft. Haduma chuckled softly, then hobbled out of the tent, leaving them alone.

Jondalar relaxed beside Noria. After a while, she sat up and looked down at him with glowing, languorous eyes.

"Jondalar man, Noria woman," she said, as though she truly felt she was a woman now, and leaned over to kiss him. He was surprised to feel a stir of excitement so soon, and wondered if Haduma's touch had anything to do with it. He forgot to wonder as he took his time showing the eager young woman ways to please him, and giving new pleasure to her.

The giant sturgeon was already beached by the time Jondalar got up. Thonolan had poked his head in the tent earlier, showing him a couple of gaffs, but Jondalar had waved him off, wrapped his arm around Noria, and gone back to sleep. When he woke up later, Noria was gone. He slipped on his trousers and walked towards the river. He watched Thonolan, Jeren, and several others laughing in newfound camaraderie, rather wishing he had fished with them.

"Well, look who decided to get up," Thonolan said when he saw him. "Leave it to blue eyes to lie around while everyone else is fighting to haul that old grandmother fish, that old Haduma out of the water."

Jeren caught the phrase. "Haduma! Haduma!" he shouted, laughing and pointing at the fish. He pranced around it, then stood in front of its primitive, sharklike head. The feelers sprouting out of the lower jaw attested to its bottom-feeding habits and harmlessness, but its size alone had made it a challenge. It was well over fifteen feet long.

With a roguish grin, the young hunter moved his pelvis back and forth in erotic mimicry at the nose of the great old fish, shouting, "Haduma! Haduma!" as though begging to be touched. The rest of them broke up in gales of bawdy laughter, and even Jondalar smiled. The others started dancing around the fish, shaking their pelvises and shouting "Haduma!" and, with high spirits, began pushing each other aside, vying for the spot at the head. One man was shoved into the river. He waded back, grabbed the nearest one, and pulled him in. Soon they were all pushing each other into the water. Thonolan right in the thick of it.

He splashed up on the bank soaking wet, spied his brother, and grabbed him. "Don't think you're going to get away dry!" he said as Jondalar resisted. "Come on, Jeren, let's give blue eyes a dunking!"

Jeren heard his name, saw the struggle, and came running. The others followed. Pulling and pushing, they dragged Jondalar to the river's edge, and all ended up in the water, laughing. They came out dripping, still grinning, until one of them noticed the old woman standing by the fish.

"Haduma, eh?" she said, fixing them with a severe stare. They gave each other surreptitious glances and looked sheepish. Then she cackled delightedly, stood at the head of the fish, and wagged her old hips back and forth. They laughed and ran towards her, each man getting down on hands and knees and begging her to get on his back.

Jondalar smiled at the game they had obviously played with her before. Her tribe not only revered their ancient ancestress, they loved her, and she seemed to enjoy their fun. Haduma looked around and, seeing Jondalar, pointed at him. The men waved him over, and he noticed the care with which they helped her onto his back. He stood up carefully. She weighed almost nothing, but he was surprised at the strength of her grip. The fragile old woman still had a certain toughness.

He started walking, but the rest were racing ahead, and she pounded his shoulder, urging him on. They ran up and down the beach until they were all out of breath, and then Jondalar got down to let her off. She straightened herself, found her staff, and, with great dignity, headed towards the tents.

"Can you believe that old woman?" Jondalar said to Thonolan with admiration. "Sixteen children, five generations, and she's still going strong. I don't doubt that she will live to see her sixth generation."

"She live see six generation, then she die."

Jondalar turned at the voice. He hadn't seen Tamen approach. "What do you mean, then she die?"

"Haduma say, Noria make blue-eye son, Zelandonii spirit, then Haduma die. She say, long time here, time go. See baby, then die. Baby name, Jondal, six generation Hadumai. Haduma happy Zelandonii man. Say good man. Pleasure woman First Rites not easy, Zelandonii man, good man."

Jondalar was filled with mixed emotions. "If it is her wish to go, she will, but it makes me sad," he said.

"Yes, all Hadumai much sad," Tamen said.

"Can I see Noria again, so soon after First Rites? Just for a while? I don't know your customs."

"Custom, no. Haduma say yes. You go soon?"

"If Jeren says the sturgeon pays our obligation for chasing off the horses, I think we should. How did you know?"

"Haduma say."

The camp feasted on sturgeon in the evening, and many hands had made short work of cutting strips for drying earlier in the afternoon. Jondalar glimpsed Noria once from a distance as she was escorted by several women to some place farther upstream. It was after dark before she was led to see him. They walked together towards the river, with two women following discreetly behind. It broke custom enough for her to see him immediately after First Rites; alone would be too much.

They stood by a tree not saying anything, her head bowed. He moved aside a tendril of hair and lifted her chin to look at him. She had tears in her eyes. Jondalar wiped a glistening drop from the corner of her eye with a knuckle, then brought it to his lips.

"Oh . . . Jondalar," she cried, reaching for him.

He held her, kissed her gently, then more passionately.

"Noria," he said. "Noria woman, beautiful woman."

"Jondalar make Noria woman," she said. "Make . . . Noria . . . Make . . ." She heaved a sob, wishing she knew the words to tell him what she wanted to say.

"I know, Noria, I know," he said, holding her. Then he stood back holding her shoulders, smiled at her and patted her stomach. She smiled through her tears.

"Noria make Zelandonyee. . . ." She touched his eyelid. "Noria make Jondal . . . Haduma. . . ."

"Yes." He nodded. "Tamen told me. Jondal, sixth-generation Hadumai." He reached into his pouch. "I have something I want to give you, Noria." He took out the stone donii and put it in her hand. He wished there were some way to tell her how special it was to him, to tell her his mother had given it to him, to tell her how old it was, how it had been passed down for many generations. Then he smiled. "This donii is my Haduma," he said. "Jondalar's Haduma. Now, it is Noria's Haduma."

"Jondalar Haduma?" she said with wonder, looking at the carved female shape. "Jondalar Haduma, Noria?"

He nodded, and she burst into tears, clutched it in both hands, and brought it to her lips. "Jondalar Haduma," she said, her shoulders shaking with sobs. Suddenly she threw her arms around him and kissed him, then ran back towards the tents, crying so hard that she could barely see her way.

The whole camp turned out to see them off. Haduma was standing beside Noria when Jondalar stopped in front of them. Haduma was smiling, nodding approval, but tears were rolling down Noria's cheeks. He reached for one, brought it to his mouth, and she smiled, though it didn't check her tears. He turned to go, but not before he saw the curly haired young man Jeren had sent as a runner looking at Noria with lovesick eyes.

She was a woman now and blessed by Haduma, assured of bringing a lucky child to a man's hearth. It was common talk that she had known pleasure at First Rites, and everyone knew such women made the best mates. Noria was eminently mateable, utterly desirable.

"Do you really think Noria is pregnant with a child of your spirit?" Thonolan asked after they left the camp behind.

"I'll never know, but that Haduma is a wise old woman. She knows more than anyone can guess. I think she does have 'big magic'. If anyone could make it happen, she could."

They walked in silence beside the river for a while, then Thonolan said, "Big Brother, there's something I'd like to ask you."

"Ask away."

"What magic do you have? I mean, every man talks about being chosen for First Rites, but it really scares a lot of them. I know a couple who have turned it down, and to be honest, I always feel clumsy. I'd never turn it down, though. But you,

you get chosen all the time. And I've never seen it fail. They all fall in love with you. How do you do it? I've watched you rut around at festivals; I can't see anything special."

"I don't know, Thonolan," he said, a little embarrassed. "I just try to be careful."

"What man doesn't? It's more than that. What was it Tamen said, 'Pleasure woman First Rites not easy.' How do you give a woman pleasure then? I'm just happy if I don't hurt her too much. And it's not like you're undersized or anything to make it easier. Come on, give your little brother some advice. I wouldn't mind a bunch of young beauties following me around."

He slowed and looked at Thonolan. "Yes you would. I think that's one of the reasons I got myself promised to Marona, so I'd have an excuse." Jondalar's forehead furrowed. "First Rites are special for a woman. They are for me, too. But a lot of young women are still girls in some ways. They haven't learned the difference between running after boys and inviting a man. How do you tactfully tell a young woman, whom you've just spent a very special night with, that you'd rather relax with a more experienced woman, when she's cornered you alone? Great Doni, Thonolan! I don't want to hurt them, but I don't fall in love with every woman I spend a night with."

"You don't fall in love at all, Jondalar."

Jondalar started walking faster. "What do you mean? I've loved a lot of women."

"Loved them, yes. That's not the same thing."

"How would you know? Have you ever been in love?"

"A few times. Maybe it hasn't lasted, but I know the difference. Look, Brother, I don't want to pry, but I worry about you, especially when you get moody. And you don't have to run. I'll shut up if you want me to."

Jondalar slowed down. "So, maybe you're right. Maybe I've never fallen in love. Maybe it's not in me to fall in love."

"What's missing? What don't the women you know have?"

"If I knew, don't you think . . ." he began angrily. Then he paused. "I don't know, Thonolan. I guess I want it all. I want a woman like she is at First Rites – I think I fall in love with every woman then, at least for that night. But I want a woman, not a girl. I want her honestly eager and willing without any pretences, but I don't want to have to be so careful with her. I want her to have spirit, to know her own mind. I want her young and old, naïve and wise, all at the same time."

"That's a lot to want, Brother."

"Well, you asked." They walked in silence for a while.

"How old would you say Zelandoni is?" Thonolan asked. "A little younger than Mother, maybe?"

Jondalar stiffened. "Why?"

"They say she was really beautiful when she was younger, even just a few years ago. Some of the older men say no one could compare to her, not even come close. It's hard for me to tell, but they say she's young to be First among Those Who Serve the Mother. Tell me something, Big Brother. What they say about you and Zelandoni, is it true?"

Jondalar stopped and slowly turned to face his brother. "Tell me, what do they say about me and Zelandoni?" he asked through gritted teeth.

"Sorry. I just went too far. Forget I asked."

5

Ayla walked out of the cave and onto the stone ledge in front of it, rubbing her eyes and stretching. The sun was still low in the east and she shaded her eyes as she looked to see where the horses were. Checking the horses when she awoke in the morning had already become a habit, though she had been there only a few days. It made her solitary existence a little more bearable to think she was sharing the valley with other living creatures.

She was becoming aware of their patterns of movement, where they went for water in the morning, the shade trees they favoured in the afternoon, and she was noticing individuals. There was the yearling colt whose grey coat was so light that it was almost white, except where it shaded darker along the characteristic stripe down the spine and the dark grey lower legs and stiff standing mane. And there was the dun mare with her hay-coloured foal, whose coat matched the stallion's. And then the proud leader himself, whose place would some day be taken by one of those yearlings he barely tolerated, or perhaps one of next year's brood, or the next. The light yellow stallion, with the deep brown feral stripe, mane, and lower legs, was in his prime, and his bearing showed it.

"Good morning, horse clan," Ayla signalled, making the gesture commonly used for any greeting purpose, with a slight nuance which shaded it to a morning greeting. "I slept late this morning. You've already had your morning drink – I think I'll get mine."

She ran lightly down to the stream, familiar enough with the steep path to be sure-footed on it. She took a drink, then doffed her wrap for her morning swim. It was the same wrap, but she had washed it and worked it with her scrapers to soften the leather again. Her own natural preference for order and cleanliness had been reinforced by Iza, whose large pharmacopoeia of medicinal herbs required order to avoid misuse, and who understood the dangers of dirt and filth and infections. It was one thing to accept a certain amount of grime while travelling, when it couldn't be avoided. But not with a sparkling stream nearby.

She ran her hands through thick blonde hair that fell in waves well below her shoulders. "I'm going to wash my hair this morning," she motioned to no one in particular. Just around the bend she had found soaproot growing, and went to pull some roots. As she strolled back looking over the stream, she noticed the large rock jutting out of the shallows with smooth saucer-shaped depressions in it. She picked up a round stone and waded out to the rock. She rinsed the roots, scooped water into a depression, and pounded the soaproot to release the rich sudsy saponin. When she had worked up the foam, she wetted her hair, rubbed it in, then washed the rest of her body and dived into the water to rinse.

A large section of the jutting wall had broken off at some time in the past. Ayla climbed out on the portion that was underwater and walked across the surface that rose above the water to a place warming in the sun. A waist-deep channel on the shoreward side made the rock an island, partly shaded by an overhanging willow whose exposed roots clutched at the stream like bony fingers. She broke a twig off a small bush whose roots had found purchase in a crack, peeled it with her teeth, and used it to pull snarls out of her hair while it dried in the sun.

She was staring dreamily into the water, humming under her breath, when a flicker of movement caught her eye. Suddenly alert, she looked into the water at the silvery shape of a large trout resting beneath the roots. I haven't had fish since I left the cave, she thought, recalling she hadn't had breakfast either.

Slipping silently into the water off the far side of the rock, she swam downstream a way, then waded towards the shallows. She put her hand in the water, letting her fingers dangle, and slowly, with infinite patience, she moved back upstream. As she approached the tree, she saw the trout with its head into the current, undulating slightly to maintain itself in its place under the root.

Ayla's eyes glistened with excitement, but she was even more cautious, placing each foot securely as she neared the fish. She moved her hand up from behind until it was just below the trout, then touched it lightly, feeling for the open gill-covers. Suddenly, she grasped the fish and, in one sure movement, lifted it out of the water and threw it on the bank. The trout flopped and struggled for a few moments, then lay still.

She smiled, pleased with herself. It had been difficult learning how to tickle a fish out of the water when she was a child, and she still felt almost as proud as she had the first time she succeeded. She would watch the spot, knowing it would be used by a succession of tenants. This one is big enough for more than breakfast, she thought, as she retrieved her catch – anticipating the taste of fresh trout baked on hot stones.

As her breakfast cooked, Ayla busied herself making a basket of beargrass she had picked the day before. It was a simple, utilitarian basket, but with small variations in the weaving she created a change in texture to please herself, giving it a subtle design. She worked quickly, but with such skill that the basket would be watertight. By adding hot rocks, it could be used for a cooking utensil, but that was not the purpose she had in mind for it. She was making a storage container, thinking about everything she had to do to make herself secure for the cold season ahead.

The currants I picked yesterday will be dry in a few days, she estimated, glancing at the round red berries spread out on grass mats on her front porch. By then, more will be ripe. There will be a lot of blueberries, but I won't get much out of that scrawny little apple tree. The cherry tree is full, but they're almost too ripe. If I'm going to get some, I'd better do it today. Sunflower seeds will be good, if the birds don't get them all first. I think those were hazelnut bushes by the apple tree, but they're so much smaller than the ones by the little cave, I'm not sure. I think those pine trees are the kind with the big nuts in the cones, though. I'll check them later. Wish that fish would cook!

I should start drying greens. And lichen. And mushrooms.

And roots. I won't have to dry all the roots, some will keep for a long time in the back of the cave. Should I get more pigweed seeds? They're so small, it never seems like much. Grain is worth the effort, though, and some seed heads in the meadow are ripe. I'll get cherries and grain today, but I'm going to need more storage baskets. Maybe I can make some containers out of birchbark. Wish I had some rawhide to make those big cases.

There always seemed to be extra skins around for rawhide when I lived with the Clan. Now I'd be happy if I had one more warm fur for winter. Rabbits and hamsters aren't big enough to make a good fur wrap, and they're so lean. If I could hunt a mammoth, I'd have plenty of fat, even enough for lamps. And nothing is as good and rich as mammoth meat. Wonder if that trout is done yet? She moved aside a limp leaf and poked at the fish with a stick. Just a little more.

It would be nice to have a little salt, but there's no sea around here. Coltsfoot tastes salty, and other herbs can add flavour. Iza could make anything taste good. Maybe I'll go out on the steppes and see if I can find some ptarmigan, and then make it the way Creb always liked it.

She felt a lump in her throat thinking about Iza and Creb, and shook her head as though she were trying to stop the thoughts, or at least the impending tears.

I need a drying rack for herbs and teas, and medicines, too. I could get sick. I can chop down some trees for posts, but I need fresh thongs to bind them together. Then, when they dry and shrink, it'll hold. With all the deadfall and driftwood, I don't think I'll have to cut down trees for firewood, and there will be dung from the horses. It burns well when it's dry. I'll start bringing wood up to the cave today, and I should make some tools soon. It's lucky I found flint. That fish must be done.

Ayla ate the trout straight off the bed of hot rocks on which it had cooked, and she thought about looking through the pile of bones and driftwood for some flat pieces of wood or bone to use for plates; pelvic or shoulder bones worked well. She emptied her small waterbag into her cooking bowl and wished she had the waterproof stomach of a larger animal to make a more capacious waterbag for the cave. She added hot stones from the fire to start the water in her cooking bowl heating, then sprinkled some dried rosehips from her medicine bag into the steaming water. She used rosehips as a remedy for minor colds, but they also made a pleasant tea.

The arduous task of collecting, processing, and storing the abundance of the valley was no deterrent; rather, she looked forward to it. It would keep her busy; she wouldn't have time to think about being lonely. She only had to preserve enough for herself, but there were no extra hands to make the task go faster, and she worried whether there was enough of the season left to lay in an adequate supply. Something else bothered her, too.

Sipping tea while she finished the basket, Ayla considered the requirements she would need to survive the long cold winter. I should have another fur for my bed this winter, she was thinking. And meat, of course. What about fat? I should have some in winter. I could make birchbark containers much faster than baskets, if only I had some hooves, bones, and hide scraps to boil for glue. And where will I get a large waterbag? Thongs to bind the post for a drying rack? I could use sinew, and intestines for storing the fat, and . . .

Her rapidly moving fingers stopped. She stared into space as though seeing the vision of a revelation. I could get all that from one large animal! Just one is all I'd need to kill. But how?

She finished the small basket and put it inside her collecting basket, which she tied to her back. She put her tools in the folds of her wrap, picked up her digging stick and sling, and headed for the meadow. She found the wild cherry tree, picked as many as she could reach, then climbed up to get more. She ate her share, too; even overripe, they were tart-sweet.

When she climbed down, she decided to get cherry bark for coughs. With her hand-axe, she chopped away a section of the tough outer bark, then scraped off the inner cambium layer with a knife. It reminded her of the time when she was a girl and had gone to collect wild cherry bark for Iza. She had spied on the men practising with their weapons in the field. She knew it was wrong, but she was afraid they might see her leaving, and she became intrigued when old Zoug began teaching the boy to use a sling.

She knew women weren't supposed to touch weapons, but

when they left the sling behind, she couldn't resist. She wanted to try it, too. Would I be alive today if I hadn't picked up that sling? Would Broud have hated me so much if I hadn't learned to use it? Maybe he wouldn't have made me leave if he didn't hate me so much. But if he hadn't hated me, he wouldn't have enjoyed forcing me, and maybe Durc would not have been born.

Maybe! Maybe! Maybe! she thought angrily. What's the sense of thinking about what might have been? I'm here now, and that sling isn't going to help me hunt a big animal. For that I need a spear!

She picked her way through a stand of young aspen to get a drink and wash the sticky cherry juice off her hands. There was something about the tall, straight young trees that made her stop. She grasped the trunk of one; then it struck her. This would work! This would make a spear.

She quailed for a moment. Brun would be furious, she thought. When he allowed me to hunt, he told me I must never hunt with anything but a sling. He'd . . .

What would he do? What could he do? What more can any of them do to me, even if they knew? I'm dead. I'm already dead. There's no one here except me.

Then, like a cord pulled so taut it breaks from the strain, something inside her snapped. She fell to her knees. Oh, how I wish there were someone here beside me. Someone. Anyone. I'd even be glad to see Broud. I'd never touch a sling again if he'd let me go back, if he'd let me see Durc again. Kneeling at the base of the slender aspen, Ayla buried her face in her hands, heaving and choking.

Her sobs fell on indifferent ears. The small creatures of meadow and woodland only avoided the stranger in their midst and her incomprehensible sounds. There was no one else to hear, no one to understand. While she had been travelling, she had nursed the hope of finding people, people like herself. Now that she had decided to stop, she had to put that hope aside, accept her solitude, and learn to live with it. The gnawing worry of survival, alone, in an unknown place through a winter of unknown severity, added to the strain. The crying relieved the tension.

When she got up, she was shaking, but she took out her hand-axe and hacked angrily at the base of the young aspen, then attacked a second sapling. I've watched the men make spears often enough, she said to herself as she stripped off the branches. It didn't look that hard. She dragged the poles to the field and left them while she gathered seed heads of einkorn wheat and rye for the rest of the afternoon, then dragged them back to the cave.

She spent the early evening stripping bark and smoothing shafts, stopping only to cook herself some grain to have with the rest of her fish, and to spread the cherries out to dry. By the time it was dark, she was ready for the next step. She took the shafts into her cave, and, remembering how the men had done it, she measured off a length on one somewhat taller than herself and marked it. Then she put the marked section in the fire, turning the shaft to char it all around. With a notched scraper, she shaved away the blackened section and continued to char and scrape until the upper piece broke off. More charring and scraping brought it to a sharp, fire-hardened point. Then she started on the next one.

When she finished, it was late. She was tired, and glad of it. It would bring sleep more easily. Nights were the worst time. Ayla banked her fire, walked to the opening, gazed out at the star-spattered sky, and tried to think of some reason to delay going to bed. She had dug a shallow trench, filled it with dry grass, and covered it with her fur. She walked towards it with slow steps. She lowered herself onto it and stared at the faint glow of the fire, listening to the silence.

There were no rustlings of people preparing for bed, no sounds of coupling from nearby hearths, no grunting or snoring; none of the many small sounds of people, not a single breath of life – except her own. She reached for the cloak she had used to carry her son on her hip, bunched it up and pressed it to her breast, and rocked back and forth crooning under her breath while tears rolled down her face. Finally, she lay down, curled herself around the empty cloak, and cried herself to sleep.

When Ayla went outside the next morning to relieve herself, there was blood on her leg. She rummaged through her small pile of belongings for the absorbent straps and her special waist thong. They were stiff and shiny despite washings, and they should have been buried the last time she used them. She wished she had some mouflon wool to pack in them. Then she spied the rabbit fur. I wanted to save that rabbit skin for winter, but I can get more rabbits, she thought.

She cut the small skin into strips before she went down for her morning swim. I should have known it was coming, I could have planned for it. Now I won't be able to do anything except . . .

Suddenly she laughed. The women's curse doesn't matter here. There are no men I have to avoid looking at, no men whose food I can't cook or gather. I'm the only one I have to worry about.

Still, I should have expected it, but the days have gone by so fast, I didn't think it was time yet. How long have I been in this valley? She tried to remember, but the days seemed to fade into each other. She frowned. I ought to know how many days I've been here – it might be later in the season than I thought. She felt a moment of panic. It's not that bad, she reminded herself. The snow won't fall before the fruits ripen and the leaves drop, but I should know. I should keep track of the days.

She recalled when, long ago, Creb had shown her how to cut a groove in a stick to mark the passage of time. He had been surprised when she caught on so quickly; he had only explained it to still her constant questions. He shouldn't have been showing a girl sacrosanct knowledge reserved for holy men and their acolytes, and he had cautioned her not to mention it. She remembered, as well, his anger another time when he caught her marking a stick to count the days between full moons.

"Creb, if you're watching me from the spirit world, don't be angry," she said with the silent sign language. "You must know why I need to do it."

She found a long smooth stick and made a notch in it with her flint knife. Then she thought a while and added two more. She fitted her first three fingers over the notches and held them up. I think it's been more days than that, but I'm sure of that many. I'll mark it again tonight, and every night. She studied the stick again. I think I'll put a little extra knick above this one, to mark the day I started bleeding.

*

The moon went through half its phases after she made the spears, but she still didn't know how she was going to hunt the large animal she needed. She was sitting at the opening of her cave looking at the wall across and the night sky. The summer was waxing into full heat and she was savouring the cool evening breeze. She had just completed a new summer outfit. Her full wrap was often too hot to wear, and although she went naked near the cave, she needed the pouches and folds of a wrap to hold things when she went very far from it. After she had become a woman, she liked to wear a leather band wrapped tightly round her full breasts when she went hunting. It was more comfortable to run and jump. And in the valley she didn't have to put up with surreptitious glances from people who thought she was odd for wearing it.

She didn't have a large hide to cut down, but she finally devised a way to wear rabbit skins, dehaired, as a summer wrap that left her bare from the waist up, and she used other skins as a breast band. She planned to make a trip to the steppes in the morning, with her new spears and hopes of finding animals to hunt.

The gradual slope of the northern side of the valley gave easy access to the steppes east of the river; the sheer wall made the western plains too difficult to reach. She saw several herds of deer, bison, horses, even a small band of saiga antelopes, but she brought back nothing more than a brace of ptarmigan and a great jerboa. She just couldn't get close enough to jab anything with her spears.

As the days passed, hunting a large animal was a constant preoccupation. She had often watched the men of the clan talk about hunting – they talked about almost nothing else – but they always hunted cooperatively. Their favourite technique, like that of a pack of wolves, was to cut an animal out of a herd and run it down in relays, until it was so exhausted, they could get close enough to make the fatal thrust. But Ayla was alone.

It was the night of the new moon when she finally got an idea she thought might work. She often thought of the Clan Gathering when the moon turned its back on the earth and bathed the far reaches of space with its reflected light. The Cave Bear Festival was always held when the moon was new.

She was thinking about the hunt re-enactments made by

the different clans. Broud had led the exciting hunt dance for their clan, and the vivid re-creation of chasing a mammoth into a blind canyon with fire had won the day. But the host clan's portrayal of digging a pit trap on the path a woolly rhinoceros usually took to water, and then surrounding it and chasing him into it, had brought them in a close second in that competition. Woolly rhinos were notoriously unpredictable and dangerous.

The next morning, Ayla looked to see if the horses were there, but she didn't greet them. She could identify each member of the herd individually. They were company, almost friends, but there was no other way, not if she was going to survive.

She spent the greater part of the next several days observing the herd, studying their movements: where they normally watered, where they liked to graze, where they spent the nights. As she watched, a plan began to take shape in her mind. She worried over details, tried to think of every contingency, and finally set to work.

It took a full day to chop down small trees and brush and drag them halfway across the field, piling them up near a break in the trees along the stream. She gathered pitchy barks and limbs of fir and pine, dug through rotted old stumps for residual hard lumps that caught fire quickly, and pulled up bunches of dry grass. In the evening, she bound the lumps and pieces of pitch to branches with grass to make torches that would start quickly and burn smoky.

The morning of the day she planned to start, she got out her hide tent and the aurochs horn. Then she scrounged through the pile at the foot of the wall for a flat sturdy bone and scraped one side until it tapered to a sharp edge. Then, with hopes she would need them, she got out every cord and thong she could find, and pulled lianas down from the trees and piled them on the rocky beach. She hauled loads of driftwood and deadfall to the beach, too, so she'd have enough for fires.

By early evening, everything was ready, and Ayla paced back and forth along the beach as far as the jutting wall, checking on the herd's movements. Anxiously, she watched a few clouds building up in the east and hoped they would not move in and obscure the moonlight she was counting on. She cooked herself some grain and picked a few berries, but couldn't eat much. She kept picking up her spears to make practice lunges and putting them down.

At the last moment, she dug through the pile of driftwood and bones until she found the long humerus from the foreleg of a deer with its knobby end. She smashed it against a large piece of mammoth ivory and winced at the recoil through her arm. The long bone was undamaged; it was a good solid club.

The moon rose before the sun set. Ayla wished she knew more about hunting ceremonies, but women had always been excluded. Women brought bad luck.

I never brought bad luck to myself, she thought, but I've never tried to hunt a big animal before. I wish I knew something that would bring good luck. Her hand went to her amulet, and she thought of her totem. It was her Cave Lion, after all, that had led her to hunt in the first place. That's what Creb said. What other reason could there be for a woman to become more skilled with her chosen weapon than any man? Her totem was too strong for a woman – it gave her masculine traits, Brun had thought. Ayla hoped her totem would bring her luck again.

Twilight was fading into darkness when Ayla walked to the bend in the river and saw the horses finally settling down for the night. She gathered up the flat bone and the tent hide, and ran through the tall grass until she came to the break in the trees where the horses watered in the morning. The green foliage was grey in the waning daylight, and the more distant trees were black silhouettes against a sky ablaze with colour. Hoping the moon would shed enough light to see, she laid the tent on the ground and began to dig.

The surface was hard-packed, but, once she broke through it, digging was easier with the sharpened bone shovel. When a pile of soil was mounded on the hide, she dragged it into the woods to dump it. As the hole became deeper, she laid the hide out on the bottom of the pit and hauled the dirt up with it. She felt her way more than seeing, and it was hard work. She had never dug a pit by herself before. The large cooking pits, lined with rocks and used to roast whole rumps, had always been a community effort by all the women, and this pit had to be deeper and longer.

The hole was about waist high when she felt water and

realized she should not have dug so close to the stream. The bottom filled quickly. She was ankle deep in mud before she gave up and climbed out, breaking down one edge as she lifted out the hide.

I hope it's deep enough, she thought. It will have to be – the more I dig, the more water comes in. She glanced at the moon, surprised at how late it was. She was going to have to work fast to finish, and she wasn't going to get the short rest she had planned.

She ran towards the place where the brush and trees were piled, and tripped on an unseen root, falling heavily. This is no time to be careless! she thought, rubbing her shin. Her knees and palms stung, and she was sure the slippery ooze down one leg was blood, though she couldn't see it.

With sudden insight, she understood how vulnerable she was, and had a moment of panic. What if I break my leg? There's no one here to help me – if anything happens. What am I doing out here at night? With no fire? What if an animal attacks? She vividly recalled a lynx that leaped at her once, and reached for her sling, imagining glowing eyes in the night.

She found the weapon still securely tucked into her waist thong. It brought reassurance. I'm dead anyway, or supposed to be. If something is going to happen, it will happen. I can't worry now. If I don't hurry, it will be morning before I'm ready.

She found her brush pile and began to drag the small trees towards the pit. She couldn't surround the horses by herself, she had reasoned, and there were no blind canyons in the valley, but, with an intuitive leap, she got an idea. It was the stroke of genius to which her brain – the brain that had differentiated her from the Clan far more than had physical appearance – was especially suited. If there were no canyons in the valley, she thought, perhaps she could make one.

It didn't matter that the idea had been thought of before. It was new to her. She didn't think of it as a great invention. It seemed only a minor adaptation to the way Clan men hunted; only a minor adaptation that might, just might, enable a lone woman to kill an animal that no man of the Clan would dream of hunting alone. It was a great invention, born of necessity.

Ayla watched the sky anxiously as she wove branches, constructing a barrier angling out from both sides of the pit. She filled in the gaps and made it higher with brush as the stars winked out in the eastern sky. The earliest birds had started their warbling greeting and the sky was lightening when she stood back and looked over her handiwork.

The pit was roughly rectangular, somewhat longer than it was wide, and muddy around the edges where the last wet loads had been hauled out. Loose piles of dirt, spilled from the hide, were strewn on the trampled grass within the triangular area defined by the two walls of brush coming together at the muddy hole. Through a gap where the pit separated the two fences, the river could be seen, reflecting the glowing eastern sky. On the other side of the rippling water, the steep southern wall of the valley loomed darkly; only near the top were its contours distinguishable.

Ayla turned around to check the position of the horses. The other side of the valley had a more gradual slope, growing steeper towards the west as it rose to form the jutting wall in front of her cave, and levelling out to rolling grassy hills far down the valley on the east. It was still dark there, but she could see the horses beginning to move.

She grabbed the hide and the flat bone shovel and raced back to the beach. The fire was down. She added wood, then fished out a hot coal with a stick and put it in the aurochs horn, grabbed the torches, the spears, and the club, and ran back to the pit. She laid a spear down on either side of the hole, the club beside one, then loped around in a wide circle to get behind the horses before they began to move.

And then, she waited.

The waiting was harder than the long night of working. She was keyed up, anxious, wondering if her plan would work. She checked her coal, and waited; looked over the torches, and waited. She thought of countless things she hadn't thought of before, that she should have done, or done differently, and waited. She wondered when the horses were going to begin their meandering move towards the stream, thought about prodding them on, thought better of it, and she waited.

The horses began to mill around. Ayla thought they seemed more nervous than usual, but she had never been this close to them, and she wasn't sure. Finally, the lead mare started towards the river and the rest followed behind, stopping to graze along the way. They definitely became nervous as they drew nearer the river and picked up Ayla's scent and the smell of disturbed earth. When the lead mare appeared to be veering off, Ayla decided it was time.

She lit a torch with the coal, then a second from the first. When they were burning well, she started after the herd, leaving the aurochs horn behind. She ran, whooping and hollering and waving the torches, but she was too far from the herd. The smell of smoke brought an instinctive fear of prairie fires. The horses picked up speed and quickly outdistanced her. They were heading towards their watering place and the brush fence, but, sensing danger, some made a break towards the east. Ayla angled in the same direction, running as fast as she could, hoping to head them off. As she drew closer, she saw more of the herd swerving to avoid the trap, and she ran into their midst yelling. They dodged around her. Ears laid back, nostrils flaring, they passed her by on either side, screaming in fear and confusion. Ayla was getting panicky, as well, afraid they were all going to get away.

She was near the eastern end of the brush barrier when she saw the dun mare coming towards her. She screamed at the horse, held her torches wide, and ran straight for what seemed a sure head-on collision. At the last moment, the mare dodged, the wrong way – for her. She found her escape blocked and galloped along the inside of the fence, trying to find a way out. Ayla pounded behind her, panting for breath, feeling her lungs were about to burst.

The mare saw the gap with its beckoning glimpse of the river and headed for it. Then she saw the open pit – too late. She gathered her legs under her to leap over the hole, but her hooves slipped on the muddy edge. She crashed into the pit with a broken leg.

Ayla dashed up, breathing hard; she picked up a spear and stood looking at the wild-eyed mare that was screaming, tossing her head, and floundering in the mud. Ayla grasped the shaft with both hands, braced her legs, and plunged the point towards the pit. Then she realized that she had driven the spear into a flank, wounding the horse, but not mortally. She raced around to the other side, slipping on the mud and nearly falling in the hole herself.

Ayla picked up the other spear and this time took more careful aim. The mare was neighing in confusion and pain, and, as the point of the second spear bored into her neck, she lurched forward in a last valiant effort. Then she sank back with a whinny that was more like a whimper, with two wounds and a broken leg. A hard blow with the club finally ended her pain.

Realization came slowly to Ayla; she was too dazed to comprehend her achievement yet. At the edge of the pit, leaning heavily on the club she still held and gasping for breath, she stared at the fallen mare in the bottom of the hole. The shaggy greyish coat was streaked with blood and covered with mud, but the animal did not move.

Then, slowly, it filled her. An urge, like none she had ever known, rose out of her depths, grew in her throat, and burst from her mouth in a primal scream of victory. She did it!

At that moment, in a lonely valley in the middle of a vast continent, somewhere near the undefined boundary of the desolate northern loess steppes and the wetter continental steppes to the south, a young woman stood with a bone club in her hand – and felt powerful. She could survive. She would survive.

But her exultation was short lived. As Ayla looked down at the horse, it suddenly occurred to her that she would never be able to drag the whole animal out of the pit; she would have to butcher it in the bottom of the muddy hole. And then she would have to get it back to the beach, quickly, with the whole skin in reasonably good condition, before too many other predators picked up the scent of blood. She would have to cut the meat into thin strips, salvage the other parts she wanted, keep the fires going, and keep watch while the meat dried.

And she was already exhausted from the gruelling night's work and the anxious chase. But she wasn't a man of the Clan who could relax, now that his exciting part was over, and leave the job of butchering and processing to the women. Ayla's work had just begun. She heaved a great sigh, then jumped down into the pit to slit the mare's throat.

She ran back to the beach for the tent hide and the flint tools, and, on her return, she noticed that the herd at the far end of the valley was still moving. She forgot them as she struggled in the cramped space of the pit, covered with blood and mud, hacking out hunks of meat and trying not to damage the hide any worse than it was.

Carion birds were picking shreds of meat off discarded bones when she had piled up as much meat on the tent hide as she thought she could haul. She dragged it to the beach, added fuel to the fire, and dumped her load as close as she could. She ran back dragging the empty hide, but had her sling out and stones flying before she reached the pit. She heard the yip of a fox and saw it limp away. She would have killed one if she hadn't run out of stones. She picked up more stones from the riverbed and took a drink before she started back to work.

The stone was sure and fatal to the wolverine that had braved the heat of the fire and was trying to drag a large hunk of meat away when Ayla returned with a second load. She dragged her meat to the fire, then went back to get the glutton, hoping she'd have time to skin it, too. Wolverine fur was particularly useful for winter wear. She added more wood to the fire and eyed the driftwood pile.

She wasn't as lucky with the hyena when she returned to the pit. It managed to make off with a whole shank. She hadn't seen so many carnivores in the valley since she arrived. Foxes, hyenas, wolverines had all got a taste of her kill. Wolves, and their fiercer, doglike relatives, dholes, paced just beyond the range of her sling. Hawks and kites were braver, only flapping wings and backing off slightly as she approached. She expected to see a lynx, or a leopard, or even a cave lion any time.

By the time she hauled the filthy hide out of the hole, the sun had passed its zenith and was starting down, but not until she had dragged her last load to the beach did she give in to her fatigue and sink to the ground. She hadn't slept all night; she hadn't eaten all day; and she didn't want to move. But the smallest of the creatures after their share of her kill finally made her get up again. The buzzing flies caused her to notice how filthy she was, and they bit. She forced herself up and walked into the stream without bothering to remove her clothes, gratefully letting the water wash over her.

The river was refreshing. Afterwards, she went up to her

cave, spread her summer wraps out to dry, and wished she had remembered to take her sling out of her waist thong before she went into the water. She was afraid it would dry stiff. She didn't have time to work it soft and flexible. She put on her full wrap and got her sleeping fur from the cave. Before she went down to the beach, she looked across the meadow from the edge of her stone porch. There were scufflings and movements near the pit, but the horses were gone from the valley.

Suddenly she remembered her spears. They were still on the ground where she had left them after pulling them out of the mare. She debated with herself about going after them, almost talked herself out of it, then admitted it was better to keep two perfectly good spears than go to the work of making new ones later. She picked up her damp sling and dropped her fur on the beach as she stopped for a pouchful of stones.

Drawing near the pit trap, she saw the carnage as though for the first time. The brush fence had fallen over in places. The pit was a raw wound in the earth and the grass trampled. Blood, scraps of meat, and bones were scattered around. Two wolves were snarling over the remains of the mare's head. Kit foxes were yipping around a shaggy foreleg with a hoof still attached, and a hyena was eyeing her warily. A flock of kites took wing as she approached, but a wolverine stood its ground beside the pit. Only the cats were still conspicuously absent.

I'd better hurry, she was thinking, as she cast a stone to make the glutton give way. I've got to get fires going around my meat. The hyena made a whooping cackle as it backed off, staying just out of range. Get out of here, you ugly thing! she thought. Ayla hated hyenas. Every time she saw one, she remembered the time a hyena had snatched Oga's baby. She hadn't stopped to think about the consequences; she had killed it. She just couldn't let the baby die that way.

As she bent to pick up her spears, her attention was caught by movement seen through the gap in the brush barrier. Several hyenas were stalking a spindly legged, hay-coloured foal.

I'm sorry for you, Ayla thought. I didn't want to kill your dam, she just happened to be the one who got caught. Ayla had no feelings of guilt. There were hunters, and there were the hunted, and sometimes the hunters were hunted. She could as easily fall prey, in spite of her weapons and her fire. Hunting was a way of life.

But she knew the little horse was doomed without its mother, and she felt sorry for a small and helpless animal. Ever since the first rabbit she had brought to Iza to heal, she had brought a succession of small wounded animals to the cave, much to Brun's dismay. He had drawn the line at carnivores, though.

She watched the hyenas circle the little filly, who was skittishly trying to stay out of their way, looking wild-eyed and scared. With no one to take care of you, maybe it's better to get it over with, Ayla reasoned. But when one hyena made a rush for the foal, slashing its flank, she didn't think. She tore through the brush, slinging stones. One hyena dropped, the others dashed away. She wasn't trying to kill them; she wasn't interested in the scruffy-looking spotted fur of hyenas; she wanted them to leave the little horse alone. The foal ran away too, but not as far. It was afraid of Ayla, but more fearful of hyenas.

Ayla approached the baby slowly, holding out her hand and crooning softly in a way that had calmed other frightened animals before. She had a natural way with animals, a sensitivity, that extended to all living creatures, developed along with her medical skills. Iza had fostered it, seen it as an extension of her own compassion that had impelled her to pick up a strange-looking girlchild because she was hurt and hungry.

The little filly reached out to sniff Ayla's outstretched fingers. The young woman moved closer, then patted, and rubbed, and scratched the foal. When the little horse noticed some familiar smell about Ayla's fingers and began sucking on them noisily, it woke an old aching hunger in Ayla.

Poor baby, she thought, so hungry and no mother to give you milk. I don't have any milk for you; I don't even have enough for Durc. She felt tears threaten and shook her head. Well, he grew strong anyway. Maybe I can think of something else to feed you. You'll have to be weaned young, too. Come on, baby. She led the young filly towards the beach with her fingers.

Just as she approached, she saw a lynx about to make off

with a hunk of her hard-won meat. A cat had finally made an appearance. She reached for two stones and her sling as the skittish foal backed away, and, as the lynx looked up, she hurled the stones with force.

"You can kill a lynx with a sling," Zoug had stoutly maintained once long ago. "Don't try anything bigger, but you can kill a lynx."

It wasn't the first time Ayla had proved him right. She retrieved her meat and dragged the tufted-eared cat back, too. Then she looked at the pile of meat, the mud-encrusted horsehide, the dead wolverine, and the dead lynx. Suddenly she laughed out loud. I needed meat. I needed furs. Now all I need is a few more hands, she thought.

The little filly had shied away from her burst of laughter and the smell of fire. Ayla got a thong, approached the young horse carefully again, then tied the thong around her neck and led her to the beach. She tied the other end to a bush, remembered she had forgotten her spears again, ran to get them, then went to soothe the little horse who had tried to follow her. What am I going to feed you she thought when the baby tried to suck her fingers again. It's not as if I don't have enough to do right now.

She tried some grass, but the little horse didn't seem to know quite what to do with it. Then she noticed her cooking bowl with the cold cooked grain in the bottom. Babies can eat the same kind of food as their mothers, she remembered, but it has to be softer. She added water to the bowl, mashed the grain to a fine gruel, and brought it to the foal, who only snorted and backed off when the woman put her muzzle in it. But then she licked her face and seemed to like the taste. She was hungry and went after Ayla's fingers again.

Ayla thought for a moment; then, with the filly still sucking, she lowered her hand into the bowl. The horse sucked in a little gruel and tossed her head, but after a few more attempts the hungry baby seemed to get the idea. When she was through, Ayla went up to the cave, brought down more grain, and started it cooking for later. Then she looked at the task ahead of her and set to work.

She was still cutting meat into thin strips when the full moon rose and the stars winked on again. A ring of fires circled the beach, and she was grateful for the large pile of driftwood nearby. Within the circle, line after line of drying meat was stretched out. A tawny lynx fur was rolled up beside a smaller roll of coarse brown wolverine, both waiting to be scraped and cured. The freshly washed grey coat of the mare was laid out on the stones, drying alongside the horse's stomach, which was cleaned and filled with water to keep it soft. There were strips of drying tendon for sinew, lengths of washed intestine, a pile of hooves and bones and another of lumps of fat waiting to be rendered and poured into the intestines for storage. She had even managed to salvage a little fat from the lynx and wolverine – for lamps and water-proofing – though she discarded the meat. She didn't much care for the taste of carnivores.

Ayla looked at the last two hunks of meat, washed off mud in the stream, and reached for one. Then she changed her mind. They could wait. She couldn't ever remember being so tired. She checked her fires, piled more wood on each, then spread out her bearskin fur and rolled up in it.

The little horse was no longer tied to the bush. After a second feeding, she seemed to have no desire to wander off. Ayla was almost asleep when the filly sniffed her and then lay down beside her. She didn't think at the time that the foal's responses would wake her if any predator came too close to dying fires, though it was so. Half asleep, the young woman put her arm around the warm little animal, felt her heart-beat, heard her breath, and cuddled closer.

6

Jondalar rubbed the stubble on his chin and reached for his pack that was propped against a stunted pine. He withdrew a small packet of soft leather, untied the cords and opened the folds, and carefully examined a thin flint blade. It had a slight curvature along its length – all blades cleaved from flint were bowed a little, it was a characteristic of the stone – but the edge was even and sharp. The blade was one of several especially fine tools he had put aside.

A sudden wind rattled the dry limbs of the lichen-scabbed old pine. The gust whipped the tent flap open, billowed through, straining the guy lines and tugging at the stakes, and slapped it shut again. Jondalar looked at the blade, then shook his head and wrapped it up again.

"Time to let the beard grow?" Thonolan asked.

Jondalar hadn't noticed his brother's approach. "One thing about a beard," he said. "In summer it may be a bother. Itches when you sweat – more comfortable to shave it off. But it sure helps keep your face warm in winter, and winter is coming."

Thonolan blew on his hands, rubbing them, then squatted down by the small fire in front of the tent and held them over the flames. "I miss the colour," he said.

"The colour?"

"Red. There's no red. A bush here and there, but everything else just turned yellow and then brown. Grass, leaves," he nodded in the general direction of the open grassland behind him, then looked towards Jondalar standing near the tree. "Even the pines look drab. There's ice on puddles and the edges of streams already, and I'm still waiting for fall."

"Don't wait too long," Jondalar said, moving over and

hunkering down in front of the fire opposite his brother. "I saw a rhino earlier this morning. Going north."

"I thought it smelled like snow."

"Won't be much yet, not if rhinos and mammoths are still around. They like it cold, but they don't like much snow. They always seem to know when a big storm is coming and head back towards the glacier in a hurry. People say 'Never go forth when mammoths go north.' It's true for rhinos, too, but this one wasn't hurrying."

"I've seen whole hunting parties turn back without throwing a single spear, just because the woollies were moving north. I wonder how much it snows around here?"

"The summer was dry. If the winter is too, mammoths and rhinos may stay all season. But we're farther south now, and that usually means more snow. If there are people in those mountains to the east, they should know. Maybe we should have stayed with the people who rafted us across the river. We need a place to stay for the winter, and soon."

"I wouldn't mind a nice friendly cave full of beautiful women right now," Thonolan said with a grin.

"I'd settle for a nice friendly Cave."

"Big Brother, you wouldn't want to spend a winter without women any more than I would."

Jondalar shrugged and stood up. "Well, we're not going to find women, or a Cave, this way. Let's break camp."

"Right!" Thonolan said eagerly, then turned his back to the fire – and froze! "Jondalar!" he gasped, then strained to sound casual. "Don't do anything to attract his attention, but if you look over the tent, you'll see your friend from this morning, or one just like him."

Jondalar peered over the top of the tent. Just on the other side, swaying from side to side as he shifted his massive tonnage from one foot to the other, was a huge, double-horned, woolly rhinoceros. With his head turned to the side, he was eyeing Thonolan. He was nearly blind directly ahead; his small eyes were set far back and his vision was poor to begin with. Acute hearing and a sharp sense of smell more than made up for his eyesight.

He was obviously a creature of the cold. He had two coats, a soft undercoat of thick downy fur and a shaggy outer one of reddish brown hair, and beneath his tough hide was a three-inch layer of fat. He carried his head low, downward from his shoulders, and his long front horn sloped forward at an angle that barely cleared the ground as he swayed. He used it for sweeping snow away from pasturage – if it wasn't too deep. And his short thick legs were easily mired in deep snow. He visited the grasslands of the south only briefly – to graze on their richer harvest and store additional fat – in late fall and early winter after it became cold enough for him, but before the heavy snows. He could not stand heat, with his heavy coats, any more than he could survive in deep snow. His home was the bitter-cold, crackling dry tundra and steppes near the glacier.

The long, tapering, anterior horn could be put to a far more dangerous use than sweeping snow, however, and there was nothing between the rhino and Thonolan but a short distance.

"Don't move!" Jondalar hissed. He ducked down behind the tent and reached for his pack with the spears.

"Those light spears won't do much good," Thonolan said, though his back was towards him. The comment stayed Jondalar's hand for a moment; he wondered how Thonolan knew. "You'd have to hit him in a vulnerable place like an eye, and that's too small a target. You need a heavy lance for rhino," Thonolan continued, and his brother realized he was guessing.

"Don't talk so much, you'll draw his attention," Jondalar cautioned. "I may not have a lance, but you don't have a weapon at all. I'm going around the back of the tent to try for him."

"Wait, Jondalar! Don't! You'll just make him angry with that spear; you won't even hurt him. Remember when we were boys, how we used to bait rhinos? Someone would run, get the rhino chasing him, then dodge away while someone else got his attention. Keep him running until he was too tired to move. You get ready to draw his attention – I'm going to run and try to make him charge."

"No, Thonolan!" Jondalar yelled, but it was too late. Thonolan was sprinting.

It was always impossible to outguess the unpredictable beast. Rather than charging after the man, the rhino made a rush for the tent billowing in the wind. He rammed it, gouged a hole in it, snapped thongs and got snared in them. When he disentangled himself, he decided he didn't like the men or their camp and left, trotting off harmlessly. Thonolan, glancing over his shoulder, noticed the rhino was gone and came loping back.

"That was stupid!" Jondalar yelled, slamming his spear into the ground with a force that broke the wooden shaft just below the bone point. "Were you trying to get yourself killed? Great Doni, Thonolan! Two people can't bait a rhino. You have to surround him. What if he had gone after you? What in Great Mother's underworld am I supposed to do if you get hurt?"

Surprise, then anger flashed across Thonolan's face. Then he broke into a grin. "You were really worried about me! Yell all you want, you can't bluff me. Maybe I shouldn't have tried it, but I wasn't going to let you make some stupid move, like going for a rhino with such a light spear. What in Great Mother's underworld am I supposed to do if you get hurt?" His smile grew, and his eyes lit up with the delight of a small boy who had succeeded in pulling off a trick. "Besides, he didn't come after me."

Jondalar looked blank in the face of his brother's grin. His outburst had been more relief than anger, but it took him a while to grasp that Thonolan was safe.

"You were lucky. I guess we both were," he said, expelling a long breath. "But we'd better make a couple of lances, even if we just sharpen points for now."

"I haven't seen any yew, but we can watch for ash or alder on the way," Thonolan remarked as he began to take down the tent. "They should work."

"Anything will work, even willow. We should make them before we go."

"Jondalar, let's get away from this place. We need to reach those mountains, don't we?"

"I don't like travelling without lances, not with rhinos around."

"We can stop early. We need to fix the tent anyway. If we go, we can look for some good wood, find a better place to camp. That rhino might come back."

"And he might follow us, too." Thonolan was always eager to start in the morning, and restless about delays,

Jondalar knew. "Maybe we should try to reach those mountains. All right, Thonolan, but we stop early, right?"

"Right, Big Brother."

The two brothers strode along the edge of the river at a steady, ground-covering pace, long since adjusted to each other's step and comfortable with each other's silences. They had grown closer, talked out each other's heart and mind, tested each other's strengths and weaknesses. Each assumed certain tasks by habit, and each depended on the other when danger threatened. They were young and strong and healthy, and unselfconsciously confident that they could face whatever lay ahead.

They were so attuned to their environment that perception was on a subliminal level. Any disturbance that posed a threat would have found them instantly on guard. But they were only vaguely aware of the warmth of the distant sun, challenged by the cold wind soughing through leafless limbs; black-bottomed clouds embracing the white-walled breastworks of the mountains before them; and the deep, swift river.

The mountain ranges of the massive continent shaped the course of the Great Mother River. She rose out of the highland north of one glacier-covered range and flowed east. Beyond the first chain of mountains was a level plain – in an earlier age the basin of an inland sea – and, farther east, a second range curved around in a great arc. Where the easternmost alpine foreland of the first range met the flysch foothills at the northwestern end of the second, the river broke through a rocky barrier and turned abruptly south.

After dropping down karstic highlands, she meandered across grassy steppes, winding into oxbows, breaking into separate channels and rejoining again as she wove her way south. The sluggish, braided river, flowing through flat land, gave the illusion of changelessness. It was only an illusion. By the time the Great Mother River reached the uplands at the southern end of the plain that swung her east again and gathered her channels together, she had received into herself the waters of the northern and eastern face of the first, massive, ice-mantled range.

The great swollen Mother swept out a depression as she

curled east in a broad curve towards the southern end of the second chain of peaks. The two men had been following her left bank, crossing the occasional channels and streams still rushing to meet her as they came to them. Across the river to the south the land rose in steep craggy leaps; on their side rolling hills climbed more gradually from the river's edge.

"I don't think we'll find the end of Donau before winter," Jondalar remarked. "I'm beginning to wonder if there is one."

"There's an end, and I think we'll find it soon. Look how big she is." Thonolan waved an expansive arm towards the right. "Who would have thought she'd get that big? We have to be near the end."

"But we haven't reached the Sister yet, at least I don't think we have. Tamen said she is as big as the Mother."

"That must be one of those stories that get bigger with the telling. You don't really believe there's another river like that flowing south along this plain?"

"Well, Tamen didn't say he'd seen it himself, but he was right about the Mother turning east again, and about the people who took us across her main channel. He could be right about the Sister. I wish we'd known the language of that Cave with the rafts; they might have known about a tributary to the Mother as big as she is."

"You know how easy it is to exaggerate great wonders that are far away. I think Tamen's 'Sister' is just another channel of the Mother, farther east."

"I hope you're right, Little Brother. Because if there is a Sister, we're going to have to cross it before we reach those mountains. And I don't know where else we're likely to find a place to stay for the winter."

"I'll believe it when I see it."

A movement, apparently at odds with the natural way of things which brought it to the level of consciousness, caught Jondalar's attention. By the sound, he identified the black cloud in the distance, moving with no regard for the prevailing wind, and he stopped to watch as the V-formation of honking geese approached. They swooped lower as a single entity, darkening the sky with their numbers, then broke up into individuals as they neared the ground with lowered feet and flapping wings, braking to a rest. The river swerved around the steep rise ahead.

"Big Brother," Thonolan said, grinning with excitement, "those geese wouldn't have set down if there wasn't a marsh up ahead. Maybe it's a lake or a sea, and I'll wager the Mother empties into it. I think we've reached the end of the river!"

"If we climb that hill, we should get a better view." Jondalar's tone was carefully neutral, but Thonolan had the impression his brother didn't quite believe him.

They climbed quickly, breathing hard when they reached the top, then caught their breath in amazement. They were high enough to see for a considerable distance. Beyond the turn the Mother widened, and her waters became choppy, and, as she approached a vast expanse of water, she rolled and spumed. The larger body of water was cloudy with mud churned up from the bottom, and filled with debris. Broken limbs, dead animals, whole trees bobbed and spun around, caught by conflicting currents.

They had not reached the end of the Mother. They had met the Sister.

High in the mountains in front of them, the Sister had begun as rivulets and streams. The streams became rivers that raced down rapids, spilled over cataracts, and coursed straight down the western face of the second great mountain range. With no lakes or reservoirs to check the flow, the tumultuous waters gained force and momentum until they gathered together on the plain. The only check to the turbulent Sister was the glutted Mother herself.

The tributary, nearly equal in size, surged into the mother stream, fighting the controlling influence of swift current. She backed up and surged again, throwing a tantrum of crosscurrents and undertows; temporary maelstroms that sucked floating debris in a perilous spin to the bottom and spewed it up a moment later downstream. The engorged confluence expanded into a hazardous lake too large to see across.

Fall flooding had peaked and a marshland of mud sprawled over the banks where the waters had recently receded, leaving a morass of devastation: upturned trees with roots reaching for the sky, waterlogged trunks and broken branches; carcasses and dying fish stranded in drying puddles. Water birds were feasting on the easy pickings; the near shore was alive with them. Nearby, a hyena was making short work of a stag, undisturbed by the flapping wings of black storks.

"Great Mother!" Thonolan breathed.

"It must be the Sister." Jondalar was too awed to ask his brother if he believed now.

"How are we going to get across?"

"I don't know. We'll have to go back upstream."

"How far? She's as big as the Mother."

Jondalar could only shake his head. His forehead knotted with concern. "We should have taken Tamen's advice. It could snow any day; we don't have time to backtrack very far. I don't want to be caught in the open when a big storm blows."

A sudden gust of wind caught Thonolan's hood and whisked it back, baring his head. He pulled it on again, closer to his face, and shivered. For the first time since they had set out, he had serious doubts about surviving the long winter ahead. "What do we do now, Jondalar?"

"We find a place to make camp." The taller brother scanned the area from their vantage point. "Over there, just upstream, near that high bank with a stand of alder. There's a creek that joins the Sister – the water should be good."

"If we tie both backframes to one log, and attach a rope to both our waists, we could swim across and not get separated."

"I know you are hardy, Little Brother, but that's foolhardy. I'm not sure I could swim across, much less pulling a log with everything we have. That river is cold. Only the current keeps it from freezing – there was ice at the edge this morning. And what if we get tangled up in the branches of some tree? We'd get swept downstream, and maybe pulled under."

"Remember that Cave that lives close to the Great Water? They dig out the centres of big trees and use them to cross rivers. Maybe we could . . ."

"Find me a tree around here big enough," Jondalar said,

flinging his arm at the grassy prairie, with only a few thin or stunted trees.

"Well . . . someone told me about another Cave that makes shells out of birchbark . . . but that seems so flimsy."

"I've seen them, but I don't know how they're made, or what kind of glue they use so they won't leak. And the birch trees in their region grow bigger than any I've seen around here."

Thonolan glanced around, trying to think of some other idea that his brother couldn't put down with his implacable logic. He noticed the stand of straight tall alders on the high knoll just to the south, and grinned. "How about a raft? All we'd have to do is tie a bunch of logs together, and there are more than enough alders on that hill."

"And one long enough, and strong enough to make a pole to reach the bottom of the river to guide it? Rafts are hard to control even on small shallow rivers."

Thonolan's confident grin crumpled, and Jondalar had to suppress a smile. Thonolan never could hide his feelings; Jondalar doubted that he ever tried. But it was his impetuous, candid nature that made him so likeable.

"That's really not such a bad idea, though," Jondalar amended, noting the return of Thonolan's smile, "once we get upstream far enough so there's no danger of getting swept into that rough water. And find a place where the river widens and gets shallower, and not so fast, and where there are trees. I hope the weather holds."

Thonolan was as serious as his brother by the time the weather was mentioned. "Let's get moving then. The tent is fixed."

"I'm going to look over those alders first. We still need a couple of sturdy spears. We should have made them last night."

"Are you still worried about that rhino? He's well behind us now. We need to get started so we can find a place to cross."

"I'm going to cut a shaft, at least."

"You might as well cut one for me then. I'll start packing."

Jondalar picked up his axe and examined the edge, then nodded to himself and started up the hill towards the alder grove. He looked over the trees carefully and selected a tall straight sapling. He had chopped it down, stripped the branches, and was looking for one for Thonolan when he heard a commotion. There was snuffling, grunting. He heard his brother shout, and then a sound more terrifying than anything he had ever heard: a scream of pain in his brother's voice. The silence as his scream was cut short was even worse.

"Thonolan! Thonolan!"

Jondalar raced back down the hill, still clutching the alder shaft and clutched by cold fear. His heart pounded in his ears when he saw a huge woolly rhinoceros, as tall at the shoulders as he, pushing the limp form of a man along the ground. The animal didn't seem to know what to do with his victim now that he was down. From the depths of his fear and anger, Jondalar didn't think, he reacted.

Swinging the alder staff like a club, the older brother rushed the beast, careless of his own safety. One hard blow landed on the rhino's snout, just below the large curving horn, and then another. The rhino backed off, undecided in the face of a berserk man charging him and causing him pain. Jondalar prepared to swing again, pulled back the long shaft – but the animal turned. The powerful whack on his rump didn't hurt much, but it urged him on, with the tall man chasing after him.

When a swing of the alder shaft whistled through the air as the animal raced ahead, Jondalar stopped and watched the rhino go, catching his breath. Then he dropped the shaft and ran back to Thonolan. His brother was lying face down where the rhino had left him.

"Thonolan? *Thonolan!*" Jondalar rolled him over. There was a rip in Thonolan's leather trousers near the groin, and a bloodstain growing larger.

"Thonolan! Oh, Doni!" He put his ear to his brother's chest, listening for a heartbeat, and was afraid he only imagined hearing it until he saw him breathing.

"Oh, Doni, he's alive! But what am I going to do?" With a grunt of effort, Jondalar picked up the unconscious man and stood for a moment, cradling him in his arms.

"Doni, O Great Earth Mother! Don't take him yet. Let him live, O please . . ." His voice cracked and a huge sob welled up in his breast. "Mother . . . please . . . let him live . . ."

Jondalar bowed his head, sobbed into his brother's limp shoulder a moment, then carried him back to the tent. He laid him down gently on his sleeping roll, and, with his bone-handled knife, cut away the clothing. The only obvious wound was a raw, jagged rip of skin and muscle at the top of his left leg, but his chest was an angry red, the left side swelling and discolouring. A close examination by touch convinced Jondalar that several ribs were broken; probably there were internal injuries.

Blood was pumping out of the gash in Thonolan's leg, collecting on the sleeping roll. Jondalar rummaged through his pack, trying to find something to sop it up with. He grabbed his sleeveless summer tunic, wadded it up, and tried to wipe up the blood on the fur, but only succeeded in smearing it around. Then he laid the soft leather on the wound.

"Doni, Doni! I don't know what to do. I'm not a zelandoni." Jondalar sat back on his heels, pulled his hand through his hair, and left bloodstains on his face. "Willowbark! I can make willowbark tea."

He went out to heat some water. He didn't have to be a zelandoni to know about the painkilling properties of willowbark; everyone made willowbark if they had a headache, or some other minor pain. He didn't know if it was used for serious wounds, but he didn't know what else to do. He paced nervously around the fire, looking inside the tent with each circuit, waiting for the cold water to boil. He piled more wood on the fire and singed an edge of the wooden frame that supported the cooking hide full of water.

Why is it taking so long! Wait, I don't have the willowbark. I'd better get it before the water boils. He put his head inside the tent and stared at his brother for a long moment, then ran to the edge of the river. After peeling bark from a bare-leafed tree whose long thin branches trailed the water, he raced back.

He looked first to see if Thonolan had roused, and saw that his summer tunic was soaked with blood. Then he noticed the overfull cooking skin boiling over and putting out the fire. He didn't know what to do first – tend to the tea, or to his brother – and he looked back and forth from the fire to the tent to the fire. Finally he grabbed a drinking cup and scooped out some water, scalding his hand, then dropped the willowbark in the hide pot. He put a few more sticks on the fire, hoping they would catch. He searched through Thonolan's backframe, dumped it out in frustration, and picked up his brother's summer tunic to replace his bloody one.

As he started into the tent, Thonolan moaned. It was the first sound he had heard from his brother. He scrambled out to scoop up a bowl of the tea, noticed there was hardly any liquid left, and wondered if it was too strong. He ducked back into the tent with a cup of the hot liquid, looked frantically for a place to set it, and saw that more was soaked with blood than his summer tunic. It was pooling under Thonolan, discolouring the sleeping roll.

He's losing too much blood! O Mother! He needs a zelandoni. What am I going to do? He was becoming more agitated and fearful for his brother. He felt so helpless. I need to go for help. Where? Where can I find a zelandoni? I can't even get across the Sister, and I can't leave him. Some wolf or hyena will smell the blood and come after him.

Great Mother! Look at all the blood on that tunic! Some animal will smell it. Jondalar snatched the blood-soaked shirt and threw it out of the tent. No, that's not any better! He dived out of the tent, picked it up again, and looked wildly for some place to put it, away from the camp, away from his brother.

He was in shock, overcome with grief, and, in the depths of his heart, he knew there was no hope. His brother needed help that he could not give, and he could not go for help. Even if he knew where to go, he couldn't leave. It was senseless to think any bloody tunic would draw carnivorous animals any more than Thonolan himself would, with his open wound. But he didn't want to face the truth in his heart. He turned away from sense and gave in to panic.

He spied the stand of alder and, in an irrational moment, raced up the hill and stuffed the leather shirt high up in a crook of one of the trees. Then he ran back. He went into the tent and stared at Thonolan, as if by sheer effort of will he could make his brother sound and whole again, and smiling.

Almost as though Thonolan sensed the plea, he moaned,

tossed his head, and opened his eyes. Jondalar kneeled closer and saw pain in his eyes, in spite of a weak smile.

"You were right, Big Brother. You usually are. We didn't leave that rhino behind."

"I don't want to be right, Thonolan. How do you feel?"

"Do you want an honest answer? I hurt. How bad is it?" he asked, trying to sit up. The halfhearted grin turned to a grimace of pain.

"Don't try to move. Here, I made some willowbark." Jondalar supported his brother's head and held the cup to his lips. Thonolan took a few sips, then lay back down with relief. A look of fear joined the pain in his eyes.

"Tell me straight, Jondalar. How bad is it?"

The tall man closed his eyes and drew a breath. "It's not good."

"I didn't think so, but how bad?" Thonolan's eyes fell on his brother's hands and opened wider with alarm. "There's blood all over your hands! Is it mine? I think you'd better tell me."

"I don't really know. You're gored in the groin, and you've lost a lot of blood. The rhino must have tossed you, too, or trampled you. I think you have a couple of broken ribs. I don't know what else. I'm not a zelandoni . . ."

"But I need one, and the only chance of finding help is across that river we can't cross."

"That's about it."

"Help me up, Jondalar. I want to see how bad it is."

Jondalar started to object, then reluctantly gave in and was immediately sorry. The moment Thonolan tried to sit, he cried out in pain and lost consciousness again.

"Thonolan!" Jondalar cried. The bleeding had slowed, but his effort caused it to flow again. Jondalar folded his brother's summer tunic and put it over the wound, then left the tent. The fire was nearly out. Jondalar added fuel more carefully and built it up again, set more water to heat, and cut more wood.

He went back to check on his brother again. Thonolan's tunic was soaked with blood. He moved it aside to look at the wound, and he grimaced remembering how he had run up the hill to get rid of the other tunic. His initial panic was gone, and it seemed so foolish. The bleeding had stopped. He found another piece of clothing, a cold-weather undergarment, laid it over the wound, and covered Thonolan, then picked up the second bloody tunic and walked to the river. He threw it in, then bent to wash the blood off his hands, still feeling ridiculous over his panic.

He didn't know that panic was a survival trait, in extreme circumstances. When all else fails, and all rational means of finding a solution have been exhausted, panic takes over. And sometimes an irrational act becomes a solution the rational mind would never have thought of.

He walked back, put a few more sticks of wood on the fire, then went to look for the alder staff, though it seemed pointless to be making a spear now. He just felt so useless, he needed to do something. He found it, then sat outside the tent, and with vicious strokes, began to shave one end.

The next day was a nightmare for Jondalar. The left side of Thonolan's body was tender to the lightest touch and deeply bruised. Jondalar had slept little. It had been a difficult night for Thonolan and every time he moaned, Jondalar got up. But all he could offer was willowbark tea, and that didn't help much. In the morning, he cooked some food and made broth, but neither man ate much. By evening, the wound was hot, and Thonolan was feverish.

Thonolan woke from a restless sleep to his brother's troubled blue eyes. The sun had just dipped below the rim of the earth, and though it was still light outside, in the tent it was harder to see. The dimness didn't keep Jondalar from noticing how glazed Thonolan's eyes were, and he had been moaning and mumbling in his sleep.

Jondalar tried to smile encouragingly. "How are you feeling?"

Thonolan hurt too much to smile, and Jondalar's worried look was not reassuring. "I don't feel much like hunting rhinos," he replied.

They were silent for a while, neither knowing what to say. Thonolan closed his eyes and sighed deeply. He was tired of fighting the pain. His chest hurt with every breath, and the deep ache in his left groin seemed to have spread to his whole body. If he had thought there was any hope, he would have endured it, but the longer they stayed, the less chance Jondalar would have of crossing the river before a storm. Just because he was going to die was no reason his brother had to die, too. He opened his eyes again.

"Jondalar, we both know without help there's no hope for me, but there's no reason you . . ."

"What do you mean, no hope? You're young, you're strong. You'll be all right."

"There's not enough time. We don't have a chance out here in the open. Jondalar, keep moving, find a place to stay, you . . ."

"You're delirious!"

"No, I . . ."

"You wouldn't be talking like that if you weren't. You worry about gaining your strength – let me worry about taking care of us. We're both going to make it. I've got a plan."

"What plan?"

"I'll tell you about it when I get all the details worked out. Do you want something to eat? You haven't eaten much."

Thonolan knew his brother wouldn't leave while he was alive. He was tired; he wanted to give up, let it end, and give Jondalar a chance. "I'm not hungry," he said, then saw the hurt in his brother's eyes. "I could use a drink of water, though."

Jondalar poured out the last of the water and held Thonolan's head while he drank. He shook the bag. "This is empty. I'll get some more."

He wanted an excuse to get out of the tent. Thonolan was giving up. Jondalar had been bluffing when he said he had a plan. He had given up hope – no wonder his brother thought it was hopeless. I have to find some way to get us across that river and find help.

He walked up a slight rise that gave him a view upriver, over the trees, and stood watching a broken branch snagged by a jutting rock. He felt as trapped and helpless as that bare limb and, on impulse, walked to the water's edge and freed it from the restraining stone. He watched the current carry it downstream, wondering how far it would go before it was snared by something else. He noticed another willow, and he peeled more inner bark with his knife. Thonolan might have a bad night again, not that the tea did much good.

Finally he turned away from the Sister and went back to

the small creek that added its tiny fraction to the rampaging river. He filled the waterbag and started back. He wasn't sure what made him look upstream – he couldn't have heard anything above the sound of the rushing torrent – but when he did, he stared in open-mouthed disbelief.

Something was approaching from upriver, heading straight for the bank where he stood. A monstrous water bird, with a long curved neck supporting a fierce crested head and large unblinking eyes, was coming towards him. He saw movement on the creature's back as it drew near, heads of other creatures. One of the smaller creatures waved.

"Ho-la!" a voice called out. Jondalar had never heard a more welcome sound.

7

Ayla wiped the back of her hand across her sweaty forehead and smiled at the little yellow horse who had nudged her, trying to insinuate her muzzle under the woman's hand. The filly didn't like to let Ayla out of her sight and followed her everywhere. Ayla didn't mind, she wanted the company.

"Little horse, how much grain should I pick for you?" Ayla motioned. The small, hay-coloured foal watched her motions closely. It made Ayla think of herself when she was a young girl just learning the sign language of the Clan. "Are you trying to learn to talk? Well, understand, anyway. You'd have trouble talking without hands, but you seem to be trying to understand me."

Ayla's speech incorporated a few sounds; her Clan's ordinary language wasn't entirely silent, only the ancient formal language was. The filly's ears perked up when she spoke a word out loud.

"You're listening, aren't you, little filly?" Ayla shook her head. "I keep calling you little filly, little horse. It doesn't feel right. I think you need a name. Is that what you are listening for, the sound of your name? I wonder what your dam called you? I don't think I could say it if I knew."

The young horse was watching her intently, knowing Ayla was paying attention to her when she moved her hands in that way. She nickered when Ayla stopped.

"Are you answering me? Whiiinneeey!" Ayla tried to mimic her and made a fair approximation of a horse's whinny. The young horse responded to the almost familiar sound with a toss of her head and an answering neigh.

"Is that your name?" Ayla motioned with a smile. The foal

tossed her head again, bounded off a way, then came back. The woman laughed. "All little horses must have the same name, then, or maybe I can't tell the difference." Ayla whinnied again and the horse whinnied back, and they played the game for a while. It made her think of the game of sounds she used to play with her son, except Durc could make any sound she could. Creb had told her she made many sounds when they first found her, and she knew she could make some no one else could. It had pleased her when she discovered her son could make them, too.

Ayla turned back to picking grain from the tall einkorn wheat. Emmer wheat grew in the valley, too, and rye grass similar to the kind that grew near the Clan's cave. She was thinking about naming the horse. I've never named anyone before, she smiled to herself. Wouldn't they think I was strange, naming a horse? Not any stranger than living with one. She watched the young animal racing and frisking playfully. I'm so glad she lives with me, Ayla thought, feeling a lump in her throat. It's not so lonely with her around. I don't know what I'd do if I lost her now. I am going to name her.

The sun was on its way down when Ayla stopped and glanced at the sky. It was a big sky, vast, empty. Not a single cloud measured its depth nor arrested the eye from infinity. Only the distant incandescence in the west, whose wavering circumference was revealed in after-image, marred the rich, uniformly blue expanse. Judging the amount of daylight left by the space between the radiance and the top of the cliff, she decided to stop.

The horse, noticing her attention was no longer on her task, whinnied and came to her. "Should we go back to the cave? Let's get a drink of water first." She put her arm around the neck of the young horse and walked towards the stream.

The foliage near the running water at the base of the steep southern wall was a slow-motion kaleidoscope of colour, reflecting the rhythm of the seasons; now deep sombre greens of pines and fir dabbed with vivid golds, paler yellows, dry browns, and fiery reds. The sheltered valley was a bright swatch amidst the muted beige of the steppes, and the sun was warmer within its wind-protected walls. For all the fall colours, it had felt like a warm summer day, a misleading illusion.

"I think I should get more grass. You're starting to eat your bedding when I put it down fresh." Walking beside the horse, Ayla continued her monologue, then unconsciously stopped the hand motions, her thoughts alone carrying on the thread. Iza always collected grass in fall for winter bedding. It smelled so good when she changed it, especially when the snow was deep and the wind blowing outside. I used to love falling asleep listening to the wind and smelling summer fresh hay.

When she saw the direction they were going, the horse trotted ahead. Ayla smiled indulgently. "You must be as thirsty as I am, little whiiinneeey," she said, making the sound out loud in response to the filly's call. That does sound like a name for a horse, but naming should be done properly.

"Whinney! Whiiinneeey!" she called. The animal perked up her head, looked towards the woman, then trotted to her.

Ayla rubbed her head and scratched her. She was shedding her prickly baby coat and growing in longer winter hair, and she always loved a scratching. "I think you like that name, and it suits you, my little horse baby. I think we should have a naming ceremony. I can't pick you up in my arms, though, and Creb isn't here to mark you. I guess I'll have to be the mog-ur and do it." She smiled. Imagine, a woman mog-ur.

Ayla started back towards the river again but veered upstream when she noticed she was near the open place where she had dug the pit trap. She had filled in the hole, but the young horse spooked around it, sniffing and snorting and pawing the ground, bothered by some lingering odour or memory. The herd had not returned since the day they raced down the length of the valley, away from her fire and her noise.

She led the filly to drink nearer the cave. The cloudy stream, engorged with fall runoff, had receded from its high point, leaving a slurry of rich brown mud at the water's edge. It squished under Ayla's feet and left a brownish red stain on her skin, and it reminded her of the red ochre paste Mog-ur used for ceremonial purposes, like namings. She swished her finger around in the mud and made a mark on her leg, then smiled and scooped up a handful.

I was going to look for red ochre, she thought, but this might do as well. Closing her eyes, Ayla tried to remember what Creb had done when he named her son. She could see his ravaged old face, with a flap of skin covering the place where an eye should have been, his large nose, his overhanging brow ridges and low sloping forehead. His beard had got thin and scraggly, and his hairline had receded, but she remembered him the way he had looked that day. Not young, but at the peak of his power. She had loved that magnificent, craggy old face.

Suddenly all her emotions came flooding back. Her fear that she would lose her son and her utter joy at the sight of a bowl of red ochre paste. She swallowed hard several times, but the lump in her throat would not go down, and she wiped a tear away, not knowing she left a smudge of brown in its place. The little horse leaned against her, nuzzling for affection, almost as though she sensed Ayla's need. The woman knelt down and hugged the animal, resting her forehead against the sturdy neck of the little filly.

This is supposed to be your naming ceremony, she thought, gaining control of herself. The mud had squeezed out between her fingers. She scooped up another handful, then reached towards the sky with the other hand, as Creb had always done with his abbreviated one-handed gestures, calling for the spirits to attend. Then she hesitated, not sure if she should invoke the Clan spirits at the naming of a horse – they might not approve. She dipped her fingers into the mud in her hand and made a streak down the foal's face, from her forehead to the end of her nose, as Creb had drawn a line with the paste of red ochre from the place where Durc's brow ridges met to the tip of his rather small nose.

"Whinney," she said aloud, and finished with the formal language. "This girl's . . . this female horse's name is Whinney."

The horse shook her head, trying to rid herself of the wet mud on her face, making Ayla laugh. "It will dry up and wear off soon, Whinney."

She washed her hands, adjusted the basketful of grain on her back, and walked slowly to the cave. The naming ceremony had reminded her too much of her solitary existence. Whinney was a warm living creature and eased her loneliness, but by the time Ayla reached the rocky beach, tears had come unbidden, unnoticed.

She coaxed and guided the young horse up the steep path to her cave, which roused her out of her grief somewhat. "Come on, Whinney, you can do it. I know you're not an ibex or a saiga antelope, but it only takes getting used to."

They reached the top of the wall that was the front extension of her cave and went in. Ayla rekindled the banked fire and started some grain cooking. The young filly was now eating grass and grain and didn't need specially prepared food, but Ayla made mashes for her because Whinney liked them.

She took a brace of rabbits, caught earlier in the day, outside to skin them while it was still light, brought them in to cook, and rolled up the skins until she was ready to process them. She had accumulated a large supply of animal skins: rabbits, hares, hamsters, whatever she caught. She wasn't sure how she was going to use them, but she carefully cured and saved them all. During the winter she might think of a use for them. If it got cold enough, she'd just pile them around her.

Winter was on her mind as the days grew shorter and the temperature fell. She didn't know how long or harsh it would be, which worried her. A sudden attack of anxiety sent her checking her stores, though she knew exactly what she had. She looked through baskets and bark containers of dried meat, fruits and vegetables, seeds, nuts, and grains. In the dark corner farthest from the entrance, she examined piles of whole, sound roots and fruits to make sure no signs of rot had appeared.

Along the rear wall were stacks of wood, dried horse dung from the field, and mounds of dry grass. More baskets of grain, for Whinney, were stashed in the opposite corner.

Ayla walked back to the hearth to check the grain cooking in a tightly woven basket and turn the rabbits, then past her bed and personal belongings along the wall near it, to examine herbs, roots, and barks suspended from a rack. She had sunk the posts for it in the packed earth of the cave not too far from the fireplace, so the seasonings, teas, and medicines would benefit from the heat as they dried, but would not be too close to the fire.

She had no clan to tend and didn't need all the medicines, but she had kept Iza's pharmacopoeia well-stocked after the old woman became too weak, and she was accustomed to gathering the medicines along with food. On the other side of the herb rack was an assortment of various materials: chunks of wood, sticks and branches, grasses and barks, hides, bones, several rocks and stones, even a basket of sand from the beach.

She didn't like to dwell too much on the long, lonely, inactive winter ahead. But she knew there would be no ceremonies with feasting and storytelling, no new babies to anticipate, no gossiping, or conversations, or discussions of medical lore with Iza or Uba, no watching the men discuss hunting tactics. She planned instead to spend her time making things – the more difficult and time-consuming, the better – to keep herself as busy as possible.

She looked over some of the solid chunks of wood. They ranged from small to large so she could make bowls of various sizes. Gouging out the inside and shaping it with a hand-axe used as an adze, and a knife, then rubbing it smooth with a round rock and sand could take days; she planned to make several. Some of the small hides would be made into hand coverings, leggings, footwear linings, others would be de-haired and worked so well that they would be as soft and pliable as baby's skin, but very absorbent.

Her collection of beargrass, cattail leaves and stalks, reeds, willow switches, roots of trees, would be made into baskets, tightly woven or looser weave in intricate patterns, for cooking, eating, storage containers, winnowing trays, serving trays, mats for sitting upon, serving or drying food. She would make cordage, in thicknesses from string to rope, from fibrous plants, barks and the sinew and long tail of the horse; and lamps out of stone with shallow wells pecked out to be filled with fat and a dried moss wick which burned with no smoke. She had kept the fat of carnivorous animals separate for that use. Not that she wouldn't eat it if she had to, it was just a matter of taste preference.

There were flat hipbones and shoulder bones to be shaped into plates and platters, others for ladles or stirrers; fuzz from various plants to be used for tinder or stuffing, along with feathers and hair; several nodules of flint and implements to shape it with. She had passed many a slow winter day making similar objects and implements, necessary for existence, but she also had a supply of materials for objects she was not accustomed to making, though she had watched men make them often enough: hunting weapons.

She wanted to make spears, clubs shaped to fit the hand, new slings. She thought she might even try a bola, although skill with that weapon took as much practice as the sling. Brun was the expert with the bola; just making the weapon was a skill in itself. Three stones had to be pecked round, into balls, then attached to cords and fastened together with the proper length and balance.

Daylight was fading and her fire was nearly out. The grain had absorbed all the water and softened. She took a bowlful for herself, then added water and prepared the rest for Whinney. She poured it into a watertight basket and brought it to the animal's sleeping place against the wall on the opposite side of the cave mouth.

For the first few days down on the beach, Ayla had slept with the little horse, but she decided the foal should have her own place up in the cave. While she used dried horse dung for fuel, she found little use for fresh droppings on her sleeping furs, and the foal seemed unhappy about it as well. The time would come when the horse would be too big to sleep with, and her bed wasn't big enough for both of them, though she often lay down and cuddled the baby animal in the place she had made for her.

"It should be enough," Ayla motioned to the horse. She was developing a habit of talking to her, and the young horse was beginning to respond to certain signals. "I hope I gathered enough for you. I wish I knew how long the winters are here." She was feeling rather edgy and a little depressed. If it hadn't been dark, she would have gone for a brisk walk. Or better, a long run.

When the horse started chewing on her basket, Ayla brought her an armload of fresh hay. "Here, Whinney, chew on this. You're not supposed to eat your food dish!" Ayla felt like paying special attention to her young companion with petting and scratching. When she stopped, the foal nuzzled her hand and presented a flank that was in need of more attention.

"You must be very itchy." Ayla smiled and began scratching again. "Wait, I have an idea." She went back to the place where her miscellaneous materials were assembled and found a bundle of dried teasel. When the flower of the plant dried, it left an elongated egg-shaped spiny brush. She snapped one from its stem, and with it gently scratched the spot on Whinney's flank. One spot led to another and before she stopped, she had brushed and curried Whinney's entire shaggy coat, much to the young animal's evident delight.

Then she wrapped her arms around Whinney's neck and lay down on the fresh hay beside the warm young animal.

Ayla woke up with a start. She stayed very still with her eyes open wide, filled with foreboding. Something was wrong. She felt a cold draft, then caught her breath. What was that snuffling noise? She wasn't sure if she had heard it, over the sound of the horse's breath and heartbeat. Did it come from the back of the cave? It was so dark, she couldn't see.

It was so dark. . . . That was it! There was no warm red glow from the banked fire in the hearth. And her orientation to the cave wasn't right. The wall was on the wrong side, and the draft. . . . There it was again! The snuffling and coughing! What am I doing in Whinney's place? I must have fallen asleep and forgotten to bank the fire. Now it's out. I haven't lost my fire since I found this valley.

Ayla shuddered and suddenly felt the hairs on the back of her neck rise. She had no word, no gesture, no concept for the presentiment that washed over her, but she felt it. The muscles of her back tightened. Something was going to happen. Something to do with fire. She knew it, as certainly as she knew she breathed.

She'd had these feelings occasionally, ever since the night she had followed Creb and the mog-urs into the small room deep in the cave of the clan that hosted the Gathering. Creb had discovered her, not because he saw her, but because he felt her. And she had felt him, inside her brain in some strange way. Then she had seen things she couldn't explain. Afterwards, sometimes, she knew things. She knew when

Broud was staring at her, though her back was turned. She knew the malignant hatred he felt for her in his heart. And she knew, before the earthquake, that there would be death and destruction in the clan's cave.

But she had not felt anything so strongly before. A deep sense of anxiety, fear – not about the fire, she realized, and not for herself. For someone she loved.

She got up, silently, and felt her way to the hearth, hoping there might be a small ember that could be rekindled. It was cold. Suddenly she had an urgent need to relieve herself, found the wall and followed it towards the entrance. A cold gust whipped her hair back from her face and rattled the dead coals in the fireplace, blowing up a cloud of ashes. She shivered.

As she stepped out, a strong wind buffeted her. She leaned into it and hugged the wall as she walked to the end of the stone ledge opposite the path, where she dumped her refuse.

No stars graced the sky, but the overcast cloud layer diffused the moonlight to a uniform glow, making the black outside less complete than the black within the cave. But it was her ears, not her eyes, that warned her. She heard snuffling and breathing before she saw the slinking movement.

She reached for her sling, but it wasn't at her waist. She hadn't brought it. She had grown careless around her cave, depending on the fire to keep unwanted intruders away. But her fire was out, and a young horse was fair game for most predators.

Suddenly, from the mouth of the cave, she heard a loud whooping cackle. Whinney neighed, and it had a note of fear. The little horse was inside the stone chamber, and its only access was blocked by hyenas.

Hyenas! Ayla thought. There was something about the mad cackling sound of their laughter, their scruffy spotted fur, the way their backs sloped down from well-developed forelegs and shoulders to smaller hind legs giving them a cowering look, that repelled her. And she could never forget Oga's scream as she watched, helpless, while her son was dragged away. This time they were after Whinney.

She didn't have her sling, but that didn't stop her. It wasn't the first time she had acted without thinking of her own safety and when someone else was threatened. She ran towards the cave, waving her fist and shouting.

"Get out of here! Get away!" They were verbal sounds, even in Clan language.

The animals scuttled off. Partly it was her assurance that made them back down, and, though the fire had gone out, its smell still lingered. But there was another element. Her scent was not commonly known to the beasts, but it was becoming familiar, and the last time it had been accompanied by hard-flung stones.

Ayla felt around inside the dark cave for her sling, angry with herself because she couldn't remember where she had put it. That won't happen again, she decided. I'm going to make a place for it and keep it there.

Instead, she gathered up her cooking stones – she knew where they were. When one bold hyena ventured close enough for his outline to be silhouetted in the cave opening, he discovered that, even without the sling, her aim was true, and the stones smarted. After a few more attempts, the hyenas decided the young horse wasn't such easy game after all.

Ayla groped in the dark for more stones and found one of the sticks she had been notching to mark the passage of time. She spent the rest of the night beside Whinney, prepared to defend the foal with only a stick, if necessary.

Fighting off sleep proved to be more difficult. She dozed for a while just before dawn, but the first streak of morning light found her out on the ledge with sling in hand. No hyenas were in sight. She went back in for her fur wrap and foot coverings. The temperature had taken a decided drop. The wind had shifted during the night. Blowing from the northeast, it was funnelled by the long valley until, baffled by the jutting wall and the bend in the river, it blasted into her cave in erratic bursts.

She ran down the steep path with her waterbag and shattered a thin transparent film which had formed at the edge of the stream. The air had that enigmatic smell of snow. As she broke through the clear crust and dipped out icy water, she wondered how it could be so cold when it had been so warm the day before. It had changed fast. She had been too comfortable in her routine. It took only a change in the weather to remind her that she couldn't afford to become complacent.

Iza would have been upset with me for going to sleep without banking the fire. Now I'll have to make a new one. I didn't think the wind would be able to blow into my cave either; it always comes from the north. That might have helped the fire go out. I should have banked it, but driftwood burns so hot when it's dry. It doesn't hold a fire well. Maybe I should chop down some green trees. They're harder to get started, but they burn slower. I should cut posts for a windscreen, too, and bring up more wood. Once it snows, it will be harder to get. I'll get my hand-axe and chop the trees before I make a fire. I don't want the wind to blow it out before I make a windscreen.

She picked up a few pieces of driftwood on her way back to the cave. Whinney was on the ledge and nickered a greeting, and butted her gently, looking for affection. Ayla smiled, but hurried into the cave, followed closely by Whinney, trying to get her nose under the woman's hand.

All right, Whinney, Ayla thought after she put the wood and water down. She patted and scratched the foal for a moment, then put some grain into her basket. She ate some cold leftover rabbit and wished she had some hot tea, but she drank cold water instead. It was cold in the cave. She blew on her hands and put them under her arms to warm them, then got out a basket of tools which she kept near her bed.

She had made a few new ones shortly after she arrived and had been meaning to make more, but something else always seemed more important. She picked out her hand-axe, the one she had carried with her, and took it outside to examine in better light. If handled properly, a hand-axe could be self-sharpening. Tiny spalls usually chipped off the edge with use, always leaving a sharp edge behind. But mishandling could cause a large flake to break off, or even break the brittle stone into fragments.

Ayla didn't notice the clop of Whinney's hooves coming up behind her; she was too accustomed to the sound. The young animal tried to put her nose in Ayla's hand.

"Oh, Whinney!" she cried, as the brittle flint hand-axe fell on the hard stone ledge and broke in several pieces. "That was my only hand-axe. I need it to chop wood." I don't know what is wrong, she thought. My fire goes out just when it turns cold. Hyenas come, as though they didn't expect to find a fire, all ready to attack you. And now, my only hand-axe breaks. She was getting worried, a streak of bad luck was not a good omen. I'll have to make a new hand-axe now, before I do anything else.

She picked up the pieces of the hand-axe – it might be possible to shape them to some other purpose – and put them near the cold fireplace. From a niche behind her sleeping place, she took out a bundle wrapped in the hide of a giant hamster and tied with a cord, and brought it down to the rocky beach.

Whinney followed, but when her nudging and butting caused the woman to push her away rather than pet her, she left Ayla to her stones and wandered around the wall into the valley.

Ayla unwrapped the bundle carefully, reverently; an attitude assimilated early from Droog, the Clan's master toolmaker. It held an assortment of objects. The first she picked up was an oval stone. The first time she worked the flint, she had searched for a hammerstone that felt good in her hand and had the right resilience when struck against flint. All stone working tools were important, but none had the significance of the hammerstone. It was the first implement to touch the flint.

Hers had only a few nicks, unlike Droog's hammerstone, battered from repeated use. But nothing could have convinced him to give it up. Anyone could rough out a flint tool, but the truly fine ones were made by expert toolmakers who cared for their implements and knew how to keep a hammerstone spirit happy. Ayla worried about the spirit of her hammerstone, though she never had before. It was so much more important now that she had to be her own master toolmaker. She knew rituals were required to avert bad luck if a hammerstone broke, to placate the stone's spirit and coax it into lodging in a new stone, and she didn't know them.

She put the hammerstone aside and examined a sturdy piece of legbone from a grazing animal for signs of splintering from the last time she used it. After the bone hammer, she looked over a retoucher, the canine tooth of a large cat dislodged from a jawbone she had found in the pile at the bottom of the wall, and then she checked the other pieces of bone and stone.

She had learned to knap flint by watching Droog and then practising. He didn't mind showing her how to work the stone. She paid attention and she knew he approved of her efforts, but she was not his apprentice. It wasn't worthwhile to consider a female; the range of tools they were allowed to make was limited. They could not make tools that were used to hunt or those used to make weapons. She had found out that the tools women used were not too different. A knife was a knife after all, and a notched flake could be used to sharpen a point on a digging stick or a spear.

She looked over her implements and picked up a nodule of flint, then put it down. If she was going to do some serious flint knapping, she needed an anvil, something to support the stone while she worked it. Droog didn't need an anvil to make a hand-axe, he only used it for more advanced tools, but Ayla found she had more control if she had support for the heavy flint, though she could rough out tools without one. She wanted a firm flat surface, not too hard or the flint would shatter under hard blows. The foot bone of a mammoth was what Droog used, and she decided to see if she could find one in the bone pile.

She climbed around the jumbled mound of bones, wood, and stone. There were tusks; there had to be foot bones. She found a long branch and used it as a lever to move heavy pieces. It snapped when she tried to pry up a boulder. Then she found a small ivory tusk of a young mammoth which proved to be much stronger. Finally, near the edge of the pile closest to the inside wall, she saw what she was looking for and managed to extricate it from the mass of rubble.

As she dragged the foot bone back to her work area, her eye was caught by a grey yellow stone that gleamed in the sunlight and flashed from facets. It looked familiar, but it wasn't until she stopped and picked up a piece of the iron pyrite that she remembered why.

My amulet, she thought, touching the small leather pouch hanging around her neck. My Cave Lion gave me a stone like this to tell me my son would live. Suddenly she noticed the beach was strewn with the brassy grey stones glittering in the sun. It made her aware, too, that the clouds were breaking up. It was the only one when I found mine. Here there's nothing special about them, they're all over.

She dropped the stone and dragged the mammoth foot bone down the beach, then sat down and pulled it between her legs. She covered her lap with the hamster hide and picked up the flint again. She turned it over and over, trying to decide where to make the first strike, but she couldn't settle down and concentrate. Something was bothering her. She thought it must be the hard, lumpy cold stones she was sitting on. She ran up to the cave for a mat, and she brought down her fire drill and platform, and some tinder. I'll be glad when I get a fire going. The morning is half gone and it's still cold.

She settled herself on the mat, put the toolmaking implements within reach, pulled the foot bone between her legs, and laid the hide across her lap. Then she reached for the chalky grey stone and positioned it on the anvil. She picked up the hammerstone, hefted it a few times to get the right grip, then put it down. What's wrong with me? Why am I so restless? Droog always asked his totem for help before he started; maybe that's what I need to do.

She clasped her hand around her amulet, closed her eyes and took several slow deep breaths to calm herself. She didn't make a specific request – she just tried to reach the spirit of the Cave Lion with her mind and with her heart. The spirit that protected her was part of her, inside her, the old magician had explained, and she believed him.

Trying to reach the spirit of the great beast who had chosen her did have a soothing effect. She felt herself relax, and, when she opened her eyes, she flexed her fingers and reached again for the hammerstone.

After the first blows broke away the chalky cortex, she stopped to examine the flint critically. It had good colour, a dark grey sheen, but the grain was not the finest. Still, there were no inclusions; about right for a hand-axe. Many of the thick flakes that fell away as she began to shape the flint into a hand-axe could be used. They had a bulge, a bulb of percussion, on the end of the flake where the hammerstone struck, but they tapered to a sharp edge. Many had semi-circular ripples that left a deep rippled scar on the core, but such flakes could be used for heavy-duty cutting implements, like cleavers to cut through tough hide and meat, or sickles to cut grass.

When Ayla had the general shape she wanted, she transferred to the bone hammer. Bone was softer, more elastic, and would not crush the thin, sharp, if somewhat wavy edge, as the stone striker would have. Taking careful aim, she struck very close to the rippled edge. Longer, thinner flakes, with a flatter percussion bulge and less rippled edges were detached with each blow. In much less time than it took her to get prepared, the tool was finished.

It was about five inches long, in outline shaped like a pear with a pointed end, but flat. It had a strong, rather thin cross section, and straight cutting edges from the point down the sloping sides. Its rounded base was made to hold in the hand. It could be used as an axe to chop wood, as an adze – perhaps to make a bowl. With it a piece of mammoth ivory could be broken to a smaller size, as could animal bones when butchering. It was a strong, sharp hitting tool with many uses.

Ayla was feeling better, looser, ready to try the more advanced and difficult technique. She reached for another chalky nodule of flint and her hammerstone, and struck the outer covering. The stone was flawed. The chalky surface extended into the dark grey interior, all the way through the core. The inclusion made it unusable and interrupted the flow of her work and concentration. It put her on edge again. She put her hammerstone down on the rocky beach.

Another piece of bad luck, another bad omen. She didn't want to believe that, didn't want to give in. She looked at the flint again, wondered if she could make some usable flakes from it, and picked up her hammerstone again. She broke off one flake, but it needed retouching, so she put her hammerstone down and reached for a stone retoucher. But she only glanced in the direction of her other implements. Her eye was on the flint when she picked up a stone from the beach – and caused an event that would change her life.

Not all inventions are wrought by necessity. Sometimes serendipity plays a part. The trick is recognition. All the elements were there, but chance alone had put them together in just the right way. And chance was the essential ingredient. No one, least of all the young woman sitting on a rocky beach in a lonely valley, would have dreamed of making such an experiment on purpose.

When Ayla's hand reached for the stone retoucher, it found instead a piece of iron pyrite of close to the same size. When she struck the exposed fresh flint from the flawed stone, the dry tinder from her cave happened to be nearby, and the spark produced when the two stones hit happened to fly into the ball of shaggy fibre. Most important, Ayla just happened to be looking in that direction when the spark flew, landed on the tinder, smouldered for a moment, and sent up a wisp of smoke before it died.

That was the serendipity. Ayla supplied the recognition and the other necessary elements: she understood the process of making fire, she needed fire, and she wasn't afraid to try something new. Even then, it took her a while to recognize, and appreciate, what she had observed. First the smoke puzzled her. She had to think about it before she made the connection between the wisp of smoke and the spark, but then the spark puzzled her more. Where had it come from? That was when she looked at the stone in her hand.

It was the wrong stone! It wasn't her retoucher, it was one of those shiny stones that were scattered all over the beach. But it was still a stone, and stone didn't burn. Yet something had made a spark that had made the tinder smoke. The tinder had smoked, hadn't it?

She picked up the ball of shaggy bark fibre, ready to believe she had imagined the smoke, but the small black hole left soot on her fingers. She picked up the iron pyrite again, and looked at it closely. How had the spark been drawn from the stone? What had she done? The flint flake, she had struck the flint. Feeling a little silly, she banged the two stones together. Nothing happened.

What did I expect? she thought. Then she banged them together again, with more force, striking sharply, and watched a spark fly. Suddenly, an idea that had been tenuously forming sprang into her mind full blown. A strange, exciting idea, and a little frightening, too.

She put the two stones down carefully on the leather lap cover, on top of the mammoth foot bone, then gathered together the materials to build a fire. When she was ready, she picked up the stones, held them close to the tinder, and struck them together. A spark flew and then died on the cold stones. She changed the angle, tried again, but the force was less. She struck harder and watched a spark land squarely in the middle of the tinder. It singed a few strands and died, but the wisp of smoke was encouraging. The next time she struck the stones, the wind gusted, and the smouldering tinder flared before it went out.

Of course! I have to blow on it. She changed her position so she could blow on the incipient flame, and made another spark with the stones. It was a strong, bright, long-burning spark, and it landed right. She was close enough to feel the heat as she blew the smouldering tinder into flame. She fed it shavings, and slivers, and, almost before she knew it, she had a fire.

It was ridiculously easy. She couldn't believe how easy. She had to prove it to herself again. She gathered together more tinder, more shavings, more kindling, and then she had a second fire, and then a third, and a fourth. She felt an excitement that was part fear, part awe, part joy of discovery, and a large dose of sheer wonder, as she stood back and gazed at four separate fires, each made from the firestone.

Whinney trotted back around the wall, drawn by the smell of smoke. Fire, once so fearful, smelled of safety now.

"Whinney!" Ayla called, running to the little horse. She had to tell someone, to share her discovery, even if just with a horse. "Look!" she motioned. "Look at those fires! They were made with stones, Whinney. Stones!" The sun broke through the clouds and suddenly the whole beach seemed to glitter.

I was wrong when I thought there was nothing special about those stones. I should have known; my totem gave one to me. Look at them. Now that I know, I can see the fire that lives inside. She grew thoughtful then. But why me? Why was I shown? My Cave Lion gave one to me once to tell me Durc would live. What is he telling me now?

She remembered the strange premonition she'd had after her fire died and, standing in the midst of four fires, she shivered, feeling it again. Then, suddenly, she felt an overwhelming sense of relief, though she didn't even know she had been worried.

8

"Hello! Hello!" Jondalar waved as he called out, running to the river's edge.

He felt an overwhelming sense of relief. He had all but given up, but the sound of another human voice filled him with a fresh surge of hope. It didn't occur to him that they might be unfriendly; nothing could be worse than the utter helplessness he had felt.

The man who had called to him held up a coil of rope, attached at one end to the strange enormous water bird. Jondalar could see that it was not a living creature, but some kind of craft. The man threw the rope at him. Jondalar dropped it and splashed in after it. A couple of other people, hauling on another rope, scrambled out and waded through water swirling up to their thighs. One of them, smiling when he saw Jondalar's expression – which managed to combine hope, relief, and perplexity over what to do with the wet rope in his hands – took the hawser from him. He hauled the craft in closer, then tied the rope to a tree and went to check on the other line snubbed to a jutting end of a broken branch of a large tree that lay half submerged in the river.

Another occupant of the watercraft hoisted himself over the side and jumped on the log to test its stability. He said a few words in an unfamiliar language, and a ladderlike gangplank was lifted up and stretched across to the log. He climbed back to help a woman assist a third person down the gangplank and along the log to the shore, though it seemed the assistance was allowed rather than needed.

The person, obviously greatly respected, had a composed, almost regal bearing, but there was an elusive quality Jondalar couldn't define, an ambiguity, and he found himself staring. Wind caught at wisps of long white hair tied at the nape of the neck, pulled back from a clean-shaven – or beardless – face lined with years, yet glowing with a soft luminous complexion. There was strength in the line of the jaw, the jut of the chin.

Jondalar realized he was standing in cold water when he was beckoned out, but the enigma did not resolve itself on closer inspection, and he felt he was missing something important. Then he stopped and looked into a face with a compassionate, questioning smile and piercing eyes of some indeterminate shade of grey or hazel. With a flush of wonder, Jondalar suddenly realized the implications of the mysterious person waiting patiently in front of him, and looked for some hint of gender.

Height was no help; a little tall for a woman, a little short for a man. Bulky shapeless clothing hid physical details; even the walk left Jondalar wondering. The more he looked and found no answer, the more relieved he felt. He knew of people like that; born into the body of one sex but with the inclinations of the other. They were neither, or both, and usually joined the ranks of Those Who Served the Mother. With powers derived from both female and male elements centred within them, they were reputed to have extraordinary skill as healers.

Jondalar was far from home and did not know the customs of these people, yet he had no doubt that the person standing in front of him was a healer. Maybe One Who Served the Mother, maybe not; it didn't matter. Thonolan needed a healer, and a healer had come.

But how had they known a healer was needed? How had they known to come at all?

Jondalar threw another log on the fire and watched a burst of sparks chase smoke into the night sky. He slid his bare backside farther down into his sleeping roll and leaned back on a boulder to stare at the undying sparks flung across the heavens. A shape floated into his field of vision, blocking out a portion of the star-splashed sky. It took a moment for his unfocused eyes to shift from the endless depths to the head of the young woman holding a cup of steaming tea out to him.

He sat up quickly and exposed a length of bare thigh and

grabbed at the sleeping roll, pulling it up with a glance at his trousers and boots hanging near the fire to dry. She grinned, and her radiant smile changed the rather solemn, shy, softly pretty young woman into a flashing-eyed beauty. He had never seen such an amazing transformation, and his smile in response reflected his attraction. But she had ducked her head to suppress a laugh of mischievous humour, not wanting to embarrass the stranger. When he looked back, only a twinkle remained in her eyes.

"You have a beautiful smile," he said when she gave him the cup of tea.

She shook her head and answered with words that he thought meant she didn't understand him.

"I know you can't understand me, but I still want to tell you how grateful I am you are here."

She watched him closely, and he had the feeling she wanted to communicate as much as he. He kept talking, afraid she would leave if he stopped.

"It's wonderful just to talk to you, just to know you are here." He sipped the tea. "This is good. What kind is it?" he asked, holding up the cup and nodding appreciatively. "I think I can taste chamomile."

She nodded back, acknowledging, then sat near the fire, answering his words with others he understood as little as she understood his. But her voice was pleasant and she seemed to know he wanted her company.

"I wish I could thank you. I don't know what I would have done if you hadn't come." He frowned with worry and tension, and she smiled understandingly. "I wish I could ask how you knew we were here, and how your zelandoni, or whatever you call your healer, knew to come."

She answered him, gesturing towards the tent that had been set up nearby, glowing from the firelight within. He shook his head with frustration. It seemed that she almost understood him; he just couldn't understand her.

"I don't suppose it matters," he said. "But I wish your healer would let me stay with Thonolan. Even without words, it was clear my brother would get no help until I left. I don't doubt the healer's ability. I want to stay with him, that's all."

He was looking at her so earnestly that she laid a hand on

his arm to reassure him. He tried to smile, but it was pained. The flap of the tent caught his attention as an older woman came out.

"Jetamio!" she called, adding other words.

The young woman got up quickly, but Jondalar held her hand to detain her. "Jetamio?" he asked, pointing to her. She nodded. "Jondalar," he said, tapping his own chest.

"Jondalar," she repeated slowly. Then she looked towards the tent, tapped herself, then him, and pointed to it.

"Thonolan," he said. "My brother's name is Thonolan."

"Thonolan," she said, repeating it as she hurried towards the tent. She had a slight limp, Jondalar noticed, though it didn't seem to hinder her.

His trousers were still damp, but he pulled them on anyway and made a dash for a wooded copse, not bothering to fasten them or put his boots on. He had been restraining his urge ever since he woke up, but his extra clothing was in his backframe, which had been left behind in the large tent where the healer was treating Thonolan. Jetamio's grin of the evening before made him think twice about casually sauntering over to the secluded patch of brush wearing nothing but his short inner shirt. Nor did he want to chance breaching some custom or taboo of these people who were helping him – not with two women in the camp.

He had first tried to get up and walk in his sleeping roll, and he had waited so long before it occurred to him to put on his trousers, wet or not, that he was close to forgetting his embarrassment and ready to make a run for it. As it was, Jetamio's laughter followed him.

"Tamio, don't laugh at him. It's not nice," the older woman said, but the force of her admonition was lost as she tried to suppress her own laughter.

"Oh, Rosharia, I don't mean to make fun of him. I just can't help it. Did you see him trying to walk in his sleeping bag?" She started giggling again, though she struggled to contain it. "Why didn't he just get up and go?"

"Maybe the customs of his people are different, Jetamio. They must have travelled a long way. I've never seen clothes like theirs before, and his language isn't even close. Most travellers have a few words that are similar. I don't think I could pronounce some of his words."

"You must be right. He must have some objection to showing his skin. You should have seen him blush last night just because I saw a little of his thigh. I never saw anyone so glad to see us, though."

"Can you blame him?"

"How is the other one?" the young woman said, serious again. "Has the Shamud said anything, Roshario?"

"I think the swelling is down, and the fever, too. At least he's sleeping quieter. The Shamud thinks he was gored by a rhino. I don't know how he lived through it. He wouldn't have much longer if that tall one hadn't signalled for help. Even so, it was luck we found them. Mudo must have smiled on them. The Mother always has favoured handsome young men."

"Not enough to keep . . . Thonolan from getting hurt. The way he was gored. . . . Do you think he'll walk again?"

Roshario smiled tenderly at the young woman. "If he has half the determination you did after your paralysis, he'll walk, Tamio."

Jetamio's cheeks reddened. "I think I'll go and see if the Shamud needs anything," she said, ducking towards the tent, and trying very hard not to limp at all.

"Why don't you bring the tall one his pack," Roshario called after her, "so he won't have to wear wet breeches."

"I don't know which one is his."

"Bring them both, it'll make more room in there. And ask the Shamud how soon we can move . . . what's his name? Thonolan?"

Jetamio nodded.

"If we're going to be here a while, Dolando will have to plan a hunt. We didn't bring much food. I don't think the Ramudoi can fish with the river like that, though I think they'd be just as happy if they never had to come to shore. I like solid ground under me."

"Oh, Rosh, you'd be saying just the opposite if you had mated a Ramudoi man instead of Dolando."

The older woman eyed her sharply. "Has one of those rowers been making advances? I may not be your real mother, Jetamio, but everyone knows you are just like a

152

daughter. If a man doesn't even have the courtesy to ask, he's not the kind of man you want. You can't trust those river men . . ."

"Don't worry, Rosh. I haven't decided to run off with a river man . . . yet," Jetamio said with a mischievous smile.

"Tamio, there are plenty of good Shamudoi men who will move into our lodging. . . . What are you laughing at?"

Jetamio had both her hands at her mouth, trying to swallow the laughter that kept bubbling forth in snorts and giggles. Rosharior turned in the direction the younger woman was looking, and slapped a hand over her mouth to keep from bursting out with laughter herself.

"I'd better get those packs," Jetamio finally managed to say. "Our tall friend needs some dry clothes." She started sputtering again. "He looks like a baby with full pants!" She made a dash for the tent, but Jondalar heard her laughter peal forth as she entered.

"Hilarity, my dear?" the healer said, cocking an eyebrow with a quizzical look.

"I'm sorry, I didn't mean to come in here laughing like that. It's just . . ."

"Either I'm in the next world, or you're a donii who's come to take me there. No earthly woman could be so beautiful. But I can't understand a word you're saying."

Jetamio and the Shamud both turned towards the wounded man. He was looking at Jetamio with a weak smile. Her smile left her face as she knelt beside him.

"I've disturbed him! How could I be so thoughtless?"

"Don't stop smiling, my beautiful donii," Thonolan said, taking her hand.

"Yes, my dear, you have disturbed him. But don't let it disturb you. I suspect he will be much more 'disturbed' before you are through with him."

Jetamio shook her head and gave the Shamud a puzzled look. "I came to ask if there was anything you needed, or if I could help in any way."

"You just did."

She looked more perplexed. Sometimes she wondered if she ever understood anything the healer said.

The piercing eyes took on a gentler look, with a touch of irony. "I've done all I can. He must do the rest. But anything that gives him more will to live can only help at this stage. You just did that with your lovely smile . . . my dear."

Jetamio blushed and bowed her head, then realized Thonolan was still holding her hand. She looked up and saw his laughing grey eyes. Her smile in response was radiant.

The healer made a throat-clearing sound, and Jetamio broke contact, a little flustered to realize she had been staring at the stranger so long. "There is something you can do. Since he's awake, and lucid, we might try giving him some nourishment. If there's any broth, I believe he would drink it, if it came from you."

"Oh. Of course. I'll get some," she said, hurrying out to cover her embarrassment. She saw Roshario attempting to talk to Jondalar, who was standing awkwardly and trying to look natural. She ducked back in to complete the rest of her errands.

"I need to get their packs, and Roshario wants to know how soon Thonolan can be moved."

"What did you say his name was?"

"Thonolan. That's what the other one told me."

"Tell Roshario a day or two yet. He's not up to a ride over rough water."

"How do you know my name, beautiful donii, and how do I ask yours?" She turned to smile at Thonolan before she hurried out with both packs. He settled back down with a self-satisfied grin, but gave a start when he noticed, for the first time, the white-haired healer. The enigmatic face held a catlike smile; wise, knowing, and a little predatory.

"Isn't young love splendid," the Shamud commented. The meaning of the words was lost on Thonolan, but not the wry sarcasm. It made him look closer.

The voice of the healer was pitched neither deep nor high, and Thonolan looked for some clue of dress or behaviour that would tell him if it was a woman's low alto or a man's high tenor. He couldn't decide, and though he wasn't exactly sure why, he relaxed a bit, feeling confident he was in the best of hands.

Jondalar's relief was so evident when he saw Jetamio come out of the tent with the backframes that she was a little ashamed she hadn't got them sooner. She knew his problem, but he was so funny. He thanked her profusely with unfamiliar words that nonetheless communicated his gratitude, and then he headed for the patch of high brush. He felt so much better with dry clothes on, he even forgave Jetamio for laughing.

I suppose I did look rather ridiculous, he thought, but those trousers were wet, and cold. Well, a little laughter is a small price to pay for their help. I don't know what I would have done . . . I wonder how they knew? Perhaps the healer has other powers – that could explain it. Right now, I'm just glad for the healing powers. He stopped. At least I think that zelandoni has healing powers. I haven't seen Thonolan. I don't know if he's better or not. I think it's time I found out. After all, he is my brother. They can't keep me away if I want to see him.

Jondalar strode back to the camp, put his pack down beside the fire, deliberately took the time to stretch out his damp clothes to dry again, and then headed for the tent.

He nearly bumped into the healer, who was leaving just as he ducked to enter. The Shamud sized him up quickly, and before Jondalar could attempt to say anything, smiled ingratiatingly, stepped aside, and waved him on with an exaggerated graceful gesture, acquiescing to the tall, powerful man.

Jondalar gave the healer an appraising look. No hint of relinquished authority showed in the piercing eyes evaluating him in return, though any further disclosure of intent was as obscure as the ambiguous colour. The smile, which had seemed ingratiating at first glance, was more ironic on second look. Jondalar sensed that this healer, like many of that calling, could be a powerful friend or a formidable enemy.

He nodded, as though reserving judgment, briefly smiled his thanks, and went in. He was surprised to see that Jetamio had arrived before he did. She was supporting Thonolan's head, holding a bone cup to his lips.

"I might have known," he said, and his smile was pure joy at seeing his brother awake, and apparently much improved. "You did it again."

Both of them looked up at Jondalar. "What did I do, Big Brother?"

"Within three heartbeats of opening your eyes, you managed to get the prettiest woman around waiting on you."

Thonolan's grin was the most welcome sight his brother could imagine. "You are right about the prettiest woman around." Thonolan looked fondly at Jetamio. "But what are you doing in the spirit world? And while I'm thinking of it, just remember, she's my own personal donii. You can keep your big blue eyes to yourself."

"Don't worry about me, Little Brother. Every time she looks at me, all she can do is laugh."

"She can laugh at me anytime she wants," Thonolan said, smiling at the woman. She smiled in return. "Can you imagine waking up from the dead to that smile?" His fondness was beginning to look adoring as he stared into her eyes.

Jondalar looked from his brother to Jetamio and back again. What is going on here? Thonolan just woke up, they can't have said one word to each other, but I'd swear he was in love. He looked at the woman again, more objectively. Her hair was a rather nondescript shade of light brown, and she was smaller and thinner than the women Thonolan was usually attracted to. She could almost be mistaken for a girl. She had a heart-shaped face with regular features and was really a rather ordinary looking young woman; pretty enough, but certainly not exceptional – until she smiled.

Then, by some unexpected alchemy, some mysterious redistribution of light and shadows, some subtle shift in arrangement, she became beautiful, completely beautiful. She had only to smile once to create that impression, yet Jondalar had the feeling she didn't usually smile often. He remembered she had seemed solemn and shy at first, though it was hard to believe now. She was radiant, vibrantly alive, and Thonolan was looking at her with an idiotic, lovesick grin.

Well, Thonolan has been in love before, Jondalar thought. I just hope she won't take it too hard when we leave.

One of the laces which held closed the smoke-hole flap in the roof of his tent was frayed. Jondalar was staring at it, but not seeing it. He was wide awake, lying in his sleeping roll wondering what had brought him out of the depths of sleep so quickly. He didn't move, but he was listening, smelling, trying to detect anything unusual that might have alerted him to some impending danger. After a few moments, he slipped out of his bedroll and looked carefully out of the opening of his tent but could find nothing wrong.

A few people were gathered around the campfire. He wandered over, still feeling restless and edgy. Something bothered him, but he didn't know what. Thonolan? No, between the skill of the Shamud and Jetamio's attentive care, his brother was doing well. No, it wasn't Thonolan that was troubling him – exactly.

"Hola," he said to Jetamio as she looked up and smiled.

She didn't find him so laughable any more. Their mutual concern for Thonolan had begun to ripen into friendship, though communication was limited to basic gestures and the few words he had learned.

She gave him a cup of hot liquid. He thanked her with the words he had learned that expressed the concept of thanks for them, wishing he could find a way to repay them for their help. He took a sip, frowned, and took another. It was a herb tea, not unpleasant, but surprising. They customarily drank a meat-flavoured broth in the morning. His nose told him the kerfed wooden cooking box near the fire had roots and grain simmering in it, but no meat. It took only a quick glance to explain the change in the morning menu. There was no meat; no one had gone hunting.

He quaffed his drink, put down the bone cup, and hurried back to his tent. While waiting, he had finished making the sturdy spears out of the alder saplings and even tipped them with flint points. He picked up the two heavy shafts that were leaning against the back of the tent, then reached inside for his backframe, took several of the lighter throwing spears, and walked back to the fire. He didn't know many words, but it didn't take many to communicate a desire to go hunting, and before the sun was much higher, an excited group was gathering.

Jetamio was torn. She wanted to stay with the wounded stranger whose laughing eyes made her feel like smiling every time he looked at her, but she wanted to go hunting, too. She never missed a hunt if she could help it, not since she had been able to hunt. Rosario urged her to go. "He'll be fine.

The Shamud can take care of him without you for a little while, and I'll be here."

The hunting party had already started out when Jetamio called after them and ran up out of breath, still tying on her hood. Jondalar had wondered if she hunted. Young Zelandonii women often did. For women, it was a matter of choice, and the custom of the Cave. Once they started having children, women usually stayed closer to home, except during a drive. When they went on *battue*, every able-bodied person was necessary to drive a herd into traps or over cliffs.

Jondalar liked women who hunted – most men of his Cave did, though he'd learned the feeling was by no means universal. It was said that women who had hunted themselves appreciated the difficulties and made more understanding mates. His mother had been noted, especially, for her tracking prowess, and she had often joined a hunt even after she had children.

They waited for Jetamio to catch up, then set off at a good pace. Jondalar thought the temperature was dropping, but they were moving so fast that he wasn't sure until they stopped beside a meandering streamlet winding its way across the flat grassland searching for a way to reach the Mother. He noticed the ice thickening along the edges when he filled up his waterbag. He pushed back his hood, the fur around his face limiting peripheral vision – but before long he wasn't alone in pulling it back on. The air was decidedly nippy.

Someone noticed tracks upstream, and they all gathered around while Jondalar examined them. A family of rhinoceroses had stopped for a drink, too, and not long before. Jondalar drew a plan of attack in the wet sand of the bank with a stick, noticing that ice crystals were hardening the ground. Dolando asked a question with a stick of his own, and Jondalar elaborated on the drawing. Understanding was reached and they were all eager to get moving again.

They broke into a jog, following the tracks. The fast pace warmed them, and hoods were loosened again. Jondalar's long blond hair crackled and clung to the fur of his hood. It took longer than he expected to catch up, but when he sighted the reddish brown woolly rhinos ahead, he understood. The animals were moving faster than usual – and straight north.

Jondalar glanced uneasily at the sky; it was a deep azure bowl inverted over them, with only a few scattered clouds in the distance. It didn't appear that a storm was brewing, but he was ready to turn back, get Thonolan, and get out. No one else seemed to have any inclination to leave, now that the rhinos were in sight. He wondered if their lore included the forecasting of snow by the northward movement of the woollies, but he doubted it.

It had been his idea to go hunting, and he'd had little difficulty communicating that; now he wanted to get back to Thonolan and get him to safety. But how was he going to explain that a snowstorm was on the way when there was hardly a cloud in the sky, and he couldn't speak the language? He shook his head; they'd have to kill a rhino first.

When he drew nearer, Jondalar dashed ahead, trying to outdistance the last straggler – a young rhino, not full grown and having a little trouble keeping up. When the tall man pulled ahead, he shouted and waved his arms, trying to get the animal's attention to make him veer or slow down. But the youngster, pushing forward towards the north with the same single-minded determination as the others, ignored the man. They were going to have trouble distracting any of them, it seemed, and it worried him. The storm was coming faster than he thought.

Out of the corner of his eye, he noticed that Jetamio had caught up with him, and he was surprised. Her limp was more noticeable, but she moved with speed. Jondalar nodded his head in unconscious approval. The rest of the hunting party were moving up, trying to surround one animal and stampede the others. But rhinoceroses were not herd animals, who were easily led or stampeded. They were independent, cantankerous creatures, who seldom mingled in groups larger than a family, and they were dangerously unpredictable. Hunters were smart to be wary around them.

By tacit agreement, the hunters concentrated on the young one lagging behind, but the shouts of the rapidly closing group neither slowed him down nor hurried him along. Jetamio finally got his attention when she took off her hood and waved it at him. He slowed, turned the side of his head toward the flutter, and seemed decidedly undecided.

It gave the hunters a chance to catch up. They deployed themselves around the beast, those with heavy lances moving in closer, those with light spears forming an outer circle, ready to rush to the defence of the more heavily armed, if necessary. The rhino came to a stop; he seemed unaware that the rest of his troupe were rapidly moving ahead. Then he started out at a rather slow run, veering towards the hood fluttering in the wind. Jondalar moved in closer to Jetamio, and he noticed Dolando doing the same.

Then a young man, whom Jondalar recognized as one who stayed on the boat, waved his hood and rushed in front of them towards the animal. The confused rhino stalled his headlong run towards the young woman and, changing his direction, started after the man. The larger moving target was easier to follow even with limited sight; the presence of so many hunters misled his acute sense of smell. Just as he was getting close, another running figure darted between him and the young man. The woolly rhino stalled again, trying to decide which moving target to follow.

He changed direction and charged after the second who was so tantalizingly close. But then another hunter interceded, flapping a large fur cloak, and, when the young rhino neared it, still another ran past, so close he gave the long reddish fur on his face a yank. The rhinoceros was getting more than confused; he was getting angry, murderously angry. He snorted, pawed the ground, and, when he saw another of those disconcerting running figures, tore after it at top speed.

The young man of the river people was having difficulty staying ahead, and, when he swerved, the rhino swerved in fast pursuit. But the animal was tiring. He had been chasing one after another of the vexatious runners, back and forth, unable to catch up with any. When yet another hood-waving hunter dashed in front of the woolly beast, he stopped, lowered his head until his large front horn touched the ground, and concentrated on the limping figure moving just beyond his reach.

Jondalar raced toward them, his lance held high. He needed to make the kill before the winded rhino caught his breath. Dolando, approaching from another direction, had the same intention, and several others were closing in. Jetamio flapped her hood, warily moving closer, trying to keep the animal's interest. Jondalar hoped he was as exhausted as he seemed.

Everyone's attention was riveted on Jetamio and the rhino. Jondalar wasn't sure what caused him to look north – perhaps a peripheral motion. "*Look out!*" he cried, spurting forward. "From the north, a rhino!"

But his actions seemed inexplicable to the others; they didn't understand his shouts. And they didn't see the enraged female rhinoceros bearing down on them full tilt.

"Jetamio! Jetamio! North!" He shouted again, waving his arm and pointing his spear.

She looked north, the way he was pointing, and she screamed a warning to the young man the she-rhino was charging. The rest of them raced to help him, forgetting the young one for the moment. It may have been that he was rested, or that the scent of the charging female had revived him, but suddenly the young male rushed the person waving a hood so provocatively close.

Jetamio was lucky he was so close. He didn't have time to build up speed or momentum, and his snort as he began his advance snapped her attention back, and Jondalar's as well. She threw herself back, dodging the rhino's horn, and ran behind him.

The rhinoceros slowed, looking for the target that had slipped away, and wasn't focusing on the tall man who closed the gap with long strides. And then it was too late. The small eye lost all ability to focus. Jondalar rammed the heavy lance into the vulnerable opening and smashed it into the brain. The next instant, all his sight disappeared when the young woman thrust her spear into the rhino's other eye. The animal seemed surprised, then stumbled, fell to his knees, and, as life ceased to sustain him, dropped to the ground.

There was a shout. The two hunters looked up and sprinted away at full speed in different directions. The full-grown female rhinoceros was hurtling towards them. But she slowed as she neared the young one, overran a few paces before she halted, then turned back to the young male lying on the ground with a spear bristling out of each eye. She nudged him with her horn, urging him to get up. Then she turned her head from side to side and shifted her weight from foot to foot as though trying to make up her mind.

Some of the hunters tried to get her attention, flapped hoods and cloaks at her, but she didn't see or chose to ignore them. She nudged the young rhino again, and then, in answer to some deeper instinct, turned north once more.

"I will tell you, Thonolan, it was close. But that female was determined to go north – she didn't want to stay at all."

"You think snow is on the way?" Thonolan asked, glancing down at his poultice, then back to his worried brother.

Jondalar nodded. "But I don't know how to tell Dolando that we'd better leave before the storm comes, when there's hardly a cloud in the sky . . . even if I could speak the language."

"I've been smelling snow on the way for days. It must be building up to a big one."

Jondalar was sure the temperature was still dropping, and knew it the next morning when he had to break a thin film of ice in a cup of tea that had been left near the fire. He tried again to communicate his concern, seemingly without success, and nervously watched the sky for more overt signs of weather change. He would have been relieved when he saw curdled clouds pouring over the mountains and filling up the blue bowl of the sky, if it weren't for the imminent threat they posed.

At the first sign that they were breaking camp, he struck his own tent and packed his and Thonolan's backframes. Dolando smiled and nodded at his readiness, then motioned him toward the river, but there was a nervousness to the man's smile and deep concern in his eyes. Jondalar's apprehension grew when he saw the swirling river and the wooden craft bobbing and jerking, straining at the ropes.

The expressions of the men who took his packs and stowed them near the cut-up frozen carcass of the rhino were more impassive, but Jondalar didn't see much encouragement either. And for all that he was anxious to get away, he was by no means comfortable about the means of transportation. He wondered how they were going to get Thonolan into the boat, and he went back to see if he could help.

Jondalar watched as the camp was dismantled with speed

and efficiency, knowing that sometimes the best assistance one could offer was simply to stay out of the way. He had begun to notice certain details in clothing that differentiated those who had set up shelters on land, and referred to themselves as Shamudoi, from the Ramudoi, the men who stayed on the boat. Yet they didn't quite seem like different tribes.

There was an ease of communication, with much joking, and none of the elaborate courtesies that usually indicated underlying tensions when two different peoples met. They seemed to speak the same language, shared all their meals, and worked well together. He noticed, though, that on land Dolando seemed to be in charge, while the men on the boat looked to another man for direction.

The healer emerged from the tent, followed by two men carrying Thonolan on an ingenious stretcher. Two shafts from the grove of alder trees on the knoll were wound over and around with extra rope from the boat, forming a support between them to which the wounded man was securely lashed. Jondalar hurried toward them, noticing that Roshario had begun taking down the tall circular tent. Her nervous glances toward the sky and the river convinced Jondalar she was not looking forward to the trip any more than he was.

"Those clouds look full of snow," Thonolan said when his brother came into sight and started walking beside the litter. "You can't see the tops of the mountains; snow must be falling up north already. I'll say one thing, you get a different view of the world from this position."

Jondalar looked up at the clouds rolling over the mountains, hiding the frozen peaks, tumbling over each other as they pushed and shoved in their hurry to fill the clear blue space above. Jondalar's frown looked almost as threatening as the sky, and his brow clouded with concern, but he tried to mask his fears. "Is that your excuse for lying around?" he said, trying to smile.

When they reached the log that was jutting out into the river, Jondalar fell back and watched the two river men balance themselves and their burden along the unsteady fallen tree and manhandle the stretcher up the even more precarious gangplank-ladder. He understood why Thonolan had been firmly lashed to the conveyance. He followed after, having trouble keeping his own balance, and looked at the men with even greater respect.

A few white flakes were beginning to sift down from a grey overcast sky when Roshario and the Shamud gave tightly bound bundles of poles and hides – the large tent – to a couple of the Ramudoi to carry on board and started across the log themselves. The river, reflecting the mood of the sky, rolled and swirled violently – the increased moisture in the mountains making its presence felt downstream.

The log was bobbing to a different motion from the boat, and Jondalar leaned over the side and reached a hand towards the woman. Roshario gave him a grateful look and took it, and was almost lifted up the last rung and into the boat. The Shamud had no qualms about accepting his assistance either, and the healer's look of gratitude was as genuine as Roshario's.

One man was still on shore. He released one of the moorings, then raced up the log and clambered aboard. The gangplank was hauled in quickly. The heaving craft that was trying to pull away and join the current was restrained by only one line and long-handled paddles in the hands of the rowers. The line was slipped with a sharp jerk, and the craft jumped at its chance for freedom. Jondalar clung tightly to the side as the craft bobbed and bounced into the mainstream of the Sister.

The storm was building rapidly and the swirling flakes reduced visibility. Floating objects and refuse travelled with them at varying speeds – heavy water-soaked logs, tangled brush, bloated carcasses, and an occasional small iceberg – making Jondalar fear a collision. He watched the shore slipping by, and his glance was held by the stand of alder on the high knoll. Something, attached to one of the trees, was flapping in the wind. A sudden gust broke its hold and carried it towards the river. As it dropped, Jondalar suddenly realized that the stiff, dark-stained leather was his summer tunic. Had it been flapping from that tree all this time? It floated for a moment before it became waterlogged and sank.

Thonolan had been released from his stretcher and was propped up against the side of the boat, looking pale, in pain, and frightened, but he smiled gamely at Jetamio who was beside him. Jondalar settled near them, frowning as he remembered his fear and his panic. Then he recalled his incredulous joy when he first saw the boat approaching, and he wondered again how they had known he was there. A thought struck him: could it have been that bloody tunic flapping in the wind that told them where to look? But how had they known to come in the first place? And with the Shamud?

The boat jounced over the rough water, and, taking a good look at its construction, Jondalar became intrigued by the sturdy craft. The bottom of the boat appeared to be made of a solid piece, a whole tree trunk hollowed out, wider at the midsection. The boat was made larger by rows of planks, overlapped and sewn together, extending up the sides and joined in front at the prow. Supports were spaced at intervals along the sides, and planks extended between them for seats for the rowers. The three of them were in front of the first seat.

Jondalar's eye followed the structure of the craft and skipped over a log that had been shoved against the prow. Then he looked back and felt his heart pound. Near the prow, caught in the tangled branches of the log in the bottom of the boat, was a leather summer tunic stained dark with blood.

9

"Don't be so greedy, Whinney," Ayla cautioned, watching the hay-coloured horse lapping up the last drops of water from the bottom of a wooden bowl. "If you drink it all, I'll have to melt more ice." The filly snorted, shook her head, and put her nose back in the bowl. Ayla laughed. "If you're that thirsty, I'll get more ice. Are you coming with me?"

Ayla's steady flow of thought directed at the young horse had become a habit. Sometimes it was no more than mental pictures, and often the expressive language of gestures, postures, and facial expressions with which she was most familiar, but since the young animal tended to respond to the sound of her voice, it encouraged Ayla to vocalize more. She mimicked the sounds of animals, invented new words out of combinations of sounds she knew, even incorporated some of the nonsense syllables from her games with her son. With no one to glare disapprovingly at her for making unnecessary sounds, her oral vocabulary expanded, but it was a language comprehensible only to her – and, in a unique sense, to her horse.

Ayla wrapped on fur leggings, a wrap of shaggy horsehair, and a wolverine hood, then tied on hand coverings. She put a hand through the slit in the palm to tuck her sling in her waist thong and tie on her carrying basket. Then she picked up an icepick – the long bone from a horse's foreleg cracked with a spiral break to get out the marrow and then sharpened by splintering and grinding against a stone – and started out.

"Well, come on, Whinney," she beckoned. She held aside the heavy aurochs hide, once her tent, attached to poles sunk into the earth floor of the cave as a windbreak at the mouth. The horse trotted out and behind her down the steep path.

Wind whipping around the bend buffeted her as she walked out on the frozen watercourse. She found a place that looked as if the crumpled crystal of the ice-locked stream could be broken, and hacked off shards and blocks.

"It's much easier to scoop up a bowl of snow than chop ice for water, Whinney," she said, loading the ice into her basket. She stopped to add some driftwood from the pile at the foot of the wall, thinking how grateful she was for the wood, for melting the ice as much as for warmth. "The winters are dry here, colder, too. I miss the snow, Whinney. The little bit that blows around here doesn't feel like snow, it just feels cold."

She piled the wood near the fireplace and dumped the ice into a bowl. She moved it near the fire to let the warmth begin to melt the ice before she put it into her skin pot, which needed some liquid so it wouldn't burn when she placed it over the fire. Then she looked around her snug cave at several projects in various stages of completion, trying to decide which one to work on that day. But she was restless. Nothing appealed to her until she noticed several new spears completed not long before.

Maybe I'll go hunting, she thought. I haven't been up on the steppes for a while. I can't take those, though. She frowned. It wouldn't do any good, I'd never get close enough to use them. I'll just take my sling and go for a walk. She filled a fold in her wrap with round stones from a pile she had brought up to the cave, just in case the hyenas returned. Then she added wood to the fire and left the cave.

Whinney tried to follow when Ayla hiked the steep slope up from her cave to the steppes above, then neighed after her nervously. "Don't worry, Whinney. I won't be gone long. You'll be all right."

When she reached the top, the wind grabbed her hood and threatened to make off with it. She pulled it back on and tightened the cord, then stepped back from the edge and paused to look around. The parched and withered summer landscape had bloomed with life compared to the sere frozen emptiness of the winter steppes now before her. The harsh wind gusted a dissonant dirge, ululating a thin penetrating whine that swelled to a wailing shriek and diminished to a hollow muffled groan. It whipped the dun earth bare, swirling the dry grainy snow out of whitened hollows and, captive of the wind's lament, flung the frozen flakes into the air again.

The driven snow felt like gritty sand that burned her face raw with its absolute cold. Ayla pulled her hood closer, bowed her head, and walked into the sharp northeast wind through dry brittle grass bent to the ground. Her nose pinched together and her throat ached as moisture was snatched away by the bitter air. A violent blast of wind caught her by surprise. She lost her breath, gulped for air, coughing and wheezing, and brought up phlegm. She spat it out and watched it freeze solid before it hit the rock-hard ground and bounced.

What am I doing up here? she thought. I didn't know it could be so cold. I'm going back.

She turned around and stopped still, for the moment forgetting the intense cold. Across the ravine a small herd of woolly mammoths was lumbering past; huge moving hummocks of dark reddish-brown fur with long curving tusks. This stark, seemingly barren, land was their home; the rough grass burned crisp with cold was life-sustaining nourishment for them. But in adapting to such an environment, they had forfeited their ability to live in any other. Their days were numbered; they would last only as long as the glacier.

Ayla watched, spellbound, until the indistinct shapes disappeared into the swirling snow, then hurried on and was only too glad to drop over the edge and out of the wind. She remembered feeling the same way when she first found her sanctuary. What would I ever have done if I hadn't found this valley? She hugged the filly when she reached the ledge in front of her cave, then walked to the edge and looked out over the valley. The snow was slightly deeper there, especially where it had blown into drifts, but just as dry, and just as cold.

But the valley did offer protection from the wind, and a cave. Without it, and fur and fire, she could not have survived; she was not a woolly creature. Standing on the ledge, the wind brought the howl of a wolf to her ears, and the yipping bark of a dhole. Below, an arctic fox walked across the ice of the frozen stream, its white fur almost hiding it from view when it stopped and held a stiff pose. She noticed movement down the valley and made out the shape of a cave lion; its tawny coat, lightened to almost white, was thick and full. Four-legged predators adapted to the environment of their prey. Ayla, and her kind, adapted the environment to themselves.

Ayla started when she heard a whooping cackle close by, and looked up to see a hyena above her at the rim of the gorge. She shivered and reached for her sling, but the scavenger moved off with its distinctive shuffling lope along the edge of the ravine, then turned back to the open plains. Whinney moved up beside her, nickered softly, and nudged her gently. Ayla pulled her dun-coloured wrap of horse fur closer around her, put her arm around Whinney's neck, and walked back to her cave.

Ayla lay on her bed of furs staring at a familiar formation of rock over her head, wondering why she was suddenly wide awake. She lifted her head and looked in Whinney's direction. Her eyes were open too, and looked toward the woman, but she displayed no anxiety. Yet, Ayla was sure something was different.

She snuggled back down in her furs, not wanting to leave their warmth, and looked around the home she had made for herself by the light shining in the hole above the mouth of the cave. Her projects were scattered around, but there was a growing stack of completed utensils and implements along the wall on the other side of the drying rack. She was hungry, and her eye was drawn back to the rack. She had poured the fat she had rendered from the horse into the cleaned intestines, giving it a pinch and a twist at intervals, and the little white sausages were dangling near a variety of dried herbs and seasonings hanging by their roots.

It made her think of breakfast. Dried meat made into a broth, a little fat added for richness, seasonings, maybe some grain, dried currants. She was too wide awake to stay in bed, and threw back the covers. She quickly tied on her wrap and foot coverings, then reached for the lynx fur from her bed, still warm from body heat, and hurried to go out and pass her urine off the far corner of the ledge. She pushed aside the windbreak and caught her breath.

The sharp angular contours of the rock ledge had been softened during the night by a thick blanket of white. It glistened in uniform brilliance, reflecting a transparent blue sky hung with mounded fluff. It took a moment longer to comprehend a more astounding change. The air was still. There was no wind.

The valley, nestled in the region where the wetter continental steppes were giving way to the dry loess steppes, partook of both climates, the south holding sway for the moment. The heavy snow resembled the winter conditions that usually prevailed around the cave of the Clan, and to Ayla it was a taste of home.

"Whinney!" she called. "Come out! It snowed! It really snowed for a change."

She was suddenly reminded of the reason she had come out of the cave, and made virgin tracks in the pure white expanse rushing to the far edge. Returning, she watched the young horse step gingerly on the insubstantial stuff, lower her head to sniff, then snort at the strange cold surface. She looked at Ayla and nickered.

"Come on, Whinney. It won't hurt you."

The horse had never experienced deep snow in such quiet abundance before; she was accustomed to it blowing in the wind or piled up in drifts. Her hoof sunk in when she took another tentative step, and she nickered at the woman again, as though asking for reassurance. Ayla led the young animal out until she felt more comfortable, then laughed at her antics when the filly's natural curiosity and sense of fun took over. It wasn't long before Ayla realized she wasn't dressed for an extended stay outside of the cave. It was cold.

"I'm going in to make some hot tea and something to eat. But I'm low on water, I'll have to get some ice . . ." She laughed. "I don't need to chip ice from the river. I can just get a bowlful of snow! How would you like a warm mash this morning, Whinney?"

After they ate, Ayla dressed warmly and went back outside. Without the wind, it felt almost balmy, but it was the familiarity of ordinary snow on the ground that delighted her most. She brought bowls and baskets of it into the cave and set them near the fireplace to melt. It was so much easier than chipping ice for water that she decided to use some for washing. It had been her custom to wash herself with melted snow regularly in winter, but it had been difficult enough to chip sufficient ice for drinking water and cooking. Washing was a forgone luxury.

She built up the fire with wood from the pile in the rear of the cave, then cleared the snow from the additional firewood stack outside and brought more in.

I wish I could stack water up like wood, she thought, looking at the containers of melting snow. I don't know how long this will last once the wind starts blowing again. She went out for another load of wood, taking a bowl out with her to clear the snow away. As she scooped up a bowlful and dumped it beside the wood, she noticed that it held its shape when she lifted the bowl away. I wonder. . . . Why couldn't I stack snow like that? Like a pile of wood?

The idea fired her with enthusiasm, and soon most of the untrodden snow from the ledge was piled against the wall near the cave entrance. Then she began on the pathway down to the beach. Whinney took advantage of the cleared trail to go down to the field. Ayla's eyes were glistening and her cheeks were rosy when she stopped and smiled with satisfaction at the mound of snow just outside her cave. She saw a small section at the end of the ledge that hadn't been entirely cleared, and she headed for it with determination. She looked out over the valley and laughed at Whinney picking her way through the unaccustomed drifts with high dainty steps.

When she glanced back at the pile of snow, she paused and a quirky grin lifted one corner of her mouth as a peculiar idea overcame her. The large pile of snow was made up of many bowl-shaped bumps and from her viewpoint suggested the contours of a face. She scooped up a bit more snow, then walked back, patted it in place, and stepped away to assess the effect.

If the nose were a little bigger, it would look just like Brun, she thought, and scooped up more snow. She packed it in place, scraped out a hollow, smoothed down a lump, and stepped back to survey her creation again.

Her eyes twinkled with a mischievous grin. "Greetings, Brun," she motioned, then felt a little chagrined. The real Brun would not appreciate her addressing a pile of snow with his name. Name-words were too important to assign them so indiscriminately. Well, it does look like him. She giggled at the thought. But maybe I should be more polite. It isn't proper for a woman to greet the leader as though he were a sibling. I should ask permission, she thought, and, elaborating on her game, sat in front of the snowpile and looked down at the ground – the correct posture for a woman of the Clan to assume when she was requesting an audience with a man.

Smiling inwardly with her playacting, Ayla sat quietly with her head bowed, just as though she really expected to feel a tap on her shoulder, the signal that she would be allowed to speak. The silence grew heavy, and the stone ledge was cold and hard. She began to think how ridiculous it was to be sitting there. The snow replica of Brun wouldn't tap her on the shoulder, any more than Brun himself had the last time she sat in front of him. Suddenly her playful mood evaporated. She got up and stared at the snow sculpture she had made.

"You're not Brun!" she gestured angrily, knocking away the part she had shaped so carefully. Rage swelled up inside her. "You're not Brun! You're not Brun!" She pummelled the mound of snow, with fists and feet, destroying every semblance to the shape of a face. "I'll never see Brun again. I'll never see Durc. I'll never see anyone again, ever! I'm all alone." A keening wail escaped her lips, and a sob of despair. "Oh, why am I all alone?"

She crumpled to her knees, lay down in the snow, and felt warm tears grow cold on her face. She hugged the frigid moisture to her, wrapping herself around it, welcoming its numbing touch. She wanted to burrow into it, let it cover her and freeze out the hurt, and anger, and loneliness. When she began shivering, she closed her eyes and tried to ignore the cold that was beginning to seep into her bones.

Then she felt something warm and wet on her face, and heard the soft nicker of a horse. She tried to ignore Whinney, too. The young animal nudged her again. Ayla opened her eyes to see the large dark eyes and long muzzle of the steppe horse. She reached up, put her arms around the filly's neck, and buried her face in the shaggy coat. When she let go, the horse neighed softly.

"You want me to get up, don't you, Whinney?" The horse shook her head up and down, as though she understood, and Ayla wanted to believe it. Her sense of survival had always been strong; it would take more than loneliness to make her give up. Growing up in Brun's clan, though she had been loved, in many ways she had been lonely all her life. She was always different. Her love for others had been the stronger force. Their need for her – Iza when she was sick, Creb as he grew old, her young son – had given reason and purpose to her life.

"You're right, I'd better get up. I can't leave you alone, Whinney, and I'm getting all wet and cold out here. I'll put on something dry. Then I'll make you a nice warm mash. You'd like that, wouldn't you?"

Ayla watched the two male arctic foxes snarling and nipping at each other, fighting over the vixen, and smelled the strong foxy odour of males in rut even from the elevation of her ledge. They are prettier in winter; in summer they're just a dull brown. If I want white fur, I should get it now, she thought, but made no move to get her sling. One male had emerged victorious and was claiming his prize. The vixen announced his act with a raucous scream as he mounted her.

She only makes that sound when they couple like that. I wonder if she likes it, or if she doesn't? I never liked it, even after it didn't hurt any more. But the other women did. Why was I so different? Just because I didn't like Broud? Why should that make any difference? Does that female fox like that male? Does she like what he's doing? She doesn't run away.

It wasn't the first time Ayla had refrained from hunting in order to observe foxes and other carnivorous animals. She had often spent long days watching the prey her totem allowed her to hunt, to learn their habits and habitats, and she had discovered they were interesting fellow creatures. The men of the Clan learned hunting by practising on herbivorous animals, food animals, and though they could track and hunt them when a warm fur was wanted, carnivores were never their favourite prey. They did not develop the special bond with them that Ayla had.

They still fascinated her, though she knew them well, but the rapidly pumping fox and the screaming vixen set her to wondering about more than hunting. Every year in late winter they come together like that. In spring, when her coat is turning brown, that vixen will have a litter. I wonder if she'll stay here under the bones and driftwood, or dig a burrow someplace else. I hope she stays. She'll nurse them, then give them baby food partly chewed from her own mouth. After that she'll bring dead prey, mice and moles and birds. Sometimes a rabbit. When her babies are bigger, she'll bring them animals still alive and teach them to hunt. By next fall, they'll be almost grown, and next winter the vixens will screech like that when the males mount.

Why do they do it? Come together like that? I think he's starting her babies. If all she has to do to have them is swallow a spirit, like Creb always told me, why do they couple like that? No one thought I'd have a baby. They said the spirit of my totem was too strong. But I did. If Durc was started when Broud did that to me, it wouldn't matter if my totem was strong.

People are not like foxes, though. They don't have babies only in spring, women can have them any time. And women and men don't couple just in winter, they do it all the time. A woman doesn't have a baby every time, though. Maybe Creb was right, too. Maybe the spirit of a man's totem has to get inside a woman, but she doesn't swallow it. I think he puts it inside her when they come together, with his organ. Sometimes her totem fights it, and sometimes it starts a new life.

I don't think I want a white fox fur. If I kill one, the rest will leave, and I want to see how many kits she'll have. I'll get that ermine I saw downstream before she turns brown. Her fur is white, and softer, and I like the black tip on her tail.

But that little weasel is so small, her pelt is hardly big enough to make one hand covering, and she'll have babies in spring too. Next winter there will probably be more ermines. Maybe I won't go hunting today. I think I'll finish that bowl instead.

It didn't occur to Ayla to wonder why she was thinking about the creatures who might be in her valley next winter, when she had planned to leave in spring. She was growing accustomed to her solitude, except in the evening when she added a new notch to a smooth stick and put it on the growing pile of them.

*

174

Ayla tried to push the stringy, oily lock of hair out of her face with the back of her hand. She was splitting a feeder root of a tree in preparation for making a large mesh basket, and couldn't let go. She had been experimenting with new weaving techniques, using various materials and combinations of them to produce different textures and meshes. The whole process of weaving, tying, knotting and the making of webbing, strands, and cords had captured her interest to the exclusion of almost everything else. Though occasionally the end products were unworkable, and sometimes laughable, she had made some startling innovations, encouraging her to try more. She found herself twining or plaiting nearly everything that came to hand.

She had been working since early morning on a particularly intricate weaving process, and it wasn't until Whinney entered, nosing aside the hide windbreak, that Ayla noticed it was evening.

"How did it get so late, Whinney? You don't even have water in your bowl," she said, getting up and stretching, stiff from sitting in one place for so long. "I should get something to eat for us, and I was going to change my bedding."

The young woman bustled about, getting fresh hay for the horse, and more for the shallow trench under her bed, dumping the old grass off the ledge. She chopped through the coating of ice to get at the snow inside the mound piled near the cave mouth, grateful again she had it there. She noticed there was not much left and wondered how long it would last before she'd have to get water below. She debated with herself about bringing in enough to wash, then, thinking she might not have the opportunity again until spring, brought in enough to wash her hair as well.

Ice melted in bowls near the fire while she prepared and cooked a meal. As she worked, her thoughts kept turning back to the processes of working with fibres that she was finding so engrossing. After she had eaten and washed, she was pulling tangles out of her wet hair with a twig and her fingers when she saw the dried teasel she had been using to comb and untangle some shaggy bark for twinning. Combing Whinney regularly had given her ideas to use the teasel on the fibres, and it was a natural step to try it on her own hair.

She was delighted with the results. Her thick golden

tresses felt soft and smooth. She had not paid particular attention to her hair before, aside from an occasional washing, and she usually wore it pushed out of the way behind her ears with a haphazard parting down the middle. Iza had often told her it was her best feature, she remembered, after she had brushed it forward to examine by firelight. The colour was rather nice, she thought, but even more appealing was the texture, the smooth long strands. Almost before she realized it, she was plaiting a section in a long braided cord.

She tied a piece of sinew to the end, then started on another section. She had a passing thought of how odd it would seem if anyone saw her making cords of her own hair, but it didn't deter her and before long her entire head was covered with many long braids. Swinging her head from side to side, she smiled at the novelty of them. She liked the braids, but she couldn't tuck them behind her ears to keep them off her face. After some experimenting, she discovered a way to coil and tie them down on her head in front, but she liked to swing them and left the sides and back hanging down.

It was the novelty that appealed to her in the beginning, but it was the convenience that persuaded her to keep her hair in braids. It stayed in place; she wasn't always tucking loose tendrils out of the way. And what did it matter if someone might think her strange? She could make cords of her hair if she wished – she had only herself to please.

She used up the snow on her ledge not long after, but it wasn't necessary to chip ice for water any more. Enough snow had accumulated in drifts. The first time she went down for it, though, she noticed that the snow below her cave had a sifting of soot and ash from her fire. She walked upstream on the frozen surface to find a cleaner location to collect it, but when she entered the narrow gorge, curiosity kept her going.

She had never swum as far upstream as she could have. The current was strong, and it hadn't seemed necessary. But walking was no effort, except for watching her footing. Along the gorge, where falling temperatures caught sprays of water or pressures built up ridges, fantasies in ice created a magical dreamland. She smiled with pleasure at the wondrous formations, but she was unprepared for the sight ahead.

She had been walking for some time and was thinking of

turning back. It was cold in the bottom of the shaded gorge, and the ice added its measure to the chill. She decided to go only as far as the next bend in the river. When she reached it, she stopped and stared in awe. Beyond the turn, the gorge walls came together forming a stone wall that reached to the steppes high above, and cascading down it were the glittering stalactite icicles of a frozen waterfall. Hard as stone but cold and white, it seemed a spectacular inversion, like a cave turned inside out.

The massive ice sculpture was breathtaking in its grandeur. The entire force of the water held by the grip of winter seemed ready to break upon her. It was dizzying in its effect, yet she was rooted to the spot, held by its magnificence. She shivered in the face of the restrained power. Before she turned away, she thought she saw a glistening drop of water at the tip of a high icicle, and shivered with a deeper chill.

Ayla awoke to cold gusting draughts and looked up to see the opposite wall out of the entrance of the cave, and the windbreak whipping against the post. After she repaired it, she stood for a while with her face to the wind.

"It's warmer, Whinney. The wind isn't as cold, I'm sure."

The horse twitched her ears and looked at the woman expectantly. But it was just conversation. There were no signals or sounds requiring a response from the young mare: no gestures beckoning her to approach or back away; no sign that food was forthcoming, or currying or patting or other forms of affection. Ayla had not been consciously training the horse; she thought of Whinney as a companion and friend. But the intelligent animal had begun to perceive that certain signals and sounds were associated with certain activities and had learned to respond to many of them appropriately.

Ayla, too, was beginning to understand Whinney's language. The horse didn't need to speak with words; the woman was accustomed to reading fine shades of meaning in nuances of expression or posture. Sounds had always been a secondary aspect of communication in the Clan. During the long winter that had enforced close association, the woman and the horse had formed a warm bond of affection and achieved a high level of communication and understanding.

Ayla usually knew when Whinney was happy, content, nervous, or upset, and responded to signals from the horse that she required attention – food, water, affection. But it was the woman who had assumed the dominant role, intuitively; she who had begun to give purposeful directions and signals to which the horse responded.

Ayla stood just inside the cave entrance examining her repair work and the condition of the hide. She'd had to make new holes along the top edge, below the ones that had ripped out, and thread a new thong through them to lash the windbreak back to the horizontal crosspiece. Suddenly she felt something wet on the back of her neck.

"Whinney, don't . . ." She turned around, but the horse had not moved. Just then another drop splatted her. She looked around, then up at a long shaft of ice hanging down from the smoke hole. The moisture from cooking steam and breath, carried up by the warmth of the fire, met the freezing cold air coming in the hole, causing ice to form. But the dry wind drew off just enough moisture to keep it from growing very long. For most of the winter, only a fringe of ice had decorated the top of the hole. Ayla was surprised to see the long dirty icicle, full of soot and ash.

A drop of water at the tip let go and splashed her forehead before she overcame her amazement enough to move out of the way. She wiped away the wetness, then let out a whoop.

"Whinney! Whinney! Spring is coming! The ice is starting to melt!" She ran to the young mare and threw her arms around the shaggy neck, calming the horse's startled nervousness. "Oh, Whinney, soon the trees will be budding, and the first greens will be starting. Nothing is as good as the first greens of spring! Wait until you taste spring grass. You'll love it!"

Ayla ran out on the broad ledge as though she expected to see a world of green instead of white. The chill wind drove her back inside quickly enough, and her excitement at the first drops of meltwater turned to dismay when spring took back its promise and the worst blizzard of the season whistled down the river gorge a few days later. But despite the mantle of glacial ice, spring inexorably followed on the heels of winter, and the warming breath of the sun melted the frozen crust of the earth. The drops of water did, indeed, herald the change from ice to water in the valley – more than Ayla ever imagined.

The early warm drops of melt were soon joined by spring rains which helped soften and wash out the accumulated snow and ice, bringing the seasonal moisture to the dry steppes. There was more than local accumulation, however. The source of the valley's river was meltwater from the great glacier itself, and during the spring melt it acquired tributaries all along its route, many that had not existed when Ayla first arrived.

Flash floods in formerly dry washes caught unsuspecting animals by surprise and churned them downstream. In the wild turbulence, whole carcasses were torn apart, battered, bashed, and bared to the bone. At times previous streambeds were ignored by the runoff. The meltwater cut new channels, tearing out by the roots brush and trees that had struggled to grow in the hostile environment for years, sweeping them away. Stones and rocks, even huge boulders, made buoyant by the water, were carried off, urged along by the scouring debris.

The narrow walls of the river gorge upstream from Ayla's cave constricted the rampaging water that poured over the high waterfall. The resistance added force to the current and, with the excess volume, the level of the river rose. The foxes had left their kennel under the former year's pile long before the rocky beach below the cave was awash.

Ayla could not keep herself in the cave. From the ledge she watched the swirling, churning, foaming river rising daily. Surging through the narrow gorge – she could see the water fall over itself as it broke free – it slammed into the jutting wall, dropping portions of its load of debris at the foot. She finally understood how the pile of bones, driftwood, and erratic stones that she had found so useful had lodged there, and she came to appreciate how fortunate she was to have found a cave so high up.

She could feel the ledge shudder when a large boulder or tree crashed against it. It frightened her, but she had developed a fatalistic view of life. If she was meant to die, she would die; she had been cursed and was supposed to be dead anyway. There must be forces more powerful than she controlling her destiny, and if the wall was going to give way while she was on top of it, there wasn't anything she could do to prevent it. And the mindless violence of nature fascinated her.

Each day presented a new aspect. One of the tall trees growing near the opposite wall gave in to the tide. It fell against her ledge but soon was swept away by the swollen stream. She watched it hurtled around the bend by the current that spread out into a long narrow lake across the lower meadow, flooding or entirely inundating vegetation that had once lined the bank of quieter waters. Limbs of trees and tangled brush, that clung to the earth beneath the turbulent river, snatched and held the fallen giant. But resistance was fruitless. The tree was torn from their grasp or they were torn out by their roots.

She knew the day winter lost its final grip on the ice falls. A crash echoing down the canyon announced the appearance of water-worn ice floes bobbing and swirling on the current. They crowded together at the wall, then careened around it, losing shape and definition as they proceeded.

The familiar beach had a different character when the waters finally receded enough for Ayla to walk down the steep path to the river's edge again. The muddy pile at the foot of the wall had taken on new dimensions, and among the bones and driftwood were carcasses and trees. The shape of the rocky bit of land had changed, and familiar trees had been washed out. But not all of them. Roots went deep in a land essentially dry, especially those of vegetation set back from the edge of the stream. The brush and trees were accustomed to the yearly inundation, and most of those that had survived several seasons were still firmly entrenched. When the first green nubs on the raspberry bushes began to show, Ayla began to think about the coming year. The first stirrings of spring had brought the need to make a decision: when to leave the valley to continue her search for the Others. It was more difficult than she imagined it would be.

She was sitting at the far end of the terrace in a favourite place. On the side facing the meadow was a flat place to sit and, at just the right distance below it, another to rest her feet. She could not see the water as it turned the bend or the rocky beach, but she had a clear view of the valley, and if she turned her head she could see the upstream river gorge. She had been watching Whinney in the meadow and had seen her head back. The mare had disappeared from view when she rounded the jutting nose of the wall, but Ayla could hear her coming up the path and was waiting for her to appear.

The woman smiled when she saw the large head of the steppe horse, with her dark ears and stiff brown mane. As she continued up, Ayla noticed the scraggly shedding coat of the yellow horse and the dark brown feral stripe down her spine ending in a full, long dark horse's tail. There was a faint suggestion of stripes on her forelegs above the dark brown lower part. The young horse looked at the woman and nickered softly, waiting to see if Ayla wanted something, then proceeded into the cave. Though not quite filled out, the yearling had reached her adult size.

Ayla turned back to the view, and to thoughts that had been occupying her for days, keeping her awake nights. I can't leave now – I need to hunt a little first and maybe wait for some fruits to ripen. And what am I going to do about Whinney? That was the crux of her problem. She didn't want to live alone, but she didn't know anything about the people whom the Clan called the Others, except that she was one. What if I find people who won't let me keep her? Brun would never let me keep a full-grown horse, especially one so young and tender. What if they wanted to kill her? She wouldn't even run away, she'd just stand there and let them. If I told them not to, would they pay attention? Broud would kill her no matter what I said. What if men of the Others are like Broud? Or worse? After all, they did kill Oda's baby, though it wasn't on purpose.

I have to find someone sometime, but I can stay a little longer. At least until I do some hunting, and maybe until some of the roots are ready. That's what I'll do. I'll stay until the roots are big enough for digging.

She felt relieved after her decision to postpone her departure, and ready to do something. She got up and walked to the other side of the ledge. The stench of rotting meat wafted up from the new pile at the base of the wall. She noticed movement below and watched a hyena crush with powerful jaws the foreleg of what had likely been a deer. No other animal, predator or scavenger, had such strength concentrated in jaw and forequarters, but it gave the hyena an ungainly disproportionate build.

She'd had to restrain herself the first time she saw the back end of one, with its low hindquarters and slightly crooked legs, nosing into the pile. But when she saw it digging out a rotting piece of carcass, she left it alone, for once grateful of the service they performed. She had studied them, as she had observed other carnivorous animals. Unlike the felines or wolves, they didn't need powerful springing hindleg muscles to attack. When they hunted, they went for the viscera, the soft underbelly and mammary glands. But their usual diet was carrion – in any condition.

They revelled in corruption. She had seen them scavenge human refuse piles, disinter bodies if they weren't carefully buried; they even ate dung, and they smelled as foul as their diet. Their bite, if not immediately fatal, often caused death later, from infection; and they went after the young.

Ayla made a face and shuddered with disgust. She hated them, and she had to resist an urge to chase off the ones below with her sling. Her attitude was irrational, but she couldn't help her revulsion at the brown-spotted scavengers. To her they had no redeeming features. She was not nearly as offended by other scavengers, though they often smelled as bad.

From the vantage point of the ledge she saw a wolverine going after a share of the offal. The glutton resembled a bear cub with a long tail, but she knew they were more like weasels, and their musk glands were as noxious as a skunk's. Wolverines were vicious scavengers. They would vandalize caves or open sites for no apparent reason. But they were scrappy, intelligent animals and absolutely fearless predators that would attack anything, even a giant deer, though they could content themselves with mice, birds, frogs, fish, or berries. Ayla had seen them drive off larger animals from their own kills. They were worthy of respect, and their unique frost-doffing fur was valuable.

She watched a pair of red kites take wing from their nest high in a tree across the stream, and fly rapidly into the sky. They spread long reddish wings and deeply forked tails and soared down to the rocky beach. Kites fed on carrion, but, like other raptors, they also preyed on small mammals and reptiles. The young woman wasn't as familiar with carnivorous birds, but she knew the females were usually larger than the males, and they were beautiful to watch.

Ayla could tolerate the vulture, despite its ugly bald head and a smell as evil as its looks. Its hooked beak was sharp and strong, built for shearing and dismembering dead animals, but there was majesty in its movements. It was breathtaking to see one gliding and soaring so effortlessly, riding air currents with large wings, then, on spying food, plummeting to the ground and running towards the corpse with outstretched neck and wings half open.

The scavengers below were having a feast, even carrion crows were getting a share, and Ayla was delighted. With the stink of decaying corpses so near her cave, she could even abide the hated hyena. The faster they cleaned it up, the happier she would be. Suddenly she felt overpowered by the fulsome reek. She wanted a breath of air untainted by malodorous emanations.

"Whinney," she called. The horse poked her head out of the cave at the sound of her name. "I'm going for a walk. Do you want to come with me?" The mare saw the beckoning signal and walked towards the woman, tossing her head.

They walked down the narrow path, gave the rocky beach and its noisome inhabitants a wide berth, and edged around the stone wall. The horse seemed to relax as they strolled along the fringe of brush that lined the small river, quietly contained within its normal banks again. The smell of death made her nervous, and her unreasoning fear of hyenas had a basis in early experience. They both enjoyed the freedom allowed by the sunny spring day after a long restricting winter, though the air still had a chilly dampness. It smelled fresher on the open meadow, too, and flying scavengers were not the only birds feasting, although other activities seemed more important.

Ayla slowed to watch a pair of great spotted woodpeckers, the male with a crimson crown, the female's white, indulge in aerial displays, drum on a dead snag, and chase each other around trees. Ayla knew woodpeckers. They would hollow out the heart of an old tree and line the nest with wood chips. But once the six or so brown-spotted eggs were laid and incubated, and the young hatched and reared, the couple would go their separate ways again to search tree trunks within their territory for insects and make the woods resound with their harsh laughing call.

Not so the larks. Only during breeding season did the sociable flocks separate into pairs and the males behave like feisty gamecocks with former friends. Ayla heard the glorious song as a pair soared straight up. It was sung with such volume that she could hear them as they hovered above, hardly more than specks in the sky. Suddenly, like a pair of stones, they dropped, then swooped up singing again the next movement.

Ayla reached the place where she had once dug a pit to hunt a dun mare; at least she thought it was the place. No trace remained. The spring flood had swept away the brush she had cut and smoothed out the depression. Farther on, she stopped for a drink and smiled at a wagtail running along the water's edge. It resembled a lark, but was slimmer with a yellow underbelly, and it held its body horizontal to keep its tail from getting wet, which caused it to wag up and down.

A flood of liquid notes brought her attention to another pair of birds who had no qualms at all about getting wet. The water ouzels were bobbing at each other in courtship display, but she always wondered how they could walk under water without getting their plumage waterlogged. When she went back to the open field, Whinney was grazing the new green shoots. She smiled again at a pair of brown wrens scolding her with their *chick-chick* when she passed too close to their shrub. Once beyond it, they changed to a loud clear flowing song that was sung first by one, and then by the other in an alternating response.

She stopped and sat on a log listening to the sweet songs of several different birds, and then was surprised when a bush warbler imitated the whole chorus in one burst of melody. She sucked in her breath at the virtuosity of the small creature, and surprised herself with the whistling sound she produced. A green bunting followed her with his characteristic note that sounded like an indrawn whistle, and the mimicking bush warbler repeated it again.

Ayla was delighted. It seemed she had become part of the avian chorus, and she tried again. Pursing her lips, she sucked in her breath but managed to produce only a faint windy whistle. The next time she got more volume, but filled her lungs so full of air that she had to expel it, making a loud whistle. It was much closer to the sound of the birds. With the next effort, she only blew air through her lips and she had no better luck with several more tries. She went back to the indrawn whistle and had more success making a whistling sound, though it lacked volume.

She kept trying, pulling in and blowing out, and occasionally she produced a sharp sound. She became so involved with the attempts that she didn't notice Whinney perking up her ears whenever the piercing whistle was made. The horse didn't know how to respond, but she was curious and took a few steps towards the woman.

Ayla saw the young mare approaching with a quizzical forward cocking of her ears. "Are you surprised that I can make bird sounds, Whinney? So am I. I didn't know I could sing like a bird. Well, maybe not quite like a bird, but if I keep practising, I think I could come close. Let me see if I can do it again."

She drew in a breath, pursed her lips, and, concentrating on it, let out a long, solid whistle. Whinney tossed her head, whinnied, and pranced to her. Ayla stood up and hugged the horse's neck, suddenly realizing how much she had grown. "You're so big, Whinney. Horses grow so fast, you're almost a grown woman horse. How fast can you run now?" Ayla gave her a sharp slap on the rump. "Come on, Whinney, run with me," she motioned, starting across the field as fast as she could.

The horse outdistanced her in a few paces and raced ahead, stretching out as she galloped. Ayla followed after, running just because it felt good. She pushed herself until she could go no farther, panting to a breathless halt. She watched the horse gallop down the long valley, then veer around in a wide circle and come cantering back. I wish I could run like you, she thought. Then we could both run together wherever we wanted.

The filly was lathered when she returned, and made Ayla laugh when she rolled in the meadow, kicking her legs up in the air and making little noises of pleasure. When she got up, she shook herself and went back to grazing. Ayla kept watching her, thinking how exciting it would be to run like a horse, then fell to practising her whistle again. The next time she managed a shrill piercing sound, Whinney looked up and cantered to her again. Ayla hugged the young horse, rather pleased that she had come at the whistle, but she couldn't get the thought of running with the horse out of her mind.

Then an idea struck her.

Such an idea would not have occurred to her if she hadn't lived with the animal all winter, thinking of her as a friend and companion. And certainly she would not have acted on such a thought if she were still living with the Clan. But Ayla had become more used to following her impulses.

Would she mind? Ayla thought. Would she let me? She led the horse to the log and climbed up on it, then put her arms around the horse's neck and lifted a leg. Run with me, Whinney. Run and take me with you, she thought, then straddled the horse.

The young mare was unaccustomed to weight on her back, and she flattened her ears back and pranced nervously. But, though the weight was unfamiliar, the woman was not, and Ayla's arms around her neck had a calming influence. Whinney almost reared to throw the weight off, then tried to run away from it instead. Breaking into a gallop, she raced down the field with Ayla clinging to her back.

When Whinney stopped, the woman slid off her back. She lifted the drooping muzzle with both hands and laid her cheek on the animal's nose; then she tucked the mare's head under her arm in a gesture of affection which she hadn't used since the horse was small. It was a special embrace, saved for special occasions.

The ride was a thrill she could hardly contain. The very idea of going along with a horse when it galloped filled Ayla with a sense of wonder. She had never dreamed such a thing was possible. No one had. She was the first.

10

Ayla could hardly keep herself off the horse's back. Riding the young mare as she galloped at top speed was an inexpressible joy. It thrilled her more than anything she had ever known. Whinney seemed to enjoy it as well, and she quickly became accustomed to carrying the woman on her back. The valley soon became too small to contain the woman and her galloping steed. They often raced across the steppes east of the river, which were easy to reach.

She knew that soon she would have to gather and hunt, process and store wild food nature provided to prepare for the next cycle of seasons. But during early spring when the earth was still awakening from the long winter, its offerings were lean. A few fresh greens added variety to a dried winter diet, but neither roots nor buds, nor bony shanks, had yet filled out. Ayla took advantage of her enforced leisure to ride the horse as often as she could, most days from early morning to late evening.

At first she just rode, sitting passively, going wherever the horse went. She didn't think in terms of directing the filly; the signals Whinney had learned to understand were visual – Ayla didn't attempt to communicate with only words – and she couldn't see them with the woman sitting on her back. But to the woman, body language had always been as much a part of speaking as specific gestures, and riding allowed close contact.

After an initial period of soreness, Ayla began to notice the play of the horse's muscles, and after her initial adjustment, Whinney could sense the woman's tension and relaxation. They had already developed an ability to sense each other's needs and feelings, and a desire to respond to them. When Ayla wanted to go in a particular direction, unknowingly she leaned that way, and her muscles communicated the change in tension to the horse. The horse began reacting to the tension and relaxation of the woman on her back by changing direction or speed. The animal's response to the barely perceptible movements caused Ayla to tense or move in the same way when she wanted Whinney to respond that way again.

It was a mutual training period, each learning from the other, and in the process deepening their relationship. But without being aware of it, Ayla was taking control. The signals between woman and horse were so subtle, and the transition from passive acceptance to active direction so natural, that Ayla didn't notice it at first, except at a subliminal level. The almost continuous riding became a concentrated and intense training course. As the relationship grew more sensitive, Whinney's reactions came to be so finely tuned that Ayla had only to *think* of where she wanted to go and at what speed and, as though the animal were an extension of her own body, the horse responded. The young woman didn't realize she had transmitted signals through nerves and muscles to the highly sensitive skin of her mount.

Ayla hadn't planned to train Whinney. It was the result of the love and attention she lavished on the animal, and the innate differences between horse and human. Whinney was curious and intelligent, she could learn and had a long memory, but her brain was not as evolved and was organized differently. Horses were social animals, normally living in herds, and they needed the closeness and warmth of fellow creatures. The sense of touch was particularly developed and important in establishing close rapport. But the young mare's instincts led her to follow directions, to go where she was led. When panicked, even leaders of herds fled with the rest.

The woman's actions had purpose, were directed by a brain in which foresight and analysis were constantly interacting with knowledge and experience. Her vulnerable position kept her survival reflexes sharp and forced her to be constantly aware of her surroundings, which together had precipitated and accelerated the training process. The sight of a hare or a giant hamster, even while she was riding for pleasure, tended to make Ayla reach for her sling and want to go after it. Whinney had quickly interpreted her desire, and her first step in that direction led ultimately to the young woman's tight, though unconscious, control of the horse. It wasn't until Ayla killed a giant hamster that she became aware of it.

It was still early in spring. They had flushed the animal inadvertently, but the moment Ayla saw it running, she leaned toward it – reaching for her sling as Whinney started racing after it. When they drew near, Ayla's shift in position, that came with a thought to jump down, brought the horse to a halt in time for her to slide off and hurl a stone.

It'll be nice to have fresh meat tonight, she was thinking as she walked back towards the waiting horse. I should do more hunting, but it's been so much fun riding Whinney . . .

I was riding Whinney! She chased after that hamster. And she stopped when I wanted her to! Ayla's thoughts raced back to the first day she had climbed on the horse's back and wrapped her arms around the young mare's neck. Whinney had reached down for a clump of tender new grass.

"Whinney!" Ayla cried. The horse lifted her head and perked up her ears expectantly. The young woman was stunned. She didn't know how to explain it. The mere idea of riding on the horse had been overwhelming enough, but that the horse would go where Ayla wanted to go was harder to understand than the process had been for both of them to learn.

The horse came to her. "Oh, Whinney," she said again, her voice cracking with a sob, though she wasn't sure why, as she hugged the shaggy neck. Whinney blew through her nostrils and arched her neck so her head was leaning over the woman's shoulder.

When she went to mount the horse, Ayla felt clumsy. The hamster seemed to get in the way. She walked to a boulder, though she had long since ceased using one, and, stopping to think about it, knew she had jumped and thrown her leg over, mounting easily before. After some initial confusion, Whinney started back to the cave. When Ayla consciously tried to govern the filly, her unconscious signals lost some of their decisiveness, as did Whinney's response. She didn't know how she had been directing the horse.

Ayla learned to rely on her reflexes again when she

discovered that Whinney responded better if she relaxed, though in the process she did develop some purposeful signals. As the season waxed, she began to hunt more. At first she stopped the horse and got off to use her sling, but it wasn't long before she made an attempt from horseback. Missing her shot only gave her reason to practise, a new challenge. She had taught herself the use of the weapon in the beginning by practising alone. It was a game then, and there was no one she could have turned to for training; she wasn't supposed to hunt.

It had been a long time since she'd had need to practise with her sling, and it again became a game, though no less serious because it was fun. She was already so skilled, however, that it wasn't long before she was as accurate from horseback as she was standing on her own two feet. But, even racing on the horse as she closed on a fleet-footed hare, the young woman still didn't comprehend, couldn't imagine, the advantages she had gained.

Initially, Ayla carried her kills home the way she always had, in a basket strapped to her neck. Laying her prey in front of her across Whinney's back was an easy step to make. Devising a pannier, a specially made basket for the young mare to carry on her back, was the next logical move. It took a little more thought to come up with a pair of baskets on either side of the horse, attached to a wide thong tied around her middle. But with the addition of the second basket, she began to perceive some of the benefits of harnessing the strength of her four-legged friend. For the first time, she was able to bring to the cave a load that was larger than she alone could carry.

Once she understood, her methods changed. The entire pattern of her life changed. She stayed out longer, ranged farther afield, and returned with more produce, or plant materials, or small animals at one time. Then she spent the next few days processing the results of her forays.

Once when she noticed wild strawberries were beginning to ripen, she searched over a large area to find as many as she could. It was nearly dark when she started back. She had a sharp eye for landmarks, but before she reached the valley, it was too dark to see them. When she found herself near the cave, she relied on Whinney's instincts to guide them, and on subsequent trips she often let the horse find their way back.

But afterward she took along a sleeping fur. One evening she decided to sleep out on the open steppes, because it was late and she thought she'd enjoy a night under the stars again. She made a fire, but cuddled up beside Whinney in her fur, hardly needing it for warmth. Rather fire was a deterrent to nocturnal wildlife. All the steppes creatures were wary of the smell of smoke. Raging grass fires sometimes burned unchecked for days, flushing out – or roasting – everything in their path.

After the first time, it was easier to spend a night or two away from the cave, and Ayla began to explore the region east of the valley more extensively.

She wasn't admitting it to herself, but she was looking for the Others – hoping she would find them, and afraid that she might. It was a way of putting off the decision to leave the valley. She would soon have to make preparations to go if she was going to take up her search again, but the valley had become her home. She didn't want to leave, and she was still worried about Whinney. If there were people living within range of her valley by horseback, she could, perhaps, observe them first before making her presence known, and learn something about them.

She couldn't remember anything of her life before living with the Clan. She was near death when Iza picked her up half starved and burning with infected cave lion gashes, and carried her with them on their search for a new cave. But whenever she tried to recall anything of her earlier life, a nauseous fear overcame her.

The earthquake that had cast a five-year-old girl alone in the wilderness, left to the mercy of fate – and the compassion of people who were much different – had been too devastating for her. She had lost all memory of the earthquake and of the people to whom she had been born. They were to her as they were to the rest of the Clan: the Others.

Like the indecisive spring, with its swift changes from icy showers to warm sun and back again, Ayla's inclination shifted from one extreme to the other. Every night she decided she would begin preparations for leaving the next day, and every morning she put it off and rode Whinney on the eastern plains instead.

Her careful and extended survey made her aware not only of the territory, but of the life that inhabited the vast prairie. Herds of grazers had begun to migrate. She began to think about hunting a large animal again. As the idea took up more of her thoughts, it displaced a measure of her preoccupation with her solitary existence.

She saw horses, though none had returned to her valley, but she had no intention of hunting horses. Though she didn't know how she might use them, she began taking her spears along on her rides. The long poles were unwieldy until she devised secure holders for them, one in each basket carried on either side of the horse.

It wasn't until she noticed a herd of female reindeer that an idea began to take shape. When she was a girl, and surreptitiously teaching herself to hunt, she often found an excuse to work near the men when they were discussing hunting. She had been more interested in the hunting lore associated with the sling – her weapon – but was intrigued no matter what kind of hunting they discussed. At first sight, she thought the herd of small-antlered reindeer were males. Then she noticed the calves and recalled that among all the varieties of deer, only female reindeer had antlers. The recollection triggered a whole set of associated memories – including the taste of reindeer meat.

More important, she remembered the men saying that when reindeer migrate north in the spring, they move in separate groups, but travel the same route, as though following a path only they could see. First the females and the young, then a herd of young males. Later in the season, the old bucks come stringing along in small groups.

Ayla rode at a leisurely pace behind a herd of antlered does and their calves. The rising sun had steamed out the morning mist clinging to low-lying hollows and dips, lending an unaccustomed moisture to the steppes. The summer hordes of gnats and flies that liked to nest in reindeer fur, especially near eyes and ears, driving the reindeer to seek cooler climates, were just appearing. Ayla absently brushed away the few that were buzzing around her head. The deer were used to other ungulates, and they ignored Whinney, and her human passenger, as long as they didn't get too close.

Ayla was thinking of hunting. If the bucks follow the does, they should be coming this way soon. I could hunt a young reindeer buck; I'll know what path they will be taking. But that won't help if I can't get close enough to use my spears. I could dig a hole again. No, they'd avoid it. There's not enough brush to build a fence. Maybe if I get them running, one would fall in.

How will I get it out? I don't want to butcher an animal in the bottom of a muddy hole again, and I'll have to dry the meat out here.

The woman and the horse followed the herd all day, stopping occasionally to eat and rest, until the clouds turned pink in a deepening blue sky. She was farther north than she had been before, in an unfamiliar area. From a distance she'd seen a line of vegetation, and, in the fading light as the sky turned vermilion, she saw the colour reflected beyond a stand of thick brush. The reindeer formed themselves into single files to pass through narrow openings to reach the water of a large stream, and they ranged along the shallow edge to drink before crossing.

Grey twilight drained the fresh green from the land while the sky blazed, as though the colour stolen by night was returned in brighter hue. Ayla wondered if it was the same stream they had crossed several times before. Rather than several rills, creeks, and streams contributing to a larger body of running water, often the same river was crossed several times as it meandered across flat grasslands, turning back on itself in oxbows and breaking into channels. If her reckoning was right, from the other side of the river she could reach her valley without having to cross any other major watercourses.

The reindeer appeared to be settling down for the night on the opposite side. Ayla decided to do the same. It was a long way back. She didn't want to cross the river and get chilled with night coming on. She slid off the horse, then removed the carrying baskets and let Whinney run loose while she made camp. Dry brush and driftwood were soon blazing with the help of her firestone and flint. After a meal of starchy groundnuts wrapped in leaves to roast, and a giant hamster, she set up her low tent. Ayla whistled the horse to her, wanting her near, then crawled into her sleeping fur, with her head outside the tent opening.

The clouds had settled against the horizon. Above, the stars were so thick that it seemed some impossibly brilliant light was straining to break through the cracked and pitted black barrier of the night sky. Creb said they were fires in the sky, she mused, hearths of the spirit world, and the hearths of totem spirits, too. Her eyes searched the heavens until they found the pattern she was looking for. There's the home of Ursus, and over there, my totem, the Cave Lion. It's strange how they can move around the sky, but the pattern doesn't change.

The bucks will be along soon. That means they should be crossing here. Whinney, smelling the presence of a four-legged predator, snorted, and moved closer to the fire and the woman.

"Is there something out there, Whinney?" Ayla asked, using sounds and signals, words not quite like any the Clan had ever used. She could make a soft nicker that was indistinguishable from the sound Whinney made. She could yip like a fox, howl like a wolf, and was quickly learning to whistle like almost any bird. Many of the sounds had become incorporated in her private language. She hardly thought about the Clan stricture against unnecessary sounds any more. The normal facile ability of her kind to vocalize was asserting itself.

The horse moved in between the fire and Ayla, drawing security from both.

"Move over, Whinney. You're blocking the heat."

Ayla got up and added another stick of wood to the fire. She put an arm around the animal's neck, sensing Whinney's nervousness. I'll stay up and keep the fire going, she thought. Whatever is over there is going to be a lot more interested in those reindeer, but it might be a good idea to have a nice big fire for a while.

She hunkered down, stared at the flames, watching sparks fly up to melt into the dark whenever she added another log. Sounds from across the river told her when a deer, or two, had fallen prey to something, probably something feline. Her thoughts turned to hunting a deer for herself. At one point, she pushed the horse aside to get more wood, and she suddenly got an idea. Later, after Whinney was more relaxed, Ayla returned to her sleeping fur, her thoughts whirling as the idea grew and expanded to other exciting possibilities. By the time she fell asleep, the major outlines of a plan had formed, using a concept so incredible that she smiled to herself at the audacity of it.

When she crossed the river in the morning, the herd of reindeer, smaller by one or two, had departed, but she was through following them. She urged Whinney to a gallop back to the valley. There was much to prepare if she was going to be ready in time.

"That's it, Whinney. See, it's not so heavy," Ayla encouraged. The horse she was patiently guiding had an arrangement of leather straps and cords around her chest and back attached to a heavy log she was dragging. Originally, Ayla had put the weight-bearing thong across Whinney's forehead, in a manner similar to the tumpline she sometimes used when she had a heavy load to carry. She quickly realized the horse needed to move her head freely and pulled better with her chest and shoulders. Still, the young animal wasn't accustomed to pulling a weight, and the harness inhibited her movements. But Ayla was determined. It was the only way her plan would work.

The idea had come to her when she was feeding the fire to fend off predators. She had shoved Whinney aside to get at the wood, thinking, with affection, of the full-grown horse who, with all her strength, had come to her for protection. A fleeting thought of wishing she were as strong had burst the next instant into a possible solution to the problem she had been turning over in her mind. Maybe the horse could haul a deer out of a pit trap.

Then she thought about processing the meat, and the novel concept grew. If she butchered the animal on the steppes, the smell of blood would draw the inevitable, and unknown, carnivores. Maybe it wasn't a cave lion she had heard attacking the reindeer, but it was some cat. Tigers, panthers, and leopards might be only half the size of cave lions, her sling was still no defence. She could kill a lynx, but the big cats were another matter, especially out in the open. But near her cave, with a wall at her back, she might be able to drive them away. A hard-flung stone might not be fatal, but they would feel it. If Whinney could drag a deer out of the trap, why not all the way back to the valley?

But first, she had to turn Whinney into a draft horse. Ayla thought she would only have to devise a way to attach ropes or thongs from the dead reindeer to the horse. It didn't occur to her that the young mare might balk. Learning to ride had been such an unconscious process that she didn't know she would have to train Whinney to haul a load. But in fitting out the harness, she found out. After a few more tries, that included a complete revision in concept and several adjustments, the horse began to accept the idea, and Ayla decided it just might work.

The reindeer bucks were not many days behind the does. They migrated at a leisurely pace. Once she spotted them, it wasn't difficult for Ayla to observe their movements and confirm that they were following the same trail, nor to gather her equipment and gallop ahead of them. She set up camp beside the river downstream of the reindeer crossing. Then, with her digging stick to loosen the ground, the sharpened hipbone to shovel and lift the dirt, and the tent hide to carry it away, she went to the crossing place of the female herd.

Two main trails and two ancillary paths cut through the brush. She chose one of the main trails for her trap, close enough to the river so that the reindeer would be using it in single file, but far enough back so she could dig a deep hole before water seeped in. By the time it was dug, the late afternoon sun was closing with the end of the earth. She whistled for the horse and rode back to see how far the herd had moved, and estimated they would reach the river sometime the next day.

When she returned to the river, light was fading, but the large gaping hole was conspicuously evident. None of those reindeer are going to fall into that hole. They'll see it and run around it, she thought, feeling discouraged. Well, it's too late to do anything tonight. Maybe I'll think of something in the morning.

But morning brought no lightening of spirit or brilliant ideas. It had clouded up overnight. She was awakened by a huge splat of water on her face to a dreary dawn of diffused light. She hadn't set up the old hide as a tent the night before, since the sky had been clear when she went to bed and the hide wet and muddy. She had spread it out to dry nearby, but it was now getting wetter. The drop on her face was only the first of many. She wrapped the sleeping fur around her and, after a search of the carrying baskets revealed she had forgotten to bring her wolverine hood, pulled an end over her head and huddled over the black wet remains of a fire.

A bright flash crackled across the eastern plains – sheet lightning that illuminated the land to the horizon. After a moment, a distant rumble growled a warning. As though it were a signal, the clouds above dumped a new deluge. Ayla picked up the wet tent hide and wrapped it around her.

Gradually daylight brought the landscape into sharper focus, driving shadows out of crevices. A grey pallor dulled the burgeoning steppes, as though the dripping nimbus cover had washed out the colour. Even the sky was a nondescript shade of nothing, neither blue nor grey nor white.

Water began to pool as the thin layer of permeable soil above the level of the subterranean permafrost became saturated. The permafrost itself was impenetrable. There was no drainage. Under certain conditions the saturated soil could turn into treacherous quicksand bogs that could swallow a full-grown mammoth. And if it happened close to the leading edge of a glacier, which shifted unpredictably, a sudden freeze could preserve the mammoth for millennia.

The leaden sky dropped large liquid blobs into the black puddle that had once been a fireplace. Ayla watched them erupt into craters, then spread out in rings, and wished she were in her dry snug cave in the valley. A bone-chilling cold was seeping up through her heavy leather foot coverings in spite of the grease she had smeared on them and the sedge grass stuffed inside. The sodden quagmire dampened her enthusiasm for hunting.

She moved up on a hummock of higher ground when the overflowing puddles cut channels of muddy water to the river, carrying twigs, sticks, grass, and last season's old leaves along. Why don't I just go back, she thought, hauling the carrying baskets with her up the rise. She peeked under the lids; the rain was running off the woven cattail leaves and the contents were dry. It's useless. I ought to load these on Whinney and go.

Ayla heaved a sigh, then pulled the fur wrap and the old tent hide up around her. I've been planning and working so long, I can't let a little rain stop me. Maybe I won't get a deer; it wouldn't be the first time a hunter returned empty-handed. Only one thing is sure – I'll never get one if I don't try.

She climbed up on a rock formation when the runoff threatened to undercut the hummock, and she squinted up through the rain to see if it was slackening. There was no shelter on the flat open prairie, no large trees or overhanging cliffs. Like the shaggy dripping horse beside her, Ayla stood in the middle of the downpour patiently waiting out the rain. She hoped the reindeer were waiting, too. She wasn't ready for them. Her resolve faltered again around midmorning, but by then she just didn't feel like moving.

With the usual erratic disposition of spring, the cloud cover broke about noon, and a brisk wind sent it streaming off. By afternoon, no trace of clouds could be seen, and the bright young colours of the season sparkled with fresh-washed brilliance in the full glory of the sun. The ground steamed in its enthusiasm to give back the moisture to the atmosphere. The dry wind that had driven off the clouds sucked it up greedily, as though it knew it would forfeit a share to the glacier.

Ayla's determination returned, if not her confidence. She shook off the heavy, waterlogged aurochs hide and draped it over high brush, hoping this time it would dry a little. Her feet were damp – everything was damp – but they were not cold, so she ignored them and went to the deer crossing. She couldn't see her hole, and her heart sank. With a closer look, she saw an overflowing muddy pool clogged with leaves, sticks, and debris where her pit had been.

Setting her jaw, she returned for a water basket to bail out the hole. On her way back, she had to look carefully to see the hole from a distance. Then suddenly, she smiled. If I have to look for it, all covered up with leaves and sticks like that, maybe a reindeer running fast wouldn't see it either. But I can't leave the water in it – I wonder if there's some other way . . .

Willow switches would be long enough to go across. Why couldn't I make a cover for the pit out of willow switches, and put leaves on it. It wouldn't be strong enough to hold up a deer, but fine for leaves and twigs. Suddenly she laughed out loud. The horse neighed in response and went to her.

"Oh, Whinney! Maybe that rain wasn't so bad after all."

Ayla bailed out the pit trap, not even minding that it was a messy, dirty job. It was not as deep, but when she tried to dig it out, she found the water table was higher. It just filled up with more water. She noticed that the river was fuller when she looked at the muddy, churning stream. And, though she didn't know it, the warm rain had softened some of the subterranean frozen earth which formed the rock-hard base underlying the land.

Camouflaging the hole was not as easy as she had thought. She had to range downstream for quite a distance to collect an armload of long switches from the stunted willow brush, supplementing them with reeds. The wide mesh mat sagged in the middle when she laid it over the pit, and she had to stake the edges. When she had strewn it with leaves and sticks, it still seemed obvious to her. She was not entirely satisfied, but she hoped it would work.

Covered with mud, she plodded back downstream, glanced longingly at the river, then whistled for Whinney. The deer were not as close as she thought they would be. Had the plains been dry they would have hurried to reach the river, but with so much water in puddles and temporary creeks, they had slowed. Ayla felt sure the herd of young bucks would not reach their accustomed crossing place before morning.

She returned to her camp and, with great relief, took off her wraps and foot coverings and waded into the river. It was cold, but she was used to cold water. She washed off the mud, then spread her wraps and footwear on the rock outcropping. Her feet were white and wrinkled from being encased in the damp leather – even her hard calloused soles had softened – and she was glad for the sun-warmed rock. It gave her a dry base for a fire, too.

Dead lower branches of pine usually stayed dry in the hardest rain, and though dwarfed to the size of brush, the pine near the river was no exception. She carried dry tinder with her, and, using a firestone and flint, she soon had a small starter fire burning. She kept it fed with twigs and small wood until the larger, slower-burning wood, leaned together in a tepee shape over the fire, dried out. She could start and keep a fire going even in rain – so long as it wasn't a downpour. It was a matter of starting small and keeping at it until the fire was established in wood large enough to dry out as it burned.

She sighed with satisfaction at her first sip of hot tea, after a meal of travelling cakes. The cakes were nourishing and filling, and they could be eaten on the move – but the hot liquid was more satisfying. Though it was still damp, she had set up the hide tent near the fire where it could dry out more while she slept. She glanced at clouds blotting out the stars in the west, and she hoped it would not rain again. Then, giving Whinney an affectionate pat, she crawled into her fur and wrapped it around her.

It was dark. Ayla lay absolutely still, ears straining to hear. Whinney moved and blew softly. Ayla propped herself up to look around. A faint glow could be seen in the eastern sky. Then she heard a sound that raised the hair on the back of her neck, and she knew what had awakened her. She had not heard them often, but she knew the snarling roar from across the river was that of a cave lion. The horse nickered nervously, and Ayla got up.

"It's all right, Whinney. That lion is far away." She added wood to the fire. "It must have been a cave lion I heard the last time we were here. They must live near the other side of the river. They'll take a buck, too. I'm glad it will be daytime when we go through their territory, and I hope they'll be full of deer before we get there. I might as well make tea – then it will be time to get ready."

The glow in the eastern sky was turning rosy when the young woman finished packing everything into the carrying baskets and tightened the cinch around Whinney. She put a long spear into the holder inside each basket and fastened them firmly, then mounted, sitting forward of the carriers, between the two sharp-pointed wooden shafts sticking up in the air.

She rode back towards the herd, circling wide until she was behind the approaching reindeer. She urged her horse forward until she caught sight of the young bucks, then slowed and followed them at a comfortable pace. Whinney fell into the migrating pattern easily. Observing the herd from the vantage point of horseback, as they approached the small river, she saw the lead deer slow, then sniff at the disturbance of mud and leaves on the path of the trap. An alert nervousness passed through the deer that even the woman could sense.

The first deer had broached the brush-choked banks to the water along the alternate trail when Ayla decided it was time to act. She took a deep breath and leaned forward in anticipation of an increase of speed, which signalled her intention, then let out a loud whoop as the horse galloped towards the herd.

The deer at the rear jumped forward, ahead of the ones in front, shoving them aside. As the horse pounded at them with a screaming woman on her back, all the deer bounded ahead in fright. But they all seemed to be avoiding the path with the pit trap. Ayla's heart sank as she watched the animals skirt around, jump over, or somehow manage to sidestep the hole.

Then she noticed a disturbance in the fast-moving herd, and thought she saw a pair of antlers drop, while others bobbed and eddied around the space. Ayla yanked the spears out of their holders and slid off the horse, running as soon as her feet touched the ground. A wild-eyed reindeer was mired in the oozing mud at the bottom of the hole, trying to jump out. This time her aim was true. She plunged the heavy spear into the deer's neck and severed an artery. The magnificent stag slumped to the bottom of the pit, his struggles at an end.

It was over. Done. So quickly, and so much more easily than she had imagined. She was breathing hard, but she was not out of breath from exertion. So much thought, worry, and nervous energy had gone into the planning that the easy execution of the hunt hadn't drained it off. She was still keyed up and had no way to spend her excess – and no one with whom to share her success.

"Whinney! We did it! We did it!" Her yelling and gesticulating startled the young horse. Then she leaped on the mare's back and took off in a dead run across the plains.

Braids flying behind her, eyes feverish with excitement, a

maniacal smile on her face, she was a wild woman. And all the more frightening – if there had been anyone around to be frightened – for sitting astride a wild animal, whose frantic eyes and laid-back ears betokened a frenzy of a somewhat different nature.

They made a wide circle, and, on the way back, she pulled the horse to a halt, slid down, and finished the circuit with a sprint on her own two legs. This time when she looked down into the muddy hole at the dead reindeer, she panted heavily with good reason.

After she caught her breath, she pulled the spear out of the deer's neck and whistled for the horse. Whinney was skittish, and Ayla tried to calm her with encouragement and affection before putting the harness on her. She walked the horse to the pit trap. With neither bridle nor halter for control, Ayla had to coax and urge the nervous horse. When Whinney finally settled down, the woman tied the trailing ropes of the harness to the antlers of the deer.

"Pull now, Whinney," she encouraged, "just like the log." The horse moved forward, felt the drag, and backed up. Then, in response to more urging, she moved forward again, leaning into the harness as the ropes became taut. Slowly, with Ayla helping in every way she could, Whinney dragged the reindeer out of the hole.

Ayla was elated. At the least, it meant she would not have to dress the meat in the bottom of a mucky pit. She wasn't sure how much more Whinney would be willing to do; she hoped the horse would lend her strength to get the deer back to the valley, but she would only take one step at a time. Ayla led the young mare to the water's edge, untangling the reindeer's antlers from the brush. Then she repacked the baskets so that one nested inside the other and strapped them to her back. It was an unwieldy load with the two spears sticking upright, but with the help of a large rock, she straddled the horse. Her feet were bare, but she hiked up her fur wrap to keep it out of the water and urged Whinney into the river.

It was normally a shallow, wide, fordable part of the river – one of the reasons the reindeer had instinctively chosen the place to cross – but the rain had raised the water level. Whinney managed to keep her footing in the swift current, and, once the deer was in the water, it floated easily. Pulling the animal across the water had one benefit Ayla hadn't thought of. It washed away the mud and blood, and by the time they reached the other side, the reindeer was clean.

Whinney balked a little when she felt the drag again, but Ayla was down by then and helped haul the deer a short distance up the beach. Then she untied the ropes. The deer was one step closer to the valley, but before they went any farther, Ayla had a few tasks yet to do. She slit the deer's throat with her sharp flint knife, then made a straight cut from the anus up the belly, chest, and neck, to the throat. She held the knife in her hand with her index finger along the back and the cutting edge up, inserted just under the skin. If the first cut was made cleanly, not cutting into the meat, skinning would be much easier later.

The next cut went deeper, to remove the entrails. She cleaned the usable parts – stomach, intestines, bladder – and put them back into the abdominal cavity along with the edible parts.

Curled around the inside of one of the baskets was a large grass mat. She opened it out on the ground, then, pushing and grunting, she moved the deer onto it. She folded the mat over the carcass and wrapped it securely with ropes, then attached the ropes from Whinney's harness. She repacked the baskets, putting a spear in each one, and fastened the long shafts firmly in place. Then, feeling rather pleased with herself, she climbed on the horse's back.

About the third time she had to get down to free the load from hindering obstructions – grass tussocks, rocks, brush – she was no longer feeling so pleased. Finally she just walked beside the horse, coaxing her along until the trussed-up deer snagged on something, then going back to extricate it. It wasn't until she stopped to put her footwear back on that she noticed the pack of hyenas following her. The first stones from her sling only showed the wily scavengers her range, which they stayed just beyond.

Stinking ugly animals, she thought, wrinkling her nose and shuddering in disgust. She knew they also hunted – only too well. Ayla had killed one such scavenger with her sling – and given her secret away. The Clan knew she hunted, and she had to be punished for it. Brun had no choice; it was the Clan way.

Hyenas bothered Whinney, too. It was more than her instinctive fear of predators. She never forgot the pack of hyenas that attacked her after Ayla killed her dam. And Whinney was edgy enough. Getting the deer back to the cave was turning out to be more of a problem than Ayla had anticipated. She hoped they would make it before nightfall.

She stopped to rest at a place where the river wound back on itself. All the stops and starts were wearying. She filled her waterbag and a large waterproof basket with water, then took the basket to Whinney, who was still attached to the dusty bundle of deer. She took out a travelling cake and sat down on a rock to eat it. She was staring at the ground, not really seeing it, trying to think of an easier way to get her kill back to the valley. It took a while before the disturbance of the dust penetrated her consciousness, but when it did, it aroused her curiosity. The earth was trampled, the grass bent down, and the tracks were fresh. Some great commotion had occurred here recently. She got up to examine the tracks closer, and gradually pieced together the story.

From the spoor in the dried mud near the river, she could tell they were in a long-established territory of cave lions. She thought there must be a small valley nearby, with sheer rocky walls and a snug cave where a lioness had given birth to a pair of healthy cubs earlier in the year. This had been a favourite resting place. The cubs had been playfully fighting over a bloody piece of meat, worrying loose small pieces with milk teeth, while the sated males lolled in the morning sun, and sleek females indulgently watched the babes at play.

The huge predators were lords of their domain. They had nothing to fear, no reason to anticipate an assault by their prey. Reindeer, under normal circumstances, would never have strayed so close to their natural predators, but the whooping, screaming horse-riding human had whipped them into a panic. The swift river had not stopped the stampeding herd. They had plunged across, and, before they knew it, they were in the midst of a pride of lions. Both were caught unawares. The fleeing deer, realizing too late that they had run from one danger into another far worse, scattered in all directions.

Ayla followed the tracks and came upon the conclusion of the story. Too late to dodge the flying hooves, one cub had been trampled by the frightened deer.

The woman knelt beside the baby cave lion, and with the experienced hand of a medicine woman she felt for signs of life. The cub was warm, probably had broken ribs. He was near death, but he still breathed. From signs in the dirt, Ayla knew the lioness had found her baby and nudged him to get up, to no avail. Then, following the way of all animals – save the one that walked on two legs – who must allow the weak to die if the rest are to survive, she turned her attention to her other offspring and moved on.

Only in the animal called human did survival depend on more than strength and fitness. Already puny compared with their carnivorous competitors, mankind depended on co-operation and compassion to survive.

Poor baby, Ayla thought. Your mother couldn't help you, could she? It wasn't the first time her heart had been moved by a hurt and helpless creature. For a moment, she thought about taking the cub back with her to the cave, then quickly dismissed the idea. Brun and Creb had allowed her to bring small animals to the Clan's cave for her to treat when she was learning the healing arts, though the first time had caused quite a stir. But Brun had not allowed a wolf pup. The lion cub was nearly as big as a wolf already. Someday he would approach Whinney in size.

She got up and looked down at the dying cub, shaking her head, then went to lead Whinney again, hoping the load she was dragging wouldn't get stuck too soon. When they started, Ayla noticed the hyenas moving to follow them. She reached for a stone, then saw that the pack had been distracted. It was only reasonable. It was the niche nature had allotted them. They had found the lion cub. But Ayla wasn't reasonable where hyenas were concerned.

"Get out, you stinking animals! Leave that baby alone!"

Ayla ran back, hurling stones. A yelp let her know one had found its mark. The hyenas backed out of range again as the woman advanced upon them, full of righteous wrath.

There! That will keep them away, she thought, standing with her feet apart, protectively straddling the cub. Then a wry grin of disbelief crossed her face. What am I doing? Why am I keeping them away from a lion cub that's going to die anyway? If I let the hyenas at him, they won't bother me any more.

I can't take him with me. I couldn't even carry him. Not all the way. I've got to worry about getting the reindeer back. It's ridiculous to think of it.

Is it? What if Iza had left me? Creb said I was put in her path by the spirit of Ursus, or maybe the Cave Lion spirit, because no one else would have stopped for me. She couldn't bear to see someone sick or hurt without trying to help. It's what made her such a good medicine woman.

I'm a medicine woman. She trained me. Maybe this cub was put in my path for me to find. The first time I brought that little rabbit into the cave because it was hurt, she said it showed I was meant to be a medicine woman. Well, here's a baby that's hurt. I can't just leave him to those ugly hyenas.

But how am I going to get this baby to the cave? A broken rib could puncture a lung if I'm not careful. I'll have to wrap him before I can move him. That wide thong I used for Whinney's puller should work. I have some with me.

Ayla whistled for the horse. Surprisingly, the load Whinney was dragging didn't snag on anything, but the young mare was edgy. She didn't like being in cave lion territory; her kind, too, were their natural prey. She had been nervous since the hunt, and stopping every few moments to untangle the heavy load, which restricted her movement, had not contributed to calming her.

But Ayla, concentrating on the baby cave lion, wasn't paying attention to the horse's needs. After she wrapped the young carnivore's ribs, the only way she could think of getting him to the cave was to put him on Whinney's back.

It was more than the filly could take. As the woman picked up the huge young feline and tried to place him on her back, the young mare reared. In a panic, she bucked and pitched, trying to rid herself of the weights and contraptions strapped to her, then vaulted across the steppes. The deer, wrapped in the grass mat, bounced and jogged behind the horse, then caught on a rock. The restraint added to Whinney's panic, bringing on a renewed frenzy of bucking.

Suddenly, the leather thongs snapped, and with the jolt the carrying baskets, overbalanced by the long heavy spear shafts, tilted up. In open-mouthed astonishment, Ayla watched the overwrought horse race furiously ahead. The contents of the carrying baskets were dumped on the ground, except for the securely fastened spears. Still attached to the baskets cinched around the mare, the two long shafts were dragging along behind her, points down, without hindering her speed at all.

Ayla saw the possibilities immediately – she'd been racking her brain trying to think of a way to get the deer carcass and the lion cub back to the cave. Waiting for Whinney to settle down took a little more time. Ayla, worried that the horse might harm herself, whistled and called. She wanted to go after her, but was afraid to leave either deer or lion cub to the tender mercies of hyenas. The whistling did have an effect. It was a sound Whinney associated with affection, security, and response. Making a large circle, she veered back towards the woman.

When the exhausted and lathered young mare finally drew near, Ayla could only hug her with relief. She untied the harness and cinch and examined her carefully to make sure she was unhurt. Whinney leaned against the woman, making soft nickers of distress, her forelegs straddled, breathing hard and quivering.

"You rest, Whinney," Ayla said when the horse stopped shaking and seemed to calm down. "I need to work on this anyway."

It didn't occur to the woman to be angry because the horse had bucked, run away, and dumped her things. She didn't think of the animal as belonging to her, or under her command. Rather, Whinney was a friend, a companion. If the horse panicked, she had good reason. Too much had been asked of her. Ayla felt she would have to learn the horse's limits, not attempt to teach her better behaviour. To Ayla, Whinney helped of her own free will, and she took care of the horse out of love.

The young woman picked up what she could find of the basket's contents, then reworked the cinch-basket-harness arrangement, fastening the two spears the way they had fallen, points down. She attached the grass mat, which had been wrapped around the deer, to both poles, thus creating a carrier platform between them – behind the horse but off the ground. She lashed the deer to it, then carefully tied down the unconscious cave lion cub. After she relaxed, Whinney seemed more accepting of the cinches and harnesses, and she stood quietly while Ayla made adjustments.

Once the baskets were in place, Ayla checked the cub again and got on Whinney's back. As they headed towards the valley, she was astounded at the efficiency of the new means of transporting. With just the ends of the spears dragging on the ground, not a dead weight snagged by every obstacle, the horse was able to haul the load with much greater ease, but Ayla did not draw an easy breath until she reached the valley and her cave.

She stopped to give Whinney a rest and a drink, and she checked on the baby cave lion. He still breathed, but she wasn't sure he would live. Why was he put in my path? she wondered. She had thought of her totem the moment she saw the cub – did the spirit of the Cave Lion want her to take care of him?

Then another thought occurred to her. If she hadn't decided to take the cub with her, she would never have thought of the travois. Had her totem chosen that way to show her? Was it a gift? Whatever it was, Ayla was sure the cub had been put in her path for a reason, and she would do everything in her power to save his life.

11

"Jondalar, you don't have to stay here just because I am."

"What makes you think I'm staying just for you?" the older brother said with more irritation than he meant to show. He hadn't wanted to seem so touchy about it, but there was more truth to Thonolan's comment than he wanted to admit.

He'd been expecting it, he realized. He just didn't want to let himself believe his brother would actually stay and mate Jetamio. Yet, he surprised himself with his immediate decision to stay with the Sharamudoi, too. He didn't want to go back alone. It would be a long way to travel without Thonolan, and there was something deeper. It had prompted an immediate response before, when he had decided to make a Journey with his brother in the first place.

"You shouldn't have come with me."

For an instant, Jondalar wondered how his brother could know his thoughts.

"I had a feeling I'd never go back home. Not that I expected to find the only woman I could ever love, but I had a feeling I'd just keep going until I found a reason to stop. The Sharamudoi are good people – I guess most people are once you get to know them. But I don't mind settling here and becoming one of them. You're a Zelandonii, Jondalar. No matter where you are, you will always be a Zelandonii. You'll never feel quite at home any other place. Go back, Brother. Make one of those women who have been after you happy. Settle down and raise a big family, and tell the children of your hearth all about your long Journey and the brother who stayed. Who knows? Maybe one of yours, or one of mine, will decide to make a long Journey to find his kin someday."

"Why am I more Zelandonii than you? What makes you think I couldn't be just as happy here as you?"

"You're not in love, for one thing. Even if you were, you'd be making plans to take her back with you, not to stay here with her."

"Why don't you bring Jetamio back with us? She's capable, strong minded, knows how to take care of herself. She'd make a good Zelandonii woman. She even hunts with the best of them – she'd get along fine."

"I don't want to take the time, waste a year travelling all the way back. I've found the woman I want to live with. I want to settle down, get established, give her a chance to start a family."

"What happened to my brother who was going to travel all the way to the end of the Great Mother River?"

"I'll get there someday. There's no hurry. You know it's not that far. Maybe I'll go with Dolando the next time he trades for salt. I could take Jetamio with me. I think she'd like that, but she wouldn't be happy away from home for long. It means more to her. She never knew her own mother, came close to dying herself with the paralysis. Her people are important to her. I understand that, Jondalar. I've got a brother a lot like her."

"What makes you so sure?" Jondalar looked down, avoiding his brother's gaze, "of my not being in love? Serenio is a beautiful woman, and Darvo," the tall blond man smiled and the worry lines on his forehead relaxed, "needs a man around. You know, he may turn out to be a good flint knapper one day."

"Big Brother, I've known you a long time. Living with a woman doesn't mean you love her. I know you're fond of the boy, but that's not reason enough to stay here and make a commitment to his mother. It's not such a bad reason to mate, but not to stay here! Go home and find an older woman with a few children if you want – then you can be sure of having a hearthful of young ones to turn into flint knappers. But go back."

Before Jondalar could reply, a boy, not yet into his second ten years, ran up to them out of breath. He was tall for his age, but slender, with a thin face and features too fine and delicate for a boy. His light brown hair was straight and limp, but his hazel eyes gleamed with lively intelligence.

"Jondalar!" he exhaled. "I've been looking all over for

you! Dolando is ready and the river men are waiting."

"Tell them we come, Darvo," the tall blond man said in the language of the Sharamudoi. The youngster sprinted ahead. The two men turned to follow, then Jondalar paused. "Good wishes are in order, Little Brother," he said, and the smile on his face made it plain he was sincere. "I can't say I haven't been expecting you to make it formal. And you can forget about trying to get rid of me. It's not every day a man's brother finds the woman of his dreams. I wouldn't miss your mating for the love of a donii."

Thonolan's grin lit up his whole face. "You know, Jondalar, that's what I thought she was the first time I saw her, a beautiful young spirit of the Mother who had come to make my Journey to the next world a pleasure. I would have gone with her, too, without a struggle . . . I still would."

As Jondalar fell in behind Thonolan, his brow furrowed. It bothered him to think his brother would follow any woman to her death.

The path zigzagged its way down a steep slope in switchbacks, which made the descent more gradual, through a deeply shaded forest. The way ahead opened up as they approached a stone wall that brought them to the edge of a steep cliff. A path around the stone wall had been laboriously hewn out of the face wide enough to accommodate two people abreast, but not with comfort. Jondalar stayed behind his brother as they passed around the wall. He still felt an aching sensation deep in his groin when he looked over the edge at the deep, wide, Great Mother River below, though they had wintered with the Shamudoi of Dolando's Cave. Still, walking the exposed path was better than the other access.

Not all Caves of people lived in caves; shelters constructed on open sites were common. But the natural shelters of rock were sought, and prized, especially during the winter's bitter cold. A cave or rock overhang could make desirable a location that would otherwise have been spurned. Seemingly insurmountable difficulties would be casually overcome for the sake of such permanent shelters. Jondalar had lived in caves in steep cliffs with precipitous ledges, but nothing quite like the home of this Cave of Shamudoi.

In a far earlier age, the earth's crust of sedimentary

sandstone, limestone, and shale had been uplifted into ice-capped peaks. But harder crystalline rock, spewed from erupting volcanoes caused by the same upheavals, was intermixed with the softer stone. The entire plain through which the two brothers had travelled the previous summer, that had once been the basin of a vast inland sea, was hemmed in by the mountains. Over long eons the outlet of the sea eroded a path through a ridge, which had once joined the great range on the north with an extension of it to the south, and drained the basin.

But the mountain gave way only grudgingly through the more yielding material, allowing just a narrow gap bounded by obdurate rock. The Great Mother River, gathering unto herself her Sister and all her channels and tributaries into one voluminous whole, passed through the same gap. Over a distance of nearly a hundred miles, the series of four great gorges was the gate to her lower course and, ultimately, her destination. In places along the way she spread out for a mile; in others, less than two hundred yards separated walls of sheer bare stone.

In the slow process of cutting through a hundred miles of mountain ridge, the waters of the receding sea formed themselves into streams, waterfalls, pools, and lakes, many of which would leave their mark. High on the left wall, close to the beginning of the first narrow passage, was a spacious embayment: a deep broad shelf with a surprisingly even floor. It had once been a small bay, a protected cove of a lake, hollowed out by the unwavering edge of water and time. The lake had long since disappeared, leaving the indented U-shaped terrace high above the existing water line; so high that not even spring floods, which could change the river level dramatically, came close to the ledge.

A large grass-covered field edged to the sheer drop-off of the shelf, though the soil layer, evidenced by a couple of shallow cooking pits that went down to rock, was not deep. About halfway back, brush and small trees began to appear, hugging and climbing the rugged walls. The trees grew to a respectable size near the rear wall, and the brush thickened and clambered up the steep back incline. Close to the back on a side wall was the prize of the high terrace: a sandstone overhang with a deep undercut. Beneath it were several shelters constructed of wood, partitioning the area into dwelling units, and a roughly circular open space, with a main hearth and a few smaller ones, that was both an entrance and gathering place.

In the opposite corner was another valuable asset. A long thin waterfall, dropping from a high lip, played through jagged rocks for a distance before spilling over a smaller sandstone overhang into a lively pool. It ran off along the far wall to the end of the terrace, where Dolando and several men were waiting for Thonolan and Jondalar.

Dolando hailed them when they appeared around the jutting wall, then began descending over the edge. Jondalar jogged behind his brother and reached the far wall just as Thonolan started down a precarious path alongside the small stream that dropped down a series of ledges to the river below. The trail would have been impossible to negotiate in places except for narrow steps tediously chiselled out of the rock, and sturdy rope handrails. As it was, the cascading water and constant spray made it treacherously slick, even in summer. In winter it was an impassable mass of frozen icicles.

In the spring, though it was inundated with heavier runoff and icy patches which threatened footing, the Sharamudoi – both the chamois-hunting Shamudoi, and the river-dwelling Ramudoi, who formed their opposite half – scampered up and down like the agile goatlike antelope that inhabited the steep terrain. As Jondalar watched his brother descend with the reckless disregard of one born to it, he thought Thonolan was certainly right about one thing. If he lived here all his life, he would never get used to this access to the high shelf. He glanced at the turbulent water of the huge river far below and felt the familiar ache in his groin, then took a deep breath, gritted his teeth, and stepped over the edge.

More than once he was grateful for the rope as he felt his foot slip on unseen ice, and he expelled a deep sigh when he reached the river. A floating dock of logs lashed together, swaying with the shifting current, was welcome stability by comparison. On a raised platform that covered more than half the dock was a series of wood structures similar to the ones under the sandstone overhang on the ledge above.

Jondalar exchanged greetings with several inhabitants of

the houseboats as he strode along the lashed logs towards the end of the dock where Thonolan was just getting into one of the boats tied there. As soon as he got in, they shoved off and began pulling upstream with long-handled oars. Conversation was kept to a minimum. The deep, strong current was urged on by spring melt, and, while the river men rowed, Dolando's men kept an eye out for floating debris. Jondalar settled back and found himself musing on the unique inter-relationship of the Sharamudoi.

People he had met specialized in different ways, and he often wondered what had led them along their particular path. With some, all the men customarily performed one function, and all the women another, until each function became so associated with a certain gender that no woman would do what she considered man's work, and no man could bring himself to perform a woman's task. With others, tasks and chores tended to fall more along lines of age – younger people performing the more strenuous tasks, and older ones the sedentary chores. In some groups, women might be in full charge of children, in others much of the responsibility of tending and teaching young children belonged to the elders, both male and female.

With the Sharamudoi, specialization had followed different lines, and two distinct but related groups had developed. The Shamudoi hunted chamois and other animals in the high crags and tors of the mountains and cliffs, while the Ramudoi specialized in hunting – for the process was more like hunting than fishing – the enormous sturgeon, up to thirty feet long, of the river. They also fished for perch, pike, and large carp. The division of labour might have caused them to split into two distinct tribes, except for mutual needs they had of each other which kept them together.

The Shamudoi had developed a process for making beautiful velvety soft leather from chamois hides. It was so unique that distant tribes in the region would trade for them. It was a closely guarded secret, but Jondalar had learned that oils from certain fish were involved in the process. It gave the Shamudoi a strong reason to maintain a close tie with the Ramudoi. On the other hand, boats were made from oak, with some beech and pine used for fittings, and the long planks of the sides were clenched with yew and willow. The river people had need of the mountain dwellers' knowledge of the forests to find the proper wood.

Within the Sharamudoi tribe, each Shamudoi family had a counterpart Ramudoi family related to it by complex kinship lines that might or might not have anything to do with blood relationship. Jondalar still hadn't sorted them all out, but after his brother mated Jetamio, he would suddenly be endowed with a score of "cousins" among both groups, related through Thonolan's mate, although she had no living blood relatives. Certain mutual obligations would be expected to be met, though for him this would involve little more than using certain titles of respect when addressing acquaintances among his new kin.

The making of boats was a joint effort for the very practical reason that it required both the products of the land and the knowledge of the water, and this gave the Shamudoi a valid claim to the craft used by the Ramudoi. Ritual reinforced the tie, since no woman of either moiety could mate a man who did not have such a claim. Thonolan would have to assist in the building, or rebuilding, of a boat before he could mate the woman he loved.

Jondalar was looking forward to the boat building, too. He was intrigued with the unusual craft; he wondered how they were made and how to propel and navigate them. He would have preferred some other reason than his brother's decision to stay and mate a Shamudoi woman as a means of finding out. But from the beginning, these people had interested him. The ease with which they travelled on the great river and hunted the huge sturgeon surpassed the abilities of any people he had ever heard of.

They knew the river in all her moods. He'd had difficulty comprehending her sheer volume until he had seen all her waters together, and she wasn't full yet. But it wasn't from the boat that her size was so apparent. During the winter when the waterfall trail was icing over and unusable, but before the Ramudoi moved in with their Shamudoi kin above, commerce between the two was accomplished by means of ropes and large woven platforms suspended over the ledge of the Shamudoi terrace and down to the Ramudoi dock.

The falls hadn't yet frozen when he and Thonolan first

arrived, but his brother was in no shape to make the precarious ascent. They were both lifted up in a basket.

When he saw Her from that perspective for the first time, Jondalar began to understand the full extent of the Great Mother River. The blood had drained from his face; his heart pounded with the shock of comprehension as he looked down at the water and the rounded mountains across the river. He was awed and overcome with a deep reverence for the Mother whose birth waters had formed the river in Her wondrous act of creation.

He had since learned there was a longer, easier, if less spectacular ascent to the high embayment. It was part of a trail that extended from west to east over the mountain passes and dropped down to the broad river plain on the eastern end of the gate. The western part of the trail, in the highlands and foothills leading to the start of the series of gorges, was more rugged, but parts of it dipped to the river's edge. They were heading to one such place.

The boat was already pulling out of midchannel towards a group of people lining a beach of grey sand waving excitedly when a gasp caused the older brother to look around.

"Jondalar, look!" Thonolan was pointing upstream.

Bearing down on them in ominous splendour, following the deep midchannel, was a large, jagged, glittering iceberg. Reflecting crystal facets of the translucent edges haloed the monolith with insubstantial shimmer, but the blue green shadowy depths held its unmelted heart. With practised skill, the men rowing the boat changed pace and direction, then, feathering the stroke, they paused to watch a wall of glistening cold glide by with deadly indifference.

"Never turn your back on the Mother," Jondalar heard the man in front of him say.

"I'd say the Sister brought that one, Markeno," the man beside him commented.

"How did . . . big ice . . . come here, Carlono?" Jondalar asked him.

"Iceberg," Carlono said, first supplying him with the word. "It could have come from a glacier on the move in one of those mountains," he went on, moving his chin in the direction of the white peaks over his shoulder, since he had resumed rowing. "Or it could have come from farther north, probably by way of the Sister. She's deeper, doesn't have as many channels – this time of year especially. There's more to that berg than the part you see. Most of it is under water."

"It is hard to believe . . . iceberg . . . so big, come so far," Jondalar said.

"We get ice every spring. Not always that big. It won't last much longer, though – the ice is rotten. One good bump and she'll break up, and there is a midchannel rock downstream, just below the surface. I don't think that iceberg will make it through the gate," Carlono added.

"One good bump from that and we would be the ones to break up," Markeno said. "That's why you never turn your back on the Mother."

"Markeno is right," Carlono said. "Never take her for granted. This river can find some unpleasant ways to remind you to pay attention to her."

"I know some women like that, don't you, Jondalar?"

Jondalar suddenly thought of Marona. The knowing smile on his brother's face made him realize that was who Thonolan had in mind. He hadn't thought of the woman who had expected him to mate her at the Summer Meeting Matrimonial for some time. With a pang of longing, he wondered if he would ever see her again. She was a beautiful woman. But then Serenio is too, he thought, maybe you ought to ask her. She's better than Marona in some ways. Serenio was older than he, but he'd often found himself attracted to older women. Why not mate when Thonolan did and just stay?

How long have we been gone? More than a year – we left Dalanar's Cave last spring. And Thonolan won't be going back. Everyone is excited about him and Jetamio – maybe you should wait, Jondalar, he said to himself. You don't want to take the attention from their day . . . and Serenio might think it was just an afterthought. . . . Later . . .

"What took you so long?" a voice called from the shore. "We've been waiting for you and we came the long way, by trail."

"We had to find these two. I think they were trying to hide," Markeno replied, laughing.

"It's too late to hide now, Thonolan. This one has hooked you!" said a man from the shore, wading in behind Jetamio to grab the boat and help beach it. He made motions of throwing out a harpoon and jerking it back to engage the hook.

Jetamio blushed, then smiled. "Well, you must admit, Barono, he's a good catch."

"You good fisher," Jondalar returned. "He always before get away."

Everyone laughed. Though his command of the language wasn't perfect, they were pleased he had joined in the banter. And he did understand better than he spoke.

"What would it take to catch a big one like you, Jondalar?" Barono asked.

"The right bait!" Thonolan quipped, with a smile at Jetamio.

The boat was pulled onto the narrow beach of gravelly sand, and, after the occupants climbed out, it was lifted and carried up a slope to a large cleared area in the midst of a dense forest of durmast oak. The place had obviously been used for years. Logs, chunks, and scraps of wood littered the ground – the fireplace in front of a large lean-to on one side had no dearth of fuel – yet some wood had been there so long it was rotting. Activity was focused in several areas, each of them containing a boat in some stage of completion.

The boat they had come in was lowered to the ground, and the new arrivals hurried towards the beckoning warmth of the fire. Several others stopped work to join them. An aromatic herb tea was steaming from a wooden trough that had been hollowed out of a log. It was quickly emptied as cups were dipped out. Round heating stones from the river's edge were heaped in a pile nearby, and a soggy lump of wet leaves, indistinguishable as to variety, sat in the middle of a muddy runnel behind the log.

The trough was well used and about to be refilled again. Two people rolled over the large log to dump the dregs of the previous batch of tea, while a third put the heating rocks in the fire. Tea was kept in the trough, available whenever anyone wanted a cup, and cooking stones were kept in the fire to warm a cup when it cooled. After more pleasantries and gibes aimed at the about-to-be-mated couple, the assemblage put down their cups of wood or tightly woven fibres and drifted back to their various tasks. Thonolan was led off to begin his initiation in the building of boats with some hard work that took less skill: the felling of a tree.

Jondalar had been having a conversation with Carlono about the Ramudoi leader's favourite topic, boats.

"Green oak is best," Carlono was explaining. "It's tough, but supple; strong, but not too heavy. It loses flexibility if it dries out, but you can cut it in winter and store logs in a pool or bog for a year, even two. More than that, it becomes waterlogged and hard to work, and the boat has trouble finding the right balance in the water. But more important is selecting the right tree." Carlono was heading into the woods as he talked.

"A big one?" Jondalar asked.

"Not only size. For the base and the planks, you want tall trees with straight trunks." Carlono led the tall Zelandonii to a grove of close-packed trees. "In dense woods, trees grow up looking for the sun . . ."

"Jondalar!" The older brother looked up with surprise at Thonolan's voice. He was standing with several others around a huge oak, surrounded by other tall straight trees whose branches started far up the stem. "Am I glad to see you! Your little brother could use your help. Do you know I can't get mated until a new boat is built, and this," he nodded expressively at the tall tree, "has to be cut down for the 'strakes', whatever they are. Look at the size of that mammoth! I didn't know trees grew that big – it will take forever to cut it down. Big Brother, I'll be an old man before I'm a mated one."

Jondalar smiled and shook his head. "Strakes are the planks that make the sides of the bigger boats. If you're going to be Sharamudoi, you ought to know about them."

"I'm going to be Shamudoi. I'll leave the boats to the Ramudoi. Hunting chamois is something I understand. I've hunted ibex and mouflon in high meadows before. Are you going to help? We need all the muscle we can get."

"If I don't want poor Jetamio to wait until you're an old man, I guess I'll have to. And besides, it will be interesting to see how it's done," Jondalar said, then turned to Carlono and added in the Sharamudoi language, "Help Jondalar chop tree. Talk more later?"

Carlono smiled in agreement, then stood back to watch the

first chips of bark cut away. But he didn't stay long. It would take most of the day before the forest giant fell, and before it did, everyone would gather around.

Starting high up and working down at a steep angle that was met by lower horizontal cuts, small chips were detached. The stone axes did not bite deep. The blade end needed a certain thickness for strength and couldn't penetrate very far into the wood. As they worked their way towards the centre of the huge tree, it appeared more gnawed than cut, but each chip that fell away dug deeper into the heart of the ancient giant.

The day was drawing to a close when Thonolan was given an axe. With everyone who had been working gathered nearby, he made a few final swings, then jumped back when he heard a crack and saw the massive trunk sway. Toppling slowly at first, the tall oak gained momentum as it fell. Tearing limbs off neighbouring giants and taking smaller ones with it, the mammoth old tree, snapping and cracking its resistance, thundered to the ground. It bounced, then shivered and lay still.

Silence pervaded the forest; as though in profound reverence, even the birds were still. The majestic old oak had been struck down, sundered from its living roots, its stump a raw scar in the muted earth shades of the woods. Then, with quiet dignity, Dolando knelt beside the ragged stump and dug a small hole with his bare hand. He dropped an acorn in it.

"May the Blessed Mudo accept our offering and bring to life another tree," he said, then covered the seed and poured a cup of water over it.

The sun was settling into a hazy horizon and making golden streamers of the clouds when they started up the long trail to the high shelf. Before they reached the ancient embayment, the colours shifted through the spectrum of golds and bronzes, then reds to a deep mauve. When they rounded the jutting wall, Jondalar was stopped by the untouchable beauty of the panorama spread out before him. He took a few steps along the edge, too preoccupied with the view to notice the precipitous drop for once. The Great Mother River, calm and full, mirrored the vibrant sky and darkened shadows of the rounded mountains across, her oily smooth surface alive with the movement of her deep current.

"It's beautiful, isn't it?"

Jondalar turned at the voice and smiled at a woman who had moved up beside him. "Yes. Beautiful, Serenio."

"Big feast tonight to celebrate. For Jetamio and Thonolan. They're waiting – you should come."

She turned to go, but he took her hand, held her there, and watched the last glimmers of the sunset reflected in her eyes.

There was a yielding gentleness about her, an ageless acceptance that had nothing to do with age – she was only a few years older than he – neither was it giving in. Rather that she made no demands, had no expectations. The death of her first mate, of a second love before there was time to mate, and the miscarriage of a second child that would have blessed the mating, had tempered her with grief. In learning to live with hers, she had developed an ability to absorb the pain of others. Whatever their sorrow or disappointment, people turned to her and always came away relieved because she imposed no burden of obligation on them for her compassion.

Because of her calming effect on distraught loved ones or fearful patients, she often assisted the Shamud and had learned some medical skills from the association. That was how Jondalar had come to know her first, when she was helping the healer nurse Thonolan back to health. When his brother was up and recovered enough to move to the hearth of Dolando and Roshario, and most especially, Jetamio, Jondalar had moved in with Serenio and her son, Darvo. He hadn't asked. She hadn't expected him to.

Her eyes always seemed to reflect, he thought, as he leaned over to kiss her lightly in greeting before they started towards the glowing fire. He never saw into their depths. He pushed away an unbidden thought that he was grateful for it. It was as though she knew him better than he knew himself; knew of his inability to give of himself completely, to fall in love as Thonolan had done. She even seemed to know that his way of making up for the lack of emotional depth was to make love to her with such consummate skill that it left her gasping. She accepted it, as she accepted his occasional black moods, without inflicting guilt on him for it.

She wasn't reserved, exactly – she smiled and talked with easy comfort – just composed and not quite reachable. The only time he caught a glimpse of something more was when she looked at her son.

"What took you so long?" the boy said with relief when he saw them coming. "We're ready to eat, but everyone's been waiting for you."

Darvo had seen Jondalar and his mother together at the far edge but didn't want to interrupt them. Initially, he had been resentful of having to share his mother's undivided attention at the hearth. But he found that rather than having to share his mother's time, there was now someone else who paid attention to him. Jondalar talked to him, told him of his adventures on his Journey, discussed hunting and the ways of his people, and listened to him with unfeigned interest. Even more exciting, Jondalar had begun to show him some techniques of toolmaking, which the lad picked up with an aptitude that surprised them both.

The youngster had been overjoyed when Jondalar's brother had decided to mate Jetamio and stay, because he fervently hoped it might mean Jondalar would decide to stay and mate his mother. He had become very conscious of staying out of the way when they were together, trying in his own way not to impede their relationship. He didn't realize that, if anything, he encouraged it.

In fact, the idea had been on Jondalar's mind all day. He found himself appraising Serenio. Her hair was lighter than her son's, more a dark blonde than brown. She wasn't thin, but so tall she gave that impression. She was one of the few women he'd met who reached his chin, and he found that a comfortable height. There was a strong resemblance between mother and son, even to the hazel of their eyes, though his lacked her impassiveness. And on her the fine features were beautiful.

I could be happy with her, he thought. Why don't I just ask her? And at that moment, he truly wanted her, wanted to live with her.

"Serenio?"

She looked at him and was held by the magnetism of his unbelievably blue eyes. His need, his desire focused on her. The force of his charisma – unconscious and all the more powerful for it – caught her unaware and broke through the defences she had so carefully erected to avoid pain. She was open, vulnerable, drawn almost against her will.

"Jondalar . . ." Her acceptance was implicit in the texture of her voice.

"I . . . think much today." He struggled with the language. He could express most concepts, but he was having trouble finding a way to speak his thoughts. "Thonolan . . . my brother . . . Travel far together. Now he love Jetamio, he want stay. If you . . . I want . . ."

"Come on, you two. Everyone's hungry, and the food is . . ." Thonolan broke off as soon as he saw them standing close, lost in the depths of each other's eyes. "Uh . . . sorry, brother. I think I just interrupted something."

They backed off; the moment had passed. "It's all right, Thonolan. We shouldn't make everyone wait. We can talk later," Jondalar said.

When he looked at Serenio, she seemed surprised and confused, as though she didn't know what had come over her – and she was struggling to repair her shield of composure.

They walked into the area under the sandstone overhang and felt the warmth of the large fire in the central hearth. At their appearance, everyone found places around Thonolan and Jetamio, who stood in a central clear space behind the fire. The Feast of Promise marked the festive beginning of a ritual period that would culminate in the Matrimonial celebration. During the interval, communication and contact between the young couple would be severely curtailed.

The warm space formed by the people, permeated with a sense of community, encircled the couple. They joined hands, and, seeing only perfection in each other's eyes, wanted to announce their joy to the world and affirm their commitment to each other. The Shamud stepped forward. Jetamio and Thonolan kneeled to allow the healer and spiritual guide to place a crown of fresh-budding hawthorn on each of their heads. They were led, still hand in hand, around the fire and the assembled group three times and then back to their place, closing a circle that embraced the Cave of Sharamudoi with their love.

The Shamud turned to face them and, with upraised arms, spoke. "A circle begins and ends in the same place. Life is as a circle that begins and ends with the Great Mother; the First

Mother who in Her loneliness created all life." The vibrant voice carried easily over the hushed gathering and the crackling flames. "Blessed Mudo is our beginning and our end. From Her we come; to Her we return. In all ways, She provides for us. We are Her children, all life springs from Her. She gives freely of Her abundance. From Her body, we take sustenance: food, water, and shelter. From Her spirit come gifts of wisdom and warmth: talents and skills, fire and friendship. But the greater Gifts come from Her all-encompassing love.

"The Great Earth Mother takes joy in Her children's happiness. She delights in our enjoyments, and therefore She has given us Her wondrous Gift of Pleasure. We honour Her, show Her reverence, when we share Her Gift. But to the Blessed among us She has given Her greatest Gift, endowed them with Her own miraculous power to create Life." The Shamud looked at the young woman.

"Jetamio, you are among the Blessed. If you honour Mudo in all ways, you may be endowed with the Mother's Gift of Life and give birth. Yet, the spirit of the Life you bring forth comes only from the Great Mother.

"Thonolan, when you make a commitment to provide for another, you become as She who provides for us all. By so honouring Her, She may endow you with creative power as well, so that a child brought forth by the woman you care for, or another of Mudo's Blessed, may be of your spirit." The Shamud looked up at the group.

"Each of us, when we care for and provide for each other, honour the Mother, and are blessed with Her fruitfulness."

Thonolan and Jetamio smiled at each other and, when the Shamud stepped back, sat down on woven mats. That was the signal for the feast to begin. The young couple were first brought a mildly alcoholic drink made of dandelion blossoms and honey that had fermented since the last new moon. Then more of the beverage was passed around to everyone.

Mouthwatering aromas made everyone realize how hard they had worked that day. Even those who had stayed back at the high terrace had been busy, as was obvious when the first wonderfully aromatic dish was brought forth. Planked whitefish, caught in fish traps that morning and baked near the open fire, was presented to Thonolan and Jetamio by

Markeno and Tholie, their counterpart family of Ramudoi. Tangy wood sorrel that had been boiled and beaten to a pulp was served as a sauce.

The taste, new to Jondalar, was one he immediately enjoyed and found a wonderful complement to the fish. Baskets of small edibles were passed around to accompany the dish. When Tholie sat down, he asked her what they were.

"Beechnuts, collected last fall," she said, and went on to explain in detail how they were stripped of their leathery outer skins with sharp little flint blades, then carefully roasted by shaking them with hot coals in flat platter-shaped baskets kept moving to prevent scorching, and finally rolled in sea salt.

"Tholie brought the salt," Jetamio said. "It was part of her bride gift."

"Many Mamutoi live near sea, Tholie?" Jondalar asked.

"No, our camp was one of the closest to Beran Sea. Most Mamutoi live farther north. The Mamutoi are mammoth hunters," she said with pride. "We travelled north every year for the hunts."

"How you mate Mamutoi woman?" the blond Zelandonii asked Markeno.

"I kidnapped her," he replied, with a wink at the plump young woman.

Tholie smiled. "It's true," she said. "Of course, it was all arranged."

"We met when I went along on a trading expedition to the east. We travelled all the way to the delta of the Mother River. It was my first trip. I didn't care if she was Sharamudoi or Mamutoi, I wouldn't come back without her."

Markeno and Tholie told about the difficulties their desire to mate had caused. It had taken long negotiations to work out the arrangements, and then he'd had to "kidnap" her to get around certain customs. She was more than willing; the mating could not have taken place without her consent. But there were precedents. Though not common, similar matings had occurred before.

Populations of humans were sparse and so widely spaced that they seldom infringed on each other's territories, which tended to make the infrequent contact with the occasional stranger a novelty. If a little wary at first, people were usually not hostile, and it wasn't uncommon to be welcomed. Most hunting peoples were accustomed to travelling long distances, often following migratory herds with seasonal regularity, and many had long traditions of individual Journeys.

Frictions developed more often from familiarity. Hostilities tended to be intra-mural – confined within the community – if they existed at all. Hot tempers were kept in check by codes of behaviour, and most often settled by ritualized customs – although these customs were not calcified. The Sharamudoi and the Mamutoi were on good trading terms, and there were similarities in customs and languages. To the former, the Great Earth Mother was Mudo, to the latter, She was Mut, but She was still the Godhead, Original Ancestor, and First Mother.

The Mamutoi were a people with a strong self-image, which came through as open and friendly. As a group, they feared no one – they were, after all, the mammoth hunters. They were brash, confident, a bit ingenuous, and convinced that everyone saw them as they viewed themselves. Though the discussions had seemed interminable to Markeno, it had not been an insurmountable problem to arrange the mating.

Tholie herself was typical of her people: open, friendly, confident that everyone liked her. In truth, few people could resist her forthright ebullience. No one even took offence when she asked the most personal questions, since it was obvious there was no malicious intent. She was just interested and saw no reason to curb her curiosity.

A girl approached them carrying an infant. "Shamio woke up, Tholie. I think she's hungry."

The mother nodded her thanks and put the baby to her breast, with hardly a break in the conversation or feasting. Other small edibles were passed: pickled ash keys that had been soaking in brine, and fresh pignuts. The small tuber resembled wild carrot, a sweet groundnut Jondalar was familiar with, and the first taste was nutty, but the hot aftertaste of radish was a surprise. Dolando and Rosharío brought the next offerings to the young couple – a rich chamois stew and a deep red bilberry wine.

"I thought the fish was delicious," Jondalar said to his brother, "but this stew is superb!"

"Jetamio says it's traditional. It's flavoured with the dried leaves of bog myrtle. The bark is used in tanning the chamois skins – that's what gives them the yellow colour. It grows in marshes, particularly where the Sister joins the Mother. It was lucky for me they were out collecting it last fall, or they never would have found us."

Jondalar's forehead creased as he recalled the time: "You're right; we were lucky. I still wish there was some way I could repay these people." His frown deepened when he remembered his brother was becoming one of them.

"This wine is Jetamio's bride gift," Serenio said.

Jondolar reached for his cup, took a sip, and nodded. "Is good. Is much good."

"Very good," Tholie corrected. "It is very good." She had no compunctions about correcting his speech; she still had a few problems with the language herself, and she assumed he would rather speak properly.

"Very good," he repeated, smiling at the short, stocky young woman with the baby at her ample breast. He liked her outspoken honesty and her outgoing nature that so easily overcame the shyness and reserve of others. He turned to his brother. "She's right, Thonolan. This wine is very good. Even Mother would agree, and no one makes finer wine than Marthona. I think she would approve of Jetamio." Jondalar suddenly wished he hadn't said that. Thonolan would never take his mate to meet his mother; it was likely he would never see Marthona again.

"Jondalar, you should speak Sharamudoi. No one else can understand when you speak in Zelandonii, and you'll learn much faster if you make yourself speak it all the time," Tholie said, leaning forward with concern. She felt she spoke from experience.

Jondalar was embarrassed, but he couldn't be angry. Tholie was so sincere, and it had been impolite of him to speak in a language no one else could understand. He reddened, but smiled.

Tholie noted Jondalar's discomfiture, and, though outspoken, she wasn't insensitive. "Why don't we learn each other's language? We may forget our own if we don't have someone else to talk to once in a while. Zelandonii has such a musical sound, I would love to learn it." She smiled at

Jondalar and Thonolan. "We'll spend a little time at it every day," she stated as though everyone obviously agreed.

"Tholie, you may want to learn Zelandonii, but they may not want to learn Mamutoi," Markeno said. "Did you think of that?"

It was her turn to blush. "No, I didn't," she said, with both surprise and chagrin, realizing her presumption.

"Well, I want to learn Mamutoi and Zelandonii. I think it's a good idea," Jetamio said firmly.

"I, too, think good idea, Tholie," Jondalar said.

"What a mixture we're bringing together. The Ramudoi half is part Mamutoi, and the Shamudoi half is going to be part Zelandonii," Markeno said, smiling tenderly at his mate.

The affection between the two was evident. They make a good match, Jondalar thought, though he couldn't help but smile. Markeno was as tall as he, though not as muscular, and when they were together, the sharp contrast emphasized each other's physical traits. Tholie seemed shorter and rounder, Markeno taller and thinner.

"Can someone else join you?" Serenio asked. "I would find it interesting to learn Zelandonii, and I think Darvo might find Mamutoi useful if he wants to go on trading journeys some time."

"Why not?" Thonolan laughed. "East or west, if you make a Journey, knowing the language helps." He looked at his brother. "But if you don't know it, it doesn't stop you from understanding a beautiful woman, does it, Jondalar? Especially if you have big blue eyes," he said in Zelandonii, grinning.

Jondalar smiled at his brother's gibe. "Should speak Sharamudoi, Thonolan," he said with a wink at Tholie. He speared a vegetable out of his wooden bowl with his eating knife, still finding it not quite natural to use his left hand for the purpose, though that was the custom of the Sharamudoi. "What is named this?" he asked her. "In Zelandonii is called 'mushroom'."

Tholie told him the word for the shaggy cap mushroom in her language and in Sharamudoi. Then he speared a green stalk and held it up questioningly.

"That's the stem of young burdock," Jetamio said, and

then realized the word itself would mean little to him. She got up and went to the refuse pile near the cooking area and brought back some wilted but still recognizable leaves. "Burdock," she said, showing him the large, downy, grey green leaf parts that had been torn from the stem. He nodded his head with understanding. Then she held out a long, broad, green leaf with an unmistakable odour.

"That's it! I knew it was some familiar flavour," he said to his brother. "I didn't know garlic grew in leaf like that." Then back to Jetamio, "What is name?"

"Ransoms," she said. Tholie had no Mamutoi name for it, but she did for the piece of dried leaf Jetamio next held out.

"Seaweed," she said. "I brought that with me. It grows in the sea, and it thickens the stew. There is not much left. It was part of my bride gift." Tholie braced the baby over her shoulder and patted her back. "Have you made your gift to the Blessing Tree yet, Tamio?"

Jetamio lowered her head, smiling demurely. It was a question not usually asked outright, but only mildly meddlesome. "I'm hoping the Mother will bless my mating with a baby as healthy and happy as yours, Tholie. Is Shamio through nursing?"

"She just likes to suck for comfort. She'd hang on all day if I let her. Would you like to hold her? I need to go outside."

When Tholie returned, the focus of conversation had shifted. Food had been cleared out of the way, more wine served, and someone was practising rhythms on a single-skin drum and improvising words to a song. When she took her infant back, Thonolan and Jetamio stood up and tried to edge their way out. Suddenly several people with broad grins ringed them.

It was usual for the couple about to be mated to leave the feast early to find some last moments alone together before their pre-Matrimonial separation. But since they were the guests of honour, they could not politely take their leave as long as anyone was talking to them. They must try to sneak away in the moment when no one would notice, but of course, everyone knew it. It became a game, and they were expected to play their parts – making dashes to get away while everyone pretended to look aside, and then making polite excuses when they were caught. After some teasing and joking, they would be allowed to go.

"You're not in a hurry to leave, are you?" Thonolan was asked.

"It get late," Thonolan evaded, grinning.

"It's early yet. Have another helping, Tamio."

"I couldn't eat another bite."

"A cup of wine then. Thonolan, you wouldn't turn down a cup of Tamio's wonderful bilberry wine, would you?"

"Well . . . little."

"Little more for you, Tamio?"

She edged closer to Thonolan and made a conspiratorial glance over her shoulder. "Just a sip, but someone will have to get our cups. They're over there."

"Of course. You'll wait right here, won't you?"

One person went to get the cups, while the rest made a pretence of watching him. Thonolan and Jetamio made a break for the darkness beyond the fire.

"Thonolan. Jetamio. I thought you were going to share a drink of wine with us."

"Oh, we are. Just need to make a trip outside. You know how it is after a large meal," Jetamio explained.

Jondalar, standing close to Serenio, was feeling a strong desire to continue their earlier conversation. They were enjoying the sham. He leaned closer to speak privately, to ask her to leave, too, as soon as everyone tired of the sport and let the young couple go. If he was going to make a commitment to her, it had to be now, before the reluctance that was already asserting itself put him off again.

Spirits were high – the blue bilberries had been especially sweet last fall, and the wine was stronger than usual. People were milling around, teasing Thonolan and Jetamio, laughing. Some were starting a question-and-response song. Someone wanted the stew reheated; someone else put water on for tea, after pouring out the last in someone's cup. Children, not tired enough for sleep, were chasing one another. Confusion marked the shifting of activities.

Then, a yelling child ran into a man who was none too steady on his feet. He stumbled and bumped into a woman who was carrying a cup of hot tea, just as an uproar of shouts accompanied the couple's dash for the outside.

No one heard the first scream, but the loud, insistent wails of a baby in pain quickly stopped everything.

"My baby! My baby! She's burned!" Tholie cried.

"Great Doni!" Jondalar gasped, as he rushed with Serenio toward the sobbing mother and her screaming infant.

Everyone wanted to help, all at the same time. The confusion was worse than before.

"Let the Shamud through. Move aside." Serenio's presence was a calming influence. The Shamud quickly removed the baby's coverings. "Cool water, Serenio, quickly! No! Wait, Darvo, you get water. Serenio, the linden bark – you know where it is?"

"Yes," she said, and hurried off.

"Roshario, is there hot water? If not, get some on. We need a tisane of the linden bark, and a lighter infusion for a sedative. They're both scalded."

Darvo ran back with a container of water from the pool, slopping over the sides. "Good, son. That was quick," the Shamud said with an appreciative smile, then splashed the cool water on the angry red burns. The burns were beginning to blister. "We need a dressing, something soothing, until the tisane is ready." The healer saw a burdock leaf on the ground and remembered the meal.

"Jetamio, what is this?"

"Burdock," she said. "It was in the stew."

"Is there some left? The leaf?"

"We only used the stem. There's a pile over there."

"Get it!"

Jetamio ran to the refuse pile and returned with two handfuls of the torn leaves. The Shamud dipped them in the water and laid them on the burns of both mother and child. The baby's demanding screams abated to hiccuping sobs, with occasional new spasms, as the soothing effect of the leaves began to be felt.

"It helps," Tholie said. She didn't know she was burned until the Shamud mentioned it. She had been sitting and talking, letting the baby suckle to keep her quiet and contented. When the scalding hot tea spilled on them, she had only realized her baby's pain. "Will Shamio be all right?"

"The burns will blister, but I don't think she'll scar."

"Oh, Tholie. I feel so bad," Jetamio said. "It's just terrible. Poor Shamio, and you, too."

Tholie was trying to get the infant to nurse again, but the association with pain was making her fight it. Finally, the remembered comfort outweighed the fear, and Shamio's cries stopped as she took hold, which calmed Tholie.

"Why are you and Thonolan still here, Tamio?" she asked. "This is the last night you can be together."

"I can't go off with you and Shamio hurt. I want to help."

The baby was fussing again. The burdock helped, but the burn was still painful.

"Serenio, is the tisane ready?" the healer inquired, replacing the leaves with fresh ones soaking in the cool water.

"The linden bark has steeped long enough, but it will take a while to cool. Maybe if I take it outside, it will cool faster."

"Cool! Cool!" Thonolan cried, and suddenly dashed out of the sheltering overhang.

"Where's he going?" Jetamio asked Jondolar.

The tall man shrugged his shoulders and shook his head. The answer was clear when Thonolan ran back, out of breath, but holding dripping wet icicles from the steep stone stairway that led down to the river.

"Will this help?" he asked, holding them out.

The Shamud looked at Jondalar. "The boy is brilliant!" There was a hint of irony in the statement, as though such genius wasn't expected.

The same qualities in the linden bark that numbed the pain made it effective as a sedative as well. Both Tholie and the baby were asleep. Thonolan and Jetamio had finally been convinced to go off by themselves for a while, but all the lighthearted fun of the Promise Feast was gone. No one wanted to say it, but the accident had cast a shadow of misfortune on their mating.

Jondalar, Serenio, Markeno, and the Shamud were sitting near the large hearth, drawing the last warmth from the dying embers and sipping wine while they talked in quiet tones. Everyone else was asleep, and Serenio was urging Markeno to turn in for the night, too.

"There's nothing more you can do, Markeno, there's no

reason for you to stay up. I'll stay with them, you go to sleep."

"She's right, Markeno," the Shamud said. "They'll be all right. You should rest, too, Serenio."

She got up to go, as much to encourage Markeno as for herself. The others stood up, too. Serenio put her cup down, briefly touched her cheek to Jondalar's, and headed towards the structures with Markeno. "If there's any reason, I'll wake you," she said as they left.

When they were gone, Jondalar scooped the last dregs of the fermented bilberry juice into two cups and gave one to the enigmatic figure waiting in the quiet dark. The Shamud took it, tacitly understanding they had more to say to each other. The young man scraped the last few coals together near the edge of the blackened circle and added wood until a small fire was glowing. They sat for a while, silently sipping wine, huddled over the flickering warmth.

When Jondalar looked up, the eyes, whose indefinable colour was merely dark in the firelight, were scrutinizing him. He felt power in them, and intelligence, but he appraised with equal intensity. The crackling, hissing flames cast moving shadows across the old face, blurring the features, but even in daylight Jondalar had been unable to define any specific characteristics, other than age. Even that was a mystery.

There was strength in the wrinkled face, which lent it youthfulness, though the long mane of hair was shocking white. And while the figure beneath the loose clothing was spare and frail, the step had spring. The hands alone spoke unequivocally of great age, but for all their arthritic knobs and blue-veined parchment skin, no palsied flutter shook the cup that was lifted to the mouth.

The movement broke eye contact. Jondalar wondered if the Shamud had done it deliberately to relieve a tension that was growing. He took a sip. "The Shamud good healer, has skill," he said.

"It is a gift of Mudo."

Jondalar strained to hear some quality of timbre or tone that would shade the androgynous healer in one direction or the other, only to satisfy his nagging curiosity. He had not yet discerned whether the Shamud was female or male, but he did have an impression that in spite of the neutrality of gender, the healer had not led a celibate life. The satirical quips were too often accompanied by knowing looks. He wanted to ask, but he didn't know how to phrase his question tactfully.

"Shamud life not easy, must give up much," Jondalar tried. "Did healer ever want mate?"

For an instant the inscrutable eyes widened; then the Shamud broke into sardonic laughter. Jondalar felt a hot flash of embarrassment.

"Whom would you have had me mate, Jondalar? Now, if *you* had come along in my younger years, I might have been tempted. Ah, but would you have succumbed to my charms? If I had given the Blessing Tree a string of beads, could I have wished you to my bed?" the Shamud said with a slight, demure bend of the head. For a moment, Jondalar was convinced it was a young woman who spoke.

"Or would I have needed to be more circumspect? Your appetites are well developed; could I have aroused your curiosity to a new pleasure?"

Jondalar flushed, sure he had been mistaken, yet strangely drawn to the look of sensuous lechery and the catlike sinuous grace the Shamud projected with a body shift. Of course, the healer was a man, but with a woman's tastes in his pleasures. Many healers drew from both the male and female principle; it gave them stronger powers. Again he heard the sardonic laugh.

"But if the life of a healer is difficult, it's worse for the mate of one. A mate should be a man's first consideration. It would be hard to leave someone like Serenio, for instance, in the middle of the night to take care of someone who was sick, and there are long periods of abstinence required . . ."

The Shamud was leaning forward, talking to him man to man, with a gleam in his eye at the thought of a woman as lovely as Serenio. Jondalar shook his head with puzzlement. Then, with a movement of the shoulders, the masculinity had a different character. One that excluded him.

". . . and I'm not sure I'd want to leave her alone with a lot of rapacious men around."

The Shamud was a woman, but not one that would ever be attracted to him, or he to her, as anything more than a friend.

It was true, the healer's power came from the principle of both sexes but was that of a woman with a man's taste.

The Shamud laughed again, and the voice had no shading of gender. With a level look of person to person that asked human understanding, the old healer continued.

"Tell me, which one am I, Jondalar? Which one would you mate? Some try to find a relationship, one way or another, but it seldom lasts long. Gifts are not an unmixed blessing. A healer has no identity, except in the larger sense. One's personal name is given back, the Shamud effaces self to take on the essence of all. There are benefits, but mating is not usually among them.

"When one is young, being born to a destiny is not necessarily desirable. It is not easy to be different. You may not want to lose your identity. But it doesn't matter – the destiny is yours. There is no other place for one who carries the essence of both man and woman in one body."

In the fire's dying light, the Shamud looked as ancient as the Earth Herself, staring at the coals with unfocused eyes as though seeing another time and place. Jondalar got up to get a few more sticks of wood, then nursed the fire back to life. As the flames took hold, the healer straightened, and the look of irony returned. "That was long ago, and there have been . . . compensations. Not the least is discovering one's talent and gaining knowledge. When the Mother calls one to Her service, it isn't all sacrifice."

"With Zelandonii, not all who serve Mother know when young, not all like Shamud. I once thought to serve Doni. Not all are called," Jondalar said, and the Shamud wondered at the tightening of his lips and the creasing of his brow that bespoke a bitterness that still galled. There were hurts buried deep within the tall young man who seemed so well favoured.

"It is true, not all who might wish are called, and not all who are called have the same talents – or proclivities. If one is not sure, there are ways to discover, to test one's faith and will. Before one is initiated, a period of time must be spent alone. It can be enlightening, but you may learn more about yourself than you wish. I often advise those considering entering the Mother's service to live alone for a while. If you cannot, you would never be able to endure the more severe tests."

"What kind of tests?" The Shamud had never been so candid with him before, and Jondalar was fascinated.

"Periods of abstinence when we must forego all Pleasures; periods of silence when we may not speak to anyone. Periods of fasting, times when we forgo sleep as long as possible. There are others. We learn to use these methods to seek answers, revelations from the Mother, particularly for those in training. After a time, one learns to induce the proper state at will, but it is beneficial to continue their use now and then."

There was a long silence. The Shamud had managed to ease the conversation around to the real issue, the answers Jondalar wanted. He had but to ask. "You know what is need. Will Shamud tell what means . . . all this?" Jondalar spread his arms in a vague all-encompassing gesture.

"Yes. I know what you want. You are concerned about your brother after what happened tonight, and in a larger sense, about him and Jetamio – and you." Jondalar nodded. "Nothing is certain . . . you know that." Jondalar nodded again. The Shamud studied him, trying to decide how much to reveal. Then the old face turned towards the fire and an unfocused look gathered in the eyes. The young man felt a distancing, as though a great space had been put between them, though neither had moved.

"Your love for your brother is strong." There was an eerie, hollow echo to the voice, an other-worldly resonance. "You worry that it is too strong, and fear that you lead his life and not your own. You are wrong. He leads you where you must go, but would not go alone. You are following your own destiny, not his; you only walk in tandem for a pace.

"Your strengths are of a different nature. You have great power when your need is great. I felt your need of me for your brother even before we found his bloody shirt on the log that was sent for me."

"I did not send log. It was chance, luck."

"It was not chance that I felt your need. Others have felt it. You cannot be denied. Not even the Mother would refuse you. It is your gift. But be wary of the Mother's gifts. It puts you in Her debt. With a gift as strong as yours, She must have a purpose for you. Nothing is given without obligation. Even her Gift of Pleasure is not largesse; there is purpose for it, whether we know it or not . . .

"Remember this: you follow the Mother's purpose. You need no call, you were born to this destiny. But you will be tested. You will cause pain and suffer for it . . ."

The young man's eyes flew open with surprise.

". . . You will be hurt. You will seek fulfilment and find frustration; you will search for certainty and find only indecision. But there are compensations. You are well favoured in body and mind, you have special skills, unique talents, and you are gifted with more than ordinary sensitivity. Your vexations are the result of your capacity. You were given too much. You must learn by your trials.

"Remember this as well: to serve the Mother is not all sacrifice. You will find what you seek. It is your destiny."

"But . . . Thonolan?"

"I sense a break; your destiny lies another way. He must follow his own path. He is a favourite of Mudo."

Jondalar frowned. The Zelandonii had a similar saying, but it didn't necessarily mean good luck. The Great Earth Mother was said to be jealous for Her favourites and called them back to Her early. He waited, but the Shamud said no more. He didn't fully understand all the talk of "need" and "power" and "Mother's purpose" – Those Who Served the Mother often spoke with a shadow on their tongue – but he didn't like the feel of it.

When the fire died down again, Jondalar got up to leave. He started towards the shelters at the back of the overhang, but the Shamud was not quite through.

"No! Not the mother and child . . ." the pleading voice cried out in the dark.

Jondalar, caught by surprise, felt a chill down his spine.

12

"Jondalar!" Markeno hailed. The tall blond man waited for the other tall one to catch up. "Find a way to delay going up tonight," Markeno said in a hushed voice. "Thonolan has had enough restriction and ritual since the Promising. It's time for a little relaxation." He removed the stopper from a waterbag and gave Jondalar a whiff of the bilberry wine, and a sly smile.

The Zelandonii nodded and smiled back. There were differences between his people and the Sharamudoi, but some customs were evidently widespread. He had wondered if the younger men would be planning a "ritual" of their own. The two men matched strides as they continued down the trail.

"How are Tholie and Shamio?"

"Tholie is worried that Shamio will have a scar on her face, but they are both healing. Serenio says she doesn't think the burn will leave a mark, but not even the Shamud can say for sure."

Jondalar's concerned expression matched Markeno's for the next few paces. They turned a bend in the trail and came upon Carlono, studying a tree. He smiled broadly when he saw them. His resemblance to Markeno was more apparent when he smiled. He was not as tall as the son of his hearth, but the thin, wiry build was the same. He looked once more at the tree, then shook his head.

"No, it's not right."

"Not right?" Jondalar asked.

"For supports," Carlono said. "I don't see the boat in that tree. None of the branches will follow the inside curve, not even with trimming."

"How you know? Boat not finished," Jondalar said.

"He knows," Markeno interjected. "Carlono always finds limbs with the right fit. You can stay and talk about trees if you want. I'm going on down to the clearing."

Jondalar watched him stride away, then asked Carlono, "How you see in tree what fit boat?"

"You have to develop a feel for it – it takes practice. You don't look for tall straight trees this time. You want trees with crooks and curves in the branches. Then you think about how they will rest on the bottom and bend up the sides. You look for trees that grow alone where they have room to go their own way. Like men, some grow best in company, striving to outdo the rest. Others need to grow their own way, though it may be lonely. Both have value."

Carlono turned off the main trail along a path not as well travelled. Jondalar followed behind. "Sometimes we find two growing together," the Ramudoi leader continued, "bending and giving only for each other, like those." He pointed to a pair of trees entwined around each other. "We call them a love pair. Sometimes if one is cut down, the other dies, too," Carlono said. Jondalar's forehead wrinkled in a frown.

They reached a clearing and Carlono led the tall man up a sunny slope towards a massive giant of a twisted, gnarled old oak. As they approached, Jondalar thought he saw strange fruit on the tree. Drawing near, he was surprised to see that it was decorated with an unusual array of objects. There were delicate tiny baskets with dyed quill designs, small leather bags embroidered with mollusc-shell beads, and cords twisted and knotted into patterns. A long necklace had been draped around the huge bole so long before that it was embedded in the trunk. On close inspection, he saw it was made of shell beads, carefully shaped with holes bored through the centres, alternating with individual vertebrae of fish backbones which had a natural centre hole. He noticed tiny carved boats hanging from branches, canine teeth suspended from leather thongs, bird feathers, squirrel tails. He had never seen anything like it.

Carlono chuckled at his wide-eyed reaction. "This is the Blessing Tree. I imagine Jetamio has made her a gift. Women usually do when they want Mudo to bless them with a child. The women think of her as theirs, but more than a few men have made her an offering. They ask for good luck on first hunts, favour on a new boat, happiness with a new mate. You don't ask often, only for something special."

"Is so big!"

"Yes. It is the Mother's own tree, but that isn't why I brought you here. Notice how curved and bent her branches are? This one would be too big, even if she wasn't the Blessing Tree, but for supports, you look for trees like this. Then you study the branches to find the ones that will fit the inside of your boat."

They walked by a different path down to the boat-making clearing and approached Markeno and Thonolan, who were working on a log that was huge in girth as well as length. They were gouging out a trough with adzes. At the present stage, the log resembled the crude trough that was used for making tea rather than one of the gracefully shaped boats, but the rough shape had been hacked out. Later a stem and stern would be carved, but first the inside had to be finished.

"Jondalar has taken quite an interest in boat making," Carlono said.

"Maybe we need to find him a river woman so he can become a Ramudoi. It's only fair since his brother will be Shamudoi," Markeno joked. "I know a couple who have been casting long glances at him. One of them might be persuaded."

"I don't think they'd get too far with Serenio around," Carlono said with a wink at Jondalar. "But then some of the best boat makers are Shamudoi. It's not the boat on the land, it's the boat in the water that makes a river man."

"If you're so eager to learn boat making, why don't you pick up an adze and help?" Thonolan said. "I think my big brother would rather talk than work." His hands were black and one cheek was smudged the same colour. "I'll even lend you mine," he added, throwing the tool to Jondalar, who caught it by reflex. The adze – a sturdy stone blade mounted at right angles to a handle – left a black mark on his hand.

Thonolan jumped down and went to check a nearby fire. It had burned down to glowing embers out of which tongues of orange flame leaped now and then. He picked up a broken section of plank, its top pocked with charred holes, and swept hot coals out of the fire onto it with a branch. He carried them back to the log and spilled them, amidst a shower of sparks and smoke, into the troughlike hole they were gouging out. Markeno laid more wood on the fire and brought over a container of water. They wanted the coals to burn into the log, not set it on fire.

Thonolan moved the coals around with a stick, then added a strategically placed sprinkle of water. A sputtering hiss of steam and a sharp smell of burning wood evidenced the elemental battle of fire and water. But, eventually, the water had its way. Thonolan scooped out the remnant pieces of wet black charcoal, then climbed into the boat trough and began to scrape away the charred wood, deepening and widening the hole.

"Let me take a turn at that," Jondalar said after he had watched for a while.

"I was wondering if you were just going to stand around all day," Thonolan remarked with a grin. The two brothers tended to slip into their native language when they talked to each other. The ease and familiarity of it was comfortable. They were both gaining competence with the new language, but Thonolan spoke it better.

Jondalar stopped to examine the stone head of the adze after the first few strokes, tried again at a different angle, checked the cutting edges again, then found the proper swing. The three young men worked together, speaking little, until they stopped for a rest.

"I not see before, use fire to make trough," Jondalar said as they walked towards the lean-to. "Always gouge out with adze."

"You could use just an adze, but fire makes it go faster. Oak is hard wood," Markeno remarked. "Sometimes we use pine from higher up. It's softer, easier to dig out. Still, fire helps."

"Take long time make boat?" Jondalar inquired.

"Depends how hard you work, and how many work on it. This boat won't take long. It's Thonolan's claim, and it must be done before he can mate Jetamio, you know." Markeno smiled. "I never saw anyone work so hard, and he's coaxing everyone else, too. Once you start, though, it is a good idea to keep at it until it's done. Keeps it from drying out. We're going to split planks this afternoon, for the strakes. Do you want to help?"

"He'd better!" Thonolan said.

The huge oak Jondalar had helped to chop down, minus its branching top, had been carried to the other side of the clearing. It had taken almost every able-bodied person to move it, and nearly as many had gathered to split it. Jondalar hadn't needed his brother's "coaxing". He wouldn't have missed it.

First, a set of antler wedges was placed in a straight line along the grain for the full length of the log. They were driven in with heavy, handheld stone mauls. The wedges forced a crack in the massive bole, but it opened reluctantly at first. Connecting splinters were severed as the thick butts of the triangular antler pieces were pounded deeper into the heart of the wood, until, with a snap, the log fell apart, split cleanly in half.

Jondalar shook his head in wonder, yet it was only the beginning. The wedges were placed again down the centre of each half, and the process repeated until they were split in half. And then each section was halved again. By the end of the day, the huge log had been reduced to a stack of radially split planks, each one tapering towards the centre, making one long edge thinner than the other. A few planks were shorter because of a knot, but they would have uses. There were many more planks than required to build up the sides of the boats. They would be used to construct a shelter for the young couple beneath the sandstone overhang on the high terrace, connected to the dwelling of Roshario and Dolando, and large enough to accommodate Markeno, Tholie, and Shamio during the coldest part of the winter. Wood from the same tree used for both house and boat was thought to add the strength of the oak to the relationship.

As the sun descended, Jondalar noticed a few of the younger men ducking into the woods, and Markeno let Thonolan persuade him to continue working on the dugout base of the boat under construction until almost everyone had gone. It was Thonolan who finally conceded that it was too dark to see.

"There's plenty of light," a voice said from behind him. "You don't know what dark is!"

Before Thonolan could turn around to see who spoke, a blindfold was thrown over his head, and his arms were grabbed and held. "What's going on?" he shouted, struggling to break away.

The only reply was muffled laughter. He was picked up and carried some distance and, when he was put down, he felt his clothes being removed.

"Stop it! What are you doing? It's cold!"

"You won't be cold for long," Markeno said when the blindfold was removed. Thonolan saw a half dozen smiling young men, all naked. The area was unfamiliar, particularly in the deep twilight, but he knew they were near water.

Around him the forest was a dense black mass, but it thinned on one side to bare the silhouette of individual trees against a deep lavender sky. Beyond them, the widened way of a path revealed reflected silver flashing sinuously from the smooth oily rolling of the Great Mother River. Nearby, light gleamed through cracks of a small, low, rectangular structure of wood. The young men climbed onto the roof, then down into the hut through a hole in the top using a log, leaning at an angle, with steps cut into it.

A fire had been built inside the hut in a central pit, and stones had been placed on top to heat. The walls stood back, making a bench of the ground, which was covered with planks sanded smooth with sandstone. As soon as everyone was in, the entrance hole at the top was loosely covered; smoke would escape through cracks. A glow of coals showed under the hot rocks, and soon Thonolan conceded that Markeno was right. He was no longer cold. Someone threw water on the stones and a billow of steam rose, making it even more difficult to see in the dim light.

"Did you get it, Markeno?" asked the man sitting beside him.

"Right here, Chalono." He held up the waterbag of wine.

"Well, let's have it. You're a lucky man, Thonolan, mating a woman who makes bilberry wine this good." There was a chorus of agreement and laughter. Chalono passed the skin of wine, then, showing a square of leather tied into a pouch, he said with a sly grin, "I found something else."

"I wondered why you weren't around today," one man remarked. "Are you sure they're the right kind?"

"Don't worry, Rondo, I know mushrooms. At least I know these mushrooms," Chalono averred.

"You should. You pick them every chance you get." There was more laughter at the pointed dig.

"Maybe he wants to be Shamud, Tarluno," Rondo added derisively.

"Those aren't the Shamud's mushrooms, are they?" Markeno asked. "Those red ones with the white spots can be deadly if you don't prepare them right."

"No, these are nice safe little mushrooms that just make you feel good. I don't like playing around with the Shamud's. I don't want a woman inside me . . ." Chalono said, then sniggering, "I'd rather get inside a woman."

"Who's got the wine?" Tarluno asked.

"I gave it to Jondalar."

"Get it away from him. He's big enough to drink it all!"

"I gave it to Chalono," Jondalar said.

"I haven't seen any of those mushrooms – are you going to keep the wine and the mushrooms, too?" Rondo asked.

"Don't rush me. I've been trying to get this bag open. Here, Thonolan, you're the guest of honour. You get first pick."

"Markeno, is it true the Mamutoi make a drink out of a plant that's better than wine or mushrooms?" Tarluno asked.

"I don't know about better, but I've only had it once."

"How about more steam?" Rondo said, splashing a cup of water on the rocks below, assuming everyone's assent.

"Some people, to west, put in steam something," Jondalar commented.

"And one Cave breathe smoke from plant. They let you try, but they not tell what it is," Thonolan added.

"You two must have tried almost everything . . . in all your travelling," Chalono said. "That's what I'd like to do, try everything there is."

"I hear flatheads drink something . . ." Tarluno volunteered.

"They're animals – they'll drink anything," Chalono said.

"Isn't that what you just said you wanted to do?" Rondo jeered. An outburst of laughter followed.

Chalono noticed Rondo's comments often provoked laughter – sometimes at his expense. Not to be outdone, he began a story that had been known to cause laughter before. "You know the one about the old man who was so blind, he caught a flathead female and thought it was a woman . . ."

"Yeah, his pizzle fell off. That's disgusting, Chalono," Rondo said. "And what man would mistake a flathead for a woman?"

"Some do not mistake. Do on purpose," Thonolan said. "Men from Cave, far to west, take Pleasure with flathead females, make trouble for Caves."

"You're joking!"

"It no joke. Whole pack of flatheads surround us," Jondalar confirmed. "They angry. Later we hear some men take flathead women, cause trouble."

"How did you get away?"

"They let," Jondalar said. "Leader of pack, he smart. Flatheads more smart people think."

"I heard of a man who got a flathead female on a dare," Chalono said.

"Who? You?" Rondo sneered. "You said you wanted to try everything."

Chalono tried to defend himself, but the laughter drowned him out. When it died down, he tried again. "I didn't mean that. I was talking about mushrooms and wine and such when I said I wanted to try everything." He was feeling some effects and becoming a bit thick-tongued. "But a lot of boys talk about flathead females before they know what women are. I heard of one who took a flathead on a dare, or said he did."

"Boys will talk about anything," Markeno said.

"What do you think girls talk about?" Tarluno asked.

"Maybe they talk about flathead males," Chalono said.

"I don't want to listen to this any more," Rondo said.

"You did your share of talking about it when we were younger, Rondo," Chalono said, beginning to take offence.

"Well, I've grown up. I wish you would. I'm tired of your disgusting remarks."

Chalono was insulted, and a little drunk. If he was going to be accused of being disgusting, he'd really give them something disgusting. "Is that so, Rondo? Well, I heard of a woman who took her Pleasure with a flathead, and the Mother gave her a baby of mixed spirits . . ."

"Eeuch!" Rondo curled his lip and shuddered with repugnance. "Chalono, that's not anything to joke about. Who asked him to this party? Get him out of here. I feel like I've just had filth thrown in my face. I don't mind a little joking around, but he's gone too far!"

"Rondo's right," Tarluno said. "Why don't you leave, Chalono?"

"No," Jondalar said. "Cold out, dark. Not make leave. True, babies of mix spirits not for joke, but why everyone know of them?"

"Half-animal, half-human abominations!" Rondo mumbled. "I don't want to talk about them. It's too hot in here. I'm getting out before I get sick!"

"This is supposed to be Thonolan's party to relax," Markeno said. "Why don't we all go out and take a swim, then come back and start all over again. There's still plenty of Jetamio's wine left. I didn't tell you, but I brought two waterbags of it."

"I don't think the stones are hot enough, Carlono," Markeno said. There was an undercurrent of tension in his voice.

"It's not good to let the water stand in the boat too long. We don't want the wood to swell, only to soften enough to give. Thonolan, are the struts close by so they'll be ready when we need them?" Carlono asked with a worried frown.

"They here," he replied, indicating the poles of alder trunks, cut to length, on the ground near the large dugout filled with water.

"We'd better start, Markeno, and hope the stones are hot."

Jondalar was still amazed at the transformation, though he had watched it take shape. The oak bole was no longer a log. The inside had been gouged out and smoothed, and the exterior had the sleek lines of a long canoe. The thickness of the shell was no more than the length of a man's knuckle, except for the solid stem and stern. He had watched Carlono shave off a skin of wood, whose thickness was no more than that of a twig, with a chisel-shaped stone adze to bring the watercraft to its final dimension. After trying it himself, Jondalar was even more astounded at the skill and dexterity of the man. The boat tapered to a sharp cutwater at the prow, which extended forward. It had a slightly flattened bottom, a less pronounced tapering stern, and it was very long in proportion to its width.

The four of them quickly transferred the cobbles that had been heating in the large fireplace to the water-filled boat, causing the water to steam and boil. The process was no different from heating stones to boil water for tea in the trough near the lean-to, but on a larger scale. And the purpose was different. The heat and steam were not to cook anything, but to reshape the container.

Markeno and Carlono, facing each other across the boat at the midsection, were already testing the flexibility of the hull, pulling carefully to widen the craft, yet not crack the wood. All the hard work of digging out and shaping the boat would have been for nothing if it cracked in expanding. It was a tense moment. As the middle was pulled apart, Thonolan and Jondalar were ready with the longest strut, and when it was wide enough they fitted the brace in crosswise, and held their breaths. It seemed to hold.

Once the centre strut was in, proportionally shorter ones were worked into place along the length of the boat. They bailed out the hot water until the four men could manage the weight, took out the rocks and tipped the canoe to pour out the rest of the water, then set the boat between blocks to dry.

The men breathed easier as they stood back to look and admire. The boat was close to fifty feet long, and more than eight feet across at the midsection, but the expansion had altered the lines in another important way. As the middle was widened, the fore and aft sections had lifted, giving the craft a graceful upward curve towards the ends. The results of the expansion were not only a broader beam for greater stability and capacity, but a raised bow and stern that would clear the water to take waves or rough water more easily.

"Now she's a lazy man's boat," Carlono said as they walked to another area of the clearing.

"Lazy man!" Thonolan exclaimed, thinking of the hard work.

Carlono smiled at the expected response. "There's a long story about a lazy man with a nagging mate who left his boat out all winter. When he found it again, it was full of water, and the ice and snow had caused it to expand. Everyone thought it was ruined, but it was the only boat he had. When it dried out, he put it in the water and discovered how much better it handled. Afterwards, according to the story, everyone made them that way."

"It's a funny story if it's told right," Markeno said.

"And there may be some truth in it," Carlono added. "If we were making a small boat, we'd be done except for fittings," he said as they approached a group of people who were boring holes along the edges of planks with bone drills. It was a tedious, difficult job, but many hands made the job go faster, and socializing eased the boredom.

"And I'd be that much closer to mating," Thonolan said, noticing Jetamio among them.

"You have smiles on your faces. That must mean it stretched all right," the young woman said to Carlono, though her eyes quickly sought Thonolan.

"We'll know better when it dries," Carlono said, careful not to tempt fate. "How are the strakes coming?"

"They're finished. We're working on the house planks now," an older woman replied. She resembled Carlono, in her way, as much as Markeno, especially when she smiled. "A young couple need more than a boat. There *is* more to life, Brother dear."

"Your brother is as anxious to get them mated as you are, Carolio," Barono said, smiling as the two young people transfixed each other with lovelorn smiles, though they said not a word. "But what good is a house without a boat?"

Carolio gave him an aggrieved stare. It was a longstanding Ramudoi aphorism, meant to be witty, that had become tiresome with the retelling.

"Ahh!" Barono exclaimed. "It broke again!"

"He's clumsy today," Carolio said. "That's the third drill he's broken. I think he's trying to get out of boring holes."

"Don't be so hard on your mate," Carlono said. "Everyone breaks drills. It can't be helped."

"She's right about one thing. Boring holes. I can't think of anything more boring," Barono said, with a wide grin at everyone's groan.

"He thinks he's funny. What can be worse than a mate who thinks he's funny?" Carolio appealed to the general company. Everyone smiled. They knew the banter only masked great affection.

"If you have spare drill, I try make holes," Jondalar said.

"Is there something wrong with this young man? No one wants to drill holes," Barono said, but he quickly got up.

"Jondalar has taken quite an interest in boat making," Carlono said. "He's tried his hand at everything."

"We may make a Ramudoi out of him yet!" Barono said. "I always thought he was an intelligent young man. I'm not so sure about the other one, though," he added, smiling at Thonolan, who hadn't paid attention to anything except Jetamio. "I think a tree could fall on him and he wouldn't know it. Don't we have something worthwhile for him to do?"

"He could gather wood for the steam box, or strip willow withes for sewing the planks," Carlono said. "As soon as the dugout is dry and we get holes drilled around the hull, we'll be ready to bend the planks to fit around it. How long do you think it will take to finish her, Barono? We should let the Shamud know, so a day can be decided for the mating. Dolando will need to send messengers to other Caves."

"What else needs to be done?" Barono asked, as they started towards an area where sturdy posts were sunk into the ground.

"The prow and stern posts still have to be scarfed on, and . . . are you coming, Thonolan?" Markeno said.

"What! Oh . . . yes, coming."

After they left, Jondalar picked up a bone drill set in an antler handle and watched Carolio use one like it. "Why holes?" he asked, when he had made a few.

Carlono's twin sister was as preoccupied with boats as her brother – for all the teasing – and as much an expert in fastenings and fittings as he was in gouging and shaping. She started to explain, then got up and led Jondalar to another work area where a boat was partially dismantled.

Unlike a raft, which depended upon the buoyancy of its

structural materials to float, the principle of the Sharamudoi watercraft was to enclose a pocket of air within a wooden shell. It was a significant innovation allowing greater manoeuverability and the capability of transporting much heavier loads. The planks, which were used to extend the basic dugout into a larger boat, were bent to fit the curved hull using heat and steam, and then literally sewn on, usually with willow through pre-drilled holes, and pegged to solid prow and stern posts. Supports, placed at intervals along both sides, were added later for reinforcement and to attach seats.

Done well, the result was a waterproof shell which could resist the tensions and stresses of hard use for several years. Eventually, though, wear and deterioration of the willow fibres required the boats to be completely torn down and rebuilt. Weakened planks were replaced then, too, which lengthened the effective life of the boats considerably.

"See . . . where the strakes have been removed," Carolio said, pointing out the dismantled boat to Jondalar, "there are holes along the top edge of the dugout." She showed him a plank with a curve that fitted the shell. "This was the first strake. The holes along the thinner edge match the base. See, it was overlapped like this, and sewn to the top of the dugout. Then the top plank was sewn to this one."

They walked around to the other side which hadn't been dismantled yet. Carolio indicated the frayed and broken fibre in some of the holes. "This boat was overdue for refitting, but you can see how the strakes overlap. For small boats, for one or two people, you don't need sides, just the dugout. They're harder to handle in rough water, though. They can get out of control before you know it."

"Someday I like learn," Jondalar said. Then, noticing the curved strake, he asked, "How you bend plank?"

"With steam and tension, like the base you expanded. The posts over there, where Carlono and your brother are, are for the guy lines to hold the strakes in place while they are sewn on. It doesn't take long with everyone working together, once the holes are drilled. Making the holes is a bigger problem. We sharpen the bone drills, but they break so easily."

Towards evening, when they were all trooping back up to the high terrace, Thonolan noticed that his brother seemed unusually quiet. "What are you thinking about, Jondalar?"

"Making boats. There's a lot more to it than I ever imagined. I've never heard of boats like these before, or seen anyone as skilled on the water as the Ramudoi. I think the youngsters are more comfortable in their small boats than they are walking. And they're so skilled with their tools . . ." Thonolan saw his brother's eyes light up with enthusiasm. "I've been examining them. I think if I could detach a large spall from the working edge of that adze Carlono was using, it would leave a smooth concave inner face, and make it much easier to use. And I'm sure I could make a burin out of flint that would bore those holes faster."

"So that's it! For a while there I thought you were really interested in boat making, Big Brother. I should have known. It's not the boats, it's the tools they use to make them. Jondalar, you'll always be a toolmaker at heart."

Jondalar smiled, realizing Thonolan was right. The boat-building process was interesting, but it was the tools that had captured his imagination. There were adequate flint knappers in the group, but no one who had made it his or her speciality. No one who could see how a few modifications could make the tools more effective. He had always taken a keen delight in making tools suited to a task, and his technically creative mind was already envisaging possibilities to improve those the Sharamudoi used. And it might be a way he could begin to repay, with his unique skill and knowledge, these people to whom he owed so much.

"Mother! Jondalar! More people just came! There are already so many tents, I don't know where they'll find room," Darvo shouted as he raced into the shelter. He dashed out again; he had only come to impart the news. He couldn't possibly stay in – the activities outside were far too exciting.

"More visitors have come than when Markeno and Tholie were mated, and I thought that gathering was large," Serenio said. "But then, most people know of the Mamutoi, even if they haven't all met any of them. No one had heard of the Zelandonii."

"They not think we have two eye, and two arm, and two leg, like they?" Jondalar asked.

He was somewhat overwhelmed himself at the number of people. A Zelandonii Summer Meeting usually saw more, but these were all strangers, except for the residents of Dolando's Cave and Carlono's Dock. Word had travelled so fast that others beside Sharamudoi had even come. Some of Tholie's Mamutoi kith and kin, plus a few others curious enough to accompany them, had been early arrivals. There were people from upriver as well, both from the Mother and the Sister.

And many of the Mating Ceremonial customs were unfamiliar. All the Caves travelled to a prearranged meeting place for a Zelandonii Matrimonial, and several couples were formally united at one time. Jondalar was not accustomed to so many people visiting the home cave of one couple to witness their mating. As Thonolan's only blood relative, he would have a conspicuous place in the ceremonies, and he was feeling nervous.

"Jondalar, you know most people would be surprised to learn that you are not always as confident as you appear. Don't worry, you'll be fine," Serenio said, moving her body close to his and putting her arms around his neck. "You always are."

She had done the right thing. Her nearness was a pleasant distraction – she took his mind off himself without being demanding – and her words were reassuring. He pulled her closer, pressed his warm mouth on hers and lingered, allowing himself the respite of a moment's sensual pleasure before his apprehensions returned.

"You think I look right? This travel clothes, not for special wear," he asked, suddenly conscious of his Zelandonii garb.

"No one here knows that. They are unique, very special. Just right for the occasion, I think. It would seem too ordinary if you wore something familiar, Jondalar. People are going to be looking for you as well as Thonolan. That's why they have come. If they can see you from a distance, they may not all feel the need to press in closer, and you know you are comfortable in those clothes. They look good on you, too."

He let her go and looked out through a crack at the throng outside, grateful he didn't have to face them yet. He walked towards the back until the sloping roof prevented him from going farther, then returned to the front and looked out again.

"Jondalar, let me make some tea for you. It's a special blend I learned from the Shamud. It will settle your nerves."

"Do I look nervous?"

"No, but you have a right to. It will only take a moment."

She poured water into a rectangular cooking box and added hot stones. He pulled up a wooden stool – one that was much too low – and sat down. His thoughts were elsewhere, and he stared absently at the geometric patterns carved into the box: a series of slanting parallel lines above another row slanting in the opposite direction, giving a herringbone effect.

The sides of the kerfed boxes were made from a single plank in which grooves, or kerfs, were cut not quite all the way through. Using steam to make the wood pliable, the planks were bent sharply at the grooves to make corners, with the last corner pegged together. A groove was also cut near the bottom edge, into which a bottom piece was fitted. The boxes were watertight, particularly after they swelled when filled. Covered with separate removable lids, they were used for many things, from cooking to storage.

The box made him think of his brother and made him wish he could be with him at this moment before his mating. Thonolan had quickly understood the Sharamudoi way of bending and shaping wood. His craft of spearmaking utilized the same principles of heat and steam to straighten a shaft, or to bend one around for a snowshoe. Thinking of a snowshoe reminded Jondalar of the beginning of their Journey, and, with a pang of nostalgia, he wondered if he would ever see his home again. Ever since he had put on his own clothes, he'd been fighting off spasms of homesickness that had a way of sneaking up on him when he least expected it with some vivid recollection or poignant memory. This time it was Serenio's kerfed cooking box that had brought it on.

He stood up quickly, knocked over the stool and lunged to right it, just missing Serenio with the cup of hot tea she was bringing him. The near accident brought to mind the unfortunate incident during the Promise Feast. Both Tholie and Shamio seemed to be fine and their burns were almost healed, but he felt a twinge of uneasiness recalling the conversation he'd had with the Shamud afterwards.

"Jondalar, drink your tea. I'm sure it will help."

He had forgotten the cup in his hand, smiled, and took a sip. The tea had a pleasant taste – he thought he detected chamomile among the ingredients – and its warmth was calming. After a while he felt some of his tension drain of.

"You right, Serenio. Feel better. Not know what wrong."

"It's not every day one's brother takes a mate. A little nervousness is understandable."

He took her in his arms again and kissed her with a passion that made him wish he wouldn't have to leave so soon. "See tonight, Serenio," he whispered in her ear.

"Jondalar, there will be a festival to honour the Mother tonight," she reminded him. "I don't think either of us should make commitments with so many visitors. Why not let the evening work out its own way. We can have each other any time."

"I forget," he said and nodded in agreement, but for some reason he felt rebuffed. It was strange; he had never felt that way before. In fact, he had always been the one to make sure he was free during a festival. Why should he feel hurt because Serenio had made it easy for him? On the spur of the moment, he decided he was going to spend the evening with her – Mother Festival or not.

"Jondalar!" Darvo came bursting in again. "They sent me for you. They want you." He was breathless with excitement to be entrusted with such an important task, and dancing with impatience. "Hurry, Jondalar. They want you."

"Be calm, Darvo," the man said, smiling at the lad. "I come. I not miss brother's Matrimonial."

Darvo smiled a little sheepishly, realizing they wouldn't start without Jondalar, but it didn't curb his impatience. He hurried out. Jondalar took a breath and followed him.

There was a surging murmur through the crowd at his appearance, and he was glad to see the two women who were waiting for him. Roshario and Tholie conducted him to the raised mound near the side wall where the others waited. Standing on the highest part of the mound, head and shoulders above the throng, was a white-haired figure whose face was partially covered by a wooden half-mask with stylized birdlike features.

As he drew near, Thonolan flashed him a nervous smile. Jondalar tried to convey understanding when he smiled back. If he had been tense, he could just imagine how Thonolan must feel, and he was sorry the Sharamudoi customs had prevented them from being together. He noticed how well his brother seemed to fit in, and he felt a sharp, poignant stab of regret. No two people could have been closer than the two brothers while they were on their Journey, but they had begun to follow separate paths. For a moment he was overwhelmed with an unexpected grief.

He closed his eyes and clenched his fists to bring himself under control. He heard voices from the crowd and thought he detected some words, "tall" and "clothes". When he opened his eyes, it struck him that one reason Thonolan fitted in so well was that his clothes were entirely Shamudoi.

No wonder there were comments about his clothes, he thought, and for a moment was sorry he had chosen to wear such an outlandish outfit. But then, Thonolan was one of them now, had been adopted to facilitate the mating. Jondalar was still Zelandonii.

The tall man joined the group of his brother's new kin. Though he was not formally a Sharamudoi, they were his kin, too, once removed. They, along with Jetamio's kin, were the ones who had contributed the food and gifts that would be distributed among the guests. As more people had arrived, more contributions had been brought forth. The large number of visitors accrued to the high regard and status of the young couple, but it would be most demeaning if they went away unsatisfied.

A sudden hush caused them all to turn their heads in the direction of a group making their way towards them.

"Do you see her?" Thonolan asked, standing on tiptoes.

"No, but she's coming, you know that," Jondalar said.

When they reached Thonolan and his kin, the protective phalanx opened a wedge to reveal its hidden treasure. Thonolan's throat went dry when he beheld the flower-bedecked beauty within, who flashed him the most radiant smile he had ever seen. His happiness was so transparent that Jondalar beamed a smile as well. As a bee is drawn towards a flower, Thonolan was drawn to the woman he loved, leading his train to the middle of her group, until Jetamio's kin surrounded Thonolan and his kin.

The two groups merged, then paired, as the Shamud began piping a repetitive series of whistles on a flageolet. The rhythm was accented by another person with a bird half-mask playing a large, single-sided hoop drum. Another Shamud, Jondalar guessed. The woman was a stranger to him, yet there was a familiar aspect, perhaps it was just a similarity shared by all Those Who Served the Mother, but she brought on thoughts of home to him.

While members of the two sets of kin formed and re-formed in patterns that appeared complicated, but were actually variations of a simple series of steps, the white-haired Shamud played the small flute. It was a long straight stick, reamed out with a hot coal, with a whistle mouthpiece, holes cut along the length, and an open-beaked bird head carved at the end. And some of the sounds emanating from the instrument mimicked exactly the sounds of birds.

The two groups ended by facing each other in two rows, with both hands joined and raised to form a long archway. As the couple passed through, the ones behind followed them, until a train of paired couples led by the Shamud was heading to the end of the terrace and around the stone wall. Jetamio and Thonolan were just behind the flute player, followed by Markeno and Tholie, then Jondalar and Roshario, as the young couple's closest kin. The rest of the kin group trailed them, and the whole crowd of Cave members and guests brought up the rear. The drum-playing visiting Shamud fell in near the people of her Cave.

The white-haired Shamud led them down the trail towards the boat-making clearing, but turned off at the side path and brought them to the Blessing Tree. While the gathering caught up and arranged themselves around the huge old oak, the Shamud spoke quietly to the young couple – giving instructions and advice to ensure a happy relationship and to invite the Mother's blessing. Only the close kin, and a few others who happened to be within ear range were a party to that portion of the ceremony. The rest of the gathering talked among themselves until they noticed the Shamud waiting quietly.

The group hushed each other, but their silence was bursting with anticipation. In the intense stillness, the raucous caw of a jay was a demanding clamour, and the staccato of a great-spotted woodpecker resounded through the woods. Then a sweeter song filled the air as a woodlark took to wing.

As though waiting for that cue, the bird-masked figure beckoned the two young people to step forward. The Shamud produced a length of cord and, with one overhand knot, made a loop. Looking at each other with eyes that had room for no one else, Thonolan and Jetamio clasped hands and put them through the loop.

"Jetamio to Thonolan, Thonolan to Jetamio, I bind you, one to the other," the Shamud said and pulled the cord tight, binding their wrists together with a secure knot. "As I tie this knot, you are bound, committed to each other, and through each other to the ties of kinship and Cave. With your joining, you complete the square begun by Markeno and Tholie." The two other young people stepped forward as their names were spoken, and all four joined hands. "As Shamudoi share the gifts of the land, and Ramudoi share the gifts of the water, so together you are now Sharamudoi, to help each other always."

Tholie and Markeno stepped back, and as the Shamud began a high-pitched piping, Thonolan and Jetamio began a slow circuit around the ancient oak tree. On the second circuit, the spectators shouted good wishes while they threw bird down, flower petals, and pine needles on them.

On the third circuit of the Blessing Tree, the spectators joined them, laughing and shouting. Someone began a traditional song, and more flutes were brought forth to accompany the singers. Others beat on drums and hollow tubes. Then one of the Mamutoi visitors produced the shoulder bone of a mammoth. She hit it with a mallet, and everyone paused for a moment. The ringing, resonating tone surprised most people, but as she continued to play, they were even more surprised. The player could change the tone and pitch by striking the bone at different places, and she matched the melody of the singer and the flute. By the end of the third circuit, the Shamud was in front again and led the group down to the clearing beside the river.

Jondalar had missed the final touches to the boat. Though he had worked on nearly every phase of its construction, the finished product was a breath-catching sight. It seemed much larger than he recalled, and it had not been small to begin with, but now its fifty-foot length was balanced with correspondingly high sides of gently curved planks and a tall jutting stern post. But it was the forward section that brought exclamations of wonder. The curved prow had been gracefully extended into a long-necked water fowl carved of wood and scarf-jointed with pegs.

The bow piece was painted with deep ochre reds and dun ochre yellows, manganese blacks, and the white earths of calcinated limestone. Eyes were painted low on the hull to see underwater and avoid hidden dangers, and geometric designs covered bow and stern. Seats for rowers spanned the breadth, and new broad-bladed, long-handled oars were in readiness. A yellow chamois-skin awning crowned the midsection as a protection from rain or snow, and the entire craft was decorated with flowers and bird feathers.

It was glorious. Awe inspiring. And Jondalar felt a surge of pride, and a lump in his throat, to think he had contributed to its creation.

All matings required a boat, either new or refitted, as part of the ceremony, but not all were graced by one of such size and splendour. It was only chance that the Cave had decided that another large boat was needed about the same time the young couple had declared their intentions. But now it seemed particularly appropriate, especially since so many visitors had come. Both Cave and couple had garnered esteem for the accomplishment.

The newly mated couple climbed into the vessel, a little awkwardly with their wrists tied together, and took the middle seat under the canopy. Many of the close kin followed them, with some taking up oars. The boat had been propped between logs to keep it from wobbling, and the logs extended to the water's edge. Cave members and visitors crowded around to push the boat into the river, and, with grunting and laughter, the new boat was launched.

They held her near shore until the new craft was declared fit, with no listing or serious leaking, and then they started downstream for the maiden voyage to the Ramudoi dock.

Several other boats of various sizes took to the water and surrounded the large new water bird like ducklings.

Those not returning by water hurried back up the trail, hoping to reach the high embayment before the young couple did. At the dock, several people climbed the steep waterfall trail and prepared to lower the large flat basket in which Thonolan and Jondalar had first been raised to the terrace – but this time it was Thonolan and Jetamio who were lifted to the top with their hands still tied together. They had agreed to bind themselves to each other and, at least for that day, they would not be separated.

Huge amounts of food were served, washed down with quantities of new-moon dandelion wine, and gifts were presented to all the visitors, returned by prestige in like measure. But as evening came on, the new dwelling that had been built for the young couple began to see visitors, as guests quietly slipped in and left a "little something" for the newly mated to wish them well. The gifts were given anonymously so as not to detract from the nuptial wealth displayed by the hosting Cave. But, in fact, the value of the gifts received would be measured against the value of the wares distributed, and mental notes tallied against a remembered record, for the gifts were not anonymous.

The shape, design, and painted or carved features announced the donor as plainly as if they had been presented openly; not the individual maker, which was of relatively small importance, but the family, or group, or Cave. By well-known and mutually understood systems of value, the given and received gifts would have a significant impact on the relative prestige, honour, and status of the various groups. Though not violent, competition for esteem was nonetheless fierce.

"He's certainly getting a lot of attention, Thonolan," Jetamio said, noticing a handful of women hovering around the tall blond man leaning casually against a tree near the overhang.

"Always like that. His big blue eyes make women come to him like . . . moth to fire," Thonolan said, helping Jetamio lift an oak box of bilberry wine out to the celebrating guests. "Have you noticed? You not ever attracted?"

"You smiled at me first," she said, and his broad grin provoked her beautiful response. "But I think I understand it. It's more than his eyes. He stands out, particularly in those clothes. They do look good on him. But it's more than that. I think women sense that he's . . . searching. Looking for someone. And he's so responsive . . . sensitive . . . tall, and so well made. Really quite handsome. And there is something to his eyes. Did you ever notice they turn violet in firelight?" she said.

"I thought you say not attracted . . ." Thonolan said with a look of dismay until she winked impishly.

"Are you envious of him?" she asked gently.

Thonolan paused. "No. Not ever. Not know why, many men envious. Look him, you think he have everything. Like you say, well made, handsome; look all beautiful women around. And more. Good with hands, best flint knapper I ever see. Good head, but not talk big. People like him; men, women, both. Should be happy, but not. He need find someone like you, Tamio."

"No, not like me. But someone. I like your brother, Thonolan. I hope he finds what he's searching for. Maybe one of those women?"

"Not think so. I see that before. Maybe he enjoy one – or more – but not find what he want." They dipped some of the wine into waterbags and left the rest for the revellers, then walked towards Jondalar.

"What about Serenio? He seems to care for her, and I know she feels more for him than she will admit."

"He care for her, care for Darvo, too. But . . . maybe not anyone for him. Maybe he look for dream, for donii." Thonolan smiled fondly. "First time you smile at me, I thought you donii."

"We say the Mother's spirit becomes a bird. She wakes the sun with Her calls, brings the spring with Her from the south. In the autumn, some stay behind to remind us of Her. The hunting birds, the storks, every bird is some aspect of Mudo." A string of running children crossed in front of them, halting their progress. "Little children don't like birds, especially if they're naughty. They think the Mother is watching them, and knows everything. Some mothers tell their children that. I've heard stories of grown men driven to confess some evil deed by the sight of certain birds. Then others say She will guide you home if you're lost."

"We say Mother spirit become donii, fly on wind. Maybe She look like bird. I never think of that before," he said, squeezing her hand. Then looking at her and feeling an upwelling of love, he whispered in a voice husky with emotion, "I never think I find you." He tried to put an arm around her, but found himself tied to her wrist, and frowned. "I glad we tie the knot, but when do we cut off? I want hold you, Tamio."

"Maybe we're supposed to be finding out that we can be tied too close," she laughed. "We can leave the celebration soon. Let's go take your brother some wine before it's all gone."

"He maybe not want. He make show of drinking, but not drink much. He not like lose control, do foolish thing." When they stepped out of the shadows of the overhang, they were suddenly noticed.

"There you are! I've been wanting to wish you happiness, Jetamio," a young woman said. She was a Ramudoi from another Cave, young and vivacious. "You're so lucky, we never get handsome visitors to winter with us." She flashed what she hoped was a winning smile at the tall man, but he was looking at another of the young women with his astounding eyes.

"You're right. I am lucky," Jetamio said, with a melting smile at her mate.

The young woman looked at Thonolan and heaved a sigh. "They're both so handsome. I don't think I could have made a choice!"

"And you wouldn't have either, Cherunio," the other young woman said. "If you want to mate, you have to settle on one."

There was an outburst of laughter, but the young woman revelled in the attention it brought her. "I just haven't found a man I want to settle on." She dimpled at Jondalar.

Cherunio was the shortest woman there, and Jondalar really hadn't seen her before. He did then. Though short, she was very much a woman, and she had a quality of vivacious enthusiasm that was inviting. She was almost the complete opposite of Serenio. His eyes showed his interest, and

Cherunio nearly quivered with delight now that she had his attention. Suddenly she turned her head, caught by a sound.

"I hear the rhythm – they're going to do a couple dance," she said. "Come on, Jondalar."

"Not know steps," he said.

"I'll show you; it's not hard," Cherunio said, eagerly tugging in the direction of the music. He yielded to the invitation.

"Wait, we're coming, too," Jetamio said.

The other woman was not too pleased that Cherunio had captured Jondalar's attention so quickly, and he heard Radonio say, "It's not hard . . . yet!" followed by peals of laughter. But as the four of them headed towards the dance, he did not hear the conspiratorial whisper.

"Here's the last water skin of wine, Jondalar," Thonolan said. "Jetamio says we are supposed to start the dance, but we don't have to stay. We're going to slip away as soon as we can."

"Don't you want to take it with you? For a private celebration?"

Thonolan grinned at his mate. "Well, it's not really the last – we have one tucked away. But I don't think we need it. Just to be alone with Jetamio will be celebration enough."

"Their language has such a nice sound. Don't you think so, Jetamio?" Cherunio said. "Can you understand any of it?"

"A little, but I'm going to learn more. And Mamutoi, too. It was Tholie's idea that we all learn one another's language."

"Tholie say best way learn Sharamudoi is talk all time. She right. I sorry, Cherunio. Not polite talk Zelandonii," Jondalar apologized.

"Oh, I don't mind," Cherunio said, though she had. She didn't like being left out of the conversation. But the apology more than appeased her, and being included in the select group with the newly mated couple and the tall, handsome Zelandonii had other compensations. She was well aware of the envious looks of several young women.

Near the back of the field, outside the overhang, a bonfire burned. They stepped into the shadows and passed the wine skin around, and then, as a group was forming, the two young women showed the men the basic movements of the dance. Flutes, drums, and rattles began a lively melody, which was picked up by the mammoth-bone player, and the tonal qualities that resembled those of a xylophone added a unique sound.

Once the dancing started, Jondalar noticed that the basic steps could be elaborated with variations limited only by the imagination and skill of the dancer, and occasionally a person or a pair displayed such exceptional enthusiasm that everyone else stopped to shout encouragement and keep time with their feet. A group gathered around the dancers, swaying and singing, and, without a conscious break, the music shifted to a different tempo. It continued like that. The music and dancing never stopped, but people joined in – musicians, dancers, singers – and dropped out at will, creating an endless variation in tone, pace, rhythm, and melody, which would continue as long as there was anyone who wished to continue.

Cherunio was a lively partner, and Jondalar, drinking more wine than usual, had got into the mood of the evening. Someone started a response chant by saying the first familiar line. He soon discovered it was a song in which the words were made up to suit the occasion by anyone, with the intention of provoking laughter, often by innuendos of Gifts and Pleasures. It soon became a competition between those who were trying to be funny and those who were trying not to laugh. Some participants were even making faces in an attempt to bring on the desired response. Then a man went to the centre of the circle that was swaying to the rhythm of the chant.

"There's Jondalar, so big and tall, he could have had his pick of all. Cherunio is sweet, but small. He'll break his back, or maybe fall."

The man's chant brought the desired results: howls of laughter.

"How will you do it, Jondalar?" someone else called out. "You'll have to break your back just to kiss her!"

Jondalar grinned at the young woman. "No break back," he said, then picked Cherunio up and kissed her to the stamping feet and applauding laughter. Literally swept off her feet, she wrapped her arms around his neck and kissed him back with feeling. He had noticed several couples leaving the group for tents, or mats in out-of-the-way nooks, and he had been thinking along those lines himself. Her remarkable enthusiasm for kissing made him think she might be agreeable.

They couldn't leave immediately – it would only cause more laughter – but they could begin to back away. Some new people joined the singers and watchers and the pace was shifting. This would be a good time to fade into the shadows. As he was easing Cherunio towards the edge of the gathering, Radonio suddenly appeared.

"You've had him all evening, Cherunio. Don't you think it's time to share him? After all, this is a festival to honour the Mother, and we're supposed to share Her Gift."

Radonio insinuated herself between them and kissed Jondalar. Then another woman embraced him, then several more. He was surrounded by young women, and at first went along with their kissing and caresses. But by the time several pairs of hands were handling him in rather personal ways, he wasn't too sure he cared for it. Pleasures were supposed to be a matter of choice. He heard a muffled struggle but was suddenly very busy fending off hands that sought to untie his trousers and reach inside. That was too much.

He shrugged them off, none too gently. When they finally understood he wouldn't allow anyone to touch him, they stood back smirking. Suddenly he noticed someone was missing.

"Where Cherunio is?" he asked.

The women looked at each other and squealed with laughter.

"Where Cherunio is?" he demanded, and when his only reply was more giggling, he took a quick step and grabbed Radonio. He was hurting her arm, but she didn't want to admit it.

"We thought she ought to share you," Radonio said, forcing a smile. "Everyone wants the big handsome Zelandonii."

"Zelandonii not want everyone. Where Cherunio is?"

Radonio turned her head away and refused to answer.

"You want big Zelandonii, you say?" He was angry, and

his voice showed it. "You get big Zelandonii!" He forced her down to her knees.

"You're hurting me! Why don't the rest of you help me?"

But the other young women were not so sure they wanted to get too close. Holding her shoulders, Jondalar pushed Radonio down to the ground in front of the fire. The music had stopped, and people were milling around, unsure if they should intervene. She struggled to get up, and he held her down with his body.

"You want big Zelandonii, you got. Now, where Cherunio?"

"Here I am, Jondalar. They were holding me over there with something in my mouth. They said they were just playing a joke."

"Bad joke," he said as he got up and then helped Radonio. She had tears in her eyes and was rubbing her arm.

"You were hurting me," she cried.

Suddenly he realized it had been meant as a joke, and he'd handled it poorly. He hadn't been hurt, and neither had Cherunio. He shouldn't have hurt Radonio. His anger evaporated, replaced by chagrin. "I . . . I not mean hurt you . . . I . . ."

"You didn't hurt her, Jondalar. Not that much," said one of the men who had been observing. "And she had it coming. She's always starting things and making trouble."

"You just wish she'd start something with you," one of the young women said, jumping to Radonio's defence, now that they were back on normal terms.

"You might think a man likes it when you all come at him like that, but he doesn't."

"That's not true," Radonio said. "You think we haven't heard you making jokes when you think you're alone, about this woman or that woman? I've heard you talk about wanting women all at one time. I've even heard you talk about wanting girls before First Rites, when you know they can't be touched, even if the Mother has made them ready."

The young man blushed, and Radonio pushed her advantage. "Some of you even talk about taking flathead females!"

Suddenly, looming large out of the shadows at the edge of the fire, a woman appeared. She wasn't so much tall as fat, hugely obese. The epicanthic fold of her eyes spoke of a

265

foreign origin, as did the tattoo on her face, though she wore a tunic of Shamudoi leather.

"Radonio!" she said. "It isn't necessary to speak filth at a festival in honour of the Mother," Jondalar recognized her now.

"I'm sorry Shamud," Radonio said, bowing her head. Her face was flushed with embarrassment and she was genuinely contrite. It made Jondalar aware that she was quite young. They were all hardly more than girls. He had behaved abominably.

"My dear," the woman said to Radonio gently. "A man likes to be invited, not invaded."

Jondalar looked more keenly at the woman; he thought much the same thing.

"But we weren't going to hurt him. We thought he'd like it . . . after a while."

"And he might have, if you'd been more subtle. No one likes to be forced. You didn't like it when you thought he might force you, did you?"

"He hurt me!"

"Did he? Or did he make you do something against your will? I think that hurt you far more. And what about Cherunio? Did any of you think you might be hurting her? You cannot force anyone to enjoy Pleasures. That does no honour to the Mother. It abuses Her Gift."

"Shamud, it's your wager . . ."

"I'm holding up the game. Come now, Radonio. It's Festival. Mudo wants Her children to be happy. It was a minor incident – don't let it spoil your fun, my dear. The dancing has started again; go join in."

As the woman returned to her gambling, Jondalar took Radonio's hands. "I . . . sorry. I not think. Not mean hurt you. Please, I feel shame . . . forgive?"

Radonio's first impulse – to pout and withdraw in anger – melted when she looked up into his earnest face and deep violet eyes. "It was silly . . . childish joke," she said, and, nearly overwhelmed by the full impact of his presence, she swayed towards him. He held her, then leaned closer and gave her a lingering, experienced kiss.

"Thank you, Radonio," he said, then turned to walk away.

"Jondalar!" Cherunio called after him. "Where are you going?"

He had forgotten her, he realized with a stab of guilt. He strode back to the short, pretty, vivacious young woman – there was no doubt she was appealing – picked her up, and kissed her with ardour, and regret.

"Cherunio, I make promise. All this not happen if I not so ready to break promise, but you make so easy to forget. I hope . . . some other time. Please, not be angry," Jondalar said, then quickly strode towards the shelters beneath the sandstone overhang.

"Why did you have to go and spoil it for everyone, Radonio?" Cherunio said as she watched him go.

The leather flap at the door of the dwelling he shared with Serenio was down, but no crossed planks barred his way. He sighed with relief. At least she wasn't inside with someone else. When he pushed the flap aside, it was dark. Maybe she wasn't there. Maybe she was with someone else after all. Come to think of it, he hadn't seen her all evening, not since the ceremonies. And she was the one who wanted no commitment; he had only promised himself that he would spend the night with her. Maybe she had other plans, or maybe she had seen him with Cherunio.

He felt his way to the rear of the dwelling where a raised platform was covered with a feather-stuffed pad and furs. Darvo's bed along the side wall was empty. That was expected. Visitors were not frequent, especially those his age. He had likely made the acquaintance of some boys and was spending the night with them, trying to keep themselves awake.

When he neared the back, he pricked up his ears. Was that breathing he heard? He reached across the platform and felt an arm, and a smile of joy warmed his face.

He went back out, picked up a hot coal from the central fire, and hurried back carrying it on a piece of wood. He lit the moss wick of a small stone lamp, then placed two planks across each other at the door, the sign that they did not wish to be disturbed. He picked up the lamp, walked quietly to the bed, and watched the sleeping woman. Should he wake her? Yes, he decided, but slowly and gently.

The idea quickened his loins. He removed his clothes and

slipped in beside her, curling around her warmth. She mumbled and rolled over towards the wall. With long gentle strokes he caressed her, feeling her sleeping warmth beneath his hand and breathing her female scent. He explored every contour: her arm to the ends of her fingers, her sharp shoulder blades and ridged spine that led to the sensitive small of her back and the rising swell of her buttocks, then her thighs and the backs of her knees, her calves and ankles. She pulled her feet away when he touched the bottoms. He reached his arm around to cup her breast, and felt the nipple contract and harden within his palm. He had an urge to suckle it, but instead covered her back with his body and began kissing her shoulders and neck.

He loved touching her body, exploring and discovering it anew. Not just hers, he knew. He loved all women's bodies, for themselves, and for the feelings they caused within his. His manhood was already throbbing and thrusting, eager, but still controllable. It was always better if he didn't give in too soon.

"Jondalar?" said a sleepy voice.

"Yes," he said.

She rolled to her back and opened her eyes. "Is it morning?"

"No." He got up on one arm and looked down at her while he fondled a breast, then bent to suckle the nipple he'd wanted to feel in his mouth before. He caressed her stomach, then reached for the warmth between her thighs and rested his hand on the hair of her mound. She had the softest, silkiest pubic hair of any woman he'd ever known. "I want you, Serenio. I want to honour Mother with you, tonight."

"You need to give me some time to wake up," she said, but a smile played at the corners of her mouth. "Is there any cold tea? I want to wash my mouth out – wine always makes it taste terrible."

"I look," he said, getting up.

Serenio smiled languidly when he walked back with a cup. Sometimes she just liked to look at him – he was so wonderfully male: the muscles rippling across his back as he moved, his powerful chest of blond curls, his hard stomach, and his legs all strength and sinew. His face was almost too perfect: strong square jaw, straight nose, sensual mouth – she knew how sensual his mouth could be. His features were so finely moulded and proportioned that he'd be thought beautiful if he wasn't so masculine, or if *beautiful* was a word usually applied to men. Even his hands were strong and sensitive, and his eyes – his expressive, compelling, impossible blue eyes, that could set a woman's heart racing with one glance, that could make her want that hard, proud, magnificent manhood jutting out in front before she ever saw it.

It had frightened her a little, the first time she saw him like that, before she understood how well he used it. He never forced it on her, only giving as much as she could take. If anything, she forced herself, wanting it all, wishing she could take it all. She was glad he had awoken her. She got up when he gave her the cup, but before she took a drink, she leaned down and took the throbbing head in her mouth. He closed his eyes and let the pleasure surge through him.

She sat up and took a drink, then got up. "I have to go out," she said. "Are many people still up? I don't want to get dressed."

"People still dancing, still early. Maybe should use box."

As she walked back to the bed, he watched her. O Mother! She was a beautiful woman, her features so lovely, her hair so soft. Her legs were long and graceful, her buttocks small but well-formed. Her breasts were small, tight, well-shaped, with high jutting nipples – a girl's breasts still. A few stretch marks on her stomach were the only sign of her motherhood, and the few lines etched at the corners of her eyes the only sign of her years.

"I thought you'd be back late – it's Festival," she said.

"Why you here? You not say 'no commitment'?"

"I didn't meet anyone interesting, and I was tired."

"You interesting . . . I not tired," he said, smiling. He took her in his arms and kissed her warm mouth, his tongue questing, and pulled her close to him. She felt a hard hot throbbing against her stomach, and a flood of warmth washed over her.

He had meant to prolong it, to keep himself controlled until she was more than ready, but he found himself hungrily at her mouth, her neck, sucking and pulling on her nipples while she held his head to her breast. His hand reached for her furry mound and found her hot and moist. A small cry escaped her lips as he touched the small hard organ within her warm folds. She raised up and pressed herself to him as he caressed the place which he knew gave her pleasure.

He sensed what she wanted this time. They shifted position – he rolled to one side, she to her back. She lifted one leg over his hip, moved the other between his legs, and, while he fondled and massaged her centre of pleasure, she reached down to guide his eager manhood into her deep cleft. She cried out with passion as he penetrated, and she felt the exquisite excitement of both sensations at once.

He felt her warmth envelop him, moving into her as she ground down on him, trying to take him all. He pulled back and surged into her again, until he could go no farther. She raised to his hand, and he rubbed harder as he plunged into her again. He was so full, so ready, and she was crying out as her tension rose. She pushed down on him; he felt his loins tighten. He massaged hard and drove in, and then again, and then surging powerful waves pulled them together as they reached an unbearable peak and were flooded with glorious release. A last few strokes extracted a shudder and complete fulfilment.

They lay still, breathing hard, their legs still entwined. She pushed herself down on him. Only now, before he became flaccid, but was no longer fully engorged, could she finally take all of him within herself. He always seemed to give her more than she could give him. He didn't want to move – he could almost go to sleep, but didn't want to sleep either. Finally he withdrew his spent member and curled up around her. She was lying still, but he knew she wasn't asleep.

He let his mind wander, and he suddenly found himself thinking about Cherunio, and Radonio, and all the other young women. What would it have been like to be with all of them? To feel all those warm, nubile, female bodies surrounding him, with their warm thighs, and their round bottoms, and their moist wells. To have the breast of one in his mouth, and each hand exploring two other women's bodies. He was feeling a renewed twinge of excitement. Why had he pushed them away? Sometimes he could really be stupid.

He looked at the woman beside him and wondered how long it would take to make her ready again, then breathed in her ear. She smiled at him. He kissed her neck, and then her mouth. It would be slower this time, he would take his time. She is a beautiful, wonderful woman . . . why can't I fall in love?

13

Ayla had a problem when she reached the valley. She had planned to butcher and dry her meat on the beach, sleeping out as she had done before. But the wounded cave lion cub could only be taken care of properly in the cave. The cub was larger than a fox and much stockier, but she could carry him. A full-grown deer was another story. The points of the two spears trailing behind Whinney, that were the support poles of the travois, were spaced too far apart to fit the narrow path up to the cave. She didn't know how she was going to get her hard-won deer up to the cave, and she didn't dare leave it unattended on the beach, with hyenas following so close.

She was right to be concerned. Just in the short span of time it took to carry the baby lion up to the cave, hyenas were snarling over the grass-mat-covered deer still on the travois, in spite of Whinney's nervous sidestepping. Ayla's sling was in action before she was halfway down, and one hard-flung stone was fatal. She dragged the hyena by a hind paw around the stone wall and into the meadow, though she hated touching the animal. He smelled of the carrion he had last fed on, and she washed her hands in the stream before she turned her attention to the horse.

Whinney was shivering and sweating, and swishing her tail in a state of nervous agitation. It had been almost more than she could abide to have the scent of cave lion so close. Even worse was the smell of hyena on her trail. She had tried to circle when the animals attempted to close in on Ayla's kill, but one leg of the travois had caught in a cleft of rock. She was close to panic.

"This has been a hard day for you, hasn't it, Whinney?" Ayla signalled, then wrapped her arms around the mare's neck and simply held her, the way she would a frightened child. Whinney leaned against her and shook, breathing hard through her nose, but the young woman's closeness finally calmed her. The horse had always been treated with love and patience, and gave trust and willing effort in return.

Ayla started dismantling the makeshift travois, still not sure how she was going to get the deer up to the cave, but as one pole was loosened, it swung closer to the other, so that the two points of the former spears were quite close. Her problem had solved itself. She refastened the pole so it would stay, then led Whinney towards the path. The load was unstable, but there was only a short distance to go.

It was more of an effort for Whinney; the reindeer and the horse were of fairly equal weight, and the path was steep. The task gave Ayla a new appreciation of the horse's strength and an insight into the benefit she had garnered in borrowing it. When they reached the stone porch, Ayla removed all the encumbrances and hugged the young mare gratefully. She went into the cave, expecting Whinney to follow, then turned back at the horse's anxious neigh.

"What's wrong?" she signalled.

The cave lion cub was exactly where she had left him. The cub! she thought. Whinney smells the cub. She went back out.

"It's all right, Whinney. That baby can't hurt you." She rubbed Whinney's soft nose and, putting an arm around the sturdy neck, gently urged the horse into the cave. Trust in the woman again overcame fear. Ayla led the horse to the small lion. Whinney cautiously sniffed, backed off and nickered, then lowered her muzzle to sniff the unmoving cub again. The smell of predator was there, but the young lion offered no harm. Whinney sniffed and nudged the cub again, then seemed to make up her mind to accept the new addition to the cave. She walked to her place and began feeding on hay.

Ayla turned her attention to the wounded baby. He was a fuzzy little creature, with faint tan spots on a lighter pale beige background. He seemed quite young, but Ayla wasn't sure. Cave lions were predators of the steppes; she had only studied carnivorous animals that lived in the wooded regions near the cave of the Clan. She had never hunted the open plains then.

She tried to remember everything the Clan hunters had

said about cave lions. This one seemed to be a lighter shade than the ones she had seen, and she recalled that the men had often warned the women that cave lions were difficult to see. They matched the colour of the dried grass and dusty ground so well that you could almost stumble over one. An entire pride, sleeping in the shade of brush, or among the stones and outcrops near their dens, looked like boulders – even from very close.

When she thought about it, the steppes in this area did seem to be a lighter shade of beige in overall tone, and the lions nearby certainly blended into the background well. She hadn't stopped to consider it before, but it seemed logical that they should have lighter-coloured fur than the ones to the south. Perhaps she ought to spend some time studying cave lions.

With a deft, knowledgeable touch, the young medicine woman probed to discover the extent of the cub's injuries. One rib was broken but didn't threaten to cause other damage. Spasms of contraction and little mewling sounds indicated where he hurt; he might have internal injuries. The worst problem was an open wound on his head, no doubt caused by a hard hoof.

Her fire had long since burned out, but it was no longer a concern. She had come to depend on her firestones, and she could start a fire very quickly if she had good tinder. She started water boiling, then wrapped a leather band smoothly and tightly round the baby cave lion's ribs. As she peeled the dark brown skin off the comfrey roots she had picked on the way back, a glutinous mucilage oozed out. She put marigold flowers in the boiling water, and, when the liquid turned golden, she dipped in a soft absorbent skin to wash the cub's head wound.

Soaking off the dried blood caused bleeding again, and she saw that his skull was cracked, but not crushed. She chopped the white comfrey root and applied the gummy substance directly to the wound – it stopped the bleeding, and would help heal the bone – then wrapped it with more soft leather. She hadn't known what use she might find for them when she cured the hides of nearly every animal she had killed, but in her wildest imagination she never would have dreamed the use to which some had just been put.

Wouldn't Brun be surprised to see me, she thought, smiling. He never allowed animals that hunted, he wouldn't even let me bring that little wolf cub into the cave. Now look at me, with a lion cub! I think I'm going to learn a lot about cave lions in a hurry – if he lives.

She set more water to boil for a comfrey-leaf and chamomile tea, though she didn't know how she was going to get the internally healing medicine into the baby lion. She left the cub then and went out to skin the reindeer. When the first thin, tongue-shaped slices of meat were ready to hang, she was suddenly at a loss. There was no layer of soil on top of the stone ledge, nothing into which she could sink the sticks she used to string her cords across. She hadn't even thought of that when she was so concerned about bringing the deer carcass up to the cave. Why was it the small things that always seemed to stymie her? Nothing could be taken for granted.

In her frustration, she couldn't think of any solution. She was tired, and overwrought, and anxious about bringing a cave lion home. She wasn't sure she should have, and what was she going to do with him? She threw down the stick and got up. Walking to the far end of the porch, she looked out over the valley while the wind blew in her face. What could she be thinking of – to bring a baby lion back that would need care, when she should be getting ready to leave and continue her search for the Others? Maybe she should just take him back out to the steppes now, and let him go the way of all weakened animals in the wild. Had living alone made her stop thinking straight? She didn't know how to take care of him, anyway. How would she feed him? And what would happen if he did recover? She couldn't send him back to the steppes then; his mother would never take him back, he would die. If she was going to keep the cub, she'd have to stay in the valley. To continue her search, she'd have to take him back to the steppes.

She went back into the cave and stood over the young cave lion. He still hadn't moved. She felt his chest. He was warm and breathing, and his fuzzy coat reminded her of Whinney's when she was a baby. He was cute, and he looked so funny with his head bandaged up that she had to smile. But that cute baby is going to become a very large lion, she reminded herself. She stood up and looked down at him again. It didn't matter. There was no way she could take that baby out to the steppes to die.

She went back out and stared at the meat. If she was going to stay in the valley, she would have to start thinking about storing food again. Especially since she had another mouth to feed. She picked up the stick, trying to think of some way to make it stay upright. She noticed a mound of crumbled rock along the back wall near the far edge, and she tried poking the stick into it. The piece of wood stayed upright, but it would never support the weight of strings of meat. It did give her an idea though. She went into the cave, grabbed a basket, and ran down to the beach.

After some experimenting, she discovered that a pyramid of beach stones would support a longer stick. She made several trips to gather stones and cut suitable pieces of wood before she was able to string several lines across the ledge to dry the meat and could go back to the business of cutting it. She built a small fire near the place she was working and spitted a rump to roast for dinner, thinking again about how she was going to feed the cub, and how she was going to get the medicine down him. What she needed was lion baby food.

Young ones could eat the same food as adults, she recalled, but it had to be softer, easier to chew and swallow. Perhaps a meat broth, with the meat cut up very fine. She had done that for Durc, why not for the cub? In fact, why not cook the broth in the tea she had infused for medicine?

She set to work immediately, cutting up the piece of deer meat she picked up next. She brought it inside to put into the wooden cooking pot, then decided to add a little of the leftover comfrey root as well. The cub hadn't stirred, but she thought he was resting easier.

Some time later, she thought she heard sounds of stirring and went back to check on him again. He was awake, mewling softly, unable to roll over and get up – but when she approached the oversize kitten, he snarled and hissed and tried to back away. Ayla smiled and dropped down beside him.

Frightened little thing, she thought. I don't blame you. Waking up in a strange den, hurting, and then seeing someone not at all like mother and siblings. She stretched out a hand. Here, I won't hurt you. *Ow!* Your little teeth are sharp! Go ahead, little one. Taste my hand, get the smell of me. It will make it easier to get used to me. I'll have to be your mother now.

She got up to check the cooking bowl. She was rather surprised at the thickened consistency of the cooled broth, and when she stirred it with a rib bone, she found the meat compacted into a lump at the bottom of the bowl. Finally, she poked it with a sharpened skewer and lifted out a congealed mass of meat, with thick viscid liquid hanging down in strings. Suddenly she understood, and she burst out laughing. It frightened the cub so much that he almost found strength enough to get up.

No wonder that comfrey root is so good for wounds. If it holds torn flesh together as well as it has glued this meat together, it's bound to help healing!

"Baby, do you think you can drink some of this?" she motioned to the cave lion. She poured some of the cooled gummy liquid into a smaller birchbark eating dish. The cub had squirmed off the grass mat and was struggling to get up. She put the dish under his nose. He hissed at her and backed away.

Ayla heard the clatter of hooves coming up the path, and a moment later Whinney came in. She noticed the cub, very much awake and moving now, and went to investigate. She lowered her head to sniff the fuzzy creature. The young cave lion, who as an adult could instil terror in one of Whinney's kind, was instead terrified by yet another unfamiliar large animal looming near. He spat and snarled and backed away until he was almost in Ayla's lap. He felt the warmth of her leg, remembered a smell a little more familiar, and huddled there. There were just too many strange new things in this place.

Ayla lifted the baby lion to her lap, cuddled him, and made humming sounds – the way she would have soothed any baby. The way she had soothed her own.

The young animal responded to Ayla's petting and cuddling by nuzzling around for a place to nurse. You are hungry, aren't you, baby? She reached for the dish of thick broth and held it under the cub's nose. He smelled it, but didn't know what to do with it. She dipped two fingers in the bowl, put them in his mouth. He knew what to do then. Like any baby, he sucked.

As she sat in her small cave, holding the cave lion cub, rocking back and forth as he suckled her two fingers, Ayla was so overcome with the memory of her son that she didn't notice the tears running down her face and dripping on the fuzzy fur.

A bond was formed in those first days – and nights when she took the baby lion to her bed to cuddle and suckle her fingers – between the lonely young woman and the cave lion cub; a bond that could never have formed between the cub and its natural mother. The ways of nature were harsh, particularly for the young of the mightiest of predators. While the lion mother would suckle her cubs during their early weeks – and even allow them to nurse, occasionally, for six months – from the time they first opened their eyes, lion cubs began eating meat. But the hierarchy of feeding in a pride of lions allowed no sentimentality.

The lioness was the hunter, and, unlike other members of the feline family, she hunted in a cooperative group. Three or four lionesses together were a formidable hunting team; they could bring down a healthy giant deer, or a bull aurochs in its prime. Only a full-grown mammoth was immune to attack, though the young and the old were susceptible. But the lioness didn't hunt for her young, she hunted for the male. The lead male always got the lion's share. As soon as he appeared, the lionesses gave way, and only after he gorged did the females take their share. The older adolescent lions were next, and only then, if there was any left, did the young cubs get a chance to squabble over scraps.

If a young cub, out of hungry desperation, tried to dash in to snatch a bite out of turn, it was likely to be dealt a fatal blow. The mother often led her young away from a kill, though they might be starving, to avoid such dangers. Three-quarters of the cubs born never reached maturity. Most of those that did were driven from the pride to become nomads, and nomads were unwelcome anywhere, particularly if they were male. Females had a slight edge. They might be allowed to stay on the fringes if a pride was short of hunters.

The only way a male could win acceptance was to fight for it, often to the death. If the pride's dominant male was aging or hurt, a younger member of the pride, or more likely a wanderer, might drive him out and take over. The male was kept to defend the pride's territory – marked by his scent glands or the lead female's urine – and to assure the continuance of the pride as a breeding group.

Occasionally a male and female wanderer would join to form the nucleus of a new pride, but they had to claw their own niche out of adjoining territories. It was a precarious existence.

But Ayla was not a lion mother, she was human. Human parents not only protected their young, they provided for them. Baby, as she continued to call him, was treated as no cave lion had ever been treated. He had to fight no siblings for scraps, nor avoid the heavy blows of his elders. Ayla provided; she hunted for him. But though she gave him his share, she did not relinquish her own. She let him suck her fingers whenever he felt the need, and she usually took him to bed with her.

He was naturally housebroken, always going outside the cave, except in the beginning when he could not. Even then, when he puddled, he made such a grimace of disgust at his mess that it brought a smile to Ayla's face. It wasn't the only time he made her smile. Baby's antics often caused outright laughter. He loved to stalk her – and he loved it more if she feigned ignorance of his intent, then acted surprised when he landed on her back, though sometimes she'd surprise him, turn at the last moment, and catch him in her arms.

Children of the Clan were always indulged; punishment seldom involved more than ignoring behaviour that was calculated to get attention. As they grew older and became more aware of the status accorded to older siblings and adults, children began to resist pampering as babyish, and to emulate adult ways. When this brought the inevitable approval, it was usually continued.

Ayla pampered the cave lion in the same way, particularly in the beginning, but, as he grew bigger, there were times when his games inadvertently caused her pain. If he scratch-

279

ed in rambunctious playfulness, or knocked her down with a mock attack, her usual response was to stop playing, often accompanied by the Clan gesture for "Stop!" Baby was sensitive to her moods. A refusal to play tug-of-war with a stick or an old hide often made him try to appease her with behaviour which usually made her smile, or he would try to reach for her fingers to suck.

He began to respond to her gesture for "stop" with the same actions. With Ayla's usual sensitivity to actions and postures, she noticed his behaviour and began using the signal for stop whenever she wanted him to cease whatever he was doing. It wasn't so much a matter of her training him as one of mutual responsiveness, but he learned fast. He would stop in midstride, or try to break a playful leap in mid air at her signal. He usually needed the reassurance of sucking her fingers when the "stop" signal was issued with imperative sharpness, as though he knew he had done something that displeased her.

On the other hand, she was sensitive to his moods and she bound him with no physical restraints. He was as free to come and go as she or the horse. It never occurred to her to pen or tie either one of her animal companions. They were her family, her clan, living creatures who shared her cave and her life. In her lonely world, they were the only friends she had.

She soon forgot how strange it would seem to the Clan to have animals living with her, but she did wonder about the relationship that developed between the horse and the lion. They were instinctive enemies, prey and predator. If she had thought about it when she found the wounded cub, she might not have brought the lion to the cave she shared with a horse. She wouldn't have thought they could live together, much less anything more.

In the beginning, Whinney had merely tolerated the cub, but once he was up and around it was hard to ignore him. When she saw Ayla pulling at one end of a piece of hide while the baby lion held the other end in his teeth, shaking his head and snarling, the horse's natural curiosity got the better of her. She had to come and find out what was going on. After sniffing at the hide, she often grabbed it in her teeth, making it a three-way pull. When Ayla let go, it became a tug-of-war between horse and lion. In time, Baby formed the habit of dragging a hide – under his body between his front legs the way he would some day drag a kill – across the path of the horse, trying to entice her to pick up an end and play tug-of-war. Whinney often complied. With no siblings to play his lion games, Baby made do with the creatures at hand.

Another game – that Whinney was not so fond of, but that Baby could not seem to resist – was catch-a-tail. In particular, Whinney's tail. Baby stalked it. Crouching he'd watch it swish and move so invitingly as he moved up with silent stealth, quivering with excitement. Then, with an anticipatory wiggle, he'd pounce, delighted with a mouthful of hair. Sometimes, Ayla was sure Whinney played along with the cub, fully aware that her tail was the object of such intense desire, but pretending not to notice. The young mare was playful too. She just hadn't had anyone to play with before. Ayla was not given to inventing games; she had never learned how.

But after a while, when she'd had enough, Whinney would turn on the attacker of her tail and nip Baby on the rump. Though she, too, was indulgent, she never conceded her dominance. Baby might be a cave lion, but he was just a baby. And if Ayla was his mother, Whinney became his nursemaid. While games between the two developed over time, the change from mere tolerance to active care was the result of one particular trait; Baby loved dung.

The droppings of carnivorous animals were of no interest, he loved only the dung of grazers and browsers, and when they were out on the steppes, he would roll in it whenever he found it. As with most of his games, this was preparation for future hunting. An animal's own dung could mask the scent of lion, but that didn't make Ayla laugh less when she watched him discover a new pile of dung. Mammoth dung was especially nice. He would embrace the big balls, break them up, and lie on them.

But no dung was as wonderful as Whinney's. The first time he found the pile of the dried droppings which Ayla used to supplement her firewood, he couldn't get enough. He carried it around, rolled in it, played in it, immersed himself in it. When Whinney came into the cave, she smelled her own scent on him. She seemed to feel it made him a part of her. From that moment on, she lost all traces of nervousness around the young cub and adopted him as her charge. She guided him, and guarded him, and if he responded in ways that were puzzling at times, it did not lessen her attentive care.

That summer, Ayla was happier than she had been since she left the Clan. Whinney had been company and more than a friend; Ayla didn't know what she would have done without her during the long lonely winter. But the addition of the cub to her fold brought a new dimension. He brought laughter. Between the protective horse and the playful cub, something was always amusing.

On a warm sunny day in midsummer, she was in the meadow watching the cub and the horse playing a new game. They were chasing each other around in a large circle. First the young lion would slow down just enough for Whinney to catch up, then he would bound ahead while she slowed until he came all the way around and behind her. Then she would sprint ahead while he checked his speed until she caught up again. Ayla thought it was the funniest sight she had ever seen. She laughed until she collapsed against a tree, holding her stomach.

As her spasms of laughter died down, for some reason, she became aware of herself. What was this sound she made when something amused her? Why did she do it? It came so easily when there was no one to remind her it wasn't proper. Why wasn't it proper? She could not remember, ever, seeing anyone in the Clan smile or laugh, except her son. Yet they understood humour, funny stories brought on nods of agreement and a pleasant expression that centred more in the eyes. People of the Clan did make a grimace somewhat similar to her smile, she recalled. But it conveyed nervous fear, or menace, not the happiness she felt.

But if laughter made her feel so good, and came out so easily, could it be wrong? Other people like her, did they laugh? The Others. Her warm happy feelings left her. She didn't like thinking of the Others. It made her aware that she had stopped looking for them, and it filled her with mixed emotions. Iza had told her to find them, and living alone could be dangerous. If she got sick or had an accident, who would help her?

But she was so happy in the valley with her animal family. Whinney and Baby didn't look at her disapprovingly when she forgot herself and ran. They never told her not to smile, or not to cry, or what she could hunt, or when, or with what weapons. She could make her own choices, and it made her feel so free. She didn't consider that the time it took to provide for her physical needs – like food, warmth, and shelter – limited her freedom, though it took most of her efforts. Just the reverse. It gave her confidence to know she could take care of herself.

With the passage of time, and particularly since Baby had come, the grief she felt for the people she loved had abated. The emptiness, her need for human contact, was such a constant pain that it seemed normal. Any lessening of it was a joy, and the two animals went a long way towards filling the void. She liked to think of the arrangement as similar to Iza and Creb and herself when she was a little girl, except she and Whinney took care of Baby. And when the lion cub, with claws retracted, wrapped his forelegs around her when she cuddled up to him at night, she could almost imagine it was Durc.

She was reluctant to leave and seek out unknown Others, with unknown customs and restrictions; Others who might take laughter away from her. They won't, she said to herself. I won't live with anyone again who won't let me laugh.

The animals had grown tired of their game. Whinney was grazing, and Baby was resting nearby, with his tongue hanging out of his mouth, panting. Ayla whistled, which brought Whinney, with the lion padding behind her.

"I have to go hunting, Whinney," she motioned. "That lion eats so much and he's getting so big."

Once the baby cave lion had recovered from his injuries, he always followed Ayla or Whinney. Cubs were never left alone in the pride, nor were babies ever left alone in the Clan, so his behaviour seemed perfectly normal. But it presented a problem. How was she going to hunt with a cave lion trailing her? When Whinney's protective instincts were aroused, however, the problem solved itself. It was customary for a lion mother to form a subgroup with her cubs and a younger female when they were small. The younger female tended the cubs when the lioness went hunting, and Baby accepted Whinney in that role. Ayla knew that no hyena, or similar animal, would brave the stomping hooves of the mare aroused to protect her charge, but it meant she had to hunt on foot again. Yet, hiking the steppes close to the cave in search of animals appropriate for her sling gave her an unexpected opportunity.

She had always avoided the pride of cave lions that roamed the territory east of her valley. But the first time she noticed a few lions resting themselves in the shade of stunted pines, she decided it was time to learn something more about the creatures that embodied her totem.

It was a dangerous occupation. Hunter though she was, she could easily become prey. But she had observed predators before and had learned ways to make herself inconspicuous. The lions knew she was watching, but after the first few times, they chose to ignore her. It didn't remove the danger. One could turn on her at any time, for no reason other than a cranky mood, but the longer she watched, the more fascinating they became.

They spent most of their time resting or sleeping, but when they hunted, they were speed and fury in action. Wolves, hunting in packs, were able to kill a large deer; a single cave lioness could do it more quickly. They hunted only when they were hungry, and might eat only once in a handful of days. They had no need to store food ahead as she did; they hunted all year long.

They tended to be nocturnal hunters in summer when the days were hot, she noticed. In winter, when nature thickened their coats, lightening the shade to ivory to blend into the lighter landscape, she had seen them hunting during the day. The severe cold kept the tremendous energy they burned during the hunt from overheating them. At night, when temperatures plummeted, they slept piled together in a cave or rock overhang out of the wind, or amidst the strewn rubble of a canyon where the stones absorbed a little heat from the distant sun during the day and gave it up to the dark.

The young woman was returning to her valley after a day of observation which had brought new respect for the animal of her totem spirit. She had watched the lionesses bring down an old mammoth with tusks so long they curved back and crossed in front. The entire pride had gorged on the kill. How had she ever escaped from one when she was only five, with only a few scars to show for it? She was thinking, understanding better the Clan's amazement. Why did the Cave Lion choose me? For a moment, she felt a strange presentiment. Nothing specific, but it left her thinking about Durc.

When she neared the valley, a quick stone brought a hare down for Baby, and she suddenly questioned her wisdom in bringing the cub to her cave, envisioning him as a full-grown male cave lion. Her misgivings lasted only until the young lion ran to her, eager and delighted to have her back, looking for her fingers to suck, and licking her with his raspy tongue.

Later in the evening, after she had skinned the hare and cut it into chunks for Baby, cleaned Whinney's place and brought her in some fresh hay, and made some dinner for herself, she sat sipping hot tea and staring at the fire, thinking about the day's events. The young cave lion was asleep toward the back of the cave, away from the direct heat of the fire. Her thoughts turned to the circumstances that had led her to adopt the cub, and she could only conclude that it had been her totem's wish. She didn't know why, but the spirit of the Great Cave Lion had sent one of his own for her to raise.

She reached for the amulet hanging from the cord around her neck and felt the objects within it, then, with the silent formal language of the Clan, she addressed her totem: "It was not understood by this woman how powerful is the Cave Lion. This woman is grateful she was shown. This woman may not ever know why she was chosen, but this woman is grateful for the baby and the horse." She paused, then added, "Some day, Great Cave Lion, this woman would know why the cub was sent . . . if her totem would choose to tell."

Ayla's usual summer workload, preparing for the cold season to come, was compounded by the addition of the cave lion. He was carnivorous, pure and simple, and required quantities of meat to satisfy the needs of his rapid growth. Hunting small animals with her sling was taking too much of her time – she needed to go after bigger game, for herself as well as the lion. But for that, she needed Whinney.

Baby knew Ayla was planning something special when she got out the harness and whistled for the horse so she could make the adjustments to enable her to drag two sturdy wooden poles behind her. The travois had proved itself, but Ayla wanted to work out a better way to attach it so she could still use the pack baskets. She also wanted to keep one pole movable so the horse could bring the load up to the cave. Drying the meat on the ledge had worked well, too.

She wasn't sure what Baby would do, or how she was going to hunt with Baby along, but she had to try it. When everything was ready, she climbed on Whinney's back and started out. Baby followed along behind, the way he would have trailed his mother. It was so much more convenient to reach the territory east of the river that, except for a few exploratory trips, she never went west. The sheer wall on the western side continued for many miles before a steep rubbly slope finally opened a way to the plains in that direction. Since she could range so much farther on horseback, she had become familiar with the eastern side, which made it easier to hunt as well.

She had learned much about the herds of those steppes, their migration patterns, customary routes, and river crossings. But she still had to dig pitfall traps along known animal trails, and it was not a job that benefited from the interference of a lively lion cub, who thought the young woman had just invented a wonderful new game only for his enjoyment.

He crept up to the hole, breaking down the edge with his paws, bounded over it, jumped in, and leaped out just as easily. He rolled in the piles of dirt she had scooped onto the old tent hide, which she still used to haul the dirt away. When she started to drag the hide away, Baby decided to drag it too, his way. It became a tug-of-war, with all the dirt spilled on the ground.

"Baby! How am I going to get this hole dug," she said, exasperated, but laughing, which encouraged him. "Here, let me get you something to drag." She rummaged through the pack baskets, which she had taken off Whinney to let her graze comfortably, and found the deerskin she had brought along as a ground cover in case it rained. "Drag this, Baby," she motioned, then pulled it along the ground in front of him.

It was all he needed. He couldn't resist a hide dragged along the ground. He was so delighted with himself, dragging the hide between his front legs, that she had to smile.

In spite of the cub's assistance, Ayla did get the hole dug and covered with an old hide brought for the purpose, and a layer of dirt. The hide was barely held in place with four pegs, and the first time she had it ready, Baby had to investigate. He fell into the trap, then jumped out with shocked indignation, but stayed away afterwards.

Once the pitfall was prepared, Ayla whistled for Whinney and circled wide to get behind a herd of onagers. She couldn't bring herself to hunt horses again, and even the onager made her uncomfortable. The half-ass looked too much like a horse, but the herd was in such a good position for a chase into a pitfall that she couldn't pass it up.

After Baby's playful antics around the hole, she was even more concerned that he would be a hindrance to the hunt, but once they got behind the herd, he assumed a different mien. He stalked the onagers, the same way he had stalked Whinney's tail, just as though he might actually bring one down, though he was far too young. She realized then that his games were cub-size versions of adult-lion hunting skills he would need. He was a hunter from birth; his understanding of the need for stealth was instinctive.

Ayla discovered, to her surprise, that the cub was actually a help. When the herd was close enough to the trap that the scent of human and lion was causing them to swerve, she urged Whinney forward, whooping and yelping to start a stampede. The cub sensed this was the signal and took off after the animals, too. The smell of cave lion added to the onager's panic. They headed straight for the pitfall.

Ayla slid off Whinney's back, spear in hand, running at full speed towards a screaming onager trying to scramble out of the hole, but Baby was ahead of her. He jumped on the back of the animal – not knowing yet the lion's fatal suffocating hold of the prey's throat – and, with milk teeth too small to have much effect, bit at the back of the onager's neck. But it was early experience for him.

If he had still lived with the pride, no adult would have allowed him to get in the way of a kill. Any attempt would have been immediately stopped with a murderous swipe. For all their speed, lions were only sprinters, while their prey were long-distance runners. If the lions' kill wasn't made in the first surge of speed, the chances were they would lose it. They couldn't afford to let a cub practise his hunting skills, except through play, until he was nearly grown.

But Ayla was human. She had the speed of neither prey nor predator, as she lacked claw and fang. Her weapon was her brain. With it she had devised means to overcome her lack of natural hunting endowments. The trap – that allowed the slower, weaker human to hunt – gave even a cub the opportunity to try.

When Ayla arrived, breathless, the onager was wild-eyed with fear, trapped in a pit with a cave-lion kitten snarling on his back trying to get a death hold with baby teeth. The woman ended the animal's struggles with a sure thrust of the spear. With the cub hanging on – his sharp little teeth had broken the skin – the onager went down. Only when all movements had stopped did Baby let go. Ayla's smile was a mother's smile of pride and encouragement as the cave lion cub, standing on top of an animal much bigger than himself, full of pride and convinced he'd made the kill, tried to roar.

Then Ayla jumped down in the pit with him, and nudged him aside. "Move over, Baby. I've got to tie this rope around his neck so Whinney can pull him out."

The cub was a bundle of nervous energy as the horse, leaning into the strap across her chest, hauled the onager out of the pit. Baby jumped into the hole and back out of it, and when the onager was finally out of the hole, the cub leaped on top of the animal, then bounded off again. He didn't know what to do with himself. The lion who made the kill was usually the first to take a share, but cubs did not make kills. By the usual dominance patterns, they were last.

Ayla spread the onager out to make the abdominal cut that started at the anus and ended at the throat. A lion would have opened the animal in a similar way, tearing out its soft underside first. With Baby watching avidly, Ayla cut through the lower part, then turned and straddled the animal to cut up the rest of the way.

Baby couldn't wait any more. He dived into the gaping abdomen and snatched at the bloody innards bulging out. His needle-sharp teeth tore through the tender internal tissue and succeeded in grabbing hold of something. He clamped down and pulled back in typical tug-of-war fashion.

Ayla finished the cut, turned around, and felt laughter bubbling up exuberantly. She shook with mirth until tears came to her eyes. Baby had clamped down on a piece of intestine, but, unexpectedly, as he backed up, there was no resistance. It kept coming. Anxiously, he had continued to pull until a long rope of uncoiled entrails was strung out for several feet, and his look of surprise was so funny that Ayla couldn't contain herself. She collapsed on the ground, holding her side, trying to regain her composure.

The cub, not knowing what the woman was doing on the ground, let the coil drop and came to investigate. Grinning as he came bounding toward her, she grabbed his head in her hands and rubbed her cheek on his fur. Then she rubbed him behind the ears and around his slightly blood-stained jowls, while he licked her hands and wriggled into her lap. He found her two fingers, and, pressing her thighs alternately with his forefeet, he suckled, making low rumbling sounds deep in his throat.

I don't know what brought you, Baby, Ayla thought, but I'm so glad you're here.

14

By fall, the cave lion was bigger than a large wolf, and his
baby chunkiness was giving way to gangly legs and muscular
strength. But for all his size, he was still a cub, and Ayla
sported an occasional bruise or scratch from his playfulness.
She never struck him – he was a baby. She did, however,
reprimand him with the signal for "Stop it, Baby!" while
pushing him away, and adding "That's enough, you're too
rough!" as she walked off.

It was sufficient to cause a contrite cub to come after her
making submissive gestures, as members of a pride did to
those more dominant. She couldn't resist, and the happy
rambunctiousness that followed her forgiveness was always
more restrained. He would sheathe his claws before he
jumped up and put his paws on her shoulders to push her
over – rather than knocking her down – so he could wrap his
forelegs around her. She had to hug him back, and though he
bared his teeth when he took her shoulder or arm in his
mouth – as he would one day bite a female he was mating –
he was gentle and never broke the skin.

She accepted his advances and gestures of affection and
returned them, but in the Clan, until he made his first kill and
reached adulthood, a son obeyed his mother. Ayla would
have it no other way. The cub accepted her as mother. It was
therefore natural for her to be dominant.

The woman and the horse were his pride; they were all he
had. The few times he had met other lions while on the
steppes with Ayla, his inquisitive advances were soundly
rejected, as the scar on his nose proved. After the scuffle that
sent Baby back with a bleeding nose, the woman avoided
other lions when the cub was with her, but when she was out
alone, she still observed.

She found herself comparing the cubs of wild prides with Baby. One of her first observations was that he was big for his age. Unlike the young of a pride, he never knew periods of hunger with his ribs sticking out like ripples in the sand, and scruffy dull fur; much less was he threatened with death by starvation. With Ayla providing constant care and sustenance, he could reach the full extent of his physical potential. Like a Clan woman with a healthy contented baby, Ayla was proud to see her cub growing sleek and huge in comparison with wild cubs.

There was another area of his development, she noticed, in which the young lion was ahead of his contemporaries. Baby was a precocious hunter. After the first time, when he had taken such delight in chasing onagers, he always accompanied the woman. Rather than playing at stalking and hunting with other cubs, he was practising on real prey. A lioness would have forcibly restricted his participation, but Ayla encouraged and in fact welcomed his assistance. His instinctive hunting methods were so compatible with hers that they hunted as a team.

Only once did he initiate the chase prematurely and scatter a herd in advance of the pit. Then, Ayla was so disgusted with him that Baby knew he'd made a grievous mistake. He watched her closely next time and held himself in check until she started. Though he hadn't succeeded in killing a trapped animal before she arrived, she was sure it would not be long before he killed something.

He discovered that hunting smaller game with Ayla and her sling was great fun, too. If Ayla was gathering food in which he had no interest, he would chase anything that moved – if he wasn't sleeping. But when she hunted, he learned to freeze when she did at the sight of game. Waiting and watching while she took out her sling and a stone, he was off as she made her cast. She often met him dragging the kill back, but sometimes she found him with his teeth around the animal's throat. She wondered if it had been her stone, or if he had finished the job by closing the windpipe, the way lions suffocated an animal to kill it. In time, she learned to look when he froze, scenting prey before she saw it, and it was a smaller animal he first opened by himself.

Baby had been playing around with a hunk of meat she

had given him, not especially interested in it, then had gone to sleep. He woke up when he heard Ayla climbing up the steep side to the steppes above her cave, hungry. Whinney was not around. Cubs left unattended in the wild were open season for hyenas and other predators; he had learned the lesson early and well. He leaped up after Ayla and reached the top ahead of her, then walked beside her. She saw him stop before she noticed the giant hamster, but it had seen them and started to run before she hurled the stone. She wasn't sure if her aim had been true.

Baby was off the next instant. When she came upon him with his jaws buried in the bloody entrails, she wanted to find out who had made the kill. She shoved him aside to see if she could find a stone mark. He resisted for only an instant – long enough for her to look at him sternly – then gave way without argument. He had eaten enough food from her hand to know she always provided. Even after examining the hamster, she wasn't sure how it had died, but she gave it back to the lion, praising him. Tearing through the skin himself was an achievement.

The first animal she was sure he killed himself was a hare. It was one of the few times her stone slipped. She knew she had made a bad throw – the stone came to rest only a few feet beyond her – but the motion of throwing had signalled the young cave lion to give chase. She found him disembowelling the animal.

"How wonderful you are, Baby!" She praised him lavishly with her unique mixture of sounds and hand signs, as all Clan boys were praised when they killed their first small animal. The lion didn't understand what she said, but he understood he had pleased her. Her smile, her attitude, her posture, all communicated her feeling. Though he was young for it, he had satisfied his own instinctive need to hunt, and he had received approval from the dominant member of his pride. He had done well and he knew it.

The first cold winds of winter brought falling temperatures, shattery ice to the edge of the stream, and feelings of concern to the young woman. She had laid in a large supply of vegetable foods and meat for herself, and an extra store of dried meat for Baby. But she knew it would not last him all winter. She had grain and hay for Whinney, but for the horse the fodder was a luxury, not a necessity. Horses foraged all winter, though when the snow lay deep they knew hunger until dry winds cleared it away, and not all survived the cold season.

Predators foraged all winter as well, culling out the weak, leaving more feed for the strong. The populations of predators and prey rose and fell in cycles, but overall maintained a balance in relation to each other. During the years when there were fewer grazers and browsers, more carnivores starved. Winter was the hardest season of all.

With the coming of winter, Ayla's worry grew more acute. She could not hunt large animals when the ground was frozen rock hard. Her method required holes to be dug. Most small animals hibernated or lived in nests on food they had stored – making them hard to find, especially without the ability to scent them out. She doubted she could hunt enough of them to keep a growing cave lion fed.

During the early part of the season, after the weather turned cold enough to keep the meat frigid and, later, freeze it, she tried to kill as many large animals as she could, storing them under caches of piled stones. But she wasn't as familiar with the herds' patterns of winter movement, and her efforts were not as successful as she hoped. Though her worries caused an occasional sleepless night, she never regretted picking up the cub and taking him home. Between the horse and the cave lion, the young woman seldom felt the introspective loneliness usually brought on by the long winter. Instead, her laughter often filled the cave.

Whenever she went out and began uncovering a new cache, Baby was there trying to get at the frozen carcass before she had hardly removed a stone.

"Baby! Get out of the way!" She smiled at the young lion trying to wriggle his way under the rocks. He dragged the stiff animal up the path and into the cave. As though he knew it had been used before by cave lions, he made the small niche in the back of the cave his own, and brought the cached animals there to thaw. He liked to worry off a frozen hunk first, gnawing at it with relish. Ayla waited until it was thawed before cutting off a piece for herself.

As the supply of meat in the caches dwindled, she began

watching the weather. When a clear, crisp, cold day dawned, she decided it was time to hunt – or at least to try. She did not have a specific plan in mind, though not for want of thinking about it. She hoped an idea would occur to her while she was out, or at least that a better look at the terrain and conditions would open up some new possibilities to consider. She had to do something, and she didn't want to wait until all the stored meat was gone.

Baby knew they were going hunting as soon as she pulled out Whinney's pack baskets, and he ran in and out of the cave excitedly, growling and pacing in anticipation. Whinney, tossing her head and nickering, was just as pleased at the prospect. By the time they reached the cold sunny steppes, Ayla's tension and worry had begun losing ground to hope and the pleasure of the activity.

The steppes were white with a thin layer of fresh snow that was hardly disturbed by a light wind. The air had a static crackle of cold so intense, the bright sun might just as well not have been there at all, but for the light it shed. They breathed out streamers of vapour with every exhalation, and the build-up of frost around Whinney's mouth dispersed in a spray of ice when she snorted. Ayla was grateful for the wolverine hood and the extra furs all her hunting had made available to wear.

She glanced down at the supple feline moving with silent grace, and with a shock she realized that Baby was nearly as long, from shoulder to shank, as Whinney, and was fast approaching the small horse in height. The adolescent male cave lion was showing the beginnings of a reddish mane, and Ayla wondered why she hadn't noticed it before. Suddenly more alert, Baby was straining ahead, his tail held stiffly out behind him.

Ayla wasn't used to tracking in winter on the steppes, but even from horseback the spoor of wolves was evident in the snow. The pawprints were clear and sharp, not eroded by wind or sun, and evidently fresh. Baby pulled ahead; they were near. She urged Whinney to a gallop and caught up with Baby just in time to see a wolf pack closing around an old male who was trailing behind a small herd of saiga antelope.

The young lion saw them too, and, unable to control his

excitement, raced into their midst, scattering the herd and disrupting the wolves' attack. The surprised and disgruntled wolves made Ayla want to laugh, but she didn't want to encourage Baby. He's just excitable, she thought, we haven't hunted for so long.

Springing in mighty leaps of panic, the saiga bounded across the plains. The wolf pack regrouped and followed at a more deliberate pace that covered ground quickly but wouldn't tire them before they caught up with the herd again. When Ayla composed herself, she gave Baby a stern look of disapproval. He fell back beside her, but he'd enjoyed himself too much to be contrite.

As Ayla, Whinney, and Baby followed the wolves, Ayla had an idea. She didn't know if she could kill a saiga antelope with her sling, but she knew she could kill a wolf. She didn't care for the taste of wolf meat, but if Baby was hungry enough, he'd eat it, and he was the reason for hunting.

The wolves had picked up their pace. The old male saiga had dropped behind the main herd, too exhausted to keep up. Ayla leaned forward and Whinney increased her speed. The wolves circled the old buck, wary of hooves and horns. Ayla moved in close to try for one of the wolves. Reaching into the pouching fold of her fur for stones, she selected a particular wolf. As Whinney's pounding hooves closed, she let fly with a stone, and then with a second in quick succession.

Her aim was true. The wolf dropped and at first she thought the ensuing commotion was the result of her kill. Then she saw the real cause. Baby had taken her sling cast as the signal to chase, but he wasn't interested in the wolf, not when the far more delectable antelope was in sight. The wolf pack relinquished the field to the galloping horse with a sling-wielding woman on her back, and to the determined charge of the lion.

But Baby wasn't quite the hunter he strove to be – not yet. His attack lacked the strength and finesse of a full-grown lion. It took her a moment to comprehend the situation. No, Baby! That's the wrong animal, she thought. Then she quickly corrected herself. Of course, he had chosen the right animal. Baby was striving for a death grip, clinging to the fleeing buck to whom stark fear had just given a new burst of strength.

Ayla grabbed a spear from the pack basket behind her. Whinney, responding to her urgency, raced after the old saiga. The antelope's spurt of speed was short-lived. He was slowing. The speeding horse quickly closed the gap. Ayla poised the spear and, just as they came abreast, she struck, not aware that she was screaming with sheer primal exuberance.

She wheeled the horse around and trotted back to find the young cave lion standing over the old buck. Then, for the first time, he proclaimed his prowess. Though it still lacked the full-throated thunder of the adult male's, Baby's triumphant roar carried the promise of its potential. Even Whinney shied at the sound.

Ayla slid off the mare's back and patted her neck reassuringly. "It's all right, Whinney. It's only Baby."

Not considering that the lion might object and could inflict serious injury, Ayla pushed him aside and prepared to gut the antelope before taking it back. He gave way to her dominance, and to something else that was uniquely Ayla, her confidence in her love for him.

She decided to find the wolf and skin it. Wolf fur was warm. Returning, she was surprised to see Baby dragging the antelope, and she realized he intended to haul it all the way to the cave. The male antelope was full grown and Baby was not. It gave her an increased appreciation of his strength – and the power he was still to gain. But if he dragged the antelope all that way, the hide would be damaged. Saiga were widespread, living in mountains as well as the plains, but they were not numerous. She had not hunted one before, and they had a special meaning for her. The saiga antelope had been Iza's totem. Ayla wanted the hide.

She signalled "Stop!" Baby hesitated only a moment before releasing "his" kill, and, guarding it, he paced anxiously around the travois all the way back to the cave. He watched with more than usual interest while she removed the hide and the horns. When she gave it to him, he dragged the entire skinned carcass to the niche in the far corner. After he gorged, he still maintained a vigil, and he slept close by.

Ayla was amused. She understood he was protecting his

kill. He seemed to feel there was something special about this beast. Ayla did, too, for other reasons. Surges of excitement still coursed through her. The speed, the chase, the hunt had been thrilling – but more important, she had a new way to hunt. With the help of Whinney, and now Baby, she could hunt any time, summer and winter. She felt powerful, and grateful, and she would be able to provide for her Baby.

Then, for no reason she could think of, she checked on Whinney. The horse was lying down, perfectly secure in spite of the proximity of a cave lion. She lifted her head as Ayla approached. The woman stroked the horse, then, feeling a need to be close, she lay beside her. Whinney blew a soft snort of air through her nostrils, content to have the woman near.

Winter hunting with Whinney and Baby, without the arduous task of digging pits, was a game. Sport. From the earliest days of practising with her sling, Ayla had loved hunting. Each new technique mastered – tracking, the double-stone throw, the pit and spear – brought an additional feeling of accomplishment. But nothing matched the sheer fun of hunting with the horse and the cave lion. They both seemed to enjoy it as much as she. While Ayla made preparations, Whinney tossed her head and danced on her toes, with her ears pricked forward and tail raised, and Baby padded in and out of the cave, making low growls of anticipation. Weather concerned her until Whinney brought her home through a blinding blizzard.

The trio usually started out shortly after daybreak. If they sighted prey early, they were often home before noon. Their usual method was to follow a likely candidate until they were in a good position. Then Ayla would signal with her sling and Baby, eager and ready, would spring forward. Whinney, feeling Ayla's urge, galloped after him. With the young cave lion clinging to the back of a panicked animal – his claws and fangs drawing blood, if not actually fatal – it seldom took long for the galloping horse to close the distance. As they came abreast, Ayla plunged the spear.

In the beginning, they weren't always successful. Sometimes the chosen animal was too fast, or Baby would fall off, unable to get a secure hold. For Ayla, learning to wield the heavy spear at full gallop took some practice, too. Many times she missed, or made only a glancing blow, and sometimes Whinney didn't get close enough. Even when they missed, it was exciting sport, and they could always try again.

With practice, they all improved. As they began understanding each other's needs and abilities, the unlikely trio became an efficient hunting team – so efficient that when Baby made his first unassisted kill, it went almost unnoticed as part of the team's efforts.

Bearing down at a hard gallop, Ayla saw the deer falter. It was down before she reached them. Whinney slowed down as they passed by. The woman jumped off and was running back before the horse came to a halt. Her spear was raised, ready to finish the job, when she found Baby had done it himself. She proceeded to make the deer ready to take back to the cave.

Then the full import struck her. Baby, as young as he was, was a hunting lion! In the Clan, that would make him an adult. Just as she had been called the Woman Who Hunts before she was a woman, Baby had reached adulthood before he attained maturity. He should have a manhood ceremony, she thought. But what kind of ceremony would have meaning for him? Then she smiled.

She unbound the doe from the travois, then put the grass mat and the poles in the pack baskets. It was his kill, and he had a right to it. Baby didn't understand at first. He paced back and forth from the carcass to her. Then, as Ayla left, he took the deer's neck in his teeth and, pulling it underneath him, he dragged it all the way back to the beach, up the steep path, and into the cave.

She didn't notice any difference, immediately after Baby's kill. They still hunted together. But more often than not, Whinney's chase was only exercise and Ayla's spear unnecessary. If she wanted some of the meat, she took it first; if she wanted the hide, she skinned it. Though, in the wild, the pride male always took the first and largest portion, Baby was still young. He'd never known hunger, as his growing size attested, and he was accustomed to her dominance.

But towards spring, Baby began leaving the cave more, exploring by himself. He was seldom gone long, but his excursions became more frequent. Once he came back with blood on his ear. She guessed he'd found other lions. It made her realize she was no longer enough; he was looking for his own kind. She cleaned the ear, and he spent the day following her so closely that he was getting in her way. At night, he crept up to her bed and searched for her two fingers to suck.

He'll be leaving soon, she thought, wanting a pride of his own, mates to hunt for him, and cubs to dominate. He needs his own kind. Iza came to mind. You're young, you need a man of your own, one of your own kind. Find your own people; find your own mate, she had said. It will be spring soon. I should think about leaving, but not yet. Baby was going to be huge, even for a cave lion. He already far exceeded lions his age in size, but he wasn't grown; he couldn't survive, yet.

Spring followed close on the heels of a heavy snow. Flooding kept them all restricted, Whinney more than the others. Ayla could climb to the steppes above, and Baby could leap there with ease, but the slope was too steep for the horse. The water finally receded, the beach and the bone pile had new contours again, and Whinney could finally go down the path to the meadow once more. But she was irritable.

Ayla first noticed something out of the ordinary when Baby yelped from an equine kick. The woman was surprised. Whinney had never been impatient with the young lion; perhaps a nip now and then to keep him in line, but certainly not enough to kick him. She thought the unusual behaviour was a consequence of her enforced inactivity, but Baby tended to stay away from her place in the cave as he got older, sensitive of Whinney's territory, and Ayla wondered what had drawn him there. She went to see, then became conscious of a strong odour she'd been vaguely aware of all morning. Whinney was standing with her head down, her hind legs spread apart, and her tail held to the left. Her vaginal opening was swollen and pulsating. She looked up at Ayla and squealed.

The series of emotions that came over Ayla in quick succession pulled her to opposite extremes. First it was relief. So that's your problem. Ayla knew about oestrus cycles in animals. In some, the time of pairing occurred more frequently, but for grazers, once a year was usual. This was the season when males often fought for the right to couple, and it was the one time when the males and females mingled, even those who normally hunted separately or herded in different groups.

Pairing season was one of those mysterious aspects of animal behaviour that puzzled her, like deer dropping their antlers and growing new and bigger ones every year. The kinds of things that made Creb complain that she asked too many questions about, when she was younger. He didn't know why animals paired, either, though he had once volunteered that it was the time for the males to show their dominance over females, or perhaps, like people, the males had to relieve their needs.

Whinney had had a pairing season the previous spring, but at the time, though she heard a stallion neighing on the steppes above, Whinney couldn't get up to him. The young mare's need seemed stronger this time, too. Ayla didn't remember so much swelling and squealing. Whinney submitted to the young woman's pats and hugs; then the horse dropped her head and squealed again.

Suddenly, Ayla's stomach churned into a knot of anxiety. She leaned against the horse, the way Whinney sometimes did against her when she was upset or frightened. Whinney was going to leave her! It was so unexpected. Ayla hadn't had time to prepare for it, though she should have. She'd been thinking about Baby's future, and her own. Instead, Whinney's pairing season had come. The filly needed a stallion, a mate.

With great reluctance, Ayla walked out of the cave and signalled Whinney to follow. When they reached the rocky beach below, Ayla mounted. Baby got up to follow them, but Ayla motioned "stop". She did not want the cave lion with her now. She was not going hunting, but Baby might not know that. Ayla had to stop the lion once more, with firm determination, before he stayed behind watching them go.

It was warm, and damply cool at the same time, on the steppes. The sun, about midway to noon, blazed out of a pale blue sky with a veiled halo; the blue seemed faded, bleached by the intensity of the glare. Melting snow steamed to a fine mist that did not limit visibility but softened sharp angles, and fog clinging to cool shadows flattened contours. Perspective was lost and the entire view was foreshortened – lending an immediacy to the landscape, a sense of present tense, here and now, as though no other time and place ever existed. Distant objects seemed only a few paces away, yet took forever to reach.

Ayla didn't guide the horse. She let Whinney take her, only subliminally noticing landmarks and direction. She didn't care where she was going, didn't know her tears were adding their salty moisture to the ambient dampness. She sat loosely, jouncing, her thoughts turning inward. She recalled the first time she saw the valley and the herd of horses in the meadow. She thought about her decision to stay, her need to hunt. She remembered leading Whinney to the safety of her fire and her cave. She should have known it couldn't last, that some day Whinney would return to her own kind, just as she herself needed to do.

A change in the horse's pace jogged her attention. Whinney had found what she was looking for. A small band of horses was ahead.

The sun had melted the snow covering a low hill and exposed tiny green shoots poking above the ground. The animals, hungry for a change from the straw of last year's forage, were nibbling the succulent new growth. Whinney stopped when the other horses looked up at her. Ayla heard the neigh of a stallion. Off to the side, on a knoll she hadn't noticed before, she saw him. He was dark reddish brown with a black mane, tail, and lower legs. She had never seen a horse so deeply coloured. Most of them were shades of grey brown, or beige dun, or, like Whinney, the yellow colour of ripe hay.

The stallion screamed, lifted his head, and curled back his upper lip. He reared and galloped towards them, then stopped short a few paces away, pawing the ground. His neck was arched, his tail was raised, and his erection was magnificent.

Whinney nickered in reply, and Ayla slid off her back. She gave the horse a hug, then backed away. Whinney turned her head to look at the young woman who had taken care of her since she was a foal.

"Go to him, Whinney," she said. "You've found your mate, go to him."

Whinney tossed her head and neighed softly, then faced the bay stallion. He circled behind her, head low, nipping her hocks, herding Whinney closer to his flock, as if she were a recalcitrant truant. Ayla watched her go, unable to leave. When the stud mounted, Ayla couldn't help remembering Broud, and the terrible pain. Later, it had only been unpleasant, but she always hated it when Broud mounted her, and was grateful when he finally grew tired of it.

But for all the screaming and squealing, Whinney was not trying to reject her stallion, and, as she watched, Ayla felt strange stirrings within herself, sensations she could not explain. She could not tear her eyes away from the bay stallion, his front legs up on Whinney's back, pumping, and straining, and screaming. She felt a warm wetness between her legs, a rhythmic pulsation in time to the stallion's pounding, and an incomprehensible yearning. She was breathing hard, felt her heart reverberating in her head, and ached with longing for something she couldn't describe.

Afterwards, when the yellow horse willingly followed the bay, without so much as a backward look, Ayla felt an emptiness so heavy that she thought she could not bear it. She realized how fragile was the world she had built for herself in the valley, how ephemeral had been her happiness, how precarious her existence. She turned and ran back towards the valley. She ran until her breath tore her throat, until pain stabbed her side. She ran, hoping somehow, if she ran fast enough, she could leave behind all the heartache and loneliness.

She stumbled down the slope that led to the meadow, and rolled, and stayed where she stopped, gasping raggedly for breath. Even after she could breathe again, she didn't move. She didn't want to move. She didn't want to cope, or try, or live. What was the use? She was cursed, wasn't she?

Why can't I just die then? Like I'm supposed to? Why do I have to lose everything I love? She felt a warm breath and a rasping tongue licking the salt from her cheek, and she opened her eyes to a huge cave lion.

"Oh, Baby!" she cried, reaching for him. He sprawled out beside her and, with claws retracted, put a heavy foreleg over her. She rolled over, hugged his furry neck, and buried her face in his lengthening mane.

When she finally cried herself out and tried to get up, she felt the result of her fall. Lacerated hands, skinned knees and elbows, a bruised hip and shin, and her right cheek was sore. She limped back to the cave. As she was treating her scrapes and bruises, she had a sobering thought. What if I'd broken a bone? That could be worse than dying, with no one to help.

I didn't though. If my totem wants to keep me alive, maybe he has a reason. Maybe the spirit of the Cave Lion sent Baby to me because he knew Whinney would leave some day.

Baby will leave, too. It won't be long before he will want a mate. He will find one, even if he isn't growing up in a regular pride. He's going to be so big that he'll be able to defend a big territory. And he's a good hunter. He won't go hungry while he's looking for a pride, or at least one lioness.

She smiled wryly. You'd think I was a Clan mother worrying about her son growing up to be a big brave hunter. After all, he's not my son. He's just a lion, an ordinary . . . No, he's not an ordinary cave lion. He is almost as big as some full-grown cave lions already, and he is an early hunter. But he will leave me . . .

Durc must be big by now. Ura is growing, too. Oda will feel sad when Ura leaves to be Durc's mate and live with Brun's clan. . . . No, it's Broud's clan now. How long will it be until the next Clan Gathering?

She reached behind the bed for the bundle of marked sticks. She still made a notch every night. It was a habit, a ritual. She untied the bundle and laid them out on the ground, then tried to count the days since she had found her valley. She fitted her hands into the notches, but there were too many marks, too many days had passed. She had a feeling the marks ought to come together and add up in some way that would tell her how long she'd been there, but she didn't know how. It was so frustrating. Then she realized she didn't need the sticks; she could think of the years by counting each spring. Durc was born the spring before the last Clan Gathering, she thought. The next spring ended his birth year. She made a mark in the dirt. Next was his walking year; she made another mark. The next spring would have been the end of his nursing year and the beginning of his weaning year – except he was already weaned. She made a third mark.

That was when I left – she swallowed hard and blinked her eyes – and that summer I found the valley, and Whinney. The next spring, I found Baby. She made a fourth mark. And this spring . . . She didn't want to think about losing Whinney as a way to remember the year, but it was a fact. She made a fifth mark.

That's all the fingers of one hand – she held up her left hand – and that's how many Durc is now. She put out the thumb and forefinger of the right hand – and this many before the next Gathering. When they get back, Ura will be with them, for Durc. Of course, they won't be old enough to mate yet. They'll know by looking at her that she is for Durc. I wonder, does he remember me? Will he have Clan memories? How much of him is me, and how much Broud . . . Clan?

Ayla gathered up her marked sticks and noticed a regularity in the number of marks between the extra notches that she made when her spirit battled and she bled. What man's totem spirit could be battling with mine here? Even if my totem was a mouse, I'd never get pregnant. It takes a man, and his organ, to start a baby. That's what I think.

Whinney! Is that what that stallion was doing? Was he getting a baby started in you? Maybe I'll see you sometime with that herd, and find out. Oh, Whinney, that would be wonderful.

Thoughts of Whinney and the stallion made her quiver. Her breath came a little faster. Then she thought of Broud, and the pleasant sensations stopped. But it was his organ that started Durc. If he'd known it would give me a baby, he would never have done it. And Durc will have Ura. She's not deformed either. I think Ura was started when that man of the Others forced Oda. Ura is just right for Durc. She's part Clan, and part that man of the Others. A man of the Others . . .

Ayla was restless. Baby was gone, and she felt the need to be moving. She went out and strolled just outside the line of brush that hugged the stream. She walked farther than she had before, though she had ridden as far on Whinney's back. She was going to have to get used to walking again, she realized, and to carrying a basket on her back. At the far end of the valley she followed the stream around the edge of the high scarp as it swung south. Just beyond the turn, the stream swirled around rocks that could have been placed on purpose, they were so neatly spaced for stepping stones. The high wall was only a steep grade at this place. She scrambled up and looked out across the western steppes.

There was no real difference between west and east, except for a slightly rougher terrain, and she was far less familiar with the west. She always knew that when she decided to leave the valley she would go west. She turned around, crossed the stream, then hiked the long valley back to the cave.

It was nearly dark when she arrived, and Baby had not returned yet. The fire was out, and the cave was cold and lonely. It seemed emptier now than it had when she first made it her home. She lit a fire, boiled some water and made tea, but didn't feel like cooking. She took a piece of dried meat and some raisined cherries and sat on her bed. It had been a long time since she was alone in her cave. She went to the place where her old carrying basket stood and rummaged around in the bottom until she found Durc's carrying cloak. Bunching it up, she crammed it to her stomach and watched the fire. When she lay down, she wrapped it around her.

Her sleep was disturbed by dreams. She dreamed of Durc and Ura, grown up and mated. She dreamed of Whinney, in a different place with a bay colt. She woke once in a sweat of fright. Not until she was fully awake did she understand that she had had her recurring nightmare of rumbling earth and terror. Why did she have that dream?

She got up and stirred the fire, then warmed her tea and sipped it. Baby still wasn't back. She picked up Durc's cloak, and recalled again Oda's story about the man of the Others who had forced her. Oda said he looked like me. A man like me, how would one look?

Ayla tried to visualize a man like her. She tried to recall her features as she had seen them reflected in the pool, but all she could remember was her hair framing her face. She wore it long then, not tied up in many braids to keep it out of the way. It was yellow, like Whinney's coat, but a richer, more golden colour.

But every time she thought of a man's face, she saw Broud,

with a gloating sneer. She could not imagine the face of a man of the Others. Her eyes grew tired and she lay down again. She dreamed of Whinney and a bay stallion. And then of a man. His features were vague, in a shadow. Only one thing was clear. He had yellow hair.

15

"You're doing fine, Jondalar! We'll make a river man out of you yet!" Carlono said. "In the big boats, it doesn't matter so much if you miss a stroke. The worst you can do is throw off the rhythm since you are not the only rower. In small boats, like this, control is important. To miss a stroke can be dangerous, or fatal. Always be aware of the river – never forget how unpredictable she can be. She's deep here, so she looks calm. But you only have to dip your paddle in to feel the power in her current. It's a hard current to fight – you have to work with it."

Carlono kept up the running commentary as he and Jondalar manoeuvred the small two-man dugout near the Ramudoi dock. Jondalar was only half listening, concentrating instead on handling the paddle properly so the boat he was guiding would go where he wanted it to, but he was understanding at the level of his muscles the meaning of the words.

"You may think it's easier to go downstream because you are not fighting her current, but that's the problem. When you are working against the flow, you have to keep your mind on the boat and the river all the time. You know if you let up you'll lose all you've gained. And you can see anything coming soon enough to avoid it.

"Going with her, it's too easy to slack up, let your mind wander and let the river take you. There are rocks midstream whose roots are deeper than the river. The current can throw you at them before you know it, or some water-soaked log lying low in the water will hit you. 'Never turn your back on the Mother.' That's the one rule never to forget. She's full of surprises. Just when you think you know what to expect and take her for granted, she'll do the unexpected."

307

The older man sat back and pulled his oar out of the water. He scrutinized Jondalar thoughtfully, noting his concentration. His blond hair was pulled back and tied with a thong at the back of his neck, a good precaution. He had adopted the clothing of the Ramudoi, which had been adapted from that of the Shamudoi to suit life near the river.

"Why don't you head back to the dock and let me out, Jondalar? I think it's time you tried it alone. There's a difference when it's just you and the river."

"Do you think I'm ready?"

"For one not born to it, you've learned fast."

Jondalar had been anxious to test himself on the river alone. Ramudoi boys usually had their own dugouts before they were men. He had long since proved himself among the Zelandonii. When he was not much older than Darvo, and hadn't even learned his trade or reached his full growth, he had killed his first deer. Now, he could throw a spear harder and farther than most men, but, though he could hunt the plains, he did not quite feel an equal here. No river man could call himself a man until he had harpooned one of the great sturgeon, and no Shamudoi of the land, until he had hunted his own chamois in the mountains.

He had decided he would not mate Serenio until he had proved to himself that he could be both a Shamudoi and a Ramudoi. Dolando had tried to convince him that it wasn't necessary for him to do either before mating; no one had any doubts. If anyone had needed proof, the rhino hunt had been sufficient. Jondalar had learned that none of the others had ever hunted a rhino before. The plains were not their usual hunting ground.

Jondalar didn't try to rationalize why he felt he had to be better than everyone else, though he had never before felt obliged to outdo other men in hunting skills. His strong interest, and the only skill in which he ever wanted to excel, was flint knapping. And his feeling wasn't competitive. He derived personal satisfaction from perfecting his techniques. The Shamud spoke later to Dolando privately and told him the tall Zelandonii needed to work out his own acceptance.

Serenio and he had lived together so long that he felt he should formalize his tie. She was almost his mate. Most people thought of them in those terms. He treated her with consideration and affection, and to Darvo he was the man of the hearth. But after the evening when Tholie and Shamio were burned, one thing or another always seemed to interfere, and the mood was never quite right. It was easy to settle into the same routine with her. Did it really matter, he asked himself?

Serenio didn't push – she still made no demands on him – and maintained her defensive distance. But recently, he had surprised her staring at him with a haunting look that came from the depths of her soul. He was the one who always felt disconcerted and turned away first. He decided to set himself the task of proving he could be a full Sharamudoi man, and he began letting his intentions be known. It was taken by some to be an announcement of Promise, though no Promise Feast was held.

"Don't go too far this time," Carlono said, getting out of the small vessel. "Give yourself a chance to get accustomed to handling it alone."

"I'll take the harpoon, though. It wouldn't hurt to get used to throwing it while I'm at it," Jondalar said, reaching for the weapon that was on the dock. He placed the long shaft in the bottom of the canoe beneath the seats, coiled the rope beside it, and put the barbed bone point in the holder attached to the side and fastened it down. The working end of the harpoon, with its sharp tip and backward-facing barbs, was not an implement to be left loose in the boat. In case of accident, it was just as difficult to pull out of a human as out of a fish – not to mention the difficulty of shaping the bone with stone tools. Dugouts that capsized seldom sank, but loose gear did.

Jondalar settled himself on the back seat while Carlono held the boat. When the harpoon was secured, he picked up the double-sided paddle and pushed off. Without the ballast of another person sitting in front, the small craft rode higher in the water. It was harder to handle. But after some initial adjustment to the change in buoyancy, he skimmed swiftly downstream with the current, using the paddle like a rudder off one side near the stern. Then he decided to paddle back upstream. It would be easier to fight the current while he was fresh and let it carry him back later.

He had slid farther downstream than he realized. When he

finally saw the dock ahead, he almost turned into it, then changed his mind and paddled by. He was determined to master all the skills he'd set for himself to learn, and they were many, but no one, least of all himself, could accuse him of stalling to put off the commitment he had promised to make. He smiled at the waving Carlono, but he didn't let up.

Upstream the river widened and the force of the current lessened, making paddling easier. He saw a shoreline on the opposite side of the river and made for it. It was a small secluded beach, overhung with willow. He pulled in close, skimming the shoals easily in the lightweight boat, relaxing a little by letting the craft glide backward while he steered with the paddle. He was watching the water in a desultory way when suddenly his attention focused on a large silent shape beneath the surface.

It was early for sturgeon. They usually swam upstream in early summer, but it had been a warm and early spring with heavy flooding. He looked closer and saw more of the huge fish gliding silently by. They were migrating! Here was his chance. He could bring in the first sturgeon of the season!

He shipped the paddle and reached for the sections of the harpoon to assemble it. With no guidance, the small boat slewed around, scudding with the current but slightly broadside to it. By the time Jondalar attached the rope to the bow, the boat was at an angle to the current, but it was steady, and he was eager. He watched for the next fish. He wasn't disappointed. A huge dark form was undulating towards him – now he knew where the "Haduma" fish had come from, but many more that size were here.

He knew from fishing with the Ramudoi that the water altered the true position of the fish. It wasn't where it seemed to be – the Mother's way to hide Her Creatures until Her secret was revealed. As the fish neared, he adjusted his aim to compensate for the refraction of the water. He leaned over the side, waited, then hurled the harpoon off the bow.

And with equal force, the small boat shot in the opposite direction along its skewed course, out towards the middle of the river. But his aim had been true. The point of his harpoon was deeply embedded in the giant sturgeon. The fish was far from disabled though. It headed for midchannel, for deeper water, moving upstream. The rope uncoiled rapidly, and, with a jerk, the slack ran out.

The boat was yanked around, nearly pitching Jondalar overboard. As he grabbed for the side, the paddle bounced up, teetered, and fell into the river. He let go to reach for it, leaning far over. The boat tipped. He clutched for the side. At that moment, the sturgeon found the current and ploughed upstream, miraculously righting the boat and knocking him back into it. He sat up, rubbing a bruise on his shin, as the small craft was towed upstream faster than he'd ever gone before.

He grabbed for the side and moved forward, round-eyed with fear and wonder, as he watched the riverbanks speeding past. He reached for the line pulled taut into the water, then jerked, thinking that might dislodge the harpoon. Instead the bow dipped so low that the boat shipped water. The sturgeon dodged, careening the small canoe back and forth. Jondalar held on to the rope, lurching from side to side.

He didn't notice when he passed the boat-building clearing, and he didn't see the people on the beach staring agape as the boat sped upstream in the wake of the huge fish, with Jondalar hanging over the side, both hands on the rope, struggling to pull out the harpoon.

"Do you see that?" Thonolan asked. "That brother of mine has a runaway fish! I think I've seen everything now." His grin turned to guffaws. "Did you see him hanging on to that rope, trying to make that fish let go?" He slapped his thigh, brimming over with laughter. "He didn't catch a fish, the fish caught him!"

"Thonolan, it's not funny," Markeno said, having difficulty keeping a straight face. "Your brother is in trouble."

"I know. I know. But did you see him? Hauled upriver by a fish? Tell me that's not funny!"

Thonolan laughed again, but he helped Markeno and Barono lift a boat into the water. Dolando and Carolio climbed in as well. They pushed off and began paddling upstream as fast as they could. Jondalar was in trouble; he could be in real danger.

The harpoon was draining the sturgeon's life away, the drag of the boat and the man weakening the fish. The headlong ride was slowing. It only gave Jondalar time to think – he still had no control over where he was going. He was far upriver; he didn't think he'd been as far since that first boat ride with snow and howling winds. It suddenly occurred to him to cut the rope. There was no point in being hauled any further upstream.

He let go of the side and reached for his knife. But as he pulled the antler-handled stone blade from the sheath, the sturgeon, in one last mortal struggle, tried to rid itself of the painful point. It thrashed and struggled with such force, the bow dipped under every time the fish dived. Overturned, the wooden canoe would still float, but upright and filled with water it would drop to the bottom. He tried to cut the rope as the boat bobbed and dipped and jerked from side to side. He didn't see the water-swelled log, cruising towards him low in the water with the speed of the current, until it bumped into the canoe, knocking the knife from Jondalar's hand.

He recovered quickly and tried to pull up on the rope to cause a little slack so the canoe wouldn't dip so dangerously. In a last desperate effort to free itself, the sturgeon lunged towards the river's edge and finally succeeded in tearing the harpoon out of its flesh. It was too late. The last of its life surged out the gaping rip in its side. The huge marine creature plunged down to the river bottom, then rose to the top and, belly up, hung on the surface of the river with only a twitch giving testimony to the prodigious struggle the primeval fish had waged.

The river, in its long and sinuous course, made a slight curve at the place where the fish chose to die, creating a whirl of conflict in the current speeding around the bend, and the last lunge of the sturgeon carried it to an eddying backwater near the shore. The boat, trailing a slack rope, bobbed and rocked, bumping into the log and the fish that shared its resting place in the undecided trough between backwater and tide.

In the lull, Jondalar had time to realize he was lucky he hadn't cut the rope. With no paddle, he couldn't control the boat if it started downstream. The shore was near: a narrow rocky beach clipped off as it rounded the bend to a steep bank, with trees crowding so close to the edge that naked roots burst through to claw at the air for support. Maybe he could find something that would serve as a paddle there. He took a deep breath to prepare for the plunge into the cold river, then slipped over the side.

It was deeper than he expected; he went in over his head. The boat, moved by the disturbance, found its way into the river current; the fish was moved closer to shore. Jondalar started to swim after the boat, grabbing for the rope, but the light canoe, barely skimming the surface, spun around and danced away more quickly than he could follow.

The icy water was numbing. He turned towards shore. The sturgeon was bumping against the bank. He headed for it, grabbed it by its open mouth, and hauled it along after him. There was no point in losing the fish now. He dragged it part way up the beach, but it was heavy. He hoped it would stay. Don't need to find a paddle, now, he thought, with no boat, but maybe I can find some wood to make a fire. He was soaking wet and cold.

He reached for his knife and found an empty sheath. He had forgotten that he had lost it, and he didn't have another. He used to keep an extra blade in the pouch he carried at his waist, but that was when he wore Zelandonii attire. He'd given up the pouch when he began wearing Ramudoi clothing. Maybe he could find materials for a platform and fire drill to make the fire. But, without a knife you can't cut wood, Jondalar, he said to himself, or shave tinder or kindling. He shivered. At least I can gather some wood.

He looked around him, and heard a scurrying in the bushes. The ground was covered with damp rotting wood, leaves, and moss. Not a dry stick anywhere. You can get dry "small wood", he thought, looking for the dead dry lower branches. But he was not in a coniferous forest like the ones near his home. The climate of this region was less severe; it was not influenced as much by the glacial ice in the north. It was cool – it could be quite cold – but damp. It was a temperate-climate forest, not boreal. The trees were the kind the boats were made of: hardwood.

Around him was a forest of oak and beech, some hornbeam and willow; trees with thick brown crusty trunks and more slender ones with grey smooth skin, but no dry "small wood". It was spring, and even the twigs were filled with sap and budding. He'd learned something about cutting down one of those hardwood trees. It wasn't easy, even with a good stone axe. He shivered again. His teeth were chattering. He rubbed his palms together, beat his arms, jogged in place – trying to warm up. He heard more scuffing in the brush and thought he must be disturbing some animal.

The seriousness of his situation struck him. Surely they would miss him and come searching for him. Thonolan would notice he was gone, or would he? Their paths crossed less and less often, particularly as he became more involved with the Ramudoi way of life and his brother was becoming more Shamudoi. He didn't even know where his brother was that day, perhaps hunting chamois.

Well, then, Carlono. Wouldn't he come looking? He watched me going upstream in the boat. Then Jondalar got a chill of a different sort. The boat! It got away. If they find an empty boat, they'll think you've drowned, he thought. Why should they come looking for you if they think you've drowned? The tall man moved around again, jumping, beating his arms, running in place, but he couldn't stop shivering, and he was getting tired. The cold was affecting his thinking, but he couldn't keep jumping around.

Out of breath, he slumped down and huddled into a ball, trying to conserve body heat, but his teeth chattered and his body shook. He heard shuffling again, closer, but he didn't bother to investigate. Then something moved into his view: two feet – two, bare, dirty, human feet.

He looked up with a start and was almost shocked out of shivering. Standing in front of him, within arm's reach, was a child, with two large brown eyes gazing at him from under the shadow of overhanging brow ridges. A flathead! Jondalar thought. A young flathead.

He was agog with wonder, and half expected the young animal to dart back into the bush now that he was seen. The youngster didn't move. He stood there and, after a few moments of mutual staring, made beckoning motions. Or at least Jondalar had the feeling they were beckoning motions, far-fetched as it seemed. The flathead made the motion again, taking a tentative step back.

What could he want? Does he want me to go with him? When the youngster made the motion again, Jondalar took a step after him, sure the creature would run away. But the child only backed away a step and motioned again. Jondalar began to follow, slowly at first, then at a faster pace, still shivering, but intrigued.

In a few moments, the youngster moved aside a screen of brush that revealed a glade. A small, nearly smokeless fire burned in the middle of it. A female looked up, startled, then backed away in fright as Jondalar headed for the flickering warmth. He hunkered down in front of it, gratefully. He was dimly aware that the young flathead and the female were waving their hands and making guttural sounds. He had an impression they were communicating, but he was much more concerned with getting warm, and wished he had a fur or a cloak.

He didn't pay attention when the woman disappeared behind him, and was caught by surprise when he felt a fur drop over his shoulders. He saw a bare glimpse of dark brown eyes before she bowed her head and scrambled away, but he sensed her fear of him.

Even wet, the soft chamois-leather clothing he wore maintained some of its heat-keeping quality, and with the fire and the fur, Jondalar finally warmed enough to stop shaking. Only then did he realize where he was. Great Mother! This is a flathead camp. He had been holding his hands out to the warming blaze, but when the implications of the fire struck him, he jerked them back as though they were burned.

Fire! They use fire? He reached a hesitant hand for the flame again as though he couldn't believe his eyes and had to use other senses to confirm it. Then he noticed the fur draped over him. He felt an end, rubbing it between his thumb and forefinger. Wolf, he decided, and well-cured. It's soft; the inner side is amazingly soft. I doubt the Sharamudoi could do much better. The fur didn't seem to be cut to any shape. It was just one whole hide of a large wolf.

The heat finally penetrated deep enough for him to stand up and turn his back to the fire. He saw the young male watching him. He wasn't sure how he knew the young one was a male. With the skin wrapped around him and tied with a long thong, it wasn't obvious. Though wary, his direct look was not fearful like the female's had been. Jondalar remembered then that the Losadunai had said flathead females wouldn't fight. They just gave in, no sport at all. Why would anyone want a flathead female?

As he continued to look at the male flathead, Jondalar decided he wasn't so young, more adolescent than child. The short stature had been deceiving, but his muscle development showed strength, and, looking closer, he saw the downy fuzz of a beginning beard.

The young male grunted and the female quickly scurried to a small woodpile and brought a few pieces to the fire. Jondalar had not seen a flathead female this close before. He turned his head toward her. She was older, perhaps the young one's dam, he thought. She seemed uncomfortable, didn't want to be looked at. She backed away with her head lowered and, when she reached the edge of the small clearing, she kept moving away from his sight. She didn't make it obvious, but before he realized it, his head was twisted around nearly backward. He looked away for an instant, and when he looked back, she had hidden herself so effectively that he couldn't see her at first. If he hadn't known she was there, he wouldn't have seen her at all.

She's frightened. I'm surprised she didn't run away instead of bringing wood as he told her.

Told her! How could he tell her? Flatheads don't talk – he couldn't tell her to bring wood. The chill must have made me light-headed. I can't be thinking clearly.

For all his denials, Jondalar couldn't get over the feeling that the young male had indeed told the female to bring wood. Some way, he had communicated. He turned his attention back to the male and received a distinct impression of hostility. He didn't know what was different, but he knew the young one had not liked his observation of the female. He was convinced he would be in deep trouble if he made one move towards her. It was not wise to pay too much attention to flathead females, he decided, not when there was a male around, of any age.

The tension slacked off when Jondalar made no overt moves and ceased looking at the female. By standing face to face with the flathead, he felt they were each taking the other's measure and, more disturbing, that he was standing man to man. Yet, this man looked like none other he knew. In all his travels, the people he had met were recognizably human. They spoke different languages, had different customs, lived in different shelters – but they were human.

This one was different, but was he human or was he animal? He was much shorter, and stockier, but those bare feet were no different from Jondalar's. He was slightly bowlegged, but he walked as straight and tall as any man. He had a little more hair than average, especially around the arms and shoulders, Jondalar thought, but he wouldn't call it a pelt. He knew some men who were as hairy. The flathead was barrel-chested, already brawny, not someone to tangle with, as young as he was. But even the full-grown males he'd seen, for all their tremendous musculature, were still built like men. The difference seemed to be in the head, and in the face. His brows are heavy, his forehead doesn't come up as high, slopes back more, but his head is big. Short neck, no chin, just a jaw that juts out some, and a large high-bridged nose. It's a human face, not like anyone I know, but it looks human. And they use fire.

But they don't talk, and all humans talk. I wonder . . . were they communicating? Great Doni! He even communicated with me! How did he know I needed fire? And why would a flathead help a man? Jondalar was baffled, but the young flathead had probably saved his life.

The young male seemed to come to some decision. He abruptly made the same motion with which he had beckoned Jondalar to the fire, then walked out of the glade back the way they had come. He seemed to expect the man to follow, and Jondalar did, glad of the wolf skin around his shoulders when he left the fire in his still-damp clothes. When they neared the river, the flathead ran forward, making sharp loud noises and waving his arms. A small animal scuttled off, but some of the sturgeon had been eaten. It was evident that, as large as it was, unguarded, the fish wouldn't last long.

The young male's anger at the scavenging animal gave Jondalar a sudden insight. Could the fish be a possible reason for the flathead to give him aid? Did he want some fish?

The flathead reached into a fold of the skin wrapped around him, took out a flake of flint with a sharp edge, and made a pass at the sturgeon as though to cut it. Then he made motions indicating some for him and some for the tall man, then waited. It was so clear. There was no doubt in Jondalar's mind that the youngster wanted a share of the fish. A flood of questions filled him.

Where did the flathead get the tool? He wanted a closer look, but he knew it didn't have the refinement of one of his – it had been made on a thicker flake, not a thin blade – but it was a perfectly serviceable sharp knife. It had been made by someone, crafted with purposeful design. But more than the tool, there were questions that disturbed him. The youngster had not talked, but he had most certainly communicated. Jondalar wondered if he could have made his wishes known as directly and easily.

The flathead was waiting expectantly, and Jondalar nodded, not sure if the motion would be understood. But his meaning had been communicated in more than gesture. Without hesitation, the young male set to work on the fish.

As the Zelandonii watched, turmoil erupted that shook deeply held convictions. His structure of beliefs – fed to him with his mother's milk and bred into his bones – was teetering. Flatheads were animals. Everyone said flatheads were animals. What was an animal? An animal might scurry in to take a bit of that fish. A more intelligent animal might consider a man dangerous and wait until he left, or died. An animal would not perceive that a man suffering from exposure needed warmth; would not have a fire and lead him to it; would not *ask* for a share of his food. That was human behaviour; human behaviour at its most humane.

Jondalar wouldn't have cared if he had taken the whole fish, but he was curious. How much would the flathead take? It needed to be cut anyway, it was too heavy to move. Four men would have trouble lifting it.

Suddenly his heart raced. He looked up. Had he heard something?

"Jondalar! Jondalar!"

The flathead looked startled, but Jondalar was pushing through trees on the bank to get a clear view of the river.

"Here! Here I am, Thonolan!" His brother *had* come looking for him. He saw a boatload of people in the middle of the river and hailed them again. They saw him, waved back, and rowed towards him.

A straining grunt brought his attention back to the flathead. He saw, on the beach, that the sturgeon had been split in half lengthwise, from the backbone to the belly, and the young male had moved half the huge fish to a large leather hide spread out beside it. While the tall man watched, the young flathead gathered up the ends of the hide and slung the entire load on his back. Then, with the half of the head and tail sticking out the top of the huge sack, he disappeared into the woods.

"Wait!" Jondalar called, running after him. He caught up as they reached the glade. The female, with a large basket on her back, slid into the shadows as he approached. There was no evidence that the glade had been used, not even a trace of the fire. If he hadn't felt its heat, he would have doubted it had ever been there.

He took the wolf fur from his shoulders and held it out. At a grunt from the male, she took it, then both moved silently into the woods and were gone.

Jondalar felt chilled in his damp clothes as he walked back to the river. He reached it as the boat was pulling in, and he smiled as his brother climbed out. They threw their arms around each other in a great bear hug of brotherly affection.

"Thonolan! Am I happy to see you! I was afraid that when they found that empty boat I'd be given up for lost."

"Big Brother, how many rivers have we crossed together? Don't you think I know you can swim? Once we found the boat, we knew you were upriver and couldn't be much farther ahead."

"Who took half this fish?" Dolando asked.

"I gave it away."

"Gave it away! Who did you give it to?" Markeno asked.

"Who *could* you give it to?" Carolio added.

"To a flathead."

"A flathead?!" many voices echoed in response. "Why would you give half a fish that size to a flathead?" Dolando asked.

"He helped me, and he asked for it."

"What kind of nonsense is that? How could a flathead ask for anything?" Dolando said. He was angry, which surprised Jondalar. The leader of the Sharamudoi seldom showed his ire. "Where is he?"

"He's gone by now, into the woods. I was soaked, and shivering so badly that I thought I'd never warm up. Then this young flathead appeared and led me to his fire . . ."

"Fire? Since when do they use fire?" Thonolan asked.

"I've seen flatheads with fire," Barono said.

"I've seen them on this side of the river before, too . . . from a distance," Carolio remarked.

"I didn't know they were back. How many were there?" Dolando asked.

"Just the young one, and an older female. Maybe his dam," Jondalar replied.

"There's more, if they have their females with them." The stocky leader glanced around the woods. "Maybe we should get up a flathead hunting party and clean the vermin out."

There was ugly menace in Dolando's tone that made Jondalar look twice. He'd picked up shades of that feeling toward flatheads in the leader's comments before, but never with such venom.

Leadership among the Sharamudoi was a matter of competence and persuasion. Dolando was tacitly acknowledged leader not because he was the best in every way, but because he was competent, and he had the ability to attract people to him and handle problems when they arose. He did not command; he cajoled, coaxed, convinced, and compromised, and in general provided the oil that smoothed the inevitable friction of people living together. He was politically astute, effective, and his decisions were usually accepted, but no one was required to abide by them. Arguments could be vociferous.

He was confident enough to push his own judgment when he felt it was right, and to defer to someone with greater knowledge or experience on a particular subject if the need arose. He tended not to interfere in personal squabbles unless they got out of hand and someone called him in. Though generally dispassionate, his ire could be raised by cruelty, stupidity, or carelessness that threatened or caused harm to the Cave as a whole, or to someone unable to defend himself. And by flatheads. He hated them. To him, they were not just animals, they were dangerous, vicious animals that should be eliminated.

"I was freezing," Jondalar objected, "and that young flathead helped me. He brought me to his fire, and they gave me a fur to use. As far as I'm concerned, he could have had the whole fish, but he only took half. I'm not about to go out on any flathead-hunting party."

"They don't usually cause that much trouble," Barono said, "But if they're around, I'm glad to know it. They're smart. It's not a good idea to let a pack catch you by surprise . . ."

"They're murderous brutes . . ." Dolando said.

Barono ignored the interjection. "You're probably lucky it was a younger one and a female. The females don't fight."

Thonolan didn't like the direction the conversation was heading. "How are we going to get this splendid half-catch of my brother's home?" He remembered the ride the fish had given Jondalar, and a grin cracked his face. "After the fight he gave you, I'm surprised you let half of him get away."

The laughter spread to the others, with nervous relief.

"Does that mean he's half Ramudoi, now?" Markeno said.

"Maybe we can take him hunting and he'll get half a chamois," Thonolan said. "Then the other half can be Shamudoi."

"Which half will Serenio want?" Barono winked.

"Half of him is more than most," Carolio quipped, and her expression left no doubt that she was not referring to his height. In the close quarters of the Cave, his skill in the furs had not gone unnoticed. Jondalar flushed, but the ribald laughter brought a final release of tension, both from the concern over him and from Dolando's reaction to the flat-heads.

They brought out a net made of fibre which held up well when wet, spread it out beside the bleeding open half of the sturgeon, and, with some grunting and straining, moved the carcass onto the net and into the water, then tied it to the stern of the boat.

While the rest were struggling with the fish, Carolio turned to Jondalar and said, quietly, "Roshario's son was killed by flatheads. He was just a young man, not yet Promised, full of fun and daring, and Dolando's pride. No one knows how it happened, but Dolando had the whole Cave out hunting them. A few were killed – then they disappeared. He didn't much care for them in the first place, but since then . . ."

Jondalar nodded, understanding.

"How did that flathead haul his half of this fish away?"

Thonolan asked as they were getting into the boat.

"He picked it up and carried it," Jondalar said.

"He? He picked it up and carried it?"

"By himself. And he wasn't even full grown."

Thonolan approached the wooden structure shared by his brother, Serenio, and Darvo. It was constructed of planks which were leaned against a ridgepole that itself sloped to the ground. The dwelling resembled a tent made of wood, with the triangular front wall higher and wider than the rear one, making trapezoids of the sides. The planks were fastened together like the strakes on the sides of the boats, with the slightly thicker edge overlapping the thinner edge and sewn together.

These were snug, sturdy structures, tight enough so that only in the older ones could light be seen through the cracks of the dried and warped wood. With the sandstone overhang to protect them from the worst elements of the weather, the dwellings were not maintained or caulked the way the boats were. They were lighted inside primarily by the stone-lined fireplace, or by opening the front.

The younger man looked in to see if his brother was still sleeping.

"Come on in," Jondalar said, sniffing. He was sitting up on the fur-covered sleeping platform, with more furs piled around him and with a cup of something steaming in his hands.

"How's your cold?" Thonolan asked, sitting on the edge of the platform.

"Cold's worse, I'm better."

"No one thought about your wet clothes, and that wind was really blowing down the river gorge by the time we got back."

"I'm glad you found me."

"Well, I'm really glad you're feeling better." Thonolan seemed strangely at a loss for words. He fidgeted, got up and walked towards the opening, then walked back to his brother. "Is there anything I can get you?"

Jondalar shook his head and waited. Something was bothering his brother, and he was trying to get it out. He just needed time.

"Jondalar . . ." Thonolan started, then paused. "You've been living with Serenio and her son for a long time now." For a moment, Jondalar thought he was going to make some reference to the unformalized status of the relationship, but he was wrong. "How does it feel to be man of your hearth?"

"You're a mated man, a man of your hearth."

"I know, but does it make any difference to have a child of your hearth? Jetamio's been trying so hard to have a baby, and now . . . she lost another one, Jondalar."

"I'm sorry . . ."

"I don't care if she ever has a baby. I just don't want to lose her," Thonolan cried, his voice cracking. "I wish she'd stop trying."

"I don't think she has a choice. The Mother gives . . ."

"Then why won't the Mother let her keep one!" Thonolan shouted, brushing past Serenio as he ran out.

"He told you about Jetamio . . . ?" Serenio asked. Jondalar nodded. "She held this one longer, but it was harder on her when she lost it. I'm glad she's so happy with Thonolan. She deserves that much."

"Will she be all right?"

"It's not the first time a woman has lost a baby, Jondalar. Don't worry about her – she'll be fine. I see you found the tea. It's peppermint, borage, and lavender, in case you were trying to guess. Shamud said it would help your cold. How are you feeling? I just came to see if you were awake yet."

"I'm fine," he said. He smiled and tried to look healthy.

"Then I think I'll go back and sit with Jetamio."

When she left, he put the cup aside and lay down again. His nose was stuffed and his head ached. He couldn't exactly say what it was, but Serenio's answer disturbed him. He didn't want to think about it any more – it gave him another ache deep in the pit of his stomach. It must be this cold, he thought.

16

Spring ripened into summer, and the fruits of the earth with it. As they matured, the young woman gathered them. It was habit more than need. She could have spared herself the effort. She already had abundance; there was food left over from the preceding year. But Ayla had no use for leisure time. She had no way to fill it.

Even with the additional activity of winter hunting, she hadn't been able to keep herself busy enough, though she had cured the hide of nearly every animal they killed, sometimes making furs, other times dehairing to make leather. She had continued making baskets, mats, and carved bowls, and had accumulated enough tools, implements, and cave furnishings to satisfy a clan. She had looked forward to the summer's food-gathering activities.

She had also looked forward to summer hunting and discovered that the method she had developed with Baby – with some adaptation to accommodate her lack of a horse – was still effective. The lion's increasing skill made up the difference. If she had wished, she could have refrained from hunting. She not only had dried meat left over, but when Baby hunted alone successfully – which was more often the case than not – she didn't hesitate to take a share of his kill. There was a unique relationship between the woman and the lion. She was mother, and therefore dominant; she was hunting partner, and therefore equal; and he was all she had to love.

Watching the wild lions, Ayla made some astute observations about their hunting habits, which Baby confirmed. Cave lions were nocturnal stalkers during the warm season, diurnal during the winter. Although he shed in spring, Baby still had a thick coat, and during the heat of a summer's day, it was too hot to hunt. The energy expended during the chase made him too warm. Baby wanted nothing more than to sleep, preferably in the cool dark recesses of the cave.

She made one decision the morning after Whinney left, when she awoke and found Baby sleeping beside her with the carcass of a dappled fawn – the young of a giant deer. She would leave, there was no question in her mind about that, but not that summer. The young lion still needed her; he was too young to be left alone. No wild pride would accept him; the pride male would kill him. Until he was old enough to mate and start his own pride, he needed the security of her cave as much as she did.

Though she wouldn't admit it, she had a deeper reason. She didn't want to leave until she was sure Whinney would not return. She missed the horse desperately. Whinney had been with her from the beginning, and Ayla loved her.

"Come on, you lazy thing," Ayla said. "Let's go for a walk and see if we can find anything to hunt. You didn't go out last night." She prodded the lion, then went out of the cave, signalling to him to follow. He lifted his head, made a huge yawn that exposed his sharp teeth, then got up and padded after her, reluctantly. Baby was no more hungry than she was, and would much rather have slept.

She had collected medicinal plants the day before, a task she enjoyed – and one filled with pleasant associations. During her young years with the Clan, gathering medicines for Iza had given her a chance to get away from the ever watchful eyes that were so quick to disapprove of improper actions. It gave her a little breathing space to follow her natural inclinations. Later, she collected the plants for the joy of learning the medicine woman's skills, and the knowledge was now part of her nature.

To her, the medicinal properties were so closely associated with each plant that she distinguished them as much by use as by appearance. The bunches of agrimony hanging head downward inside the warm dark cave were an infusion of the dried flowers and leaves useful for bruises and injuries to internal organs, as much as they were tall slender perennials with toothed leaves and tiny yellow flowers growing on tapering spikes.

Coltsfoot leaves, which resembled their name, spread out on woven drying racks, were asthma relief when smoke from the burning dried leaves was breathed, and a cough remedy with other ingredients in tea, and a pleasant seasoning for food. Bone mending and wound healing came to mind when she saw the large downy comfrey leaves beside the roots drying outside in the sun, and the colourful marigolds were healing for open wounds, ulcers, and skin sores. Chamomile was an aid to digestion and a mild wash for wounds, and the wild rose petals floating in a bowl of water in the sun were a fragrant astringent skin lotion.

She had gathered them to replace with fresh material herbs that had not been used. Though she had very little need for the full pharmacopoeia she maintained, she enjoyed it, and it kept her skills sharp. But with leaves, flowers, roots, and barks in various stages of preparation spread out everywhere, there was no point in gathering more – there was no room for them. She had nothing to do just then and she was bored.

She strolled down to the beach, then around the jutting wall and along the brush that bordered the stream, with the huge cave lion padding beside her. As he walked, he grunted the *hnga, hnga* sound that Ayla had learned was his normal speaking voice. Other lions made similar sounds, but each was distinctive, and she could recognize Baby's voice from a long way off, just as she could identify his roar. It started deep in his chest with a series of grunts, then rose to a sonorous thunder at its full bass range that made her ears ring if she was too close.

When she came to a boulder that was a usual resting place, she stopped – not really interested in hunting, but not sure what she wanted to do. Baby pushed against her, looking for attention. She scratched around his ears and deep in his mane. His coat was a shade darker than it had been in winter, though still beige, but his mane had grown in rufous, a deep rusty tan not far from the colour of red ochre. He lifted his head so she could get under his chin, making a low rumbling growl of contentment. She reached to scratch the other side, then looked at him with new awareness. The level of his back reached just below her shoulder. He was nearly the height of Whinney but much more massive. She hadn't realized he'd grown so big.

The cave lion that roamed the steppes of that cold land broached by glaciers lived in an environment ideal for the style of hunting to which he was best suited. It was a continent of grassland crowded with a great abundance and variety of prey. Many of the animals were huge – bison and cattle half as large again as their later counterparts; giant deer with eleven-foot racks; woolly mammoth and woolly rhinoceros. Conditions were favourable for at least one species of carnivore to develop to a size capable of hunting such large animals. The cave lion filled that niche, and filled it admirably. The lions of later generations were half the size, puny by comparison; the cave lion was the largest feline that ever lived.

Baby was a superior example of that supreme predator – huge, powerful, his coat sleek with youthful health and vigour – and totally complaisant under the delightful scratching of the young woman. She would have been defenceless had he chosen to attack, yet she didn't think of him as dangerous; he was no more menacing than an overgrown kitten – and that was her defence.

Her control over him was unconscious, and he accepted it on those terms. Lifting and moving his head aside to show her where, Baby submitted to the sensuous ecstasy of her scratching, and she was enjoying it because he did. She stepped up on the boulder to reach over to his other side and was leaning over his back when another thought occurred to her. She didn't even stop to consider it; she simply put her leg over and straddled his back as she had done so often with Whinney.

It was unexpected, but the arms around his neck were familiar and her weight was negligible. For a while, neither moved. As they hunted together, Ayla had adapted her signal from casting a stone with a sling to an arm motion and her word for "go". The moment she thought of it, without hesitation, she made the signal and shouted the word.

Feeling his muscles bunch beneath her, she grasped his mane as he sprang ahead. With the sinewy grace of his kind, he sped down the valley with the woman on his back. She squinted at the wind in her face. Tendrils of hair that had escaped her braids streamed behind her. She had no control. She did not direct Baby as she had Whinney – she went where he took her, and went gladly, feeling an exhilaration beyond anything she had ever known.

The quick burst of speed was short lived, as was his way even in the attack. He slowed down, made a wide circle, and loped back to the cave. With the woman still on his back, he climbed the steep path and stopped at her place in the cave. She slid off and hugged him, knowing no other way to express the deep unnamable emotions she felt. When she let go, he flicked his tail, then headed for the back of the cave. He found his favourite spot, stretched out, and very quickly went to sleep.

She watched him, smiling. You've given me my ride and now you're through for the day, is that it? Baby, after that, you can sleep as long as you want.

Towards the end of summer, Baby's hunting absences became longer. The first time he was gone for more than a day, Ayla was beside herself with worry, and so anxious that she didn't sleep the second night. She was as tired and bedraggled as he looked when he finally appeared the next morning. He brought no kill with him, and when she gave him dried meat from her stored supply, he tore into it, though usually he toyed with the brittle strips. As tired as she was, she went out with her sling and brought back two hares. He awoke from his exhausted sleep, ran to the cave entrance to greet her, and took one hare to the rear of the cave. She carried the other to the back, then went to her own sleeping place.

The time he was gone three days, she didn't worry as much – but as the empty days passed, her heart grew heavier. He returned with gashes and scratches, and she knew he had skirmished with other lions. She suspected he was mature enough to be aware of females. Unlike horses, lionesses had no special season; they could come into heat any time of the year.

The young cave lion's longer absences became still more frequent as fall progressed, and when he did return it was usually to sleep. Ayla was sure he was sleeping elsewhere as well, but didn't feel as secure there as he did in her cave. She never knew when to expect him, or from which direction. He would just appear, either padding up the narrow path from the beach or, more dramatically, in a sudden leap down from the steppes above her cave to the ledge in front.

She was always happy to see him, and his greetings were always affectionate – sometimes a little too affectionate. After he leaped up to put heavy forepaws on her shoulders and knocked her down, she was quick to signal "stop" if he seemed a little too enthusiastically delighted to see her.

Usually, he'd stay a few days; sometimes they would hunt together, and he still brought a kill back to the cave now and then. Then he'd get restless again. She was sure Baby was hunting for himself and defending his kills against the hyenas, or wolves, or carrion birds that would try to steal them. She learned that once he started pacing, she could expect him to leave shortly afterwards. The cave felt so empty when the lion was gone that she began to dread the coming of winter. She was afraid it was going to be a lonely one.

The fall was unusual – warm and dry. Leaves turned yellow, then brown, skipping over the bright hues that a kiss of frost could bring. They clung to the trees in drab withered clusters that rattled in the wind long beyond the time they would usually have littered the ground. The peculiar weather was unsettling – autumn should be wet and cool, full of blustery winds and sudden showers. Ayla couldn't avoid a sense of dread, as though summer would hold off the seasonal change until overcome by the sudden onslaught of winter.

Every morning she went outside, expecting some drastic change, and was almost disappointed to see a warm sun rising in a remarkably clear sky. Evenings she spent outside on the ledge, watching the sun drop below the edge of the earth with only a haze of dust glowing dull red instead of a glorious display of colour on water-laden clouds. When the stars winked on, they filled the darkness so that the sky looked shattered and cracked with their profusion.

She had been staying close to the valley for days, and when yet another day dawned warm and clear, it seemed foolish to have wasted the beautiful weather when she could have been out enjoying it. Winter would come soon enough to keep her confined to a lonely cave.

Too bad Baby's not here, she thought. It would be a good day to go hunting. Maybe I can go hunting myself. She hefted a spear. No. Without Baby or Whinney, I'll have to find a new way to hunt. I'll just take my sling. I wonder if I should take a fur? It's so warm, I'd just sweat in it. I could carry it, maybe take the gathering basket. But I don't need anything – I've got more than enough. All I want is a nice long walk. I don't need to carry a basket for that, and I won't need a fur either. A brisk walk will keep me warm enough.

Ayla started down the steep trail feeling strangely unencumbered. She had no burdens to carry, no animals to be concerned for, a well-stocked cave. She had nothing to worry about but herself, but she wished she had. The utter lack of responsibility gave her mixed feelings: an unaccustomed sense of freedom and an unaccountable frustration.

She reached the meadow and climbed the easy grade to the eastern steppes, then set herself a fast pace. She had no particular destination in mind and walked wherever her whim took her. The dryness of the season was accentuated on the steppes. The grass was so withered and parched that, when she held a brittle blade in her hand and crumpled it, it shattered to dust. The wind scattered it from her open palm.

The ground beneath her feet was cemented into rock hardness and cracked in a chequered pattern. She had to watch her footing to avoid stumbling on clods or twisting an ankle in a hole or furrow. She had never seen it so arid. The atmosphere seemed to suck the moisture from her breath. She had taken only a small waterbag with her, expecting to fill it at known streams and watering places, but several of them were dry. Her bag was more than half empty before the morning was half gone.

When she came to a stream that she was sure would have water and found only mud, she decided to turn back. Hoping to fill her bag, she walked along the streambed for a way and came to a muddy puddle, all that remained of a deep watering hole. When she bent down to taste, to see if it was drinkable, she noticed fresh hoofprints. A herd of horses had obviously been there not long before. Something about one of the prints made her look closer. She was an experienced tracker, and though she hadn't thought of it, she had seen Whinney's hoofprints too many times not to know the minor variations in outline and pressure that made her prints unique. When she looked, she was certain Whinney had been there, and not long before; she must be close by. Ayla's heart beat faster.

It wasn't hard to find the trail. The broken edge of a crack where a hoof had slipped in as the horses left the mud, loose dust newly settled, bent grass – all pointed the way the horses had gone. Ayla followed with breathless excitement; even the still air seemed to be holding its breath with anticipation. It had been so long – would Whinney remember her? Just to know she was alive would be enough.

The herd was farther away than she thought they would be. Something had given chase, sending them galloping across the plains. She heard snarls and commotion before she came upon the feeding wolf pack, and she should have backed off. But she had to go closer to make sure the fallen animal was not Whinney. The sight of a deep brown coat relieved her, but it was the same uncommon colour as the stallion, and she felt sure the horse was from the same herd.

As she continued to track, she thought about horses in the wild and how vulnerable they were to attack. Whinney was young and strong, but anything could happen. She wanted to bring the young mare back with her.

It was almost noon before she finally sighted the horses. They were still nervous from the chase, and Ayla was upwind. As soon as they caught her scent, they moved. The young woman had to circle wide to come upon them downwind. As soon as she was close enough to see individual horses, she identified Whinney, and her heart pounded. She swallowed hard a few times, trying to hold back tears that insisted on coming.

She looks healthy, Ayla thought. Fat. No, she's not fat. I think she's pregnant! Oh, Whinney, how wonderful. Ayla was so pleased that she could hardly contain it. Then she couldn't stand it; she had to see if the horse would remember her. She whistled.

Whinney's head came up instantly and looked in Ayla's direction. The woman whistled again, and the horse started towards her. Ayla couldn't wait; she ran to meet the hay-coloured horse. Suddenly a beige mare galloped between them and, nipping at Whinney's hocks, herded her away. Then rounding up the rest of the herd, the lead mare drove them all away from the unfamiliar and possibly dangerous woman.

Ayla was heartbroken. She couldn't keep chasing after the herd. She was already much farther away from the valley than she had planned to come, and they could move so much faster than she. As it was, if she was going to make it back before dark, she'd have to hurry. She whistled one more time, loud and long, but she knew it was too late. She turned away, disheartened, and, pulling her leather wrap higher up around her shoulders, she bent her head into the cold wind.

She was so dejected that she wasn't paying attention to anything except her sorrow and disappointment. A snarl of warning brought her up short. She had stumbled into the wolf pack, muzzle deep in blood, gorging on the deep brown horse.

I'd better watch where I'm going, she thought, backing off. It's my fault. If I hadn't been so impatient, maybe that mare wouldn't have driven the herd away from me. She glanced again at the fallen animal as she circled around. That is a dark colour for a horse. It looks as brown as the stallion of Whinney's herd. She took a closer look. A quality to the head, the colouring, the conformation, sent a shiver through her. It was the bay stallion! How could a stallion in his prime fall prey to wolves?

The left foreleg bent at an abnormal angle gave her the answer. Even a magnificent young stud can break a leg when racing over treacherous ground. A deep crack in the dry earth had given the wolves their taste of prime stallion. Ayla shook her head. It's too bad, she thought. He would have had many good years in him yet. As she turned away from the wolves, she finally noticed her own danger.

The sky that had been so clear in the morning was now a curdled mass of ominous clouds. The high pressure that had been holding off winter had yielded, and the cold front that had been waiting rushed in. Wind was flattening the dry grass and whipping bits of it around in the air. Temperature was falling fast. She could smell snow on its way, and she was a long distance from the cave. She looked around, took her bearings, and started off at a run. It was going to be a race to see if she could get back before the storm struck.

She didn't have a chance. She was more than half a day's brisk walk from the valley, and winter had been held back too long. By the time she reached the dry stream, big, wet snowflakes were falling. They became penetrating needles of ice as the wind picked up again, then turned to the dryer siftings of a full-blown blizzard. Drifts were building on the solid base of wet snow. Swirling winds, still fighting cross-currents of shifting air streams, buffeted her first from one direction and then another.

She knew her only hope was to keep going, but she wasn't sure if she was still going the right way. The shape of landmarks was obscured. She stopped, trying to get a sense of her location, and trying to control her rising panic. How stupid she had been to leave without her fur. She could have taken her tent in her carrying basket, then, at least, she'd have had shelter. Her ears were freezing, her feet were numb, her teeth were chattering. She was cold. She could hear the wind whistling.

She listened again. That wasn't wind, was it? There it was again. She cupped her hands around her mouth and whistled as loud as she could, and listened.

The high-pitched screaming whinny of a horse sounded closer. She whistled once more, and when the shape of the yellow horse loomed like a wraith out of the storm, Ayla ran to her with tears freezing her face.

"Whinney, Whinney, oh, Whinney." She cried the horse's name over and over again, wrapping her arms around the sturdy neck and burying her face in the shaggy winter coat. Then she climbed up on the horse's back and bent low over her neck for as much warmth as she could get.

The horse followed her own instincts and headed for the cave. It was the place she had been going. The unexpected death of the stallion had disrupted the herd. The lead mare was holding them together, knowing another stallion would eventually be found. She might have kept the yellow horse as well – if it hadn't been for the familiar whistle, and memories of the woman and security. For the mare not raised in a herd, the lead horse had less influence. When the storm broke, Whinney remembered a cave that was shelter from fierce winds and blinding snows and the affection of a woman.

Ayla was shivering so hard by the time they finally reached the cave that she could hardly start a fire. When she did, she didn't huddle near it. Instead, she grabbed up her sleeping furs, brought them to Whinney's side of the cave, and curled up next to the warm horse.

But she could hardly appreciate the return of her beloved friend for the next few days. She woke up with a fever and a deep hacking cough. She lived on hot medicinal teas, when she could remember to get up and make them. Whinney had saved her life, but the horse could do nothing to help her overcome pneumonia.

She was weak and delirious most of the time, but the moment of confrontation when Baby returned to the cave brought her out of it. He had leaped down from the steppes above, but was stopped as he entered by Whinney's ringing challenge. The scream of fright and defence pierced Ayla's stupor. She saw the horse with her ears laid back in anger and then pitching forward in fear, prancing nervously, and the cave lion poised to spring with bared teeth and a low growl in his throat. She leaped out of bed and ran between predator and prey.

"Stop it, Baby! It frightens Whinney. You should be glad she's back." Ayla turned then to the horse. "Whinney! It's only Baby. You don't have to be afraid of him. Both of you stop it now," she scolded. She believed there was no danger; both animals had been raised together in the cave, and both belonged.

The scents in the cave were familiar to both animals, particularly the woman's. Baby rushed to greet Ayla, rubbing against her, and Whinney came forward to nuzzle her share of attention. Then the horse nickered, not in fear or anger, but with a sound she had used for the baby lion in her care, and the cave lion recognized his nursemaid.

"I told you it was only Baby," she said to the horse, then was overcome with coughing.

Stirring up the fire, Ayla reached for the waterbag and discovered it was empty. Wrapping her sleeping fur around her, she went outside and scooped up a bowl of snow. She tried to control the deep spasms from her chest that tore at her throat while she waited for water to boil. Finally, with a decoction of elecampane roots and wild cherry bark to help, the cough quieted and she returned to her bed. Baby had made himself comfortable in the far corner, and Whinney relaxed in her place by the wall.

Eventually, Ayla's natural vitality and hardiness overcame the illness, but she was a long time recovering. She was beside herself with joy to have her animal family back together again, though it was not quite the same. Both animals had changed. Whinney was heavy with foal and had lived with a wild herd who understood the dangers of predators. She was more reserved around the lion with whom she had played in the past, and Baby was not a funny little cub any more. He left the cave again soon after the blizzard blew itself out, and, as the winter deepened, he returned less and less.

Over-exertion often brought on fits of coughing until well past midwinter, and Ayla babied herself. She pampered the horse too, feeding her grain she had picked and winnowed for herself and only taking short rides. But when a day dawned cold and clear, and she woke up full of energy, she decided a little exercise might be good for both of them.

She strapped the pack baskets onto the horse, and took along spears and travois poles, emergency food, extra water-bags and clothing, carrying basket, tent – everything she could think of for every possible emergency. She did not want to get caught short again. The one time she had been careless was almost fatal. Before she mounted, she laid a soft leather hide over Whinney's back, an innovation since the horse's return. It had been so long since she had ridden that her thighs became chapped and sore, and the leather blanket made a difference.

Enjoying the feeling of being out, and a sense of well-being at the absence of the terrible cough, Ayla let the horse walk at her own pace once they reached the steppes. She was riding comfortably, day dreaming about the end of winter, when she felt Whinney's muscles tense. It snapped her to attention. Something was moving toward them, something that moved with the stealth of a predator. Whinney was more vulnerable now – she was nearing the time when she would give birth.

Ayla reached for her spear, though she had never tried to kill a cave lion before.

As the animal neared, she saw a rufous mane and a familiar scar on the lion's nose. She slipped off the horse and ran toward the huge predator.

"Baby! Where have you been? Don't you know I worry if you stay away so long?"

He seemed just as excited to see her and greeted her with an affectionate rub that almost knocked her over. She wrapped her arms around his neck, and scratched behind his ears and under his chin the way he loved it, while he purred a low growl of contentment.

Then she heard the distinctive grunting voice of another cave lion not far away. Baby stopped his contented growl and stiffened into a posture she had not seen him in before. Over his shoulder a lioness approached cautiously. She stopped at a sound from Baby.

"You've found a mate! I knew you would – I knew you'd have your own pride someday." Ayla looked for more lionesses. "Only one, so far, probably a nomad, too. You'll have to fight for a territory, but it's a beginning. You're going to have a wonderful big pride someday, Baby."

The cave lion relaxed a bit and came towards her again, butting her with his head. She scratched his forehead and gave him a last quick hug. Whinney was very nervous, she noticed. Baby's scent might have been familiar, but not that of the strange lioness. Ayla mounted and, when Baby approached them again, she signalled "stop". He stayed for a moment and then, with a *bnga, bnga,* turned away. Followed by his mate, Baby left.

He's gone now, living with his own kind, she thought on the way back. He might come for a visit, but he'll never come back to me like Whinney did. The woman reached down and patted the mare affectionately. I'm so glad you're back, she thought.

Seeing Baby with his lioness reminded the young woman of her own uncertain future. Baby has a mate now. You had one, too, Whinney. I wonder, will I ever have one?

17

Jondalar stepped out from under the sandstone overhang and looked down the snow-covered terrace that ended abruptly with a sheer drop. The high side walls framed the white rounded contours of the eroded hills on the other side of the river. Darvo, who had been waiting for him, waved. He was standing beside a stump next to the wall some distance down the length of the field, in the place Jondalar had chosen to work his flint. It was out in the open where the light was good, and out of the way so there would be less chance of someone stepping on a sharp chip. He started towards the boy.

"Jondalar, wait a moment."

"Thonolan," he said, smiling, and waited for his brother to catch up. They strolled together across the packed snow. "I promised Darvo I'd show him some special techniques this morning. How's Shamio?"

"She's fine; getting over her cold. She had us worried – her coughing was even keeping Jetamio awake. We're talking about making more room before next winter."

Jondalar gave Thonolan an appraising look, wondering if the responsibilities of a mate and extended family were weighing heavily on his carefree younger brother. But Thonolan had a settled, contented look about him. Suddenly, he flashed a self-satisfied grin.

"Big Brother, I have something to tell you. Had you noticed that Jetamio was putting a bit of flesh on her bones? I thought she was just getting a healthy settled look. I was wrong. She's been blessed again."

"That's wonderful! I know how much she wants a baby."

"She's known for a long time, but she didn't want to tell

me. Afraid I'd worry. She seems to be holding it this time, Jondalar. Shamud says not to count on anything, but if everything continues to go well, she'll give birth in spring. She says she's sure it is a child of my spirit."

"She must be right. Just think, my foot-loose little brother – a man of his own hearth, with his mate expecting a child."

Thonolan's grin broadened. His happiness was so transparent that Jondalar had to smile, too. He looks so pleased with himself, you'd think he was having a baby, Jondalar thought.

"There, to the left," Dolando said softly, pointing to a rocky prominence jutting out from the flank of the rugged crest rising up before them and filling the entire view.

Jondalar looked, but he was too overwhelmed to focus his vision on anything less than the full expanse. They were at timberline. Behind was the forest through which they had ascended. It had begun with oak at the lower elevations; then beech predominated. Farther up were the conifers that were more familiar to him, mountain pine, fir, and spruce. He had seen, from a distance, the hardened crust of the earth upthrust in far grander peaks, but, as they left the trees behind, his breath caught at the unexpected grandeur. As many times as he had seen the view, it still affected him the same way.

The closeness of the mounting height stunned him; the sense of immediacy, as though he could reach out and touch it. In silent awe it spoke of elemental upheavals, of gravid earth straining to birth naked rock. Unclothed by forest, the primordial bone of the Great Mother lay exposed in the tilted landscape. Beyond it the sky was unearthly blue – flat and deep – a featureless backdrop to the blinding reflections of sunlight fracturing off crystals of glacial ice that clung to spines and cracks above windswept alpine meadows.

"I see it!" Thonolan cried. "A little more to the right, Jondalar. See? On that outcrop."

The tall man shifted his gaze and saw the small, graceful chamois poised on the precipice. Its thick black winter coat still clung in patches on the flanks, but the beige grey summer pelt blended into the rock. Two small horns rose straight up from the forehead of the goatlike antelope, curving back only at the tips.

"I see him now," Jondalar said.

"That may not be a 'him'. Females have horns, too," Dolando corrected.

"They do resemble ibex, don't they, Thonolan? They're smaller – horns, too. But from a distance . . ."

"How do the Zelandonii hunt ibex, Jondalar?" a young woman asked, her eyes glistening with curiosity, excitement, and love.

She was only a few years older than Darvo and had developed an adolescent infatuation with the tall blond man. She had been born Shamudoi, but had grown up on the river when her mother mated a second time to a Ramudoi, and had moved back up when the relationship came to a stormy end. She hadn't grown accustomed to the mountain crags as most Shamudoi youngsters did and hadn't shown an inclination to hunt chamois until recently, after she discovered Jondalar's strong feeling of approval for women who hunted. To her surprise, she found it exciting.

"I don't know much about it, Rakario," Jondalar replied, smiling gently. He had seen the signs in young women before, and though he couldn't help but respond to her attention, he didn't want to encourage her. "There are ibex in the mountains south of us, and more in the eastern ranges, but we didn't hunt the mountains. They were too far. Occasionally a group would get together at the Summer Meeting and arrange a hunting party. But I just went along for the fun, and I followed the directions of the hunters who knew how. I'm still learning, Rakario. Dolando is the expert hunter of mountain animals."

The chamois leaped from the precipice to a pinnacle, then calmly surveyed the view from its new vantage.

"How do you hunt an animal that can jump like that?" Rakario breathed with hushed wonder at the effortless grace of the sure-footed creature. "How can they hold on to such a small place?"

"When we get one, Rakario, take a look at the hooves," Dolando said. "Only the outer edge is hard. The inner part is flexible, like the palm of your hand. That's why they don't slide or lose their footing. The soft part grips, the outer edge holds. To hunt them, it's most important to remember that they always look down. They always watch where they're going, and they know what is below them. Their eyes are far back on the sides of their heads, so they can see around to the side, but they can't see up behind them. That's your advantage. If you move up around them, you can get them from behind. You can get close enough to touch them, if you're careful and don't lose patience."

"What if they move before you get there?" she asked.

"Look up there. See the tinge of green on the pastures? That spring grass is a real treat after winter forage. The one up there is a look-out. The rest of them – males, females, and kids – are down among rocks and bushes staying out of sight. If the grazing is good, they won't move much, as long as they feel safe."

"Why are we standing around here talking? Let's go," Darvo said.

He was annoyed at Rakario for hanging around Jondalar all the time and impatient to begin the hunt. He'd accompanied the hunters before – Jondalar always took him along when he started hunting with the Shamudoi – though only to track, watch, and learn. This time he had been given permission to try for the kill. If he succeeded, it would be a first kill for him, and he would be the recipient of special attention. But no extraordinary pressures were imposed on him. He did not have to make the kill this time; there would be other times to try. Hunting such agile prey, in an environment to which they were uniquely adapted, was difficult at best. Whoever got close enough to try made the attempt, and that required stealth and care. No one could follow the chamois from crag to outcrop, across deep chasms, once they were frightened and started to run.

Dolando started up around a rock formation whose parallel lines of strata were skewed at an angle. Softer layers of the sedimentary deposits had worn away on the exposed face, leaving convenient step-like footholds. The steep hike to get up behind and around the herd of chamois would be arduous, but not perilous. No real mountain climbing would be required.

The rest of the hunting party fell in behind the leader. Jondalar was waiting to bring up the rear. Nearly everyone had started up the stepped rock when he heard Serenio call out to him. He turned around in surprise. Serenio was not a woman who cared for hunting, and she seldom went much beyond the vicinity of the shelters. He couldn't imagine what she was doing so far away, but the look on her face when she caught up to him sent a chill of fear down his back. She had been hurrying and had to catch her breath before she could talk. "Glad . . . reached you. Need Thonolan . . . Jetamio . . . labour . . ." she managed to get out after a moment.

He cupped his hands around his mouth and shouted: "Thonolan! Thonolan!"

One of the figures moving on ahead turned around, and Jondalar waved him back.

The silence as they waited was uncomfortable. He wanted to ask if Jetamio was all right, but something held him back.

"When did labour start?" he finally asked.

"She was having back pains last night but didn't say anything to Thonolan. He'd been looking forward to the chamois hunt, and she was afraid he wouldn't go if she told him. She said she wasn't sure it was labour, and I think she had some idea of surprising him with a baby when he got back," Serenio said. "She didn't want him to worry, or be nervous waiting, while she laboured."

That was like Jetamio, he thought. She would want to spare him. Thonolan doted on her so much. Suddenly Jondalar had an ominous thought. If it was Jetamio's wish to surprise Thonolan, why had Serenio rushed up the mountain to get him?

"There's a problem, isn't there?"

Serenio looked at the ground, closed her eyes, and breathed deep before she answered. "The baby is breech; she's too narrow and won't give. Shamud thinks it's the fault of the paralysis she had, and told me to get Thonolan. . . . You, too . . . for his sake."

"Oh, no! Good Doni, oh, no!"

"No! No! No! She can't be! Why? Why would the Mother bless her with a child, and then take them both?"

Thonolan was pacing furiously within the confines of the dwelling he had shared with Jetamio, pounding one fist into the other hand. Jondalar stood by helplessly, unable to offer more than the comfort of his presence. Most could not offer that much. Thonolan, wild with grief, had screamed at everyone to get away.

"Jondalar, why her? Why would the Mother take her? She had so little, she suffered through so much. Was it so much to ask? A child? Someone of her own flesh and blood?"

"I don't know, Thonolan. Not even a zelandoni could answer you."

"Why like that? With such pain?" Thonolan stopped in front of his brother, appealing to him. "She hardly knew me when I came. Jondalar, she was hurting. I could see it in her eyes. Why did she have to die?"

"No one knows why the Mother gives life, and then takes it back."

"The Mother! The Mother! She doesn't care. Jetamio honoured Her, I honoured Her. What did it matter? She took Jetamio anyway. I hate the Mother!" He started pacing again.

"Jondalar . . ." Roshario called from the entrance, hesitating to come in.

Jondalar stepped out, "What is it?"

"Shamud cut in to take the baby, after she . . ." Roshario blinked back a tear. "He thought he might be able to save the baby – sometimes that will work. It was too late, but it was a boy. I don't know if you want to tell him or not."

"Thank you, Roshario."

He could see she had been grieving. Jetamio had been a daughter. Roshario had raised her, cared for her through a paralyzing illness and a long recovery, and had been with her from the beginning to the agonizing end of her ill-fated labour. Suddenly Thonolan pushed past them, struggling into his old travelling backframe and heading towards the pathway around the wall.

"I don't think now is the time. I'll tell him later," Jondalar said, running after his brother.

"Where are you going?" he asked, catching up to him.

"I'm leaving. I never should have stopped. I haven't reached the end of my Journey."

"You can't leave now," Jondalar said, putting a restraining hand on his arm. Thonolan shrugged it off violently.

"Why not? What's to keep me here?" Thonolan sobbed.

Jondalar stopped him again, spun him around, and looked into a face so lacerated with grief that he hardly recognized him. The pain was so deep, it burned his own soul. There had been times when he had envied Thonolan's joy in his love for Jetamio, wondering at the defect in his own character that prevented him from knowing such love. Was it worth it? Was the love worth this anguish? This bitter desolation?

"Can you leave Jetamio and her son to be buried without you?"

"Her son? How do you know it was a son?"

"Shamud took it. He thought he might save at least the baby. It was too late."

"I don't want to see the son that killed her."

"Thonolan. Thonolan. She asked to be blessed. She wanted to be pregnant, and she was so happy about it. Would you have taken that happiness from her? Would you rather she had lived a long life of sorrow? Childless, and despairing of ever having one? She had love and happiness, first mated to you, then blessed by the Mother. It was only a short time, but she told me she was happier than she ever dreamed possible. She said nothing gave her more joy than you, and knowing she was carrying a child. Your child, she called it, Thonolan. The child of your spirit. Maybe the Mother knew it had to be one or the other, and chose to give her the joy."

"Jondalar, she didn't even know me. . . ." Thonolan's voice cracked.

"Shamud gave her something at the end, Thonolan. There was no hope that she would give birth, but she didn't suffer so much. She knew you were there."

"The Mother took everything when She took Jetamio. I was so full of love, and now I am empty, Jondalar. I have nothing left. How can she be gone?" Thonolan swayed. Jondalar reached for him, supported him as he crumpled, and held him against his shoulder while he sobbed his despair.

"Why not back home, Thonolan? If we leave now, we can make it to the glacier by winter and be home next spring. Why do you want to go east?" Jondalar's voice held longing.

"You go home, Jondalar. You should have gone long ago.

I always said you're a Zelandonii and will always be one. I'm going east."

"You said you were going to make a Journey to the end of the Great Mother River. Once you reach Beran Sea, what will you do?"

"Who knows? Maybe I'll go around the sea. Maybe I'll go north and hunt mammoth with Tholie's people. The Mamutoi say there is another mountain range far to the east. Home has nothing for me, Jondalar. I'd rather look for something new. It's time for us to go different ways, Brother. You go west, I'll go east."

"If you don't want to go back, why not stay here?"

"Yes, why not stay here, Thonolan?" Dolando said, joining them. "And you too, Jondalar. Shamudoi or Ramudoi, it doesn't matter. You belong. You have family here, and friends. We would be sorry to see either of you leave."

"Dolando, you know I was ready to live here for the rest of my life. I can't now. Everything is too full of her. I keep expecting to see her. Every day I'm here I have to remember all over again that I will never see her again. I'm sorry. I will miss many people, but I must go."

Dolando nodded. He didn't push them to stay, but he had wanted to let them know they were family. "When will you leave?"

"Soon. A few days at most," Thonolan replied. "I'd like to arrange a trade, Dolando. I'll be leaving everything behind, except travelling packs and clothes. I'd like a small boat, though."

"I'm sure it can be arranged. You'll be going downstream, then. East? Not back to the Zelandonii?"

"I'm going east," Thonolan said.

"And you, Jondalar?"

"I don't know. There's Serenio and Darvo . . ."

Dolando nodded. Jondalar may not have made the tie formal, but he knew the decision would not be any easier for it. The tall Zelandonii had reasons to go west, to stay, or to go east, and which way he would choose was anyone's guess.

"Roshario's been cooking all day. I think she's doing it to keep herself busy, so she won't have time to think," Dolando said. "It would please her if you'd join us for a meal. Jondalar, she'd like Serenio and Darvo, too. It would please

344

her even more if you would just eat something, Thonolan. She worries about you."

It must be hard on Dolando, too, Jondalar realized. He had been so worried about Thonolan that he hadn't thought of the grief of the Cave. This had been Jetamio's home. Dolando must have cared for her as he would any child of his hearth. She had been close to many. Tholie and Markeno were her family, and he knew Serenio had been crying. Darvo was upset, not wanting to talk to him.

"I'll ask Serenio," Jondalar said. "I'm sure Darvo would like to go. Maybe you should just count on him. I'd like to have a talk with Serenio."

"Send him over," Dolando said, reminding himself to keep the lad overnight to give his mother and Jondalar some time to reach a decision.

The three men walked together back to the sandstone overhang, then stood near the fire in the central hearth for a few moments.

Shadows of the terrace walls had already brought an evening chill, though from the front end sunlight could be seen streaming down the river gorge. Standing by the fire together, they could almost feel that nothing had changed, could almost forget the devastating tragedy. They stayed long into twilight, wanting to hold the moment, each thinking private thoughts that, had they shared them, they would have found remarkably similar. Each was thinking of the events that had brought the Zelandonii men to the Cave of the Sharamudoi, and each was wondering if he would ever see either of the other two again.

"Aren't you ever coming in?" Roshario asked, finally unable to wait longer. She had sensed their need for this last silent communion and hadn't wanted to disturb them. Then Shamud and Serenio came out of a shelter, Darvo detached himself from a group of youngsters, other people came to the central fire, and the mood was irrevocably lost. Roshario herded everyone towards her dwelling, including Jondalar and Serenio, but they left soon after.

They walked in silence to the edge, then around the wall to a fallen log. It made a comfortable seat from which to watch the sunset upriver. Nature conspired to keep them silent by the sheer beauty of the setting sun; a panorama presented in metallic hues. With the molten orb's descent, lead-grey clouds were highlighted in silver, then spread out in gleaming gold that shattered on the river. Fiery red transformed the gold to shining copper, which flattened to bronze, then faded to silver again.

As the silver leadened, then tarnished to darker shades, Jondalar came to a decision. He turned to face Serenio. She was certainly beautiful, he thought. She wasn't hard to live with; she made his life comfortable. He opened his mouth to speak.

"Let's go back, Jondalar," she said, first.

"Serenio . . . I . . . we have lived . . ." he started. She held a finger to his mouth to silence him.

"Don't talk now. Let's go back."

He heard the urgency in her voice this time, saw the desire in her eyes. He reached for her hand, held it, fingers to his lips, then turned her hand around, opened it, and kissed her palm. His warm seeking mouth found her wrist, then followed her arm to the inside of her elbow, pushing back her sleeve to reach it.

She sighed, closed her eyes, and tilted her head back, inviting him. He held the back of her neck to support her head, and kissed the pulse in her throat, found her ear and searched out her mouth. She was waiting, hungry. He kissed her then, slowly, lovingly, tasting the softness under her tongue, touching the ridges of her palate, and drew her tongue into his mouth. When they pulled apart, she was breathing heavily. Her hand found his warm and throbbing response.

"Let's go back," she said again, her voice husky.

"Why go back? Why not here?" he said.

"If we stay here it will be over too soon. I want the warmth of fire and furs so we won't need to rush."

Their lovemaking had become, not stale, but a little perfunctory recently. They knew what satisfied each other, and then tended to fall into a pattern, exploring and experimenting only rarely. This night, he knew, she wanted more than routine, and he was eager to comply. He took her head in both his hands, kissed her eyes and the end of her nose, the softness of her cheek, and breathed into her ear. He nibbled at an earlobe, then sought her throat again. When he found her mouth once more, he took it fiercely and held her to him.

"I think we should go back, Serenio," he breathed into her ear.

"That's what I've been saying."

Side by side, his arm over her shoulder and hers around his waist, they walked back around the jutting wall. For once, he didn't step back to allow passage around the outside edge in single file. He did not even notice the precipitous fall-off.

It was dark, the deep black of both night and shadow, in the open field. The moon's light was stopped by the high side walls; only a few scattered stars could be seen between clouds above. It was later than they realized when they reached the overhang. No one was out around the fire of the central hearth, though logs still burned with licking flames. They saw Roshario, Dolando, and several others inside their shelter, and as they passed the entrance, they saw Darvo throwing carved pieces of bone with Thonolan. Jondalar smiled. It was a game he and his brother had often played on long winter nights, one that could take half a night to resolve, and it held the attention – making forgetting easier.

The dwelling Jondalar shared with Serenio was dark when they entered. He piled wood in the stone-lined fireplace, then got a piece of burning wood from the main hearth to light it. He leaned two planks across each other at the entrance, then stretched the leather drape across, making a warm private world.

He shrugged out of his outer garment, and, while Serenio brought out drinking cups. Jondalar got the skin of fermented bilberry juice and poured for both. The immediacy of his ardour had passed, and the walk back had given him time to think. She's as lovely and passionate a woman as any I've ever known, he thought, sipping the warming liquid. I should have formalized our union long ago. Perhaps she'd be willing to come back with me, and Darvo, too. But whether we stay here, or go back, I want her for my mate.

There was relief in the decision, and one less undecided factor to cope with, and it pleased him that he felt so good about it. It was proper, right. Why had he held back so long?

"Serenio, I've made a decision. I don't know if I've ever told you how much you mean to me . . ."

"Not now," she said, putting her cup down. She reached her arms around his neck, brought his lips to hers, and pressed close. It was a long, slow, lingering kiss that reminded him quickly of his passion. She's right, he thought, we can talk later.

As the intensity of his heat reasserted itself, he led her to the fur-covered sleeping platform. The forgotten fire burned low while he explored and rediscovered her body. Serenio had never been unresponsive, but she opened herself to him as she never had before. She couldn't get enough of him, though she was satisfied and satisfied again. Surge after surge filled them, and when he thought he had reached his limit, she experimented with his techniques and slowly encouraged him again. With a last ecstatic effort, they reached a joyous release and lay together exhausted, finally sated.

They slept for a while, as they were, naked on top of the furs. When the fire died, the chill of pre-dawn woke them. She started a fresh fire from the last embers, while he put on a tunic and slipped out to fill the waterbag. The warmth inside the dwelling was welcome when he returned; he had taken a quick dip in the cold pool as well. He felt invigorated, refreshed, and so thoroughly satisfied that he was ready for anything. After Serenio started stones heating, she slipped out to relieve herself and came back as wet as he.

"You're shivering," Jondalar said, wrapping her in a fur.

"You seemed to enjoy your dunking so much, I thought I'd try it. It was cold!" She laughed.

"The tea is almost ready. I'll bring you a cup. You sit here," he said, urging her back to the sleeping platform and piling more furs around her, until only her face could be seen. Spending my life with a woman like Serenio would not be at all bad, he thought. I wonder if I could persuade her to come home with me? An unhappy thought intruded itself. If only I could persuade Thonolan to come home with me. I can't understand why he wants to go east. He took Serenio a cup of hot betony tea, and one for himself, and settled on the edge of the platform.

"Serenio, have you ever thought of making a Journey?"

"Do you mean travel to someplace I've never been before, to meet new people who speak a language I wouldn't understand? No, Jondalar, I've never had an urge to make a Journey."

"But you do understand Zelandonii. Very well. When we decided to learn each other's language with Tholie and the rest, I was surprised how quickly you learned. It wouldn't be as though you had to learn a new language."

"What are you trying to say, Jondalar?"

He smiled. "I'm trying to persuade you to travel with me back to my home after we are mated. You'd like the Zelandonii . . ."

"What do you mean, 'after we are mated'? What makes you think we are going to mate?"

He was abashed. Of course, he should have asked her first, not just blurted out questions about Journeys. Women like to be asked, not taken for granted. He gave her a sheepish grin.

"I've decided it's time to make our arrangement formal. I should have done it long before. You're a beautiful, loving woman, Serenio. And Darvo is a fine boy. To have him as the true child of my hearth would make me very proud. But I was hoping you might consider travelling with me, back home . . . back to the Zelandonii. Of course, if you don't . . ."

"Jondalar, you can't decide to make our arrangement formal. I'm not going to mate you. I decided that long ago."

He flushed, truly embarrassed. It hadn't occurred to him that she wouldn't want to mate him. He'd only thought of himself, the way he felt, not that she might not consider him worthy. "I'm . . . I'm sorry, Serenio. I thought you cared about me, too. I shouldn't have presumed. You should have told me to leave . . . I could have found another place." He got up and started gathering up some of his things.

"Jondalar, what are you doing?"

"Getting my things together so I can move out."

"Why do you want to move out?"

"I don't want to, but if you don't want me here . . ."

"After tonight, how can you say I don't want you? What does that have to do with mating you?"

He came back, sat down on the edge of the sleeping platform, and looked into her enigmatic eyes. "Why won't you mate me? Am I not . . . not man enough for you?"

"Not man enough . . ." Her voice caught in her throat. She

closed her eyes, blinked a few times, and took a deep breath. "Oh, Mother, Jondalar! Not man enough! If you aren't, no man on earth is man enough. That's just the problem. You're too much man, too much everything. I couldn't live with that."

"I don't understand. I want to mate you, and you say I'm too good for you?"

"You really don't understand, do you? Jondalar, you've given me more . . . more than any man. If I were to mate you, I'd have so much, I'd have more than any other woman I know. They'd be envious. They would wish their men would be as generous, as caring, as good as you. They already know a touch from you can make a woman feel more alive, more . . . Jondalar, you are every woman's desire."

"If I'm . . . all you say, why won't you mate me?"

"Because you don't love me."

"Serenio . . . I do . . ."

"Yes, in your way, you love me. You care about me. You would never do anything to hurt me, and you would be so wonderful, so good to me. But I'd always know. Even if I convinced myself otherwise, I'd know. And I'd wonder what was wrong with me, what I lacked, why you couldn't love me."

Jondalar looked down. "Serenio, people mate who don't love each other like that." He looked at her earnestly. "If they share other things, if they care about each other, they can have a good life together."

"Yes, some people do. I may mate again someday, and if we share other things, it may not be necessary to love each other. But not you, Jondalar."

"Why not me?" he asked, and the pain in his eyes was almost enough to make her reconsider.

"Because I would love you. I couldn't help it. I would love you and die a little every day knowing you didn't love me the same way. No woman can keep from loving you, Jondalar. And every time we would make love, like we did tonight, I would wither inside more. Wanting you so much, loving you so much, and knowing that as much as you might want to, you didn't love me back. After a while, I'd dry up, be an empty shell, and find ways to make your life as miserable as mine. You'd go on being your wonderful, caring, generous self, because you'd know why I had become like that. But you'd hate yourself for it. And everyone would wonder how you could stand such a carping, bitter old woman. I won't do that to you, Jondalar. And I won't do it to me."

He got up and paced to the entrance, then turned around and came back. "Serenio, why can't I love? Other men fall in love – what's wrong with me?" He looked at her with such anguish, she ached for him, loved him even more, and wished there were some way she could make him love her.

"I don't know, Jondalar. Maybe you haven't found the right woman. Maybe the Mother has someone special for you. She doesn't make many like you. You are really more than most women could bear. If all your love were concentrated on one, it would overwhelm her, if she wasn't one to whom the Mother gave equal gifts. Even if you did love me, I'm not sure I could live with it. If you loved a woman as much as you love your brother, she would have to be very strong."

"I can't fall in love, but if I could, no woman could bear it," he said with a laugh of dry irony and bitterness. "Be wary of gifts from the Mother." His eyes, deep violet in the red glow of the fire, filled with apprehension. "What did you mean, 'if I loved a woman as much as I love my brother'? If no woman is strong enough to 'bear' my love, are you thinking I need a . . . man?"

Serenio smiled, then chuckled. "I don't mean you love your brother like a woman. You are not like Shamud, with the body of one and the inclinations of the other. You would have known it by now and sought your calling and, like the Shamud, you would have found a love there. No," she said, and felt a flush of warmth thinking about it, "you like a woman's body too well. But you love your brother more than you have ever loved any woman. That's why I wanted you so much tonight. You'll be leaving when he goes, and I won't see you again."

As soon as she said it, he knew she was right. No matter what he thought he had decided, when the time came, he would have left with Thonolan.

"How did you know, Serenio? I didn't. I came here thinking I was going to mate you, and settle down with the Sharamudoi if I couldn't take you back with me."

"I think everyone knows you will follow him, wherever he goes. Shamud says it is your destiny."

Jondalar's curiosity about Shamud had never been satisfied. On impulse, he asked, "Tell me, is Shamud a man or a woman?"

She looked at him a long time. "Do you really want to know?"

He reconsidered. "No, I don't suppose it matters. Shamud didn't want to tell me – maybe the mystery is important to . . . Shamud."

In the silence that followed, Jondalar stared at Serenio, wanting to remember her as she was then. Her hair was still damp, and in disarray, but she had warmed and pushed most of the furs away. "What about you, Serenio? What will you do?"

"I love you, Jondalar." It was a simple declarative statement. "It won't be easy to get over you, but you gave me something. I was afraid to love. I lost so many loves that I pushed all feelings of love away. I knew I would lose you, Jondalar, but I loved you anyway. Now I know I can love again, and if I lose it, it doesn't take away the love that was. You gave that to me. And maybe something more." The mystery of a woman came into her smile. "Soon, perhaps, someone will come into my life that I can love. It's a little early to tell for sure, but I think the Mother has blessed me. I didn't think it was possible after the last one I lost – I've been many years without Her blessing. It may be a child of your spirit. I'll know if the baby has your eyes."

The familiar furrows appeared on his forehead. "Serenio, I must stay then. You have no man at your hearth to provide for you and the child," he said.

"Jondalar, you don't have to worry. No mother or her children ever lack for care. Mudo has said all those She blesses must be succoured. That's why She made men, to bring to mothers the gifts of the Great Earth Mother. The Cave will provide, as She provides for all Her children. You must follow your destiny, and I will follow mine. I won't forget you, and if I have a child of your spirit, I will think of you, just as I remember the man I loved when Darvo was born."

Serenio had changed, but she still made no demands,

placed no burden of obligation on him. He put his arms around her. She looked into his compelling blue eyes. Her eyes hid nothing, not the love she felt, or her sadness in losing him, and not her joy in the treasure she hoped she carried. Through a crack, they could see the faint light that heralded a new day. He got up.

"Where are you going, Jondalar?"

"Just outside. I've had too much tea." He smiled, and it reached his eyes. "But keep the bed warm. The night isn't over yet." He bent over and kissed her. "Serenio" – his voice was husky with feeling – "you mean more to me than any woman I have ever known."

It wasn't quite enough. He would leave, though she knew if she asked he would stay. But she did not ask, and in return he gave her the most he could. And that was more than most women would ever get.

18

"Mother said you wanted to see me."

Jondalar could see tension in the set of Darvo's shoulders and the wary look in his eyes. He knew the boy had been avoiding him, and he suspected the reason. The tall man smiled, trying to seem casual and relaxed, but the hesitancy in his usual warm fondness made Darvo more nervous; he didn't want his fears confirmed. Jondalar had not been looking forward to telling the boy, either. He took down a neatly folded garment from a shelf and shook it out.

"I think you are almost big enough for this, Darvo. I want to give it to you."

For a moment the boy's eyes lit with pleasure at the Zelandonii shirt with its intricate and exotic decoration; then the wariness returned. "You're leaving, aren't you?" he accused.

"Thonolan is my brother, Darvo . . ."

"And I'm nothing."

"That's not true. You must know how much I care about you. But Thonolan is so full of grief, he's not reasonable. I fear for him. I can't let him go alone, and if I don't look after him, who will? Please try to understand, I don't want to go farther east."

"Will you come back?"

Jondalar paused. "I don't know. I can't promise. I don't know where we're going, how long we'll travel." He proffered the shirt. "That's why I want to give you this, so you'll have something to remember the 'Zelandonii man'. Darvo, listen to me. You will always be the first son of my hearth."

The boy looked at the beaded tunic; then tears welled and threatened to break. "I'm not the son of your hearth!" he cried, then turned and ran from the dwelling.

Jondalar wanted to run after him. Instead, he placed the shirt on Darvo's sleeping platform and walked slowly out.

Carlono frowned at the lowering clouds. "I think the weather will hold," he said, "but if she really starts gusting, pull over to the shore, though you won't find many places to land until you are through the gate. The Mother will split into channels when you reach the plain on the other side of the gate. Remember, keep to the left bank. She'll swing north before you reach the sea, and then east. Soon after the turn, she is joined by a large river on the left, her last major tributary. A short distance beyond is the beginning of the delta – the outlet to the sea – but you still have a long way to go. The delta is huge, and dangerous; marsh and bogs and sand bars. The Mother separates again, usually into four, but sometimes more, main channels and many small ones. Keep to the left channel, the northern one. There's a Mamutoi Camp on the north bank, close to the mouth."

The experienced river man had gone over it before. He had even drawn a map in the dirt to help guide them to the end of the Great Mother River. But he believed repetition would reinforce their memory, especially if they had to make quick decisions. He wasn't happy about the two young men travelling on the unfamiliar river without an experienced guide, but they insisted; or rather, Thonolan did, and Jondalar wouldn't let him go alone. At least the tall man had gained some skill in handling boats.

They were standing on the wooden dock with their gear loaded in a small boat, but their departure lacked the usual excitement of such adventures. Thonolan was leaving only because he could not stay, and Jondalar would much rather have been setting out in the opposite direction.

The spark had gone out of Thonolan. His former outgoing friendliness was replaced by moodiness. His generally morose disposition was punctuated by a flaring temper – often leading to increased recklessness and careless disregard. The first real argument between the two brothers had not come to blows only because Jondalar had refused to fight. Thonolan had accused his brother of wet-nursing him like an infant, demanding the right to his own life without being followed around. When Thonolan heard of Serenio's possible pregnancy, he was furious that Jondalar would consider leaving a woman who probably carried the child of his spirit, to follow a brother to some unknown destination. He insisted that Jondalar stay and provide for her as any decent man would.

In spite of Serenio's refusal to mate, Jondalar couldn't help feeling Thonolan was right. It had been drilled into him since birth that a man's responsibility, his sole purpose, was to provide support for mothers and children, particularly a woman who had been blessed with a child that in some mysterious way might have absorbed his spirit. But Thonolan would not stay, and Jondalar, afraid his brother would do something irrational and dangerous, insisted upon accompanying him. The tension between them was still oppressive.

Jondalar didn't quite know how to say goodbye to Serenio, was almost afraid to look at her. But she had a smile on her face when he bent to kiss her, and though her eyes seemed a little swollen and red, she allowed no emotion to show in them. He searched for Darvo and was disappointed that the boy was not among those who had come down to the dock. Nearly everyone else was there. Thonolan was already in the small boat when Jondalar climbed in and settled himself in the rear seat. He took up his oar and, while Carlono untied the rope, he looked up one last time at the high terrace. A boy was standing near the edge. The shirt he was wearing would take a few years for him to fill out, but the pattern was distinctly Zelandonii. Jondalar smiled, then waved with his oar. Darvo waved back as the tall blond Zelandonii man dipped the double-ended paddle into the river.

The two brothers pulled into midstream and looked back at the dockful of people – friends. As they headed downstream, Jondalar wondered if they would ever see the Sharamudoi again, or anyone he knew. The Journey that had begun as an adventure had lost its edge of excitement, yet he was being drawn, almost against his will, farther away from home. What could Thonolan hope to find going east? And what could there possibly be for him in that direction?

The great river gorge was foreboding under the grey overcast sky. Naked rock reared out of the water from deep roots and rose in towering bulwarks on both sides. On the left bank, a series of ramparts of sharp, angular rock climbed in rugged relief all the way to the distant glaciered peaks; on the right, weathered and eroded, the rounded mountain tops gave the illusion of mere hills, but their height was daunting from the small boat. Large boulders and pinnacles broke the surface, parting the current into curls of white water.

They were a part of the medium in which they travelled, propelled by it like the debris floating on its skin and the silt within its silent depths. They did not control their speed or direction; they only steered a course around obstructions. Where the river stretched out more than a mile in width, the swells lifted and dipped the small craft, and it seemed more like a sea. When the sides drew together, they could feel the change in energy as the flow was resisted; the current was stronger when the same volume of water surged through the constricted gates.

They had travelled more than a quarter of the way through, perhaps twenty-five miles, when the threatened rain broke forth in a furious squall, whipping up waves they feared would swamp the little wooden boat. But there was no shore, only the steep wet rock.

"I can steer if you bail, Thonolan," Jondalar said. They hadn't talked much, but some of the tension between them had dissipated as they paddled in harmony to keep the craft on course.

Thonolan shipped his oar and, with a square wooden scooplike implement, tried to empty the small vessel. "It's filling as fast as I can bail," he called over his shoulder.

"I don't think this will last long. If you can keep up with it, I think we'll make it," Jondalar replied, struggling through the choppy water.

The heavy weather lifted, and, though clouds still menaced, they made their way through the entire gorge without further incident.

Like the relaxation that comes with the removal of a tight belt, the swollen muddy river spread out when she reached the plains. Channels twined around islands of willow and reed; nesting grounds for cranes and herons, transitory geese and ducks, and innumerable other birds.

They camped the first night on the flat grassy prairie of the left bank. The foot of the alpine peaks was pulling back from the river's edge, but the rounded mountains of the right bank held the Great Mother River to her eastward course.

Jondalar and Thonolan settled into a travelling routine so quickly that it seemed they had not stopped for those years while they were living with the Sharamudoi. Yet it wasn't the same. Gone was the light-hearted sense of adventure, seeking whatever lay around the bend for the simple joy of discovery. Instead, Thonolan's drive to keep moving was tainted with desperation.

Jondalar had attempted once more to talk his brother into turning back, but it led to a bitter argument. He didn't bring it up again. They spoke mostly to exchange necessary information. Jondalar could only hope that time would assuage Thonolan's grief, and that someday he would decide to return home and take up his life again. Until then, he was determined to stay with him.

The two brothers travelled much faster on the river in the small dugout than they could have walking along the edge. Riding on the current, they sped along with ease. As Carlono had predicted, the river turned north when it reached a barrier of ancient mountain stumps, far older than the raw mountains around which the great river flowed. Though ground down with their hoary age, they intervened between the river and the inland sea she strove to reach.

Undeterred, she sought another way. Her northward strategy worked, but not until, when she made her final swing to the east, one more large river brought a contribution of water and silt to the overburdened Mother. With her way finally clear, she could not hold herself to one path. Though she had many miles to go, she split up once again into many channels in a fan-shaped delta.

The delta was a morass of quicksand, salt marsh, and insecure little islands. Some of the silty islets stayed in place several years, long enough for small trees to send down tenuous roots, only to be washed away at the vicissitude of seasonal flood or eroding seepage. Four major channels – depending on season and happenstance – cut through to the sea, but their courses were inconstant. For no apparent reason, the water would suddenly switch from a deeply worn bed to a new path, tearing up brush and leaving a sinkhole of soft wet sand.

The Great Mother River – eighteen hundred miles and

two glacier-covered mountain ranges of water – had nearly reached her destination. But the delta with its hundreds of square miles of mud, silt, sand, and water was the most dangerous section of the entire river.

By following the deepest of the left channels, the river had not been hard to navigate. The current had taken the small log boat around its sweeping northward turn, and even the final large tributary had only pushed them to midstream. But the brothers didn't anticipate that she would break into channels so soon. Before they realized it, they were swept into a middle channel.

Jondalar had gained considerable skill in handling the small craft, and Thonolan could manage one, but they were far from being as capable as the expert boatmen of the Ramudoi. They tried to turn the dugout around, retreat back upstream, and re-enter the proper channel. They would have done better to reverse the direction they were rowing – the shape of the stern was not so different from the shape of the prow – but they didn't think of it.

They were crosswise against the current, Jondalar shouting instructions to Thonolan to get the front end turned around, and Thonolan becoming impatient. A large log with an extensive root system – heavy, water-soaked, and lying low in the water – was washing down the river, the sprawling roots raking along everything in their path. The two men saw it – too late.

With a splintering crash, the jagged end of the huge log, brittle and blacker where it had once been struck by lightning, rammed broadside into the thin-walled dugout. Water rushed in through a hole punched into the side and quickly swamped the small canoe. As the snag bore down on them, one long root finger just below the water's surface jabbed Jondalar in the ribs and knocked him breathless. Another barely missed Thonolan's eye, leaving a long scratch across his cheek.

Suddenly immersed in the cold water, Jondalar and Thonolan clung to the snag and watched with dismay as a few bubbles rose while the little craft, with all their possessions lashed firmly to it, sank to the bottom.

Thonolan had heard his brother's grunt of pain. "Are you all right, Jondalar?"

"A root jabbed me in the ribs. Hurts a bit, but I don't think it's serious."

With Jondalar following slowly, Thonolan started working his way around the snag, but the force of the current as they were swept along kept pushing them back into the log with the rest of the debris. Suddenly, the snag caught on a sand bar under the water. The river, flowing around and through the open network of roots, pushed out objects that had been held under by the force of the current, and a whole bloated reindeer carcass rose to the surface in front of Jondalar. He moved to get out of its way, feeling the pain in his side.

Free of the log, they swam to a narrow island in mid-channel. It supported a few young willows, but it was not stable and would be washed away before long. The trees near the edge were already partly submerged, drowned, with no green buds of spring leaves on the branches, and, with roots losing their hold, some were leaning over the rushing flow. The ground was a spongy bog.

"I think we should keep on going and try to find a drier place," Jondalar said.

"You are in a lot of pain – don't tell me you aren't."

Jondalar admitted to some discomfort, "But we can't stay here," he added.

They slid into the cold water across the narrow island bar. The current was swifter than they expected, and they were swept much farther downstream before they reached dry land. They were tired, cold, and disappointed when they found themselves to be on still another narrow islet. It was wider, longer, and somewhat higher than the level of the river, but soggy, with no dry wood to be found.

"We can't make a fire here," Thonolan said. "We'll have to keep going. Where did Carlono say that Mamutoi Camp was?"

"At the north end of the delta, close to the sea," Jondalar replied, and he looked with longing in that direction as he spoke. The pain in his side had become more intense and he wasn't sure if he could swim across another channel. All he could see was surging water, tangled pockets of debris, and a few trees marking an occasional island. "No telling how far that is."

They squelched through the mud to the north side of the narrow strip of land and plunged into the cold water. Jondalar noted a stand of trees downstream and made for it. They staggered up a beach of grey sand at the far side of the channel, breathing heavily. Rivulets of water ran from their long hair and soaked leather clothing.

The late-afternoon sun broke through a rift in the overcast sky with a wash of golden brilliance but little warmth. A sudden gust from the north brought a chill that quickly penetrated wet clothes. They had been warm enough while they were active, but the effort had sapped their reserves. They shivered in the wind, then plodded towards the scant shelter of a sparse stand of alder.

"Let's make camp here," Jondalar said.

"It's still light. I'd rather keep going."

"It will be dark by the time we make a shelter and try to get a fire started."

"If we keep going, we could probably find the Mamutoi Camp before dark."

"Thonolan, I don't think I can."

"How bad is it?" Thonolan asked. Jondalar lifted his tunic. A wound on his rib was discolouring around a gash that had no doubt bled, but had been closed off by water-swelled tissue. He noticed the hole punctured in the leather then, wondering if his rib was broken.

"I wouldn't mind a rest and a fire."

They looked around them at the wild expanse of swirling muddy water, shifting sand bars, and an unkempt profusion of vegetation. Tangled tree limbs attached to dead trunks were pulled by the current unwillingly towards the sea, digging in wherever they could find purchase in the fluctuating bottom. In the distance a few stands of greening brush and trees were anchored to some of the more stable islands.

Reeds and marsh grasses took hold anywhere they could root. Nearby, three-foot tussocks of sedge, whose clumps of sprawling grassy leaves looked sturdier than they were, matched in height by the straight sword-shaped leaves of sweetflag, grew between mats of spike rush that was barely an inch tall. In the marsh near the water's edge, ten-foot-tall scouring rushes, cattails, and bulrushes dwarfed the men.

Soaring over all, stiff-leafed phragmite reeds with tops of purple plumes reached thirteen feet or more.

The men had only the clothes on their backs. They had lost everything when the boat went down, even the backframes they had travelled with from the beginning. Thonolan had adopted the dress of the Shamudoi, and Jondalar wore the Ramudoi variation, but after his dunking in the river when he met the flatheads, he had kept a pouch of tools tied to his belt. He was grateful for it now.

"I'm going to see if there are some old stalks on those cattails that are dry enough for a fire drill," Jondalar said, trying to ignore the pain in his side. "See if you can find some dry wood."

The cattails provided more than an old-growth woody stalk for a fire drill. The long leaves woven around an alderwood frame made a lean-to, which helped contain the heat from the fire. The green tops and young roots, baked in the coals along with the sweet rhizomes of the sweetflag and the underwater base of the bulrushes, supplied the beginning of a meal. A slender alder sapling, sharpened to a point and hurled with the accuracy of hunger, brought a couple of ducks to the fire as well. The men made flexible mats of the large, soft-stemmed bulrushes, then used them to extend the lean-to and to wrap around themselves while they dried their wet clothes. Later, the men slept on the mats.

Jondalar did not sleep well. His side was sore and tender, and he knew there was something wrong inside, but he couldn't think of stopping now. They had to find their way to solid ground first.

In the morning, they seined fish out of the river with wide mesh baskets made of cattail leaves and alder branches and cords made of stringy bark. They rolled the fire-making materials and flexible baskets inside the sleeping mats, tied them with the cord, and slung them over their backs. Taking their spears, they started out. The spears were only pointed sticks, but they had provided one meal – and the fish baskets had supplied another. Survival depended not so much on equipment as knowledge.

The two brothers had a small difference of opinion over which direction to go in. Thonolan thought they were across the delta and wanted to go east, towards the sea. Jondalar wanted to go north, sure there was yet another channel of the river to cross. They compromised and headed northeast. Jondalar was proved right, though he would have been much happier if he had been wrong. Near noon they reached the northernmost channel of the great river.

"Time to go swimming again," Thonolan said. "Are you able?"

"Do I have any choice?"

They started for the water, then Thonolan stopped. "Why don't we tie our clothes to a log, the way we used to. Then we won't have to dry clothes."

"I don't know," Jondalar said. Clothes, even wet, would keep them warmer, but Thonolan had been trying to be reasonable, though his voice betrayed frustration and exasperation. "But, if you want . . ." Jondalar shrugged acquiescence.

It was chilly standing naked in the cool damp air. Jondalar was tempted to re-tie his tool pouch around his bare waist, but Thonolan had already wrapped it in his tunic and was tying everything to a log he had found. On his bare skin, the water felt colder than he remembered, and he had to grit his teeth to keep from crying out when he plunged in and tried to swim, but water numbed the pain of his wound somewhat. He favoured his side while swimming and lagged behind his brother, though Thonolan was pulling the log.

When they crawled out of the water and stood on a sand bar, their original destination – the end of the Great Mother River – was in sight. They could see the water of the inland sea. But the excitement of the moment was lost. The Journey had lost its purpose, and the end of the river was no longer their goal. Nor were they yet on solid ground. They were not quite across the delta. The sand bar where they stood had once been in midchannel, but the channel had shifted. An empty riverbed still had to be crossed.

A high wooded bank, with exposed roots dangling from the underside where a swift current had once undercut, beckoned from the other side of the vacated channel. It had not been vacated long. Water still puddled in the middle, and vegetation had barely taken root. But insects had already discovered the stagnant pools, and a swarm of mosquitoes had discovered the two men.

Thonolan untied the clothes from the log. "We still have to get through those puddles down there, and the bank looks muddy. Let's wait until we get across before we put these back on."

Jondalar nodded agreement, in too much pain to argue. He thought he'd strained something while swimming, and he was having trouble standing up straight.

Thonolan slapped a mosquito as he stared down the gentle gradient which had once been the slope leading from the bank into the river channel.

They'd been told often enough. Never turn your back on the river; never underestimate the Great Mother River. Though She had left it for a time, the channel was still Hers, and, even in Her absence, She left a surprise or two behind. Millions of tons of silt were brought down to the sea and spread over the thousand or more square miles of Her delta every year. The vacated channel, subject to tidal inundation from the sea, was a soggy salt marsh with poor drainage. The new green grass and reeds had set roots in wet silty clay.

The two men slid and slipped down the slope on the fine-grained sticky mud, and, when they reached level ground, it sucked at their bare feet. Thonolan hurried ahead, forgetting that Jondalar was not quite up to his usual long-strided pace. He could walk, but the slippery descent had hurt. He was picking his way carefully, feeling a bit foolish to be wandering through the marsh naked, making an offering of his tender skin to the hungry insects.

Thonolan had got so far ahead that Jondalar was about to call out to him. But he looked up just as he heard his brother's cry for help and saw him go down. Pain forgotten, Jondalar ran toward him. Fear clutched when he saw Thonolan floundering in quicksand.

"Thonolan! Great Mother!" Jondalar cried, rushing to him.

"Stay back! You'll get caught too!" Thonolan, struggling to free himself from the mire, was sinking deeper instead.

Jondalar looked around frantically for something to help Thonolan out. His shirt! He could throw him an end, he thought, then remembered that was impossible. The bundle of clothes was gone. He shook his head, then saw the dead stump of an old tree half buried in the muck and ran to see if he could break off one of the roots, but any roots that might have come free had long since been torn off in the violent journey downstream.

"Thonolan, where is the clothes bundle? I need something to pull you out!"

The desperation in Jondalar's voice had an unwanted effect. It filtered through Thonolan's panic to remind him of his grief. A calm acceptance came over him. "Jondalar, if the Mother wants to take me, let Her take me."

"No! Thonolan, no! You can't give up like that. You can't just die. Oh Mother, Great Mother, don't let him die like that!" Jondalar sank to his knees and, stretching out full, reached out his hand. "Take my hand, Thonolan, please, take my hand," he begged.

Thonolan was surprised at the grief and pain on his brother's face, and something more that he'd seen before only in infrequent passing glances. In that instant, he knew. His brother loved him, loved him as much as he had loved Jetamio. It was not the same, but as strong. He understood at an instinctive level, by intuition, and he knew as he reached for the hand stretching towards him that, even if he couldn't get out of the mire, he had to clasp his brother's hand.

Thonolan didn't know it, but when he ceased struggling, he didn't sink as fast. When he stretched out to reach for his brother's hand, he spread out into a more horizontal position, displacing his weight over the water-filled loose, silty sand, almost as though floating on water. He reached until they touched fingers. Jondalar inched forward until he had a firm grasp.

"That's the way! Hold on to him! We're coming!" said a voice speaking Mamutoi.

Jondalar's breath exploded, his tension punctured. He discovered he was shaking but held Thonolan's hand firmly. In a few moments, a rope was passed to Jondalar to tie around his brother's hands.

"Relax now," Thonolan was instructed. "Stretch out, like swimming. You know how to swim?"

"Yes."

"Good! Good! You relax, we will pull."

Hands pulled Jondalar back from the edge of the quick-sand and soon had Thonolan out as well. Then they all followed a woman who prodded the ground with a long pole to avoid other sinkholes. Only after they reached solid ground did anyone seem to notice that the two men were entirely naked.

The woman who had directed the rescue stood back and scrutinized them. She was a big woman, not so much tall or fat as burly, and she had a bearing that commanded respect. "Why do you have nothing on?" she asked finally. "Why are two men travelling naked?"

Jondalar and Thonolan looked down at their nude, mud-caked bodies.

"We got in the wrong channel; then a log hit our boat," Jondalar began. He was feeling uncomfortable, unable to stand straight.

"After we had to dry our clothes, I thought we might as well take them off to swim the channel, and then to cross the mud. I was carrying them, ahead because Jondalar was hurt, and . . ."

"Hurt? One of you is hurt?" the woman asked.

"My brother," Thonolan said. At the mention of it, Jondalar became acutely aware of the aching, throbbing pain.

The woman saw him blanch. "Mamut must see to him," she said to one of the others. "You are not Mamutoi. Where did you learn to speak?"

"From a Mamutoi woman living with the Sharamudoi, my kin," Thonolan said.

"Tholie?"

"Yes, you know her?"

"She is my kin, too. The daughter of a cousin. If you are her kin, you are my kin," the woman said. "I am Brecie, of the Mamutoi, leader of the Willow Camp. You are both welcome."

"I am Thonolan, of the Sharamudoi. This is my brother, Jondalar, of the Zelandonii."

"Zel-an-don-yee?" Brecie said the unfamiliar word. "I have not heard of these people. If you are brothers, why are you Sharamudoi, and he this . . . Zelandonii? He does not look well," she said, briskly dismissing further discussion until a more appropriate time. Then she said to one of the others, "Help him. I'm not sure he can walk."

"I think I can walk," Jondalar said, suddenly dizzy with pain, "if it's not too far."

Jondalar was grateful when one of the Mamutoi men took an arm while Thonolan supported the other.

"Jondalar, I would have gone long ago if you hadn't made me promise to wait until you were well enough to travel. I'm leaving. I think you should go home, but I won't argue with you."

"Why do you want to go east, Thonolan? You've reached the end of the Great Mother River. Beran Sea, it's right there. Why not go home now?"

"I'm not going east, I'm going north, more or less. Brecie said they will all be going north to hunt mammoth soon. I'm going ahead, to another Mamutoi Camp. I'm not going home, Jondalar. I'm going to travel until the Mother takes me."

"Don't talk like that! You sound like you want to die!" Jondalar shouted, sorry the instant he said it for fear the mere suggestion would make it true.

"What if I do?" Thonolan shouted back. "What do I have to live for . . . without Jetamio." His breath caught in his throat, and her name came out with a soft sob.

"What did you have to live for before you met her? You're young, Thonolan. You have a long life ahead of you. New places to go, new things to see. Give yourself a chance to meet another woman like Jetamio," Jondalar pleaded.

"You don't understand. You've never been in love. There is no other woman like Jetamio."

"So you're going to follow her to the spirit world and drag me along with you!" He didn't like saying it, but if the only way to keep his brother alive was to play on his guilt, he'd do it.

"No one asked you to follow me! Why don't you go home and leave me alone?"

"Thonolan, everyone grieves when they lose people they love, but they don't follow them to the next world."

"Someday it will happen to you, Jondalar. Someday you'll love a woman so much, you'd rather follow her to the world of the spirits than live without her."

"And if it were me, now, would you let me go off alone? If I had lost someone I loved so much I wanted to die, would you abandon me? Tell me you would, Brother. Tell me you'd go home if I was sick to death with grief."

Thonolan looked down, then into the troubled blue eyes of his brother. "No, I guess I wouldn't leave you if I thought you were sick to death with grief. But you know, Big Brother" – he tried to grin but it was a contortion on his pain-ravaged face – "if I decide to travel for the rest of my life, you don't have to follow me forever. You are sick to death of travelling. Sometime you have to go home. Tell me, if I wanted to go home, and you didn't, you'd want me to go, wouldn't you?"

"Yes, I'd want you to go. I want you to go home now. Not because you want to, or even because I do. You need your own Cave, Thonolan, your family, people you've known all your life, who love you."

"You don't understand. That's one way we're different. The Ninth Cave of the Zelandonii is your home, it always will be. My home is wherever I want to make it. I am just as much Sharamudoi as I ever was Zelandonii. I just left my Cave, and people I loved as much as my Zelandonii family. That doesn't mean I don't wonder if Joharran has any children at his hearth yet, or if Folara has grown up to be as beautiful as I know she will be. I'd like to tell Willomar about our Journey and find out where he plans to go next. I still remember how excited I was when he returned from a trip. I'd listen to his stories and dream about travelling. Remember how he always brought something back for everyone? Me, and Folara, and you too. And always something beautiful for Mother. When you go back, Jondalar, take her something beautiful."

The mention of familiar names filled Jondalar with poignant memories. "Why don't you take her something beautiful, Thonolan? Don't you think Mother wants to see you again?"

"Mother knew I wasn't coming back. She said 'good journey' when we left, not 'until you return'. It's you who must have upset her, perhaps more than you upset Marona."

"Why would she be more upset about me than you?"

"I'm the son of Willomar's hearth. I think she knew I'd be a traveller. She might not have liked it, but she understood. She understands all her sons – that's why she made Joharran leader after her. She knows Jondalar is a Zelandonii. If you made a Journey alone, she'd know you would return – but you left with me, and I wasn't going back. I didn't know it when I left, but I think she did. She would want you to return; you're the son of Dalanar's hearth."

"What difference does that make? They severed the knot long ago. They're friends when they see each other at Summer Meetings."

"They may be just friends now, but people still talk about Marthona and Dalanar. Their love must have been very special to be so long remembered, and you are all she has to remind her, the son born to his hearth. His spirit, too. Everyone knows that; you look so much like him. You have to go back. You belong there. She knew it, and so do you. Promise you'll go back someday, Brother."

Jondalar was uneasy about such a promise. Whether he continued to travel with his brother or decided to return without him, he would be giving up more than he wanted to lose. As long as he made no commitment either way, he felt he could still have both. A promise to return implied that his brother would not be with him.

"Promise me, Jondalar."

What reasonable objection could he make. "I promise," he acquiesced. "I will go home – someday."

"After all, Big Brother," Thonolan said with a smile, "someone has to tell them we made it to the end of the Great Mother River. I won't be there, so you'll have to."

"Why won't you be there? You could come with me."

"I think the Mother would have taken me at the river – if you hadn't begged Her. I know I can't make you understand, but I know She will come for me soon, and I want to go."

"You are going to try to get yourself killed, aren't you?"

"No, Big Brother." Thonolan smiled. "I don't have to try. I just know the Mother will come. I want you to know I'm ready."

Jondalar felt a knot tightening inside him. Ever since the quicksand accident, Thonolan had had a fatalistic certainty he was going to die soon. He smiled, but it wasn't his old grin. Jondalar preferred the anger to this calm acceptance. There was no fight in him, no will to live.

"Don't you think we owe something to Brecie and the Willow Camp? They've given us food, clothing, weapons, everything. Are you willing to take it all and not offer anything in return?" Jondalar wanted to make his brother angry, to know there was something left. He felt he'd been tricked into a promise that relieved his brother of his final obligation. "You are so sure the Mother has some destiny for you that you have stopped thinking of anyone but yourself! Just Thonolan, right? No one else matters."

Thonolan smiled. He understood Jondalar's anger and could not blame him. How would he have felt if Jetamio had known she was going to die, and had told him?

"Jondalar, I want to tell you something. We were close . . ."

"Aren't we still?"

"Of course, because you can relax with me. You don't have to be so perfect all the time. Always so considerate . . ."

"Yes, I'm so good, Serenio wouldn't even be my mate," he said with bitter sarcasm.

"She knew you were leaving and didn't want to get hurt any worse. If you had asked her sooner, she would have mated you. If you had even pushed her a little when you did ask, she would have — even knowing you didn't love her. You didn't want her, Jondalar."

"So how can you say I'm so perfect? Great Doni, Thonolan, I wanted to love her."

"I know you did. I learned something from Jetamio, and I want you to know it. If you want to fall in love, you can't hold everything in. You have to open up, take that risk. You'll be hurt sometimes, but if you don't, you'll never be happy. The one you find may not be the kind of woman you expected to fall in love with, but it won't matter, you'll love her for exactly what she is."

"I wondered where you were," Brecie said, approaching the two brothers. "I've planned a little farewell feast for you since you're determined to leave."

"I feel an obligation, Brecie," Jondalar said. "You've taken care of me, given us everything. I don't think it's right to leave without making some repayment."

"Your brother has done more than enough. He hunted every day while you were recovering. He takes a few too many chances, but he's a lucky hunter. You leave with no obligation."

Jondalar looked at his brother, who was smiling at him.

19

Spring in the valley was a flamboyant outbreak of colour dominated by vernal green, but an earlier break had been frightening and had subdued Ayla's usual enthusiasm for the new season. After its late start, the winter was hard with heavier than normal snow. The early-spring flooding carried off the melt with raging violence.

Surging through the narrow upstream gorge, the torrent crashed into the jutting wall with such force it shook the cave. The water level nearly reached the ledge. Ayla was concerned for Whinney. She could scramble up to the steppes if necessary, but it was too steep a climb for the horse, especially one so pregnant. The young woman spent several anxious days watching the seething stream creep higher as it surged against the wall, then eddied back and swirled around the outer edge. Downstream, half the valley was submerged and the brush along the small river's usual course was completely inundated.

During the worst of the rampaging flood, Ayla sprang up with a jolt in the middle of the night, awakened by a muffled crack, like thunder, coming from beneath her. She was petrified. She didn't know the cause until the flood subsided. The concussion of a large boulder colliding with the wall had sent shock waves through the stone of the cave. A piece of the rock barrier had broken under the impact, and a large section of the wall lay across the stream.

Forced to find a new way around the obstruction, the course of the stream changed. The breach in the wall became a convenient bypass, but it narrowed the beach. A large portion of the accumulated bones, driftwood, and beach stones had been washed away. The boulder itself, which seemed to be made of the same rock as the gorge, had lodged not far beyond the wall.

Yet, for all the rearranging of rock and uprooting of trees and brush, only the weakest had succumbed. Most perennial growth burst forth from established roots, and new sproutings filled every vacant niche. Vegetation quickly covered the raw scars of freshly exposed rock and soil, giving them the illusion of permanence. Soon, the recently altered landscape seemed as though it had always been that way.

Ayla adjusted to the changes. For every boulder or piece of driftwood used for a special purpose, she found a replacement. But the event left its mark on her. Her cave, and the valley, lost a measure of security. Each spring she went through a period of indecision – for if she was going to leave the valley and continue her search for the Others, it would have to be in spring. She needed to allow herself time to travel, and to look for some other place to settle for the winter if she did not find anyone.

This spring the decision was more difficult than ever. After her illness, she was afraid to get caught in late fall or early winter, but her cave didn't seem as safe as it once had. Her illness had not only sharpened her perceptions of the danger of living alone, it had made her conscious of her lack of human companionship. Even after her animal friends had returned, they hadn't filled the void in the same way. They were warm and responsive, but she could communicate with them only in simple terms. She could not share ideas or relate an experience; she could not tell a story or express wonder at a new discovery or a new accomplishment and receive an answering look of recognition. She had no one to allay her fears or console her griefs, but how much of her independence and freedom was she willing to exchange for security and companionship?

She hadn't fully realized how constrained her life had been until she tasted freedom. She liked making her own decisions, and she knew nothing of the people she had been born to, nothing before she was adopted by the Clan. She hadn't known how much the Others would want; she only knew there were some things she was not willing to give. Whinney was one of them. She was not going to give up the horse again. She didn't know if she would be willing to give up hunting, but what if they wouldn't let her laugh?

There was a bigger question, and though she tried not to recognize it, it made all the others insignificant. What if she did find some Others, and they didn't want her at all? A clan of Others might not be willing to take in a woman who insisted upon a horse for companionship, or who wanted to hunt, or to laugh, but what if they rejected her even if she was willing to give up everything? Until she found them, she could hope. But what if she had to live alone all her life?

Such thoughts preyed on her mind from the time the first snows started to melt, and she was relieved that circumstances delayed a decision. She would not take Whinney away from the familiar valley until after she gave birth. She knew horses usually gave birth sometime in spring. The medicine woman in her, who had assisted with enough human deliveries to know it could be any time, kept a watchful eye on the mare. She didn't attempt any hunting forays, but she went riding frequently for exercise.

"I think we've missed that Mamutoi Camp, Thonolan. We seem to be too far east," Jondalar said. They were following the trail of a herd of giant deer to replenish supplies that were running low.

"I don't. . . . Look!" They had suddenly come upon a stag with an eleven-foot rack of palmate antlers. Thonolan pointed to the skittish animal. Wondering if the stag sensed danger, Jondalar expected to hear the deep belling of an alarm, but before the buck could sound a warning, a doe broke and ran right to them. Thonolan hurled the flint-tipped spear, the way he had learned from the Mamutoi, so the wide flat blade would slide in between the ribs. His aim was true; the doe fell almost at their feet.

But before they could claim their kill, they discovered why the buck had been so nervous, and why the doe had all but run into the spear. Tensing, they watched a cave lioness loping towards them. The predator seemed confused by the fallen doe for a moment. She wasn't accustomed to her prey dropping dead before she attacked. She didn't hesitate for long. Nosing the deer to make sure it was dead, the lioness got a good hold of the neck with her teeth, and, trailing the doe underneath her body, she started dragging it away.

Thonolan was indignant. "That lioness stole our kill!"

"That lioness was stalking the deer, too, and if she thinks it's her kill, I'm not going to argue with her."

"Well, I am."

"Don't be ridiculous," Jondalar snorted. "You're not going to take a deer away from a cave lioness."

"I'm not going to give up without trying."

"Let her have it, Thonolan. We can find another deer," Jondalar said, following his brother who had started after the lioness.

"I just want to see where she takes it. I don't think she's a pride lioness – the rest would be here on top of that deer by now. I think she's a nomad, and she's hauling it off to hide it from other lions. We can see where she takes it. She'll leave sooner or later, and then we can get some fresh meat for ourselves."

"I don't want fresh meat from a cave lion's kill."

"It's not her kill. It's my kill. That doe still has my spear in her."

It was useless to argue. They followed the lioness to a blind canyon, littered with rock from the walls. They waited and watched, and, as Thonolan predicted, the lioness left shortly after. He started for the canyon.

"Thonolan, don't go down there! You don't know when that lioness will come back."

"I just want to get my spear, and maybe a little of the meat." Thonolan made his way over the edge and scrambled down loose rubble into the canyon. Jondalar followed him, reluctantly.

Ayla had become so familiar with the territory east of the valley that she was bored with it, particularly since she wasn't hunting. It had been grey and rainy for days, and, when a warm sun burned off morning clouds by the time she was ready to ride, she couldn't stand the thought of covering the same ground again.

After she fastened on travelling baskets and travois poles, she led the horse down the steep path and around the shorter wall. She decided to head down the long valley rather than out on the steppes. At the end, where the stream turned south, she noticed the steep gravelly slope she had climbed before to look towards the west, but she thought the footing was too unsure for the horse. It did encourage her, however, to ride farther to see if she could find a more accessible exit to the west. As she continued south, she looked around with eager curiosity. She was in new territory, and she wondered why she hadn't ridden this way before. The high wall was easing into a gentler slope. When she saw a shallow crossing, she turned Whinney and urged her across.

The landscape was the same kind of open grasslands. Only the detail was different, but that made it interesting. She rode until she found herself in somewhat rougher country, with rugged canyons and abruptly sheared mesas. She was farther than she had planned to go, and, as she approached a canyon, she was thinking she ought to turn back. Then, she heard something that chilled her blood and set her heart racing: the thundering roar of a cave lion – and a human scream.

Ayla stopped, hearing her blood pounding in her ears. It had been so long since she had heard a human sound, yet she knew it was human, and something else. She knew it was her kind of human. She was so stunned that she couldn't think. The scream pulled at her – it was a cry for help. But she couldn't face a cave lion, nor expose Whinney to one.

The horse sensed her acute distress and turned towards the canyon, though Ayla's body-contact signal had been tentative at best. Ayla approached the canyon slowly, then dismounted and looked in. It was blind, only a wall of rubble at the other end. She heard the growling of the cave lion and saw its reddish mane. Then she realized Whinney had not been nervous, and she knew why.

"That's Baby! Whinney, that's Baby!"

She ran into the canyon, forgetting there might be other cave lions around and not even considering that Baby was no longer her young companion but a full-grown lion. He was Baby – that was all that mattered. She had no fear of this cave lion. She climbed up some jagged rocks towards him. He turned and snarled at her.

"Stop it, Baby!" she commanded with signal and sound. He paused only a moment, but by then she was beside him and pushing him out of the way so she could see his prey. The woman was too familiar, her attitude too certain for him to resist. He moved aside, as he had always done before when she came upon him with a kill and wanted to save the skin or take a piece of meat for herself. And he wasn't hungry. He had fed on the giant deer brought by his lioness. He had only attacked to defend his territory – and then he had hesitated. Humans were not prey to him. Their scent was too much like that of the woman who had raised him, a scent of both mother and hunting companion.

There were two of them, Ayla saw. She knelt to examine them. Her main concern was as a medicine woman, but she was astonished and curious as well. She knew they were men, though they were the first men of the Others she could remember seeing. She had not been able to visualize a man, but the moment she saw these two, she recognized why Oda had said men of the Others looked like her.

She knew immediately that the man with the darker hair was beyond hope. He lay in an unnatural position, his neck broken. The toothmarks on his throat proclaimed the cause. Though she had never seen him before, his death upset her. Tears of grief welled in her eyes. It wasn't that she loved him, but that she felt she had lost something beyond value before she ever had a chance to appreciate it. She was devastated that the first time she saw someone of her own kind, he was dead.

She wanted to acknowledge his humanity, to honour him with a burial, but a close look at the other man made her realize that it would be impossible. The man with the yellow hair still breathed, but his life was pumping out of him through a gash in his leg. His only hope was to get him back to the cave as quickly as possible so she could treat him. There was no time for a burial.

Baby sniffed the darker-haired man while she worked to staunch the flow of blood out of the other man's leg with a tourniquet made of her sling and a smooth stone for pressure. She pushed the lion away from the body. I know he's dead, Baby, but he's not for you, she thought. The cave lion jumped down from the ledge and went to make sure his deer was still in the cleft in the rock where he had left it. Familiar growls told Ayla he was preparing to feed.

When the pumping blood slowed to a seepage, she whistled for Whinney and then jumped down to set up the travois. Whinney was more nervous now, and Ayla remembered that Baby had a mate. She patted and hugged the horse for reassurance. She examined the sturdy woven mat between the two poles that dragged the ground behind the horse and decided it would hold the man with the yellow hair, but she didn't know what to do about the other one. She didn't want to leave him there for the lions.

When she climbed back up, she noticed that the loose rock at the back of the blind canyon looked very unstable – much of it had piled up behind a larger boulder that was none too stable itself. Suddenly, she remembered Iza's burial. The old medicine woman had been carefully laid in a shallow depression in the floor of the cave, then rocks and boulders had been piled over her. It gave Ayla an idea. She dragged the dead man to the back of the blind canyon near the slide of loose rock.

Baby came back to see what she was doing, his muzzle bloody from the deer. He followed her back to the other man and sniffed at him while Ayla dragged him to the edge of the rock, below which waited the skittish mare and the travois.

"Move out of the way now, Baby!"

As she tried to ease the man down to the travois, his eyelids fluttered and he moaned with pain, then closed his eyes again. She was just as glad he was unconscious. He was heavy, and the struggle to move him would be painful to him. When she finally got him wrapped into the travois, she returned to the stone ledge with a long sturdy spear and went to the rear. She looked down at the dead man and felt sorrow for the fact of his death. Then she leaned the spear against the rock and, with the formal silent motions of the Clan, addressed the world of the spirits.

She had watched Creb, the old Mog-ur, consign the spirit of Iza to the next world with his eloquent flowing movements. She had repeated the same gestures when she found Creb's body in the cave after the earthquake, though she had never known the full meaning of the holy gestures. That wasn't important – she knew the intent. Memories rushed back and tears came to her eyes as she moved through the beautiful silent ritual for the unknown stranger, and sent him on his way to the spirit world.

Then, using the spear as a lever, in much the same way as she would have used a digging stick to turn over a log or pry out a root, she prized free the large stone and jumped back out of the way as a cascade of loose rock covered the dead man.

Before the dust settled, she had led Whinney out of the canyon. Ayla got on the horse's back and began the long return trip to the cave. She stopped a few times to tend to the man, and once to dig fresh comfrey roots, although she was torn between hurrying to get him back and taking it a little easy for Whinney's sake. She breathed easier when she got the injured man across the stream and around the bend, and saw the jutting rock wall far ahead. But not until she stopped to change the position of the travois poles, just before starting up the narrow path, did she let herself believe she had reached the cave with the man still alive.

She led Whinney into the cave with the travois, then got a fire going to heat water before she untied the unconscious man and dragged him to her sleeping place. She unharnessed the horse, hugged her with gratitude, then looked over her store of medicinal herbs and selected those she wanted. Before beginning the preparations, she took a deep breath and reached for her amulet.

She couldn't clarify her thoughts enough to address her totem with a particular plea – she was too filled with inexplicable anxieties and confusing hopes – but she wanted help. She wanted to bring the force of her powerful totem to bear on her efforts to treat this man. She had to save him. She wasn't exactly sure why, but nothing had ever been more important. Whatever she had to do, this man must not die.

She added wood and checked the temperature of the water in the leather pot which was slung directly over the fire. When she saw steam rise, she added marigold petals to the pot. Then finally she turned to the unconscious man. From the tears in the leather he wore, she knew he had other gashes besides the wound on his right thigh. She needed to take his clothes off, but he was not wearing a wrap tied on with thongs.

When she looked closely to find out how to remove them, she saw that leather and fur had been cut, shaped into pieces, and joined together with cords to encase his arms and legs and body. She examined the joinings carefully. She had cut through his trousers to treat his leg, and she decided that was still the best way. She was more surprised when she cut through his outer garment and found another unlike anything she had ever seen. Bits of shell, bone, animal teeth, and colourful bird feathers had been attached to it in some orderly fashion. Was it a kind of amulet, she wondered? She hated to cut it, but there was no other way to get it off. She did it carefully, trying to follow the pattern to disturb it as little as possible.

Under the decorated garment was another one that covered the lower part of his body. It wrapped around each leg individually and was joined with cord, then came together and tied around his waist like a drawstring pouch, overlapping in front. She cut that off as well, and noted in passing that he was most definitely male. She removed the tourniquet and gently eased the stiff, blood-soaked leather away from the lacerated leg. She had loosened the tourniquet a few times en route, while manually applying pressure to both control the bleeding and allow some circulation in the leg. The use of a tourniquet could mean the loss of the limb if proper measures were not understood and applied.

She stopped again when she came to the footwear which was also shaped and joined to conform to the shape of his foot; then she slashed through the laces and wrapped thongs and pulled them off. His leg wound was seeping again, but not pumping, and she examined him quickly to learn the extent of his injuries. The other lacerations and scratches were superficial, but there could be danger from infection. Cuts from lion's claws had a nasty tendency to fester; even the minor scratches Baby had inflicted on her often did. But infection was not her immediate concern; his leg was. And she almost overlooked another injury: a large swelling on the side of his head, probably from the fall when he was attacked. She wasn't sure how serious it was, but she couldn't take the time to find out. Blood had started coming from the gash again.

She applied pressure to the groin while she washed the wound using the cured skin of a rabbit, scraped and stretched until it was soft and absorbent, dipped in the warm infusion of marigold petals. The liquid was astringent as well as antiseptic, and she would later use it to check the minor bleeding of the other wounds as well. She cleaned thoroughly, flushing the injury inside out. Under the deep external gash, a section of his thigh muscle was ripped. She sprinkled geranium-root powder liberally onto the wound and noticed the immediate coagulating effect.

Holding the pressure point with one hand, Ayla dipped comfrey root in water to rinse it. Then she chewed it to a pulp, and spat it into the hot marigold-petal solution to use for a wet poultice directly on the open wound. She held the gash closed and repositioned the torn muscle, but when she took her hands away, the wound gaped open and the muscle slipped out of place.

She held it closed again but knew it wouldn't stay. She didn't think wrapping it firmly would hold it together properly, and she didn't want the man's leg to heal badly and cause a permanent weakness. If only she could sit there and hold it together while it healed, she thought, feeling helpless and wishing Iza were there. She was sure the old medicine woman would have known what to do, though Ayla could not remember any instructions ever given to her about how to treat a situation like this.

But then she remembered something else, something Iza had told her about herself when she had asked how she could be a medicine woman of Iza's line. "I'm not really your daughter," she had said. "I don't have your memories. I don't really understand what your memories are."

Iza had explained then that her line had the highest status because they were the best; each mother had passed on to her daughter what she knew and learned, and she had been trained by Iza. Iza had given her all the knowledge she could, perhaps not all she knew, but enough, because Ayla had something else. A gift, Iza had said. "You don't have the memories, child, but you have a way of thinking, a way of understanding . . . and a way of knowing how to help."

If only I could think of a way to help this man now, Ayla thought. Then she noticed the pile of clothing she had cut off the man, and something occurred to her. She let go of his leg and picked up the garment that had covered the lower part of his body. Pieces had been cut, and then joined together with fine cord; a cord made of sinew. She examined the way they were attached, pulling them apart. The cord was put through a hole on one side, and then through a hole on the other, and pulled together.

She did something similar to shape dishes of birchbark, piercing holes and tying the ends together with a knot. Could she do something like that to hold the man's leg closed? To hold the gash until it healed together?

Quickly, she got up and brought back what appeared to be a brown stick. It was a long section of deer tendon, dried and hard. With a round smooth rock, Ayla rapidly pounded the dried tendon, breaking it down to long strands of white collagen fibres. She pulled it apart, then worked out a fine strand of the tough connective tissue and dipped it in the marigold solution. Like leather, sinew was flexible when wet, and if untreated it stiffened as it dried. When she had several pieces ready, she looked over her knives and borers, trying to find the best one with which to cut small holes in the man's flesh. Then she remembered the packet of slivers she had got from the tree struck by lightning. Iza had used such slivers to pierce boils, blisters, and swellings that needed to be drained. They would work for her purpose.

She washed away seeping blood, but wasn't quite sure how to begin. When she jabbed a hole with one of the slivers, the man moved and mumbled. She was going to have to do this quickly. She threaded the stiffened piece of sinew through the hole made with the sliver, then through the hole opposite, then carefully pulled them together and tied a knot.

She decided not to make too many knots, since she wasn't sure about pulling them out later. She finished four knots along the gash and added three more to hold the torn muscle in place. When she was through, she smiled at the knots of sinew holding a man's flesh together, but it had worked. The gash no longer gaped, the muscle stayed in place. If the injury healed clean without festering, he might have good use of his leg. At least the chances of it were much better.

She made a poultice of the comfrey root and wrapped the leg in soft leather. Then she carefully washed the rest of the scratches and gashes, mostly around his right shoulder and chest. The lump on his head bothered her, but the skin was not broken – it was just swollen. In fresh water, she made an infusion of arnica flowers, then made a wet compress for the swelling and tied it on with a leather strip.

Only then did she sit back on her heels. When he woke, there were medicines she could give him, but for now, she had treated everything she could treat. She straightened a minute wrinkle in the leather wrappings on his leg, and then, for the first time, Ayla really looked at him.

He was not as robust as men of the Clan, but muscular, and his legs were incredibly long. The golden hair, curled on his chest, became a downy halo on his arms. His skin was pale. His body hair was lighter and finer than that of men she had known; he was longer and leaner, but not much different. His flaccid maleness rested on soft golden curls. She reached out to feel the texture, then held back. She noticed a fresh scar and not quite faded bruise on his ribs. He must have recovered from a previous injury only recently.

Who had taken care of him? And where had he come from?

She leaned closer to see his face. It was flat in comparison with the faces of Clan men. His mouth, relaxed, was full-lipped, but his jaws did not protrude as much. He had a strong chin, with a cleft. She touched hers, and remembered that her son had one, but no one else in the Clan did. The shape of this man's nose was not much different from Clan noses – high-bridged, narrow – but it was smaller. His closed eyes were wide spaced and seemed prominent; then she realized he had no heavy brow ridges to shadow them. His forehead, creased with the slight indentation of worry wrinkles, was straight and high. To her eyes, conditioned to seeing only people of the Clan, his forehead seemed to bulge. She laid her hand on his brow, then felt her own. They were the same. How strange she must have looked to the Clan.

His hair was long and straight – part of it still held by a thong in the back, but most a tangled mass – and yellow. Like hers, she thought, but lighter. Familiar somehow. Then, with a shock of recognition, she remembered. Her dream! Her dream about a man of the Others. She couldn't see his face, but his hair had been yellow!

She covered the man, then quickly walked out to the ledge, surprised that it was still daytime, early afternoon by the sun. So much had happened, and so much concentrated mental, physical, and emotional energy had been expended with such intensity, that it seemed it should have been much later. She tried to sort out her thoughts, put them in some kind of order, but they caromed in confusion.

Why had she decided to ride west that day? Why should she have been right there just when he screamed? And, of all the cave lions on the steppes, how did it happen that the one she found in the canyon was Baby? Her totem must have led her there. What about her dream of the man with yellow hair? Was this the man? Why was he brought here? She wasn't sure what significance he would have in her life, but she knew it would never be the same. She had seen the face of the Others.

She felt Whinney nuzzle her hand from behind, and she turned. The horse put her head over the woman's shoulder, and Ayla reached up and put both arms around Whinney's neck, then laid her head on it. She stood there clinging to the animal, hanging on to her familiar, comfortable way of life, a bit fearful of the future. Then she stroked the mare, patting and caressing, and felt the movement of the young she was carrying.

"It can't be much longer, Whinney. I'm glad you helped me bring the man back, though. I would never have been able to carry him here alone."

I'd better go back in and make sure he's all right, she thought, nervous that something might happen to him if she left him alone for even a moment. He hadn't even moved, but she stayed beside him, watching him breathe, unable to take her eyes away. Then, she noticed an anomaly: he had no beard! All the men of the Clan had beards, bushy brown beards. Did men of the Others have no beards?

She touched his jaw and felt the rough stubble of new growth. He had some beard, but it was so short. She shook her head, perplexed. He looked so young. For all that he was big and muscular, he suddenly seemed more boy than man.

He turned his head, moaned, and muttered something. His words were unintelligible, yet there was a quality to them that made her feel she ought to be able to understand them. She put her hand on his forehead and then his cheek, and she felt the growing warmth of fever. I'd better see if I can get him to take some willowbark, she thought, getting up again.

She stood for a moment, still watching the man, and felt an

upwelling of emotion that struck her with surprising force. One thought filled her: *This man must live!*

She looked over her stock of medicinal herbs while she was getting the willowbark. She hadn't stopped to question why she maintained a complete pharmacopoeia when she had no one to treat but herself. It had just been habit. Now she was glad.

Besides the willowbark, she took down a plant with a hairy stem, that seemed to be growing out of the middle of wide double-pointed leaves. When she had picked it, the clusters of withered brown flowers were white. She thought of it as a variation of agrimony – but one of the other medicine women at the Clan Gathering had called it boneset, and used it for that purpose. Ayla used it, boiled down to a thick syrup, to reduce fever. It brought on a profuse sweat, but it was strong and she didn't want to use it on the man – weakened by loss of blood – unless she had to. It was best to be prepared, though. She remembered seeing alfalfa in the field. Fresh leaves steeped in hot water helped the blood clot, and a good meaty broth would give him strength. The medicine woman in her was thinking again, pushing back the confusion she had felt earlier.

She managed to get him to swallow some willowbark tea, cradling his head in her lap. His eyes fluttered, and he mumbled but remained unconscious. His scratches and gashes had developed a warmth and a redness, and his leg was visibly swelling. She replaced the poultice and made a new compress for his head injury. At least there the swelling was down. As evening came on, her worry grew, and she wished Creb were there to call upon the spirits to help her as he used to do for Iza.

By the time it was dark, the man was tossing and thrashing, calling out words. One in particular he used over and over again, mixed in with sounds that had the urgency of warning. She thought it might be a name, perhaps the name of the other man. With a deer rib bone whose end she had hollowed out to make a small depression, she fed him the agrimony concentration in small sips sometime near midnight. While fighting the bitter taste, his eyes flew open, but there was no recognition within their dark depths. It was easier to get him to take the datura tea afterwards – as though

385

he wanted to wash his mouth of the other bitter taste. She was glad she had found the pain-relieving and sleep-inducing datura near the valley.

She kept a vigil all night, hoping the fever would break, but it was near morning before the peak was reached. After she washed his perspiration-soaked body with cool water and changed his bed coverings and dressings, he slept more quietly. She dozed then on a fur beside him.

Suddenly, she was staring towards the bright sunshine coming in through the opening, wondering why she was wide awake. She rolled over, saw the man, and the entire previous day flashed in her mind. The man seemed relaxed and sleeping normally. She lay still and listened, then heard Whinney's heavy breathing. She got up quickly and went to the other side of the cave.

"Whinney," she said with excitement, "is it time?" The mare didn't have to answer.

Ayla had helped deliver babies before, had given birth to one of her own, but it was a new experience to help the horse. Whinney knew what to do, but she seemed to welcome Ayla's comforting presence. It was only toward the end, with the foal partially delivered, that Ayla helped pull him out the rest of the way. She smiled with pleasure when Whinney started licking the brown fuzzy fur of her newborn colt.

"That's the first time I've ever seen anyone midwife a horse," Jondalar said.

Ayla spun around at the sound and looked at the man propped up on one elbow, watching her.

20

Ayla stared at the man. She couldn't help herself, though she knew it was discourteous. It was one thing to observe him while he was unconscious or sleeping, but to see him wide awake made an altogether unexpected difference. He had blue eyes!

She knew her eyes were blue: it was one of the differences she had been reminded of often enough, and she had seen them in the reflection of the pool. But the eyes of the people of the Clan were brown. She had never seen another person with blue eyes, particularly blue of such a vivid shade that she could hardly believe it was real.

She was held by those blue eyes; she could not seem to move until she discovered she was shaking. Then she realized she had been looking directly at the man, and she felt the blood rise in her face as she tore her eyes away in embarrassment. It was not only impolite to stare, a woman was never supposed to look directly at a man, especially a stranger.

Ayla looked down at the ground, struggling to regain her composure. What must he think of me! But it had been so long since she had been around anyone, and this was the first time she could remember seeing one of the Others. She wanted to look at him. She wanted to fill her eyes, to drink in the sight of another human being, and one so unusual. But it was also important to her that he think well of her. She did not want to start out wrong because of her improper curious actions.

"I'm sorry. I didn't mean to embarrass you," he said, wondering if he had offended her or if she was just shy. When she didn't respond, he smiled wryly and realized he had been talking in Zelandonii. He switched to Mamutoi, and, when that elicited no answer, tried Sharamudoi.

She had been watching him with furtive glances, the way women did when they were waiting for a man's signal to approach. But he made no gestures, at least none she could understand. He just made words. Only none of the words were anything like the sounds people of the Clan made. They weren't guttural and distinct syllables; they flowed together. She couldn't even tell where one stopped and the other started. His voice made a pleasant, deep, rumbling tone, but it frustrated her. She felt at some basic level that she ought to understand him, and she could not.

She kept waiting for him to signal, until the waiting became embarrassing. Then she recalled, from her early days with the Clan, that Creb had had to teach her to talk properly. He had told her she only knew how to make sounds, and he had wondered if the Others communicated that way. But didn't this man know any signs? Finally, when she realized he wasn't going to signal, she knew she had to find some other way to communicate with him, if only to make sure he took the medicine she had prepared for him.

Jondalar was at a loss. Nothing he had said evoked any response from her at all. He wondered if she was unable to hear, then remembered how quickly she had turned to look at him the first time he spoke. What a strange woman, he thought, feeling uncomfortable. I wonder where the rest of her people are. He glanced around the small cave, saw the hay-coloured mare and her bay colt, and was struck by another thought. What was that horse doing in a cave? And why did it allow a woman to midwife? He'd never seen a horse give birth before, not even out on the plains. Did the woman have some kind of special powers?

This whole thing was beginning to have the unreal quality of a dream, yet he didn't think he was sleeping. Maybe it's worse. Maybe she's a donii who's come for you, Jondalar, he thought with a shudder, not at all sure she was a benevolent spirit . . . if she was a spirit. He was relieved when she moved, if rather hesitantly, towards the fire.

Her manner was diffident. She moved as though she did not want him to see her; she reminded him of . . . something. Her clothing was rather odd, too. It seemed to be nothing more than a leather hide wrapped around her and tied with a thong. Where had he seen something like that before? He couldn't recall.

She had done something interesting with her hair. It was separated into orderly sections all over her head and braided. He had seen braided hair before, though never worn in a style quite like hers. It was not unattractive but unusual. He had thought she was rather pretty the first time he looked at her. She'd seemed young – there was an innocence in her eyes – but as closely as he could tell with such a shapeless wrap, she had a mature woman's body. She seemed to be avoiding his inquiring gaze. Why? he wondered. He was beginning to be intrigued – she was a strange enigma.

He didn't notice he was hungry until he smelled the rich broth she brought him. He tried to sit up, and the deep pain in his right leg made him aware that he had other injuries as well. He hurt, all over. Then, for the first time, he wondered where he was and how he had got there. Suddenly he remembered Thonolan going into the canyon . . . the roar . . . and the most gigantic cave lion he had ever seen.

"Thonolan!" he cried, looking around the cave in panic. "Where's Thonolan?" There was no one else in the cave except the woman. His stomach churned. He knew, but he did not want to believe. Maybe Thonolan was in some other cave nearby. Maybe someone else was taking care of him. "Where's my brother? Where's Thonolan?!"

That word sounded familiar to Ayla. It was the one he had repeated so often when he called out with alarm from the depths of his dreams. She guessed he was asking for his companion, and she put her head down to show respect for the young man who was dead.

"Where's my brother, woman?" Jondalar shouted, grabbing her arms and shaking her. "Where is Thonolan?"

Ayla was shocked by his outburst. The loudness of his voice, the anger, the frustration, the uncontrolled emotions she could hear in his tone and see in his actions, all disturbed her. Men of the Clan would never have displayed their emotions so openly. They might feel as strongly, but manliness was measured by self-control.

There was grief in his eyes, though, and she could read from the tension in his shoulders and the tightening of his jaw that he was fighting the truth he knew but did not want to accept. The people she had grown up among communicated by more than simple hand signs and gestures. Stance, posture, expression, all gave shades of meaning that were part of the vocabulary. The flexion of a muscle could reveal a nuance. Ayla was accustomed to reading the language of the body, and the loss of a loved one was a universal affliction.

Her eyes, too, conveyed her feelings, told of her sorrow, her sympathy. She shook her head and bowed it again. He could no longer deny to himself what he knew. He let go of her, and his shoulders slumped with acquiescence.

"Thonolan . . . Thonolan . . . why did you have to keep on going? O Doni, why? Why did you take my brother," he called out, his voice tight and strained. He tried to resist the crush of desolation, giving in to his pain, but he had never known such profound despair. "Why did you have to take him and leave me with no one? You knew he was the only person I ever . . . loved. Great Mother. . . . He was my brother . . . Thonolan . . . Thonolan . . ."

Ayla understood grief. She had not been spared its ravages, and she ached for him with empathy, wanting to comfort him. Without knowing how it happened, she found herself holding the man, rocking with him as he cried out the name in anguish. He didn't know this woman, but she was human, and compassionate. She saw his need and responded to it.

He clung to her and heaved a powerful sob; his body shook with convulsive spasms. Great deep cries were torn from his throat, and each ragged breath cost him an agony of effort.

Not since he was a child had he let go so completely. It was not his nature to reveal his innermost feelings. They were too overpowering, and he had learned early to keep them in check – but the outflowing brought on by Thonolan's death exposed the raw edges of memories buried deep.

Serenio had been right, his love was too much for most people to bear. His anger, let loose, could not be contained until it had run its course either. Growing up, he had once wreaked such havoc with righteous anger that he had caused someone serious injury. All his emotions were too powerful. Even his mother had felt forced to put a distance between them, and she had watched with silent sympathy when friends backed off because he clung too fiercely, loved too hard, demanded too much of them. She had seen similar traits in the man to whom she had once been mated, and to whose hearth Jondalar was born. Only his younger brother seemed able to handle his love, to accept with ease and deflect with laughter the tensions it caused.

When he became too much for her to handle, and the whole Cave was in an uproar, his mother had sent him to live with Dalanar. It had been a wise move. By the time Jondalar returned, he had not only learned his craft, he had learned to keep his emotions under control, and he had grown into a tall, muscular, remarkably handsome man, with extraordinary eyes and an unconscious charisma that was a reflection of his depth. Women, in particular, sensed there was more to him than he was willing to show. He became an irresistible challenge, but no one could win him. As deep as they could go, they could not touch his deepest feelings; as much as they could take, he had more to give. He learned quickly how far to go with each, but to him the relationships were superficial and unsatisfactory. The one woman in his life able to meet him on his terms had made her commitment to another calling. They would have been a mismatch in any case.

His grief was as intense as the rest of his nature, but the young woman who held him had known grief as great. She had lost everything – more than once; she had felt the cold breath of the spirit world – more than once; yet she persevered. She sensed that his passionate outpouring was more than the keening of ordinary sorrow, and, from her own loss, gave him surcease.

When his racking sobs slackened, she discovered she was crooning under her breath as she held him. She had soothed Uba, Iza's daughter, to sleep with her crooning; she had watched her son close his eyes to the sound; and she had nursed her own grief and loneliness with the same tuneless lulling tone. It was appropriate. Finally, drained and exhausted, he released his hold. He lay back with his head to the side, staring at the stone walls of the cave. When she turned his face to wipe away the tears with cool water, he closed his eyes. He would not – or could not – look at her. Soon, his body relaxed and she knew he slept.

She went to see how Whinney was doing with her new foal,

then walked outside. She felt drained as well, yet relieved. At the far end of the ledge, she looked down the valley and remembered her anxious ride with the man on the travois, her fervent hope that he would not die. The thought made her nervous; the man must live. She hurried back into the cave and reassured herself that he still breathed. She brought the cold soup back to the fire – he had needed other sustenance more – made sure the medicinal preparations were ready for him when he woke, and then sat quietly beside him on the fur.

She could not get enough of looking at him, and she studied his face as though she were trying to satisfy, all at one time, her years of yearning for the sight of another human. Now that some of the strangeness was wearing off, she saw his face as more of a whole, not just as the individual features. She wanted to touch it, to run her finger along his jaw and chin, to feel his light smooth eyebrows. Then it struck her.

His eyes had watered! She had wiped wetness from his face; her shoulder was still damp from it. It's not just me, she thought. Creb could never understand why my eyes watered when I was sad – no one else's did. He thought my eyes were weak. But the man's eyes watered when he grieved. The eyes of all the Others must water.

Ayla's all-night vigil and intense emotional reactions finally caught up with her. She fell asleep on the fur beside him, though it was still afternoon. Jondalar woke up towards dusk. He was thirsty and looked for something to drink, unwilling to wake the woman. He heard the sounds of the horse and her newborn, but could only make out the yellow coat of the mare, who was lying down near the wall on the other side of the cave entrance.

He looked at the woman then. She was on her back, facing the other way. He could see only the line of her neck and jaw, and the shape of her nose. He remembered his emotional outbreak and felt a little embarrassed, then remembered the reason for it. His pain drove out all other feelings. He could feel his eyes filling and closed them tightly. He tried not to think about Thonolan; he tried not to think about anything. Soon, he succeeded, and didn't wake again until the middle of the night, and then his moans woke Ayla as well.

It was dark; the fire was out. Ayla felt her way to the

fireplace, got tinder and kindling from the place she kept her supply, then the firestone and flint.

Jondalar's fever was up again, but he was awake. He thought he must have dozed off, though. He couldn't believe the woman had made a fire so fast. He hadn't even seen the glow of coals when he awakened.

She brought the man cold willowbark tea she had made earlier. He raised himself on one elbow to reach for the cup, and, though it was bitter, he drank for his thirst. He recognized the taste – everyone seemed to know the use of willowbark – but he wished for a drink of plain water. He was feeling an urge to urinate as well, but he didn't know how to communicate either need. He picked up the cup which had held the willowbark tea, turned it over to show it was empty, then brought it to his lips.

She understood immediately, brought a waterbag, filled his cup, and then left it beside him. The water assuaged his thirst, but it added to his other problem, and he began to squirm uncomfortably. His actions made the young woman aware of his need. She picked a stick of wood out of the fire for a torch and went to the storage section of the cave. She wanted a container of some sort, but once there found some other useful items.

She had made stone lamps, nicking a shallow well into a stone that would hold melted fat and a moss wick, though she hadn't used them much. Her fire usually provided sufficient light. She picked up a lamp, found the moss wicks, then looked for the bladders of congealed fat. When she saw the empty bladder beside them, she took that, too.

She put the full one near the fire to soften and took the empty one to Jondalar – but she could not explain what it was for. She unfolded the pouring end, showed him the opening. He looked puzzled. There was no other way. She pulled back the cover, but when she reached between his legs with the open waterbag, he quickly got the idea and took it from her.

He felt ridiculous lying flat on his back rather than standing up to let his stream flow. Ayla could see his discomfort and went to the fire to fill the lamp, smiling to herself. He's not been hurt before, she thought, at least not so badly that he couldn't walk. He smiled a little sheepishly when she took

393

the waterbag and went out to empty it. She returned it to him, to use when he needed, then finished putting oil in the lamp and lit the moss wick. She carried it to the bed and pulled the cover back from his leg.

He tried to sit up to see, though it hurt. She propped him up. When he saw the lacerations on his chest and arms, he understood why it hurt more to use his right side, but it was the deep pain in his leg that concerned him more. He wondered how skilled the woman was. Willowbark tea did not make a healer.

When she removed the bloody root-poultice, he worried even more. The lamp did not illuminate the way sunlight did, but it left no doubt as to the seriousness of his injury. His leg was swollen, bruised, and raw. He looked closer and thought he saw knots holding his flesh together. He wasn't versed in the healing arts. Until recently, he hadn't been any more interested than most healthy young men, but had any zelandonii ever tied and knotted someone together?

He watched carefully while she prepared a new poultice, this time of leaves. He wanted to ask her what the leaves were, talk to her, try to get a measure of her skill. But she didn't know any of the languages he knew. In fact, now that he thought of it, he hadn't heard her talk at all. How could she be a healer if she didn't talk? But she did seem to know what she was doing, and whatever it was she put on his leg, it did ease the pain.

He let himself relax – what else could he do? – and watched her sponge a soothing wash onto his chest and arms. It wasn't until she untied the strip of soft leather holding the compress that he knew his head had been injured. He reached up and felt a swelling and a sore spot before she bound on a fresh compress.

She returned to the fireplace to heat the soup. He watched her, still trying to fathom who she was. "That smells good," he said, when the meaty aroma wafted toward him.

The sound of his voice seemed out of place. He wasn't sure why, but it was something more than knowing he would not be understood. When he had first met the Sharamudoi, neither he nor they understood a word of each other's language, yet there had been speech – immediate and voluble speech – as each strove to exchange words that would begin the process of communication. This woman made no attempt to begin a mutual exchange of words, and she responded to his efforts with only puzzled looks. She seemed not only to lack an understanding of the languages he knew, but to have no desire to communicate.

No, he thought. That wasn't quite true. They had communicated. She had given him water when he wanted it, and she had given him a container to make his stream, though he wasn't sure how she knew he needed one. He didn't form a specific thought for the communication they had shared when he gave vent to his grief – the pain was still too fresh – but he had felt it and included it in his wonderings about her.

"I know you can't understand me," he said, rather tentatively. He didn't know quite what to say to her, but he felt a need to say something. Once he started, words came easier. "Who are you? Where are the rest of your people?" He could not see much beyond the circle of light shed by the fire and the lamp, but he had not seen any other people, nor any evidence of them. "Why don't you want to talk?" She looked at him but said nothing.

A strange thought then began to insinuate itself into his mind. He recalled sitting near a fire in the dark before with a healer, and he remembered the Shamud talking about certain tests Those Who Served the Mother had to put themselves through. Wasn't there something about spending periods of time alone? Periods of silence when they could not speak to anyone? Periods of abstinence and fasting?

"You live here alone, don't you?"

Ayla glanced at him again, surprised to see a look of wonder on his face – as though he were seeing her for the first time. For some reason, it made her conscious of her discourtesy again, and she quickly looked down at the broth. Yet he had seemed unaware of her indiscretion. He was looking around at her cave and making his mouth sounds. She filled a bowl, then sat down in front of him with it and bowed her head, trying to give him the opportunity to tap her shoulder and acknowledge her presence. She felt no tap, and when she looked up, he was gazing at her questioningly and speaking his words.

He doesn't know! He doesn't see what I'm asking. I don't

think he knows any signals at all. With sudden insight, a thought occurred to her. How are we going to communicate if he doesn't see my signals, and I don't know his words?

She was jarred by a memory of the time Creb had been trying to teach her to talk, but she didn't know he was talking with his hands. She didn't know people could talk with their hands; she had only spoken with sounds! She had spoken the language of the Clan for so long that she could not remember the meaning of words.

But I am not a woman of the Clan any more. I am dead. I was cursed. I can never go back. I must live with the Others now, and I must speak the way they speak. I must learn to understand words again, and I must learn to speak them, or I will never be understood. Even if I had found a clan of Others, I would not have been able to talk to them, and they would not have known what I was saying. Is that why my totem made me stay? Until this man could be brought? So he could teach me to speak again? She shuddered, feeling a sudden cold, but there had been no draught.

Jondalar had been rambling on, asking questions for which he didn't expect answers, just to hear himself talk. There had been no response from the woman, and he thought he knew the reason. He felt sure she was either training to be, or in the Service of the Mother. It answered so many questions: her healing skills, her power over the horse, why she was living alone and would not speak to him, perhaps even how she had found him and brought him to this cave. He wondered where he was, but for the moment it didn't matter. He was lucky to be alive. He was troubled, though, by something else the Shamud had said.

He realized now, that if he had paid attention to the old white-haired healer, he would have known Thonolan was going to die – but hadn't he also been told that he followed his brother because Thonolan would lead him where he would not otherwise go? Why had he been led here?

Ayla had been trying to think of some way to begin to learn his words, and then she remembered how Creb had begun, with the name sounds. Steeling herself, she looked directly in his eyes, tapped her chest, and said, "Ayla."

Jondalar's eyes opened wide. "So you have decided to talk

after all! Was that your name?" He pointed at her. "Say it again."

"Ayla."

She had a strange accent. The two parts of the word were clipped, the insides pronounced back in her throat as though she were swallowing them. He had heard many languages, but none had the quality of the sounds she made. He couldn't quite say them, but tried for the closest approximation: "Aaay-lah."

She almost couldn't recognize the sounds he made as her name. Some people in the Clan had had great difficulty, but none said it the way he did. He strung the sounds together, altered the pitch so that the first syllable rose and the second dropped. She couldn't ever remember hearing her name said that way, yet it seemed so right. She pointed at him and leaned forward expectantly.

"Jondalar," he said. "My name is Jondalar of the Zelandonii."

It was too much; she couldn't get it at all. She shook her head and pointed again. He could see she was confused.

"Jondalar," he said, then slower, "Jondalar."

Ayla strained to make her mouth work the same way. "Duh-dah," was as close as she could come.

He could tell she was having trouble making the right sounds, but she was trying so hard. He wondered if she had some deformity in her mouth that kept her from speaking. Is that why she hadn't been talking? Because she couldn't? He said his name again, slowly, making each sound as clear as he could, as though he were speaking to a child, or someone lacking adequate intelligence, "Jon-da-lar . . . Jonnn-dah-larrr."

"Don-da-lah," she tried again.

"Much better!" he said, nodding approvingly and smiling. She had really made an effort that time. He wasn't so sure if his analysis of her as someone who was studying to Serve the Mother was correct. She didn't seem bright enough. He kept smiling and nodding.

He was making the happy face! No one else in the Clan ever smiled like that, except Durc. Yet it had come so naturally to her, and now he was doing it.

Her look of surprise was so funny that Jondalar had to

suppress a chuckle, but his smile deepened and his eyes sparkled with amusement. The feeling was contagious. Ayla's mouth turned up at the corners and, when his answering grin encouraged her, she responded with a full, wide, delighted smile.

"Oh, woman," Jondalar said. "You may not talk much, but you are lovely when you smile!" The maleness in him began to see her as a woman, as a very attractive woman, and he looked at her that way.

Something was different. The smile was still there, but his eyes. . . Ayla noticed that his eyes in the firelight were deep violet, and they held more than amusement. She didn't know what it was about his look, but her body did. It recognized the invitation and responded with the same drawing, tingling sensations deep inside that she had felt when she was watching Whinney and the bay stallion. His eyes were so compelling that she had to force herself to look away with a jerk of her head. She fumbled around straightening his bed coverings, then picked up the bowl and stood up, avoiding his eyes.

"I believe you're shy," Jondalar said, softening the intensity of his gaze. She reminded him of a young woman before her First Rites. He felt the gentle but urgent desire he always had for a young woman during that ceremony, and the eager pull in his loins. And then the pain in his right thigh. "It's just as well," he said with a wry grin. "I'm in no shape for it anyway."

He eased himself back down on the bed, pushing aside and smoothing out the furs she had used to prop him up, feeling drained. His body hurt, and when he remembered why, he hurt deeper. He didn't want to remember or think. He wanted to close his eyes and forget, sink into the oblivion that would end all his pain. He felt a touch on his arm and opened his eyes to see Ayla holding a cup of liquid. He swallowed it, and before long he felt the pain ease and a drowsiness overcome him. She had given him something that had caused it, he knew, and was grateful, but he wondered how she had known what he needed without his saying a word.

Ayla had seen his grimace of pain and knew the extent of his injuries. She was an experienced medicine woman. She had prepared the datura before he even woke up. She watched the wrinkles on his forehead smooth out and his body relax, then put out the lamp and banked the fire. She arranged the fur she was using beside the man, but she was far from sleepy.

By the glow of the banked coals, she made her way towards the mouth of the cave, then, hearing Whinney nicker softly, she crossed over to her. She was pleased to see the mare lying down. The strange scent of the man in the cave had made her nervous after she foaled. She was accepting the man's presence if she felt relaxed enough to lie down. Ayla sat down below Whinney's neck and in front of her chest, so she could stroke her face and scratch around her ears. The foal, who had been lying near his dam's teats, got curious. He nuzzled between them. Ayla patted and scratched him too, then extended her fingers. She felt the suction, but he let go when he discovered she had nothing for him. His need to suck was satisfied by his mother.

He's a wonderful baby, Whinney, and he'll grow up strong and healthy, just as you did. You have someone now, like you, and so do I. It's hard to believe. After all this time. I'm not alone any more. Unexpected tears came to her eyes. How many, many moons have passed since I was cursed, since I've seen anyone. And now someone is here. A man, Whinney. A man of the Others, and I think he's going to live. She wiped her tears with the back of her hand. His eyes made water like this, too, and he smiled at me. And I smiled back.

I am one of the Others, just like Creb said. Iza told me to find my own kind, to find my mate. Whinney! Is he my mate? Was he brought here for me? Did my totem bring him?

Baby! Baby gave him to me! He was chosen, just as I was chosen. Tested and marked, by Baby, by the cave lion cub my totem gave me. And now his totem is the Cave Lion, too. It means he could be my mate. A man with a Cave Lion totem would be powerful enough for a woman with a Cave Lion totem. I could even have more babies.

Ayla frowned. But babies aren't really made by totems. I know Broud started Durc when he put his organ inside me. Men start babies, not totems. Don-da-lah is a man. . . .

Suddenly Ayla thought of his organ, stiffened with the need to lose his water, and she remembered his disconcerting blue eyes. She felt a strange pulsing inside that made her feel restless. Why did she have these strange feelings? They had started when she watched Whinney and the dark brown horse . . .

A dark brown horse! And now she has a dark brown foal. That stallion did start a baby in her. Don-da-lah could start a baby in me. He could be my mate. . . .

What if he doesn't want me? Iza said men do that if they like a woman. Most men. Broud didn't like me. I wouldn't hate it if Don-da-lah. . . . Suddenly she flushed. I'm so big and ugly! Why should he want to do that to me? Why should he want me for a mate? He might have a mate. What if he wants to leave?

He can't leave. He has to teach me to make words again. Would he stay if I could understand his words?

I'll learn them. I'll learn all his words. Then maybe he'll stay, even if I am big and ugly. He can't go now. I've been alone too long.

Ayla jumped up, almost in a panic, and went out of the cave. Black was shading into deep velvet blue; night was nearly over. She watched shapes of trees and familiar landmarks take on definition. She wanted to go in and look at the man again, and fought the urge. Then she thought about getting him something fresh for breakfast and started in for her sling.

Maybe he won't like it if I hunt? I already decided I wasn't going to let anyone stop me, she remembered, but did not go in to get her sling. Instead she walked down to the beach, doffed her wrap, and took a morning swim. It felt especially good and seemed to wash away her emotional turmoil. Her favourite fishing place no longer existed after the spring flood, but she had discovered another place downstream a short way and headed in that direction.

Jondalar woke up to the smell of food cooking, which made him know he was famished. He used the waterbag to empty his bladder and managed to prop himself up so he could look around. The woman was gone, and so were the horse and her foal, but the place they had occupied was the only other place in the cave that looked remotely like a sleeping place, and there was only one hearth. The woman did live here alone, except for the horses, and they could not be considered people.

But then, where were her people? Were there other caves nearby? Were they on an extended hunting trip? In the storage area were cave furnishings, furs and leathers, plants hanging from racks, meat and food storage enough for a large Cave. Was it just for her? If she lived alone, why did she need so much? And who carried him here? Perhaps her people brought him and left him with her.

That must be it! She's their zelandoni, and they brought me here for her to take care of. She's young for it – at least she seems young – but she is competent. No doubt of that. She probably came here to impose some test on herself, to develop some special skill – maybe with animals – and her people found me, and there wasn't anyone else, so she let them leave me here. She must be a very powerful zelandoni to have such control over animals.

Ayla came into the cave, carrying a dried and bleached pelvic-bone platter, with a large, freshly baked trout on it. She smiled at him, surprised to find him awake. She put the fish down, then rearranged the furs and straw-stuffed leather pads so that he could sit more comfortably. She gave him a willowbark tea to start with, to keep down the fever and alleviate pain. She put the platter across his lap, then went out and returned with a bowl of cooked grain, fresh peeled thistle stalks and cow parsley, and the first wild strawberries.

Jondalar was hungry enough to eat anything, but after the first few bites, he slowed down to appreciate the taste. Ayla had learned Iza's way with herbs, not only as medicines, but as seasonings. Both trout and grain were enhanced by her deft hand. The fresh stalks were crisp and at the right stage of tenderness, and the wild strawberries, though few, brought their own reward of sweetness with no assistance from anyone but the sun. He was impressed. His mother was acknowledged as a fine cook, and though the flavours were not the same, he understood the subtleties of food well prepared.

It pleased Ayla that he took time to savour the meal. When he was through, she brought him a cup of mint tea and prepared to change his dressings. She left the head compress off. The swelling was down and only a little soreness remained. The slashes on his chest and arms were healing. He might carry some slight scarring, but no impairment. It was the leg. Would it heal properly? Would he regain full use? Some use? Or would he be a cripple?

She removed the poultice, relieved to see that the wild cabbage leaves had reduced the festering, as she had hoped. There was definite improvement, though no way to tell yet how much use he would have of it. Tying the wounds together with sinew seemed to be working. Considering the damage, the leg was close to its original shape, though there would be extensive scarring and perhaps some deformation. She was quite pleased.

It was the first time Jondalar really had a look at his leg, and he was not pleased. It looked much more seriously damaged than he had imagined. He blanched at the sight and swallowed hard a few times. He could see what she had attempted to do with the knots. It might make a difference, but he wondered if he would ever walk again.

He talked to her and asked her where she had learned healing, not expecting an answer. She recognized her name, but nothing else. She wanted to ask him to teach her the meaning of his words, but she didn't know how. She went out to get wood for the fireplace in the cave, feeling frustrated. She was hungry to learn to talk, but how could they even begin?

He thought about the meal he had just eaten. Whoever supplied her, she was well provisioned, but she obviously knew how to take care of herself. The berries, stalks, and trout had been fresh. The grains, though, must have been harvested the previous fall, which meant surplus from winter storage. That spoke well for planning; no late-winter or early-spring famine. It also meant the area was probably well known, and therefore settled for some duration. There were some other indications that the cave had been used for some time: the black soot around the smokehole and the well-trodden floor in particular.

While she was well-supplied with cave furnishings and implements, close inspection revealed they were totally lacking in carvings or decoration, and rather primitive. He looked at the wooden cup out of which he had been drinking tea. But not crude, he thought. In fact, very well made. The cup had been carved out of a gnarl, judging from the pattern of the wood grain. As Jondalar examined it closely, it seemed to him that the cup had been formed to take advantage of a shape suggested by the grain. It would not be hard to imagine the face of a small animal in the knots and curves. Had she done that on purpose? It was subtle. He liked it better than some implements he had seen with more blatant carvings.

The cup itself was deep, with a flaring lip, symmetrical, and finished to a fine smoothness. Even the inside showed no gouging ridges. A gnarled piece of wood was hard to work; this cup must have taken many days to make. The closer he looked, the more he realized the cup was unquestionably a fine piece of workmanship, deceiving in its simplicity. Marthona would like this, he thought, remembering his mother's ability to arrange even the most utilitarian implements and storage containers in a pleasing way. She had a knack for seeing beauty in simple objects.

He looked up when Ayla brought in a load of wood and shook his head at her primitive leather wrap. Then he noticed the pad on which he was lying. Like her wrap, it was just the hide, not cut to shape, wrapped around fresh hay and tucked under in a shallow trench. He pulled out an end to examine it closer. The very outside edge was a bit stiff, and a few deer hairs still clung, but it was very pliable and velvety soft. Both the inner grain and the tough outer grain along with the fur had been scraped off, which helped to account for the supple texture. But her furs impressed him more. It was one thing to stretch and pull a skin with the grain removed to make it flexible. It was far more difficult with furs since only the inner grain was removed. Furs usually tended to be stiffer, yet the ones on the bed were as pliant as the skins.

There was a familiarity to the feel of them, but he could not think why.

No carvings or decorations on implements, he was thinking, but made with the finest workmanship. Skins and furs cured with great skill and care – yet no clothing was cut or shaped to fit, sewn or laced together, and no item was beaded, or quilled, or dyed, or decorated in any way. Yet she had fitted and sewn his leg together. They were peculiar inconsistencies, and the woman was a mystery.

Jondalar had been watching Ayla as she prepared to make a fire, but he really had not been paying attention. He'd seen fire made many times. He had wondered in passing why she didn't just bring in a coal from the fire she used to cook his meal, and then he supposed it had gone out. He saw, without seeing, the woman gather together quick-starting tinder, pick up a couple of stones, strike them together, and blow a flame to life. It was done so quickly that the fire was burning well before it occurred to him what she had done.

"Great Mother! How did you get that fire started so fast?" Ayla turned at his outburst with a quizzical look.

"How did you start that fire?" he asked again, sitting forward. "Oh, Doni! She doesn't understand a word I'm saying." He threw his hands up in exasperation. "Do you even know what you've done? Come here, Ayla," he said, beckoning to her.

She went to him immediately; it was the first time she had seen him use a hand motion in any purposeful way. He was greatly concerned about something, and she frowned, concentrating on his words, wishing she could understand.

"How did you make that fire?" he asked again, saying the words slowly and carefully as though, somehow, that would enable her to understand – and flung his arm towards the fire.

"Fy . . . ?" she made a tentative attempt to repeat his last word. Something was important. She was shaking with concentration, trying to will herself to understand him.

"Fire! Fire! Yes, fire," he shouted, gesticulating towards the flames. "Do you have any idea what it could mean to make a fire that fast?"

"Fyr . . . ?"

"Yes, like that over there," he said, jabbing his finger in the air at the fireplace. "How did you make it?"

She got up, went to the fireplace and pointed to it. "Fyr?" she said.

He heaved a sigh and leaned back on the furs, suddenly realizing he had been trying to force her to understand words she didn't know. "I'm sorry, Ayla. That was stupid of me. How can you tell me what you did when you don't know what I'm asking?"

The tension was gone. Jondalar closed his eyes feeling drained and frustrated, but Ayla was excited. She had a word. Only one, but it was a beginning. Now, how could she keep it going? How could she tell him to teach her more, that she had to learn more.

"Don-da-lah . . . ?" He opened his eyes. She pointed to the fireplace again, "Fyr?"

"Fire, yes, that's fire," he said nodding affirmatively. Then he closed his eyes again, feeling tired, a little silly for getting so excited, and in pain, physically and emotionally.

He wasn't interested. What could she do to make him understand? She felt so thwarted, so angry that she couldn't think of some way to communicate her need to him. She tried one more time.

"Dona-da-lah," she waited until he opened his eyes again, "Fyr . . . ?" she said with hopeful appeal in her eyes.

What does she want? Jondalar thought, his curiosity aroused. "What about that fire, Ayla?"

She could sense he was asking a question, in the set of his shoulders and the expression on his face. He was paying attention. She looked around, trying to think of some way to tell him, and she saw the wood beside the fire. She picked up a stick, brought it to him, and held it up with the same hopeful look.

His forehead knotted in puzzlement, then smoothed as he thought he was beginning to understand. "Do you want the word for that?" he asked, wondering at her sudden interest in learning his language, when she seemed not to have any interest in speaking before. Speaking! She wasn't exchanging a language with him, she was trying to speak! Could that be why she was so silent? Because she didn't know how to speak?

He touched the stick in her hand. "Wood," he said.

Her breath exploded out; she didn't know she had been holding it. "Ud . . . ?" she tried.

"Wood," he said slowly, exaggerating his mouth to enunciate clearly.

"Ooo-ud," she said, trying to make her mouth mimic his.

"That's better," he said, nodding.

Her heart was pounding. Did he understand? She searched again, frantically, for something to keep it going. Her eyes fell on the cup. She picked it up and held it out.

"Are you trying to get me to teach you to talk?"

She didn't understand, shook her head, and held the cup up again.

"Who are you, Ayla? Where do you come from? How can you do . . . everything you do, and not know how to talk? You are an enigma, but if I'm ever going to learn about you, I think I'm going to have to teach you to talk."

She sat on her fur beside him, waiting anxiously, still holding the cup. She was afraid that with all the words he was saying he would forget the one she asked for. She held the cup out to him once again.

"What do you want, 'drink' or 'cup'? I don't suppose it matters." He touched the vessel she was holding. "Cup," he said.

"Guh," she responded, then smiled with relief.

Jondalar followed through on the idea. He reached for the waterbag of fresh water she had left for him and poured some into the cup. "Water," he said.

"Ahddah."

"Try it again, water," he encouraged.

"Ooo-ah-dah."

Jondalar nodded, then held the cup to his lips and took a sip. "Drink," he said. "Drink water."

"Drrringk," she replied, quite clearly except for rolling the *r* and swallowing the word somewhat. "Drringk ooahdah."

21

"Ayla, I can't stand it in this cave any more. Look at that sunshine! I know I'm healed enough to move a little, at least outside the cave."

Ayla didn't understand everything Jondalar said, but she knew enough to understand his complaint – and sympathize with it. "Knots," she said, touching one of the stitches. "Cut knots. Morning see leg."

He smiled as though he had won a victory. "You're going to take out the knots, and then tomorrow morning I can go out of the cave."

Language problems or not, Ayla was not going to be committed to more than she intended. "See," she repeated emphatically. "Ayla look . . ." She struggled to express herself with her limited ability. "Leg no . . . heal, Don-da-lah no out."

Jondalar smiled again. He knew he had overstated her meaning, hoping she would go along with him, but he was rather pleased that she was not taken in by his ploy and insisted on making herself understood. He might not get out of the cave tomorrow, but it meant that ultimately she would learn faster.

Teaching her to speak had become a challenge, and her progress pleased him, though it was uneven. He was intrigued by the way she learned. The extent of her vocabulary was already astounding, she seemed able to memorize words as fast as he could give them to her. He had spent the better part of one afternoon telling her the names of everything she and he could think of, and when they were through, she had repeated every word back to him with its correct association. But pronunciation was difficult for her. She could not produce some sounds right no matter how hard she tried, and she did try hard.

He liked the way she spoke, though. Her voice was low-pitched and pleasing, and her strange accent made her sound exotic. He decided not to bother yet about correcting the way she put the words together. Proper speech could come later. Her real struggle became more apparent once they progressed beyond words that named specific things and actions. Even the simplest abstract concepts were a problem – she wanted a separate word for every shade of colour and found it hard to understand that the deep green of pine and the pale green of willow were both described by the general word *green*. When she did grasp an abstraction, it seemed to come as a revelation, or a memory long forgotten.

He commented favourably on her phenomenal memory once, but she found it difficult to understand – or believe – him.

"No, Don-da-lah. Ayla not good remember. Ayla try, little girl Ayla want good . . . memory. Not good. Try, try, all time try."

Jondalar shook his head, wishing his memory were as good as hers, or his desire to learn as strong and relentless. He could see improvement every day, though she was never satisfied. But as their ability to communicate expanded, the mystery of her deepened. The more he learned about her, the more questions he was burning to have answered. She was incredibly skilled and knowledgeable in some ways, and totally naïve and ignorant in others – and he was never sure which would be which. Some of her abilities – such as making fire – were far more advanced than any he had seen anywhere, and some were primitive beyond belief.

Of one thing he had no doubt, though: whether or not any of her people were nearby, she was entirely capable of taking care of herself. And of him, as well, he thought, as she moved his covers back to look at his injured leg.

Ayla had an antiseptic solution ready, but she was nervous as she prepared to take out the knots that held his flesh together. She didn't think the wound would fall apart – it seemed to be healing well – but she had not used the technique before and she wasn't sure. She had been considering removing the knots for several days, but it had taken Jondalar's complaint to make the decision.

The young woman bent over the leg, looking closely at the knots. Carefully, she pulled up one of the knotted pieces of deer sinew. Skin had grown attached to it and pulled up with it. She wondered if she should have waited so long, but it was too late to worry now. She held the knot with her fingers, and, with her sharpest knife, one that had not been used, she cut one side as close to the knot as possible. A few experimental tugs proved it was not going to pull out easily. Finally, she took the knot in her teeth and, with a quick jerk, pulled it out.

Jondalar winced. She was sorry to cause him discomfort, but no gap had opened. A little trickle of blood showed where the skin had torn slightly, but the muscles and flesh had healed together. Discomfort was a small price to pay. She took out the remaining stitches as quickly as she could, to get it over with, while Jondalar gritted his teeth and clenched his fists to keep from yelping every time she pulled one out. They both leaned closer to see the result.

Ayla decided that, if there was no deterioration, she would let him put weight on it and allow him to go outside the cave. She picked up the knife, and the bowl with the solution, and started to get up. Jondalar stopped her. "Let me see the knife?" he asked, pointing to it. She gave it to him and looked on while he examined it.

"This is made on a flake! It's not even a blade. It's been worked with some skill, but the technique is so primitive. It doesn't even have a handle – just retouched on the back so it won't cut you. Where did you get this, Ayla? Who made it?"

"Ayla make."

She knew he was commenting on the quality and workmanship, and she wanted to explain that she was not as skilled as Droog, but that she had learned from the Clan's best toolmaker. Jondalar studied the knife in depth, and it seemed with some surprise. She wanted to discuss the merits of the tool, the quality of the flint, but she could not. She did not have the vocabulary of the proper terms, or an understanding of how to express the concepts. It was frustrating.

She yearned to talk to him, about everything. It had been so long since she had anyone to communicate with, but she didn't know how much she missed it until Jondalar had arrived. She felt as though a feast had been set down before her, and she was starving and wanted to devour it, but she could only taste.

Jondalar gave the knife back to her, shaking his head in wonder. It was sharp, certainly adequate, but it heightened his curiosity. She was as well trained as any zelandoni, and used advanced techniques – like the stitches – but such a primitive knife. If only he could ask her and make her understand; if only she could tell him. And why couldn't she talk? She was learning rapidly now. Why hadn't she learned before? Ayla's learning to speak had become a driving ambition for both of them.

Jondalar woke early. The cave was still dark, but the entrance and the hole above it showed the deep blue of pre-dawn. It grew perceptibly lighter as he watched, bringing out the shape of every bump and hollow of the rock walls. He could see them as clearly when he closed his eyes; they were etched on his brain. He had to get outside and look at something else. He felt a growing excitement, sure this would be the day. He could hardly wait and was going to shake the woman sleeping beside him. He paused before he touched her, then changed his mind.

She slept on her side, curled up with her furs piled around her. He was in her usual sleeping place, he knew. Her furs were on a mat drawn up beside him, not in a shallow trench covered with a hay-stuffed pad. She slept in her wrap, ready to jump up at a moment's notice. She rolled over on her back, and he studied her carefully, trying to see if there were any distinguishing characteristics that would give some hint of her origins.

Her bone structure, the shape of her face and her cheekbones had a foreign quality compared with Zelandonii women, but there was nothing out of the ordinary about her, except that she was extraordinarily pretty. It was more than mere prettiness, he decided, now that he was taking a good look at her. There was a quality to her features that would be recognized as beauty by anyone's standards.

The style of her hair, bound into a regular pattern of braids, left long at the sides and back and tucked under themselves in front, was not familiar, but he had seen hair arranged in ways much more unusual. Some long strands had worked their way loose and were pushed back behind her ears or hanging in disarray, and she had a smudge of charcoal on one cheek. It occurred to him that she had not left his side for more than a moment since he regained consciousness, and probably not before. No one could fault her care. . . .

His train of thought was interrupted when Ayla opened her eyes and squealed with surprise.

She wasn't used to opening her eyes to a face, especially one with brilliant blue eyes and a scraggly blond beard. She sat up so quickly that she was dizzy for a moment, but she soon regained her composure and got up to stir the fire. It was out; she had forgotten to bank it again. She gathered the materials to start a new one.

"Would you show me how you start a fire, Ayla?" Jondalar asked when she picked up the stones. This time she understood.

"Not hard," she said, and brought the fire-making stones and burning materials closer to the bed. "Ayla show." She demonstrated hitting the stones together, then piled shaggy bark fibre and fireweed fuzz together and gave him the flint and iron pyrite.

He recognized the flint immediately – and he thought he had seen stones like the other one, but he would never have attempted to use them together for anything, particularly not for making fire. He struck them together the way she had. It was only a glancing blow, but he thought he saw a tiny spark. He struck again, still not quite believing he could draw fire from stones, in spite of seeing Ayla do it. A large flash jumped from the cold stones. He was stunned and then excited. After a few more tries and a little assistance from Ayla, he had a small fire going beside the bed. He looked at the two stones again.

"Who taught you to make fire this way?"

She knew what he was asking, but she didn't know how to tell him. "Ayla do," she said.

"Yes, I know you do, but who showed you?"

"Ayla . . . show." How could she tell him about that day when her fire went out, and her hand-axe broke, and she had discovered the firestone? She put her head in her hands for a moment, trying to find a way to explain, then looked at him and shook her head. "Ayla no talk good."

He could see her sense of defeat. "You will, Ayla. You can tell me then. It won't be long – you're an amazing woman." He smiled then. "Today I go outside, right?"

"Ayla see . . ." She pulled back his covers and checked the leg. The places where the knots had been had small scabs, and the leg was well on the way towards healing. It was time to get him up on the leg and try to assess the impairment. "Yes, Don-da-lah go out."

The biggest grin she'd ever seen cracked his face. He felt like a boy setting out for the Summer Meeting after a long winter. "Well, let's go, woman!" He pulled back the furs, eager to be up and out.

His boyish enthusiasm was infectious. She smiled back, but added a note of restraint. "Don-da-lah eat food."

It didn't take long to prepare a morning meal of food cooked the evening before, plus a morning tea. She brought grain to Whinney, and spent a few moments currying her with a teasel and scratching the little colt with it as well. Jondalar watched her. He'd watched her before, but this was the first time he noticed that she made a sound remarkably like that of a horse's nicker, and some clipped, guttural syllables. Her hand motions and signs meant nothing to him – he didn't see them, didn't know they were an integral part of the language she spoke to the horse – but he knew that in some incomprehensible way, she was talking to the mare. He had an equally strong impression that the animal understood her.

As she fondled the mare and her foal, he wondered what magic she had used to captivate the animals. He was feeling a bit captivated himself, but he was surprised and delighted when she led the horse and her colt to him. He had never patted a living horse before, nor got so close to a fuzzy new foal, and he was slightly overwhelmed by their total lack of fear. The colt seemed particularly drawn to him after his first cautious pats led to strokes and scratches that unerringly found the right places.

He remembered he had not given her the name for the animal, and he pointed to the mare. "Horse," he said.

But Whinney had a name, a name made with sounds, just

like hers, and his. Ayla shook her head. "No," she said, "Whinney."

To him, the sound she made was not a name – it was a perfect imitation of a horse's whinny. He was astonished. She couldn't speak any human languages, but she could talk like a horse? Talk to a horse? He was awed; that was powerful magic.

She mistook his dazed look for lack of understanding. She touched her chest and said her name, trying to explain. Then she pointed at him and said his name. Next she pointed to the horse and made the soft neigh again.

"Is that the mare's name? Ayla, I can't make a noise like that. I don't know how to talk to horses."

After a second, and more patient explanation, he made an attempt, but it was more like a word that sounded like it. That seemed to satisfy her, and she led the two horses back to the mare's place in the cave. "He's teaching me words, Whinney. I'm going to learn all his words, but I had to tell him your name. We'll have to think of a name for your little one. . . . I wonder, do you think he'd like to name your baby?"

Jondalar had heard of certain zelandonii who were said to have the ability to lure animals to hunters. Some hunters could even make a good imitation of the sounds of certain animals, which helped them get closer. But he'd never heard of anyone who could talk with an animal, or who had convinced one to live with her. Because of her, a wild mare had foaled right before his eyes, and had even let him touch her baby. It suddenly struck him, with wonder and a little fear, what the woman had done. Who was she? And what kind of magic did she possess? But as she walked towards him with a happy smile on her face, she seemed no more than an ordinary woman. Just an ordinary woman, who could talk to horses but not to people.

"Don-da-lah go out?"

He had almost forgotten. His face lit up with eagerness, and, before she could reach him, he tried to get up. His enthusiasm paled. He was weak, and it was painful to move. Dizziness and nausea threatened, then passed. Ayla watched his expression change from an eager smile to a grimace of pain and then a sudden blanching.

"I may need a little help," he said. His smile was strained, but earnest.

"Ayla help," she said, offering her shoulder for support and her hand for assistance. At first he didn't want to put too much weight on her, but as he saw that she was bearing up under it, had the strength, and knew how to pull him up, he took her help.

When he finally stood on his good leg, braced against a post of the drying rack, and Ayla looked up at him, her jaw dropped and her eyes opened wide. The top of her head barely reached his chin. She knew his body was longer than men of the Clan, but she hadn't projected that length into height, hadn't perceived how he would appear standing up. She had never seen anyone so tall.

Not since she was a child could she remember looking up to anyone. Even before she had reached womanhood, she was taller than everyone in the Clan, including the men. She had always been big and ugly; too tall, too pale, too flat faced. No man would have her, not even after her powerful totem was defeated and they would all have liked to think their totem had overcome her Cave Lion and made her pregnant; not even when they knew that if she wasn't mated before she gave birth, her child would be unlucky. And Durc was unlucky. They weren't going to let him live. They said he was deformed, but then Brun accepted him anyway. Her son had overcome his bad luck. He would overcome the bad luck of losing his mother, too. And he was going to be tall – she had known that before she left – but not as tall as Jondalar.

This man made her feel positively little. Her first impression of him had been that he was young, and young implied small. He had looked younger, too. She looked up at him from her new perspective and noticed his beard had been growing in. She didn't know why he hadn't had one when she had first seen him, but seeing the coarse golden hair now sprouting from his chin made her realize that he was not a boy. He was a man – a tall, powerful, fully mature man.

Her look of amazement made him smile, though he didn't know the cause. She was taller than he had guessed, too. The way she moved and held herself gave the effect of someone of much shorter stature. Actually, she was quite tall, and he liked tall women. They were the ones that usually caught his eye, though this one would catch anyone's eye, he thought. "We got this far, let's go out," he said.

Ayla was feeling conscious of his closeness, and his nakedness. "Don-da-lah need . . . garment," she said, using his word for her wrap, although she meant one for a man. "Need cover . . ." she pointed to his genitals; he had not told her that word, either. Then for some unexplainable reason, she blushed.

It was not modesty. She had seen many men unclothed, and women, too – it was not a matter for concern. She thought he would need protection, not from the elements, but from malicious spirits. Though women were not included in their rituals, she knew that men of the Clan did not like to leave their genitals exposed if they were going out. She didn't know why that thought made her feel flustered, or why her face felt hot, or why it seemed to bring on those pulling, tightening, pulsing sensations.

Jondalar looked down at himself. He had superstitions about his genitals, too, but they did not involve covering them for protection from evil spirits. If malicious enemies had induced a zelandoni to call down harm, or if a woman had just cause and cast a curse on him, it would take a great deal more than an article of clothing to protect him.

But he had learned that while a stranger might make a social blunder and be forgiven, it was wise when travelling to pay attention to subtle hints so that he would offend as seldom as possible. He had seen where she pointed – and her blush. He took it to mean she thought he should not go out with his genitals exposed. And in any case, sitting with bare skin on bare rock could get uncomfortable, and he wouldn't be able to move much.

Then he thought about himself standing there on one leg, hanging on to a post, so eager to get out of the cave that he hadn't even noticed he was completely naked. The humour in the situation suddenly struck him, and he burst out with a hearty laugh.

Jondalar had no way of knowing the effect of his laughter on Ayla. To him, it was as natural as breathing. Ayla had grown up with people who did not laugh, and who viewed her laughter with such suspicion that she had learned to curtail it so she would fit in more easily. It was part of the price she paid for survival. Only after her son was born did she discover the joy of laughter again. It was one of the qualities he had acquired from her half of his heritage. She knew encouraging him would be disapproved, but when they were alone, she couldn't resist playful tickling when he responded with giggles of delight.

To her, laughter was charged with more meaning than just a simple spontaneous response. It represented the unique bond she had with her son, the part of herself she could see in him, and was an expression of her own identity. The laughter inspired by the cave lion cub which she loved had strengthened that expression, and she would not give it up. It would not only have meant giving up memory sensations of her son, but giving up her own developing sense of self.

But she hadn't considered that someone else might laugh. Except for her own and Durc's, she could not recall hearing laughter before. The special quality of Jondalar's laugh – the hearty, jubilant freedom of it – invited response. There was unrestrained delight in his voice as he laughed at himself, and, from the moment she heard it, she loved it. Unlike the Clan adult-male reproof, Jondalar's laughter bestowed approval by its very sound. It was not only all right to laugh, it was invited. It was impossible to resist.

And Ayla did not resist. Her first shocked surprise turned to a smile, and then to laughter on her own. She didn't know what was so funny; she laughed because Jondalar did.

"Don-dah-lah," Ayla said when the moment passed. "What is word . . . ha-ha-ha-ha?"

"Laugh? Laughter?"

"What is . . . right word?"

"They're both right. When we do it, you say, 'we laugh'. When you talk about it, you say 'the laughter'," he explained.

Ayla thought for a while. There was more in what he said than the way to use that word; there was more to speaking than words. She already knew many words, but she was frustrated over and over again when she tried to express her thoughts. There was a way they were put together, and a meaning she couldn't quite grasp. Though she understood Jondalar for the most part, the words were only giving her a hint. She was understanding as much from her perceptive ability to read his unintentional body language. But she felt the lack of precision and depth in their conversation. Worse, though, was the sense that she *knew*, if she could just remember, and the unbearable tension, like a hard painful knot trying to burst apart, that she felt whenever she came close to recalling.

"Don-da-lah laugh?"

"Yes, that's right."

"Ayla laugh. Ayla like laugh."

"Right now, Jondalar 'like go out'," he replied. "Where are my clothes?"

Ayla got the pile of clothing she had cut off him. They were in shreds from the lion's claws and discoloured with brown stains. Beads and other elements of the design were coming off the decorated shirt.

The sight of them was sobering to Jondalar. "I must have been hurt bad," he said, holding up the trousers stiff with his own dried blood. "These are not fit to wear."

Ayla was thinking the same thing. She went to the storage area and brought back an unused skin and long strips of thong, and started to wrap it around his waist, in the manner of men of the Clan.

"I'll do it, Ayla," he said, putting the soft leather between his legs and pulling it up front and back for a breechclout. "But I could use a little help," he added, struggling to tie a thong around his waist to hold it on.

She helped him tie it, and then, lending her shoulder for support, she indicated that he should put pressure on the leg. He put his foot down firmly and leaned foward gingerly. It was more painful than he expected, and he began to doubt that he could make it. But, strengthening his resolve, he leaned heavily on Ayla and took a small hopping step, then another. When they reached the mouth of the small cave, he beamed at her and looked out at the stone ledge and the tall pine trees growing near the opposite wall.

She left him there, holding on to the firm rock of the cave while she went for a woven grass mat and a fur and put them near the far edge where he could get the best view of the valley. Then she went back to help him again. He was tired, in pain, and altogether pleased with himself when he finally

417

settled down on the fur and had his first look around.

Whinney and her colt were in the field; they had left shortly after Ayla had brought them to meet Jondalar. The valley itself was a green and lush paradise tucked into the arid steppes. He would not have guessed such a place existed. He turned towards the narrow gorge upstream and the portion of the rock-strewn beach not hidden from view. But his attention was drawn back to the green valley that extended downstream all the way to the far turn.

The first conclusion he reached was that Ayla lived here alone. There was no indication of any other human habitation. She sat with him a while, then went into the cave and returned with a handful of grain. She pursed her lips, made a warbling, melodic trill, and broadcast the seed around the ledge nearby. Jondalar was puzzled until a bird landed and began pecking at the seeds. Soon a host of birds of various sizes and colours whirred down around her with fluttering wings, and with quick jerky motions they pecked at the grains.

Their songs – warbles, trills, and squawks – filled the air as they squabbled for position with a display of puffed-up feathers. Jondalar had to look twice when he discovered that many of the bird songs he was hearing were made by the woman! She could make the whole range of sounds and, when she settled on one particular voice, a certain bird would climb on her finger and stay there when she lifted it and they warbled a duet. A few times, she brought one close enough for Jondalar to touch before it fluttered away.

When the seeds were gone, most of the birds left, but one blackbird stayed to exchange a song with Ayla. She mimicked the thrush's rich musical medley perfectly.

Jondalar took a deep breath when it flew away. He'd been holding it in, trying not to disturb the avian show Ayla was putting on. "Where did you learn that? It was exciting, Ayla. I've never been so close to living birds before."

She smiled at him, not sure exactly what he said, but aware that he was impressed. She trilled another bird song hoping he would tell her the name of the bird, but he only smiled in appreciation of her expertise. She tried another and still another before she gave up. He didn't understand what she wanted, but another thought caused a frown to crease his forehead. She could make bird sounds better than the Sha-mud could with a flute! Was she perhaps communing with Mother spirits in the form of birds? A bird swooped down and landed at her feet. He eyed it warily.

The fleeting apprehension passed quickly in the joy of being outside to soak up sunshine, feel the breeze, and look at the valley. Ayla was full of joy, too, because of his company. It was so hard to believe he was sitting on her ledge that she did not want to blink; if she shut her eyes, he might be gone when she opened them. When she finally convinced herself of his substantiality, she closed her eyes to see how long she could deny herself – just for the pleasure of seeing him still there when she opened them. The deep rumbling sound of his voice, if he happened to speak while her eyes were closed, was a windfall delight.

As the sun rose and made its warm presence felt, the glinting stream below drew Ayla's attention. She had forgone her usual morning swim, unable to leave Jondalar alone for fear some unexpected need might arise. But he was much better now, and he could call out if he needed her.

"Ayla go water," she said, making swimming motions.

"Swim," he said, making similar motions. "The word is 'swim', and I wish I could go with you."

"Sssvim," she said slowly.

"Swim," he corrected.

"Su-im," she tried again, and, when he nodded, she started down. It will be some time before he can walk this path – I'll bring some water up for him. But the leg is healing well. I think he'll be able to use it. Maybe a small limp, but not enough to slow him down, I hope.

When she reached the beach and untied the thong of her wrap, she decided to wash her hair as well. She went downstream for soaproot. She looked up, saw Jondalar, and waved at him, then walked back to the beach, out of his sight. She sat on the edge of a huge chunk of rock that until the spring before had been part of the wall, and began to uncoil her hair. A new pool that had not been there before the rearrangement of rocks had become her favourite bathing place. It was deeper, and in the rock nearby was a basinlike depression which she used to pound the saponin out of the soaproots.

Jondalar saw her again after she rinsed and swam upstream, and he admired her clean strong strokes. She lazily paddled back down to the rock and, sitting on it, let the sun dry her while she used a twig to pull tangles out of her hair, then brushed it with a teasel. By the time her thick hair dried, she was feeling warm, and though Jondalar hadn't called to her, she began to worry about him. He must be getting tired, she thought. One look at her wrap made her decide she wanted a clean one. She picked it up and carried it up the path.

Jondalar was feeling the sun, much more than Ayla. It had been spring when he and Thonolan had set out, and the small amount of protective tan he had acquired after they left the Mamutoi Camp had been lost during the time inside Ayla's cave. He still had a winter pallor, or he did until he came out to sit in the sun. Ayla was gone when he first became uncomfortably aware of his sunburn. He tried to ignore it, not wanting to disturb the woman enjoying a few moments for herself after her attentive care. He began wondering what was taking her so long, wishing she would hurry, glancing towards the top of the path, then up and down the stream, thinking she might have decided to take another swim.

He was looking the other way when Ayla arrived at the top of the wall, and one look at his angry red back was enough to fill her with shame. Look at that sunburn! What kind of medicine woman am I, leaving him out here so long? She hurried towards him.

He heard her and turned around, grateful that she had finally come, and a bit annoyed that she hadn't returned sooner. But when he saw her, he didn't feel his sunburn any more. He gasped in open-mouthed wonder at the naked woman walking toward him in the bright sunlight.

Her skin was golden tawny, and flowed as she moved with flat sinewy muscles of hard use. Her legs were perfectly moulded, marred only by four parallel scars on her left thigh. From his angle he could see rounded firm buttocks, and above the dark blonde fuzz of pubic hair, the curve of a stomach traced with the slight puckers of stretch marks from pregnancy. Pregnancy? Her breasts were ample, but well shaped and as high as a girl's, with dark pink aureolae and jutting nipples. Her arms were long and graceful and declared her strength unselfconsciously.

Ayla had grown up among people – men and women – who were inherently strong. To fulfil the tasks required of women of the Clan – lifting, carrying, working hides, chopping wood – her body had to develop the necessary muscular strength. Hunting had given her wiry resilience, and living alone had demanded efforts of strength to survive.

She was probably, Jondalar thought, the strongest woman he had ever seen; no wonder she was able to pull him up and support his weight. He knew, without doubt, that he had never seen a woman with a more beautifully sculptured body, but there was more than her body. From the beginning he had thought she was rather pretty, but he'd never seen her in the full light of day.

She had a long neck, with a small scar at the throat, a graceful jaw line, full mouth, straight narrow nose, high cheekbones, and wide-set blue grey eyes. Her finely chiselled features were combined in elegant harmony, and her long lashes and arching eyebrows were light brown, a shade darker than her loosely falling waves of golden hair gleaming in the sun.

"Great Bountiful Mother!" he breathed.

He strove to think of words to describe her; the total effect was dazzling. She was lovely, stunning, magnificent. He had never seen a more breathtakingly beautiful woman. Why did she hide that spectacular body under a shapeless wrap? Keep such glorious hair tied up in braids? And he had thought she was merely pretty. Why hadn't he seen her?

It wasn't until she crossed the distance of the stone ledge and drew near that he felt himself becoming aroused, but then it came upon him with insistent, throbbing demand. He wanted her with an urgency he'd never known before. His hands itched to caress that perfect body, to discover her secret places; he longed to explore, to taste, to give her Pleasures. When she leaned closer and he smelled her warm skin, he was ready to take her, without even asking, if he had been able. But he sensed that she wasn't someone who could be taken easily.

"Don-da-lah! Back is . . . fire . . ." Ayla said, searching for the right words for his glowing sunburn. Then she hesitated – stopped by the animal magnetism of his gaze. She looked into his intense blue eyes and felt drawn in deeper. Her heart pounded, her knees were weak, her face grew warm. Her body quivered, bringing a sudden dampness between her legs.

She didn't know what was wrong with her, and, wrenching her head aside, she tore her eyes away from his. They dropped to his rearing manhood outlined by his breech-clout, and she felt an overpowering urge to touch, to reach for it. She closed her eyes, breathed in deeply, and tried to still her quaking. When she opened them, she avoided his look.

"Ayla help Don-da-lah go cave," she said.

The sunburn was painful, and the time outside had left him tired, but, as he leaned on her during the short difficult walk, her naked body was so close that it kept his fierce desire inflamed. She settled him down on the bed, hurriedly looked over her store of medicine, then suddenly ran out.

He wondered where she had gone and understood when she returned with hands full of large grey green downy burdock leaves. She stripped the leaves from the heavy middle vein, tore them in shreds into a bowl, added cool water, and pounded them to a mash with a rock.

He had been feeling the discomfort and heat of the sunburn more, and when he felt the soothing cool mash on his back, he was again grateful she was a woman of healing.

"Ahhh, that's much better," he said.

Then, with her hands gently smoothing on the cool leaves, he became conscious that she had not stopped to put on a wrap. As she kneeled beside him, he felt her nearness. The smell of warm skin and other mysterious female odours encouraged him to reach for her. He ran his hand along her thigh from her knee to her buttocks.

Ayla froze at his touch and stopped the motion of her hand, acutely aware of his hand caressing her. She held herself rigid, unsure of what he was doing, or what she was supposed to do. Only sure that she did not want him to stop. But when he reached up to touch a nipple, she gasped at the unexpected jolt that coursed through her.

Jondalar was surprised at her shocked look. Wasn't it perfectly natural for a man to want to touch a beautiful woman? Especially when she was so near they almost touched anyway? He pulled his hand away, not knowing what to think. She acts like she's never been touched before, he thought. But she was a woman, not a young girl. And from the stretch marks, she had given birth, though he saw no evidence of children. Well, she wouldn't be the first woman to lose a child, but she must have had First Rites to make her ready to receive the Mother's blessing.

Ayla could still feel the tingling aftermath of his touch. She didn't know why he had stopped, and, confused, she got up and walked away.

Maybe she doesn't like me, Jondalar thought. But then why had she come so close, especially when his desire was so obvious? She couldn't help his desire, she had been treating his sunburn. And there had been nothing suggestive in her manner. In fact, she seemed oblivious to her effect on him. Was she so accustomed to that response to her beauty? She didn't behave with the callous disregard of an experienced woman, yet how could any woman who looked like that not know her effect on men?

Jondalar picked up a mashed piece of wet leaf that had fallen off his back. The Sharamudoi healer had used burdock for burns, too. She is skilled. Of course! Jondalar, you can be so stupid, he said to himself. The Shamud told you about the tests of Those Who Serve the Mother. She must be forgoing Pleasures, too. No wonder she wears that shapeless wrap to hide her beauty. She would not have come close to you if you hadn't been sunburned, and then you grab like some adolescent boy.

His leg was throbbing and, although the medication had helped, the sunburn was still uncomfortable. He eased down, tried lying on his side, and shut his eyes. He was thirsty, but he didn't want to roll over to get the waterbag just when he had found an almost bearable position. He was feeling miserable, not only because of his aches and pains, but because he thought he had committed some gross indiscretion, and he was embarrassed.

He hadn't felt the humiliation of social blunders for a long time, not since he was a boy. He had practised smooth self-control until it was an art. He had gone too far again and been rejected. This beautiful woman, this woman he had wanted more than any, had rejected him. He knew how it would go. She would act as though nothing had happened, but she would avoid him whenever she could. When she couldn't stay away, she would still put a distance between them. She would be cool, aloof. Her mouth might smile but her eyes would tell the truth. There would be no warmth in them, or worse, there would be pity.

Ayla had put on a clean wrap and was twining her hair, feeling ashamed that she had allowed Jondalar to get sunburned. What would Iza think of such carelessness, such lack of feeling for her patient? Ayla was mortified. He had been so badly wounded, was still in great pain, and she had added more pain.

But there was more to her discomfiture. He had touched her. She could still feel his warm hand on her thigh. She knew exactly where it had reached and where it had missed, as though he had burned her with his gentle caress. Why had he touched her nipple? It tingled still. He had been full in his manhood, and she knew what that meant. How many times had she seen men give the signal to a woman when they wanted to relieve their needs. Broud had done it to her – she shuddered – she had hated seeing him hard in his manhood then.

She didn't feel that way now. She'd even like it if Jondalar would give her the signal . . .

Don't be ridiculous. He couldn't, not with his leg. It was barely healed enough to put weight on.

But he had been hard in his manhood when she got back from swimming, and his eyes. . . .

She shivered thinking about his eyes. They are so blue, and so full of his need, and so . . .

She couldn't express it to herself, but she stopped twining her hair, closed her eyes, and let herself feel his pull. He had touched her.

But then he stopped. She sat up straight. Had he given her a signal? Had he stopped because she had not acquiesced? A woman was always supposed to be available to a man in his need. Every woman of the Clan was taught that, from the first time her spirit battled and she bled. Just as she was taught the subtle gestures and postures that might encourage a man to want to satisfy his need with her. She had never understood why a woman would want to use them before. Now, she suddenly realized, she did.

She wanted this man to relieve his needs with her, but she didn't know his signal! If I don't know his signal, he won't know my ways either. And if I refused him without knowing, he might never try again. But did he really want me? I'm so big and ugly.

Ayla finished tucking her last braid under itself, then went to stir up the fire to make some pain medicine for Jondalar. When she brought it to him, he was on his side resting. In bringing him something for pain so he could rest, she did not want to disturb him if he had already found some comfort. She sat down with crossed legs beside his sleeping place and waited for him to open his eyes. He didn't move, but she knew he was not sleeping. His breathing lacked the regularity, and his forehead showed discomfort he would not have if he was deep in sleep.

Jondalar had heard her coming and shut his eyes to feign sleep. He waited, muscles tensed, fighting an urge to open his eyes to see if she was there. Why was she so quiet? Why didn't she leave? The arm he was lying on started to tingle from lack of circulation. If he didn't move it soon, it would go numb. His leg throbbed. He wanted to shift it to ease the strain of holding it in one position so long. His face itched with the stubble of new beard; his back burned. Maybe she wasn't even there. Maybe she had gone and he just hadn't heard her move. Was she just sitting there staring at him?

She had been watching him intently. She had looked directly at this man more than she had ever looked at any man. It wasn't proper for women of the Clan to look at men, but she had indulged in many improprieties. Had she forgotten all the manners Iza had taught her, as well as proper care of a patient? She stared down at her hands holding the cup of datura in her lap. That was the correct way for a woman to approach a man, sitting on the ground with head bowed, waiting for him to acknowledge her with a tap on the shoulder. Perhaps it was time to remember her training, she thought.

Jondalar opened his eyes a crack, trying to see if she was there without letting her know he was awake. He saw a foot and quickly closed his eyes again. She was there. Why was she sitting there? What could she be waiting for? Why didn't she go and leave him alone with his misery and humiliation? He peeked again through lowered eyelids. Her foot hadn't moved. She was sitting cross-legged. She had a cup of liquid. Oh, Doni! He was thirsty! Was it for him? Had she been waiting there for him to wake up to give him some medicine? She could have shaken him; she didn't have to wait.

He opened his eyes. Ayla was sitting with her head bowed, looking down. She was dressed in one of those shapeless wraps, and her hair was tied up in multiple rows of braids. She had a fresh-scrubbed look. The smudge on her cheek was gone; her wrap was a clean, unworn skin. She had such a guileless quality, sitting with her head bowed. There was no artifice, no coy mannerisms or suggestive sidelong glances.

Her tight braids contributed to the impression, as did the wrap with its folds and bulges which camouflaged her so well. That was the trick, the artful concealing of her ripe woman's body and rich lustrous hair. She couldn't hide her face, but her habit of looking down or aside tended to divert attention. Why did she keep herself hidden? It must be the test she was undergoing. Most women he knew would have flaunted that magnificent body, worn such golden glory to show off to its best advantage, given anything for a face so beautiful.

He watched her without moving, his discomfort forgotten. Why was she so still? Maybe she didn't want to look at him, he thought, bringing back his embarrassment and his pain as well. He couldn't stand it, he had to move.

Ayla looked up when he rolled off his arm. He couldn't tap her shoulder to acknowledge her presence no matter how well mannered she wanted to be. He didn't know the signal. Jondalar was amazed to see contrite shame in her face, and the honest open appeal in her eyes. There was no condemnation, no rejection, no pity. Rather she seemed embarrassed. What did she have to be embarrassed about?

She gave him the cup. He took a sip, made a face at the bitter medicine, then drank it down and reached for the waterbag to wash the taste out of his mouth. Then he lay back down, not quite able to get comfortable. She motioned for him to sit up, then straightened, smoothed, and rearranged the furs and skins. He did not lie back down immediately.

"Ayla, there's so much about you I don't know and wish I did. I don't know where you learned your healing arts – I don't even know how I got here. I only know I'm grateful to you. You saved my life, and, more important, you saved my leg. I'd never get back home without my leg even if I had lived.

· "I'm sorry I made such a fool of myself, but you are so beautiful, Ayla. I didn't know – you hide it so well. I don't know why you want to, but you must have your reasons. You are learning fast. Maybe when you can talk more you will tell me, if you are free to. If not, I'll accept that. I know you don't understand everything I'm saying, but I want to say it. I won't bother you again, Ayla. I promise."

22

"Say me right . . . 'Don-da-lah'."

"You say my name just fine."

"No. Ayla say wrong," she shook her head vehemently. "Say me right."

"Jondalar. Jon-da-lar."

"Zzzon . . ."

"Juh," he showed her, articulating carefully, "Jondalar."

"Zh . . . dzh . . ." She struggled with the unfamiliar sound. "Dzhon- da- larrr," she finally got out, rolling the *r*.

"That's good! That's very good," he said.

Ayla smiled with her success; then her smile changed to a sly grin. "Dzhon-da-jarr ob da Zel-ann-do-nee." He had said the name of his people more often than he said his own name, and she had been practising in private.

"That's right!" Jondalar was genuinely surprised. She hadn't said it quite right, but only a Zelandonii would know the difference. His pleased approval made all her effort worth it, and Ayla's smile of success was beautiful.

"What means 'Zelandonee'?"

"It means my people. Children of the Mother who live in the southwest. Doni means the Great Earth Mother. Earth's Children, I guess that's the easiest way to say it. But all people call themselves Earth's Children, in their own language. It just means the people."

They were facing each other, leaning against opposite boles of a birch clump whose stalks had grown into several sturdy trunks of a tree with a common base. Though he used a staff and still had a pronounced limp, Jondalar was grateful to be standing in the green meadow of the valley. From his first tentative steps, he had pushed himself each day. His initial trip down the steep path had been an ordeal – and a triumph. Climbing back up turned out to be easier than going down.

He still didn't know how she had got him up to the cave in the beginning, without help. But if others had helped her, where were they? It was a question he had long wanted to ask, but first she would not have understood him, and then it seemed inappropriate to blurt it out just to satisfy his curiosity. He had been waiting for the right moment, and this seemed to be it.

"Who are your people, Ayla? Where are they?"

The smile left her face; he was almost sorry he asked. After a long silence, he began to think she had not understood him.

"No people. Ayla of no people," she answered finally, pushing herself away from the tree and moving out of its shade. Jondalar grabbed his staff and hobbled after her.

"But you had to have some people. You were born to a mother. Who took care of you? Who taught you healing? Where are your people now, Ayla? Why are you alone?"

Ayla walked ahead slowly, staring at the ground. She was not trying to avoid replying – she had to answer him. No woman of the Clan could refuse to answer a direct question asked by a man. In fact, all members of the Clan, male and female, responded to direct questions. It was simply that women didn't ask men searching personal questions, and men seldom posed them to each other. Women were the ones usually asked. Jondalar's questions brought up many memories, but she did not know the answer to some and did not know how to answer others.

"If you don't want to tell me . . ."

"No." She looked at him and shook her head. "Ayla say." Her eyes were troubled. "Not know words."

Jondalar wondered again if he should have brought it up, but he was curious. They stopped again at the large jagged chunk of rock that had knocked out part of the wall before coming to rest in the field. Jondalar sat on an edge where the stone had been cleaved to form a seat at a convenient height with a sloping back rest.

"What do your people call themselves?" he asked.

Ayla thought for a moment. "The people. Man . . . woman . . . baby." She shook her head again, not knowing how to explain. "The Clan." She made the gesture for the concept at the same time.

"Like family? A family is a man, woman and her children, living at the same hearth. . . . Usually."

She nodded. "Family . . . more."

"A small group? Several families living together is a Cave," he said, "even if they don't live in one."

"Yes," she said, "clan small. And more. Clan mean all people."

He hadn't quite heard her say the word the first time, and he did not perceive the hand signal she used. The word was heavy, guttural, and there was that tendency that he could only explain as swallowing the insides of the words. He would not have thought it was a word. She had not spoken any words other than the ones she learned from him, and he was interested.

"Glun?" he said, trying to copy her.

It wasn't quite right, but it was close. "Ayla no say Jondalar words right, Jondalar no say Ayla words right. Jondalar say fine."

"I didn't know you knew any words, Ayla. I've never heard you speak in your language."

"Not know many words. Clan not speak words."

Jondalar didn't understand. "What do they speak if not words?"

"They speak . . . hands," she said, knowing that was not completely accurate.

She noticed she had been making the gestures unintentionally in an effort to express herself. When she saw Jondalar's puzzled look, she took his hands and moved them with the proper motions while she repeated herself.

"Clan not speak many words. Clan speak . . . hands."

His forehead of puzzlement slowly smoothed out as comprehension took its place. "Are you telling me your people talk with their hands? Show me. Say something in your language."

Ayla thought for a moment, then began. "I want to say so much to you, but I must learn to say it in your language. Your way is the only way left to me now. How can I tell you who my people are? I'm not a woman of the Clan any more. How can I explain that I am dead? I have no people. To the

430

Clan, I walk the next world, like the man you travelled with. Your sibling, I think, your brother.

"I would like to tell you I made the signs over his grave to help him find his way, so the grief in your heart will be eased. I would like to tell you I grieved for him, too, though I did not know him.

"I don't know the people I was born to. I must have had a mother, and a family, who looked like me . . . and you. But I only know them as the Others. Iza is the only mother I remember. She taught me the healing magic and she made me a medicine woman, but she is dead now. And so is Creb.

"Jondalar, I ache to tell you about Iza, and Creb, and Durc . . ." She had to stop and take a deep breath. "My son is gone from me too, but he lives. That much I have. And now the Cave Lion has brought you. I was afraid men of the Others would be like Broud, but you are more like Creb, gentle and patient. I want to think you will be my mate. When you first came, I thought that was why you were brought here. I think I wanted to believe that because I was so lonely for company, and you are the first man of the Others I have seen . . . that I can remember. It would not have mattered who you were, then. I wanted you for a mate, just to have a mate.

"Now, it is not the same. Every day you are here, my feeling for you grows stronger. I know that Others are not too far, and there must be other men who could be a mate. But I don't want any other, and I am afraid you will not want to stay here with me once you are well. I'm afraid I will lose you, too. I wish I could tell you, I am so . . . so . . . grateful you are here, sometimes I cannot bear it." She stopped, not able to go on, but feeling in some way that she wasn't finished.

Her thoughts had not been entirely incomprehensible to the man watching her. Her movements – not just of her hands, but her features, her eyes, her whole body – were so expressive that he was deeply moved. She reminded him of a silent dancer, except for the rough sounds that, strangely, fitted together with the graceful movements. He perceived only with his emotions, and he could not quite believe that what he felt was what she had communicated – but when she stopped, he knew she *had* communicated. He knew, too, that her language of motions and gestures was not, as he had supposed, a simple extension of the gestures he sometimes used for added emphasis to his words. Rather, it seemed, the sounds she made were used for emphasis to her motions.

When she stopped, she stood a few moments, pensively, then gracefully dropped to the ground at his feet and bowed her head. He waited, and when she didn't move, he began to feel uncomfortable. She seemed to be waiting for him, and it made him feel she was paying homage. Such deference to the Great Earth Mother was fine, but She was known to be jealous and did not take kindly to one of Her children receiving veneration that was Her due.

Finally, he reached down and touched her arm. "Get up, Ayla. What are you doing?"

A touch on the arm was not exactly a tap on the shoulder, but it was as close as she thought he would come to giving her the Clan signal to speak. She looked up at the seated man.

"Clan woman sit, want talk. Ayla want talk Jondalar."

"You don't have to sit on the ground to talk to me." He reached forward and tried to lift her up. "If you want to talk, just talk."

She insisted on remaining where she was. "Is Clan way." Her eyes pleaded for him to understand. "Ayla want say . . ." Tears of frustration began to well. She started over. "Ayla no talk good. Ayla want to say, Jondalar give Ayla *talk*, want say . . ."

"Are you trying to say thank you?"

"What mean, thank you?"

He paused. "You saved my life, Ayla. You have taken care of me, treated my wounds, given me food. For that I would say thank you. I would say more than thank you."

Ayla frowned. "Not same. Man hurt, Ayla take care. Ayla take care all man. Jondalar give Ayla talk. Is more. Is more thank you." She looked at him earnestly, willing him to understand.

"You may not 'talk good', but you communicate very well. Get up, Ayla, or I'll have to get down beside you. I understand that you are a healer, and it is your calling to take care of anyone who needs help. You may not think it is anything special that you saved my life, but that doesn't make me less grateful. To me, it is a small matter to teach you my language, to teach you to talk, but I'm beginning to under-

432

stand that to you it is very important, and you are grateful. It is always difficult to express gratitude, in any language. My way is to say thank you. I think your way is more beautiful. Please get up now."

She sensed that he understood. Her smile conveyed more gratitude than she knew. It had been a difficult, but important, concept for her to communicate, and she stood up feeling elated that she had succeeded. She sought to express her exuberance in action, and when she saw Whinney and her colt, she whistled, loud and shrill. The mare perked her ears and galloped to her, and when she neared, Ayla made a running leap and landed lightly on the horse's back.

They made a large circuit of the meadow, with the colt following closely. Ayla had been staying so close to Jondalar that she hadn't ridden much since she found him, and to ride now gave her an exhilarating sense of freedom. When they returned to the rock, Jondalar was standing waiting for them. His mouth was no longer agape, though it had been when she started out. For a moment, a chill had crawled down his back, and he wondered if the woman was supernatural, perhaps even a donii. He vaguely remembered a dream of a mother spirit in the form of a young woman turning aside a lion.

Then he recalled Ayla's all too human frustration over her inability to communicate. Certainly no spirit form of the Great Earth Mother would have such problems. Still, she had an uncommonly gifted way with animals. Birds came at her call and ate out of her hand, and a nursing mare ran to her whistle and allowed the woman to ride on her back. And what about these people who spoke not with words, but with motions? Ayla had given him much to think about that day, he mused, as he scratched the colt. The more he thought about her, the deeper her mystery.

He could understand why she didn't speak, if her people did not speak. But who were these people? Where were they now? She said she had no people, and she did live in the valley alone, but who had taught her healing, or the magic way she had with animals? Where had she got the firestone? She was young to be such a gifted zelandoni. Usually it took many years to reach her abilities, often at special retreats . . .

Could that be who her people were? He knew of special

433

groups of Those Who Served the Mother that devoted themselves to gaining deep insights into profound mysteries. Such groups were greatly esteemed; Zelandoni had spent several years with one. The Shamud had spoken of tests that were self-imposed to gain insights and skills. Could Ayla have lived with such a group that did not speak except with motions? And was she now living alone to perfect her abilities?

And you were thinking of having Pleasures with her, Jondalar. No wonder she reacted the way she did. But what a shame. To give up Pleasures, as beautiful as she is. You will certainly respect her wishes, Jondalar, beautiful or not.

The brown colt was butting and rubbing against the man, looking for more attentive scratching from the sensitive hands that always managed to find just the right places in the itchy process of shedding newborn fuzz. Jondalar was delighted when the foal sought him out. Horses had never before been more than sustenance to him, and it had never occurred to him that they might be warm responsive animals that would enjoy his petting.

Ayla smiled, pleased at the attachment developing between the man and Whinney's foal. She recalled an idea she'd had, and spontaneously mentioned it.

"Jondalar give name colt?"

"Name the colt? You want me to name the colt?" He was unsure, and pleased. "I don't know, Ayla. I've never thought about naming anything, much less a horse. How do you name a horse?"

Ayla understood his dismay. It had not been an idea she had accepted immediately. Names were fraught with significance; they gave recognition. Recognizing Whinney as a unique individual apart from the concept of *horse* had certain consequences. She was no longer just an animal of the herds who roamed the steppes. She associated with humans, drew her security from and gave her trust to a human. She was unique among her kind. She had a name.

But it imposed obligations on the woman. The comfort and well-being of the animal required considerable effort and concern. The horse could never be very far from her thoughts; their lives had become inextricably entwined.

Ayla had come to recognize the relationship, especially

after Whinney's return. Though it wasn't planned or calculated, there was an element of that recognition in her desire to have Jondalar name the colt. She wanted him to stay with her. If he became attached to the young horse, it could be additional reason to stay where the colt would need to stay – at least for some time – in the valley with Whinney, and with her.

There was no need to rush the man, though. He wouldn't be going anywhere for a while, not until his leg healed.

Ayla woke up with a start. The cave was dark. She lay on her back, peering into the dense unfocusable black, and tried to go back to sleep. Finally, she slipped quietly out of her bed – she had dug a shallow trench in the earth floor of the cave beside the bed now used by Jondalar – and felt her way to the cave mouth. She heard Whinney blow an acknowledgement of her presence as she passed by on her way out.

I let the fire go out again, she thought, walking along the wall to the edge. Jondalar isn't as familiar with the cave as I am. If he needs to get up in the middle of the night, he should have more light.

When she was through, she stayed outside for a while. A quarter moon, setting in the west, was close to the lip of the wall above, across on the upstream side of the ledge, and would soon disappear behind it. It was closer to morning than middle of the night. Below was darkness except for the silvery shimmer of starshine reflected in the whispering stream.

The night sky made a barely perceptible shift from black to deep blue, but it was noticed at some unconscious level. Without knowing why, Ayla decided not to return to bed. She watched the moon deepen in colour before the black edge of the opposite wall swallowed it. She felt an ominous shiver when the last glimmer of light was snuffed out.

Gradually the sky lightened, and the stars faded into the luminous blue. At the far end of the valley, the horizon was purple. She watched the sharply defined arc of a blood-red sun swell up from the edge of the earth and cast a lurid shaft of light into the valley.

"Must be a prairie fire to the east," Jondalar said.

Ayla spun around. The man was bathed in the livid glow of

the fiery orb, which turned his eyes to a shade of lavender never seen by firelight. "Yes, big fire, much smoke. I not know you up."

"I've been awake for a while, hoping you'd come back. When you didn't, I thought I might as well get up. The fire is out."

"I know. I careless. Not make right to burn for night."

"Bank, you didn't bank it so it would not go out."

"Bank," she repeated. "I go start."

He followed her back into the cave, ducking his head as he went through the entrance. It was apprehension more than necessity. The cave opening was high enough for him, but not by much. Ayla got out the iron pyrite and flint and gathered tinder and kindling.

"Didn't you say you found that firestone on the beach? Are there more?"

"Yes. Not many. Water come, take."

"A flood? The stream flooded and washed out some of the firestones? Maybe we should go and collect as many as we can find."

Ayla nodded absently. She had other plans for the day, but she wanted Jondalar's help and didn't know how to bring it up. She was running low on meat, and she didn't know if he would object to her hunting. She had occasionally gone out with her sling, and he had not questioned where the jerboas, hares, and giant hamsters came from. But even the men of the Clan had allowed her to hunt small game with her sling. She needed to hunt larger game, though, and that meant going out with Whinney and digging a pit trap.

She wasn't looking forward to it. She would have preferred hunting with Baby, but he was gone. The absence of her hunting partner was the least of her worries, however. Jondalar concerned her more. She knew that, even if he objected, he couldn't stop her. It wasn't as though she were part of his clan – this was her cave, and he wasn't fully recovered. But he seemed to enjoy the valley, Whinney, and the colt; he even seemed to like her. She didn't want that to change. It had been her experience that men did not like women to hunt, but she had no choice.

And she wanted more than his acquiescence – she wanted his support, his help. She did not want to take the foal hunting. She was afraid he might get caught in the stampede and be hurt. He'd stay behind when she left with Whinney, if Jondalar would keep him company, she was sure. She wouldn't be gone long. She could scout a herd, dig a trap, and return, then hunt the next day. But how could she ask the man to keep a foal company while she hunted? Even if he himself wasn't able to hunt yet?

When she made a broth for the morning meal, a good look at her dwindling supply of dried meat convinced her something had to be done soon. She decided the way to begin was to expose her hunting proclivities in a small way first, by showing him her skill with her favourite weapon. His reaction to her sling hunting would give her some idea if it would be worthwhile to ask his help.

They had formed the habit of walking together in the morning alongside the brush lining the stream. It was good exercise for him, and she enjoyed it. On that morning, she tucked her sling in her waist thong when they left. All she would need was the cooperation of some creature willing to come within range.

Her hopes were more than fulfilled when a walk into the field away from the stream flushed a pair of willow grouse. She reached for sling and stones when she saw one. As she knocked the first out of the sky, the second took to wing, but her second stone brought it down. Before she retrieved them, she glanced at Jondalar. She saw astonishment, but more important, she saw a smile.

"That was amazing, woman! Is that how you've been catching those animals? I thought you had snares set. What is that weapon?"

She gave him the leather strap with a bulge in the middle, then went to get the birds.

"I think this is called a sling," he said when she returned. "Willomar told me about a weapon like this. I couldn't quite imagine what he was talking about, but this must be it. You're good with it, Ayla. That had to take a lot of practice, even with some natural ability."

"You like I hunt?"

"If you didn't hunt, who would?"

"Clan man not like woman hunt."

Jondalar studied her. She was anxious, worried. Perhaps

437

the men didn't like women who hunted, but it hadn't stopped her from learning. Why had she chosen this day to demonstrate her skill? Why did he feel she was looking for approval from him?

"Most Zelandonii women hunt, at least when they're young. My mother was noted for her tracking skill. I don't see any reason why women shouldn't, if they want. I like women who hunt, Ayla."

He could see her tension evaporate; he had obviously said what she wanted to hear, and it was the truth. He wondered, though, why it was so important to her.

"I need go hunt," she said. "Need help."

"I'd like to, but I don't think I'm up to it yet."

"Not help hunt. I take Whinney, you keep colt?"

"So that's it," he said. "You want me to mind the colt while you go hunting with the mare?" He chuckled. "That's a change. Usually, after she has a child or two, a woman stays to mind them. It's a man's responsibility to hunt for them. Yes, I'll stay with the colt. Someone has to hunt, and I don't want the little fellow to get hurt."

Her smile was one of relief. He didn't mind, he really didn't seem to mind.

"You might investigate that fire to the east before you plan your hunt, though. One that big can do your hunting for you."

"Fire hunt?" she said.

"Whole herds have been known to die from the smoke alone. Sometimes you'll find your meat cooked! Storytellers have a funny fable about a man finding cooked meat after a prairie fire, and the problems he had trying to convince the rest of his Cave to try meat he burned on purpose. It's an old story."

A smile of comprehension crossed her face. A fast-raging fire could overcome a whole herd. I might not have to dig a pit after all.

When Ayla got out the basket-harness-travois arrangement, Jondalar was intrigued, not able to understand the purpose of the complicated equipment.

"Whinney take meat to cave," she explained, showing him the travois while adjusting the straps on the mare. "Whinney take you to cave," she added.

"So that's how I got here! I've been wondering for a long time. I didn't think you carried me here alone. I thought perhaps some other people found me and left me here with you."

"No . . . other people I find . . . you . . . other man."

Jondalar's expression became strained and bleak. The reference to Thonolan caught him by surprise, and the pain of his loss gripped him. "Did you have to leave him there? Couldn't you have brought him, too?" he flung out at her.

"Man dead, Jondalar. You hurt, Much hurt," she said, feeling frustration well up inside her. She wanted to tell him she had buried the man, that she sorrowed for him, but she could not communicate. She could exchange information, but she could not explore ideas. She wanted to speak to him of thoughts she wasn't even sure could be expressed in words, but she felt stifled. He had spent his grief on her the first day, and now she couldn't even share his sorrow.

She longed for his ease with words, his ability to marshal them spontaneously into the proper order, his freedom of expression. But there was a vague barrier she couldn't cross, a lack that she often felt on the verge of breeching, which eluded her. Intuition told her she ought to know – that the knowledge was locked inside her, if only she could find the key.

"I'm sorry, Ayla. I shouldn't have shouted at you like that, but Thonolan was my brother . . ." The word was almost a cry.

"Brother. You and other man . . . have same mother?"

"Yes, we had the same mother."

She nodded and turned back to the horse, wishing she could tell him she understood the closeness of siblings and the special tie that could exist between two men born of the same mother, Creb and Brun had been brothers.

She finished loading the pack baskets, then picked up her spears to carry them outside to load after they were through the low cave opening. As he watched her making final preparations, he began to see that the horse was more than a strange companion to the woman. The animal gave her a decided advantage. He hadn't realized how useful a horse could be. But he was puzzled by another set of contradictions she posed: she used a horse to help her hunt and to carry back the meat – an advancement he'd never heard of before – yet she used a spear more primitive than any he'd seen.

He had hunted with many people, and each group had its own variation of hunting spear, but none was as radically different as hers. Yet there was something familiar about it. Its point was sharp and fire-hardened, and the shaft was straight and smooth, but it was so clumsy. There was no question that it was not meant to be thrown; it was larger than the one he used to hunt rhino. How did she hunt with it? How could she get close enough to wield it? When she came back, he'd have to ask her. It would take too much time now. She was learning the language, but it was still difficult.

He led the colt into the cave before Ayla and Whinney left. He scratched, stroked, and talked to the young horse until he was sure Ayla and his dam were far away. It felt odd to be in the cave alone, knowing the woman would be gone most of the day. He used the staff to pull himself up, and then, succumbing to his curiosity, he found a lamp and lit it. Leaving the staff behind – he didn't need it inside the cave – he held the hollowed-out stone lamp in one palm and started following the walls of the cave to see how big it was and where it led. There were no surprises in the size – it was about as big as he had thought, and, except for the small niche, there were no side passages. But the niche held a surprise: every indication of recent cave lion occupation, including a pug-mark, a big one!

After he had looked over the rest of the cave, he was convinced Ayla had been there for years. He had to be wrong about the cave lion spoor, but when he went back and examined the niche even more carefully, he was certain a cave lion had dwelled in that corner some time within the past year.

Another mystery! Would, he ever find an answer to all the perplexing questions?

He picked up one of Ayla's baskets – unused as far as he could tell – and decided to look for firestones on the beach. He might as well try to be useful. While the colt bounded ahead, Jondalar worked his way down the steep path with the help of the staff, then leaned it against the wall near the bone pile. He'd be grateful when he wouldn't have to use it at all.

He stopped to scratch and fondle the foal who was nosing his hand, and then laughed when the young horse rolled with exuberant delight in the wallow he and Whinney both used. Squealing with intense pleasure, the colt, with his legs in the air, wriggled in the loose, giving earth. He got up and shook himself, throwing dirt in all directions, then found a favourite spot in the shade of a willow and settled down to rest.

Jondalar walked slowly on the rocky beach, bent over to scan each rock. "I found one!" he shouted in excitement, which startled the colt. He felt a bit foolish. "Here's another!" he said again, then smiled sheepishly. But as he picked up the brassy grey stone, he was stopped by the sight of another stone, much larger. "There's flint on this beach!"

She gets the flint to make her tools right here! If you could find a hammerstone, and make a punch, and. . . . You could make some tools, Jondalar! Good sharp blades, and burins. . . . He straightened up and appraised the pile of bones and rubble which the stream had thrown against the wall. It looks like there is good bone around here, too, and antler. You could even make her a decent spear.

She might not want a "decent spear", Jondalar. She might have a reason for using the one she does. But that doesn't mean you can't make a spear for yourself. It would be better than sitting around all day. You might even do some carving. You used to have a fair hand for carving, before you gave it up.

He rummaged through the heap of bones and driftwood piled against the wall, then went around to her midden on the other side of it and searched through the overgrown brush to find disarticulated bones, skulls, and antler among the refuse. He found several handfuls of firestones while searching for a good hammerstone. When he broke off the cortex of the first nodule of flint, he was smiling. He hadn't realized how much he missed practising his craft.

He thought about everything he could do, now that he had some flint. He wanted a good knife, and an axe, with handles. He wanted to make spears, and now he could fix his clothes with some good awls. And Ayla might like his kind of tools; at least he could show her.

The day had not dragged the way he had feared, and

twilight was settling before he carefully gathered his new flint-knapping tools, and the new flint tools he had made with them, into the hide he had borrowed from Ayla. When he returned to the cave, the colt was nudging and looking for attention, and he suspected the young animal was hungry. Ayla had left behind some cooked grains in a thin gruel – which the colt had refused at first, then took later, but that had been at midday. Where was she?

By the time it was dark, he was definitely worried. The colt needed Whinney, and Ayla should be back. He stood out on the far side of the ledge watching for her, then decided to build a fire, thinking she might see it in case she had lost her way. She wouldn't lose her way, he said to himself, but he made the fire anyway.

It was late when she finally returned. He heard Whinney and started down the path to meet them, but the colt was ahead of him. Ayla dismounted on the beach, dragged a carcass off the travois, adjusted the poles to accommodate the narrow trail, and led the mare up as Jondalar reached the bottom and stepped aside. She came back with a stick from the fire for a torch. Jondalar took it while Ayla loaded a second carcass back on the travois. He hobbled over to help, but she had moved it already. Watching her handle the dead weight of the deer gave him an appreciation of her strength, and an insight into how she had acquired it. The horse and travois were useful, perhaps even indispensable, but she was still only one person.

The colt was eagerly searching for his dam's teat, but Ayla pushed him aside until they reached the cave.

"You right, Jondalar," she said as he reached the ledge. "Big, big fire. I not see before so big fire. Far away. Many, many animals."

Something in her voice made him look closer. She was exhausted, and the carnage she had seen had left its imprint in the strained hollowness of her eyes. Her hands were black, her face and wrap were smudged with soot and blood. She unfastened the harness and travois, then put an arm around Whinney's neck and leaned her forehead against the mare in weariness. The horse was standing with her head down and front legs straddled while her colt eased the fullness of her udders. She looked as tired.

"That fire must have been far away. It's late. Have you been riding all day?" Jondalar asked.

She pulled her head up and turned to him. For a moment, she had forgotten he was there. "Yes, all day," she said, then took a deep breath. She couldn't give in to her fatigue yet, she had too much to do. "Many animal die. Many come take meat. Wolf. Hyena. Lion. Other I not see before. Big teeth," she demonstrated an open mouth and her two index fingers hanging down like elongated canines.

"You saw a dirk-toothed tiger! I didn't know they were real! One old man used to tell stories to the youngsters at Summer Meetings about seeing one when he was young, but not everyone believed him. You really saw one?" He was wishing he could have been with her.

She nodded and shivered, tightening her shoulders and shutting her eyes. "Make Whinney fright. Stalk. Sling make go. Whinney, I run."

Jondalar's eyes opened wide at her halting recitation of the incident. "You drove off a dirk-toothed tiger with your sling? Good Mother, Ayla!"

"Much meat. Tiger . . . not need Whinney. Sling make go." She wanted to say more, to describe the incident, to express her fear, to share it with him, but she didn't have the means. She was too tired to visualize the motions and then try to think how the words fitted in.

No wonder she's exhausted, Jondalar thought. Maybe I shouldn't have suggested checking the fire, but she did get two deer. That took nerve, though, facing down a dirk-toothed tiger. She is quite a woman.

Ayla looked at her hands, then headed down the path to the beach again. She took the torch which Jondalar had left stuck in the ground, carried it to the stream, and held it up to look around. Pulling up a stalk of pigweed, she crushed the leaves and roots in her hand, wet the mixture, and added a bit of sand. Then she scoured her hands, cleaned the travel grime off her face, and went back up.

Jondalar had started cooking rocks heating, and she was grateful. A cup of hot tea was just what she wanted. She had left food behind for him and hoped he wasn't expecting her to cook. She couldn't worry about meals now. She had two deer to skin and cut up into pieces for drying.

She had searched for animals that were not scorched, since she wanted the hides. But when she started to work, she remembered that she had planned to make some new sharp knives. Knives dulled with use – tiny spalls breaking off along the cutting edge. It was usually easier to make new ones and then turn the old into some other tool, such as a scraper.

The dull knife pushed her beyond her limit. She hacked at the hide while tears of weariness and defeat filled her eyes and spilled over.

"Ayla, what's wrong?" Jondalar asked.

She only hacked more violently at the deer. She couldn't explain. He took the dull knife out of her hand and pulled her up. "You're tired. Why don't you go lie down and rest for a while?"

She shook her head, though she desperately wanted to do as he said. "Skin deer, dry meat. No wait, hyena come."

He didn't bother to suggest they bring the deer in; she wasn't thinking clearly. "I'll watch it," he said. "You need some rest. Go in and lie down, Ayla."

Gratitude filled her. He would watch it! She hadn't thought to ask him; she wasn't used to having someone else to help. She stumbled into the cave, shaking with relief, and fell onto her furs. She wanted to tell Jondalar how grateful she was, and she felt tears rise again, knowing that her attempt would be ineffectual. She couldn't talk!

Jondalar came in and went out of the cave several times during the night, occasionally standing and watching the sleeping woman, his brow furrowed with concern. She was restless, flailing her arms and mumbling unintelligibly in her dreams.

Ayla was walking through fog, crying for help. A tall woman, shrouded in mist, her face indistinct, held out her arms. "I said I'd be careful, Mother, but where did you go?" Ayla muttered. "Why didn't you come when I called you. I called and called, but you never came. Where have you been? Mother? Mother! Don't go away again! Stay here! Mother, wait for me! Don't leave me!"

The vision of the tall woman faded, and the mists cleared. In her place stood another woman, stocky and short. Her strong muscular legs were slightly bowed with an outward curvature, but she walked straight and upright. Her nose was large and aquiline, with a high prominent bridge, and her jaw, jutting forward, was chinless. Her forehead was low and sloped back, but her head was very large, her neck short and thick. Heavy brow ridges shaded large brown intelligent eyes that were filled with love and sorrow.

She beckoned. "Iza!" Ayla cried out to her. "Iza, help me! Please help me!" But Iza only looked at her quizzically. "Iza, don't you hear me? Why can't you understand?"

"No one can understand you if you don't talk properly," said another voice. She saw a man using a staff to help him walk. He was old and lame. One arm had been amputated at the elbow. The left side of his face was hideously scarred, and his left eye was missing, but his good right eye held strength, wisdom, and compassion. "You must learn to talk, Ayla," Creb said with his one-handed gestures, but she could hear him. He spoke with Jondalar's voice.

"How can I talk? I can't remember! Help me, Creb!"

"Your totem is the Cave Lion, Ayla," the old Mog-ur said.

With a tawny flash, the feline sprang for the aurochs and wrestled the huge reddish-brown wild cow to the ground bawling in terror. Ayla gasped, and the dirk-toothed tiger snarled at her, fangs and muzzle dripping blood. He came for her, his long sharp fangs growing longer, and sharper. She was in a tiny cave trying to squeeze herself into the solid rock at her back. A cave lion roared.

"No! No!" she cried.

A gigantic paw with claws outstretched reached in and raked her left thigh with four parallel gashes.

"No! No!" she called out. "I can't! I can't!" The mist swirled around her. "I can't remember!"

The tall woman held out her arms. "I'll help you . . ."

For an instant the mist cleared, and Ayla saw a face not unlike her own. An aching nausea shook her, and a sour stench of wetness and rot issued from a crack opening in the ground.

"Mother! *Motherrr!*"

"Ayla! Ayla! What's wrong?" Jondalar shook her. He had been out on the ledge when he heard her scream in an unfamiliar language. He hobbled in faster than he thought he could move.

She sat up and he took her in his arms. "Oh, Jondalar! It was my dream, my nightmare," she sobbed.

"It's all right, Ayla. It's all right now."

"It was an earthquake. That's what happened. She was killed in an earthquake."

"Who was killed in an earthquake?"

"My mother. And Creb, too, later. Oh, Jondalar, I *hate* earthquakes!" She shuddered in his arms.

Jondalar took her by both shoulders and pushed her back so he could look at her. "Tell me about your dream, Ayla," he said.

"I've had those dreams as long as I can remember – they always come back. In one, I am in a small cave, and a claw reaches in. I think that is how my totem marked me. The other I could never remember, but I always woke up shaking and sick. Except this time, I saw her, Jondalar. I saw my mother!"

"Ayla, do you hear yourself?"

"What do you mean?"

"You're talking, Ayla. You're talking!"

Ayla had known how to speak once, and, though the language was not the same, she had learned the feel, the rhythm, the sense of spoken language. She had forgotten how to speak verbally because her survival depended upon another mode of communication, and because she wanted to forget the tragedy that had left her alone. Though it wasn't a conscious effort, she had been hearing and memorizing more than the vocabulary of Jondalar's language. The syntax, grammar, stress, were part of the sounds she heard when he spoke.

Like a child first learning to speak, she was born with the aptitude and the desire, and she needed only the constant exposure. But her motivation was stronger than a child's, and her memory more developed. She learned faster. Though she could not reproduce some of his tones and inflections exactly, she had become a native speaker of his language.

"I am! I can! Jondalar, I can think in words!"

They both noticed then that he was holding her, and both

446

became self-conscious about it. He let his arms drop.

"Is it morning already?" Ayla said, noticing the light streaming in through the cave opening and the smoke hole above it. She threw back the covers. "I didn't know I would sleep so long. Great Mother! I've got to start that meat drying." She had picked up his epithets as well. He smiled. It was rather awe-inspiring to hear her suddenly speaking, but hearing his phrases coming out of her mouth, spoken with her unique accent, was funny.

She hurried to the entrance, then stopped cold when she looked out. She rubbed her eyes and looked again. Lines of meat cut in neat little tongue-shaped pieces were strung out from one end to the other of the stone porch, with several small fires spaced in the midst of them. Could she still be dreaming? Had all the women of the Clan suddenly appeared to help her?

"There is some meat from a haunch I spitted at that fireplace, if you're hungry," Jondalar said, with assumed casualness, and a big smug smile.

"You? You did that?"

"Yes. I did it." His grin was even wider. Her reaction to his little surprise was better than he'd hoped. Maybe he wasn't quite up to hunting yet, but at least he could skin the animals she brought and start the meat drying, especially since he had just made new knives.

"But . . . you're a man!" she said, stunned.

Jondalar's little surprise was more staggering than he knew. It was only by drawing on their memories that members of the Clan acquired the knowledge and skills to survive. For them, instinct had evolved so that they could remember the skills of their forebears and pass them down to their progeny, stored in the backs of their brains. The tasks that men and women performed had been differentiated for so many generations that Clan members had sex-differentiated memories. One sex was unable to perform the functions of the other; they did not have the memories for it.

A man of the Clan could have hunted or found deer and brought them back. He could even have skinned them, though somewhat less efficiently than a woman. If pressed, he might have hacked out some hunks. But he would never have considered cutting up the meat to start it drying, and, even if he had, he wouldn't have known how to begin. He could certainly not have produced the neat, properly shaped pieces that would dry uniformly that Ayla saw in front of her eyes.

"Isn't a man allowed to cut up a little meat?" Jondalar asked. He knew some people had different customs concerning woman's work and man's work, but he had only meant to help her. He didn't think she would be offended.

"In the Clan, woman cannot hunt, and men cannot . . . make food," she tried to explain.

"But you hunt."

His statement gave her an unexpected jolt. She had forgotten she shared with him the differences between the Clan and the Others.

"I . . . I am not a Clan woman," she said, disconcerted. "I . . ." She didn't know how to explain. "I'm like you, Jondalar. One of the Others."

23

Ayla pulled up, slid off Whinney, and gave the dripping waterbag to Jondalar. He took it and drank in large thirsty gulps. They were far down the valley, almost on the steppes, and quite a distance from the stream.

The golden grass rippled in the wind around them. They had been collecting grains of broomcorn millet and wild rye from a mixed stand that also included the nodding seed heads of unripe two-row barley, and both einkorn and emmer wheat. The tedious job of pulling the hand along each stalk to strip off the small hard seeds was hot work. The small round millet, put into one side of a divided basket which hung from a cord around the neck to free the hands, broke off easily, but it would need additional winnowing. The rye, which went into the other side of the basket, threshed free.

Ayla put the cord of her basket around her neck and went to work. Jondalar joined her shortly afterwards. They pluck-ed the grains side by side for a while, then he turned to her. "What is it like to ride a horse, Ayla?" he asked.

"It's hard to explain," she said, pausing to think. "When you go fast it's exciting. But so is riding slow. It makes me feel good to ride Whinney." She turned back to her task again, then stopped. "Would you like to try?"

"Try what?"

"Riding Whinney."

He looked at her, trying to determine how she really felt about it. He had wanted to try riding the horse for some time, but she seemed to have such a personal relationship with the animal that he didn't know how to ask tactfully. "Yes. I would. But will Whinney let me?"

"I don't know." She glanced towards the sun to see how

late it was, then swung the basket to her back. "We can see."

"Now?" he asked. She nodded, already starting back. "I thought you went to get the water so we could pick more grain."

"I did. I forgot, the picking goes faster with two sets of hands. I was only looking at my basket – I'm not used to the help."

The man's range of skills was a constant surprise to her. He was not only willing, he was able to do anything she could, or he could learn to. He was curious and interested in everything, and particularly liked to try anything new. She could see herself in him. It gave her a new appreciation for just how unusual she must have seemed to the Clan. Yet they had taken her in and tried to fit her into their pattern of life.

Jondalar flipped his picking basket to his back and fell in beside her. "I'm ready to give this up for today. You've got so much grain already, Ayla, and the barley and wheat aren't even ripe yet. I don't understand why you want more."

"It's for Whinney and her baby. They'll need grass, too. Whinney feeds outside in winter, but when the snow is deep, many horses die."

The explanation was sufficient to quell any objection he might have had. They walked back through the tall grass, enjoying the warm sun on bare skin – now that they weren't working in it. Jondalar wore only his breechclout, and his skin was as tanned as hers. Ayla had changed to her short summer wrap that covered her from waist to thigh, but more importantly, provided pouches and folds for carrying tools, sling, and other objects. Her only other piece of apparel was the small leather pouch around her neck. Jondalar had found himself admiring her firm supple body more than once, but he made no overt gestures, and she invited none.

He was anticipating the ride on the horse, wondering what Whinney would do. He could get out of her way in a hurry if he had to. Except for a slight limp, his leg was fine, and he thought the limp would work its way out in time. Ayla had made a miraculous job of treating his wound; he had so much to thank her for. He had begun to think about leaving – there was no reason for him to stay any more – but she seemed in no hurry for him to go, and he kept putting it off. He wanted to help her prepare for the coming winter; he owed her that much at least.

And she had to worry about the horses, too. He hadn't thought of that. "It takes a lot of work to store feed for the horses, doesn't it?"

"Not so much," she said.

"I was just thinking, you said they needed grass, too. Couldn't you cut whole stalks and take them to the cave? Then, instead of gathering grain in these," he indicated the picking baskets, "you could shake the seeds into a basket. And have grass for them besides."

She paused, frowning, to consider the idea. "Maybe. . . . If the stalks are left to dry after they're cut, the seeds might shake loose. Some better than others. There's still wheat and barley . . . worth a try." A big smile spread across her face. "Jondalar, I think it might work!"

She was so genuinely excited that he had to smile, too. His approval of her, his attraction, his sheer delight in her were all apparent in his wonderfully seductive eyes. Her response was open and spontaneous.

"Jondalar, I like it so much when you smile . . . to me, with your mouth, and with your eyes."

He laughed – his unexpected, unconstrained, exuberantly wanton laugh. She is so honest, he thought. I don't think she's ever been anything but completely forthright. What a rare woman she is.

Ayla was caught up by his outburst. Her smile gave in to the contagion of his merriment, collapsed into a chuckle, then grew into a full, uninhibited exultation of delight.

They were both breathless when they regained control, relapsing into new spasms, then taking deep breaths and wiping their eyes. Neither of them could say what had been so outrageously funny; their laughter had fed on itself. But it was as much a release of tensions that had been accumulating, as the mirthfulness of the situation.

When they started walking again, Jondalar put an arm around Ayla's waist. It was an affectionate reflex to the shared laughter. He felt her stiffen and jerked his arm away immediately. He had promised himself, and her, even if she hadn't understood him at the time, that he would not impose himself on her. If she had made vows to abstain from

Pleasures, he was not going to put himself in a position that would force her to refuse him. He had been very careful to respect her person.

But he had smelled the female essence of her warm skin, felt the turgid fullness of her breast on his side. He remembered, suddenly, how long it had been since he had lain with a woman, and the breechclout did nothing to hide the evidence of his thoughts. He turned away in an attempt to conceal his obvious tumescence, but it was all he could do to keep from tearing off her wrap. His stride lengthened until he was nearly running ahead of her.

"Doni! How I want that woman!" he muttered under his breath.

Tears squeezed out of the corners of Ayla's eyes as she watched him bolt ahead. What did I do wrong? Why does he pull away from me? Why won't he give me his signal? I can see his need, why doesn't he want to relieve it with me? Am I so ugly? She quivered with the remembered feel of his arm around her; her nostrils were full of his masculine scent. She dragged her feet, not wanting to face him, feeling the way she had when she was a little girl and had done something she knew was wrong – only this time, she didn't know what it was.

Jondalar had reached the cool shade of the wooded strip near the stream. His urgency was so strong that he could not constrain himself. Only moments after he was out of sight behind a screen of dense foliage, spasms of viscous white spurted to the ground, and then, still holding himself, he leaned his head against the tree, shaking. It was release, nothing more, but at least he could face the woman without trying to throw her down and force her.

He found a stick to loosen the soil and covered the essence of his Pleasures with the earth of the Mother. Zelandoni had told him it was a waste of the Mother's Gift to spill it, but if it was necessary, it should be given back to Her, spilled on the ground and covered. Zelandoni was right, he thought. It was a waste, and there had been no pleasure in it.

He walked alongside the stream, embarrassed to come out in the open. He saw her waiting by the large boulder with her arm around the colt and her forehead pressed on Whinney's neck. She looked so vulnerable, clinging to the animals for support and comfort. She should be leaning on him for support, he thought; he should be comforting her. He was sure he had caused her distress, and he felt ashamed, as though he had committed some reprehensible act. With reluctance, he came out of the woods.

"There are times when a man can't wait to make his stream," he lied, with a weak smile.

Ayla was surprised. Why should he make words that were not true? She knew what he had done. He had relieved himself.

A man of the Clan would have asked for the leader's mate before he would have relieved himself. If he couldn't control his need, even she, as ugly as she was, would have been signalled, if there was no other woman. No adult male would relieve himself. Only adolescents, who had reached physical maturity but had not yet made their first kill, would consider it. But Jondalar had preferred to take care of himself rather than signal her. She was beyond hurt; she was humiliated.

She ignored his words and avoided a direct look. "If you want to ride Whinney, I'll hold her while you get up on the rock and put your leg over. I will tell Whinney you want to ride. Maybe she will let you."

That was the reason they had stopped picking, he recalled. What had happened to his enthusiasm? How could so much change in the course of walking from one end of the field to the other? Trying to give the impression that everything was normal, he climbed up on the seat-like indentation of the large boulder while Ayla guided the horse closer, but he avoided eye contact, too.

"How do you make her go where you want?" he asked.

Ayla had to consider the question. "I do not make her go, she wants to go where I want to go."

"But how does she know where you want to go?"

"I don't know . . ." She didn't; she hadn't thought about it.

Jondalar decided he didn't care. He was willing to go wherever the horse would take him, if she was willing to take him at all. He put a hand on her withers to steady himself, then gingerly straddled the horse.

Whinney cocked her ears back. She knew it wasn't Ayla, and the load was heavier and lacked the immediate sense of guidance, the muscle tension of Ayla's thighs and legs. But Ayla was close, holding her head, and the man was familiar. The mare pranced with uncertainty but settled down after a few moments.

"What do I do now?" Jondalar asked, seated on the small horse with his long legs dangling on either side – not quite knowing what to do with his hands.

Ayla patted the horse with familiar reassurance, then addressed her in a language that was part gesture, part clipped Clan words, and part Zelandonii. "Jondalar would like you go give him a ride, Whinney."

Her voice had the urging-forward tone, and her hand exerted gentle pressure; cue enough to the animal so attuned to the woman's directions. Whinney started forward.

"If you need to hold on, put your arms around her neck," Ayla advised.

Whinney was used to carrying a person on her back. She didn't jump or buck, but without guidance, she moved with hesitancy. Jondalar leaned forward to pat her neck, as much to reassure himself as the horse, but the movement had a similarity to Ayla's direction to move faster. The unexpected forward jolt caused the man to follow Ayla's advice. He wrapped his arms around the mare's neck, leaning far forward. To Whinney, it was a signal to increase speed.

The horse broke into an all-out gallop straight across the field, with Jondalar hanging on to her neck for all he was worth, his long hair streaming behind him. He could feel the wind in his face, and, when he finally dared open his eyes a crack, he saw the land moving past at an alarming speed. It was frightening – and thrilling! He understood Ayla's inability to describe the feeling. It was like sliding down an icy hill in winter, or the time he was pulled up the river by the big sturgeon, but more exciting. His eye was drawn by a blur of movement to his left. The bay colt was racing beside his mother, matching her pace.

He heard a distant whistle, sharp and piercing, and suddenly the horse wheeled around in a tight turn and galloped back.

"Sit up!" she called to Jondalar as they approached. When the horse slowed, nearing the woman, he sat up straighter. Whinney cantered to a halt beside the stone.

Jondalar was shaking a bit when he dismounted, but his eyes glistened with excitement. Ayla patted the mare's sweaty flanks, then followed her more slowly when Whinney trotted towards the beach near the cave.

"Do you know that colt kept up with her the whole way? What a racer he is!"

From the way Jondalar used it, Ayla sensed there was more to the word than its meaning. "What is a 'racer'?" she asked.

"At Summer Meetings there are contests – all kinds – but the most exciting are the Races, the running contests," he explained. "The runners are called racers, and the word has come to mean anyone who strives to win, or tries to achieve some goal. It is a word of approval and encouragement – praise."

"The colt is a racer; he likes to run."

They continued walking in silence, which grew more painful with each step. "Why did you tell me to sit up?" Jondalar finally asked, trying to fill it. "I thought you said you didn't know how you told Whinney what you wanted. She did slow down when I sat up."

"I never thought about it before, but when I saw you coming, I suddenly thought, 'sit up'. I didn't know how to tell you at first, but when you needed to slow down, I just knew."

"You do give the horse signals, then. Some kind of signals. I wonder if the colt could learn signals," he mused.

They reached the wall that extended out towards the water and rounded it to the spectacle of Whinney rolling in the mud at the edge of the stream to cool down, groaning with exquisite pleasure. Near her was the colt with his legs in the air. Jondalar, smiling, stopped to watch, but Ayla kept walking with her head down. He caught up with her as she started up the path.

"Ayla . . ." She turned around, and then he didn't know what to say. "I . . . I, ahhh . . . I want to thank you."

It was still a word she had some difficulty comprehending. There was no direct parallel in the Clan. The members of each small clan were so dependent on each other for survival, mutual assitance was a way of life. Thanks were no more offered than a baby would thank its mother for care, or a mother expect it. Special favours or gifts imposed obligations to return them in kind, and they were not always received with pleasure.

The closest anyone in the Clan came to thanks was a form of gratitude from someone of lower status to someone with more rank, usually a woman towards a man, for a special dispensation. It seemed to her that Jondalar was trying to say he was grateful to her for riding on Whinney.

"Jondalar, Whinney allowed you to sit on her back. Why do you thank me?"

"You helped me ride her, Ayla. And besides, I have so much more to thank you for. You've done so much for me, taken care of me."

"Would the colt say thank you to Whinney for taking care of him? You were in need, I took care of you. Why . . . 'thank you'?"

"But you saved my life."

"I am a woman who heals, Jondalar." She tried to think of a way to explain that when someone saved another's life, a piece of the life spirit was claimed, and, therefore, the obligation of protecting that person in return; in effect, the two became closer than siblings. But she was a medicine woman, and a piece of everyone's spirit had been given to her with the piece of black manganese dioxide that she carried in her amulet. No one was obligated to give her more. "Thank you is not necessary," she said.

"I know it is not necessary. I know you are a Woman Who Heals, but it is important to me that you know how I feel. People say thank you to each other for help. It's courtesy, a custom."

They ascended the path single file. She didn't answer him, but his comment made her think of Creb, trying to explain that it was discourteous to look past the boundary stones into another man's hearth. She had had more difficulty learning the customs than the language of the Clan. Jondalar was saying it was a custom to express gratitude to each other among his people, a courtesy, but that confused her more.

Why would he want to express gratitude when he had just shamed her? If a man of the Clan had offered her such contempt, she would cease to exist for him. His customs were going to be hard to learn, too, she realized, but that did not make her feel less humiliated.

He tried to get through the barrier that had sprung up between them and stopped her before she went into the cave. "Ayla, I'm sorry if I've offended you in some way."

"Offended? I don't understand that word."

"I think I have made you angry, made you feel bad."

"Not angry, but yes, you have made me feel bad."

The admission startled him. "I'm sorry," he said.

"Sorry. That is courtesy, right? Custom? Jondalar, what good are words like *sorry*? It doesn't change anything, it doesn't make me feel any better."

He pulled his hand through his hair. She was right. Whatever he had done – and he thought he knew what it was – being sorry didn't help. It also didn't help that he had been evading the issue, not facing it directly for fear he would open himself to further embarrassment.

She went into the cave, took off her picking basket, and stirred up the fire to begin an evening meal. He followed her, put his basket next to hers, and pulled up a mat to the fireplace to sit and watch her.

She used some of the tools he had given her after he cut up the deer, and liked them, but for some tasks she preferred to use the handheld knife she was accustomed to. He thought she wielded the crude knife, shaped on flake of flint, that was much heavier than his blades, with as much skill as anyone he knew used with the smaller, finer, hafted knives. His flint-knapper mind was judging, evaluating, comparing the merits of each type. It's not so much that one is easier to use than the other, he was thinking. Any sharp knife will cut, but think how much more raw flint it must take to make tools for everyone. Just hauling the stone could be a problem.

It made Ayla nervous to have him sitting there watching her so closely. Finally she got up to get some chamomile for tea, hoping it would divert his attention, and to calm herself. It only made him realize he had been putting off facing the problem again. He gathered up his fortitude and decided on a direct approach.

"You're right, Ayla. Saying I'm sorry doesn't mean much, but I don't know what else to say. I don't know what I did that offended you. Please tell me, why do you feel bad?"

He must be saying words that were untrue again, she thought. How could he not know? Yet he seemed troubled. She looked down, wishing he hadn't asked. It was bad enough having to suffer such humiliation, without having to talk about it. But he had asked.

"I feel bad because . . . because I'm not acceptable." She said it to the hands in her lap holding her tea.

"What do you mean you are not acceptable? I don't understand."

Why was he asking her these questions? Was he trying to make her feel worse? Ayla glanced up at him. He was leaning forward, and she read sincerity and anxiety in his posture and eyes.

"No man of the Clan would ever relieve his need himself if there was an acceptable woman around." She blushed with the recitation of her failing and looked down at her hands. "You were full with need, but you ran away from me. Should I not feel bad if I am not acceptable to you?"

"Are you saying you're offended because I didn't . . ." He sat back and looked up. "Oh, Doni! How could you be so stupid, Jondalar?" he asked the cave at large.

She looked up at him, startled.

"I thought you didn't want me to annoy you, Ayla. I was trying to respect your wishes. I wanted you so much, I couldn't stand it, but every time I touched you, you stiffened up. How could you think any man would not find you acceptable?"

A surge of understanding welled up inside her that dissolved the taut aching heart. He wanted her! He thought she didn't want him! It was custom again, different custom. "Jondalar, you only had to make the signal. Why did it matter what I wanted?"

"Of course it matters what you want. Don't you . . ." suddenly he flushed. "Don't you want me?" There was hesitation in his eyes, and fear of rejection. She knew the feeling. It surprised her to see it in a man, but it melted any residual doubt she might have harboured and drew forth a warmth and tenderness.

"I want you Jondalar. I wanted you when I first saw you. When you were so hurt I wasn't sure you would live, I would look at you and feel. . . . Inside would come this feeling. But you never gave me the signal . . ." She looked down again. She had said more than she intended. Women of the Clan were more subtle in their inviting gestures.

"And all this time I've been thinking. . . . What is this signal you keep talking about?"

"In the Clan, when a man wants a woman, he makes the signal."

"Show me."

She made the gesture and blushed. It was not a signal usually made by a woman.

"That's all? I just do that? Then what do you do?" He was a little stunned when she got up, kneeled, and presented.

"Are you saying a man does this, and a woman does that, and that's it? They're ready?"

"A man doesn't make the signal if he's not ready. Weren't you ready today?"

It was his turn to blush. He had forgotten how ready he was, what he had done to keep from forcing himself on her. He would have given anything then to have known this signal.

"What if a woman doesn't want him? Or she's not ready?"

"If a man makes the signal, a woman must assume the position." She thought of Broud, and her face clouded with remembered pain and degradation.

"Anytime, Ayla?" He saw the pain, and wondered. "Even her first?" She nodded. "Is that how it happened for you? Some man just gave you a signal?" She closed her eyes and swallowed, then nodded again.

Jondalar was aghast, and indignant. "Do you mean to say there were no First Rites? No one to watch and make sure a man didn't hurt you too much? What kind of people are they? Don't they care about a young woman's first time? They just leave it to any man to take her when he's high in his heat? To force her whether she's ready or not? Whether it hurts or not?" He was up and angrily pacing. "That's cruel! That's inhuman! How could anyone allow it? Don't they have any compassion? Don't they care at all?"

His outburst was so unexpected that Ayla just sat staring wide-eyed, watching Jondalar work himself up into a fever of righteous wrath. But as his words became more vituperative, she started shaking her head, negating his statements. "No!"

she said, finally giving voice to her dissent. "That's not true, Jondalar. They do care! Iza found me – she took care of me. They adopted me, made me part of the Clan, even though I was born to the Others. They didn't have to take me in.

"Creb didn't understand that Broud hurt me, he never had a mate. He didn't know about women that way and it was Broud's right. And when I got pregnant, Iza took care of me. She made herself sick getting medicine for me so I wouldn't lose my baby. Without her, I would have died when Durc was born. And Brun accepted him, even though everyone thought he was deformed. But he wasn't. He's strong and healthy . . ." Ayla stopped when she saw Jondalar staring at her.

"You have a son? Where is he?"

Ayla hadn't spoken of her son. Even after so long a time, it was painful to talk about him. She knew any mention would cause questions, though eventually it would have come up.

"Yes, I have a son. He is still with the Clan. I gave him to Uba when Broud made me leave."

"Made you leave?" He sat back down. So she had a son. He had been right in suspecting that she had been pregnant. "Why would someone make a mother leave her child? Who is this . . . Broud?"

How could she explain? She closed her eyes for a moment. "He's the leader. Brun was the leader when they found me. He allowed Creb to make me Clan, but he was getting old, so he made Broud leader. Broud always hated me, even when I was a little girl."

"He's the one who hurt you, isn't he?"

"Iza told me about the signal when I became a woman, but she said men relieved their needs with women they liked. Broud did it because it made him feel good to know he could make me do something I hated. But I think my totem led him to do it. The spirit of the Cave Lion knew how much I wanted a baby."

"What does this Broud have to do with your baby? The Great Earth Mother blesses when She chooses. Was your son of his spirit?"

"Creb said spirits made babies. He said a woman swal-

460

lowed the spirit of a man's totem. If it was strong enough, it would overcome the spirit of her totem, take its life force, and start a new life growing in her."

"That's an odd way of looking at it. It's the Mother who chooses the man's spirit to mix with the woman's spirit when She blesses a woman."

"I don't think spirits make babies. Not spirits of totems, or spirits mixed by your Great Mother. I think life starts when a man's organ is full and he puts it inside a woman. I think that's why men have such strong needs, and why women want men so much."

"That can't be, Ayla. Do you know how many times a man can put his manhood inside a woman? A woman couldn't have that many children. A man makes a woman, with the Mother's Gift of Pleasure; he opens her so the spirits can enter. But the Mother's most sacred Gift of Life is given only to women. They receive the spirits and create life, and become mothers like Her. If a man honours Her, appreciates Her Gifts, and makes a commitment to take care of a woman and her children, Doni may choose his spirit for the children of his hearth."

"What is the Gift of Pleasure?"

"That's right! You've never known Pleasures, have you?" he said, amazed when he considered the idea. "No wonder you didn't know when I. . . You're a woman who's been blessed with a child without ever having First Rites. Your Clan must be very unusual. Everyone I met on my Journey knew about the Mother and Her Gifts. The Gift of Pleasure is when a man and a woman feel they want each other, and give themselves to each other."

"It is when a man is full and must relieve his needs with a woman, isn't that right?" Ayla said. "It's when he puts his organ in the place where babies come out. That is the Gift of Pleasure?"

"It's that, but it's much more."

"Perhaps, but everyone told me I'd never have a baby because my totem was too strong. They were all surprised. He wasn't deformed, either. He just looked a little like me, and a little like them. But it was only after Broud kept giving me the signal that I became pregnant. No one else wanted me – I'm too big and ugly. Even at the Clan Gathering there wasn't a man who would take me, though I had Iza's status when they accepted me as her daughter."

Something about her story began to bother Jondalar, nagged at him, but floated just out of reach.

"You said the medicine woman found you – what was her name? Iza? Where did she find you? Where did you come from?"

"I don't know. Iza said I was born to the Others, other people like me. Like you, Jondalar. I don't remember anything before I lived with the Clan – I didn't even remember my mother's face. You are the only man I've seen who looks like me."

Jondalar was feeling an uneasiness in the pit of his stomach as he listened.

"I learned about a man of the Others from a woman at the Clan Gathering. It made me afraid of them, until I met you. She had a baby, a girl that resembled Durc so much, she could have been mine. Oda wanted to arrange a mating between her daughter and my son. They said her baby was deformed, too, but I think that man of the Others started her baby when he forced her to relieve his needs with him."

"The man forced her?"

"And killed her first daughter, too. Oda was with two other women, and many of the Others came, but they didn't give the signal. When one of them grabbed her, Oda's first baby fell and hit her head on a rock."

Suddenly Jondalar remembered the gang of young men from a Cave far to the west. He wanted to reject the conclusions he was beginning to draw. Yet, if one gang of young men would do it, why not another? "Ayla, you keep saying you are not like the Clan. How are they different?"

"They're shorter – that's why I was so surprised when you stood up. I've always been taller than everyone, including the men."

"What else?" He didn't want to ask, but he couldn't stop himself. He had to know.

"Their eyes are brown. Iza thought something was wrong with my eyes because they were the colour of the sky. Durc has their eyes, and the . . . I don't know how to say it, the big brows, but his forehead is like mine. Their heads are flatter . . ."

"Flatheads!" His lips pulled back in disgust. "Good Mother, Ayla! You've been living with those animals! You let one of their males . . ." He shuddered. "You gave birth to . . . an abomination of mixed spirits, half human and half animal!" As though he had touched something filthy, Jondalar backed away and jumped up. It was a reaction born of irrational prejudice, of harsh, unthinking assumptions, never questioned by most people he knew.

Ayla didn't comprehend at first, and she looked at him with a puzzled frown. But his expression was filled with loathing, just as hers was when she thought of hyenas. Then his words took on meaning.

Animals! He was calling the people she loved animals! Stinking hyenas! Gentle loving Creb, who was nonetheless the most awesome and powerful holy man of the Clan – Creb was an animal? Iza, who had nursed her and mothered her, who taught her medicine – Iza was a stinking hyena? And Durc! Her son!

"What do you mean, animals?" Ayla cried, on her feet and facing him. She had never raised her voice in anger before and she surprised herself at the volume – and the venom. "Creb and Iza, animals? My son, half human? People of the Clan are not some kind of awful stinking hyenas.

"Would animals pick up a little girl who was hurt? Would they accept her as one of them? Would they take care of her? Raise her? Where do you think I learned to find food? Or cook it? Where do you think I learned healing? If it were not for those animals, I would not be alive today, and neither would you, Jondalar!

"You say the Clan are animals, and the Others are human? Well, remember this: the Clan saved a child of the Others, and the Others killed one of theirs. If I could make a choice between human and animal, I'd take the stinking hyenas!"

She stormed out of the cave and down the path, then whistled for Whinney.

24

Jondalar was dumbfounded. He followed her out and watched her from the ledge. She mounted the horse with a practised leap and galloped down the valley. Ayla had always been so complaisant, had never showed anger. The contrast made her outburst all the more astounding.

He had always thought of himself as fair and open-minded about flatheads. He thought they should be left alone, not bothered or baited, and he would not have intentionally killed one. But his sensibilities had been grossly offended by the idea of a man using a flathead female for Pleasures. That one of their males should have used a human female the same way had exposed a deeply buried nerve. The woman would be defiled.

And he had been so eager for her. He thought of the vulgar stories told by sniggering boys and young men and felt a shrinking in his loins, as though he were already contaminated and his member would shrivel up and rot off. By some grace of the Great Earth Mother, he had been spared.

But worse, she had birthed an abomination, a whelp of malignant spirits who couldn't even be discussed in decent company. The very existence of such issue was hotly denied by some, yet talk of them had persisted.

Ayla certainly had not denied it. She openly admitted it, stood there and defended the child . . . as vehemently as any mother would if her child had been maligned. She was insulted, angry that he had spoken of any of them in derogatory terms. Had she really been raised by a pack of flatheads?

He'd met a few flatheads on his Journey. He'd even questioned in his own mind whether they were animals. He recalled the incident with the young male and the older female. Come to think of it, hadn't the youngster used a knife made on a heavy flake to cut the fish in half, *just like the one Ayla used*? And his dam wore a hide wrapped around her, as Ayla did. Ayla even had the same mannerisms, especially in the beginning; that tendency to look down, to efface herself so she wouldn't be noticed. The furs on her bed, they had the same soft texture as the wolf skin they had given him. And her spear! That heavy primitive spear – wasn't it like the spears carried by that pack of flatheads he and Thonolan had met coming off the glacier?

It was right there in front of him all the time, if he'd only looked. Why had he made up that story about her being One Who Serves the Mother testing herself to perfect her skills? Had Ayla really learned her healing skill from a flathead?

He watched her riding off in the distance. She had been magnificent in her rage. He knew many women who raised their voices at the least provocation. Marona could be a shrill, contentious, foul-tempered shrew, he recalled, thinking about the woman to whom he had been promised. But there was a strength in someone so demanding that had appealed to him. He liked strong women. They were a challenge, and they could hold their own and not be so easily overwhelmed by his own passions on the rare occasions when they were expressed. He'd suspected there was a rock-hard core to Ayla in spite of her composure. Look at her on that horse, he thought. She is a remarkable, beautiful woman.

Suddenly, like a splash of icy water, he realized what he had done. The blood drained from his face. She had saved his life, and he had drawn away from her as if she were filth! She had lavished care on him, and he had repaid her with vile disgust. He had called her child an abomination, a child she obviously loved. He was mortified by his insensitivity.

He ran back into the cave and threw himself on the bed. Her bed. He had been sleeping on the bed of a woman from whom he had just cringed in contempt.

"Oh, Doni!" he cried. "How could you let me do it? Why didn't you help me? Why didn't you stop me?"

He buried his head under the furs. He hadn't felt so wretched since he was young. He thought he was over that. He'd acted without thinking then, too. Would he never learn? Why hadn't he exercised some discretion? He would be leaving soon; his leg was healed. Why couldn't he have controlled himself until he left?

In fact, why was he still here? Why hadn't he thanked her and gone? There was nothing holding him. Why had he stayed and pressed her for answers to questions that were not his concern? Then he could have remembered her as the beautiful, mysterious woman who lived alone in a valley, and charmed animals, and saved his life.

Because you could not walk away from a beautiful, mysterious woman, Jondalar, and you know it!

Why should it bother you so much? What difference does it make that she . . . lived with flatheads?

Because you wanted her. And then you thought she wasn't good enough for you because she had . . . she had let . . .

You idiot! You weren't listening. She didn't *let* him, he forced her! With no First Rites. And you blame her! She was telling you, opening up and reliving the hurt, and what did you do?

You are worse than he was, Jondalar. At least she knew how he felt. He hated her, he wanted to hurt her. But you! She trusted you. She told you how she felt about you. You wanted her so much, Jondalar, and you could have had her any time. But you were afraid to hurt your pride.

If you'd been paying attention to her, and not worrying about yourself so much, you might have noticed she wasn't behaving like an experienced woman. She was acting like a scared young girl. Haven't you had enough of them to know the difference? But she doesn't look like a scared young girl.

You only thought she was assured, she doesn't even know she's beautiful. She really thinks she's big and ugly. How can anyone think she's ugly?

She grew up with flatheads, remember? Who would imagine they'd think about the difference? But then, who would imagine they'd take in a strange little girl? Would we take in one of theirs?

And healed by a flathead! How could a flathead know healing? But she learned from them, and she's good. Good enough to make you think she was One Who Serves the Mother. You ought to give up flint knapping and become a storyteller! You didn't want to see the truth. Now that you know, does it make a difference? Are you less alive because

466

she learned her healing from flatheads? Is she less beautiful because . . . because she gave birth to an abomination? What makes her child an abomination?

You still want her, Jondalar.

It's too late. She'll never believe you again, never trust you. A new surge of shame rose up. He balled his fists and hit the furs. You idiot! You stupid, stupid, idiot! You spoiled it for yourself. Why don't you go away?

You can't. You have to face her, Jondalar. You don't have clothes, you don't have weapons, you don't have food, you can't travel with nothing.

Where are you going to get supplies? Where else? This is Ayla's place – you have to get them from her. You'll have to ask her, at least for some flint. With tools, you can make spears. Then you can hunt for food, and skins to make clothes, and a sleeping roll, and a backframe. It's going to take time to get ready, and a year to get back, or more. It's going to be lonely without Thonolan.

Jondalar burrowed deeper into the furs. Why did Thonolan have to die? Why didn't that lion kill me instead? Tears squeezed out of the corners of his eyes. Thonolan wouldn't have done anything so stupid.

He heard a clatter of hooves on the rocky path up from the beach and thought it was Ayla coming back. But it was the colt. He got up, went out on the ledge, and looked down the valley. Ayla was not in sight.

What's the matter, little fellow? Did they leave you behind? It's my fault, but they'll be back . . . if only for you. Besides, Ayla lives here . . . alone. I wonder how long she's been here? Alone.

Here you are, crying over your stupidities, and look at what she's been through. She's not crying about it. She's such a remarkable woman. Beautiful. Magnificent. And you've lost it all, Jondalar, you idiot! Oh Doni! I wish I could make it right.

Jondalar was wrong: Ayla was crying, crying as she'd never cried before. It didn't make her less strong, it only made it easier to bear. She pushed Whinney until the valley was far behind, then stopped at an oxbow meander of a stream that was a tributary of the one near her cave. The land within the loop of the oxbow flooded often, leaving alluvial silt that provided a fertile base for lusher growth. It was a place she had hunted willow grouse and ptarmigan, and an assortment of animals from marmot to giant deer, who found the enticing spot of green impossible to resist.

She threw her leg over and slid off Whinney's back, took a drink and washed her tear-streaked and dirty face. She felt as if she'd had a bad dream. The entire day had been a dizzying series of giddy emotional highs and oppressive lows, with each swing reaching greater peaks and dips. She didn't think she could stand another swing, in either direction.

The morning had started well. Jondalar had insisted on helping her pick grain. It was more than the extra pair of hands that helped, though. It was the company; having someone near made her realize how much she had missed it.

Then there was a small disagreement. Nothing serious. She wanted to keep picking and he wanted to quit when the waterbag ran out. But when she returned from the stream and understood he wanted to try horse riding, she thought it might be a way to keep him there with her. He liked the colt, and if he liked riding he might want to stay until the colt was grown. When she offered, he had jumped at the chance.

Then the laughter started. She had not laughed like that since Baby left. She loved Jondalar's laugh.

Then he touched me, she thought. No one in the Clan touches like that, at least not outside the boundary stones. Who knows what a man and his mate might do at night, under furs. Maybe they touch the way he touches. Do all the Others touch like that outside the hearth? I liked it when he touched me. Why did he run away?

Ayla had wanted to die with shame, sure she was the ugliest woman on earth, when he relieved himself. Then, in the cave, when he said he wanted her, that he didn't think she wanted him, she almost cried with happiness. The way he looked at her, she could feel the warmth starting inside, the wanting, drawing-in feeling. He was so angry when she told him about Broud that she was sure he liked her.

But she would never forget the way he looked at her, like some disgusting piece of rotten flesh. He even shuddered.

Iza and Creb are *not* animals! They are people. People who

took care of me and loved me. Why does he hate them? This was their land first. His kind came later . . . my kind. Is that what my kind are like?

I'm glad I left Durc with the Clan. They might think he is deformed, Broud might hate him because he is my son, but my baby will not be some animal . . . some abomination. That was the word he said. He doesn't have to explain it.

Tears started again. My baby, my son . . . He is not deformed – he is healthy and strong. And he is not an animal, not . . . abomination.

How could he change so fast? He was looking at me, with his blue eyes, he was looking. . . . Then he pulled away as though I would burn him, or as if I were an evil spirit whose name only mog-urs know. It was worse than a death curse. They only turned away and didn't see me any more. I was just dead and belonged to the next world. They didn't look at me as if I were . . . abomination.

The setting sun brought the chill of evening. Even during the hottest part of the summer, the steppes were cold at night. She shivered in her summer wrap, and realized she had to return. If I had thought to bring a tent and a fur . . . No, Whinney would get anxious for the colt, and she needs to nurse.

When Ayla got up from the bank of the stream, Whinney raised her head from the lush grass, trotted to her, and flushed a pair of ptarmigan. Ayla's reaction was almost instinctive. She pulled the sling from her waist and stooped to pick up pebbles in one motion. The birds had barely lifted off the ground before one, and then the other, plummeted back. She retrieved them, searched for the nest, and then stopped.

Why am I looking for eggs? Am I going to make Creb's favourite dish for Jondalar? Why should I cook anything for him, especially Creb's favourite? But when she spied the nest – hardly more than a depression scratched out of the hard ground containing a clutch of seven eggs – she shrugged and collected them carefully.

She set the eggs down near the stream beside the birds, then picked long reeds growing near the water's edge. The loosely woven basket she made took only a few moments; it would be used only to transport the eggs and then be thrown away. She used more reeds to fasten together the feathered feet of the brace of ptarmigan. The dense winter snowshoe feathers were already growing in.

Winter. Ayla shivered. She didn't want to think about winter, cold and bleak. But winter was never entirely out of mind. Summer was only the time to get ready for winter.

Jondalar was going to leave! She knew it. It was silly to think he would stay with her in the valley.

"Why did he come?"

She startled herself with her voice. She wasn't used to hearing herself talk when she was alone. "But I can talk. That much Jondalar did. At least, if I see people, I can talk to them now. And I know people live to the west. Iza was right, there must be many people, many Others."

She draped the ptarmigan over the mare's back, one dangling on either side, and held the basket of eggs between her legs. I was born to the Others . . . Find a mate, Iza told me. I thought Jondalar was sent for me by my totem, but would one my totem sent look at me like that?

"How could he look at me like that?" she cried with a convulsive sob. "O Cave Lion, I don't want to be alone any more." Ayla slumped down, giving in to tears again. Whinney noticed the lack of direction, but it didn't matter. She knew the way. After a while Ayla sat up. No one is making me stay here. I should have been looking before this. I can talk now . . .

" . . . and I can tell them Whinney is not a horse to hunt," she continued out loud after reminding herself. "I'll get everything ready, and next spring I will leave." She knew she would not put it off again.

Jondalar won't leave right away. He will need clothes and weapons. Maybe my Cave Lion sent him here to teach me. Then I must learn all I can before he goes. I will watch him, and ask him questions, no matter how he looks at me. Broud hated me all the years I lived with the Clan. I can stand it if Jondalar . . . if he . . . hates me. She closed her eyes to squeeze back tears.

She reached for her amulet, remembering what Creb had told her long ago: when you find a sign your totem has left for you, put it in your amulet. It will bring you luck. Ayla had put them all in her amulet. Cave Lion, I've been alone so long, put luck in my amulet.

*

The sun had fallen behind the upstream gorge wall by the time she rode down towards the stream. Darkness always followed quickly. Jondalar saw her coming and ran down to the beach. Ayla had urged Whinney to a gallop, and, as she rounded the jutting wall, she almost collided with him. The horse shied, nearly unseating the woman. Jondalar reached up a steadying hand, but when he felt bare flesh, he jerked his hand away, sure she must despise him.

He hates me, Ayla thought. He can't stand to touch me! She swallowed a sob and signalled Whinney forward. The horse crossed the rocky beach and clattered up the path with Ayla on her back. She dismounted at the cave entrance and dashed in, wishing she had some other place to go. She wanted to hide. She dropped the egg basket beside the hearth, scooped up an armful of furs, and carried them to the storage area. She dumped them on the ground on the other side of the drying rack, amidst unused baskets, mats, and bowls, then jumped into them and pulled them over her head.

Ayla heard Whinney's hooves a moment later, and then the colt. She was shaking, fighting back tears, acutely conscious of the movements of the man in the cave. She wished he would leave so at least she could cry.

She didn't hear his bare feet on the dirt floor as he approached, but she knew he was there and tried to stop her shaking.

"Ayla?" he said. She didn't answer. "Ayla, I brought you some tea." She held herself stiff. "Ayla, you don't have to stay back here. I'll move. I'll go to the other side of the fireplace."

He hates me! He can't stand to be near me, she thought, stifling a sob. I wish he'd go away, I wish he'd just go away.

"I know it doesn't do any good, but I have to say it. I'm sorry, Ayla. I'm more sorry than I can say. You didn't deserve what I did. You don't have to answer me, but I have to talk to you. You have always been honest with me — it's time for me to be straightforward with you for a change.

"I've been thinking about it since you rode off. I don't know why I did . . . what I did, but I want to try to explain. After that lion attacked and I woke up here, I didn't know where I was, and I couldn't understand why you wouldn't talk to me. You were a mystery. Why were you here alone? I began to imagine a story about you, that you were a zelandoni testing yourself, a sacred woman answering a call to Serve the Mother. When you didn't respond to my gross attempts to share Pleasures with you, I thought you were forgoing them as part of your testing. I thought the Clan was a strange group of zelandonii you lived with.''

Ayla had stopped shaking and was listening, but not moving.

"I was only thinking of myself, Ayla." He hunkered down. "I'm not sure if you'll believe this, but I, ahhh . . . I've been considered a . . . an attractive man. Most women have . . . wanted my attention. I had my choice. I thought you were rejecting me. It hurt my pride, but I wouldn't admit it.

"If I'd been paying attention, I would have known you weren't an experienced woman rejecting me, but more like a young woman before her First Rites – unsure, and a little scared, and wanting to please. If anyone ought to recognize that, I should – I've had . . . never mind. That doesn't matter."

Ayla had let the covers fall back, listening so intensely that she could hear her heart pounding her ears.

"All I could see was Ayla the woman. And, believe me, you don't look like a girl. I thought you were teasing me when you talked of yourself as big and ugly. Maybe to fl. . . the people who raised you, you were too tall, and different, but Ayla, you need to know, you are *not* big and ugly. You are beautiful. You are the most beautiful woman I've ever seen.''

She had rolled over and was sitting up. "Beautiful? Me?" she said. Then with a stab of disbelief, she dived back into the furs, afraid of being hurt again. "You're making fun of me.''

He reached over to touch her, then hesitated and pulled his hand back. "I can't blame you for not believing me. Not after . . . today. Maybe I should face up to that, and try to explain.

"You need to know how people feel about the ones you call Clan. I thought the same way – people think of them as animals . . .''

"They are not animals!"

"But I didn't know, Ayla. Some people hate your Clan. I don't know why. When I think about it, animals – real animals that are hunted – aren't hated. Maybe, in their hearts, people know that flatheads – they are called that too, Ayla – are human. But they're so different. It's frightening, or maybe threatening. Yet, some men will force flathead women to – I can't say share Pleasures. That is hardly the word. Maybe your way – 'relieve their needs'. You should also know that for a man to force a *Clan* woman is one thing – not approved, but overlooked. For a woman to 'share Pleasures' with a flathead male is . . . unforgivable to many people."

"Abomination?"

Jondalar blanched, but pressed on. "Yes, Ayla. Abomination."

"I am not abomination!" she flared. "And Durc is not abomination! I did not like what Broud did to me, but it was not abomination. If it had been some other man who did it just to relieve his needs, and not with hatred, I would have accepted it like any Clan woman. There is no shame to being a woman of the Clan. I would have stayed with them, even as Broud's second woman, if I could have. Just to be near my son. I don't care how many people do not approve!"

He had to admire her, but it was not going to be easy for her. "Ayla, I'm not saying you should feel shame. I am only telling you what to expect. Perhaps you could say you come from some other people."

"Jondalar, why do you tell me to say words that are not true? I don't know how. In the Clan, no one makes untruths – it would be known. It could be seen. Even if one refrains from mentioning something, it is known. It is allowed sometimes, for . . . courtesy, but it is known. I can see when you say words that are not true. Your face tells me, and your shoulders, and your hands."

He flushed. Were his lies so apparent? He was glad he had decided to be scrupulously honest with her. Maybe he could learn something from her. Her honesty, her forthrightness, were part of her inner strength.

"Ayla, you don't have to learn to lie, but I thought I should tell you these things before I leave."

Ayla felt a tight knot forming in her stomach, and her throat constricted. He is going to leave. She wanted to dive back into the furs and hide her head again. "I thought you would," she said. "But you have nothing for travelling. What do you need?"

"If I could have some of your flint, I can make tools, and some spears. And if you will tell me where the clothes are that I was wearing, I'd like to repair them. The haversack should be in good shape, if you brought it from the canyon."

"What is a haversack?"

"It's something like a backframe, but worn over one shoulder. There is no word for it in Zelandonii; the Mamutoi use it. Those are Mamutoi clothes I was wearing . . ."

Ayla shook her head. "Why is this a different word?"

"Mamutoi is a different language."

"A different language? What language did you teach me?"

Jondalar had a sinking feeling. "I taught you my language Zelandonii. I didn't think . . ."

"Zelandonii – they live west?" Ayla felt uneasy.

"Well, yes, but far to the west. The Mamutoi live nearby."

"Jondalar, you taught me a language spoken by people who live far away, but not one spoken by people who live nearby. Why?"

"I . . . didn't think about it. I just taught you my language," he said, suddenly feeling terrible. He hadn't done anything right.

"And you are the only one who can speak it?"

He nodded. Her stomach churned. She thought he had been sent to teach her to speak, but she could only speak to him. "Jondalar, why didn't you teach me the language everyone knows?"

"There is no language everyone knows."

"I mean the one you use when you speak to your spirits, or maybe to your Great Mother."

"We don't have a language just for speaking to Her."

"How do you talk to people who don't know your language?"

"We learn each other's. I know three languages, and a few words in some others."

Ayla was shaking again. She thought she would be able to leave the valley and speak to the people she would meet. What was she going to do now? She got up, and he stood also. "I wanted to know all your words, Jondalar. I have to know how to speak. You must teach me. You must."

"Ayla, I can't teach you two more languages now. It takes time. I don't even know them perfectly – it's more than words . . ."

"We can start with words. We will have to start from the beginning. What is the word *fire* in Mamutoi?"

He told her and started to object again, but she kept on, one word after another in the order in which she had learned them in the Zelandonii language. After she had run through a long list, he stopped her again. "Ayla, what good does it do to say a lot of words. You can't remember them all just like that."

"I know my memory could be better. Tell me which words are wrong."

She went back to the word *fire* and repeated all the words back to him in both languages. By the time she was through, he was staring at her in awe. He recalled that it had not been the words she had trouble with when she was learning Zelandonii, but the structure and concept of the language.

"How did you do that?"

"Did I miss any?"

"No, none at all!"

She smiled with relief. "When I was young, I was much worse. I had to go over everything so many times. I don't know how Iza and Creb were so patient with me. I know some people thought I was not very intelligent. I am better now, but it has taken practice, and still everyone in the Clan remembers better than I do."

"Everyone in your Clan can remember better than the demonstration you just gave me?"

"They don't forget anything, but they are born knowing almost everything they need to know, so they don't have much to learn. They only have to remember. They have . . . memories – I don't know what else you would call them. When a child is growing up, he only has to be reminded – told once. Adults don't have to be reminded any more, they know how to remember. I didn't have the Clan memories. That's why Iza had to repeat everything until I could remember without mistake."

Jondalar was stunned by her mnemonic skill, and he was

finding it difficult to grasp the concept of Clan memories.

"Some people thought I could not be a medicine woman without Iza's memories, but Iza said I would be good even though I couldn't remember as well. She said I had other gifts that she didn't quite understand, a way of knowing what was wrong, and of finding the best way to treat it. She taught me how to test new medicines, so I could find ways to use them without a memory of the plants.

"They have an ancient language, too. It has no sounds in it, only gestures. Everyone knows the Old Language, they use it for ceremonies and for addressing spirits, and also if they don't understand another person's ordinary language. I learned it, too.

"Because I had to learn everything, I made myself pay attention and concentrate so I would remember after only one 'reminding', so people wouldn't get so impatient with me."

"Do I understand you right? These . . . Clan people all know their own language, and some kind of ancient language that is commonly understood. Everyone can talk . . . communicate with everyone else?"

"Everyone at the Clan Gathering could."

"Are we talking about the same people? Flatheads?"

"If that is what you call the Clan. I told you how they look," Ayla said, then looked down. "That's when you said I was abomination."

She remembered the icy stare that had drained the warmth from his eyes before, the shudder when he pulled away – the contempt. It had happened just when she was telling him about the Clan. Suddenly she felt uneasy; she had been talking too comfortably. She walked quickly towards the fire, saw the ptarmigan where Jondalar had put them beside the eggs, and started plucking feathers, to be doing something.

Jondalar had watched her suspicion grow. He had hurt her too much and he'd never regain her trust, though for a while he had hoped. The contempt he felt now was for himself. He picked up her furs and carried them back to her bed, then took the ones he had been using and moved them to a place on the other side of the fire.

Ayla put the birds down – she didn't feel like plucking

feathers — and hurried to her bed. She didn't want him to see the water that filled her eyes.

Jondalar tried to arrange the furs around him in a comfortable way. Memories, she had said. Flatheads have some special kind of memories. And a language of signs that they all know? Was it possible? It was hard to believe, except for one thing: Ayla did not tell untruths.

Ayla had grown accustomed to quiet and solitude over the past years. The mere presence of another person, while relished, required some adjustment and accommodation, but the emotional upheavals of the day had left her drained and exhausted. She did not want to feel, or think about, or react to, the man who shared her cave. She only wanted to rest.

Yet sleep would not come. She had felt so confident of her ability to talk. She had put all her effort and concentration into it, and she felt cheated. Why did he teach her the language he grew up with? He was leaving. She would never see him again. She would have to leave the valley in spring and find some people who lived closer, and perhaps some other man.

But she didn't want some other man. She wanted Jondalar, with his eyes, and his touch. She remembered how she had felt in the beginning. He was the first man of her people she had seen, and he stood for all of them in a generalized way. He wasn't quite an individual. She didn't know when he ceased being an example and became, uniquely, Jondalar. All she knew was that she missed the sound of his breathing and his warmth beside her. The emptiness of the place he had occupied was more than matched by the aching void she felt inside.

Sleep came no more easily to Jondalar. He couldn't seem to get comfortable. His side, that had been next to her, felt cold, and his guilt stung. He couldn't remember when he'd had a worse day, and he hadn't even taught her the right language. When would she ever use Zelandonii? His people lived a year's travel from this valley, and only that if no stops of any length were made.

He thought about the Journey he had made with his brother. It all seemed so useless. How long ago had they left? Three years? That meant at least four years before he could get back. Four years of his life gone. For no purpose. His brother dead. Jetamio dead, and the child of Thonolan's spirit. What was left?

Jondalar had struggled to keep his emotions under control since he was young, but he wiped away wetness with his furs, too. His tears were not only for his brother, they were for himself: for his loss and sorrow, and for the lost chance that might have been wonderful.

25

Jondalar opened his eyes. His dream of home had been so vivid that the rough walls of the cave seemed unfamiliar, as though the dream was reality and Ayla's cave a figment of dream. The dregs of sleep began to clear, and the walls seemed displaced. Then he woke up and realized he had been looking from a different perspective, from the far side of the fireplace.

Ayla was gone. Two naked ptarmigan and the covered basket in which she saved loose feathers were beside the hearth; she had been up for some time. The cup he customarily used – the one fashioned so that the wood grain gave the impression of a small animal – was set out. Beside it was the tightly woven basket in which she steeped his morning tea, and a freshly peeled birch twig. She knew he liked to chew the end of a twig to a fibrous bristle and use it to clean his teeth of the coating that accumulated overnight, and she had formed the habit of having one ready for him in the morning.

He got up and stretched, feeling stiff from the unaccustomed hardness of his bed. He had slept on hard ground before, but a padding of straw could make a big difference to comfort, and it smelled clean and sweet. She changed the straw regularly, so unpleasant odours did not accumulate.

The tea in the pot-basket was hot – she could not have been gone long. He poured some and sniffed the warm minty aroma. He made a game of trying to identify which herbs she used each day. Mint was one of his favourites and was usually one component. He sipped and thought he detected the taste of raspberry leaf, and perhaps alfalfa. He took the cup and twig outside with him.

Standing at the edge of the shelf facing the valley, he chewed on the twig and watched his stream arc down and water the cliff wall. He still wasn't fully awake. His actions were the mechanical movements of habit. When he was through, he scrubbed his teeth with the gnawed stick of wood, then swished his mouth out with the tea. It was a ritual and always refreshed him, and it usually led him to thinking about plans for the day.

It wasn't until he drank the last of the tea that he felt himself flush and his complacency slip away. This was not like every other day. His actions of the day before had seen to that. He was about to throw the twig away, then noticed it and held it up, twirling it between his thumb and forefinger, thinking about its implications.

It had been easier to fall into the habit of letting her take care of him; she did it with such subtle grace. He never had to ask, she anticipated his wishes. The twig was a good example. Obviously, she had got up before him, gone down to get one, peeled it, and put it there for him. When had she started doing it? He recalled that when he was first able to walk down, he had found one for himself one morning. The next morning, when a twig was beside his cup, he had been very grateful. He still had difficulty with the steep path, then.

And the hot tea. No matter what time he woke up, hot tea was ready. How did she know when to start it? The first time she had brought him a cup in the morning, he had been warm in his appreciation. When was the last time he thanked her? How many other thoughtful acts had she done for him so unobtrusively? She never makes an issue of it. Marthona is like that, he thought, so gracious with her gifts and her time that no one ever feels obligated. Whenever he offered to help, Ayla seemed surprised, and was so grateful – as though she genuinely expected nothing in return for everything she had done for him.

"I gave her worse than nothing," he said aloud. "And even after yesterday . . ." He held up the twig, gave it a twirl, and pitched it over the edge.

He noticed Whinney and the colt in the field, racing around in a large circle, full of high spirits, and he felt a twinge of excitement at seeing the running horses. "Look at him go! That colt can really run! In a sprint, I think he could outrace his dam!"

"In a sprint, young stallions often do, but not in the long run," Ayla said, appearing at the top of the path. Jondalar spun around, his eyes glowing and his smile full of pride for the colt. His enthusiasm was hard to resist; she smiled in spite of her misgivings. She had hoped the man would develop an affection for the young horse – not that it mattered any more.

"I was wondering where you were," he said. He felt awkward in her presence and his smile faded.

"I started a fire in the roasting pit earlier, for the ptarmigan. I went to see if it was ready." He doesn't seem very happy to see me, she thought, turning to go into the cave. Her smile vanished, too.

"Ayla," he called, hurrying after her. When she turned back, he didn't know what to say. "I . . . uh . . . I was wondering . . . uh . . . I'd like to make some tools. If you don't mind, that is. I don't want to use up your flint."

"I do not mind. Every year the floods take some away and bring more," she said.

"Must be washing down from a chalk deposit upstream. If I knew it wasn't far, I'd get some from the source. It's so much better when it's freshly mined. Dalanar mines his from a deposit near his Cave, and everyone knows the quality of Lanzadonii flint."

The enthusiasm returned to his eyes, as it always did when he talked about his craft. Droog was like that, Ayla thought. He loved toolmaking, and everything connected with it. She smiled to herself remembering the time Droog discovered Aga's young son, the one born after they were mated, pounding rocks together. Droog was so proud, he even gave him a hammerstone. He liked teaching the skill; he didn't even mind showing me, though I was a girl.

Jondalar noticed her inward look and the hint of a smile. "What are you thinking about, Ayla?" he asked.

"Droog. He was a toolmaker. He used to let me watch him if I was very quiet and didn't disturb his concentration."

"You can watch me, if you want," Jondalar said. "In fact, I was hoping you'd show me the technique you use."

"I am not an expert. I can make the tools I need, but Droog's are much better than mine."

"Your tools are perfectly serviceable. It's the technique I'd like to see."

Ayla nodded and went into the cave. Jondalar waited, and when she didn't come out immediately, he wondered if she had meant now or later. He started in after her just as she was coming out, then jumped back so fast that he almost tripped. He didn't want to offend her with an inadvertent touch.

Ayla took a breath, straightened her shoulders, and lifted her chin. Maybe he couldn't stand to be near her, but she was not going to let him know how much it hurt. He'd be gone soon enough. She started down the path carrying both ptarmigan, the basket with the eggs, and a large bundle wrapped in a hide and tied with a cord.

"Let me help you carry something," Jondalar said, hurrying after her. She paused long enough to give him the basket of eggs.

"The ptarmigan should be started first," she said, putting the bundle down on the beach. It was just a statement, but Jondalar had the impression she was waiting for his consent, or at least acknowledgement. He was not far off. Despite her years of independence, the ways of the Clan still governed many of her actions. She was not accustomed to doing something else when a man had commanded, or requested, her to do something for him.

"Of course, go ahead. I need to get my implements before I can work the flint," he said.

She carried the plump birds around the wall to the hole she had dug earlier and lined with rocks. The fire was out in the bottom of the pit, but the stones sizzled when she sprinkled drops of water on them. She had searched up and down the valley for the right combination of greens and herbs, and had brought them to the stone oven. She collected coltsfoot for its slightly salty taste; nettles, pigweed, and sprightly wood sorrel for greens; wild onions, garlicky-tasting ramsons, basil, and sage were for flavour. Smoke would add its touch of flavour as well, and wood ashes a taste of salt.

She stuffed the birds with their own eggs nested in the greens – three eggs in one bird and four in the other. She had always wrapped grape leaves around the ptarmigan before they were lowered into the pit, but grapes did not grow in the valley. She remembered fish was sometimes cooked wrapped in fresh hay, and decided that would work for fowl. After the birds were resting in the bottom of the pit, she piled more grass on top, then rocks, and covered it all with dirt.

Jondalar had an array of antler, bone, and stone flint-knapping implements spread out, some of which Ayla recognized. Some, though, were totally unfamiliar. She opened her bundle and arranged her implements within easy reach, then sat down and spread the leather over her lap. It was good protection; flint could shatter into very sharp slivers. She glanced at Jondalar. He was looking over the pieces of bone and stone she had set out with great interest.

He moved several nodules of flint closer to her. She noticed two within easy reach – and thought of Droog. A good toolmaker's ability began with selection, she recalled. She wanted stone with a fine grain, looked them over, then chose the smaller one. Jondalar was nodding his head in unconscious approval.

She thought of the youngster who had shown an inclination for toolmaking before he was hardly toddling. "Did you always know you would work the stone?" she asked.

"For a while I thought I might be a carver, perhaps even serve the Mother, or work with Those Who Serve Her." A touch of pain and poignant yearning crossed his features. "Then I was sent to live with Dalanar and learned to be a stone knapper instead. It was a good choice – I enjoy it and have some skill. I would never have been a great carver."

"What is a 'carver', Jondalar?"

"That's it! That's what is missing!" Ayla jumped with startled consternation. "There are no carvings, no paintings, no beads, no decorations at all. Not even colours."

"I don't understand . . ."

"I'm sorry, Ayla. How could you know what I'm talking about? A carver is someone who makes animals out of stone."

Ayla frowned. "How can someone make an animal out of stone? An animal is blood and meat; it lives and breathes."

"I don't mean a real animal. I mean an image, a representation. A carver makes the likeness of an animal out of stone – makes the stone look like an animal. Some carvers make images of the Great Earth Mother, too, if they receive a vision of Her."

"A likeness? Out of stone?"

"Out of other things, too. Mammoth ivory, bone, wood, antler. I've heard that some people make images out of mud. For that matter, I've seen some pretty good likenesses out of snow."

Ayla had been shaking her head, struggling to understand, until he said snow. Then she remembered one winter day when she had piled bowls of snow against the wall near the cave. Hadn't she, for a while, imagined the likeness of Brun in that pile of snow?

"A likeness out of snow? Yes," she nodded, "I think I understand."

He wasn't sure if she did, but he could think of no way to make it plainer with no carving to show her. How drab her life must have been, he thought, growing up with flatheads. Even her clothes are no more than serviceable. Did they just hunt and eat and sleep? They don't even appreciate the Gifts of the Mother. No beauty, no mystery, no imagination. I wonder if she can understand what she missed.

Ayla picked up the small boulder of flint and examined it closely, trying to decide where to start. She would not make a hand axe – even Droog considered them rather simple tools, though very useful. But she didn't think that was the technique Jondalar wanted to see. She reached for an item missing from the man's tool kit: the foot bone of a mammoth – the resilient bone that would support the flint while she worked it, so the stone would not shatter. She pulled it around until it was comfortably between her legs.

Next she picked up her hammerstone. There was no real difference between her stone striker and his, except hers was smaller to fit her hand better. Holding the flint firmly on the mammoth-bone anvil, Ayla struck with force. A piece of the cortex, the outer covering, fell away, exposing the dark grey material inside. The pieces she had flaked off had a thick bulge where the hammerstone had struck – the bulb of percussion – and tapered to a thin edge on the opposite end. It could have been used as a cutting implement, and the first knives ever made were just such sharp-edged flakes, but the tools Ayla wanted to make required a far more advanced and complex technique.

She studied the deep scar left on the core, the negative impression of the flake. The colour was right; the texture was smooth, almost waxy; there was no foreign matter imbedded within it. Good tools could be made from this stone. She struck off another piece of the cortex.

As she continued to chip away, Jondalar could see she was shaping the stone as she removed the chalky coating. When it was off, she continued to knock off a bit here, an unwanted bump there, until the nucleus of flint was shaped like a somewhat flattened egg. Then she exchanged the hammerstone for a sturdy length of bone. Turning the core on its side, and working from the edge toward the centre, she struck off pieces from the top end with the bone hammer. The bone was more elastic and the pieces of flint that fell away were longer and thinner with a flatter bulb of percussion. When she was through, the large stone egg had a rather flat oval top, as though the tip had been sliced off.

Then she stopped, and, reaching for the amulet hanging around her neck, she closed her eyes and sent a silent thought to the spirit of the Cave Lion. Droog had always called upon the help of his totem to accomplish the next step. Luck was needed as well as skill, and she was nervous with Jondalar watching her so closely. She wanted to do it right, sensing there was more importance to the making of these tools than to the tools themselves. If she spoiled the stone, it would cast doubt on the ability of Droog and the entire Clan, no matter how many times she might explain that she was not an expert.

Jondalar had noticed her amulet before, but, watching her hold it in both her hands with closed eyes, he wondered what significance it held. She seemed to handle it with reverence, almost as he would handle a donii. But a donii was a carefully sculpted figure of a woman in all her motherly abundance, a symbol of the Great Earth Mother, and the wondrous mystery of creation. Certainly no lumpy leather pouch could hold the same meaning.

Ayla took up the bone hammer again. In order to cleave a flake from the core that would have the same dimension as the flat oval top, but with sharp straight edges, there was one important preliminary step – a striking platform. She had to detach a small chip that would leave a dent at the edge of the flat face that had a surface perpendicular to the flake she ultimately wanted.

Grasping the nucleus of the flint firmly to hold it steady, the woman took careful aim. She had to gauge the force as well as the placement: not enough and the chip would have the wrong angle, too much and she would shatter the carefully shaped edge. She took a breath and held it, then brought the bone hammer down with a sharp tap. The first was always important. If it went well, it presaged good luck. A small chip flew away, and she let herself breathe again when she saw the indentation.

Changing the angle at which she held the core, she struck again, with more force. The bone hammer landed squarely in the dent, and a flake fell away from the prefabricated core. It had the shape of a long oval. One side was the flat surface she had made. The reverse side was the inner bulbar face, which was smooth, thicker at the end that was struck, and narrowed down to a razor-sharp edge all the way around.

Jondalar picked it up. "That is a difficult technique to master. You need strength and precision both. Look at the edge! This is not a crude tool."

Ayla expelled a tremendous sigh of relief and felt the warm glow of accomplishment – and something more. She had not let the Clan down. In truth, she represented them better because she was not born to the Clan. Though he would have tried, this man, so skilled in the craft himself, had he been observing a member of the Clan, would have been too aware of the performer to judge the performance objectively.

Ayla watched him turning the flake of stone over in his hand, then, suddenly, felt a peculiar inner shift. She was gripped by an uncanny chill, and seemed to be observing the two of them from a distance, as though she were outside herself.

A vivid memory burst upon her of a time when she had experienced a similar disorientation. She was following lighted stone lamps deep into a cave and she watched herself clutching at the damp stone as she was inexplicably drawn towards a small lighted space screened by thick columns of stalactites in the heart of the mountain.

Ten mog-urs were sitting in a circle around a fire, but it was The Mog-ur – Creb himself – whose powerful mind, amplified and assisted by the drink Iza had told Ayla how to make for the magicians, discovered her presence. She had consumed the powerful substance too, unintentionally, and her mind was reeling out of control. It was The Mog-ur who drew her back from the deep abyss within, and took her with him on a frightening and fascinating journey of the mind back to primordial beginnings.

In the process, the greatest holy man of the Clan, whose brain was unique even among his own kind, forged new pathways in her brain where only vestigial tendencies had been. But while it resembled his, her brain was not the same. She could move back with him and his memories to their mutual beginning, and through each stage of development, but he could not go as far when she came back to herself – and went a step beyond.

Ayla did not understand what had hurt Creb so deeply, she only knew it had changed him, and their relationship. Nor did she understand the changes he had wrought, but for an instant she felt with utter certainty that she had been sent to the valley for a purpose that included the tall blond man.

As she saw herself and Jondalar on the rocky beach of the remote valley, aberrant currents of light and motion, forming out of a numinous thickening of the air and disappearing into emptiness, surrounded them, joining them. She felt a vague sense of her own destiny as a pivotal nexus of many strands linking past, present, and future through a crucial transition. A deep cold swept over her, she gasped, and, with a startled jerk, she was looking at a furrowed brow and a concerned face. She shuddered to dispel an eerie sense of unreality.

"Are you all right, Ayla?"

"Yes. Yes, I'm fine."

An unaccountable chill had raised gooseflesh and the hair on the back of his neck. He felt a strong urge to protect her, but he didn't know what threatened. It lasted only an instant, and he tried to shrug it off, but uneasiness lingered.

"I think the weather is about to change," he said. "I felt a cold wind." They both looked up at the clear blue sky unmarked by clouds.

"It's the season for thunderstorms – they can blow up fast."

He nodded, and then, to grasp at substance, he turned the subject back to the hard practicalities of toolmaking.

"What is your next step, Ayla?"

The woman bent back to her task. With careful concentration, she flaked off five more sharp-edged ovals of flint, and after a final examination of the butt of stone to see if one more usable flake might be detached, she threw it aside.

She turned then to the six flakes of grey flint and picked up the thinnest of them. With a smooth, flattened round stone, she retouched one long sharp edge, blunting it for a back and shaping a point at the narrow end opposite the bulge made by the impact of percussion. When she was satisfied, she held it out to Jondalar in the flat of her palm.

He took it and inspected it carefully. In cross section it was rather thick, but tapered to a thin, sharp cutting edge along its length. It was wide enough to be held in the hand comfortably, and the back was dulled so it would not cut the user. In some ways it resembled a Mamutoi spear point, he thought, but it was never intended to be hafted to shaft or handle. It was a handheld knife, and from observing her using a similar one, he knew it was surprisingly efficient.

Jondalar put it down and nodded to her to continue. She picked up another thick stone flake, and, using the canine tooth of an animal, she chipped off fine splinters from the end of the oval. The process dulled it only slightly, enough to strengthen the edge so the sharp rounded end would not crush when used to scrape hair and grain from hides. Ayla put it down and picked up another piece.

She put a large smooth beach stone on the mammoth-foot-bone anvil. Then, using pressure with the pointed tooth retoucher against the stone, she made a V-shaped notch in the middle of one long sharp edge, large enough to shave the end of a spear shaft to a point. On a longer oval flake, using a similar technique, she made a tool which could be used to pierce holes in leather, or bore holes in wood, antler, or bone.

Ayla didn't know what other kinds of tools she might need, and she decided to leave the last two stone flakes as blanks for later. Pushing the mammoth bone out of the way, she gathered up the ends of the hide and carried it to the midden around the wall to shake it out. Splinters of flint were sharp enough to cut even the toughest of bare feet. He hadn't said anything about her tools, but she noticed Jondalar turning them over and holding them in his hand as though to try them.

"I'd like to use your lap cover," he said.

She gave it to him, glad her demonstration was over and anticipating his. He spread the leather hide over his lap, then closed his eyes and thought about the stone, and what he would do with it. Then he picked up one of the flint nodules he had brought to the site and inspected it.

The hard siliceous mineral had been torn loose from chalk deposits laid down during the Cretaceous period. It still bore traces of its origin in the chalky outer covering, though it had been disgorged with the raging flood through the narrow canyon upstream and flung onto the rocky beach. Flint was the most effective material, occurring naturally, for making tools. It was hard, and yet, due to its minute crystal structure, it could be worked; its shape was limited only by the skill of the knapper.

Jondalar was looking for the distinctive characteristics of chalcedony flint, the purest and clearest. Any stones with cracks or fissures he discarded, as well as those that made a sound when tapped with another stone – indicating, to his ear, flaws of inclusions. He finally selected one.

Supporting it with his thigh, he held it with his left hand, and, with his right, he reached for the hammerstone and juggled it to get the right feel. It was new, still unfamiliar, and each hammerstone had its own individuality. When it felt right, he held the flint firmly, and struck. A large piece of the greywhite cortex fell away. Inside, the flint was a paler shade of grey than the one Ayla had worked, with a bluish sheen. Finegrained. A good stone. A good sign.

He struck again, and again. Ayla was familiar enough with the process to recognize his expertise immediately. He far surpassed any skill she had. The only one she'd ever seen who could shape the stone with such certain confidence was Droog. But the shape Jondalar was giving to his stone was not like any made by the Clan toolmaker. She bent closer to watch.

Rather than egg-shaped, Jondalar's core was becoming

more cylindrical, but not exactly circular. By flaking pieces from both sides, he was creating a ridge which ran the length of the cylinder. The ridge was still rough and wavy when the cortex was removed, and he put the hammerstone down to pick up a solid length of antler that had been cut off below the first fork to eliminate all branches.

With the antler hammer, he chipped off smaller pieces to make the ridge straight. He was preparing the core also, but he was not planning to remove thick flakes with a predetermined shape – that much was obvious to Ayla. When he was finally satisfied with the ridge, he picked up another implement, one she had been curious about. This was also made from a section of a big antler, longer than the first, and, rather than being cut off below the fork, two branches projected from the central stem, and the bottom of it had been shaped into a point.

Jondalar got up and held the flint core with his foot. Then he placed the point of the forked antler just above the ridge he had so carefully shaped. He held the upper protruding branch so that the lower one faced front and jutted out. Then, with a heavy length of a long bone, he tapped the jutting tine.

A thin blade fell away. It was as long as the cylinder of stone, but only about a sixth as wide as the length. He held it up to the sun and showed it to Ayla. Translucent light filtered through. The ridge he had so carefully shaped ran down the centre of the outside face for the full length, and it had two very sharp cutting edges.

With the point of the antler punch placed directly on the flint, he had not had to aim as carefully or gauge distance as closely. The force of the percussion was directed exactly where he wanted it, and with the force of the blow dispersed between two intermediate resilient objects – the bone hammer and the antler punch – there was almost no percussion bulge. The blade was long and narrow, and uniformly thin. Without having to judge the strength of his strike as carefully, he had far more control over the results.

Jondalar's stone-working technique was a revolutionary improvement, but as important as the blade it produced was the scar it left behind on the core. The ridge he had made was gone. In its place was a long trough with two ridges on either side. That had been the purpose of the careful pre-working.

He moved the tip of the punch over so that it was above one of the new ridges, then tapped again with the bone hammer. Another long narrow blade fell off, leaving two more ridges behind. He moved the punch again, above another of the ridges, detached another blade, and created more ridges.

When he finally ran out of usable material, not six, but twenty-five blades were lined up in a row – more than four times the useful cutting edge from the same amount of stone: more than four times the number of blanks. Long and thin, with surgically sharp edges, the blades were usable as cutting implements as they were, but they were not his finished product. They would be further shaped for a multitude of uses, primarily to make other tools. Depending on the shape and quality of the flint nodule, not four, but up to six or seven times the usable number of blanks for tools could be made from stones of the same size with the more advanced technique. The new method not only gave the toolmaker more control, it gave his people an unparalleled advantage.

Jondalar picked up one of the blades and gave it to Ayla. She checked the sharpness of the edge lightly with her thumb, exerted some pressure to test its strength, and turned it over in her hand. It curved up at the ends; it was the nature of the material, but more noticeable in the long thin blade. She held her palm out flat and watched it rock on its bowed back. The shape did not, however, limit its function.

"Jondalar, this is . . . I don't know the word. It's wonderful . . . important. You made so many . . . You are not through with these, are you?"

He smiled. "No, I'm not through."

"They are so thin and fine – they are beautiful. They might break more easily, but I think with the ends retouched, they'd be strong scrapers." Her practical side was already imagining the blanks into tools.

"Yes, and like yours, good knives – though I'd want to put a tang on it for a handle."

"I don't know what 'tang' is."

He picked up a blade to explain. "I can blunt the back of this and shape a point, and I would have a knife. If I pressure off a few flakes on the inner face, I can even straighten out the curve somewhat. Now, about halfway down the blade, if I use pressure to break off the edge and make a shoulder, and leave just a prong on the lower end, that is a tang."

He picked up a small segment of antler. "If I fit the tang into a piece of bone, or wood, or antler like this, the knife will have a handle. It's easier to use with a handle. If you boil antler for a while, it will swell and soften, and then you can force the tang into the middle where it's softer. When the antler dries, it shrinks and tightens around the tang. Often it will hold without binding or glue for a long time."

Ayla was excited about the new method, and wanted to practise it as she had always done after watching Droog, but she wasn't sure if it would violate Jondalar's customs or traditions. The more she learned about the ways of his people, the less sense they made. He didn't seem to mind her hunting, but he might not want her to make his kind of tools.

"I would like to try . . . Is there . . . objection to women making tools?"

Her question pleased him. It took skill to make her kind of tools. He was sure even the best toolmaker had inconsistent results, though the worst could probably turn out some that were usable – even smashing a flint boulder by accident usually produced a few pieces that were usable. But he would have understood if she had tried to justify her method. Instead, she seemed to recognize his technique for what it was – a vast improvement – and wanted to try it. He wondered how he would feel if someone showed him as radical an improvement.

I'd want to learn it, he said to himself with a wry grin.

"Women can be good flint knappers. Joplaya, my cousin, is one of the best. But she's a terrible tease – so I would never tell her that. She'd never let me forget it." He smiled at the memory.

"In the Clan, women can make tools, but not weapons."

"Women make weapons. After they have children, Zelandonii women seldom hunt, but if they learned when they were young, they understand how weapons are used. Many tools and weapons are lost or broken on a hunt. A man whose mate knows how to make new ones always has a fresh supply. And women are closer to the Mother. Some men think women-made weapons are luckier. But if a man has bad luck – or lacks skill – he'll always blame the toolmaker, especially if it's a woman."

"Could I learn?"

"Anyone who can make tools the way you did can certainly learn to make them this way."

He answered her question in a slightly different sense than she meant it. She knew she was capable of learning – she had been trying to assure herself that it was allowable. But his answer made her stop and think.

"No . . . I don't think so."

"Of course you can learn."

"I know I can learn, Jondalar, but not anyone who makes tools the Clan way can learn to make them your way. Some could, I think Droog could, but anything new is difficult for them. They learn from their memories."

He thought at first she was joking, but she was serious. Could she be right? Given the opportunity, would fla . . . Clan toolmakers be, not unwilling, but unable to learn?

Then it occurred to him that he would not have thought them capable of making tools at all not so long ago. They made tools, they communicated, and they took in a strange orphan child. He had learned more about flatheads in the past few days than anyone knew, except Ayla. It could be useful to know more about them, perhaps. There seemed to be more to them than anyone realized.

Thinking about flatheads suddenly made him recall the day before; an unexpected flush of embarrassment rushed him. With their concentration on toolmaking, he had forgotten. He had been looking at the woman, but not really seeing her golden braids shining in the sunlight, offering marked contrast to her deep rich tan; or her eyes, blue-grey and clear, like the translucent colour of fine flint.

O Mother, she was beautiful! He became acutely conscious of her sitting so close to him and felt a movement in his groin. He could not have kept his sudden shift of interest out of his eyes if he'd tried. And he didn't try.

Ayla felt his change in mood; it washed over her, caught her unprepared. How could anyone's eyes be so blue? Not the sky, not the blue gentians growing in the mountain meadows near the Clan's cave were so deeply, vibrantly hued. She could feel that . . . that feeling starting. Her body tingled, ached for him to touch her. She was leaning forward, pulled, drawn to him, and only with supreme effort of will did she close her eyes and pull away.

Why does he look at me that way when I'm . . . abomination? When he can't touch me without jerking away as if he were burned? Her heart was pounding; she was panting as though she had been running, and she tried to slow her breaths.

She heard him get up before she opened her eyes. The leather lap cover had been flung aside and his carefully wrought blades were scattered. She watched him walking away with stiff movements, his shoulders hunched, until he was around the wall. He seemed miserable, as miserable as she was.

Once he cleared the wall, Jondalar broke into a run. He raced down the field until his pumping legs ached and his breath raled in ragged sobs; then he slowed and jogged to a halt, heaving great gasps.

You stupid fool, what does it take to convince you? Just because she's decent enough to let you get some supplies together doesn't mean she wants any part of you . . . particularly that part! Yesterday, she was hurt and offended because you didn't. . . . That was before you ruined it for yourself!

He didn't like to think about it. He knew what he had felt, what she must have seen, the revulsion, the disgust. So, what is different now? She lived with flatheads, remember? For years. She became one of them. One of their males . . .

He was purposely bringing out everything loathsome, defiled, unclean that was part of his way of life. Ayla was all of them! When he was a young boy hiding with the other young boys behind bushes, telling each other the foulest words they knew, "flathead females" was among them. When he was older – not much older, but enough to know what "woman-maker" meant – the same boys gathered in dark corners of the cave to talk in hushed voices about girls, and to plot with sneering laughter to get a flathead female, and to scare each other about the consequences.

Even then the thought of a flathead male and a woman was unthinkable. Only when he was a young man was it mentioned, and then not so any elder might hear. When young men wanted to be snickering boys again and told each other the coarsest, filthiest stories they could think of, it was of flathead males and women, and what would happen to a man who shared Pleasures with such a woman afterwards, even unknowingly – especially unknowingly. That was the joke.

But they did not joke about abominations – or the women who bore them. They were polluted mixtures of spirits, an evil let loose upon the land that even the Mother, the creator of life, abhorred. And the women who bore them, untouchable.

Could Ayla be that? Could she be defiled? Unclean? Filth? Evil? Honest, straightforward Ayla? With her Gift of healing? So wise, and fearless, and gentle, and beautiful. Could anyone that beautiful be unclean?

I don't think she would even understand the meaning! But what would someone think who didn't know her? What if they met her and she just told them who raised her? Told them about the . . . child? What would Zelandoni think? Or Marthona? And she would tell them, too. She'd tell them about her son and stand up to them. I think Ayla could stand up to anyone, even Zelandoni. She could almost be a zelandoni herself, with her skill in healing and her way with animals.

But if Ayla is not evil, then everything about flatheads is not true! No one will believe that.

Jondalar had not been paying attention to where he was going and was startled when he felt a soft muzzle in his hand. He hadn't seen the horses. He stopped to scratch and stroke the young colt. Whinney gradually moved towards the cave, grazing as she went. The colt bounded ahead to her when the man gave him a final pat. Jondalar was not in a hurry to face Ayla again.

But Ayla was not at the cave. She had followed him around the wall and watched him run down the length of the valley. She felt like running sometimes, but she wondered what made him suddenly need to run so hard. Was it she? She put a hand on the warm dirt over the roasting pit, and then she walked to the large rock. Jondalar, distracted again by his thoughts, was surprised when he looked up to see both animals clustered around her.

"I . . . I'm sorry, Ayla. I shouldn't have run off like that."

"Sometimes I need to run. Yesterday, I let Whinney run for me. She goes farther."

"I'm sorry about that, too."

She nodded. Courtesy again, she thought, custom. What does it really mean? In silence, she leaned against Whinney and the horse dropped her head over the woman's shoulder. Jondalar had seen them in a similar pose before, when Ayla was upset. They seemed to be drawing support from each other. He was finding satisfaction in stroking the colt, himself.

But the young horse was too impatient to put up with such inaction for long, as much as he loved attention. He tossed his head, raised his tail and bounded off. Then with a bucking jump, he turned around, came back, and bumped the man, as though asking him to come and play. Ayla and Jondalar both laughed, breaking the tension.

"You were going to name him," she said. It was just a statement, carrying no urging tones. If he didn't name the colt, she most probably would.

"I don't know what to name him. I've never had to think of a name before."

"I never did either, until Whinney."

"What about your . . . son? Didn't you name him?"

"Creb named him. Durc was the name of a young man in a legend. It was my favourite of all the legends and stories, and Creb knew it. I think he chose the name to please me."

"I didn't know your Clan had legends. How do you tell a story without talking?"

"The same way you'd tell one with words, except, in some ways, it's easier to show something than to tell it."

"I suppose that's true," he said, wondering what kind of stories they were told, or rather, showed. He wouldn't have thought flatheads were capable of imagining stories.

They were both watching the colt, tail out, head reaching forward, enjoying a good run. What a stallion he's going to be, Jondalar thought. What a racer!

"Racer!" he said. "What do you think of naming him Racer?" He had used the word so often in reference to the colt that it fitted him.

"I like it. It's a good name. But if it is to be his, he should be named properly."

"How do you name a horse properly?"

"I'm not sure if it is proper for a horse, but I named

Whinney the way children of the Clan are named. I'll show you."

With the horses following them, she led him to a draw on the steppes that had once been a riverbed, but had been dry for so long that it was partially filled in. One side had eroded to show the horizontal layers of strata. To Jondalar's surprise, she loosened a layer of red ochre with a stick and gathered up the deep brownish-red earth in both hands. Back at the stream, she mixed the red earth with water to a muddy paste.

"Creb mixed the red colour with cave bear grease, but I don't have any, and I think plain mud is better for a horse. It dries and brushes off. It's the naming that counts. You'll have to hold his head."

Jondalar beckoned. The colt was full of lively antics but understood the gesture. He stood still while the man put an arm around his neck and scratched. Ayla made some movements in the Old Language requesting the attention of the spirits. She did not want to make it too serious. She still wasn't sure if spirits were offended by the naming of a horse, though naming Whinney had produced no ill effects. Then she picked up a handful of red mud.

"The name of this male horse is Racer," she said, making the gestures at the same time. Then she smeared the wet red earth down his face, from the tuft of white hair on his forehead to the end of his rather long nose.

It was done quickly, before the colt could wriggle out of Jondalar's grasp. He pranced away, tossing his head, trying to rid himself of the unaccustomed wetness, then butted up against Jondalar, leaving a red streak on his bare chest.

"I think he just named me." the man said, smiling. Then, true to his name, Racer sped down the field. Jondalar brushed at the reddish smear on his chest. "Why did you use this? The red earth?"

"It is special . . . holy . . . for spirits." she said.

"Sacred? We call it sacred. The blood of the Mother."

"The blood, yes. Creb . . . the Mog-ur rubbed a salve of red earth and cave bear grease on Iza's body after her spirit left. He called it the blood of birth, so Iza could be born into the next world." The memory still brought her pain.

Jondalar's eyes widened. "Flatheads . . . I mean, your

497

Clan uses the sacred earth to send a spirit to the next world? Are you sure?"

"No one is buried properly without it."

"Ayla, we use the red earth. It is the blood of the Mother. It is put on the body and the grave so she will take the spirit back into Her womb to be born again." A look of pain came into his eyes. "Thonolan had no red earth."

"I had none for him, Jondalar, and I couldn't take the time to get it. I had to get you back here, or I would have needed to make a second grave. I did ask my totem, and the spirit of Ursus, the Great Cave Bear, to help him find his way."

"You buried him?! His body was not left to scavengers?"

"I put his body next to the wall and loosened a rock so the gravel and stones covered him. But I had no red earth."

Jondalar found the idea of flathead burials the hardest to comprehend. Animals did not bury their dead. Only humans thought about where they came from, and where they were going after this life. Could her Clan spirits guide Thonolan on his way?

"It is more than my brother would have had if you hadn't been there, Ayla. And I have so much more – I have my life."

26

"Ayla, I can't remember when I've tasted anything this good. Where did you learn to cook like this?" Jondalar said, reaching for another piece of the rich, delicately seasoned ptarmigan.

"Iza taught me. Where else would I have learned? This was Creb's favourite dish." Ayla didn't know why, but his question irritated her a little. Why shouldn't she know how to cook? "A medicine woman knows herbs, Jondalar, those that flavour as well as those that heal."

He detected the tone of annoyance in her voice and wondered what had brought it on. He had only meant to compliment her. The meal was good. Excellent, in fact. When he thought about it, everything she prepared was delicious. Many of the foods were unusual to his taste, but new experiences were one reason for travelling, and though unfamiliar, the quality was evident.

And she did it all. Like the hot tea in the morning, she makes it so easy to forget how much she does. She hunted, foraged, cooked this meal. She provided everything. All you've done is eat it, Jondalar. You haven't contributed a thing. You've taken it all and given nothing back . . . less than nothing.

And now you give her compliments, words. Can you blame her for being annoyed? She'll be glad to see you go, you just make more work for her.

You could do some hunting, repay some of the meat you've eaten, at least. That seems so little, after everything she's done for you. Can't you think of something more . . . lasting? She hunts well enough herself. How worthwhile is a little hunting?

How she does it, though, with that clumsy spear? I wonder

. . . would she think I was insulting her Clan if I offered . . .

"Ayla . . . I, um . . . I want to say something, but I don't want to offend you."

"Why do you worry now about offending me? If you have something to say, say it." The prickles of her irritation were still showing, and his chagrin almost stopped him.

"You're right. It is a little late. But, I was wondering . . . ahhh . . . how do you hunt with that spear?"

She was puzzled by his question. "I dig a hole, and run, no, stampede, a herd towards it. But last winter . . ."

"A pit trap! Of course, so you can get close enough to use that spear. Ayla, you've done so much for me, I want to do something for you before I leave, something worthwhile. But I don't want you to feel offended by my suggestion. If you don't like it, just forget I said anything, all right?"

She nodded, a little apprehensive, but curious.

"You are . . . you are a good hunter, especially considering your weapon, but I think I can show you a way to make it easier, a better hunting weapon, if you'll let me."

Her annoyance evaporated. "You want to show me a better hunting weapon?"

"And an easier way to hunt – unless you'd rather not. It will take some practice . . ."

She shook her head with disbelief. "Clan women do not hunt, and no man wanted me to hunt – not even with a sling. Brun and Creb only allowed it to appease my totem. The Cave Lion is a powerful male totem, and he made them know it was his choice that I should hunt. They dared not defy him." Suddenly she recalled a vivid scene. "They made a special ceremony." She reached for the small scar in the hollow of her throat. "Creb drew my blood as sacrifice to the Ancient Ones So I could become the Woman Who Hunts.

"When I found this valley, the only weapon I knew was my sling. But a sling is not enough, so I made spears like the ones the men used, and I learned to hunt with them, the best I could. I never thought any man would want to show me a better way." She stopped and looked down at her lap, suddenly overcome. "I would be most grateful, Jondalar. I cannot tell you how much."

The wrinkles of tension on the man's forehead smoothed

out. He thought he glimpsed a tear glistening. Could it mean that much to her? The more he learned about her, the less he seemed to know. She taught herself?

"I will need to make some special tools. And some bone, the deer leg bones I found will work fine, but I'll need to soak them. Do you have a container I can use to soak bones?"

"How big does it need to be? I have many containers," she said, getting up.

"It can wait until you finish eating, Ayla."

She didn't feel like eating now; she was too excited. But he wasn't through. She sat back down and picked at her food until he noticed she wasn't eating.

"Do you want to go look at containers now?" he asked.

She leaped up and headed for the storage area, then went back for the stone lamp. It was dark in the back of the cave. She gave the lamp to Jondalar while she uncovered baskets, bowls, and birchbark containers that were stacked and nested within each other. He held the lamp high to shed more light and looked around. There was so much, far more than she could use.

"Did you make all this?"

"Yes," she replied, sorting through the stacks.

"It must have taken days . . . moons . . . seasons. How long did it take?"

Ayla tried to think of a way to tell him. "Seasons, many seasons. Most were made during the cold seasons. I had nothing else to do. Are any of these the right size?"

He looked over the containers she had spread out and picked up several, more to examine the workmanship than to select one. It was hard to believe. No matter how skilled she was, or how fast she worked, the finely woven baskets and smoothly finished bowls had taken time to make. How long had she been here? Alone.

"This one will be fine," he said, selecting a large trough-shaped wooden bowl with high sides. Ayla piled everything back neatly while he held the lamp.

They walked down the path. Jondalar filled the bowl with water and inspected the leg bones he had found in her midden. "This one has a crack I didn't notice before," he mentioned, showing her the bone before he discarded it. He placed the rest in the water. As they went back up to the cave, he tried to estimate Ayla's age. She had an ageless quality, a certain ingenuousness, that was at odds with her full, ripe woman's body. *I wonder how old she is? She can't be too young – she's too skilled a healer. Yet can she be as old as I am?*

"Ayla, how long have you been here?" he asked as they started into the cave, unable to contain his curiosity.

She halted, not sure how to respond, or if she could make him understand. Her counting sticks came to mind, but although Creb had shown her how to make the marks, she wasn't supposed to know. *Jondalar might disapprove. But he's leaving,* she thought.

She got out a bundle of the sticks she had marked every day, untied it and laid them out.

"What are these?" he asked.

"You want to know how long I've been here. I don't know how to tell you, but since I found this valley I have cut a mark on a stick every night. I have been here as many nights as there are marks on my sticks."

"Do you know how many marks there are?"

She remembered the frustration she had felt when she had tried to make some meaning of her marked sticks before. "As many as there are," she said.

Jondalar picked up one of the sticks, intrigued. She did not know the counting words, but she had some sense of them. Not even everyone in his Cave could comprehend them. The powerful magic of their meaning was not given to everyone to know. Zelandoni had explained some to him. He didn't know all the magic they contained, but he knew more than most who were not of the calling. Where had Ayla learned to mark the sticks? How could someone raised by flatheads have any understanding of counting words?

"How did you learn to do this?"

"Creb showed me. Long ago. When I was a little girl."

"Creb? He knew what they meant? He wasn't just making marks?"

"Creb was . . . Mog-ur . . . holy man. The Clan looked to him to know the proper time for certain ceremonies, like naming days or Clan Gatherings. This was how he knew. I don't think he believed I would understand – it is difficult even for mog-urs. He did it so I wouldn't ask so many questions. Afterwards, he told me not to mention it again. He caught me once, when I was older, marking the days of the moon's cycle and was very angry."

"This ... Mog-ur." Jondalar had difficulty with the pronunciation. "He was someone holy, sacred, like a zelandoni?"

"I don't know. You say zelandoni when you mean healer. Mog-ur was not a healer. Iza knew the plants and herbs – she was medicine woman. Mog-ur knew spirits. He helped her by talking to them."

"A zelandoni can be a healer, or can have other Gifts. A zelandoni is someone who has answered the call to Serve the Mother. Some have no special Gifts, just a desire to Serve. They can talk to the Mother."

"Creb had other gifts. He was most high, most powerful. He could ... he did ... I don't know how to explain."

Jondalar nodded. It was not always easy to explain a zelandoni's Gifts either, but they were also the keepers of special knowledge. He looked back at the sticks. "What does this mean?" he asked, pointing to the extra marks.

Ayla blushed. "It's ... it is my ... my womanhood," she answered, groping for a way to explain.

Women of the Clan were supposed to avoid men during their menses, and men totally ignored them. Women suffered the partial ostracism – the woman's curse – because men feared the mysterious life force that enabled a woman to bring forth life. It imbued the spirit of her totem with extraordinary strength which fought off the impregnating essences of the spirits of men's totems. When a woman bled, it meant her totem had won and had wounded the essence of the male totem – had cast it out. No man wanted his totem spirit to be drawn into the battle at that time.

But Ayla had been faced with a dilemma shortly after she brought the man to the cave. She could not keep herself in strict isolation when her bleeding started, not when he was barely clinging to life and needed close attention. She had to ignore the stricture. Later, she tried to make her contact with him during those times as brief as possible, but she couldn't avoid him when just two of them shared the cave. Nor could she attend only to women's tasks then, as was the Clan practice. There were no other women to take her place. She had to hunt for the man, and cook for the man, and he wanted her to share meals with him.

All she could do to maintain some semblance of womanly decorum was to avoid any reference to the subject, and take care of herself in private to keep the fact as inconspicuous as possible. How then could she answer his question?

But he accepted her statement with no apparent qualms or misgivings. She could detect no sign that he was disturbed at all.

"Most women keep some kind of record. Did Creb or Iza teach you to do that?" he asked.

Ayla bowed her head to hide her discomfiture. "No, I did it, so I would know. I didn't want to be away from the cave unprepared."

His nod of understanding surprised her. "Women tell a story about the counting words," he continued. "They say the moon, Lumi, is the lover of the Great Earth Mother. On the days when Doni bleeds, She will not share Pleasures with him. That makes him angry and hurts his pride. He turns away from Her and hides his light. But he cannot stay away for long. He gets lonely, misses Her warm full body, and peeks back to see Her. By then, Doni is upset, and will not look on him. But as he turns around and shines for Her in all his splendour, She cannot resist him. She opens Herself to him once more, and they are both happy.

"That is why many of Her festivals are held when the moon is full. Women say their phases match the Mother's – they call their time of bleeding the moon time, and they can tell when to expect it by watching Lumi. They say Doni gave them the counting words so they would know even when the moon is hidden by clouds, but they are used in many important ways now."

Though she was disconcerted to hear a man talk so casually about intimate female matters, Ayla was fascinated by the story. "Sometimes I watch the moon," she said, "but I mark the stick, too. What are counting words?"

"They are . . . names for the marks on your sticks, for one thing, for other things too. They are used to say the number of . . . anything. They can say how many deer a scout has seen, or how many days away they are. If it is a large herd, such as bison in the fall, then a zelandoni must scout the herd, one who knows the special ways to use counting words."

An undercurrent of anticipation coursed through the woman; she could almost understand what he meant. She felt on the edge of resolving questions whose answers had previously eluded her.

The tall blond man spied the pile of round cooking stones and scooped them up in both hands. "Let me show you," he said. He lined them up in a row, and, pointing to each in turn, began to count, "One, two, three, four, five, six, seven . . ."

Ayla watched with rising excitement.

When he finished, he looked around for something else to count, and he picked up a few of Ayla's marked sticks. "One," he said, putting down the first, "two," laying the next down beside it, "three, four, five . . ."

Ayla had a vivid recollection of Creb telling her, "Birth year, walking year, weaning year . . ." as he pointed to her outstretched fingers. She held up her hand, and, looking at Jondalar, she pointed to each finger. "One, two, three, four, five," she said.

"That's it! I knew you were close when I saw your sticks."

Her smile was gloriously triumphant. She picked up one of the sticks and began counting the marks. Jondalar continued with the counting words beyond the ones she knew, but even he had to stop a few marks beyond the second extra mark. His brow knotted in concentration. "Is this how long you've been here?" he asked, indicating the few sticks she had brought out.

"No," she said, and got the rest. Untying the bundles, she spread out all the sticks.

Jondalar looked closer, and paled. His stomach turned. Years! The marks represented years! He lined them up so he could see all the marks, then studied them for a while. Though Zelandoni had explained some ways to tally large numbers, he had to think.

Then he smiled. Rather than try to count the days, he would count the extra marks, the ones that represented a complete cycle of the moon's phases as well as the beginning of her moon times. Pointing to each mark, he made a mark in the dirt floor as he said the counting word aloud. After thirteen marks, he started another row, but skipped the first, as Zelandoni had explained, and made only twelve marks. Moon cycles did not match the seasons of the years exactly. He came to the end of her marks at the end of the third row, then looked at her with awe.

"Three years! You've been here three years! That's how long I've been on my Journey. Have you been alone all that time?"

"I've had Whinney, and up until . . ."

"But you haven't seen any people?"

"No, not since I left the Clan."

She thought of the years the way she had tallied them. The beginning, when she left the Clan, found the valley, and adopted the little filly, she called Whinney's year. The next spring – the beginning of the cycle of regrowth – she found the lion cub, and thought of that as Baby's year. From Whinney's year to Baby's year was Jondalar's one. Next was the stallion's year, two. And three was the year of Jondalar and the colt. She remembered the years better her way, but she liked the counting words. The man had made her marks tell him how long she had been in the valley, and she wanted to learn to do it.

"Do you know how old you are, Ayla? How many years you have lived?" Jondalar suddenly asked.

"Let me think about it," she said. She held up one hand with her fingers outstretched. "Creb said Iza thought I was about this many . . . five years . . . when they found me." Jondalar made five marks on the ground. "Durc was born, the spring of the year we went to the Clan Gathering. I took him with me. Creb said there are this many years between Clan Gatherings." She held up two fingers in addition to the full hand.

"That's seven," Jondalar said.

"There was a Clan Gathering the summer before they found me."

"That's one less – let me think," he said, making more marks in the dirt. Then he shook his head. "Are you sure? That means your son was born when you were eleven!"

"I'm sure, Jondalar."

"I've heard of a few women giving birth that young, but not many. Thirteen or fourteen is more usual, and some think that's too young. You were hardly more than a child your-self."

"No, I was not a child. I had not been a child for several years by then. I was too big to be a child, taller than everyone, including the men. And I was already older than most Clan girls are when they become women." Her mouth drew up in a skewed smile. "I don't think I could have waited any longer. Some thought I would never become a woman because I have such a strong male totem. Iza was so glad when . . . when the moon times started. So was I, until . . ." Her smile faded. "That was Broud's year. The next one was Durc's year."

"The year before your son was born – ten! Ten years when he forced you? How could he do it?"

"I was a woman, taller than most women. Taller than he."

"But not bigger than he! I've seen some of those flatheads! They may not be tall, but they're powerful. I wouldn't want to fight one hand to hand."

"They are men, Jondalar," she corrected gently. "They are not flatheads – they are men of the Clan."

It stopped him. For all her soft-spoken tones, there was a stubborn set to her jaw.

"After what happened, you still insist he isn't an animal?"

"You might say Broud was an animal for forcing me, but then what do you call the men who force women of the Clan?" ·

He hadn't thought of it in quite that way.

"Not all the men were like Broud, Jondalar. Most of them were not. Creb was not – he was gentle and kind, even though he was a powerful mog-ur. Brun was not, even though he was leader. He was strong-willed, but he was fair. He accepted me into his clan. Some things he had to do – it was the Clan way – but he honoured me with his gratitude. Men of the Clan do not often show gratitude to women in front of everyone. He let me hunt; he accepted Durc. When I left, he promised to protect him."

"When did you leave?"

She stopped to think. Birth year, walking year, weaning year. "Durc was three years when I left," she said.

Jondalar added three more lines. "You were fourteen? Only fourteen? And you've lived here alone since then? For three years?" He counted up all the lines. "You are seventeen years, Ayla. You have lived a lifetime in your seventeen years," he said.

Ayla sat silently for a time, pensively – then she spoke. "Durc is six years now. The men will be taking him with them to the practice field by now. Grod will make him a spear, his size, and Brun will teach him to use it. And if he's still alive, old Zoug will show him how to use a sling. Durc will practise hunting small animals with his friend, Grev – Durc is younger but he's taller than Grev. He always was tall for his age – he gets that from me. He can run fast; no one can run faster. And he's good with the sling. And Uba loves him. She loves him as much as I do."

Ayla didn't notice the tears falling until she took a breath that was a sob, and she didn't know how she found herself in Jondalar's arms with her head on his shoulder.

"It's all right, Ayla," the man said, patting her gently.

Ayla felt wrung out when she finally lifted her head from the man's shoulder, but she felt lighter, too, as though her grief rested less heavily on her. It was the first time since she had left the Clan that she had shared her loss with another human soul. She smiled at him with gratitude.

He smiled back with tenderness and compassion, and something more that welled up from the unconscious source of his inner self and showed in the blue depths of his eyes. It found a responsive chord within the woman. They spent a long moment locked in the intimate embrace of outspoken eyes, declaring in silence that which they would not say aloud.

The intensity was too much for Ayla; she was still not entirely comfortable with a direct stare. She wrenched her eyes away and began gathering up her marked sticks. It took a moment for Jondalar to gather himself together and help her tie the sticks into bundles. Working beside her made him more aware of her warm fullness and pleasant female scent than when he was comforting her in his arms. And Ayla felt an after-sense of the places their bodies had met, where his gentle hands had touched her, and the taste of the salt of his skin mingled with her tears.

They both realized they had touched each other and neither had been offended, but they carefully avoided looking too directly at each other or brushing too close, fearful that it might disturb their unplanned moment of tenderness.

Ayla picked up her bundles, then turned to the man. "How many years are you, Jondalar?"

"I was eighteen years when I started my Journey. Thonolan was fifteen . . . and eighteen when he died. So young." His face showed his pain; then he continued: "I am twenty and one years now . . . and I've yet to mate. I'm old for an unmated man. Most men have found a woman and made a hearth at a much younger age. Even Thonolan. He was sixteen at his Matrimonial."

"I found only two men, where is his mate?"

"She died. While giving birth. Her son died, too." Compassion filled Ayla's eyes. "That's why we were travelling again. He couldn't stay there. This was his Journey more than mine from the beginning. He was always the one after adventure, always reckless. He'd dare anything, but everyone was his friend. I just travelled with him. Thonolan was my brother, and the best friend I had. After Jetamio died, I tried to convince him to go back home with me, but he wouldn't. He was so full of grief that he wanted to follow her to the next world."

Ayla recalled the depth of Jondalar's desolation when he had first comprehended that his brother was dead, and she saw the ache that still lingered. "Perhaps he's happier, if it's what he wanted. It's difficult to go on living when you lose someone you love so much," she said gently.

Jondalar thought of his brother's inconsolable sorrow and understood it more now. Maybe Ayla was right. She ought to know; she had suffered enough grief and hardship. But she chose to live. Thonolan had courage, rash and impetuous; Ayla's is the courage to endure.

Ayla didn't sleep well, and the turnings and shufflings she heard from the other side of the fireplace made her wonder if Jondalar was lying awake, too. She wanted to get up and go to him, but the mood of caring tenderness that had grown out of shared griefs seemed so fragile that she was afraid to spoil it by wanting more than he was willing to give.

In the dim red light of the banked fire, she could see the shape of his body wrapped in sleeping furs with a tanned arm flung out and a muscular calf with a heel in the dirt. She saw him more distinctly when she closed her eyes than when she opened them to the breathing mound across the hearth. His straight yellow hair tied back with a piece of thong, his beard, darker and curly; his startling eyes that said more than his words, and his large, sensitive, long-fingered hands went deeper than vision. They filled her with inner sight. He always knew what to do with his hands, whether holding a piece of flint, or finding just the right place to scratch the colt. Racer. It was a good name. The man had named him.

How could a man so tall, so strong, be so gentle? She had felt his hard muscles, felt them move when he comforted her. He was . . . unashamed to show care, to show sorrow. Men of the Clan were more distant, more reserved. Even Creb, as much as she knew he loved her, had not shown his feelings so openly, not even within the boundary stones of his hearth.

What would she do when he was gone? She didn't want to think about it. But she had to face it – he was going to leave. He said he wanted to give her something before he left – he said he was leaving.

Ayla tossed and turned through the night, catching glimpses of his bare torso, deeply tanned; the back of his head and broad shoulders; and once, his right thigh with a jagged scar but nothing worse. Why had he been sent? She was learning the new words – was it to teach her to talk? He was going to show her a new way to hunt, a better way. Who would imagine that a man would be willing to teach her a new hunting skill? Jondalar was different from men of the Clan in that way, too. Maybe I can do something special for him, to remember me.

Ayla dozed off thinking how much she wanted him to hold her again, how much she wanted to feel his warmth, his skin next to hers. She awoke just before dawn with a dream of him walking across the winter steppes, and she knew what she wanted to do. She wanted to make something for him that would always be close to his skin, something that would keep him warm.

She got up quietly and found the clothes she had cut off him that first night, and she brought them closer to the fireplace. They were still stiff with dried blood, but if she soaked it out, she could see how they were made. The shirt, with the fascinating design, could be salvaged, she thought, if she replaced the arm sections. The trousers would have to be re-made from new material, but she could save some of the parka. The foot coverings were undamaged; they only needed new thongs.

She leaned close to the red coals, examining the seams. Small holes had been poked through the skins along the edges, then pulled together with sinew and thin leather strips. She had looked at them before, the night she had cut them off. She wasn't sure if she could reproduce them, but she could try.

Jondalar stirred, and she held her breath. She didn't want him to see her with his clothes; she didn't want him to know until they were ready. He settled down again, making the heavy breathing sounds of deep sleep. She bundled up the clothes once more and put them under her sleeping fur. Later, she could go through her pile of finished skins and furs and select the ones to use.

As faint light began to filter in through the cave openings, a slight change in his movements and breathing signalled to Ayla that he would wake soon. She added wood to the fire along with heating stones, then set out the pot-basket. The waterbag was nearly empty, and tea was better made with fresh water. Whinney and her colt were standing on their side of the cave, and Ayla stopped on her way out when the mare blew softly.

"I have a wonderful idea," she said to the horse in silent sign language, smiling. "I'm going to make Jondalar some clothes, his kind of clothes. Do you think he'll like that?" Then her smile left her. She put an arm around Whinney's neck, the other around Racer, and leaned her forehead on the mare. Then he'll leave me, she thought. She could not force him to stay. She could only help him leave.

She walked down the path by the first light of dawn, trying to forget her bleak future without Jondalar, and trying to draw some comfort from the thought that the clothes she would make would be close to him. She slipped out of her wrap for a brisk morning swim, then found a twig of the right size and filled the waterbag.

I'll try something different this morning, she thought: sweet grass and chamomile. She peeled the twig, put it beside the cup, and started the tea steeping. The raspberries are ripe. I think I'll pick some.

She set the hot tea out for Jondalar, selected a picking basket, and went back out. Whinney and Racer followed her out and grazed in the field near the patch of raspberries. She also dug up wild carrots, small and pale yellow, and white, starchy groundnuts that were good raw or cooked.

When she returned, Jondalar was outside on the sunny ledge. She waved when she washed the roots, then brought them up and added them to a broth she had started using dry meat. She tasted it, sprinkled in some dried herbs, and divided the raspberries into two portions, then poured herself a cup of cool tea.

"Chamomile," Jondalar said, "and I don't know what else."

"I don't know what you call it, something like grass that is sweet. I'll show you the plant sometime." She noticed his toolmaking implements were out, along with several of the blades he had made the previous time.

"I thought I'd start early," he said, seeing her interest. "There are certain tools I need to make first."

"It is time to go hunting. Dried meat is so lean. The animals will have some fat built up this late in the season. I'm hungry for a fresh roast with rich drippings."

He smiled. "You make it sound delicious just talking about it. I meant it, Ayla. You are a remarkably good cook."

She flushed and put her head down. It was nice to know he thought so, but strange that he should take notice of something that ought to be expected.

"I didn't mean to embarrass you."

"Iza used to say compliments make the spirits jealous. Doing a task well should be enough."

"I think Marthona would have liked your Iza. She's impatient with compliments, too. She used to say, 'The best compliment is a job well done'. All mothers must be alike."

"Marthona is your mother?"

"Yes, didn't I tell you?"

"I thought she was, but I wasn't sure. Do you have siblings? Other than the one you lost?"

"I have an older brother, Joharran. He's the leader of the Ninth Cave now. He was born to Joconan's hearth. After he

512

died, my mother mated Dalanar. I was born to his hearth. Then Marthona and Dalanar severed the knot, and she mated Willomar. Thonolan was born to his hearth, and so was my young sister, Folara."

"You lived with Dalanar, didn't you?"

"Yes, for three years. He taught me my craft – I learned from the best. I was twelve years when I went to live with him, and already a man for over a year. My manhood came to me young, and I was big for my age, too." A strange, unreadable expression crossed his face. "It was best that I left."

He smiled then. "That was when I got to know my cousin, Joplaya. She is Jerika's daughter, born to Dalanar's hearth after they were mated. She's two years younger. Dalanar taught both of us to work the flint at the same time. It was always a competition – that's why I would never tell her how good she is. She knows it, though. She has a fine eye and a steady hand – she'll match Dalanar some day."

Ayla was silent for a while. "I don't quite understand something, Jondalar. Folara has the same mother as you, so she is your sister, right?"

"Yes."

"You were born to Dalanar's hearth, and Joplaya was born to Dalanar's hearth, and she is your cousin. What is the difference between sister and cousin?"

"Sisters and brothers come from the same woman. Cousins are not as close. I was born to Dalanar's hearth – I am probably of his spirit. People say we look alike. I think Joplaya is of his spirit, too. Her mother is short, but she is tall, like Dalanar. Not quite as tall, but a little taller than you, I think.

"No one knows for sure whose spirit the Great Mother will choose to mix with a woman's, so Joplaya and I may be of Dalanar's spirit, but who knows? That's why we are cousins."

Ayla nodded. "Perhaps Uba would be a cousin, but to me she was a sister."

"Sister?"

"We were not true siblings. Uba was Iza's daughter, born after I was found. Iza said we were both her daughters." Ayla's thoughts turned inward. "Uba was mated, but not to

513

the man she would have chosen. But the other man would have only his sibling to mate, and in the Clan, siblings may not mate."

"We don't mate our brothers or sisters," Jondalar said. "We don't usually mate our cousins, either, though it is not absolutely forbidden. It is frowned on. Some kinds of cousins are more acceptable than others."

"What kind of cousins are there?"

"Many kinds, some closer than others. The children of your mother's sisters are your cousins; the children of the mate of your mother's brothers; the children of . . ."

Ayla was shaking her head. "It's too confusing! How do you know who is a cousin and who isn't? Almost everyone could be a cousin. . . . Who is left in your Cave to mate with?"

"Most people don't mate with people from their own Cave. Usually it's someone met at a Summer Meeting. I think mating with cousins is allowed sometimes because you may not know the person you want to mate is a cousin until you name your ties . . . your relationships. People usually know their closest cousins, though, even if they live at another Cave."

"Like Joplaya?"

Jondalar nodded assent, his mouth full of raspberries.

"Jondalar, what if it isn't spirits that make children? What if it's a man? Wouldn't that mean children are just as much from the man as from the woman?"

"The baby grows inside a woman, Ayla. It comes from her."

"Then why do men and women like to couple?"

"Why did the Mother give us the Gift of Pleasure? You'd have to ask Zelandoni that."

"Why do you always say 'Gift of Pleasure'? Many things make people happy and give them pleasure. Does it give a man such pleasure to put his organ in a woman?"

"Not only a man, a woman . . . but you don't know, do you? You didn't have First Rites. A man opened you, made you a woman, but it's not the same. It was shameful! How could those people let it happen?"

"They didn't understand, they only saw what he did. What he did was not shameful, only the way he did it. It was not done for Pleasure – Broud did it with hatred. I felt pain

514

and anger, but not shame. And no pleasure, either. I don't know if Broud started my baby, Jondalar, or made me a woman so I could have one, but my son made me happy. Durc was my pleasure.''

"The Mother's Gift of Life is a joy, but there is more to the joining of man and woman. That, too, is a Gift, and should be done with joy for Her honour.''

There may be more than you know, too, she thought. Yet he seemed so certain. Could he be right? Ayla didn't quite believe him, but she was wondering.

After the meal, Jondalar moved over to the broad flat part of the ledge where his implements were laid out. Ayla followed and settled herself nearby. He spread out the blades he had made so he could compare them. Minor differences made some more appropriate for certain tools than others. He picked out one blade, held it up to the sun, then showed it to the woman.

The blade was more than four inches long and less than an inch wide. The ridge down the middle of its outer face was straight, and tapered evenly from the ridge to edges so thin that light shone through. It curved upward, towards its smooth inner bulbar face. Only when held up to the sun could the lines of fracture raying out from a very flat bulb of percussion be seen. The two long cutting edges were straight and sharp. Jondalar pulled a hair of his beard straight and tested an edge. It cut with no resistance. It was as close to a perfect blade as was possible to get.

"I'm going to keep this one for shaving," he said.

Ayla didn't know what he meant, but she had learned from watching Droog to accept whatever comments and explanations were given without asking questions that might interrupt concentration. He put the blade off to one side and picked up another. The two cutting edges on this one tapered together, making it narrower at one end. He reached for a smooth beach rock, about twice the size of his fist, and laid the narrow end against it. Then, with the blunted tip of an antler, he tapped the end into a triangular shape. Pressing the triangle's edges against the stone anvil, he detached small chips which gave the blade a sharp, narrow point.

He pulled an end of his leather breechclout taut and poked a small hole in it. "This is an awl," he said, showing it to

Ayla. "It makes a little hole for sinew to be drawn through to sew clothes."

Had he seen her examining his clothes, Ayla suddenly wondered. He seemed to know what she had been planning.

"I'm going to make a borer, too. It's like this, but bigger and sturdier, to make holes in wood, or bone, or antler."

She was relieved; he was just talking about tools.

"I've used an . . . awl, to make holes for pouches, but none so fine as that."

"Would you like it?" he grinned. "I can make another for myself."

She took it, then bowed her head, trying to express gratitude the Clan way. Then she remembered. "Thank you," she said.

He flashed a big pleased smile. Then he picked up another blade and held it against the stone. With the blunted antler hammer, he squared off the end of the blade, giving it a slight angle. Then, holding the squared-off end so that it would be perpendicular to the blow, he struck one edge sharply. A long piece fell away – the burin spall – leaving the blade with a strong, sharp, chisel tip.

"Are you familiar with this tool?" he asked. She inspected it, then shook her head and gave it back.

"It's a burin," he said. "Carvers use them, and sculptors – theirs are a little different. I'm going to use this for the weapon I was telling you about."

"Burin, burin," she said, getting used to the word.

After making a few more tools similar to the one he had made, he shook the lap cover over the edge and pulled the trough-shaped bowl closer. He took a long bone out and wiped it off, then turned the foreleg over in his hands, deciding where to start. Sitting down, he braced the bone against his foot and, using the burin, he scratched a long line down the length of it. Then he etched a second line which joined the first at a point. A third short scratch connected the base of an elongated triangle.

He retraced the first line and brushed away a long curl of bone shavings, then continued tracing over the lines with the chisel point, each time cutting deeper into the bone. He retraced until he had cut through to the hollow centre, and, going around one last time to make sure no small section was not free, he pressed down on the base. The long tip of the triangle flipped up and he lifted the piece out. He put it aside, then returned to the bone and etched another long line that made a point with one of the recently cut sides.

Ayla watched closely, not wanting to miss anything. But after the first time, it was repetition, and her thoughts wandered back to their breakfast conversation. Jondalar's attitude had changed, she realized. It wasn't any specific comment he had made, rather a shift in the tenor of his comments.

She remembered his saying, "Marthona would have liked your Iza," and something about mothers being alike. His mother would have liked a flathead? They were alike? And later, even though he had been angry, he had referred to Broud as a man – a man who had opened the way for her to have a child. And he said he didn't understand how those "people" could let it happen. He hadn't noticed, and that pleased her more. He was thinking of the Clan as people. Not animals, not flatheads, not abominations – people!

Her attention was drawn back to the man when he changed activities. He had picked up one of the bone triangles and a sharp-edged, strong flint scraper and begun smoothing the sharp edges of the bone, scraping off long curls. Before long he held up a round section of bone that tapered to a sharp point.

"Jondalar, are you making a . . . spear?"

He grinned. "Bone can be shaped to a sharp point like wood, but it's stronger and doesn't splinter, and bone is lightweight."

"Isn't that a very short spear?" she asked.

He laughed, a big hearty laugh. "It would be, if that was all there was to it. I'm just making points now. Some people make flint points. The Mamutoi do, especially for hunting mammoth. Flint is brittle and it breaks, but with knife-sharp edges a flint spear point will pierce a tough mammoth hide more easily. For most hunting, though, bone makes a better point. The shafts will be wood."

"How do you put them together?"

"Look," he said, turning the point around to show her the base. "I can split this end with a burin and a knife, then shape the end of the wooden shaft to fit inside the split." He demonstrated by holding the forefinger of one hand between the thumb and forefinger of the other. "Then, I can add some glue or pitch, and wrap it tight with wet sinew or thong. When it dries and shrinks up, it will hold the two together."

"That point is so small. The shaft will be a twig!"

"It will be more than a twig, but not as heavy as your spear. It can't be, if you're going to throw it."

"Throw it! Throw a spear?"

"You throw stones with your sling, don't you? You can do the same with a spear. You won't have to dig pitfalls, and you can even make a kill on the run, once you develop the skill. As accurate as you are with that sling, I think you'll learn fast."

"Jondalar! Do you know how often I've wished I could hunt deer or bison with a sling? I never thought about throwing a spear." She frowned. "Can you throw with enough force? I can throw much harder and farther with a sling than I can by hand."

"You won't have quite the force, but you still have the advantage of distance. You're right, though. It's too bad you can't throw a spear with a sling, but . . ." He paused in mid-sentence. "I wonder . . ." His brow furrowed at a thought so startling that it demanded immediate attention. "No, I don't think so . . . Where can we find some shafts?"

"By the stream. Jondalar, is there any reason I can't help make those spears? I'd learn faster if you're still here to tell me what I'm doing wrong."

"Yes, of course," he said, but he felt a heaviness as he descended the path. He had forgotten about leaving and was sorry she had reminded him.

27

Ayla crouched low and looked through a screen of tall golden grass, bent with the weight of ripened seed heads, concentrating on the contours of the animal. She held a spear, poised for flight, in her right hand, and another ready in her left. A strand of long blonde hair, escaped from a tightly plaited braid, whipped across her face. She shifted the long shaft slightly, searching for the balance point, then, squinting, gripped it and took aim. Bounding forward, she hurled the spear.

"Oh, Jondalar! I'll never get any accuracy with this spear!" Ayla said, exasperated. She marched towards a tree, padded with a grass-stuffed hide, and retrieved the still quivering spear from the rump of a bison Jondalar had drawn with a piece of charcoal.

"You're too hard on yourself, Ayla," Jondalar said, beaming with pride. "You are much better than you think you are. You are learning very fast, but then I've seldom seen such determination. You practise every spare moment. I think that may be your problem right now. You're trying too hard. You need to relax."

"The way I learned to use a sling was to practise."

"You didn't gain your skill with that weapon overnight, did you?"

"No. It took several years. But I don't want to wait years before I can hunt with this spear."

"You won't. You could probably hunt right now and manage to bring something down. You don't have the thrust and speed you're used to, Ayla, but you never will. You have to find your new range. If you want to keep practising, why don't you switch to your sling for a while."

"I don't need to practise with the sling."

"But you need to relax, and I think it would help you loosen up. Give it a try."

She did feel her tension dissipate with the familiar feel of the leather strap in her hands, and the rhythm and movement of handling the sling. She enjoyed the warm satisfaction of skilled expertise, though it had been a struggle to learn. She could hit anything she aimed for, particularly practice targets that did not move. The man's obvious admiration encouraged her to put on a demonstration showing off her ability.

She picked up a few handfuls of pebbles from the edge of the stream, then walked across to the far side of the field to display her true range. She exhibited her rapid-fire double-stone technique, and then showed how quickly she could follow through with an additional two stones.

Jondalar joined in, setting up targets that tested her accuracy. He set four stones in a row on the large boulder; she knocked them off with four rapid casts. He threw two stones into the air one after the other; she hit them in mid-flight. Then he did something that surprised her. He stood in the middle of the field, balanced a rock on each shoulder, and looked at her with a grin on his face. He knew that she hurled a stone from her sling with such force that it could, at the least, be painful – fatal if it happened to hit a vulnerable spot. This test showed his trust in her, but more, it tested her confidence in her skill.

He heard the whistling of wind and the dull clink of stone hitting stone; at first one, and then, an instant later, the other stone was knocked away. He didn't get away with nothing to show for his dangerous trick. A tiny chip flew off one stone and embedded itself in his neck. He didn't flinch, but a small trickle of blood, which smeared when he picked the stone sliver out, gave him away.

"Jondalar! You're hurt!" Ayla exclaimed when she saw him.

"Just a chip, it's nothing. But you are good with that sling, woman. I've never seen anyone handle a weapon like that."

Ayla had never seen anyone look at her the way he did. His eyes sparkled with respect and admiration; his voice was husky with warm praise. She blushed, filled with such a flood of emotion that it brought tears for lack of any other outlet.

"If you could throw a spear like that . . ." He stopped and closed his eyes, straining to see something with his mind's eye. "Ayla, can I use your sling?"

"Do you want to learn to use a sling?" she asked, giving it to him.

"Not exactly."

He picked up a spear, one of several on the ground, and tried to fit the butt end into the pocket of the sling, worn to the shape of the round stones it usually held. But he was not familiar enough with the techniques of handling a sling, and, after a few clumsy attempts, he gave it back, along with the spear.

"Do you think you could throw this spear with your sling?"

She saw what he was trying, and she managed an unwieldy arrangement – the butt of the spear stretching out of the sling, while she held the ends of it and the shaft of the spear at the same time. She could not reach a good balance – had little force and less control over the long missile when it left her hand – but she did succeed in casting it.

"It would need to be longer, or the spear shorter," he said, trying to visualize something he had never seen. "And the sling is too flexible. The spear needs more support. Something to rest on . . . maybe wood or bone . . . with a backstop so it won't slide off. Ayla! I'm not sure, but I think it might work. I think I could make a . . . spear thrower!"

Ayla watched Jondalar constructing and experimenting, fascinated as much by the concept of making something from an idea as by the process of making it. The culture in which she was raised was not given to such innovation, and she didn't realize that she had invented hunting methods and a travois from a similar wellspring of creativity.

He used materials to suit his needs and adapted tools to new requirements. He asked her advice, drawing from her years of experience with her hurling weapon, but it soon became apparent that the contrivance he was making, though its impetus had come from her sling, was a new and unique device.

Once he had the basic principles worked out, he devoted time to modifications to improve the performance of the spear, and she was no more experienced with the finer points of hurling a spear than he was with the operation of a sling. Jondalar warned her, with a gleam of delight, that once he had good working models, they would both need to practise.

Ayla decided to let him use the tools he knew best to finish the two working models. She wanted to experiment with another of his tools. She had not progressed very far in making the clothes for him. They were together so much that the only time she could find was early morning or the middle of the night when he was sleeping.

While he was finishing and refining, she brought his old clothing and her new materials out to the ledge. In the daylight, she could see how the original pieces were stitched together. She found the process so interesting, and the garments so intriguing, that she thought she would make an adaptation of them to fit herself. She didn't try to match the elaborate beading and quillwork of the shirt, but she studied it carefully, thinking it might be a good challenge to attempt during the next long quiet winter.

From her vantage, she could watch Jondalar on the beach and in the field, and put her project away before he returned to the cave. But on the day he ran up the path, proudly displaying two finished spear throwers, Ayla barely had time to crumple the garment she was working on into an inconspicuous pile of leather. He was too full of his accomplishment to see anything else.

"What do you think, Ayla! Will it work?"

She took one from him. It was a simple, though ingenious, device: a flat narrow wooden platform, about half as long as the spear, with a groove in the middle where the spear rested, and a backstop carved into a hook-shape. Two leather-thong loops for the fingers were fastened on either side near the front of the spear thrower.

The thrower was held first in a horizontal position, with two fingers through the front loops, holding the thrower and the spear, which was resting in the long groove, butt against the backstop. When hurling, holding the front end by the loops caused the back end to flip up, in effect increasing the length of the throwing arm. The additional leverage added to the speed and force with which the spear left the hand.

"I think, Jondalar, it's time to start practising."

*

Practising filled their days. The padded leather around the target tree fell apart from constant puncturings, and a second one was put up. This time Jondalar drew the outline of a deer. Minor adaptations suggested themselves as they both gained in proficiency. Each of them borrowed from the techniques of the weapon with which he or she was most familiar. His strong overhand casts tended to have more lift; hers, angling more to the side, had a flatter trajectory. And each made a few adjustments on the thrower to suit his or her individual style.

A friendly competition developed between them. Ayla tried but could not match Jondalar's mighty thrusts which gave him greater range; Jondalar could not match Ayla's deadly accuracy. They were both astounded by the tremendous advantage of the new weapon. With it, Jondalar could hurl a spear more than twice as far, with greater force and perfect control, once a measure of skill was achieved. But one aspect of the practice sessions with Jondalar had greater effect on Ayla than the weapon itself.

She had always practised and hunted alone. First playing in secret, fearful of being found out. Then practising in earnest, but no less secretly. When she was allowed to hunt, it was only grudgingly. No one ever hunted with her. No one ever encouraged her when she missed, or shared a triumph when her aim was true. No one discussed with her the best way to use a weapon, advised her of alternate approaches, or listened with respect and interest to a suggestion of hers. And no one had ever teased, or joked, or laughed with her. Ayla had never experienced the camaraderie, the friendship, the fun, of a companion.

Yet, with all the easing of tensions practising brought about, a distance remained between them that they could not seem to close. When their talk was about such safe subjects as hunting or weapons, their conversations were animated; but the introduction of any personal element caused uncomfortable silences and halting courteous evasions. An accidental touch was like a jolting shock from which they both sprang apart; followed always by stiff formality and lingering afterthoughts.

"Tomorrow!" Jondalar said, retrieving a twanging spear. Some of the hay stuffing came with it through a much enlarged and ragged hole in the leather.

"Tomorrow what?" Ayla asked.

"Tomorrow we go hunting. We've played long enough. We're not going to learn any more, dulling points on a tree. It's time to get serious."

"Tomorrow," Ayla agreed.

They picked up several spears and started walking back. "You know the area around here, Ayla. Where should we go?"

"I know the steppes to the east best, but maybe I should scout it first. I could go on Whinney." She looked up to check the placement of the sun. "It's still early."

"Good idea. You and that horse are better than a handful of foot scouts."

"Will you hold Racer back? I'll feel better if I know he's not following."

"What about tomorrow when we go hunting?"

"We'll have to take him with us. We need Whinney to bring the meat back. Whinney is always a little bothered by a kill, but she's used to it. She will stay where I want her to, but if her colt gets excited and runs, and maybe gets caught in a stampede . . . I don't know."

"Don't worry about it now. I'll try to think of something."

Ayla's piercing whistle brought the mare and the colt. While Jondalar put an arm around Racer's neck, scratched his itchy places, and talked to him, Ayla mounted Whinney and urged her to a gallop. The young one was comfortable with the man. After the woman and the mare were well gone, Jondalar picked up the armload of spears and both throwers.

"Well, Racer, shall we go to the cave to wait for them?"

He laid the spears down outside the entrance to the small break in the canyon wall, then went in. He was restless and didn't quite know what to do with himself. He stirred the fire, brought the coals together, and added a few sticks, then went out to the front edge of the shelf and looked down the valley. The colt's soft muzzle reached for his hand, and he absently caressed the shaggy young horse. As he pulled his fingers through the animal's thickening coat, he thought of winter.

He tried to think of something else. The warm summer

days had an unending quality, one so like the next that time seemed held in suspension. Decisions were easy to put off. Tomorrow was soon enough to think about the coming cold . . . to think about leaving. He noticed the simple breechclout he wore.

"I don't grow a winter coat like you, little fellow. I ought to make myself something warm soon. I gave that sewing awl to Ayla and never made another one. Maybe that's what I should do – make a few more tools. And I need to think of a way to keep you from getting hurt."

He went back into the cave, stepped over his sleeping furs, and cast a longing look at Ayla's side of the fireplace. He rummaged through the storage area for some thong or heavy cordage and found some skins that had been rolled up and put away. That woman certainly knows how to finish skins, he thought, feeling the velvety soft texture. Maybe she'd let me use some of these. I hate to ask her, though.

If those spear throwers work, I should get enough hides to make something to wear. Maybe I could carve a charm on them for good luck. It wouldn't hurt. Here's a coil of thong. Maybe I can make something for Racer out of this. He's such a runner – wait until he's a stallion. Would a stallion let someone ride on his back? Could I make him go where I wanted him to?

You'll never know. You won't be here when he's a stallion. You're leaving.

Jondalar picked up the coiled thong, stopped off to get his bundle of flint-knapping tools, and went down the path to the beach. The stream looked inviting, and he felt hot and sweaty. He took off his breechclout and waded in, then started pulling upstream, against the current. He usually turned back when he reached the narrow gorge. This time he decided to explore further. He made it past the first rapids and around the last bend, and saw a roaring wall of white water. Then he headed back.

The swim invigorated him, and the feeling that he had made a discovery encouraged a desire for change. He pulled his hair back, squeezed it out, and then his beard. You've worn this all summer, Jondalar, and it's almost over. Don't you think it's time?

First I'll shave, then make something to keep Racer out of

the way. I don't want just to put a rope around his neck. Then I'll make an awl, and a burin or two so I can carve a charm on the throwers. And I think I'll make the meal tonight. A man could forget how, around Ayla. I may not be up to her standards, but I think I can still put a meal together. Mother knows, I did it often enough on the Journey.

What kind of carvings should I put on the spear throwers? A donii would bring the best luck, but I gave mine to Noria. I wonder if she ever had a baby with blue eyes? That certainly is a strange idea Ayla has, about a man making a baby start. Who would have thought that was what that old Haduma wanted. First Rites. Ayla's never had First Rites. She's been through so much, and she's a wonder with that sling. Not bad with a spear thrower either. I think I'll put a bison on hers. Will they really work? Wish I had a donii. Maybe I could make one . . .

Jondalar started watching for Ayla from the ledge as the evening sky darkened. When the valley became a black bottomless pit, he built a fire on the ledge so she could find her way, and he kept thinking he heard her coming up the path. Finally he made a torch and headed down. He followed the edge of the stream around the jutting wall, and he would have gone farther if he hadn't heard the pounding of hooves approaching.

"Ayla! What took you so long?"

She was taken aback by his peremptory tone. "I've been scouting for herds. You know that."

"But it's after dark!"

"I know. It was almost dark before I started back. I think I've found the place, a herd of bison southeast . . ."

"It was nearly dark and you were still chasing bison! You can't see a bison in the dark!"

Ayla couldn't understand why he was so excited, or his demanding questions. "I wasn't looking at bison in the dark, and why do you want to stand here talking?"

With a high-pitched nicker, the colt appeared in the circle of light from the torch and butted up against his dam. Whinney responded, and before Ayla could dismount, the young horse was nuzzling under the mare's hind legs. It occurred to Jondalar then that he had been acting as if he had some right to question Ayla, and he turned away from the torchlight, grateful for the dark that hid his red face. He followed behind while she plodded up the path, so embarrassed that he didn't notice her weary exhaustion.

She grabbed a sleeping fur and, wrapping it around her, squatted near the fire. "I forgot how cold it gets at night," she said. "I should have taken a warm wrap, but I didn't think I'd be gone this long."

Jondalar saw her shiver and was more chagrined. "You're cold. Let me get you something hot to drink." He poured some hot broth into a cup for her.

Ayla hadn't been paying very close attention to him either – she had been too eager to get to the fire, but when she looked up to take the cup, she nearly dropped it.

"What happened to your face?" she said with equal parts of shock and concern.

"What do you mean?" he asked, worried.

"You're beard . . . it's gone!"

The shock which had mirrored hers gave way to a smile. "I shaved it off."

"Shaved?"

"Cut it off. Close to the skin. I usually do it in summer. It gets itchy when I'm hot and sweaty."

Ayla couldn't resist. She reached for his face to feel the smoothness of his cheek, then, rubbing against the grain, an incipient roughness; scratchy, like a lion's tongue. She recalled he had no beard when she first found him, but after it grew she forgot about it. He seemed so young without a beard, appealing in a childlike way, but not as a man. She wasn't accustomed to full-grown men without beards. She ran her finger along his strong jaw and the slight cleft of his firm chin.

Her touch held him motionless. He couldn't pull away. He felt the light tracery of her fingertips with every nerve. Though she had intended no erotic implications, just gentle curiosity, his response was from a deeper source. The insistent, straining throbbing in his groin was so immediate, so powerful, that it caught him by surprise.

The way his eyes looked at her compelled a rush of desire to know him as a man, in spite of his almost too youthful appearance. He moved to reach for her hand, to hold it to his face, but with an effort, she pulled it away, picked up the cup, and drank without tasting. It was more than being self-conscious about touching him. She had a sudden vivid memory of the last time they had sat face to face near the fire and that look had come into his eyes. And this time she had been touching him. She was afraid to look at him, afraid she'd see that horrible, degrading look again. But her finger-tips remembered his smooth-rough face, and tingled.

Jondalar was distressed at his instant, almost violent reaction to her gentle touch. He couldn't keep his eyes away from her though she avoided his look. Looking down like that, she seemed so shy, so fragile, yet he knew the strength at her core. He thought of her as a beautiful blade of flint, perfect as it fell from the stone, its thin edges delicate and translucent, yet so hard and sharp that it could cut the toughest leather in one clean stroke.

O Mother, she is so beautiful, he thought! O Doni, Great Earth Mother, I want that woman. I want her so much . . .

Suddenly he jumped up. He couldn't stand just looking at her. Then he remembered the meal he had made. Here she is, cold and tired, and I'm just sitting. He went to get the mammoth-hipbone platter she used.

Ayla heard him get up. He had jumped up so abruptly, she was convinced he had suddenly been overcome with revulsion again. She started shaking, and clenched her teeth trying to stop. She could not face that again. She wanted to tell him to leave so she would not have to see him, to see his eyes naming her . . . abomination. She sensed, though her eyes were closed, when he was in front of her again, and she held her breath.

"Ayla?" He could see her shivering, even with the fire and her fur wrap. "I thought it might be late when you got back, so I went ahead and made something for us to eat. Would you like some? If you're not too tired?"

Had she heard him right? She opened her eyes, slowly. He was holding a platter. He put it down in front of her, then pulled up a mat and sat down beside her. There was a hare, spitted and roasted, some boiled roots in a broth of dried meat he had already given her, and even some blueberries.

"You . . . cooked this . . . for me?" Ayla said, incredulous.

"I know it's not as good as you would make, but I hope it's

all right. I thought it might be bad luck to use the spear thrower yet, so I just used a spear. It takes a different casting technique, and I wasn't sure if all that practice with the thrower would spoil my aim, but I guess you don't forget. Go ahead, eat."

Men of the Clan did not cook. They could not – they had no memories for it. She knew Jondalar was more versatile in his abilities, but it never occurred to her that he would cook; not when there was a woman around. Even more than that he could, and that he did, was that he had thought of it in the first place. In the Clan, even after she was allowed to hunt, she was still expected to perform her usual tasks. It was so unexpected, so . . . considerate. Her fears had been entirely unfounded, and she didn't know what to say. She picked up a leg he had cut off and took a bite.

"Is it all right?" he asked, a bit anxious.

"It's wonderful," she said with her mouth full.

It was fine, but it wouldn't have mattered if it had been burned crisp – it would have been delicious to her. She had a feeling she was going to cry. He scooped out a ladleful of long thin roots. She picked one up and took a bite. "Is this . . . clover root? It's good."

"Yes," he said, pleased with himself. "They are better with some oil to dip them in. It's one of those foods women usually make for the men for special feasts because it's a favourite. I saw the clover upstream and thought you might like it." It had been a good idea to make a meal, he thought, enjoying her surprise.

"It's a lot of work to dig them. There's not much to eat on one, but I didn't know they'd be so good. I only use the roots for medicine, as part of a tonic in the spring."

"We usually eat them in spring. It's one of the first fresh foods."

They heard a clatter of hooves on the stone ledge and turned as Whinney and Racer came in. After a while, Ayla got up and settled them in. It was a nightly ritual that consisted of greetings, shared affection, fresh hay, grain, water, and, particularly after a long ride, a rub down with absorbent leather and a currying with a teasel. Ayla noticed the fresh hay, grain, and water had already been put out.

"You remembered the horses, too," she said when she sat

down to finish her blueberries. Even if she hadn't been hungry she would have eaten them.

He smiled. "I didn't have much to do. Oh, I have something to show you." He got up and returned with the two spear throwers. "I hope you don't mind, it's for luck."

"Jondalar!" She was almost afraid to touch hers. "Did you make this?" Her voice was full of awe. She had been surprised when he drew the shape of an animal on the target, but this was so much more. "It's . . . like you took the totem, the spirit of the bison, and put him there."

The man was grinning. She made surprises so much fun. His spear thrower had a giant deer with huge palmate antlers, and she marvelled at it as well. "It is supposed to capture the spirit of the animal, so it will be drawn to the weapon. I'm not really a very good carver, you should see the work of some, and that of the sculptors, and engravers, and the artists who paint the sacred walls."

"I'm sure you have put powerful magic in these. I did not see deer, but a herd of bison is southeast. I think they are beginning to move together. Will a bison be drawn to a weapon that has a deer on it? I can go out again tomorrow and look for deer."

"This will work for bison. Yours will be luckier, though. I'm glad I put a bison on yours."

Ayla didn't know what to say. He was a man, and had given her more hunting luck than himself, and he was glad.

"I was going to make a donii for luck, too, but I didn't have time to finish it."

"Jondalar, I am confused. What is 'donii'? Is it your Earth Mother?"

"The Great Earth Mother is Doni, but She takes other forms and they are all donii. A donii is usually Her spirit form, when She rides on the wind, or sends Herself into dreams – men often dream of Her as a beautiful woman. A donii is also the carved figure of a woman – usually a bountiful mother – because women are Her blessed. She made them in Her likeness, to create life as She created all life. She rests most easily in the likeness of a mother. A donii is usually sent to guide a man to Her spirit world – some say women don't need a guide, they know the way. And some women claim they can change themselves into a donii when they

530

want – not always to a man's benefit. The Sharamudoi who live west of here say the Mother can take the form of a bird."

Ayla nodded. "In the Clan, only the Ancient Ones are female spirits."

"What about your totems?" he asked.

"The protective totem spirits are all male, for both men and women, but women's totems are usually the smaller animals. Ursus, the Great Cave Bear, is the great protector of all the Clan – everyone's totem. Ursus was Creb's personal totem. He was chosen, just as the Cave Lion chose me. You can see my mark." She showed him the four parallel scars on her left thigh, where she had been clawed by a cave lion when she was five.

"I had no idea fl . . . your Clan understood the spirit world at all, Ayla. It is still hard to believe – I do believe you – but it's hard for me to comprehend that the people you talk about are the same ones I've always thought of as flatheads."

Ayla put her head down, then looked up. Her eyes were serious, and concerned. "I think the Cave Lion has chosen you, Jondalar. I think he is your totem now. Creb told me a powerful totem is not easy to live with. He gave up an eye in his testing, but he gained great power. Next to Ursus, the Cave Lion is the most powerful totem, and it has not been easy. His tests have been difficult, but once I understood the reason, I have never been sorry. I think you should know, in case he is your totem now." She looked down, hoping she hadn't said too much.

"They meant very much to you, your Clan, didn't they?"

"I wanted to be a woman of the Clan, but I could not. I could not make myself be one. I am not like them. I am of the Others. Creb knew it, and Iza told me to leave and find my own kind. I didn't want to go, but I had to leave and I can never go back. I am cursed with death. I am dead."

Jondalar wasn't sure what she meant, but a chill raised his small hairs when she said it. She drew a deep breath before she continued.

"I did not remember the woman I was born to, or my life before the Clan. I tried, but I could not imagine a man of the Others, a man like me. Now, when I try to imagine Others, I can only see you. You are the first of my own kind I have ever seen, Jondalar. No matter what happens, I will never forget you." Ayla stopped, feeling she had said too much. She got up. "If we are going hunting in the morning, I think we should get some sleep."

Jondalar knew she had been raised by flatheads and lived alone in the valley after she left them, but until she said it, he didn't fully understand that he was the first. It disturbed him to think he represented all his people, and he wasn't proud of the way he had done it. Yet, he knew how everyone felt about flatheads. If he had just told her, would it have made the same impression? Would she have really known what to expect?

He went to bed with unsettled, ambivalent feelings. He stared at the fire after he lay down, thinking. Suddenly he felt a distorting sensation, and something like vertigo without the dizziness. He saw a woman as though reflected in a pond into which a stone had dropped; a wavering image from which ripples spread out in larger and larger circles. He did not want the woman to forget him – to be remembered by her was significant.

He sensed a divergence, a path splitting, a choice, and he had no one to guide him. A current of warm air raised the hair on the back of his neck. He knew She was leaving him. He had never consciously felt Her presence, but he knew when She was gone, and the void She left behind ached. It was the beginning of an ending: the ending of the ice, the end of an age, the end of the time when Her nourishment provided. The Earth Mother was leaving Her children to find their own way, to carve out their own lives, to pay the consequences of their own actions – to come of age. Not in his lifetime, not in many lifetimes to come, but the first inexorable step had been taken. She had passed on Her parting Gift, Her Gift of Knowledge.

Jondalar felt an eerie keening wail, and he knew he heard the Mother cry.

Like a thong stretched taut and released, reality snapped back into place. But it had been stretched too far and could not fit back into its original dimension. He felt that something was out of place. He looked across the fire at Ayla and saw tears flowing down her face.

"What's wrong, Ayla?"

"I don't know."

*

"Are you sure she can take both of us?"

"No. I'm not sure," Ayla said, leading Whinney, loaded with her carrying baskets. Racer trailed behind, led by a rope that was tied to a sort of halter made of leather thongs. It gave him freedom to graze and to move his head, and it would not tighten up around his neck and choke him. The halter had bothered the colt at first, but he was getting used to it.

"If we can both ride, travelling will be faster. If she doesn't like it, she will let me know. Then we can ride her in turns, or both walk."

When they reached the large boulder in the meadow, Ayla climbed on the horse, moved up a bit, and held the mare steady while Jondalar mounted her. Whinney flicked her ears back. She felt the extra weight and wasn't accustomed to it, but she was a sturdy rugged horse and she started out at Ayla's urging. The woman kept her to a steady pace and was sensitive to the horse's change in gait that signalled it was time to stop and rest.

The second time they started out, Jondalar was more relaxed and then wished he was still nervous. Without the tense worry, he became entirely aware of the woman riding in front of him. He could feel her back pressing up against him, her thighs against his, and Ayla became sensitive to more than the horse. A hot, hard pressure had risen behind her, over which Jondalar had no control, and every movement of the horse jogged them together. She wished it would go away – and yet at the same time she didn't.

Jondalar was beginning to feel a pain he had not experienced before. He had never forced himself to hold in his aroused desire so much. From the first days of manhood, there had always been some means for release, but there was no other woman here except Ayla. He refused to bring it about himself again and just tried to bear it.

"Ayla," his voice was strained. "I think . . . I think it's time to rest," he blurted out.

She stopped the horse and got off as quickly as she could. "It's not far," she said. "We can walk the rest of the way."

"Yes, it will give Whinney a rest."

Ayla didn't argue, although she knew that was not why she was walking. They walked three abreast, with the horse between them, talking over her back. Even then, Ayla could hardly keep her mind on landmarks and directions, and Jondalar walked with aching loins, grateful for the screen the horse provided.

As they came in sight of a herd of bison, the anticipation of actually hunting with the spear thrower began to drain off a measure of their stifled ardour, though they took care not to stand too close together, and preferred to keep one or the other of the horses between them.

The bison were milling around a small stream. The herd was larger than when Ayla had first seen it. Several other small groupings had joined it and more would follow. Eventually, tens of thousands of densely packed, shaggy, brownish black animals would crowd across acres of rolling hills and river valleys; a lowing, thundering, living carpet. Within that throng, any one individual animal had little significance; their survival strategy depended on numbers.

Even the smaller number that had accumulated near the stream had subjugated their prickly individualities to the herding instinct. Later, survival would demand splintering again into small family herds to disperse and search for fodder during the lean seasons.

Ayla took Whinney to the edge of the stream near a tenacious wind-bent pine. In the sign language of the Clan, she told the horse to stay nearby, and, seeing the mare herd her young one close to her, Ayla knew she need not have worried about Racer. Whinney was entirely capable of guiding her foal away from danger. But Jondalar had gone to some trouble to find a solution to a problem she had envisaged, and she was curious to see how it would work.

The woman and man each took a spear thrower and a holder of long spears, and proceeded on foot towards the herd. Hard hooves had broken down the dry crust of the steppes and kicked up a haze of dust that settled in a fine coating on the dark shaggy fur. The movement of the herd was marked by the choking dust, the way smoke from a smouldering prairie fire showed the course of the blaze – and a similar devastation was left in the wake.

Jondalar and Ayla circled to get downwind of the slowly moving herd, squinting to pick out individual animals as the wind, laden with the hot rangy odour of bison, blew fine grit in their faces. Bawling calves straggled after cows, and butting yearlings tested the patience of hump-backed bulls.

One old bull, rolling in a dust wallow, heaved up to regain his feet. His massive head hung low as though weighted down by the enormous black horns. Jondalar's six-foot-six inches topped the height of the bison at his humped shoulders – by not much. The animal's powerful, thickly furred front quarters tapered to low, lean hindquarters. The huge old beast, probably just past his prime, was too tough and stringy for their needs, but they knew he could be formidable when he stopped to eye them suspiciously. They waited until he moved on.

As they moved in closer, the variously pitched bawling and lowing of the herd rose and fell. Jondalar pointed out a young female. The heifer was nearly full grown, ready to bear young, and fattened from summer grazing. Ayla nodded agreement. They fitted the spears into their spear throwers and Jondalar signalled his intention to circle to the other side of the young cow.

By some unknown instinct, or perhaps because she had seen the man moving, the animal sensed she had been marked as prey. Nervously, she edged closer to the main body of the herd. Several others were moving to close around her, and Jondalar's attention was distracted by them. Ayla was sure they were going to lose the cow. Jondalar's back was towards her, she couldn't signal, and the heifer was moving out of range. She couldn't shout; even if he could hear her, it might warn the bison.

She made a decision and took aim. He glanced back as she was ready to hurl, took in the situation, and readied his thrower. The fast-moving heifer was stirring up the other animals, as were they. The man and woman had thought the cloud of dust would be sufficient cover, but the bison were used to it. The young cow had almost reached the safety of the crowd, with others moving in.

Jondalar dashed toward her and heaved his spear. Ayla's followed an instant later, finding its mark in the shaggy neck of the bison after his tore into her soft underbelly. The bison's momentum carried her forward, then her pace slowed. She wavered, staggered, and slumped to her knees, cracking Jondalar's spear as she collapsed on it. The herd smelled blood. A few sniffed at the downed heifer, lowing uneasily.

Others picked up their dirge, jostling and eddying, the air tense and panicky.

Ayla and Jondalar ran toward the kill from opposite directions. Suddenly he started shouting and waving his arms at her. She shook her head, not understanding his signals.

A young bull, who had been playing at butting, had finally elicited a response from the old patriarch and dodged away, running into a nervous cow. The young male moved back, indecisive and agitated, but his evasive action was cut off by the big bull. He didn't know which way to turn until his attention was caught by a moving bipedal figure. He lowered his head and ran toward it.

"Ayla! Look out!" Jondalar shouted, running toward her. He had a spear in his hand and pointed it.

Ayla turned and saw the young bull coming at her. Her first thought was her sling, an almost instinctive reaction. It had always been her immediate means of defence. But she dismissed it quickly and slapped a spear into her thrower.

Jondalar launched his spear by hand a moment before her, but the spear thrower imparted greater speed. Jondalar's weapon found a flank, which turned the bison momentarily. When he looked, Ayla's spear, still quivering, was lodged in the young bull's eye; the animal was dead before he fell.

The running, shouting and new source of blood smell started the aimlessly milling animals in a concerted direction – away from the disturbing activity. The last stragglers bypassed their fallen members to join the herd in a ground-shaking stampede. The rumble could still be heard after the dust settled.

The man and woman were struck dumb for a moment as they stood looking at the two dead bison on the empty plain.

"It's over," Ayla said, stunned. "Just like that."

"Why didn't you run?" Jondalar shouted, giving in to his fear for her now that it was over. He strode toward her. "You could've been killed!"

"I couldn't turn my back on a charging bull," Ayla countered. "He would have gored me for sure." She looked again at the bison. "No, I think your spear would have stopped him . . . but I didn't know that. I never hunted with anyone before. I always had to watch out for myself. If I didn't, no one would have."

Her words jogged a final piece into place, and suddenly he saw what her life must have been. She had survived more than anyone would believe. No, she could not have run away, just as she had not run away from anything. Even faced with him at his worst, she stood her ground.

"Ayla, you beautiful, wild, wonderful woman, look what a hunter you are!" He smiled. "Look what we've done! Two of them. How are we going to get them both back?"

As the full significance of their achievement filled her, she smiled, with satisfaction, triumph, and joy. It made Jondalar aware that he had not seen that smile often enough. She was beautiful, but when she smiled like that, she glowed, as though a fire was lit from within. A laugh rose up in him unexpectedly – uninhibited and infectious. She joined him; she couldn't help it. It was their shout of victory, of success.

"Look what a hunter you are, Jondalar," she said.

"It's the spear throwers – they made the difference. We walked into this herd, and before they knew what happened . . . two of them! Think what that can mean!"

She knew what it would mean to her. With the new weapon she would always be able to hunt for herself. Summer. Winter. No pit traps to dig. She could travel and hunt. The spear thrower had all the advantages of her sling, and so many more.

"I know what it means. You said you would show me a better way to hunt, an easier way, and you did. I don't know how to tell you . . . I am so . . ."

There was only one way she knew to express her gratitude, the way she had learned in the Clan. She sat at his feet and bowed her head. Perhaps he would not tap her shoulder to give her permission to tell him, in the proper way, but she had to try.

"What are you doing?" he said, reaching down to urge her up. "Don't sit there like that, Ayla."

"When a woman of the Clan wants to tell a man something important, this is how she asks for his attention," she said, looking up. "It is important for me to tell you how much this means, how grateful I am for the weapon. And for teaching me your words, for everything."

"Please, Ayla, get up," he said, lifting her to her feet. "I didn't give this weapon to you, you gave it to me. If I hadn't seen you use your sling, I would not have thought of it. I am grateful to you, for more than this weapon."

He was holding her arms, feeling her body close to his. She was looking into his eyes, unable and unwilling to turn her eyes aside. He bent closer and put his mouth on hers.

Her eyes opened wide in surprise. It was so unexpected. Not only his action, but her reaction, the jolt that flushed through her, when she felt his mouth on hers. She did not know how to respond.

And, finally, he understood. He wouldn't push her beyond that gentle kiss – not yet.

"What is that mouth on mouth?"

"It's a kiss, Ayla. It's your first kiss, isn't it? I keep forgetting, but it's very hard to look at you and . . . Ayla, sometimes, I am a very stupid man."

"Why do you say that? You are not stupid."

"I am stupid. I can't believe how stupid I have been." He let go of her. "But right now, I think we'd better find a way to get those bison back to the cave, because if I stay here standing next to you like this, I'll never be able to do it right for you. The way it should be done for your first time."

"The way what should be done?" she said, not really wanting him to move away.

"First Rites, Ayla. If you will allow me."

28

"I don't think Whinney could have hauled them both back here if we hadn't left the heads behind," Ayla said. "It was a good idea." She and Jondalar dragged the carcass of the bull off the travois and onto the ledge. "There is so much meat! It will take a long time to cut it up. We should start right away."

"They'll keep for a while, Ayla." His smile and his eyes filled her with warmth. "I think your First Rites are more important. I'll help you take the harness off Whinney – then I'm going for a swim. I'm sweaty, and bloody."

"Jondalar . . ." Ayla hesitated. She was feeling excited, and yet shy. "It is a ceremony, this First Rites?"

"Yes, it is a ceremony."

"Iza taught me to prepare myself for ceremonies. Is there a . . . preparation for this ceremony?"

"Usually older women help young women prepare. I don't know what they say or do. I think you should do whatever is appropriate for you."

"Then I will find the soaproot and purify myself, the way Iza taught me. I will wait until you are through with your swim. I should be alone when I prepare." She flushed and looked down.

She seems so young, and shy, he thought. Just like most young women at First Rites. He felt the familiar surge of tenderness and excitement. Even her preparations were right. He lifted her chin and kissed her again, then firmly moved himself away. "I'd like a little soaproot myself."

"I'll get some for you," she said.

He was grinning as he walked along the stream behind Ayla, and after she dug the soaproot and went back up to the cave, he flung himself into the water with a tremendous splash, feeling better about himself than he had for a long time. He pounded the soapy foam from the roots, rubbed it on his body, then took off the leather thong and worked it into his hair. Sand usually worked well enough, but soaproot was better.

He dived into the water and swam upstream, almost as far as the falls. When he returned to the beach, he put his breechclout on and hurried up to the cave. A roast was on, smelling delicious. He was so relaxed and happy, he couldn't believe it.

"I'm glad you're back. It will take some time to purify myself properly, and I didn't want it to get too late." She picked up a bowl of steaming liquid with horsetail ferns in it, for her hair, and a newly cured skin for a fresh wrap.

"Take as long as you need," he said, kissing her lightly.

She started down, then stopped and turned around. "I like that mouth on mouth, Jondalar. That kiss," she said.

"I hope you like the rest," he said after she left.

He walked around the cave, seeing everything with new eyes. He checked the haunch of roasting bison and turned the spit, noticed she had wrapped some roots in leaves and put them near coals, and then found the hot tea she had ready for him.

He saw his sleeping furs on the other side of the fireplace, frowned, and then, with great delight, picked them up and brought them back to the empty place beside Ayla's. After straightening them, he went back for the bundle that held his tools, then remembered the donii he had begun to carve. He sat on the mat that had kept his sleeping furs off the ground and opened the deerskin-wrapped package.

He examined the piece of mammoth-tusk ivory he had started to shape into a female figure and decided to finish it. Maybe he wasn't the best of carvers, but it didn't seem right to have one of the Mother's most important ceremonies without a donii. He picked out a few carving burins and took the ivory outside.

He sat at the edge, carving, shaping, sculpting, but he realized the ivory was not turning out to be ample and motherly. It was taking on the shape of a young woman. The hair that he had intended to resemble the style of the ancient donii he had given away – a ridged form covering the face as well as the back – was suggestive of braids, tight braids all over the head, except for the face. The face was blank. No face was ever carved on a donii: who could bear to look upon the face of the Mother? Who could know it? She was all women, and none.

He stopped carving and looked upstream and then down, hoping he might see her, though she said she wanted to be alone. Could he bring her Pleasure? he wondered. He had never doubted himself when he was called upon for First Rites at Summer Meetings, but those young women understood the customs and knew what to expect. They had older women to explain it to them.

Should I try to explain? No, you don't know what to say, Jondalar. Just show her. She will let you know if she doesn't like anything. That's one of her most appealing qualities, her honesty. No coy little ways. It's refreshing.

What would it be like to show the Mother's Gift of Pleasure to a woman with no pretences? Who would neither hold back nor feign enjoyment?

Why should she be any different from any other woman at First Rites? Because she's not like any other woman at First Rites. She has been opened, with great pain. What if you can't overcome that terrible beginning? What if she can't enjoy the Pleasures, what if you can't make her feel them? I wish there was some way to make her forget. If I could draw her to me, overcome her resistance and capture her spirit.

Capture her spirit?

He looked at the figure in his hand, and suddenly his mind was racing. Why did they engrave the image of an animal on a weapon, or on the Sacred Walls? To approach the Mother-Spirit of it, to overcome her resistance and capture the essence.

Don't be ridiculous, Jondalar. You can't capture Ayla's spirit that way. It wouldn't be right, no one puts a face on a donii. Humans were never pictured – a likeness might capture a spirit's essence. But to whom would it be captive?

No one should hold another person's spirit captive. Give the donii to her! She'd have the spirit back then, wouldn't she? If you kept it for just a while, then gave it to her . . . afterwards.

If you put her face on it, would it turn her into a donii? You almost think she is one, with her healing, and her magic way with animals. If she's a donii, she might decide to capture your spirit. Would that be so bad?

You want a piece to stay with you, Jondalar. The piece of the spirit that always stays in the hands of the maker. You want that part of her, don't you?

O Great Mother, tell me, would it be such a terrible thing to do? To put her face on a donii?

He stared at the small ivory figure he had carved. Then he took up a burin and began to carve the shape of a face, a familiar face.

When it was done, he held the ivory figurine up and turned it around slowly. A real carver might have done it better, but it wasn't bad. It resembled Ayla, but more in the feeling than the actual likeness; his feeling of her. He went back inside the cave and tried to think of a place to put it. The donii should be nearby, but he didn't want her to see it, yet. He saw a bundle of leather wrapped up near the wall by her bed, and he tucked the ivory figure in a flap of it.

He went back out and looked off the far edge. What's taking her so long? He looked over the two bison that were laid out side by side. They would keep. The spears and spear throwers were leaning against the stone wall near the entrance. He picked them up and carried them into the cave, and then he heard the sound of gravel pattering on stone. He turned around.

Ayla adjusted the tie on her new wrap, put her amulet around her neck, and pushed her hair, just brushed with teasel but not quite dry, back from her face. Picking up her soiled wrap, she started up the path. She was nervous, and excited.

She had an idea of what Jondalar meant by First Rites, but she was touched because of his desire to do it for her and share it with her. She didn't think the ceremony would be too bad – even Broud hadn't hurt after the first few times. If men give the signal to women they liked, did it mean Jondalar had grown to care?

As she neared the top, Ayla was startled out of her thoughts by a tawny blur of swift motion.

"Stay back!" Jondalar shouted. "Stay back, Ayla! It's a cave lion!"

He was at the mouth of the cave, a spear in his hand poised for throwing at a huge cat, crouched, ready to spring, a deep snarl rumbling in his throat.

"No, Jondalar!" Ayla screamed, rushing between them. "No!"

"Ayla don't! O Mother stop her!" the man cried when she jumped in front of him, in the path of the charging lion.

The woman made a sharp, imperative motion, and in the guttural language of the Clan, shouted, "Stop!"

The huge rufous-maned cave lion, with a wrenching twist, pulled his leap short and landed at the woman's feet. Then he rubbed his massive head against her leg. Jondalar was thunderstruck.

"Baby! Oh, Baby. You came back," Ayla said in motions, and without hesitation, without the least fear, she wrapped her arms around the huge lion's neck.

Baby knocked her over, as gently as he could, and Jondalar watched with mouth agape while the biggest cave lion he had ever seen draped forepaws around the woman in the closest equivalent to an embrace he could imagine a lion to be capable of. The feline lapped salty tears from the woman's face with a tongue that rasped it raw.

"That's enough, Baby," she said, sitting up, "or I won't have a face left."

She found the places behind his ears and around his mane that he loved to have scratched. Baby rolled over on his back to bare his throat to her ministrations, growling a deep rumble of contentment.

"I didn't think I'd ever see you again, Baby," she said when she stopped and the cat rolled over. He was bigger than she remembered and, though a bit thin, seemed healthy. He had scars she hadn't seen before, and she thought he might be fighting for territory, and winning. It filled her with pride. Then Baby noticed Jondalar again, and snarled.

"Don't snarl at him! That's the man you brought me. You have a mate . . . I think you must have many by now." The lion got up, turned his back to the man, and padded toward the bison.

"Is it all right if we give him one?" she called over to Jondalar. "We really have too much."

He still held the spear in his hand, standing in the mouth of the cave, stunned. He tried to answer, but only a squeak came out. Then he recovered his voice. "All right? You're asking me if it's all right? Give him both of them. Give him anything he wants!"

"Baby doesn't need both of them." Ayla used the word for his name in the language Jondalar didn't know, but he guessed it was a name. "No, Baby! Don't take the heifer," she said in sounds and gestures the man still didn't quite perceive as language, but elicited a gasp from him when she took one bison away from the lion and shoved him towards the other. He clamped huge jaws around the severed neck of the young bull and pulled it away from the edge. Then, getting a better grip, he started down the familiar path.

"I'll be right back, Jondalar," she said. "Whinney and Racer might be down there, and I don't want Baby to scare the colt."

Jondalar watched the woman follow behind the lion until she was out of sight. She appeared again on the valley side of the wall, walking casually beside the lion who was dragging the bison under his body between his legs.

When they reached the large boulder, Ayla stopped and hugged the lion again. Baby dropped the bison, and Jondalar shook his head in disbelief when he saw the woman climb on the fierce predator's back. She lifted an arm and flung it forward, and held on to the rufous mane while the huge feline leaped forward. He raced off with all his great speed, Ayla clinging tight, her hair streaming behind her. Then he slowed and turned back to the stone.

He got a grip on the young bison again and dragged it down the valley. Ayla stayed by the large rock, watching after him. Far down the field, the lion dropped the bull once more. He began a series of speaking grunts, his familiar *hnga hnga*, and built up to a roar so loud that it shook Jondalar's bones.

When the cave lion was gone, Jondalar took a deep breath and leaned against the wall, feeling weak. He was awestruck, and a little fearful. What is this woman? he thought. What kind of magic does she have? Birds, maybe. Even horses. But a cave lion? The biggest cave lion he'd ever seen?

Was she a . . .donii? Who but the Mother could make animals do her bidding? What about her healing powers? Or her phenomenal ability to speak so well already? For all that she had an unusual accent, she had learned most of his Mamutoi, and some words in Sharamudoi. Was she an aspect of the Mother?

He heard her coming up the path and felt a shiver of fear. He half expected her to declare she was the Great Earth Mother incarnate, and he would have believed it. He saw a woman with dishevelled hair and tears rolling down her face.

"What's wrong?" he asked, tenderness overcoming his imagined fears.

"Why do I have to lose my babies?" she sobbed.

He paled. Her babies? That lion was her baby? With a shock, he remembered a feeling of the Mother crying, the Mother of all.

"Your babies?"

"First Durc, and then Baby."

"Is that a name for the lion?"

"Baby? It means little one, infant," she answered, trying to translate.

"Little one!" he snorted. "That's the biggest cave lion I've ever seen!"

"I know." A smile of maternal pride gleamed through her tears. "I always made sure he had enough to eat, not like pride cubs. But when I found him, he was little. I called him Baby and never got around to naming him anything else."

"You found him?" Jondalar asked, still hesitant.

"He'd been left for dead. I think a deer trampled him. I was chasing them into my pit trap. Brun used to let me bring little animals into the cave sometimes, if they were hurt and needed my help, but never meat-eating animals. I wasn't going to pick up that baby cave lion, but then the hyenas went after him. I chased them away with my sling and brought him back."

Ayla's eyes took on a far-away look and her mouth assumed a lopsided grin. "Baby was so funny when he was little, always making me laugh. But it took a lot of time to hunt for him until the second winter, when we learned to hunt together. All of us, Whinney, too. I haven't seen Baby since . . ." She suddenly realized when.

"Oh, Jondalar, I am so sorry. Baby is the lion that killed your brother. But if it had been any other lion, I would not have been able to get you away from him."

"You are a donii!" Jondalar exclaimed. "I saw you in my dream! I thought a donii had come to take me to the next world, but she made the lion leave instead."

"You must have revived a little, Jondalar. Then when I moved you, you probably passed out from the pain. I had to get you away in a hurry. I knew Baby wouldn't hurt me – he's a little rough at times, but he doesn't mean to be. He can't help it. But I didn't know when his lioness would be back."

The man was shaking his head in wonder and disbelief. "Did you really hunt with that lion?"

"It was the only way I could keep him fed; at first, before he was able to make a kill himself, he'd bring an animal down and I'd ride up on Whinney and kill it with a spear. I didn't know about throwing spears then. When Baby got big enough to make the kill, sometimes I'd take a piece before he chewed it up, or else I'd want to save the hide . . ."

"So you pushed him away, like that bison? Don't you know it's dangerous to take meat away from a lion? I've seen one kill its own cub for that!"

"So have I. But Baby is different, Jondalar. He wasn't raised in a pride. He grew up here, with Whinney and me. We hunted together – he's used to sharing with me. I'm glad he found a lioness, though, so he can live like a lion. Whinney went back to a herd for a while, but she wasn't happy and came back . . ."

Ayla shook her head and looked down. "That's not true. I want to believe it. I think she was happy with her herd and her stallion. I was not happy without her. I am so glad she was willing to come back after her stallion died."

Ayla picked up the soiled wrap and headed into the cave. Jondalar, noticing he was still holding the spear, leaned it against the wall and followed. Ayla was pensive. Baby's return had evoked so many memories. She looked at the bison roast, turned the spit, and stirred up the coals. Then she poured water into a cooking basket from the large onager-stomach waterbag that was hanging on a post, and she put some cooking stones in the fire to heat.

Jondalar just watched her, still dazed by the cave lion's visit. It had been shock enough to see the lion leap down to the ledge, but the way Ayla had stepped out in front of him and stopped the massive predator . . . no one would believe it.

As he stared, he had the feeling something was different about her. Then he noticed her hair was down. He remembered the first time he saw her with her hair free, gleaming golden in the sun. She had come up from the beach, and he had seen her, all of her, for the first time with her hair down and her magnificent body.

" . . . good to see Baby again. Those bison must have been in his territory. He probably scented the kill, then picked up our trail. He was surprised to see you. I don't know if he remembered you. How did you get trapped in that blind canyon?"

"Wha . . . ? I'm sorry, what did you say?"

"I was wondering how you and your brother got trapped in that canyon with Baby," she said, looking up. Luminous violet eyes were watching her, sending a flush to her face.

With an effort he focused his mind on her question. "We were stalking a deer. Thonolan killed it, but a lioness had been after the same one. She dragged it away and Thonolan went after it. I told him to let her have it, but he wouldn't listen. We saw the lioness go into the cave, and then leave. Thonlan thought he could get the spear back, and some of the meat before she returned. The lion had other ideas."

Jondalar closed his eyes for a moment. "I can't blame him. It was stupid to go after that lioness, but I couldn't stop him. He was always reckless, but after Jetamio died, he was more than reckless. He wanted to die. I suppose I shouldn't have gone after him, either."

Ayla knew he still sorrowed for his brother and changed the subject. "I didn't see Whinney in the field. She must be out on the steppes with Racer. She's been going there lately. The way you fixed those straps around Racer's head worked well, but I don't know if it was necessary to keep him tied to Whinney."

"The rope was too long. I didn't think it might be caught

in a bush. It held them, though. That might be something to remember, if you want them to stay someplace. At least Racer. Does Whinney always do what you want?"

"I guess she does, but it's more like she wants to. She knows what I want, and she does it. Baby just takes me where he wants to go, but he goes so fast." Her eyes sparkled with the memory of her recent ride. It was always a thrill to ride the lion.

Jondalar recalled her clinging to the back of the cave lion, her hair, more golden than the reddish mane, flying in the wind. Watching her had made him afraid for her, but it was exciting – as she was. So wild and free, so beautiful . . .

"You're an exciting woman, Ayla," he said. His eyes carried his conviction.

"Exciting? Exciting is . . . the spear thrower, or riding fast on Whinney . . . or Baby, is that right?" She was flustered.

"Right. And so is Ayla exciting, to me . . . and beautiful."

"Jondalar, you are making a joke. A flower is beautiful or the sky when the sun drops over the edge. I am not beautiful."

"Can't a woman be beautiful?"

She turned aside from the intensity of his look. "I . . . I don't know. But I am not beautiful. I am . . . big and ugly."

Jondalar got up and, taking her hand, urged her up too. "Now, who is bigger?"

He was overpowering standing so close. He had shaved his face again, she noticed. The short beard hairs could only be seen up close. She wanted to touch his rough-smooth face, and his eyes made her feel they could reach inside her.

"You are," she said, softly.

"Then you are not too big, are you? And you are not ugly, Ayla." He smiled, but she only knew it because his eyes showed it. "It's funny, the most beautiful woman I have ever seen thinks she's ugly."

Her ears heard, but she was too lost in the eyes that held her, too moved by her body's response, to notice his words. She saw him bend closer, then put his mouth on hers, and she felt him put his arms around her and draw her close.

"Jondalar," she breathed. "I like that . . . mouth on mouth."

"Kiss," he said. "I think it's time, Ayla." He took her hand and led her toward the sleeping furs.

"Time?"

"First Rites," he said.

They sat down on the furs. "What kind of ceremony is it?"

"It is the ceremony that makes a woman. I can't tell you all about it. The older women tell a girl what to expect and that it may hurt, but that it is necessary to open the passage for her to become a woman. They choose the man for it. Men want to be chosen, but some are afraid."

"Why are they afraid?"

"They're afraid they will hurt a woman, afraid they will be clumsy, afraid they won't be able, that their woman-maker won't rise."

"That means a man's organ? It has so many names."

He thought of all the names, many vulgar or humorous. "Yes, it has many names."

"What is the real name?"

"Manhood, I guess," he said after a moment's thought, "the same as for a man, but 'woman-maker' is another."

"What happens if the manhood won't rise?"

"Another man has to be brought in – it's very embarrassing. But most men want to be chosen for a woman's first time."

"Do you like being chosen?"

"Yes."

"Are you chosen often?"

"Yes."

"Why?"

Jondalar smiled and wondered if all her questions were the result of curiosity or nervousness. "I think because I like it. A woman's first time is special to me."

"Jondalar, how can we have a ceremony of First Rites? I am past my first time, I am already open."

"I know, but there is more to First Rites than just opening."

"I don't understand. What more can there be?"

He smiled again, then leaned closer and put his mouth on hers. She leaned towards him, but was startled when his mouth opened and she felt his tongue try to reach inside her mouth. She backed off.

"What are you doing?" she asked.

"Don't you like it?" His forehead creased with consternation.

"I don't know."

"Do you want to try again and see?" Slow down, he said to himself. Don't rush this. "Why don't you lie back and relax?"

He pushed her with gentle pressure, then stretched out beside her, resting on one elbow. He looked down at her, then put his mouth on hers again. He waited until her tension was gone, then lightly flicked his tongue along her lips. He lifted up and saw her mouth smiling and her eyes closed. When she opened them, he bent to kiss her again. She strained to reach him. He kissed with more pressure, and an open mouth. When his tongue sought entrance, she opened her mouth to receive it.

"Yes," she said. "I think I like it."

Jondalar grinned. She was questioning, tasting, testing, and he was pleased she had not found him wanting.

"What now?" she asked.

"More of the same?"

"All right."

He kissed her again, gently exploring her lips, and the roof of her mouth, and under her tongue. Then his lips traced her jaw. He found her ear, breathed his warm breath in it, nibbled her lobe, and then covered her throat with kisses and his questing tongue. Then he returned to her mouth again.

"Why does that make me feel like a fever, and shivers?" she said. "Not like a sickness, nice shivers."

"You don't have to be a medicine woman now, it's not a sickness," he said. Then after a moment, "If you're warm, why don't you open your wrap, Ayla?"

"That's all right. I'm not that warm."

"Would you mind if I open your wrap?"

"Why?"

"Because I want to." He kissed her again, trying to undo the knot in the thong that held her wrap closed. He was not successful, and expected more discussion from her about it.

"I'll open it," she whispered, when he lifted his mouth from hers. Deftly, she untied the knot, then arched up to unwind the thong. The leather wrap fell away, and Jondalar caught his breath.

"Oh, woman!" His voice was husky with need, and his loins tightened. "Ayla, O Doni, what a woman!" He kissed her open mouth fiercely, then buried his face in her neck and sucked warmth to the surface. Breathing hard, he backed off and saw the red mark he had made. He took a deep breath, reaching for control.

"Is anything wrong?" Ayla asked, with a worried frown.

"Only that I want you too much. I want to make it right for you, but I don't know if I can. You are . . . so beautiful, so much woman."

Her frown smoothed to a smile. "Whatever you do will be right, Jondalar."

He kissed her again, more gently, wanting more than ever to give her Pleasure. He caressed the side of her body, feeling the fullness of her breast, the dip of her waist, the smooth curve of her hip, the taut muscle of her thigh. She quivered under his touch. His hand brushed the golden curls of her mound, and across her stomach to the turgid swelling of her breast, and felt her nipple harden in his palm. He kissed the tiny scar at the base of her throat; then he sought the other breast and sucked her nipple into his mouth.

"It doesn't feel the same as a baby," she said.

It broke the tension. Jondalar sat up, laughing. "You are not supposed to be analyzing this, Ayla."

"Well, it doesn't feel the same as when a baby sucks and I don't know why. I don't know why a man wants to suckle like a baby at all," she said, feeling a bit defensive.

"Don't you want me to? I won't if you don't like it."

"I didn't say I don't like it. It feels good when a baby sucks. It doesn't feel the same when you do it, but it feels good. I feel it all the way down inside me. A baby doesn't make you feel that way inside."

"That's why a man does it, to make a woman feel that way, and to make himself feel that way. That's why I want to touch you, to give you Pleasure, and me too. It is the Mother's Gift of Pleasure to Her children. She created us to know this Pleasure, and we know her when we accept her Gift. Will you let me give you Pleasure, Ayla?"

He was looking at her. Her golden hair, tousled on the fur, framed her face. Her dilated eyes, deep and soft, glowed with hidden fire, and seemed full, as though they might spill over. Her mouth trembled when she opened it to answer; she nodded instead.

He kissed one eye closed, and then the other, and saw a tear. He tasted the salty drop with the tip of his tongue. She opened her eyes and smiled. He kissed the tip of her nose, then her mouth, then each nipple. Then he got up.

She watched him walk to the hearth and move the spitted roast away from the fire and push the leaf-wrapped roots away from the coals. She waited, beyond thinking, only anticipating she did not know what. He had made her feel more than she ever imagined her body was capable of feeling, yet had awakened an inexpressible yearning.

He filled a cup with water and brought it back. "I don't want anything to interrupt us," he said, "and I thought you might want a drink of water."

She shook her head. He took a sip and put the cup down, then untied the cord of his breechclout and stood looking at her with his prodigious manhood extended. Her eyes held only trust and desire, none of the fear that his size often inspired in younger women, and some not so young, when they first saw him.

He lay down beside her, filling his eyes with the sight of her. Her hair, soft, rich, luxuriant; her eyes, brimming and expectant; her magnificent body; all of this beautiful woman, waiting for his touch, waiting for him to awaken in her those feelings he knew were there. He wanted it to last, this first awareness for her. He felt more excited than he ever had at the First Rites for a newly fledged woman. Ayla did not know what to expect; no one had described it in vivid, expanded detail. She had only been abused.

O Doni, help me do it right, he thought, feeling for the moment that he was undertaking some awesome responsibility, rather than a joyful Pleasure.

Ayla lay still, not moving a muscle, yet quivering. She felt as though she had been waiting forever for something she could not name, but which he could give. His eyes alone could touch inside her; she could not explain the pulsing, throbbing delirious effects of his hands, his mouth, his tongue, but she ached for more. She felt unfinished, incomplete. Until he gave her the taste, she hadn't known her hunger, but once aroused, it had to be satisfied.

When his eyes had had their fill, he closed them and kissed her once more. Her mouth was parted, waiting. She drew his seeking tongue in, and tentatively experimented with her own. He pulled up and smiled encouragement. He brought a rich lustrous strand of her hair to his lips, then rubbed his face in a thick, soft pile of her golden crown. He kissed her forehead, her eyes, her cheeks, wanting to know all of her.

He found her ear, and his warm breath sent shivers of delight through her once more. He nibbled her earlobe, then suckled it. He found the tender nerves on her neck and throat that excited chills in internal places never touched. His large, expressive, sensitive hands explored her, felt the silky texture of her hair, cupped her cheek and jaw, traced the contours of her shoulder and arm. When he reached her hand, he brought it to his mouth, kissed her palm, stroked each finger, then followed the inside curve of her arm.

Her eyes were closed, giving in to the sensation with rhythmic surges. His warm mouth found the scar in the hollow of her throat, then followed the path between her breasts and curved underneath one. He described decreasing circles with his tongue and felt the texture of her skin change when he reached the aureole. She gasped when he drew her nipple into his mouth, and he felt a flush of heat throbbing in his loins.

His hand matched his tongue's movement with her other breast, and his fingers found her nipple hardened and erect. He suckled gently at first, but when she pushed herself up to him, he increased the suction. She breathed hard, moaned softly. His breath matched her wanting; he wasn't sure he could wait. He stopped then, to look at her again. Her eyes were closed, her mouth open.

He wanted all of her, all at once. He took her mouth, drew her tongue inside his. When he released it, she drew in his, following his example, and felt the warm inside of his. He found her throat again, and drew wet circles around her other full breast until he reached the nipple. She pushed herself up to him, wanting, and shuddered when he answered with a deep pull.

His hand caressed her stomach, her hip, her leg, then

reached for her inner thigh. Her firm muscles rippled as she tensed a moment, then she separated her legs. He cupped his hand over her mound of dark gold curls and felt a sudden damp warmth. The answering jolt in his groin caught him by surprise. He stayed as he was, fighting for control, and almost lost it when he felt another surge of wetness in his hand.

His mouth left her nipple and circled her stomach and her navel. When he reached her mound, he looked up at her. She was breathing in mewing gasps, her back arched and tensed with anticipation. She was ready. He kissed the top of her mound, felt crinkly hair, and inched lower. She was quivering and, when his tongue found the top of her narrow slot, she sprang up with a cry, then lay back moaning.

His manhood was throbbing eagerly, impatiently, as he shifted position to slide down between her legs. Then he spread open her folds and took a long, loving taste. She could not hear her own sounds as she lost herself to the flood of exquisite sensations coursing through her as his tongue explored every fold, every ridge.

He concentrated on her to keep his own demanding need in check, found the nodule that was her small but erect centre of delight, and moved it firmly and rapidly. He feared he had reached the limit of his self-control when she writhed and sobbed with an ecstasy unknown before. With two long fingers, he entered her moist passage and applied pressure up, from inside.

Suddenly she arched her back and cried out, and he tasted a new wetness. Her hands clenched and unclenched convulsively in unconscious beckoning motions that matched her spasmodic breaths.

"Jondalar," she cried out to him. "Oh, Jondalar, I need . . . need you . . . need something . . ."

He was on his knees, gritting his teeth in an effort to hold back, trying to enter her carefully. "I'm trying . . . to be easy," he said, almost painfully.

"It . . . won't hurt me, Jondalar . . ."

It was true! It wasn't really her first time. As she arched up to receive him, he let himself enter. There was no blockage. He pressed farther, expecting to find her barrier, but he felt himself drawn in, felt her warm, moist depths opening and enfolding him until, to his wonder, she embraced him fully. He drew back and plunged deeply into her again. She wrapped legs around him to pull him into her. He withdrew again, and, as he penetrated once more, he felt her wonderous throbbing passage caress his full length. It was more than he could bear. He dived in again, and again, with unrestrained abandon, for once giving in entirely to his own need.

"Ayla! . . . Ayla! . . . Ayla!" he cried out.

The tension was reaching its peak. He could feel it gathering in his loins. He drew back once more. Ayla raised up to him with every nerve and muscle taut. He surged into her, revelling in the sheer sensual pleasure of burying his full proud manhood completely in her eager warmth. They strained together, Ayla cried his name, and, giving her his final fraction, Jondalar filled her.

For an eternal instant, his deeper, throatier cries rose in harmony with her breathless sobs repeating his name as paroxysms of inexpressible pleasure shuddered through them. Then, with exquisite release, he collapsed on top of her.

For a long moment, only their breathing could be heard. They could not move. They had given all to each other, every fibre to their shared experience. After a time, they didn't want to move, didn't want it to end, though they knew it was over. It had been Ayla's awakening: she had never known the pleasures a man could give her. Jondalar knew his pleasure would be to awaken her, but she had given him an unexpected surprise, adding immeasurably to his excitement.

Only few women had depth enough to take in all of him; he had learned to control his penetration to suit and did it with sensitivity and skill. It would never be quite the same again – but to enjoy the excitement of First Rites, and the rare and glorious release of full penetration at the same time, was unbelievable.

He always did put forth greater efforts for First Rites; there was something about the ceremony that brought out the best in him. His care and concern were genuine, his efforts were to please the woman, and his satisfaction came from her enjoyment as much as his own. But Ayla had pleased him, satisfied him beyond his wildest fantasy. Not ever had he felt so profoundly fulfilled. For a moment, it seemed, they had become one.

"I must be getting heavy," he said, pulling himself up to support partially his weight on an elbow.

"No," she said in a soft voice. "You're not heavy at all. I don't think I ever want you to get up."

He bent down to nuzzle an ear and kiss her neck. "I don't want to get up either, but I think I should." He disengaged himself slowly, then lay down beside her, fitting an arm under her so that her head rested in the hollow beneath his shoulder.

Ayla was dreamily content, completely relaxed, and acutely aware of Jondalar. She felt his arm around her, his finger caressing her lightly, the play of pectoral muscles under her cheek; she could hear his heartbeat, or perhaps her own, in her ear; she smelled the warm musky scent of his skin, and their Pleasures. And she had never felt so cared for or so coddled.

"Jondalar," she said after a while, "how do you know what to do? I didn't know those feelings were in me. How did you?"

"Someone showed me, taught me, helped me to know what a woman needs."

"Who?"

She felt his muscles tense, detected a change in the tone of his voice.

"It's customary for older, more experienced women to teach young men."

"You mean like First Rites?"

"Not quite. It's more informal. When young men start coming into their heat, the women always know. One, or more, who understands he is nervous and unsure of himself will be there for him, and will help him over it. But it's not a ceremony."

"In the Clan, when a boy makes his first kill – on a real hunt, not just little animals – then he is a man and has a manhood ceremony. Coming into his heat doesn't matter. It's hunting that makes him a man. That's when he must assume adult responsibilities."

"Hunting is important, but some men never hunt. They have other skills. I suppose I wouldn't have to hunt if I didn't

556

want to. I could make tools and trade them for meat or skins, or whatever I wanted. Most men hunt, though, and a boy's first kill is very special."

Jondalar's voice took on the warm tones of memory. "There is no real ceremony, but his kill is distributed to everyone in the Cave – he doesn't eat any of it. When he walks by, they remark to each other so he can hear, how big and wonderful his kill is, and how tender and delicious. The men invite him to join them for gaming or talking. The women treat him like a man instead of a boy, and make friendly jokes with him. Almost any woman will make herself available to him, if he's old enough and that's what he wants. A first kill makes him feel very much a man."

"But no manhood ceremony?"

"Each time a man makes a woman, opens her, let's the life force flow into her, he reaffirms his manhood. That's why his tool, his manhood, is called woman-maker."

"It might do more than make a woman. It might start a baby."

"Ayla, the Great Earth Mother blesses a woman with children. She brings them into the world and to a man's hearth. Doni created men to help her, to provide for her when she is heavy with child, or nursing and caring for an infant. And to make her a woman. I can't explain it any better. Maybe Zelandoni can."

Maybe he's right, Ayla thought, snuggling down beside him. But if he isn't, a baby could be growing in me now. She smiled. A baby like Durc, to cuddle and nurse, and take care of, a baby that would be part Jondalar.

But who will help me when he's gone, she thought with a stab of anguish. She recalled her difficult previous pregnancy, her brush with death during delivery. Without Iza, I wouldn't be alive. And if I did manage to have a baby alone, how could I hunt and take care of a baby? What if I got hurt, or killed? Who would take care of my baby then? He'd die, all alone.

I can't have another baby now! She bolted up. What if one has started? What should I do? Iza's medicine! Tansy or mistletoe, or . . . not mistletoe. That only grows on oak, and there is no oak here. But there are several plants that will work – I'll have to think about it. It could be dangerous, but better to lose the baby now, than lose him to some hyena after he's born.

"Is anything wrong, Ayla?" Jondalar asked, reaching up to cup a full firm breast, because he knew he could and that made him want to.

She leaned into his hand, remembering his touch. "No, nothing is wrong."

He smiled, recalled his deep satisfaction, and felt renewed stirrings. Soon, he thought. I think she has Haduma's touch!

She saw warmth and desire in his blue eyes. Maybe he'll want to make Pleasure with me again, Ayla thought, smiling back. Then her smile faded. If a baby hasn't started, and we do Pleasures again, one could start. Maybe I should take Iza's secret medicine, the one she said not to mention to anyone.

She remembered when Iza told her about the plants – golden thread and root of antelope sage – that had such potent magic, they could add strength to a woman's totem to fight off the man's impregnating essences, and prevent life from starting. Ayla had just learned she was pregnant. Iza had not told her about the medicine before – no one thought she would ever have a baby, and it hadn't come up in her training. Strong totem or not, I had a baby, and I might again. I don't know if it's spirits or men, but the medicine worked for Iza, and I think I'd better take it, or I may have to take something else to lose one.

I wish I didn't have to, I wish I could keep it. I would like to have a baby from Jondalar. Her smile was so tender and inviting that he reached up and pulled her down on him. The amulet, hanging around her neck, banged his nose.

"Oh, Jondalar! Did that hurt?"

"What do you have in that thing? It must be full of rocks!" he said, sitting up and rubbing his nose. "What is it?"

"It is . . . for my totem spirit, so he can find me. It holds the part of my spirit he recognizes. When he has given me signs, I keep them in there, too. Everyone in the Clan has one. Creb said if I lose it, I will die."

"It's a charm, or an amulet," he said. "Your Clan does understand the mysteries of the spirit world. The more I learn about them, the more like people they seem, though not like any I know." His eyes filled with contrition. "Ayla, it was my ignorance that made me behave as I did when I first understood whom you meant by Clan. It was shameful, and I'm sorry."

"Yes, it was shameful, but I am not angry or hurt any more. You have made feel . . . I want to make a courtesy, too. For today, for First Rites, I want to say . . . thank you."

He grinned. "I don't think anyone ever thanked me before." The grin left, but a smile lingered though his eyes were serious. "If anyone should say it, I should. Thank you, Ayla. You don't know what experience you gave me. It hasn't been that gratifying for me since . . ." He stopped and she saw a frown of pain. ". . . since Zolena."

"Who is Zolena?"

"Zolena is no more. She was a woman I knew when I was young." He lay back down and stared up at the roof of the cave, silent for so long that Ayla did not think he would say any more. Then, to himself more than her, he began speaking.

"She was beautiful then. All the men talked about her, and all the boys thought about her, but none more than I, even before the donii came to me in my sleep. The night my donii came, she came as Zolena, and when I woke my sleeping furs were full of my essence, and my head full of Zolena.

"I remember following her, or finding a place to wait where I could watch her. I begged the Mother for her. But I couldn't believe it when she came to me. It could have been any one of the women, but the only one I wanted was Zolena – oh, how I wanted her – and she came to me.

"First, I just took my pleasure in her. Even then, I was big for my age – in many ways. She taught me how to control, how to use it, and she taught me what a woman needed. I learned I could get pleasure from a woman, even if she wasn't quite deep enough, if I held myself back as long as possible, and made her ready. Then I wouldn't need as much depth, and she could take more.

"With Zolena, I didn't have to worry. Yet, she could make men happy who were smaller – she had ways of control, too. There wasn't a man who didn't want her – and she chose me. After a while, she chose me all the time, though I was hardly more than a boy.

"But there was one man who kept after her, though he

knew she didn't want him. It made me angry. When he saw us together, he'd tell her to pick a man for a change. He wasn't as old as Zolena, but older than I. I was bigger, though."

Jondalar closed his eyes, but kept on. "It was so stupid! I shouldn't have done it, it only called attention to us, but he wouldn't let her alone. He made me so furious. One day I hit him, and then I couldn't stop.

"They say it's not good for a young man to be with one woman too much. With more women, there's less chance that he will form an attachment. Young men are supposed to mate young women; older women are only supposed to teach them. They always blame the woman if a young man grows to feel too much for her. But they shouldn't have blamed her. I didn't want any of those other women, I wanted only Zolena.

"Those women seemed so crude then, insensitive, teasing, making fun of the men all the time, especially the young men. Perhaps I was insensitive, too, chasing them away from me, calling them names.

"They're the ones who choose the men for First Rites. All the men want to be chosen – they always talk about it. It's an honour, and it's exciting, but they worry about being too rough, or too hasty, or worse. What good is a man if he can't even open a woman? Any time a man passes a group of women, they tease."

He shifted his voice to a falsetto and mimicked. "'Here's a handsome one. Would you like me to teach you a thing or two?' Or, 'I haven't been able to teach this one anything, anyone else willing to try?'"

Then in his own voice, "Most men learn to give it back and enjoy the banter as much as the women, but it's hard on young men. Any man passing a group of laughing women wonders if they are laughing at his expense. Zolena wasn't like that. The other women didn't like her much, maybe because the men liked her too much. On any of the Mother's holidays or festivals, she was first choice . . .

"The man I hit lost several teeth. It's hard on a man that young to lose teeth. He can't chew, and women don't want him. I've been sorry ever since. It was so stupid! My mother made compensation for me, and he moved to another Cave.

But he comes to Summer Meetings, and I wince every time I see him.

"Zolena had been talking about serving the Mother. I thought I would be a carver and serve Her in that way. That was when Marthona decided I might have an aptitude for stone working and sent word to Dalanar. Not long afterwards, Zolena left to take special training, and Willomar took me to live with the Lanzadonii. Marthona was right. It was best. When I returned after three years, Zolena was no more."

"What happened to her?" Ayla asked, almost afraid to speak.

"Those Who Serve the Mother give up their own identity and take on the identity of the people for whom they intercede. In return, the Mother gives them Gifts unknown to Her ordinary children: Gifts of magic, skill, knowledge – and power. Many who go to Serve never progress beyond acolytes. Of those who receive Her call, only a few are truly talented, but they rise in the ranks of Those Who Serve very quickly.

"Just before I left, Zolena was made High Priestess Zelandoni, First among Those Who Serve the Mother."

Suddenly Jondalar jumped up and saw the scarlet and gold western sky through the cave openings. "It's still daylight. I feel like going for a swim," he said, striding quickly out of the cave. Ayla picked up her wrap and long thong and followed him. By the time she reached the beach, he was in the water. She took off her amulet, walked in a few feet, then kicked off. He was far upstream. She met him on his way back.

"How far did you go?" she asked.

"To the falls," he said. "Ayla, I have never told that to anyone before. About Zolena."

"Do you ever see Zolena?"

Jondalar's explosive laugh was bitter. "Not Zolena, Zelandoni. Yes, I've seen her. We are good friends. I have even shared Pleasures with Zelandoni," he said. "But she doesn't choose just me any more." He started swimming downstream, fast and hard.

Ayla frowned and shook her head, then followed him back to the beach. She slipped her amulet on and tied on her wrap as she trailed him up the path. He was standing by the fireplace looking down at barely glowing coals when she walked in. She made a last adjustment to her wrap, then picked up some wood and fed it to the fire. He was still wet and she saw him shiver. She went to get his sleeping fur.

"The season is changing," she said. "Evenings are cool. Here, you might get a chill."

He held the fur around his shoulders awkwardly. It wasn't right for him, she thought, a fur wrap. And if he's going to leave, he should start before the season turns. She went to her sleeping place and picked up a bundle that was beside the wall.

"Jondalar . . . ?"

He shook his head to bring himself back to the present and smiled at her, but it didn't reach his eyes. When she started to untie the bundle, something fell out. She picked it up.

"What is this?" she asked in tones of frightened wonder. "How did it get here?"

"It's a donii," Jondalar said when he saw the piece of carved ivory.

"A donii?"

"I made it for you, for your First Rites. A donii should always be present at First Rites."

Ayla bent her head to hide a sudden rush of tears. "I don't know what to say, I have never seen anything like this. She is beautiful. She looks real, like a person. Almost like me."

He lifted her chin, "I meant her to look like you, Ayla. A real carver would have done it better . . . no. A real carver would not have made a donii like this. I'm not sure if I should have. A donii does not usually have a face – the face of the Mother is unknowable. To put your face on that donii may have trapped your spirit there. That's why she is yours, to keep in your possession, my gift to you."

"I wonder why you put your gift here," Ayla said as she finished untying the bundle. "I made this for you."

He shook out the leather, and saw the garments, and his eyes brightened. "Ayla! I didn't know you could do sewing or beadwork," he said, examining the clothing.

"I didn't do the beadwork. I just made new parts for the shirt you were wearing. I took apart the other clothes so I'd know what size and shape to make the pieces, and I looked at the way they were put together so I could see how it was done. I used the sewing awl you gave me – I don't know if I used it right, but it worked."

"It's perfect!" he said, holding the shirt up to himself. He tried on the trousers and then the shirt. "I've been thinking about making clothes for myself that would be more appropriate for travelling. A breechclout is fine for here, but . . ."

It was out. Spoken aloud. Like the evil ones Creb had talked about, whose power came only from the recognition they were given when their names were spoken aloud, Jondalar's leaving had become a fact. No longer was it a vague thought that would some day come about – it had substance now. And it drew more weight as their thoughts concentrated on it, until an oppressive physical presence seemed to have entered the cave, and would not go away.

Jondalar quickly took the clothes off and folded them into a pile. "Thank you, Ayla. I can't tell you how much these mean. When it gets colder, they will be perfect, but I don't need them yet," he said, and he put the breechclout on.

Ayla nodded, not trusting herself to speak. She felt a pressure in her eyes, and the ivory figurine blurred. She brought it to her breast; she loved it. It had been made with his hands. He called himself a toolmaker, but he could do so much more. His hands were skilled enough to make an image that gave her the same feeling of tenderness she had felt when he made her know what it was to be a woman.

"Thank you," she said, remembering the courtesy.

He frowned. "Don't ever lose it," he said. "With your face on it, and maybe your spirit in it, it might not be safe if someone else found it."

"My amulet holds a part of my spirit and my totem's spirit. Now this donii holds a part of my spirit and your Earth Mother's spirit. Does that make it my amulet, too?"

He hadn't considered that. Was she part of the Mother now? One of Earth's Children? Maybe he shouldn't have tampered with forces beyond his ken. Or had he been an agent of them?

"I don't know, Ayla," he answered. "But don't lose it."

"Jondalar, if you thought it might be dangerous, why did you put my face on this donii?"

He took her hands that were holding the figure. "Because I wanted to capture your spirit, Ayla. Not to keep, I meant to give it back. I wanted to give you Pleasure, and I didn't know if I could. I didn't know if you would understand; you were not raised to know Her. I thought putting your face on this might draw you to me."

"You didn't need to put my face on a donii for that. I would have been happy if you had just wanted to relieve your needs with me, before I knew what Pleasures were."

He enfolded her in his arms, donii and all. "No, Ayla. You may have been ready, but I needed to understand that it was your first time, or it would not have been right."

She was losing herself in his eyes again. His arms tightened and she gave herself up to him, until all she knew was his arms holding her, his hungry mouth on her mouth, his body against hers, and a dizzying, demanding need. She didn't know when he swept her up and moved her away from the fireplace.

Her bed of furs reached up to accept her. She felt him fumble with the knot in her thong, then give up and simply raise her wrap. She opened herself to him eagerly, felt his rigid manhood search, and then find.

Fiercely, almost desperately, he sank his shaft deeply, as though to convince himself again that she was there for him, that he did not have to hold back. She raised to meet him, taking him in, wanting as much as he.

He drew back and plunged again, feeling the tension mount. Urged by the excitement of her total embrace, and the reckless delight of giving in entirely to the force of his passion, he rode the rising surge with furious joy. She met him at every crest, matching him thrust for thrust, arching to guide the pressure of his movement.

But the sensations she felt went beyond the push and pull within her cleft. Each time he filled her, she was conscious only of him; her body – nerves, muscles, sinews – was filled with him. He felt the pulling in his loins building, mounting, surging – then an unbearable crescendo as the pressure broke with a shuddering eruption as he bore down to fill her one last time. She rose to meet his final frantic drive, and the explosion diffused through her body with voluptuous release.

29

Ayla rolled over, not quite awake, but aware of some discomfort. The lump under her would not go away until she finally woke up to reach for it. She held up the object and, in the dim red light of a fire almost out, saw the silhouette of the donii. With a flash of recognition, the day before sprang vividly to mind, and she knew the warmth lying with her in the bed was Jondalar.

We must have fallen asleep after we made Pleasures, she thought. In a happy glow she snuggled close to him and shut her eyes. But sleep eluded her. Snatches of scenes formed patterns and textures which she sorted through with her inner sense. The hunt, and Baby's return, and First Rites, and, overlaid on all, Jondalar. Her feelings about him were beyond any words she knew, but they filled her with inexpressible joy. She thought of him as she lay beside him, until it became too much to contain – then she quietly slipped out of bed, taking the ivory figurine with her.

She walked to the mouth of the cave and saw Whinney and Racer standing together, leaning close. The mare blew a quiet nicker of recognition and the woman veered toward them.

"Was it like that for you, Whinney?" she said in soft tones. "Did your stallion give you Pleasures? Oh, Whinney, I didn't know it could be like that. How could it have been so terrible with Broud and so wonderful with Jondalar?"

The young horse nuzzled in for his share of attention. She scratched and stroked, then hugged him. "No matter what Jondalar says, Whinney, I think your stallion gave you Racer. He's even the same colour, and there are not many brown horses. I suppose it could have been his spirit, but I don't think so.

"I wish I could have a baby. Jondalar's baby. I can't — what would I do after he goes?" She blanched with a feeling close to terror. "Goes! Oh, Whinney, Jondalar is going to leave!"

She raced out of the cave and down the steep path, more by feel than sight. Her eyes were blinded by tears. She dashed across the rocky beach until she was stopped by the jutting wall, then huddled near it, sobbing. Jondalar is leaving. What will I do? How can I stand it? What can I do to make him stay? Nothing!

She hugged herself and hunkered down, leaning into the stone barrier as if trying to fend off some ravaging blow. She would be alone again when he left. Worse than alone: without Jondalar. What will I do here without him? Maybe I should leave too, find some Others and stay with them. No, I can't do that. They will ask where I come from, and Others hate the Clan. I will be abomination to them, unless I make words that are untrue.

I cannot. I cannot shame Creb or Iza. They loved me, cared for me. Uba is my sister, and she is taking care of my son. The Clan is my family. When I had no one, the Clan took care of me, and now the Others don't want me.

And Jondalar is leaving. I will have to live here alone, all my life. I might as well be dead. Broud cursed me; he has won after all. How can I live without Jondalar?

Ayla cried until she had no tears left, only a desolate emptiness inside. She wiped her eyes with the backs of her hands, and she noticed she still held the donii. She turned it around, marvelling as much at the concept of making a piece of ivory into a small woman as the figurine itself. In the moonlight, it resembled her even more. The hair carved into braids, the eyes in shadow, the nose and shape of the cheek, reminded her of her own reflection in a pool of water.

Why had Jondalar put her face on this symbol of the Earth Mother whom the Others revered? Was her spirit captured, linked with the one he called Doni? Creb had said her spirit was held with the Cave Lion's by her amulet, and by Ursus, the Great Cave Bear, the Clan's totem. She had been given a piece of the spirit of each member of the Clan when she became a medicine woman, and they had not been taken back after her death curse.

Clan and Others, totems and the Mother, all had some claim to that invisible part of her called spirit. I think my spirit must be confused, she thought – I know I am.

A cool wind urged her back up to the cave. Moving the cold spitted roast out of the way, she built up a small fire, trying not to disturb Jondalar, and started water heating for a tea to help her relax. She couldn't go to sleep yet. She stared at the flames while she waited, and she thought about the many times she had stared at flames to see a semblance of life. The hot tongues of light danced along the wood, leaping for the taste of a new piece, then drawing back and leaping again, until they claimed it, and devoured it.

"Doni! It's you! It's you!" Jondalar cried out in his sleep. Ayla jumped up and went to him. He was tossing and thrashing, obviously dreaming. She wondered if she should wake him. Suddenly his eyes flew open, looking startled.

"Are you all right, Jondalar?" she asked.

"Ayla? Ayla! Is it you?"

"Yes, it's me."

His eyes closed again, and he mumbled something incoherent. He hadn't been awake, she realized. It had been part of his dream, but he was calmer. She watched him until he relaxed, and then she went back to the fire. She let the flames die down as she sipped her tea. Finally feeling sleepy again, she removed her wrap and crawled in beside Jondalar and pulled the furs around her. The man's sleeping warmth made her think how cold it would be when he was gone – and from her vast reservoir of emptiness, new tears emerged. She cried herself to sleep.

Jondalar ran, panting to catch his breath, trying to reach the opening in the cave ahead. He glanced up and saw the cave lion. No, no! Thonolan! Thonolan! The cave lion was after him, crouched, then leaped. Suddenly the Mother appeared, and, with a command, she turned the lion away.

"Doni! It's you! It's you!"

The Mother turned around, and he saw Her face. The face was the donii carved to resemble Ayla. He called out to Her.

"Ayla? Ayla? Is it you?"

The carved face came to life; Her hair was a golden halo surrounded by a red glow.

"Yes, it's me."

The Ayla-donii grew and changed shape, became the ancient donii he had given away, the one that had been in his family for so many generations. She was ample and motherly and kept expanding until she was the size of a mountain. Then She began giving birth. All the creatures of the sea flowed out of Her deep cavern in a gush of birth waters, then all the insects and birds of the air flew out in a swarm. Then the animals of the land – rabbits, deer, bison, mammoth, cave lions – and in the distance, he saw through a misty haze the vague forms of people.

They drew near as the mists cleared, and suddenly he could see them. They were flatheads! They saw him and ran away. He called after them, and one woman turned around. She had Ayla's face. He ran towards her, but the mists closed around her and enveloped him.

He groped through a red fog and heard a distant roar, like a rushing waterfall. It grew louder, bore down on him. He was overwhelmed by a torrent of people emerging from the capacious womb of the Earth Mother, a huge mountainous Earth Mother with Ayla's face.

He pushed his way through the people, struggling to get to Her, and finally reached the great cavern, Her deep opening. He entered Her, and his manhood was probing Her warm folds until they enclosed him in their satisfying depths. He was pumping furiously, with unrestrained joy; then he saw Her face, awash with tears. Her body was shaking with sobs. He wanted to comfort Her, to tell Her not to cry, but he could not speak. He was pushed away.

He was in the midst of a great crowd flowing out of Her womb, all wearing beaded shirts. He tried to fight his way back, but the great press of people carried him away like a log caught in the flood of birth water; a log carried by the Great Mother River with a bloody shirt clinging to it.

He craned his neck to look back, and he saw Ayla standing in the mouth of the cavern. Her sobs echoed in his ears. Then, with resounding thunder, the cavern collapsed in a great rain of rocks. He stood alone, crying.

Jondalar opened his eyes to darkness. Ayla's small fire had used up the wood. In the absolute black, he wasn't sure if he was awake. The cave wall had no definition, no familiar focus to establish his place within his surroundings. For all his eyes could tell him, he might have been suspended in a fathomless void. The vivid shapes of his dreams were more substantial. They played across his mind in remembered bits and pieces, reinforcing their dimensions in his conscious thoughts.

By the time the night had faded enough to give bare outline to stone and cave openings, Jondalar had begun to attribute meaning to his sleeping images. He didn't often remember his dreams, but this one had been so strong, so tangible, that it had to be a message from the Mother. What was She trying to tell him? He wished for a zelandoni to help him interpret the dream.

As faint light penetrated the cave, he saw a tumult of blonde hair framing Ayla's sleeping face, and he noticed the warmth of her body. He watched her in silence as shadows lightened. He had an overwhelming desire to kiss her, but he didn't want to waken her. He brought a long golden tress to his lips. Then, quietly, he got up. He found the tepid tea, poured himself a cup, and walked out to the stone porch of the cave.

It was chilly in his breechclout, but he ignored the temperature, though a thought about the warm clothes Ayla had made for him passed through his mind. He watched the eastern sky lighten and the details of the valley sharpen, and he dredged up his dream again, trying to follow its tangled strands to unravel its mystery.

Why should Doni show him that all life came from Her? He knew it; it was an accepted fact of his existence. Why should She appear in his dream giving birth to all the fish and birds and animals and . . .

Flatheads! Of course! She was telling him the people of the Clan were Her Children too. Why had no one made that clear before? No one ever questioned that *all* life came from Her, why were those people so vilified? They were called animals as though animals were evil.

But they were *not* animals. They were human, a different kind of human! That's what Ayla has been saying all along. Is that why one of them had Ayla's face?

He could understand why her face would be on the donii he had made, the one who had stopped the lion in his dream – no one would believe what Ayla had actually done;

it was more incredible than the dream. But why was her face on the ancient donii? Why should the Great Earth Mother Herself bear the likeness of Ayla?

He knew he would never understand all of his dream, but he felt he was still missing an important part. He went over it again, and when he recalled Ayla standing in the cave that was about to collapse, he almost shouted to her to get away.

He was staring at the horizon, his thoughts inward, feeling the same desolation and loneliness as in his dream when he had been standing alone, without her. Tears wet his face. Why did he feel such utter despair? What was he not seeing?

People in beaded shirts came to mind, leaving the cavern. Ayla had fixed the beaded shirt for him. She had made clothes for him, and she hadn't even known how to sew before. Travelling clothes that he would wear when he left.

Left? Leave Ayla? The fiery light rose over the edge. He closed his eyes and saw a warm golden glow.

Great Mother! What a stupid fool you are, Jondalar. Leave Ayla? How can you possibly leave her? You love her! Why have you been so blind? Why should it take a dream from the Mother to tell you something so plain that a child could have seen it?

A sense of great weight lifting from his shoulders made him feel a joyous freedom, a sudden lightness. I love her! It has finally happened to me! I love her! I didn't think it was possible, but I love Ayla!

He was filled with exuberance, ready to shout it to the world, ready to rush in and tell her. I have never told a woman that I love her, he thought. He hurried into the cave, but Ayla was still sleeping.

He went back out and brought in some wood, and using flint and a firestone – it still amazed him – quickly had a fire going. For once, he'd managed to wake up before her, and he wanted to surprise her with hot tea for a change. He found her mint leaves, and soon had the tea steeped and ready, but Ayla still slept.

He watched her, breathing, turning – he loved her hair long and free like that. He was tempted to wake her. No, she must be tired. It's daylight and she's not up.

He went down to the beach, found a twig to clean his teeth, then took a morning swim. It left him refreshed, full of energy, and famished. They had never got around to eating. He smiled to himself, remembering the reason; the thought caused a rising.

He laughed. You deprived him all summer, Jondalar. You can't blame your woman-maker for being so eager, now that he knows what he's missed. But don't push her. She may need to rest – she's not used to it. He raced up the path and entered the cave quietly. The horses were out to pasture. They must have gone while I was swimming, and she's still not awake. Is she all right? Maybe I should wake her. She rolled over and exposed a breast, adding impulse to his earlier thoughts.

He contained his urge and went to the fireplace to pour himself more tea, and wait. He noticed a difference in her random motions, then saw her groping for something.

"Jondalar! Jondalar! Where are you?" she cried, bolting up.

"Here I am," he said, rushing to her.

She clung to him. "Oh, Jondalar, I thought you were gone."

"I'm here, Ayla, I'm right here." He held her until she quieted. "Are you all right now? Let me get you some tea."

He poured the tea and brought her a cup. She took a sip, and then a bigger drink. "Who made this?" she asked.

"I did. I wanted to surprise you with hot tea, but it's not so hot any more."

"You made it? For me?"

"Yes, for you. Ayla, I have never said this to a woman before. I love you."

"Love?" she asked. She wanted to be sure he meant what she hardly dared hope he might mean. "What does 'love' mean?"

"What does . . . ! Jondalar! You pompous fool!" He stood up. "You, the great Jondalar, the one every woman wants. You believed it yourself. So careful to withhold the one word you thought they all wanted to hear. And proud that you've never said it to a woman. You finally fall in love – and you couldn't even admit it to yourself. Doni had to tell you in a dream! Jondalar is finally going to say it, going to admit he loves a woman. You almost expected her to faint with

571

surprise, and she doesn't even know the meaning of the word!"

Ayla watched him with consternation, pacing back and forth, ranting to himself about love. She had to learn that word.

"Jondalar, what does 'love' mean?" She was serious, and she sounded a trifle annoyed.

He knelt down in front of her. "It's a word I should have explained long ago. Love is the feeling you have for someone you care for. It is what a mother feels for her children, or a man for his brother. Between a man and a woman, it means they care for each other so much that they want to share their lives together, not ever be apart."

She closed her eyes and felt her mouth tremble as she heard his words. Did she hear him right? Did she really understand?

"Jondalar," she said, "I did not know that word, but I know the meaning of the word. I have known the meaning of that word since you came, and the longer you were here, the more I knew it. So many times I have wished for the word to say that meaning." She closed her eyes, but the tears of relief and joy would not stay back. "Jondalar, I . . . love, too."

He stood up, bringing her with him, and kissed her tenderly, holding her like some new-found treasure that he didn't want to break or lose. She put her arms around his chest and held him as though he were a dream that might fade if she let go. He kissed her mouth, and her face salty with tears, and, when she laid her head against him, he buried his face in her tangled golden hair to dry his own eyes.

He could not speak. He could only hold her and marvel at his incredible luck in finding her. He'd had to travel to the far ends of the earth to find a woman he could love, and nothing was going to make him let her go now.

"Why not just stay here? This valley has so much. With two of us, it will be so much easier. We have the spear throwers, and Whinney is a help. Racer will be, too," Ayla said.

They were walking through the field for no purpose other than to talk. They had picked all the seeds she wanted to pick; hunted and dried enough meat to last through the winter; gathered and stored the ripening fruits, and roots, and other plants for food and medicine; and collected a variety of materials for winter projects. Ayla wanted to try decorating clothing, and Jondalar thought he'd carve some gaming pieces and teach Ayla how to play. But the true joy for Ayla was that Jondalar loved her – she would not be alone.

"It is a beautiful valley," Jondalar said. Why not stay here with her? Thonolan was willing to stay with Jetamio, he thought. But it wasn't just the two of them. How long could he stand it with no one else? Ayla had lived alone, for three years. They wouldn't have to be alone. Look at Dalanar. He started a new Cave, but in the beginning he had only Jerika, and her mother's mate, Hochaman. More people joined them later, and children were born. They are already planning a Second Cave of the Lanzadonii. Why can't you found a new Cave, like Dalanar? Maybe you can, Jondalar, but whatever you do, it won't be without Ayla.

"You need to know other people, Ayla, and I want to take you home with me. I know it would be a long Journey, but I think we could make it in a year. You'd like my mother, and I know Marthona would like you. And so would my brother, Joharran, and my sister, Folara – she must be a young woman by now. And Dalanar."

Ayla bowed her head, then looked up again. "How much will they like me when they find out my people were the Clan? Will they welcome me when they learn I have a son who was born when I lived with them, who is abomination to them?"

"You can't hide from people for the rest of your life. Didn't the woman . . . Iza . . . didn't she tell you to find your own kind? She was right, you know. It won't be easy – I can't keep the truth from you. Most people don't know the Clan people are human. But you made me understand, and there are others who wonder. Most people are decent, Ayla. Once they get to know you, they will like you. And I'll be with you."

"I don't know. Can't we think about it?"

"Of course we can," he said. We can't start on a long Journey until spring, he was thinking. We could get as far as the Sharamudoi before winter sets in, but we can winter here as well. It would give her some time to get used to the idea.

Ayla smiled with genuine relief and stepped up her pace. She had been dragging her feet physically as well as mentally. She knew he was missing his family, and his people, and if he decided to go, she would go with him no matter where he went. She hoped, though, that after settling down for the winter he might want to stay and make his home in the valley with her.

They were far from the stream, almost up the slope to the steppes, when Ayla stooped to pick up a vaguely familiar object.

"It's my aurochs horn!" she said to Jondalar, brushing off the dirt and noticing the charred inside. "I used it to carry my fire. I found it while I was travelling, after I left the Clan." Memories flooded back. "And I carried a coal in it to light the torches to help me chase the horses into my first pit trap. It was Whinney's dam that was caught, and when the hyenas went after her foal, I chased them away and brought her to the cave. So much has happened since then."

"Many people carry fire when they travel, but with the firestones, we don't have to worry about it." His brow suddenly furrowed, and Ayla knew he was thinking. "We're stocked up, aren't we? There's nothing more we need to do."

"No, we don't need anything."

"Then why don't we make a Journey? A short Journey," he added when he saw her distress. "You haven't explored the area to the west. Why don't we take some food and tents and sleeping furs, and look it over? We don't have to go far."

"What about Whinney and Racer?"

"We'll take them with us. Whinney can even carry us part of the time, and maybe the food and gear. It would be fun, Ayla. Just the two of us," he said.

Travelling for fun was new to her, and hard to accept, but she couldn't think of any objections. "I suppose we could," she said. "Just the two of us . . . why not?" It might not be a bad idea to explore more of the country to the west, she thought.

"The dirt is not as deep back here," Ayla said, "but it's the best place for a cache, and we can use some of the fallen rocks."

Jondalar held the torch higher to spread the flickering light farther. "Several small caches, don't you think?"

"So if an animal breaks into one, he won't get everything. Good idea."

Jondalar moved the light to see into some of the crannies among the fallen rocks in the far corner of the cave. "I looked back here once. I thought I saw signs of cave lion."

"This was Baby's place. I saw cave lion signs before I moved in, too. Much older. I thought it was a sign from my totem to stop travelling and stay for the winter. I didn't think I would stay so long. Now I think I was supposed to wait here for you. I think the Cave Lion spirit guided you here, and then chose you so your totem would be strong enough for mine."

"I always thought of Doni as my guiding spirit."

"Maybe She guided you, but I think the Cave Lion chose you."

"You may be right. The spirits of all creatures are Doni's, the cave lion is Hers, too. The ways of the Mother are mysterious."

"The Cave Lion is a hard totem to live with, Jondalar. His tests have been difficult – I wasn't always sure I would live – but his gifts have made them worth it. I think his greatest gift to me is you," she finished in a soft voice.

He stuffed the torch in a crack, then took the woman he loved in his arms. She was so open, and honest, and when he kissed her she responded so eagerly that he almost gave in to his wanting of her.

"We have to stop this," he said, holding her shoulders to put a space between them, "or we'll never get ready to leave. I think you have Haduma's touch."

"What is Haduma's touch?"

"Haduma was an old woman we met, the mother of six generations, and greatly revered by her descendants. She had many of the Mother's powers. The men believed that if she touched their manhood, it would make them able to rise as often as they wished, to satisfy any woman, or many of them. Most men wish for that. Some women know ways to encourage men. All you have to do is get close to me, Ayla. This morning, last night. How many times yesterday? And the day before? I've never been able, or wanted to so much.

But if we stop now, we'll never finish the caches this morning."

They cleared away rubble, levered aside some large boulders, and decided where to establish caches. As the day progressed, Jondalar thought Ayla seemed unusually quiet and withdrawn, and he wondered if it was anything he had said or done. Maybe he shouldn't seem so eager. It was hard to believe she was so ready for him every time he wanted her.

He knew many women held back and made a man work for his Pleasures, though they liked them, too. It had seldom been a problem for him, but he'd learned not to seem too eager: there was more challenge for a woman if a man seemed a bit restrained.

When they began moving the stored food to the rear of the cave, Ayla seemed even more reserved, bowing her head often and kneeling in quiet repose before picking up a rawhide-wrapped package of dried meat or a basket of roots. By the time they started making trips down to the beach to bring up more stones to pile around their winter supplies, Ayla was noticeably upset. Jondalar was sure it was his fault, but he didn't know what he had done. It was late afternoon when he saw her angrily trying to pick up a boulder much too heavy for her.

"We don't need that stone, Ayla. I think we should take a rest. It's warm, and we've been working all day. Let's go for a swim."

She stopped tugging at the rock, pushed her hair out of her eyes, undid the knot in her thong, and pulled off her amulet as her wrap fell away. Jondalar felt a familiar stirring in his loins. It happened every time he saw her body. She moves like a lion, he thought, admiring her sleek, sinewy grace as she ran into the water. He doffed his breechclout and raced in after her.

She was churning upstream so hard that Jondalar decided to wait until she came back downstream, and let her use up some of her irritation in effort. She was floating easily on the current when he caught up to her, and she did seem more relaxed. When she turned over to swim, he ran his hand along the curve of her back, from her shoulder, following the dip of her waist, and over her smooth rounded buttocks.

She shot ahead of him and was out of the water with her

amulet back on and reaching for her wrap when he waded out.

"Ayla, what am I doing wrong?" he asked, standing in front of her, dripping.

"It's not you. I'm the one who's doing it wrong."

"You're not doing anything wrong."

"Yes, I am. I've been trying all day to encourage you, but you don't understand Clan gestures."

When Ayla had first become a woman, Iza had explained not only how to care for herself when she bled, but how to clean herself after she had been with a man, and the gestures and postures that would encourage a man to give her the signal, though Iza had doubted she would need the information. Men of the Clan were not likely to find her attractive no matter what gestures she used.

"I know when you touch me in certain ways, or put your mouth on mine, that is your signal, but I don't know the ways to encourage you," she continued.

"Ayla, all you have to do is to be there to encourage me."

"That's not what I mean," she said. "I don't know how to tell you when I want you to make Pleasures with me. I don't know the ways. . . . You said some women know ways to encourage a man."

"Oh, Ayla, is that what's bothering you? You want to learn how to encourage me?"

She nodded and put her head down, feeling a surge of embarrassment. Clan women were not so forward. They exhibited their desire for a man with excessive modesty, as though they could hardly bear the sight of such an overwhelmingly masculine male – yet with demure glances and innocent postures that resembled the proper position for a female to assume, they let him know he was irresistible.

"Look how you've encouraged me, woman," he said, knowing he had developed an erection while talking to her. He couldn't help it, and he couldn't hide it. Seeing him so obviously encouraged brought a smile to the woman's lips; she couldn't help it. "Ayla," he said, and swept her up in both arms, "don't you know you encourage me just by being alive?"

Carrying her, he started across the beach toward the path. "Do you have any idea how it encourages me just to look at you? The first time I saw you, I wanted you." He continued up the path with a very surprised Ayla. "You are so much woman, you don't need ways to encourage – you don't have to learn a thing. Everything you do makes me want you more." They reached the entrance. "If you want me, all you have to do is say so, or better yet, this." He kissed her.

He carried her into the cave and put her down on the bed of furs. Then he kissed her again with open mouth and gently probing tongue. She felt his manhood, hard and hot between them. He sat up then and had a teasing grin on his face.

"You said you were trying all day. What makes you think you weren't encouraging me?" he said. Then he did something totally unexpected: he made a gesture.

Her eyes flew open with surprise. "Jondalar! That's . . . that's the signal!"

"If you're going to make your Clan signals to me, I think it's only fair to give them back."

"But . . . I . . ." She was at a loss for words – if not actions. She got up, turned around and went down on her knees, spreading them apart, and presented.

He had meant the signal as a joke; he didn't expect to be stimulated so quickly. But the sight of her round, firm buttocks, and her exposed female opening, deep pink and inviting, were irresistible. Before he knew it, he was on his knees behind her, entering her warm, pulsating depths.

From the moment she assumed the position, memories of Broud crowded her thoughts. For the first time, she would have refused Jondalar – if she could have. But as strong as the repellent associations were, her early conditioning to obey the signal was stronger.

He mounted and plunged. She felt Jondalar fill her, and she cried out with the unexpected pleasure. The posture made her feel pressures in new places, and when he drew back, the rubbing and friction excited in new ways. She backed to meet him when he dived in again. As he hovered over her, pumping and straining, she was suddenly reminded of Whinney and her bay stallion. The thought brought on a shudder of delicious warmth, and a pulsing, tingling pull. She reared up and backed to him, matching his pace, moaning and squealing.

The pressure was mounting quickly; her actions and his

need drove him faster. "Ayla! Oh, woman," he cried out. "Beautiful, wild, woman," he breathed as he thrust and thrust and thrust again. He held her hips, pulled her to him, and, as he filled her, she reared back to meet him as he surged into her with a shudder of delight.

They stayed there for a moment, shaking. Ayla's head hanging down. Then taking her with him, he rolled them both over on their sides, and then they lay there unmoving. Her back nestled against him, and with his manhood still in her, he curled around her and reached one hand over to cup her breast.

"I must admit," he said after a while, "that signal isn't so bad." He nuzzled the back of her neck and reached for her ear.

"I wasn't sure at first, but with you, Jondalar, everything is right. Everything is Pleasure," she said, snuggling back into him closer.

"Jondalar, what are you looking for?" Ayla called down from the ledge.

"I was trying to see if I could find any more firestones."

"I have hardly marked the first one I started using. It will last a long time – we don't need any more."

"I know, but I saw one, and thought I'd see how many more I could find. Are we ready?"

"I can't think of anything else we need. We can't stay too long – the weather changes so fast this time of year. It can be hot in the morning and a blizzard by evening," she said, coming down the path.

Jondalar put the new stones in his pouch, looked around once more, then looked up at the woman. Then he looked at the woman again.

"Ayla! What are you wearing?"

"Don't you like it?"

"I like it! Where did you get it?"

"I made it, when I was making yours. I copied yours to fit me, but I wasn't sure if I should wear it. I thought it might be something only a man should wear. And I didn't know how to bead a shirt. Is it all right?"

"I think so. I don't recall that the woman's outfit was much different. The shirt was a little longer, maybe, and the decorations might be different. This is Mamutoi clothing. I lost mine when we reached the end of the Great Mother River. It looks wonderful on you, Ayla, and I think you'll like it better. When it gets cold, you'll notice how warm it is, and comfortable."

"I'm glad you like it. I wanted to dress . . . your way."

"My way . . . I wonder if I know what my way is any more. Look at us! A man and a woman and two *horses*! One of them loaded with our tent and food and extra clothing. It feels strange to be starting on a Journey so unencumbered, to be carrying nothing except spears – and a spear thrower! And my pouch full of firestones. I think we'd be quite a surprise if anyone were to see us. But I'm not surprised at myself. I am not the same man I was when you found me. You have changed me, woman, and I love you for it."

"I, too, am changed, Jondalar. I love you."

"Well, which way do we go?"

Ayla felt a disquieting sense of loss as they walked the length of the valley, followed by the mare and her colt. When she reached the turn at the far end, she looked back.

"Jondalar! Look! Horses have come back to the valley. I haven't seen horses here since I first came. They left when I chased them and caught Whinney's dam. I am glad to see them back. I always did think this was their valley."

"Is it the same herd?"

"I don't know. The stallion was yellow, like Whinney. I don't see the stallion, only the lead mare. It's been a long time."

Whinney had seen the horses, too, and she gave a loud neigh. The greeting was returned, and Racer's ears turned toward them with interest. Then the mare followed the woman, and her colt trotted behind.

Ayla followed the river south and crossed when she saw the steep slope on the other side. She stopped at the top, and both she and Jondalar mounted Whinney. The woman found her landmarks and headed southwest. The terrain became rougher, more broken and folded, with rocky canyons and steep slopes leading to flat rises. When they neared an opening between jagged rock walls, Ayla dismounted and examined the ground. It held no fresh spoor. She led the way into a blind canyon, then climbed up on a rock that had split from the wall. As she walked to a rockslide at the back, Jondalar followed her.

"This is the place, Jondalar," she said, and, withdrawing a pouch from her tunic, she gave it to him.

He knew the place. "What is this?" he asked, holding up the small leather bag.

"Red earth, Jondalar. For his grave."

He nodded, unable to speak. He felt the pressure of tears and made no effort to check them. He poured the red ochre into his hand and broadcast it on the rocks and gravel, then spread a second handful. Ayla waited while he stared at the rocky slope with wet eyes, and, when he turned to go, she made a gesture over Thonolan's grave.

They rode for some time before Jondalar spoke. "He was a favourite of the Mother. She wanted him back."

They went a little farther, and then he asked, "What was that gesture you made?"

"I was asking the Great Cave Bear to protect him on his journey, to wish him luck. It means 'walk with Ursus'."

"Ayla, I didn't appreciate it when you told me. I do now. I am grateful to you for burying him, and for asking the Clan totems to help him. I think that, because of you, he will find his way in the spirit world."

"You said he was brave. I don't think the brave need help to find their way. It would be an exciting adventure for those who are fearless."

"He was brave, and he loved adventure. He was so full of life – as though he was trying to live it all at once. I would not have made this Journey if it hadn't been for him." His arms were around Ayla as they rode double. He tightened them, pulling her closer. "And I would not have found you.

"That's what the Shamud meant by saying it was my destiny! 'He leads where you would not otherwise go,' were the words. Thonolan led me to you . . . and then followed his love to the next world. I didn't want him to go, but I can understand him now."

As they continued west, the broken land gave way to flat open steppes again, crossed by the rivers and streams of runoff from the great northern glacier. The waterways cut through occasional high-walled canyons and meandered down gently sloping valleys. The few trees that graced the steppes were dwarfed by their struggle to live, even alongside the waters that fed their roots, and their shapes were tortured, as though frozen in the act of bending away from a violent gust.

They kept to the valleys when they could, for shelter from the wind, and for wood. Only there, protected, did birch, willow, pine, and larch grow in any abundance. The same was not true for animals. The steppes were a massive reserve of wildlife. With their new weapon, the man and woman hunted at will, whenever they wanted fresh meat, and they often left the remains of their kills for other predators and scavengers.

They had been travelling for half a moon's cycle of phases when a day dawned hot and unusually still. They had walked most of the morning, and they mounted when they saw a rise in the distance with a hint of green. Jondalar, prodded by Ayla's warmth and closeness, had worked his hand under her tunic to fondle her. They topped the hill and looked down at a pleasant valley watered by a large river. They reached the water when the sun was high.

"Should we go north or south, Jondalar?"

"Let's not do either. Let's make camp," he said.

She started to object, only because she was not accustomed to stopping so early for no reason. Then, when Jondalar nibbled at her neck and gently squeezed her nipple, she decided they had no reason to go on, and more than enough to stop.

"All right, let's make camp," she said. She threw a leg over and slid down. He dismounted and helped her remove the pack baskets from Whinney, so the horse could rest and graze. Then he took her in his arms and kissed her, reaching under her tunic again.

"Why don't you let me take it off," she said.

He smiled while she pulled the tunic over her head and undid the waist tie of the lower garment and stepped out of it. He pulled his tunic over his head, then heard her giggle. When he looked up, she was gone. She laughed again, then jumped into the river.

"I decided to go swimming," she said.

He grinned, took off his trousers, and followed her in. The

river was deep and cold and the current swift, but she was swimming upstream so hard that he had difficulty catching up with her. He grabbed her and, treading water, kissed her. She ducked out of his arms and raced for the shore, laughing.

He went after her, but, by the time he reached the shore, she had raced up the valley. He took off after her, and, just as he reached her, she dodged away again. He chased her again, putting forth all his effort, and finally caught her around the waist.

"You're not getting away this time, woman," he said, pulling her close. "You'll tire me out chasing you – then I won't be able to give you Pleasures," he said, delighted with her playfulness.

"I don't want you to give me Pleasures," she said.

His jaw dropped, and lines creased his forehead. "You don't want me . . ." He let go of her.

"I want to give you Pleasures."

His heart started beating again. "You do give me Pleasures, Ayla," he said, taking her back in his arms.

"I know it pleases you to give me Pleasures – that's not what I mean." Her eyes were serious. "I want to learn to Pleasure you, Jondalar."

He couldn't resist her. His manhood was hard between them as he held her close, and he kissed her as though he couldn't get enough of her. She kissed him back, following his example. They lingered over the kiss, tasting, touching, exploring each other.

"I will show you how to please me, Ayla," he said, and, taking her hand, he found a place of green grass near the water. When they sat down, he kissed her again, then reached for her ear and kissed her neck, pushing her back. His hand was on her breast, and he was reaching for it with his tongue, when she sat up.

"I want to Pleasure you," she said.

"Ayla, it pleases me so much to give you Pleasure – I don't know how it could possibly please me more for you to Pleasure me."

"Will it please you less?" she asked.

Jondalar threw back his head, laughed, and took her in his arms. She smiled but wasn't sure what had delighted him so.

"I don't think anything you did could please me less."

Then, looking at her with his vibrant blue eyes, he said, "I love you, woman."

"I love you, Jondalar. I feel love when you smile like that, with your eyes like that, and so much when you laugh. No one laughed in the Clan, and they did not like it when I did. I don't ever want to live with people who will not let me smile or laugh."

"You should laugh, Ayla, and smile. You have a beautiful smile." She couldn't help smiling at his words. "Ayla, oh, Ayla," he said, burying his face in her neck and caressing her.

"Jondalar, I love when you touch me, and kiss in my neck, but I want to know what you like."

He made a wry grin. "I can't help myself – you 'encourage' me too much. What do you like, Ayla? Do to me what feels good to you."

"Will you like it?"

"Try it."

She pushed him back, then bent over to kiss him, opening her mouth and using her tongue. He responded, but held himself in check. Then she kissed his neck, flicking her tongue lightly. She felt him shiver a bit, and she looked at him, wanting confirmation.

"Does it please you?"

"Yes, Ayla, it pleases me."

It did. Restraining himself under her tentative advances fired him more than he dreamed. Her light kisses seared through him. She was unsure of herself, as inexperienced as a girl who had reached puberty, but had not yet had First Rites – and no one was more desirable. Such tender kisses had more power to arouse than the most ardent and sensual caresses of more experienced women – because they were forbidden.

Most women were available to some degree; she was untouchable. The untried young woman could drive men, young and old, to a frenzy with secret caresses in dark corners of the cave. A mother's worst fear was that her daughter would come into her womanhood just after the Summer Meeting, with a long winter to face before the next. Most girls had some experience by First Rites with kissing and fondling, and Jondalar had known it was not the first time for a few, though he would not disgrace them by revealing it.

He knew the appeal of those young women – it was part of his enjoyment of First Rites – and it was that appeal Ayla was exerting on him. She kissed his neck. He quivered and, closing his eyes, gave himself up to it.

She moved lower and made ticklish wet circles on his body, feeling her own excitement rising. It was almost torture for him, exquisite torture, part tickle and part searing stimulation. When she reached his navel, he couldn't stop himself. He put his hands on her head and gently pushed her lower until she felt his hot shaft on her cheek. She was breathing hard, and drawing, pulling sensations reached deep. Her tickling tongue was more than he could bear. He guided her head to his outstretched rigid organ. She looked up at him.

"Jondalar, do you want me to . . ."

"Only if you want to, Ayla."

"It would please you?"

"It would please me."

"I want."

He felt a moist warmth enclose the end of his throbbing manhood, and then more than the end. He groaned. Her tongue explored the smooth round head, probed the small fissure, discovered the texture of the skin. When her first actions brought expressions of pleasure, she grew more confident. She was enjoying her explorations and felt her own throbbing inside. She circled his shape with her tongue. He called out her name, and she moved her tongue faster and felt wetness between her own legs.

He felt suction, and moist warmth moving up and down. "Oh Doni! Oh, woman! Ayla, Ayla! How did you learn to do that!"

She tried to discover how much she could hold, and she drew him in until she nearly gagged. His cries and moans encouraged her to try again, and again, until he was rising to meet her.

Then, sensing his need for her depths – and her own need as well – she rose, moved her leg over to straddle him, impaled herself on his full-girthed and extended member, and drew it into her. She arched her back and felt her Pleasure, as he penetrated deep.

He looked up at her and gloried in the sight. The sun

behind her turned her hair into a golden nimbus. Her eyes were closed, her mouth open, and her face suffused with ecstasy. As she leaned back, her shapely breasts jutted forward, her slightly darker nipples pointing out. Her sinuous body glistened in the sun; his own manhood buried deep within was ready to burst with rapture.

She raised up along his shaft, and came down as he raised to meet her, and his breath caught. He felt a surge he couldn't have controlled if he'd tried. He cried out when she rose again. She pushed against him, feeling a spurting wetness, as he shook with release.

He reached up and pulled her down, his mouth finding her nipple. After a while of drained contentment, Ayla rolled over. Jondalar got up, bent over to kiss her, then reached for both her breasts to nuzzle between them. He suckled one, then the other, and kissed her again. Then he relaxed beside her, cradling her head.

"I like to give you Pleasures, Jondalar."

"No one has ever pleased me better, Ayla."

"But you like it better when you Pleasure me."

"Not better, exactly, but . . . how do you know me so well?"

"It is what you learned to do. It is your skill, like tool-making." She smiled, then giggled. "Jondalar has two skills. He is a toolmaker and a woman-maker," she said, looking pleased with herself.

He laughed. "You just made a joke, Ayla," he said, smiling askance. It was a little too close to the truth, and the joke had been made before. "But you are right. I love to give you Pleasures, I love your body, I love all of you."

"I like it when you Pleasure me, too. It makes love fill up inside me. You can Pleasure me as much as you want, only, sometimes, I want to Pleasure you."

He laughed again. "Agreed. And since you want to learn so much, I can teach you more. We can Pleasure each other, you know. I wish it was my turn to make 'love fill up inside you'. But you did it so well, I don't think even Haduma's touch could raise me."

Ayla was silent for a moment. "It would not matter, Jondalar."

"What wouldn't matter?"

"Even if your manhood never rose again – you still make love fill up inside me."

"Don't ever say it!" He grinned, but gave a small shudder.

"Your manhood will rise again," she said with great solemnity, then giggled.

"What makes you so full of salt, woman? There are some things you shouldn't make jokes about," he said with mock offence, then laughed. He was surprised and pleased at her playfulness and new understanding of humour.

"I like to make you laugh. Laughing with you feels almost as good as loving you. I want you always to laugh with me. Then I think you won't ever stop loving me."

"Stop loving you?" he said, sitting up a bit and looking down at her. "Ayla, I looked for you all my life and didn't know I was looking. You are everything I ever wanted, everything I ever dreamed of in a woman, and more. You are a fascinating enigma, a paradox. You are totally honest, open; you hide nothing; yet you are the most mysterious woman I've ever met.

"You are strong, self-reliant, entirely able to take care of yourself and of me: yet you would sit at my feet – if I'd let you – with no shame, no resentment, as easily as I would honour Doni. You are fearless, courageous; you saved my life, nursed me back to health, hunted for my food, provided for my comfort. You don't need me. Yet you make me want to protect you, watch over you, make sure no harm comes to you.

"I could live with you all my life and never really know you; you have depths it would take many lifetimes to explore. You are wise and ancient as the Mother, and as fresh and young as a woman at First Rites. And you are the most beautiful woman I have ever seen. I can't believe how lucky I am to get so much. I didn't think I was able to love anyone; now I know I was only waiting for you. I didn't think it was possible for me to love, Ayla, and I love you more than life itself."

Ayla had tears in her eyes. He kissed both eyelids, and he held her close, as though he was afraid he might lose her.

When they woke up the next morning, there was a thin layer of snow on the ground. They let the tent opening fall back and snuggled into the sleeping furs, but they both felt a sense of sadness.

"It's time to turn back, Jondalar."

"I suppose you're right," he said, watching his breath rise in a slight puff of steam. "It's still early in the season. We shouldn't run into any bad storms."

"You never know; the weather can surprise you."

They finally got up and started breaking camp. Ayla's sling brought down a great jerboa emerging from its subterranean nest in rapid bipedal jumps. She picked it up by a tail that was nearly twice as long as its body, and slung it over her back by hoof-like hind claws. At the campsite, she quickly skinned and spitted it.

"I'm sad to be going back," Ayla said, while Jondalar built up the fire. "It has been . . . fun. Just travelling, stopping where we wanted. Not worrying about bringing anything back. Making camp at noon just because we wanted to swim, or have Pleasures. I'm glad you thought of it."

"I'm sad it's over, too, Ayla. It's been a good trip."

He got up to get more wood, walking down towards the river. Ayla helped him. They rounded a bend and found a pile of rotted deadfall. Suddenly, Ayla heard a sound. She looked up and reached for Jondalar.

"Heyooo!" a voice called.

A handful of people were walking towards them, waving. Ayla clung to Jondalar; his arm was around her, protective, reassuring.

"It's all right, Ayla. They're Mamutoi. Did I ever tell you they call themselves the mammoth hunters? They think we are Mamutoi, too," Jondalar said.

As the group neared, Ayla turned to Jondalar, her face full of surprise and wonder. "Those people, Jondalar, they are smiling," she said. "They are smiling at me."

IT'S HERE!

**Millions worldwide feared it was an era
lost forever in the mists of time.
Now at last, the hour has come.**

The fifth book in Jean Auel's spectacular
Earth's Children® series is published on 30th April 2002
It's called THE SHELTERS OF STONE and it more
than justifies even the unprecedented excitement
with which it has been anticipated.

The journey continues at all good bookshops.

THE SHELTERS OF STONE 0 340 82195 7
Hodder & Stoughton

www.madaboutbooks.com

THE CLAN OF THE CAVE BEAR · THE VALLEY OF HORSES ·
THE MAMMOTH HUNTERS · THE PLAINS OF PASSAGE ·
THE SHELTERS OF STONE